雙解
英語近義詞
辨異詞典

Martin Manser

商務印書館

© 2009 by Martin H. Manser
www.martinmanser.com
This translation of *English-Chinese Learner's Thesaurus* is published by
arrangement with Martin H. Manser.
本書繁體版經商務印書館授權出版。

雙解英語近義詞辨異詞典

主　　編：Martin Manser

編　　者：Stephen Collins　Alice Grandison

審　　訂：鄒曉玲

翻　　譯：梅玉華　馮巨瀾

責任編輯：黃家麗　Eddy Wong

封面設計：張　毅

出　　版：商務印書館 (香港) 有限公司
　　　　　香港筲箕灣耀興道 3 號東滙廣場 8 樓
　　　　　http://www.commercialpress.com.hk

發　　行：香港聯合書刊物流有限公司
　　　　　香港新界荃灣德士古道 220–248 號荃灣工業中心 16 樓

印　　刷：中華商務彩色印刷有限公司
　　　　　香港新界大埔汀麗路 36 號中華商務印刷大廈

版　　次：2023 年 3 月第 5 次印刷
　　　　　© 2010 商務印書館 (香港) 有限公司
　　　　　ISBN 978 962 07 0297 6
　　　　　Printed in Hong Kong

Contents

目　　錄

How to use this book
使用説明

First, look up the word for which you want to find a synonym in the index. For example, if you want to find a word to use instead of **stubborn**, you could look that up in the index. In the index, the word **stubborn** is in bold, which means it is one of the main keywords in the dictionary. If you then look up **stubborn** in the main dictionary part of the book, you will find a list of alternative words. By looking at the definitions and examples, you can choose the one that most closely matches what you want to express.

如果想為一個詞查找近義詞，請首先在索引中找到該詞。例如，你希望找一個詞來代替 **stubborn**，可以先在索引中找 **stubborn** 這個詞。若該詞是黑體，表明它是主詞條。該詞的正文下面有一系列的近義詞選項，你可參照該等近義詞的釋義和例證，挑選出最貼切的詞。

Alternatively, if you look up a word that is in italics in the index, you will be directed to the main bold keyword where other similar words are discussed. For example, if you look up *study* in the index, this will direct you to the keyword **learn**, where *study* is one of the synonyms listed in alphabetical order. By looking up **learn** in the main dictionary part of the book, you are given a wider range of alternatives. By looking at the definitions and examples you can choose the word that most closely matches what you want to express.

另外，如果你在索引中查到的詞是斜體，請按指引找到黑體主詞條。例如：在索引中查到單詞 *study* 它會提示你查閱 **learn**，在該詞條下有一組依照字母順序排列的近義詞，*study* 就在其中。通過查閱正文的詞條 **learn**，你會得到大量的近義詞選項。然後參照釋義與例證，你就能選擇表達最貼切的詞。

Index 索引

The definitions are intended to show the various shades of meaning of the group of synonyms. The examples show the context in which a word is used and which other words typically occur with each synonym.

釋義幫助了解每一組同義詞詞義的細微差別；例證提供每一個近義詞最常出現的語言環境。

restrain *verb* not to allow something, someone, or yourself to become too violent or forceful or to express themselves openly, or to prevent someone, for example a prisoner, from behaving violently by holding them, handcuffing them, etc. 抑制，遏制（以防變得過於激烈、強硬或直白）；（通過拘留、上手銬等方式）阻止，限制（囚犯等的暴力行為）：*I couldn't restrain my self any longer and burst out laughing.* 我再也忍不住，突然大笑起來。

control not to allow something, someone, or yourself to act freely, especially to limit or restrain something or someone（尤指）限制，限定（行動自由）：*Government efforts to control immigration have so far failed.* 政府限制外來移民的努力迄今未獲成功。

curb to keep something under strict control and, usually, to reduce it 嚴格控制；抑制：*He should try to curb his enthusiasm and act more rationally.* 他應該設法抑制自己的衝動，做事更理智一些。

hold back to restrain something such as tears or laughter, or to stop something from progressing or developing as fast as it would like 抑制（淚水或笑聲等）；阻止（某事的進程或發展）：*Business is being held back by government restrictions.* 商業正受到政府限制性政策的制約。

inhibit to prevent an event or process from developing 約束，阻止（事件或過程的發展）：*Does the Internet encourage or inhibit learning?* 互聯網是促進還是妨礙學習呢？

Guidance on usage is given in two ways: showing context of use by style markers in round brackets, e.g., *(informal)*, *(formal)* and by means of brief usage notes introduced by*.

近義詞用法指南：圓括號標註語體類型，如（非正式）、（正式）等；星號標註簡要的用法說明。

clanger *(informal)* a stupid or embarrassing mistake（愚蠢或令人困窘的）錯誤：*What a clanger – Linda said the capital of Belgium was Amsterdam!* 多麼愚蠢的錯誤，琳達把比利時的首都説成了阿姆斯特丹！

intransigent *(formal)* completely unwilling to change your mind about something 毫不妥協的；不讓步的：*Senior party members remained intransigent in their opposition to any change in the constitution.* 政黨高層人員仍然堅決反對修訂憲法。

engaged* not free to speak to someone because you are speaking to someone or doing something else 忙着的；繁忙的：*Mike is engaged at the moment. Shall I ask him to phone you when he's free?* 邁克此時正忙。我讓他有空給你打電話好嗎？

* In British English a telephone line is said to be when someone is speaking on it; in US English, it is said to be busy. 電話佔線在英國英語中用；在美國英語中則用 busy。

Cross-references are given at the end of many entries to show additional words with a related meaning.

許多詞條後都有參見提示 ➋ see also，以幫助讀者了解更多意義相關的詞。

Index 索引

xiv

A

abandon[1] *verb* to go away from a person, place, or thing, usually hurriedly or without warning（通常指慌忙地、無先兆地）拋棄，遺棄：*She was abandoned by her parents when she was a baby.* 她還是嬰孩時便被父母遺棄了。

desert to leave or to stop supporting someone or something that you have a duty to stay with or help（不顧責任地）背棄，離棄，撇下不管：*All his friends deserted him when he was in trouble.* 當他處於困境時，所有朋友都棄他而去。

dump (*informal*) to end a romantic relationship with someone suddenly in a way that hurts their feelings 甩掉（某人，以結束戀情）：*He dumped his girlfriend when he met someone else.* 他有了新歡便把女朋友給蹬了。

jilt to end a romantic relationship suddenly with someone, especially someone who expects you to marry them 拋棄（欲與之成婚的人）：*Her fiancé jilted her the day before the wedding.* 婚禮前一天，她的未婚夫拋棄了她。

leave to stop living with your husband or wife 遺棄，拋棄（配偶）：*She left her husband after twelve years of marriage.* 婚後 12 年她離開了丈夫。

leave in the lurch (*informal*) to leave someone to cope with a difficult situation 棄（某人）於艱難之中：*The speaker cancelled at the last minute and left me in the lurch.* 演講人在最後時刻放棄演講，令我無所適從。

vacate to leave a place that you have been staying in 空出，騰出（住所）：*They vacated the premises on Friday.* 他們在星期五搬出了營業場所。

abandon[2] *verb* to stop doing something 停止進行：*She abandoned her attempts to help and left them to sort the mess out for themselves.* 她不再設法幫助他們，而是讓他們自己去收拾爛攤子。

chuck (in) (*informal*) to stop doing a job or task, especially because you are tired of it（尤指因厭倦而）放棄（工作或任務）：*He chucked the job in, because he was fed up with all the paperwork.* 他放棄這份工作是因為厭倦了所有的文書工作。

give up to stop doing something, especially something that you have been doing for a long time or that has become a habit 放棄（尤指長期進行的或習以為常的事）：*When I tried to give up smoking, I put on a lot of weight.* 在我努力戒煙的過程中，體重增加了許多。

leave behind to stop being involved in an activity permanently, especially because you are older and wiser or have new interests（尤指因年齡增長而諳於世事或興趣轉移而永久性地）忍住不做，放棄（某項活動）：*I had to leave my acting career behind and concentrate on being a diplomat's wife.* 我不得不放棄我的演藝生涯，專心做外交官夫人。

refrain (from) not to do something that you want, or are intending, to do 忍住不做，放棄（打算做的事情）：*I was sorely tempted to tell the boss exactly what was wrong with his management style, but decided it was wiser to refrain.* 我很想告訴老闆他的管理方式究竟錯在哪裏，但決定還是不說為妙。

renounce to stop holding a belief or opinion, or give up a particular type of behaviour, especially by making a formal declaration that you now consider it to be wrong (尤指正式) 宣佈放棄 (信念、觀點或行為方式)：*The regime agreed to renounce all forms of violence.* 政府同意宣佈放棄使用任何形式的暴力。

able *adjective* having above average skill or intelligence (指超出平均水平) 有才能的，有才智的：*an able student* 能幹的學生

capable very good at dealing with situations or people 能幹的，有能力的 (指善於應付各種情況或與不同的人打交道)：*I will leave you in the hands of my capable assistant.* 我會把你託付給我能幹的助手。

clever showing a lot of intelligence or skill 聰明的；精明的；靈巧的：*She deceived her opponent with a clever trick.* 她用巧妙的計謀蒙騙了對手。

competent having the skill necessary to do a particular job or activity well 有能力的；能勝任的：*He's not a computer expert, but he's perfectly competent to carry out ordinary tasks on a computer.* 他不是電腦專家，但在電腦上完成一些基本任務還是完全能夠勝任的。

expert having a thorough knowledge of a particular subject or great skill in a particular type of work 老練的；內行的；專家的：*It took me two days to do a job that an expert dressmaker would have finished in two hours.* 我花了兩天時間才完成一個裁縫高手兩小時就能做完的工作。

gifted born with a high degree of skill or intelligence 有天賦的；天資聰慧的：*She thinks that she's naturally gifted and that she doesn't need to study or practise.* 她自認為有天賦，毋須學習和實踐。

skilful having or showing a lot of skill 有技巧的；熟練的：*A more skilful driver would have avoided the obstacle.* 技術更嫻熟的駕駛員完全可以避開這個障礙物。

talented naturally very good at something, especially in the arts or sport (尤指在藝術或體育方面) 有天賦的：*His art teacher realized that he was an exceptionally talented painter.* 他的美術老師認識到他是個極具天賦的繪畫者。

➲ see also 參見 **clever**

abolish *verb* to take official action to stop a practice or ensure that a law or regulation is no longer in effect (採取官方行為) 廢止，廢除 (習俗、法律、規章制度等)：*Slavery was abolished a long time ago.* 奴隸制在很久以前就被廢止了。

cancel to decide that something that has been arranged will not after all take place 取消 (已經安排之事)：*The party has been cancelled.* 晚會已經取消了。

discontinue to stop something after it has been going on for some time 終止，中斷 (進行中的事)：*The doctor discontinued my treatment.* 醫生終止了對我的治療。

do away with to stop a practice or remove something completely 廢除 (習俗)；取消 (某事)：*The government did away with free school milk.* 政府取消了學校免費提供的牛奶。

eradicate to stop or remove something harmful permanently and make sure that it cannot start again 根除 (有害的事物)；杜絕：*The school aims to eradicate bullying.* 學校力爭杜絕以強凌弱的現象。

get rid of to remove something that causes problems 擺脫，清理掉（引起問題的事情）: *Isn't it time that we finally got rid of all restrictions on free trade?* 現在不正是我們最終擺脫所有自由貿易限制的時機嗎？

put an end to to prevent something from continuing 結束，終止（事物的繼續發展）: *The accident put an end to her dancing career.* 這次意外事故結束了她的舞蹈生涯。

quash to state officially that a decision or punishment is wrong or unjust 宣佈（裁決或懲處）不當或不公平；撤銷: *His drink-driving conviction was quashed.* 對他酒後駕車的定罪被撤銷了。

terminate to end an agreement 終止，結束（協議）: *Your contract has been terminated.* 你的合同已經終止了。

accept[1] *verb* to be willing to take, or say yes to, something that is offered to you 認可，接受（某事）: *She accepted his proposal of marriage.* 她接受了他的求婚。

receive to be given something 收到，接到（某物）: *I received a beautiful bouquet of flowers.* 我收到了一束漂亮的花。

take to receive or make use of something when it is offered to you 接收，使用（所提供之物）: *If they offer me the job, I shall definitely take it.* 如果他們給我這份工作，我肯定會接受。

take on to agree to be responsible for doing something 承擔（某工作）: *They have taken on too much work.* 他們承擔了過多的工作。

welcome to receive something or someone gladly 欣然接受，樂意接納: *I welcome this opportunity to give my side of the story.* 我很高興有機會陳述我方觀點。

accept[2] *verb* to be willing to allow yourself to be governed by something such as a decision, a rule, or someone else's right to do something 承認，接受（指願意受某項決定、規章或他人權利的約束）: *Tick this box to show that you accept the company's terms and conditions.* 請在方框內打勾，以示接受公司的各項條款。

abide by to obey a rule 遵守（規則）: *You must abide by the rules of the game.* 你必須遵守遊戲規則。

agree to to say that you are willing to do what is required by a suggestion or proposal 允諾，同意（按照建議或提議行事）: *They agreed to the terms of the house sale .* 他們同意房屋的銷售條款。

assent to (*formal*) to agree to do what someone asks you to do 同意，贊成（他人的請求）: *I assented to their request to give a slide show.* 我答應了給他們播放幻燈的請求。

comply with to do what is required by a rule or expressed in a wish 遵從，遵照: *Your car must be fitted with seatbelts to comply with the laws on vehicle safety.* 遵照車輛安全法，你的汽車必須配備安全帶。

⊃ see also 參見 **admit**[1],**admit**[2]

accidental *adjective* happening without anyone planning or wishing it should happen 意外的；偶然發生的: *Can you prove that the damage was* *accidental and not inflicted on purpose?* 你能證明這次損失屬於意外而非故意造成的嗎？

casual unexpected and of little importance 偶然的；不經意的：*a casual encounter with a stranger* 與陌生人的邂逅

chance happening unexpectedly 偶然的；意想不到的：*a chance remark* 不經意的一句話

fortuitous not planned but having a happy outcome 偶然發生的，巧合的（但有好結果的）：*a fortuitous meeting with a new business contact* 與新業務夥伴的不期而遇

inadvertent done by mistake 未留心的；疏忽造成的：*his inadvertent revelation of the winner's name* 他無意洩露優勝者的姓名。

random not selected according to a plan or system 隨機的；任意的：*a random sample of viewers* 對電視觀眾的隨機抽樣

unintentional not deliberate 非蓄意的；無心的：*If I offended you, it was unintentional.* 如果我冒犯了你，那一定是無心的。

unplanned happening without being planned 未籌劃而發生的；無意的：*an unplanned pregnancy* 意外懷孕

unwitting doing something without realizing that you are doing it 不知情的：*He became an unwitting accomplice in her plan.* 他糊裏糊塗地成了她計劃中的幫兇。

accompany *verb* to go with a person to a place or an event 陪伴，陪同（某人去某地）：*Will you accompany me to the concert?* 你可以陪我去聽音樂會嗎？

associate with to spend a lot of time with someone（花大量時間）與（某人）在一起；交往：*I mostly associate with work colleagues.* 我大部分時間都和同事在一起。

attend to go with and look after someone as a servant（作為僕人）陪同，侍候：*The princess was attended by her lady-in-waiting.* 這位公主由她的侍女陪同。

chaperone to go somewhere, especially to a social event, with a young person in order to make sure that they do not get into trouble（尤指在社交場所）做（未成年人的）保護人：*She chaperoned her daughter when she was invited to her first ball.* 女兒第一次受邀參加舞會時，她陪伴在女兒左右。

conduct to lead someone to or around a place that they do not know 為（某人）導遊：*The guide conducted us to the monastery.* 導遊帶着我們參觀了修道院。

escort to go somewhere with someone either as a guard or as their partner at a social occasion（作為警衛或同伴）護送，護衛（某人）：*The security guard escorted her out of the building.* 保安護送她出了大樓。

partner to act as a partner to someone, especially in a game or dance（尤指在競賽或舞會上與某人）結成夥伴，成為拍檔：*Will you partner me in the bowling competition?* 這次保齡球比賽你和我拍檔好嗎？

tag along with (*informal*) to go somewhere with someone, especially when you have not been invited to go with them（尤指未經邀請而）跟隨，尾隨（某人）：*My little sister always wants to tag along with me and my friends.* 我妹妹總是想跟隨我和我的朋友。

usher to show someone where they have to go or sit, usually in a very polite way (常指彬彬有禮地) 引領 (客人入座)：*The head waiter ushered us to a small table in a quiet corner of the restaurant.* 樓面部長把我們引領到餐館安靜一角的小桌旁。

accurate *adjective* conforming to fact, reality, or the actual state of affairs 與 (實際情況) 完全相符的；準確的；精確的：*an accurate description* 準確的描述

   correct without error 無誤的；正確的：*the correct answer* 正確的答案

   exact correct in every detail 確切的；準確無誤的；精確的：*an exact copy* 精確的副本

   perfect having no faults 完美的；完全正確的；無缺點的：*perfect grammar* 地道的語法

   precise exactly as specified 精確的；準確的；恰好的：*at that precise time* 恰好在那個時候

   right correct, or correct in what you say or think (所説或所思) 正確的：*You were right about her, she isn't a very nice person.* 你對她的看法是正確的，她不是一個很友善的人。

   spot-on (*informal*) absolutely correct or true to life 完全正確的；逼真的：*Yesterday's weather forecast was spot-on.* 昨天的天氣預告很準確。

   strict not allowing for any deviation or vagueness 嚴密的；嚴格的；精確的：*in the strict sense* 從嚴格意義上説

   true not a lie and not invented 真實的；非虛構的：*a true story* 一個真實的故事

   ➲ see also 參見 **true**

achieve *verb* to gain something through effort or ability (憑藉努力或能力) 獲得，達到，實現 (某事)：*He achieved worldwide fame as a rock guitarist.* 他是世界有名的搖滾結他手。

   accomplish to be successful in finishing a task or reaching a goal, especially one that you have set yourself 達到，實現 (目標，尤指自己設立的目標)：*She accomplished her goal of winning an Olympic gold medal.* 她實現了贏得奧運會金牌的目標。

   carry out to put an idea or a plan into action 貫徹；履行；實施：*We carried out my father's wish to have his ashes scattered at sea.* 我們履行了父親的遺願，將他的骨灰撒到大海。

   complete to finish a task 完成 (任務)：*Julia completed the crossword puzzle.* 朱莉婭完成了這個填字遊戲。

   do (*informal*) to perform a task or an action successfully (成功地) 執行，完成 (任務或行動)：*We did it! We did it! We won the UEFA Cup!* 我們成功了！我們成功了！我們贏得了聯盟盃！

   pull off (*informal*) to be unexpectedly successful in doing something 出乎意料地獲得成功：*Nobody thought Lawrie had a chance of winning but somehow he pulled it off!* 誰也沒想到勞利有可能贏，可他居然贏了。

   reach to manage to get to a level, standard, or goal that you have been working towards 實現，達到 (一直為之奮鬥的目標)：*She reached her target weight loss of ten pounds.* 她終於達到了減少 10 磅體重的目標。

realize to fulfil an ambition, hope or dream 實現 (夢想或希望)：*I finally realized my ambition to visit China.* 我終於實現了到中國旅遊的心願。

succeed to manage to do what you wanted or planned to do 取得成功：*Janet succeeded in being elected a Member of Parliament.* 珍妮特成功當選國會議員。

➲ see also 參見 **get**

active *adjective* able and eager to move about and do things 好動的；活躍的：*an active 70-year-old who plays golf four times a week* 一個每週打 4 次高爾夫球，70 歲依然活躍的老人

busy dealing with work or involved in an activity so that you cannot stop to do anything else 忙碌的；沒空的：*I was too busy to take a day off.* 我忙得沒有一天空閒。

energetic having or requiring a lot of energy 精力充沛的；充滿活力的；需要能量的：*an energetic dance routine* 活潑的舞步

hyperactive having a medical condition that makes you unable to sit still, be quiet or concentrate on something 患有多動症的；好動的：*Looking after a hyperactive child can be very tiring.* 照顧一個好動的孩子有時真夠累的。

industrious (*formal*) working hard and steadily 勤勉的；勤奮的；刻苦的：*an industrious student* 一個勤勉的學生

lively cheerful and full of energy 生氣勃勃的；充滿生機活力的：*lively youngsters running about the place* 四處亂跑，生氣勃勃的少年

on the go (*informal*) extremely busy 忙個不停的；忙得不可開交的：*She is always on the go, looking after her six kids.* 她總是在馬不停蹄地照顧着她的 6 個孩子。

vigorous having or requiring great strength and energy 充滿力量的；精力旺盛的；高度的：*a vigorous workout* 高度的訓練

➲ see also 參見 **vigour**

admire *verb* to feel that someone or something is worthy of respect and praise 讚賞，欽佩 (某人)：*I really admire you for standing up to the bullies.* 我真的很欽佩你不畏強暴的行為。

appreciate to enjoy something, such as an art form, and understand what makes it good 欣賞，鑒賞 (藝術等)：*He doesn't appreciate opera.* 他不欣賞歌劇。

approve of to think that an action or a person's behaviour is morally good or is sensible and correct 同意，贊成 (合乎道德或明智正確的行為)：*I don't approve of teenagers smoking.* 我不贊成青少年抽煙。

idolize to have an unrealistically high opinion of someone, usually a famous person 崇拜 (常指名人)：*Many young girls idolize pop stars.* 許多年輕女孩都崇拜流行明星。

look up to to have respect for someone, usually an older person, who is a model of how you would like to be 尊敬，景仰 (常指德高望重的長者)：*She looked up to her older sister and wanted to be like her.* 她仰慕自己的姐姐，希望將來和她一樣優秀。

respect to have a high opinion of someone or their actions 尊敬，尊重：*I respect him for sticking to his principles.* 我尊重他堅持自己的原則。

take your hat off to (*informal*) to think that someone has done something that deserves praise or admiration 佩服，欽佩（某人）：*Well, I take my hat off to him. I wouldn't have dared to try anything so risky myself.* 嗨，我真佩服他。我本人肯定沒有膽量冒這種險。

think the world of (*informal*) to be very fond of someone 喜愛，喜歡（某人）：*He thinks the world of his wife and kids.* 他非常喜愛他的妻子和孩子。

value to consider a person or a quality important 重視，珍視，看重：*I really value your friendship.* 我很看重你的友誼。

venerate (*formal*) to regard someone with deep almost religious feelings of respect, because of their age or their achievements 崇敬，敬仰，仰慕：*She is venerated as a leader of the Women's Movement.* 作為婦女解放運動的領袖，她備受人們的尊重。

⊃ see also 參見 **appreciate; respect**

admit¹ *verb* to say that something is true, especially that it is true that you have done something wrong or made a mistake 承認（某事屬實，尤指承認錯誤）：*I admit that I was rather drunk when I said that.* 我承認我說那話時是有些醉了。

accept to regard what someone says as true 認可，相信（某人的說法屬實）：*The police accepted his version of events.* 警察相信了他對事件的陳述。

acknowledge to say, sometimes reluctantly, that you realize that something is true（有時指不情願地）承認（某事屬實）：*He finally acknowledged that my advice had been helpful.* 他最終承認我的忠告是有用的。

agree to say that something that someone else has said is right, often before adding a comment about something that you think is not so good（常指在給予負面評價之前）承認（某事的正確性）：*They agreed that the meeting had been useful, but wished that more time had been spent discussing the budget for the following year.* 他們承認這次會議是卓有成效的，但希望用更多的時間討論來年的預算問題。

allow (*formal*) to say that someone or something may be right, but in a rather cautious or reluctant way（謹慎地、有保留地）同意，認可：*She allowed that she might have been somewhat hasty.* 她承認她可能有些草率。

come clean (*informal*) to admit to some wrongdoing that you have been keeping secret 招供，招認，坦白（不願說出的錯誤）：*In the end he decided to come clean about cheating on his wife.* 最後他決定坦白自己對妻子的不忠行為。

concede to say that a point or an argument made by someone who is arguing against you is right 承認（對方觀點正確）：*I concede your point that it may be difficult to complete the work in the time available.* 我承認你的觀點，在現有時間內完成這項工作可能有困難。

confess to tell someone, especially the police or a priest, that you have done something wrong（尤指對警察或牧師）坦白，懺悔（所做的錯事）：*She confessed to killing her husband.* 她承認殺死了自己的丈夫。

own up to admit that you are responsible for some wrongdoing（為錯誤行為）承擔責任；坦白；供認：*Unless the person who stole the money owns up, the whole class will be punished.* 除非偷錢的人坦白，否則全班同學都會受到懲罰。

recognize to say that you realize that something is true or possible 認可，認識到（某事的真實性或可能性）：*I recognize that her intentions were good.* 我認為她的意圖是好的。

admit² *verb* to allow someone to enter a building or place, especially because they have something such as a ticket that gives them the right to enter（尤指因持有入場券等）准許進入：*You won't be admitted if you haven't got a valid ticket.* 如果沒有有效入場券，你會被禁止入內。

accept to allow someone to join a group or organization 接納，接受（成員）：*The golf club is not accepting new members at the moment.* 本高爾夫俱樂部目前不接納新會員。

let in to allow someone to enter a building or other place 允許（某人）進入（建築物等）：*He came home drunk, and his wife would not let him in.* 他醉酒後回家，妻子不讓他進門。

receive to greet and welcome a guest or visitor as they enter a place 迎接，接待（客人）進入（某地）：*The host and hostess were standing at the door to receive their guests.* 男女主人站在門口迎接客人。

take in to give someone shelter and a place to stay 收留，留宿：*After their parents died, relatives took the children in.* 這些孩子的父母去世後，親戚們便收留了他們。

welcome to greet a guest or newcomer warmly 歡迎（客人或新來者）：*We had a party to welcome the new neighbours.* 我們舉行了一個聚會歡迎新鄰居。

adventure *noun* a journey or activity that is exciting and unusual for you and perhaps slightly risky（異乎尋常或令人激動的）冒險經歷，冒險活動：*I live in a very quiet little village, so a trip to London is always a bit of an adventure.* 我住在一個安靜的小村莊，因此倫敦之旅總有些令人激動的冒險經歷。

enterprise an attempt to do something important or exciting, which shows you have initiative or courage but also involves a risk of failure（指需要進取心或勇氣，並且要冒險的）事業，計劃：*The enterprise was so badly planned that many people thought it was doomed from the start.* 糟糕的策劃使許多人認為這項事業從一開始就注定會失敗。

escapade an act that is exciting, but often comical or foolish（通常指滑稽或愚蠢的）惡作劇：*They recalled some daring escapades from their schooldays.* 他們回想起學生時代所搞的一些大膽的惡作劇。

exploit an act of bravery 英勇行為：*the heroic exploits of the mountain rescue service* 山區拯救隊的英勇行為

exploration the activity of making journeys to unknown places in order to learn about them（對陌生地帶的）探險，探索：*rockets for space exploration* 用於太空探險的火箭

quest a journey to search for something important or valuable（對重要或有價值事物的）追求，探索：*They set out on a quest to find the hidden treasure.* 他們開始探尋隱藏的寶藏。

undertaking an action or a task that involves a lot of effort and often an element of risk（需要耗費精力且具冒險性的）行動，任務：*Going into the mountains without a guide was a risky undertaking.* 沒有嚮導領路就進入山區是冒險的行動。

venture an attempt to achieve success or make a profit, usually in the world of business or finance（通常指商界或金融界為盈利而進行的）冒險事業，經營項目：*I have invested in a new business venture.* 我投資了一個新的商業項目。

advertise *verb* to give information about something, or display it, in order to make people want to buy it or go to it 為…做廣告：*The concert was advertised in all the newspapers.* 這場音樂會在各家報紙上都登了廣告。

announce to make a piece of information known to a lot of people 宣佈，宣告（某信息）：*The winner of the art competition will be announced tomorrow at morning assembly.* 藝術比賽的獲勝者將在明天的早會上公佈。

broadcast to make information publicly known, for example on television or radio 廣播，播放（消息）：*The Prime Minister's speech will be broadcast in full.* 總理的演講將全文播放。

hype up (*informal*) to make exaggerated claims about how good or exciting someone or something is（誇大地）吹捧，宣揚（某人或某事）：*This new band has been so hyped up that people are expecting it to be as good as U2.* 這個新樂隊被吹捧得天花亂墜，人們還以為它和 U2 樂隊一樣出色。

market to advertise a product in a way that is designed to appeal to a specific section of the public 推銷，促銷（某產品以吸引特定的公眾群）：*This new drink is being marketed as a young person's drink.* 這種新飲料正面向年輕人做促銷。

plug (*informal*) to give an interview on television or radio or in the press, in order to promote your latest recording, film, book, etc.（通過媒體）宣傳，推廣（新唱片、影片、圖書等）：*Not another actor is plugging his autobiography!* 沒有哪位演員像他那樣宣傳自己的自傳！

promote to present a product or an idea to the public in such a way as to encourage interest in it 推銷，宣傳（產品或觀點）：*a campaign to promote breast-feeding* 提倡母乳育嬰的宣傳活動

publicize to make the public aware of a certain product or event by advertising it on television or radio or on posters（通過媒體或廣告）推廣（某產品），宣傳（某事件）：*The actors paraded through the street in costume to publicize the show.* 演員們穿着戲服遊行，為這次演出做宣傳。

push (*informal*) to give a product a lot of publicity to try to convince the public to buy it 宣傳促銷，推銷（產品）：*They are really pushing this new magazine, with loads of TV adverts and posters.* 他們正利用大量的電視廣告和海報推銷這本新雜誌。

advice *noun* an opinion on something that is meant to be helpful to someone（有益的）忠告，建議：*Can I ask your advice on how to remove ink stains?* 對於如何去除墨跡，請問你有甚麼建議？

counsel (*formal*) advice about a serious matter from a wise or knowledgeable person（有識之士對某嚴肅事件的）建議，忠告：*In despair, he sought counsel from the parish priest.* 絕望之餘，他向教區牧師尋求建議。

counselling professional advice given by a trained counsellor to people who have a specific type of problem 專業諮詢，專家意見：*They went for counselling when their marital problems got really serious.* 他們在婚姻出現嚴重問題時去尋求專家意見。

guidance help and advice that might be offered to a person who is undecided about something, such as which career to pursue（為就業等問題所提供的）指導，建議：*The careers teacher will give you guidance on which subjects to study if you want to become a lawyer.* 如果你想成為一名律師，就業指導老師會就學科的選擇為你提供指導。

instruction a direction to do something that people are expected to follow 操作指南；使用說明（書）：*I followed the instructions on how to install the new software in my computer.* 我按照操作指南給電腦安裝新軟件。

opinion someone's personal view on a subject, which the person hearing it may or may not agree with（個人的）看法，主張：*I would value your opinion on which car I should buy.* 關於購買哪一款汽車，我會重視你的意見。

recommendation a statement saying that a particular thing or course of action is definitely good and that you think a person should try it 推薦；建議：*On my sister's recommendation, we visited Barcelona.* 在姐姐的推薦下，我們參觀了巴塞隆拿。

suggestion a statement putting forward an idea that you think may be good or helpful 建議，提議：*Do you have any suggestions as to what I could give Mum for her birthday?* 我該送媽媽甚麼生日禮物，你有甚麼建議嗎？

⊃ see also 參見 **guide; opinion; suggest¹**

affect¹ *verb* to have an effect on someone or something 影響（人或物）：*The flooding doesn't seem to have affected the bus service in this area.* 這次洪災似乎並沒有影響這一地區的公共汽車服務。

alter to make changes to something, such as a garment 修改（衣服等）：*My trousers were too long, so I had them altered.* 我的褲子太長了，所以讓人改了改。

change to make someone or something different in some way 改變；使不同：*His mother's death when he was a child changed his whole life.* 孩提時母親的去世改變了他的整個人生。

concern to be relevant to someone 關係到，涉及到（某人）：*The state of my finances does not concern you.* 我的財政狀況與你無關。

impinge on (*formal*) to be an external factor that has an influence on something, especially by restricting it in some way 對⋯有外在影響；妨礙；侵犯：*Any form of censorship necessarily impinges on the ordinary citizen's freedom of speech.* 任何形式的審查制度必然影響普通公民的言論自由。

influence to use power or persuasion to change someone's thoughts, feelings, or action（用權力或說服力）影響，支配，左右（某人的想法、情感或行為）：*He tried to influence the way other members voted.* 他試圖左右其他成員的投票方式。

modify to change something, usually in quite a small way, in order to create an improvement or advantage 對⋯稍作修改；調整：*The design may have to* *be modified to suit the new customer's requirements.* 這個設計也許要修改以滿足新客戶的要求。

affect^2 *verb* to cause an emotional reaction in someone, especially sadness 打動，感動；使悲傷：*I was deeply affected by the famine reports.* 關於饑荒的報道深深地打動了我。

disturb to make someone feel worried and upset 使煩惱；使不安：*His obsessive behaviour disturbs me.* 他的癡迷行為令我焦慮不安。

faze (*informal*) to make someone feel uneasy and lose their composure 使困窘；使慌亂；使不安：*She was totally fazed by his rudeness.* 他的粗魯無禮使她驚慌失措。

move to make someone feel strong emotion, especially sadness 使感動；（尤指）使悲痛：*Her speech moved me to tears.* 她的演講讓我很感動，我不禁流淚。

touch to make someone feel an emotion such as love, gratitude, or sympathy（使）感動；觸動，打動：*I was touched by my colleagues' concern.* 我被同事的關心所感動。

upset to cause someone to feel distressed or offended 使煩惱；使生氣：*It upsets me to see cruelty to children.* 看到孩子被虐待我感到氣憤。

⊃ see also 參見 **moving**

afraid *adjective* feeling fear in a particular situation, or worried about something because you think it may harm you（在特定情況下感到）害怕的；（對可能受到傷害）擔心的：*Louise is afraid of spiders.* 路易斯害怕蜘蛛。

anxious worried and tense 焦慮不安的：*I start to feel anxious if she's more than ten minutes late.* 只要她遲到超過 10 分鐘我就開始感到焦慮不安了。

apprehensive worried because you feel that something that you are going to do will be bad experience for you（對將要做的事）憂慮的：*She felt apprehensive about driving again so soon after the accident.* 車禍不久就重新駕車，她心有餘悸。

fearful (*formal*) nervous about doing something that other people might dislike or disapprove of（對做別人不喜歡或不同意的事而）擔心的，害怕的：*Fearful of offending her guests, she restricted her conversation to the weather and similarly safe topics.* 因害怕得罪客人，她將談話局限在天氣以及諸如此類穩妥的話題上。

frightened in a state of fear 受驚嚇的；恐懼的：*Don't be frightened if you hear a loud noise. It's only me drilling a hole in the floor.* 如果你聽到尖銳的噪音不要驚恐，那只是我在地板上鑽孔。

nervous being worried and having physical symptoms such as trembling hands and an uneasy feeling in your stomach because of something you are about to do（因為將要做某事而）擔憂的，神經緊張的：*I always get terribly nervous just before I have to go on stage.* 我上台前總是緊張得要命。

petrified so afraid that you are almost unable to move 嚇呆的：*The thunderstorm left the child petrified.* 這場雷雨把孩子嚇呆了。

scared afraid of someone or something 害怕的，恐懼的：*scared of the dark* 害怕黑暗

terrified extremely frightened 極其恐懼的：*The terrified child was hiding behind the sofa.* 極度驚恐的孩子躲到了沙發背後。

⊃ see also 參見 **cowardly; fear**

agree¹ *verb* to say that you will do something that someone has asked you to do 同意，答應（做別人請求之事）：*She agreed to reconsider her decision.* 她同意重新考慮她的決定。

acquiesce (*formal*) to say that you will do what someone else wants, although you have reservations 勉強同意；默許，默認：*She acquiesced in the group's decision, even though she had her doubts.* 雖然有疑惑，她還是勉強同意了小組裏的決定。

assent (*formal*) to say that you are willing to accept a request, proposal or suggestion 同意，贊成（請求或建議）：*The Prime Minister assented to their request for an interview.* 首相同意了他們的採訪請求。

consent to give someone permission to do something 同意，准許，允許（做某事）：*He reluctantly consented to have his photograph taken.* 他勉強同意了讓人給他拍照。

go along with (*informal*) to be willing to accept something such as opinion or suggestion or what someone says 贊同，接受（意見、建議或看法）：*I went along with the suggestion, because I couldn't think of anything better to do.* 我接受這個提議，因為我想不出更好的方法。

agree² *verb* to have the same opinion about something as someone else（與別人）意見一致：*I agree with Katie. It's too cold to go swimming.* 我同意凱蒂的意見，天氣太冷不宜游泳。

be of one mind (*formal*) said about two or more people: to have the same opinion on a subject（二人或二人以上）意見一致，同一想法：*The prime minister and I are of one mind on this issue.* 我和首相在這個問題上意見一致。

concur (*formal*) to accept that someone else's statement or decision is correct 同意，贊同（他人的陳述或決定的正確性）：*I concur with Mr Justice Smythe in holding the case against the defendant to be unproven.* 我同意法官斯邁思先生的看法，對被告的指控缺乏證據。

see eye to eye (*with*) (*informal*) to have the same or similar views on a subject（在某個問題上與某人）看法一致，觀點相同：*Politics is one subject on which I don't exactly see eye to eye with my father.* 在政治觀點這一問題上，我和父親並不完全一致。

agree³ *verb* to be the same as, or compatible with, one another 相符合；相一致：*Their accounts of the incident agree on some points and differ on others.* 他們對這個事件的敘述有些方面是一致的，有些方面則有分歧。

accord (*formal*) to be consistent with what someone else has said or found out（與他人所説或發現）一致，相符：*This accords with the findings of the original investigation.* 這與最初的調查結果是一致的。

fit to be the same as, or exactly adapted to, something 與⋯⋯一致；和⋯相稱：*His face fits the description given by the police.* 他的外貌與警察的描述一致。

match to be the same as something, very like it, or a good accompaniment to it 與…相配；與…相似：*The curtains don't match the carpet.* 這些窗簾與地毯不相配。

tally to be consistent with one another; to accord with something 相一致；相吻合：*The two witnesses' statements about the incident do not tally.* 兩位目擊證人對事件的陳述不一致。

‚ see also 參見 **accept²; admit¹**

alone¹ *adverb* without anyone else being with you 單獨；獨自：*He prefers to travel alone.* 他更喜歡獨自旅遊。

by yourself without anyone else being with you or helping you 獨自地；憑自己的力量：*I decorated the room all by myself.* 我獨自一人把屋子裝飾了一番。

off your own bat (*informal*) without anyone else telling you what to do 獨立地；主動地；自覺地：*He gave me a ring to say sorry off his own bat.* 他主動給我打電話表達歉意。

on your own without anyone else being with you or helping you 獨自地；憑自己的力量：*She has been living on her own since her husband died.* 丈夫過世後，她一直獨自一人生活。

on your tod (*informal*) with no one else present 單獨地；獨自地：*They all shoved off and left me on my tod.* 他們都離開了，留下我獨自一人。

unaccompanied without an escort 無陪伴地：*Claire went to the wedding unaccompanied.* 克萊爾獨自一人參加婚禮。

unaided without the help or support of someone or something, such as a walking stick 無外援的；無支撐的：*Can the old lady walk unaided?* 這位老婦人能獨自行走嗎？

alone²* *adjective* not with anyone else 獨自一人：*I was alone in the office.* 我獨自一人留在辦公室。

* Not used before a noun. 不用於名詞前。

deserted abandoned by a partner, parent, or friend 被拋棄的；被遺棄的：*a deserted wife* 棄婦

forlorn sad and lonely because you have been deserted (因被遺棄而) 孤苦伶仃的，孤獨淒涼的：*a forlorn figure all alone on the beach* 海灘上孤獨淒涼的身影

isolated feeling lonely because you have no friends nearby（由於沒有朋友而感覺）孤獨的，孤立的：*I felt isolated when I moved from the city to the country.* 我從城市搬到鄉下時感到很孤獨。

lonely unhappy because you are alone (因為形單影隻而感到) 孤獨的，寂寞的：*It can be very lonely at first when you go away to university.* 離家上大學之初，你會感到很寂寞。

angry *adjective* having a strong negative feeling about something and a wish to do something, possibly something violent, to change things or take revenge 生氣的；憤怒的：*I was so angry about the way the shop assistant treated me, I complained to the manager.* 商店店員的態度使我十分生氣，於是向經理投訴。

annoyed feeling mildly angry and impatient 惱怒的；不耐煩的：*She was annoyed by his persistence.* 他的固執使她感到惱火。

cross (*informal*) moderately angry 惱怒的；生氣的：*My mum was cross with me for breaking a vase.* 媽媽對我打碎花瓶的行為相當生氣。

enraged feeling intensely angry and likely to do something violent 非常憤怒的；激怒的：*He was so enraged by their refusal to let him in that he threatened to break down the door.* 他們拒絕讓他進去使他憤怒至極，他甚至威脅説要破門而入。

furious feeling or showing extreme anger 狂怒的；暴怒的：*Furious at being ignored, she stormed out.* 因為沒人理睬，她怒不可遏，氣沖沖地離開了。

heated in which angry words are spoken（言辭）激烈的：*a heated argument* 激烈的爭論

incensed feeling extremely angry because you feel that a moral wrong has been done（因為犯道德錯誤而）極端憤怒的：*Incensed by his brother's treachery, the king ordered his immediate execution.* 兄弟的背信棄義令國王勃然大怒，於是下令立即處死他。

indignant feeling or showing anger and resentment because of something that seems unfair or unjust（因為不公平的事情而）憤慨的，憤憤不平的：*She got very indignant when I suggested that it was her fault that we had to cancel the party.* 當我暗示説是她的過失使我們不得不取消聚會時，她大為光火。

irate (*formal*) very angry and upset 極其憤怒的；暴怒的：*appeasing an irate customer* 安撫一個憤怒的顧客

mad (*informal*) feeling anger 感到生氣的：*He went mad just because I was ten minutes late!* 我不過遲到了 10 分鐘他就非常生氣。

➲ see also 參見 **annoy**

annoy *verb* to make someone feel mildly angry 使惱怒；使生氣：*It annoys me when you leave the lid off the toothpaste.* 你不蓋上牙膏蓋讓我不高興。

aggravate (*informal*) to annoy and provoke someone deliberately（故意）激怒，惹惱（某人）：*He's only playing that stupid drum because he knows it aggravates me!* 他一個勁兒地敲打那破鼓，因為他知道那樣做能激怒我。

bother to hinder or prevent someone from doing something by persistently trying to get their attention 煩擾，打擾（某人）：*Stop bothering your dad when he's trying to rest!* 你爸爸要休息時別打擾他！

displease (*formal*) to make someone mildly unhappy and annoyed by what you do 使不悦；使惱怒：*He didn't voice his misgivings for fear of displeasing the President.* 因害怕總統生氣，他沒有説出自己的疑慮。

exasperate to make someone feel more and more annoyed and frustrated, usually because you will not or cannot do what they want you to do（通常因沒有按他人要求辦事而）使煩惱，使惱怒：*I was exasperated by his failure to understand my point of view.* 他不理解我的觀點讓我非常惱火。

get on someone's nerves (*informal*) to make someone irritable or cause them to lose patience, usually by doing something annoying again and again or over a long period of time（因反覆或長時間做惱人之事而）使人惱怒，使

人煩燥：*It really gets on my nerves when you repeat everything I say.* 你這樣鸚鵡學舌真使我心煩。

hack off (*informal*) to make someone feel frustrated and impatient 使沮喪；使心煩：*I'm getting seriously hacked off with that racket from upstairs.* 樓上的喧嘩聲令我不勝其煩。

irritate to cause someone to feel a mild degree of anger and impatience 使惱怒；使心煩：*His whiney voice really irritates me.* 他嘀嘀咕咕的牢騷聲真讓我心煩。

vex to make someone feel angry and upset 使惱怒；使憂慮：*It vexed him to see the old lady struggling to make ends meet.* 看到老婦人艱難地維持生計，他憂心忡忡。

➲ see also 參見 **angry**

answer¹ *verb* to say something in reaction to question that you have been asked 回答（問題）：*She refused to answer any questions about her marriage break-up.* 她拒絕回答任何關於她婚姻破裂的問題。

acknowledge to show that you have received something such as a letter, or noticed something such as a greeting, by doing something in return 告知收悉；（以某種方式）致意：*I am writing to acknowledge receipt of your message sent yesterday.* 特此致函告知昨日所發信息已收悉。

get back to (*informal*) to contact someone again to give your response to a subject previously discussed 以後再回覆：*I'll get back to you later about the stag night.* 關於男子婚前聚會的情況我以後再回覆你。

reply to say in response to a question or remark 回答，答覆（問題或話）：*'No, thank you. I've had enough,' he replied.* "不，謝謝你。我已經飽了。"他回答道。

respond to react to what someone has said or done（對某人所說或所為）作出回應；回答：*She responded to his threat by calling his bluff.* 面對他的威脅，她說她奉陪到底。

answer² *noun* something said in reaction to a question that has been asked（對問題的）回答，答案：*The answer to your question is 'No'.* 對於你的問題，答案是"不"。

rejoinder (*formal*) a clever reply, usually spoken and made during an argument or discussion in response to another person's reply to a question（爭論或討論中對他人回答的）反駁，回應：*Simpson's brilliant rejoinder brought their witty repartee to a close.* 辛普森絕妙的反駁結束了這場機智的辯論。

reply a spoken or written response to what someone has said or written（口頭或書面的）回覆：*I am waiting for a reply to my job application.* 我正等着求職申請的回覆。

response a reaction to an event or to what someone says（對事件或言論的）反應，回應：*Her only response to his comment was a coy smile.* 她對於他的評論僅報以靦腆的一笑。

retort a spoken reply that is made in a sharp tone and attacks the person who asked the original question（對提問人尖銳的）反駁，口頭還擊：*I'll start* *minding my own business, when you stop letting your business go to rack and ruin' was Stephen's witty retort.* "你的事情不再一團糟的時候便是我少管閒事之時。"史提芬如此反駁。

riposte a quick witty spoken response made in retaliation 機敏的回答；巧妙的反駁：*Joan's quick-witted riposte silenced her detractors.* 瓊機智敏銳的應答讓詆毀者閉上了嘴。

anxiety *noun* a feeling of worry about possible harm that may happen to you or to someone or something else (對可能發生的傷害的) 焦慮，擔憂：*The thought of driving in the snow filled her with anxiety.* 一想到在雪地裏駕車她就憂心忡忡。

anguish intense mental suffering 極度的精神痛苦：*Having to report her own son to the police caused her great anguish.* 她不得不向警察告發自己的兒子，這讓她感到極度痛苦。

apprehension a feeling of nervousness and fear that something bad may be about to happen (對可能發生的不祥之事感到的) 擔心，恐懼：*Sue was filled with apprehension about her first parachute jump.* 蘇珊對自己第一次跳傘擔心不已。

care something that causes you to worry because you feel an emotional involvement or responsibility (因情感上的瓜葛或責任而產生的) 煩惱事，操心事：*She seemed weighed down with cares.* 她顯得憂心忡忡。

concern a state of worry combined with caring about someone's wellbeing (對他人的) 關心，擔憂，掛念：*I appreciate your concern for my safety.* 我感激你記掛着我的安全。

foreboding a strong feeling that something bad is going to happen in the future, often quite soon (對即將發生的不祥之事的) 強烈預感：*The house was unusually quiet, and I had a terrible sense of foreboding as I walked up the path to the front door.* 房子裏異乎尋常的安靜，當我沿着小道走到前門時，便有了一種可怕的不祥之感。

stress a state of being under mental or emotional pressure (精神或情感的) 壓力：*She is under stress because of the exams.* 她因為考試而產生心理壓力。

unease a feeling that something is wrong or that there may be danger or difficulty, which makes you uncomfortable and nervous (因擔心出錯、危險或困難而產生的) 心神不安：*His obvious unease was because he had a guilty conscience.* 良心上的內疚使他表現出明顯的不安。

worry a troubled state of mind arising from a difficult situation or from something bad that you fear might happen (對困難的處境或可能發生的不祥而產生的) 憂慮，擔憂：*Her husband's gambling has caused her a great deal of worry.* 她丈夫好賭使她憂慮重重。

➲ see also 參見 **fear**

appreciate *verb* to enjoy something because you understand what makes it good 欣賞，鑒賞 (某物)：*You don't appreciate good music.* 你不會欣賞好音樂。

cherish to hold dear something such as a gift, memento or memory that is important to you on a personal level 珍愛，愛惜 (禮物、紀念品、記憶等)：*I cherish every little gift she ever gave me.* 我珍愛她給我的每一件小禮物。

enjoy to get great pleasure from an activity or an object 享受（某項活動）的樂趣；喜愛（某物）；樂於（某事）: *He has always enjoyed fine wine.* 他總是喜歡品嚐好酒。

prize to place a high value on something, such as a possession or a quality 珍視，重視，看重（某物品、品質等）: *He prizes that battered old guitar above any other item in his collection.* 在他的收藏品中，他最看重那支又破又舊的結他。

savour to take the time and enjoy something pleasurable, especially a taste or smell, fully 品味，體味，細品（尤指令人愉悅的味道、氣味等）: *I like to eat slowly and savour my food.* 我喜歡細嚼慢嚥，細細品味食物。

treasure to consider something, such as a memory, precious 珍視，珍愛，珍重（回憶等）: *I treasure the time we spent together.* 我珍視我們在一起的時光。

value to hold something, such as someone's opinion or a quality, in high esteem 尊重，重視，珍視（某人的觀點、品質等）: *My grandmother is one person whose opinion I value.* 我很重視我祖母的觀點。

welcome to accept gratefully something such as an opportunity or a break 感激地接受（機會、好運等）: *I welcome the opportunity to present my side of the story.* 我很感激能有機會陳述我對此事的看法。

appropriate *adjective* of the right kind or nature to suit a particular event or situation （對特定事件或場合）合適的，恰當的: *an outfit appropriate for a wedding* 適合婚禮穿的一套服裝

applicable that concerns or has to do with a particular person or a particular case （對特定的人或情況）適用的，合適的: *These sections are only applicable if you are applying for a passport for the first time.* 這些條款只適用於第一次申請護照。

apposite (*formal*) that is relevant, made at the right time, and comments interestingly on the subject （時間或評論）適當的，恰當的: *a most apposite remark* 恰如其分的評論

apt that suits the circumstances or describes something very well （環境或描述）適合的，貼切的: *an apt description* 恰當的描述

correct in accordance with the rules or conventions, especially those that deal with social behaviour 恰當的；合乎（規範、習俗或社交行為）的: *He's never been taught the correct way to behave at a formal dinner.* 從來沒有人教過他在正式宴會上恰當的禮儀。

fitting particularly suitable or well deserved 特別適合的；相稱的: *a fitting tribute to a courageous woman* 對一個勇敢的婦女恰如其分的褒獎

proper being the only one that is considered right for a particular purpose （對特定目的）適當的，唯一適合的: *That's not the proper place for that CD.* 把那隻光碟放在那裏並不合適。

relevant to do with the matter that is being discussed or dealt with and not with something else 相關聯的；切題的: *If what you have to say is relevant to the discussion, say it; if it isn't, don't.* 如果你要說的與討論有關，就說出來；不然就別說。

right that is needed in or is best for a particular situation（特定情形下）適宜的：*There's no doubt that she's the right person for the job.* 毫無疑問她是這份工作的最佳人選。

seemly (*old-fashioned*) correct in a particular situation, according to convention（特定情形下）適宜的，得體的，符合習俗的：*His remarriage so soon after his wife's death was not considered seemly.* 他在妻子死後很快再婚被認為是不恰當的。

suitable right for a particular purpose or occasion（對特定目的或某種場合）合適的，適宜的：*She was not considered suitable for the job.* 人們認為她不適合幹這份工作。

approval *noun* the act of stating that you think something is good or that you will allow something to take place 同意；贊成；批准：*The matter has been settled, subject to approval by the board of directors.* 這事已確定了，就等董事會的正式批准了。

agreement the act of saying or showing that you give permission for a course of action（對某做法的）贊同，許可：*He is making this journey with his doctor's agreement.* 他這次旅行是徵得醫生同意的。

authorization official permission to do something, for example to enter a private area（正式的）批准，授權：*Do you have authorization to go beyond this barrier?* 你有穿越這道關卡的授權嗎？

blessing warm approval of a proposed course of action, such as a marriage（對所提出的某種做法的）贊同，贊成：*We don't need your permission to get married but we would like your blessing.* 我們結婚雖然不需要經過你的許可，但我們還是希望得到你的同意。

endorsement support for someone's course of action or opinion（對某種做法或觀點的）支持：*Your silence on the matter will be seen as endorsement of their view.* 你對此事態度沉默會被看作是支持他們的觀點。

go-ahead (*informal*) permission to proceed with a plan（對某一計劃的）批准，許可：*We finally got the go-ahead to take on extra staff.* 我們最終得到許可僱用額外的人手。

permission the act of allowing someone to do something they want to do 准許，許可，批准（做想做之事）：*I have my son's permission to show you his letter.* 我徵得兒子的同意給你看他的信件。

sanction official permission to follow a particular course of action（正式的）批准，許可，同意：*This information was made public with the Government's sanction.* 經過政府的批准，這條消息得以公開。

argument *noun* a situation in which two or more people disagree about something and try to change each other's views, often getting angry in the process 爭論；爭吵：*She stormed out after an argument with her boyfriend.* 與男友吵架後，她氣沖沖地出門了。

altercation (*formal*) an angry exchange of words 口角；爭執：*There was a vehement altercation between an irate customer and the restaurant manager.* 惱羞成怒的顧客與飯店經理之間發生了激烈的爭執。

dispute a difference of opinion between individuals or groups about a matter that is considered serious, often resulting in hostility（常導致敵對的）

爭論，爭吵：*an industrial dispute between management and the union* 勞資雙方的工業糾紛

feud a long-running disagreement or hostile relationship, especially between two families（尤指家族間的）長期不和，世仇，夙怨：*a bitter five-year feud with our next-door neighbours* 我們與隔壁鄰居長達 5 年的夙怨

fight (*informal*) an angry disagreement, especially between partners, friends, or members of a family（尤指夥伴、朋友或家庭成員間的）爭吵，吵架：*We had another fight about money last night.* 昨晚我們又為錢發生了爭吵。

quarrel an angry disagreement between friends（朋友間的）爭吵，口角：*The two girls had a quarrel but made up soon after.* 這兩個女孩發生了口角，但很快就和解了。

row a noisy disagreement, usually between partners or family members（通常指夥伴或家庭成員間）嘈雜的爭論；爭吵：*My brother and his wife had a huge row at the dinner table.* 我兄弟和他妻子吃飯時大聲地爭吵起來。

squabble an argument over something trivial（由瑣事引起的）爭吵：*a squabble over whose turn it is to take the rubbish out* 由誰該倒垃圾引起的爭吵

➲ see also 參見 **disagree; quarrel**

arrive *verb* to reach a place, especially after a journey（尤指經過一段旅程後）到達：*After a long trek through the mountains, we arrived safely in the village.* 我們長途跋涉穿越越山區後安全到達村莊。

appear to come into view or to be present in a place 出現；出席：*When I fell over, a nice young man appeared as if from nowhere and helped me to my feet.* 在我跌倒時，不知從哪兒冒出了一個好心的小伙子扶起我。

come to move towards the place where you are 來，走到（所在的位置）：*What time are the children coming home?* 孩子們甚麼時候回家？

enter to come into a place 進入（某地）：*The Prime Minister entered the building, surrounded by police officers.* 總理在警員們的簇擁下進入大樓。

land to come to the end of a journey by air（飛機）着陸：*We land at Miami Airport at 10.00 am.* 上午 10 點我們在邁阿密機場着陸。

put in an appearance to attend a social event for a short time only, although you may not be keen to attend at all（儘管無興趣仍然短暫地）出席，露面，到場：*Simon put in an appearance at the wedding reception just before the bride and groom left.* 西蒙趕在新郎、新娘離開前到婚宴上露了一面。

reach to arrive at a place, especially at the end of a journey 到達（尤指終點）：*The climbers reached the top of the mountain without mishap.* 登山者都順利地到達了山頂。

show up (*informal*) to arrive at a place as arranged or expected（按計劃或預期）來到，露面：*I was expecting ten guests but only eight showed up.* 我原指望有 10 位客人，結果只來了 8 位。

turn up (*informal*) to appear somewhere, often unexpectedly（常指出乎意料地）出現，露面：*My aunt's ex-husband turned up unexpectedly at her funeral.* 我姑媽的前夫意外地出現在她的葬禮上。

artificial *adjective* not natural, but made by human beings – often to look like something natural 人造的，非天然的（但通常看上去很自然的）: *artificial flowers* 假花

counterfeit made to look like something genuine, especially money, but false and intended to defraud（尤指以詐騙為目的的錢幣）偽造的，假冒的: *He was arrested trying to use a counterfeit £20 note.* 他因試圖使用一張 20 英鎊的假鈔而被捕。

fake not genuine, especially because manufactured using non-natural ingredients to produce the effect of something natural 假的，冒充的（尤指採用非天然材料達到天然產品的效果）: *fake fur* 假毛皮

false manufactured to look like and take the place of something such as a part of the body or of a structure 假的，人造的（與真品一樣的替代品，如身體或某構造部分的替代品）: *false teeth* 假牙

imitation manufactured to look like something natural, but usually regarded as inferior to the natural version 仿製的，仿造的（但通常在質量上遜於自然品）: *imitation leather* 人造皮革

man-made not produced naturally but manufactured, usually from non-natural materials, and sometimes having advantages over the natural version 人造的（通常指採用非天然材料生產，但有時在質量上卻優於天然品）: *man-made fibres* 人造纖維

mock made in imitation of something and generally regarded as inferior to the genuine article 仿造的，仿製的（通常在質量上遜於真品）: *mock-Tudor beams* 仿都鐸式房樑

simulated done in such a way as to imitate a natural action or recreate conditions in the real world 模擬的；仿真的: *Police cadets have to deal with simulated riot conditions as part of their training.* 警校的學生們必須處理模擬騷亂場景，作為訓練課之一。

synthetic produced by combining chemical substances and used as a substitute for something natural 人造的；合成的: *synthetic rubber* 合成橡膠

ashamed *adjective* having a strong feeling of guilt and embarrassment about something wrong that you have done（因做錯事而感到）慚愧的，羞恥的: *I was deeply ashamed of the way I had treated her.* 我對自己以那種方式對待她深感羞愧。

abashed feeling embarrassed, self-conscious, or rather humiliated, usually because someone has called attention to a mistake you made or a wrong you did（通常指因被提醒所犯錯誤而感到）尷尬的，窘迫的，羞愧的: *She was not in the least abashed, though it was perfectly plain that she was the cause of all this unnecessary trouble.* 很顯然所有這些不必要的麻煩都是她引起的，但她卻沒有絲毫的羞愧。

conscience-stricken feeling very guilty about some wrongdoing（因做壞事而）內疚的，良心不安的: *Beth was conscience-stricken about having offended her hostess.* 貝絲因惹惱了她的女房東而感到內疚。

embarrassed feeling shy or uncomfortable in a particular situation, e.g., when talking about sex（在特定情況下，如談論性問題時）尷尬的，不好意思

的：*I was so embarrassed when I forgot my lines in the play.* 我在演出中忘掉台詞，感到非常尷尬。

guilty knowing that you did something wrong and feeling rather bad about it（知道自己做錯事而）內疚的，有犯罪感的：*I felt guilty about not including Jackie in our plans.* 沒把積奇納入我們的計劃，我感到內疚。

humbled feeling that someone else's actions show great goodness or generosity and that you might not be as good or generous in the same situation 自愧不如的：*He felt humbled by the generosity of these people who had so little but were willing to share what they had.* 這些人雖擁有不多但卻樂於與人分享的慷慨行為使他感到自愧不如。

humiliated having been made, often deliberately, that you are very bad or very unimportant person 羞辱的，丟臉的：*I felt humiliated when the whole class laughed at my answer.* 全班人都嘲笑我的回答，這讓我感到很丟臉。

sheepish looking embarrassed or self-conscious, for example because you have been caught doing something wrong（如因被發現做錯事而）窘迫的，難為情的：*She looked rather sheepish as I caught her taking the last biscuit.* 我撞見她拿最後一塊餅乾時，她顯得非常尷尬。

➲ see also 參見 **disgrace**

ask *verb* to direct a question or request at someone 問；詢問：*'What time is it?' he asked.* "現在幾點了？"他問道。

beg to ask someone earnestly to give you something or to do something for you 懇求；祈求：*The dying woman begged her friend to make sure her children were looked after.* 這位婦人臨終懇求朋友一定要讓她的孩子們得到照顧。

demand to ask for information insistently or forcefully 一再查問；強烈要求：*'Where's your purse?' the burglar demanded.* "你的錢包在哪兒？"竊賊一再追問道。

enquire* to try to find out information about something 問明；探究：*I'm enquiring about the availability of flights to Barcelona.* 我在打聽到巴塞隆拿的航班情況。

* The spelling enquire is commoner in British English, but in US English the word is usually spelt inquire. Enquire 在英國英語的拼寫中更常見，但在美國英語中通常寫為 inquire。

grill (*informal*) to question someone very thoroughly, sometimes in a hostile way, to find out how much they know, what they think, etc.（有時指充滿敵意地詳細）盤問，追問，審問：*They grilled me on my reasons for wanting to work for the company.* 他們仔細盤問我願意為這家公司效勞的原因。

interrogate to ask someone a series of probing questions, especially in some official capacity（尤指通過官方）審問，盤問，訊問：*The murder suspect was interrogated by the police.* 這個謀殺案疑犯受到警察盤問。

invite to ask someone to join you at a social event 邀請：*We have been invited to a party on Saturday.* 我們被邀請參加週六的聚會。

question to ask someone a series of questions, especially during an interview or an investigation（尤指在面試或調查中）質詢，詢問：*Police*

questioned the man for several hours, but eventually released him. 警察查問了
這位男子好幾個小時，但最終還是將他釋放了。

quiz to ask someone a lot of questions 詢 問 ， 盤 問：*Her grandmother quizzed her about her new boyfriend.* 她祖母仔細詢問了她新男友的情況。

request to ask if you can have something 要求；請求：*I have requested a window seat.* 我已經要求了一個靠窗的座位。

assistant *noun* a person whose job or task is to help someone 助理；助手：
The director would be totally disorganized without his personal assistant. 要是沒
有私人助理，主管會亂得一塌糊塗。

accomplice a person who helps someone to commit a crime 幫兇；同謀者：
The thief stole my purse while his accomplice distracted me. 趁同夥轉移了我
的注意力，小偷把我的錢包偷走了。

aide a person whose job is to assist an important person（重要人物的）助
理，隨從：*The President arrived, surrounded by his aides.* 總統在隨從的簇擁
下到達。

auxiliary an untrained person who assists trained colleagues, especially in a hospital or in the armed forces（尤指在醫院或軍隊的）輔助工，輔助人員：*a nursing auxiliary* 護理輔助人員

colleague a person who works for the same organization or in the same department as you 同事：*She has gone out for dinner with her colleagues from the office.* 她和公司的同事一起出去吃晚飯了。

deputy a person who substitutes for a superior when he or she is absent 副 手；代 理：*While the head teacher is away having an operation, her deputy will take over her duties.* 校長離開工作崗位接受手術時，她的副手代
行其職。

helper any person who helps another 幫手；助手：*I am looking for a helper to tidy up after the party.* 我要找一個幫手在聚會後幫我收拾整理一下。

right-hand man or woman a person who assists someone in authority and on whom they rely heavily 左右手，左膀右臂；得力助手：*The prime minister often called his press assistant his right-hand man.* 首相常把他的新聞助理稱作
他的左右手。

second-in-command the person who has second most authority in an organization 副手；副官：*The manager has had invaluable support from his second-in-command.* 經理從他的副手那兒得到了寶貴的支持。

assume *verb* to accept that something is true without checking that it is true 假設；假定；以為：*I assumed the woman he was with was his wife.* 我以為
跟他在一起的女人是他妻子。

believe to think quite strongly that something is true, even though you cannot be certain about it or prove that it is true 相信；認為：*I believe the new neighbours are American.* 我想這些新鄰居是美國人。

guess *(informal)* to suppose something is the case without knowing or thinking very much about it 猜測；猜想：*I guess we must have been a bit drunk at the time.* 我猜想當時我們肯定有些醉了。

imagine to think that something is the case, based on a certain amount of information plus imagination 想像；設想：*I imagine that must have been a frightening experience.* 我想像那肯定是一次令人恐懼的經歷。

presume to act as if something is the case, without knowing for certain that it is, unless or until it is proven not to be 假設；假定；推定：*Legally you are presumed innocent until proven guilty.* 從法律上講，在證明你有罪之前，你被假定為無罪。

suppose to think that something is likely to be the case, but realizing that you could quite easily be wrong 推斷；料想：*I suppose the heavy rain must have caused the car to skid.* 我料想肯定是這場大雨導致跌車。

take for granted to believe something to be the case without questioning it 想當然地認為：*The singer took it for granted that everyone would pander to her wishes.* 這位歌手想當然地認為每個人都會迎合她的心願。

think to have an idea or opinion about something, often a rather vague one and always without being sure about it 認為，以為（常指不明確的或不確定的想法）：*I took my umbrella because I thought it was going to rain.* 我帶了傘，因為我以為會下雨。

⊃ see also 參見 **guess**

attack[1] *verb* to use force to try to harm or capture someone or something 襲擊，攻擊（人或物）：*He was attacked by a mountain lion.* 他遭到一隻山獅的襲擊。

ambush to attack someone after hiding and waiting for them to come by 伏擊（某人）：*The travelers were ambushed by bandits.* 遊客們遭到了土匪的伏擊。

assault to attack someone violently 暴力襲擊，猛烈攻擊（某人）：*The old Lady was assaulted by a strange man in her own home.* 老太太在家裏遭到一個陌生人的襲擊。

beat up (*informal*) to hit or kick someone repeatedly 毒打，痛毆（某人）：*He got beaten up by a gang of thugs.* 他被一伙暴徒痛毆了一頓。

mug to attack someone physically and rob them 行兇搶劫，打劫（某人）：*She was mugged on her way home from the bank.* 她在從銀行回家的路上被打劫了。

storm to make a swift and sudden attack on a building or other place with a large force, in order to capture it or the people inside it 突然襲擊，攻佔（某處）：*The army stormed the citadel.* 軍隊突襲了這座城堡。

vilify (*formal*) to say bad things about a person's character in a vicious way 污衊；誹謗；中傷；詆毀：*He was vilified by the media for his association with prominent figures in the world of organized crime.* 他被媒體污衊與犯罪集團的頭目有聯繫。

attack[2] *verb* to use words to show your negative feelings or opinions about someone or something（用語言）抨擊，非難：*The right-wing press attacked the government's policy on immigration.* 右翼傳媒抨擊政府的移民政策。

berate (*formal*) to scold someone angrily 嚴厲指責；痛斥：*I was berated for being obstructive.* 我因固執己見而受到嚴厲指責。

blast (*informal*) to criticize someone severely 嚴厲批評，激烈抨擊（某人）: *He was blasted in the tabloids for his racist remarks.* 他因發表種族主義言論而受到小報的嚴厲抨擊。

criticize to say that someone has behaved badly or that something is bad or faulty 批評；指責，責備: *She was heavily criticized for putting her career before her family.* 她因把事業放在比家庭更重要的位置而受到嚴厲指責。

scold to use angry words to show your disapproval of someone or their behavior 責罵，訓斥: *My mother scolded me for coming home so late.* 我因回家太晚受到媽媽的訓斥。

attack³ *noun* an attempt, using force, to harm or capture someone or something: （武力）襲擊，攻擊: *The city is under attack from the air.* 這座城市正在遭受空襲。

assault a sudden violent attack on a person or on enemy territory 人身傷害；襲擊；攻擊: *a serious assault on a homeless man* 對一名無家可歸者的嚴重傷害

offensive an attack or series of attacks on a military target （對軍事目標的）進攻，攻擊: *The latest offensive has resulted in heavy casualties among the allies.* 最近一次進攻給聯軍帶來了巨大傷亡。

onslaught a violent and forceful physical or verbal attack （身體或語言的）猛烈攻擊: *Few of his colleagues thought he would survive the onslaught from the media.* 他的同事幾乎都認為他抵受不住傳媒的抨擊。

raid a sudden small-scale attack by military forces into enemy territory, or an unexpected attack on a building or other place by police or criminals （部隊小規模的）突然襲擊；（警察的）突然搜查；（罪犯的）搶劫: *a bank raid* 一宗銀行搶劫案

strike a military attack on a place, usually from the air 軍事行動；襲擊（通常指空襲）: *an air strike on the capital* 一次對首都的空襲

➲ see also 參見 **invade**

avoid *verb* not to hit an object, not to meet a person, or not to become involved in a situation 避免，迴避（某物、某人或捲入某事）: *She crossed the road to avoid her ex-boyfriend.* 她橫過馬路，避免遇見前男友。

dodge to move aside quickly in order to avoid being hit；to avoid doing something, especially in a dishonest way 閃開；躲開；（尤指以欺騙方式）逃避: *The boy dodged out of the way of the oncoming car.* 男孩躲開了迎面駛來的汽車。

duck out of (*informal*) to avoid doing something you have arranged to do 推脫，迴避（已經安排之事）: *He ducked out of taking the kids swimming.* 他借故不帶孩子們去游泳。

elude to avoid being caught or discovered by someone 躲避；避開；避免（被抓住或發現）: *The singer eluded the paparazzi by slipping out by the back door.* 那歌星為避開狗仔隊從後門溜走了。

escape to succeed in avoiding an unpleasant situation or outcome 逃脫，擺脫: *The boys escaped punishment by giving each other alibis.* 男孩們通過互相證明不在事發現場，逃脫了懲罰。

eschew (*formal*) not to do something or become involved in something that you think is undesirable 避開，迴避（不願意做的事）：*an artistic genius who eschews commercialism* 一個拒絕商業化的藝術天才

evade to deliberately avoid doing something that you should do（有意）逃避，規避（應做之事）：*He was arrested for evading income tax.* 他因逃避所得稅而被捕。

shun to deliberately avoid someone because you do not like them or are displeased with them（因不喜歡或不滿而刻意）迴避，避開（某人）：*She was shunned by her family when she married a gangster.* 她和一個歹徒結婚後，家人都躲着她。

sidestep to skillfully avoid dealing with a subject you don't want to deal with（巧妙地）迴避，規避（不想處理的問題）：*The prime minister sidestepped all questions about the war.* 首相迴避了所有關於戰爭的問題。

➲ see also 參見 **prevent**

aware *adjective* having knowledge or consciousness of something 知道的；意識到的：*Are you aware that Sam has a black belt in karate?* 你知道森姆有一條空手道黑腰帶嗎？

acquainted well informed about a subject 熟悉的；了解的：*fully acquainted with the rules of backgammon* 熟知百家樂的規則

alert watching and concentrating, so as to notice anything unusual, especially danger, immediately（尤指對危險等不尋常之事）警覺的，注意的：*alert to the dangers of windsurfing* 慎防風帆運動的危險

clued up (*informal*) having detailed knowledge about a subject（對某事）所知甚多的，很熟悉的：*He is well clued up on hip-hop.* 他非常熟悉嘻哈文化。

cognizant (*formal*) having full knowledge and understanding of a subject 知曉的；熟知的：*Are you cognizant of the terms of the contract?* 你對合同的條款熟悉嗎？

conscious noticing or feeling something that is happening 意識到的；注意到的：*conscious of being stared at* 覺察到有人盯着自己

informed having a lot of information about a particular subject 有學問的；有見識的：*politically informed* 對政治熟悉的

knowledgeable knowing a lot about a particular subject 知識淵博的；博學的；有見識的：*We need someone who is knowledgeable about civil rights.* 我們需要一個精通民權的人。

mindful bearing in mind the importance of something 留心的；不忘記的：*ever mindful of the need for caution* 隨時記着要小心謹慎

B

back *verb* to give help and encouragement to someone, or to show approval and support for something 支持，幫助（某人）；贊成（某事）：*If you decide to oppose the management on this issue, we'd back you all the way.* 如果你決定在這個問題上與資方針鋒相對，我們自始至終都支持你。

advocate to argue in favor of a course of action or a cause 提倡，倡導：*an MP who advocates capital punishment* 一個提倡死刑的國會議員

champion to support and defend a person or a cause 捍衛，擁護（某人或事業）：*He championed the Cubist movement.* 他擁護立體主義藝術運動。

encourage to give someone emotional support and boost their confidence 鼓勵，激勵，鼓舞：*He could always depend on his wife to encourage him when he felt low.* 他感到消沉時妻子總是鼓勵他。

endorse to show strong approval of someone's course of action or opinion （對某人的行為或主張）極力贊成，支持：*I heartily endorse your views on complementary medicine.* 我由衷地贊成你關於輔助性療法的觀點。

promote to speak or take action in order to encourage other people to adopt a particular course of action or to support a cause 促進；推進；推動：*The local authority promotes recycling by providing households with separate containers for different types of refuse.* 地方當局為家庭提供分類垃圾箱分裝不同類型的垃圾，以此推動回收再用。

second to speak in support of a motion made by a previous speaker in a meeting or debate（在會議或辯論中）附議，贊成：*Kathy proposed that we accept the company's offer, and Paul seconded the motion.* 凱西建議我們接受公司的提議，保羅對此表示贊成。

support to take action to help someone or something that you approve of 捍衛，支援（人或事）：*We support various charities, not only by giving money, but also by taking part in fund-raising events.* 我們支持各種形式的慈善活動，不僅提供現金，還參加一些籌款活動。

uphold to defend a belief or a decision, often against opposition 捍衛，維護，維持（信念或決定）：*She always upheld the cause of women's rights.* 她始終支持女權事業。

⊃ see also 參見 **support**

bad[1] *adjective* doing things that are wicked or harmful 邪惡的；有害的：*The bad fairy cast a spell on the princess.* 邪惡的魔女對公主施了咒語。

corrupt committing acts that are morally wrong, usually for money 腐敗的；貪污的：*a corrupt police officer who accepts bribes* 一個收受賄賂的貪污警察

criminal committing acts that are against the law 犯罪的；犯法的：*He is known to have criminal tendencies.* 人們知道他有犯罪傾向。

evil capable of committing extremely wicked acts, such as murder 極端邪惡的；罪惡的：*an evil dictator* 一個罪惡的獨裁者

immoral committing acts that are generally considered morally wrong 不道德的；道德敗壞的：*Many people consider prostitution immoral.* 許多人認為賣淫是不道德的。

malicious intending to cause people harm 懷有惡意的；惡毒的：*malicious gossip* 惡毒的流言蜚語

mischievous deliberately causing trouble, but not of a serious nature 惡作劇的；淘氣的：*The mischievous child rang the doorbell and ran away.* 那淘氣的小孩按了門鈴就跑了。

nasty unpleasant and cruel 令人厭惡的；兇惡的：*By betraying his best friend, Craig has shown that he has a nasty streak.* 克雷格出賣了他最好的朋友，顯露出他卑鄙的性格。

naughty badly behaved, but not in a serious way 頑皮的；調皮搗蛋的：*Tom was sent to bed early because he had been a naughty boy.* 湯姆因為調皮搗蛋被早早地送上了牀。

wicked deliberately causing harm to people（故意）造成傷害的，傷天害理的：*Stealing your sister's boyfriend was a wicked thing to do.* 搶走你姐姐的男朋友是傷天害理的事。

bad² *adjective* having a harmful effect 不利的；有害的：*Smoking is bad for your health.* 吸煙有害健康。

adverse causing difficulties or problems, or unfavorable to what you want to do 不利的；反面的；有害的：*The adverse effects of using the drug were not pointed out in the report.* 報告中沒有指出使用那種藥的副作用。

damaging causing usually non-physical damage,e.g.,to someone's health or reputation（對健康或名譽等）造成損害的，有害的：*This story could be seriously damaging to your chances of promotion.* 這個報道可能會嚴重破壞你晉升的機會。

detrimental having a harmful effect 有害的；不利的：*Living in a damp flat would be detrimental to the children's health.* 生活在潮濕的房子裏對孩子們的健康有害。

harmful causing danger to people or damage to objects 有害的；導致損害的：*substances that are harmful to the environment* 對環境有害的物質

unhealthy harmful to your health 不健康的；對健康有害的：*unhealthy living conditions* 有礙健康的生活條件

bad³ *adjective* causing a lot of trouble, pain, or worry 煩惱的；疼痛的：*She went to bed with a bad headache.* 她頭痛得厲害就上牀睡了。

dreadful (*informal*) very unpleasant or severe 令人不快的；嚴重的：*I had dreadful toothache.* 我牙疼得厲害。

major large in scale and causing great difficulties 主要的；較嚴重的：*major problems* 主要問題

nasty unpleasant and troublesome, but not necessarily serious 令人不悅的，令人厭惡的，麻煩的（但不一定嚴重的）：*a nasty cold* 令人討厭的感冒

serious causing, or likely to cause, a great deal of harm or trouble 嚴重的；有危險的：*a serious illness* 嚴重的疾病

severe worse than serious, very threatening to people's well-being 十分嚴重的，極為惡劣的（以至威脅健康的）：*The man sustained severe burns in the explosion.* 那個男人在爆炸中被嚴重燒傷。

terrible (*informal*) very unpleasant or severe 令人極不愉快的；非常討厭的；十分嚴重的：*He had a terrible hangover the morning after the party.* 他在聚會後第二天早晨出現嚴重的宿醉。

bad⁴ *adjective* of low quality or lacking in skill 劣質的；蹩腳的：*Bill is a really bad singer.* 比爾唱歌唱得真差。

defective having a fault or defect 有缺陷的；有毛病的：*I returned the hairdryer to the shop because it was defective.* 電風筒有毛病，我把它退回商店。

imperfect containing mistakes or flaws 不完美的；有缺點的；有缺陷的：*He seemed to understand my imperfect French.* 他似乎聽懂了我蹩腳的法語。

poor of a low standard or low quality 劣質的；拙劣的：*The leading man gave a poor performance on opening night.* 男主角在首演那晚的表演很拙劣。

shoddy done or made without skill 手工粗糙的；粗製濫造的：*shoddy workmanship* 粗糙的工藝

substandard not reaching the required or expected standard 未達到標準的；不合格的：*an excellent CD with no substandard tracks* 歌曲質量全部達標的優質光碟

⮑ see also 參見 **inferior**

ban *verb* to forbid someone, officially, to do something（尤指官方）明令禁止（某人做某事）：*She has been banned from driving for a year.* 她被禁止駕駛一年。

bar to forbid someone to enter a place, such as a pub or club 阻止，禁止（某人進入酒吧或俱樂部等）：*Wayne has been barred from the rugby club for starting a fight.* 韋恩因為引發一場打鬥被禁止進入欖球俱樂部。

disallow to reject something, such as a score in a game, as being invalid because it breaks a rule 不准許，不接受（某事）；（比賽中）判（得分）無效：*The last goal was disallowed because it was offside.* 最後一個入球因為越位被判無效。

disqualify to stop a competitor from taking part in a race or competition because they have broken a rule 使喪失資格（尤指競賽中違反規則）：*Johnson was disqualified after two false starts.* 莊遜因兩次起跑犯規被取消參賽資格。

exclude to prevent someone from entering a place, especially a school, often as a punishment（常出於處罰目的）禁止（某人）進入，阻止（某人）參加：*Matthew was excluded from school for a week for persistent bad behavior.* 馬修因為長期的不良行為而被停學一週。

forbid not to allow someone to do something or to go somewhere 禁止（某人做某事或去某處）：*Children are forbidden to use the swimming pool unless accompanied by an adult.* 如無大人陪同，兒童禁止在游泳池游泳。

prohibit not to allow an activity 禁止，阻止（某項活動）：*Smoking is prohibited in the cinema.* 電影院禁止吸煙。

veto to prevent something, such as a piece of legislation, being passed（對法律等）行使否決權，拒絕認可：*The President vetoed the welfare-reform bill.* 總統否決了福利改革法案。

banish *verb* to send a person away, especially to another country, because of something bad that they have done 放逐，流放；驅逐出境：*The king banished the duke to Ireland following his involvement in a murder.* 公爵因捲入一椿謀殺案被國王流放到了愛爾蘭。

deport to force someone to leave the country where they are living, especially to return to their country of origin 驅逐出境，遣送回國：*She was deported because her working visa had expired.* 她因工作簽證到期被驅逐出境。

eject to remove someone by force from a place, such as a night club or a party（將某人從夜總會或聚會等地）逐出，驅逐，趕出：*The man was ejected from the theatre for causing a disturbance.* 那個男人因為引發一場騷亂被逐出戲院。

evict to force someone to leave their home, for example because they have broken a contract（因違反合約等將某人從房屋）逐出，驅逐，趕出：*The family was evicted because they had not been paying their rent.* 那家人因為一直不付房租而被趕走了。

exile to force someone to leave their country and go and live in another country, often for political reasons（常因政治原因）流放，放逐（某人）：*Napoleon was exiled to St Helena for the rest of his life.* 拿破崙被流放到聖赫勒拿島，在那裏度過餘生。

expel to force someone to leave a place, especially to force a pupil to leave a school as punishment for very bad behavior（尤指因違反校規）開除，除名：*John was expelled for setting fire to the school.* 約翰因在校內縱火被開除。

basic *adjective* simple but necessary and important, especially as a starting point for expansion or development（尤指作為發展的起點）基本的，初步的：*the basic qualifications for the job* 這份工作的基本入職要求

central being the main and most important one among several 處於中心的；最重要的：*the central theme of the film* 這部電影的中心主題

elementary very simple and easy to understand, or dealing with the simplest aspects of something 初級的；基礎的：*an evening class in elementary motor mechanics* 講授初級車輛機械學課程的夜校

essential very important because it plays a part in determining the nature or identity of something（在決定事物的性質或特性方面）極其重要的，必不可少的，必需的：*all the essential ingredients of a great party* 一個盛大聚會所有必需的要素

fundamental very important, often because it serves as a basis for other things（作為其他事物的基礎）非常重要的，根本的，基本的：*Food and shelter are fundamental human rights.* 食物和住所是最基本的人權。

indispensable so important or so highly valued that you could not manage without it or them 不可或缺的；必需的：*an indispensable aid to navigation* 航行所不可或缺的輔助設備

key being the most important person or thing in a particular situation（在特定形勢下）關鍵的，至關重要的：*the key witness at a murder trial* 謀殺案審理中的關鍵證人

necessary which is needed in order to enable something to happen（做某事）必要的，必需的：*They did not have the necessary funding to make an offer for the property.* 他們沒有出價購買這個物業所必需的資金。

primary coming first in order of importance（在重要性上）首要的，主要的：*Alcohol abuse is the primary cause of his health problems.* 酗酒是他健康問題的元兇。

rudimentary very simple, especially because it has not been developed 簡單的；初步的；（尤指）未充分發展的：*With my rudimentary knowledge of*

Polish, I had great difficulty understanding what she said. 我對波蘭語的了解粗淺，很難聽懂她説的話。

vital very important and hard to do without 至關重要的；必不可少的：*We think of you as a vital member of the department.* 我們認為你是我們部門中必不可少的一份子。

basis *noun* something, e.g., a fact, reason, or situation, that underlies and supports something else such as a claim or argument（主張、論點等的）基礎，依據，根據：*It's an exciting story, but it has no basis in history.* 這是個令人激動的故事，可惜沒有歷史依據。

core the central or most important part of a problem or an issue（問題的）核心，精髓：*We must tackle the core of the problem, not just the details.* 我們必須解決問題的核心而不只是枝節。

essentials the basic and most important parts of something, especially all the things that you need to know if you want to be able to understand a subject sufficiently to be able to proceed（理解某事物必須的）基本要素，要點：*Some of the details of what she said were rather obscure, but I think I grasped the essentials.* 她所説的一些細節相當含糊，不過我相信基本要點我是理解的。

foundation a strong background element on which to base something important, such as a relationship or a belief（某種關係或信仰等的）基礎，基石：*You need a solid foundation of love and trust on which to build a marriage.* 你必須把婚姻建立在牢固的愛和信任的基礎之上。

fundamentals the basic and most important principles of something, such as a system or a subject（某體系或學科等的）基本原則，基本原理：*The artist taught me the fundamentals of portrait painting.* 那位畫家教我畫肖像畫的基本原理。

grounds a justifiable reason for a course of action, such as divorce or dismissal from a job（離婚或解僱某人等行為的）充分理由，根據：*Stealing is regarded as grounds for instant dismissal.* 偷竊被認為是立即免職的充分理由。

groundwork preliminary work done in preparation for something more important 準備工作；基礎工作：*At today's meeting we laid the groundwork for the pay negotiations.* 我們在今天的會議上為工資談判問題做了準備。

heart the essential or most important part of something, such as a problem（問題等的）核心，實質，重點：*Jealousy was at the heart of the matter.* 嫉妒是這件事的問題所在。

starting point something that serves as a beginning for something else, such as a discussion（討論等的）起點，基礎：*The company's pay offer was the starting point for negotiations.* 該公司的工資提議是談判的基礎。

bear *verb* to be able to experience something without either suffering or getting angry 承受，忍受，忍耐：*She couldn't bear to be parted from her children.* 她無法忍受和孩子們分離。

abide* to remain calm and not get angry when faced with someone or something that is extremely trying 默默忍受，容忍（極端令人厭煩的人或事）：*One thing he could never abide was rudeness.* 他決不能容忍的一件事就是粗魯無禮。

*Only used in the negative. 只用於否定句。

endure to experience physical or emotional pain or hardship, especially with courage or without complaining（尤指勇敢或無怨言地）忍耐，忍受（身體或精神上的痛苦或磨難）：*Paula bravely endured the other children's taunts.* 葆拉勇敢地忍受了其他孩子的奚落。

put up with to cope patiently with a difficult person, situation, or type of behaviour（耐心地）容忍，忍受（難相處的人、困難的處境或某種行為）：*I don't know how she puts up with her boyfriend's jealousy.* 我不知道她是怎麼容忍男朋友的嫉妒心的。

stand to bear someone or something that you find very unpleasant or annoying 容忍，忍受（令人不快的或討厭的人或事）：*I couldn't stand his arrogant attitude a minute longer.* 我一分鐘也不能再容忍他那傲慢的態度。

stomach (*formal*) to tolerate something that you find very unpleasant or unacceptable 容忍，忍受（令人不快的或難以接受的事情）：*Cruelty to animals was something George simply could not stomach.* 虐待動物是佐治完全不能容忍的事。

tolerate to accept someone or something even though you do not like them or do not approve of them 接受，忍受，容忍（不喜歡或不贊同的人或事）：*I tolerate my sister's husband for her sake, but I don't like him.* 我看在姐姐的面上接受了姐夫，但我並不喜歡他。

⊃ see also 參見 **carry**

beat¹ *verb* to hit someone or something repeatedly with hard blows of your fists or hands or a weapon or tool, especially a stick（用拳頭、手、武器或工具，尤其是棍棒等反覆用力地）擊打，敲打：*The man was beaten senseless by a gang of youths.* 那個男人被一伙年輕人打得不省人事。

batter to hit someone or something hard and repeatedly, usually implying greater and more concentrated and destructive force than 'beat'（連續用力地）擊打，猛擊（通常比 beat 更用力、更具傷害性）：*They picked up a bench and used it to batter down the door.* 他們拾起一條凳子砸向那扇門。

hammer to strike against something with heavy blows, as if using a hammer 用力捶打（某物）：*She hammered on the door to be let in.* 她用力捶打門要求進去。

hit to make hard and harmful contact with something or someone once 用力碰撞，撞擊（以造成傷害）：*The man hit the burglar over the head with a baseball bat.* 那男子用棒球棒擊打竊賊的頭部。

pummel to punch someone repeatedly 連續猛擊，反覆拳打（某人）：*The toddler threw a tantrum, pummelling his mother's legs in frustration.* 那個蹣跚學步的孩子耍起了脾氣，氣惱地用拳頭不斷打媽媽的腿。

punch to hit someone with a clenched fist 以拳痛擊，拳打（某人）：*He drew back his fist and punched me right in the face.* 他縮回拳頭，然後一拳正擊在我臉上。

strike to hit someone or something sharply, either with the hand or with a weapon（用手或武器）痛擊，猛烈擊打：*It's against the law for a teacher to strike a pupil.* 老師打學生是違法的。

tap to hit someone or something lightly, either with the open hand or with an object（用手掌或物體）輕拍，輕打：*She tapped him lightly on the hand with a ruler.* 她用尺子輕輕地打他的手。

thrash to strike someone hard and repeatedly, especially as a punishment （尤指作為懲罰）痛打，連續擊打（某人）：*His father thrashed him with a belt buckle until he bled.* 父親用皮帶扣狠狠抽他，直到流血。

beat² *verb* to win a contest, battle, game, or race (which may be a friendly one or one where there is not much at stake) against someone or something（在友誼賽或風險小的比賽中）獲勝，打敗：*England beat Australia at cricket.* 英格蘭隊在板球比賽中打敗了澳大利亞隊。

conquer to defeat an enemy in a war or battle and take control of them and their territory 征服（敵人）；攻克，佔領（某地）：*The Roman emperor conquered Sicily.* 羅馬帝國佔領了西西里島。

crush to beat someone easily, or comprehensively so that they are no longer able to resist（輕鬆徹底地）制服，鎮壓（某人）：*The new ruler's purges effectively crushed all opposition to his regime.* 新統治者的肅反運動有效地平息了所有反政府勢力。

defeat to beat someone in a contest, fight, race, etc., usually where there is something serious at stake（通常指在嚴肅而有風險的賽事中）擊敗，戰勝（某人）：*Octavius Caesar defeated the combined naval forces of Antony and Cleopatra at the Battle of Actium.* 在亞克興戰役中，奧克塔維厄斯·凱撒擊敗了安東尼和克萊奧帕特拉的海軍聯盟。

get the better of to gain an advantage over someone 佔（某人的）上風；勝過（某人）：*Because she is more intelligent than him, she always gets the better of him in an argument.* 她比他更聰明，因此在辯論中總是佔上風。

outdo to do better than someone else at some activity（在活動中）勝過，優於（某人）：*Val can always outdo the rest of us when it comes to witty repartee.* 只要是智力應答，瓦爾總能勝過我們所有的人。

overcome to defeat someone or something, usually after a long struggle （經過長期鬥爭）克服，戰勝（人或事）：*In the end the army was overcome by a superior force.* 最後這支軍隊敗給了一支更精銳的部隊。

vanquish (*formal*) to defeat an army or a leader thoroughly in a war or battle（在戰鬥中）徹底擊敗，完全征服（軍隊或首領）：*Their foes were vanquished in a bloody battle.* 他們的敵人在一場血戰中被徹底擊敗。

↪ see also 參見 **attack¹**，**attack²**

beautiful *adjective* very pleasing to the senses, especially sight or hearing, or very satisfying when judged by aesthetic criteria (mostly used when making a serious assessment of something or someone) 漂亮的；美麗的；美妙的（多用於認真評價）：*a beautiful woman* 一個漂亮的女人

attractive having an appearance or character that appeals to people（相貌或性格）有魅力的，有吸引力的：*She has a very attractive warm personality.* 她有着充滿魅力的熱情性格。

fine beautiful because well made, done, or performed（製作）精美的，精湛的；（表演）精彩的：*There is some fine singing on this disc.* 這張唱片裏有一些很動聽的歌曲。

good-looking having a very pleasing appearance 漂亮的；好看的：*For his age, he is a very good-looking man.* 以他的年齡來看，他算得上是非常英俊的男人。

gorgeous extremely attractive in personal appearance, or rich and splendid in colour and decoration（外表）華麗的；（色彩和裝飾）燦爛的；吸引人的：*a gorgeous evening dress* 一套華麗的晚禮服

handsome having attractive, regular, and usually masculine features（通常指男性）帥氣的，英俊的：*She is in love with a handsome film star.* 她迷上了一個英俊的電影明星。

lovely beautiful or attractive (but often used in a more casual way than 'beautiful')美麗的，可愛的（常不如 beautiful 正式）：*Katie has a lovely singing voice.* 凱蒂有一副甜美的歌喉。

picturesque (*said about a place or scene*) so pleasing in appearance as to make a beautiful picture（用於形容某處或某景色）如圖畫般的：*a picturesque village in the foothills* 山腳下風景如畫的村莊

pretty pleasing in appearance (but without the more striking qualities that make a person or thing 'beautiful'): 漂亮的，招人喜愛的（但程度不及 beautiful）: a *pretty* little girl 一個俊俏的小女孩

radiant looking beautiful and very happy 容光煥發的：*The bride looked positively radiant.* 新娘看上去容光煥發。

stunning extraordinarily beautiful or impressive 格外美麗的；給人以深刻印象的：*When we reached the top of the hill, we had a stunning view of the coastline.* 我們到達山頂時，看到了美麗壯觀的海岸線。

beg *verb* to ask for something earnestly and humbly 乞求；哀求：*The hostages begged their captors for mercy.* 人質央求綁架者放過他們。

appeal to to ask someone earnestly and urgently for something, such as help or co-operation 呼籲，懇求（幫助或合作等）：*The murdered girl's parents appealed to the public to come forward if they know anything that might help find the killer.* 被害女孩的父母呼籲公眾中對案件偵破有幫助的知情人能夠站出來。

beseech (*literary*) to ask someone earnestly and anxiously to do something for you（真誠、焦慮地）懇求，請求：*We beseech Thee to hear us, good Lord.* 尊敬的大人，懇請您聽我們説。

crave to ask someone earnestly to grant you something such as indulgence or understanding 懇求，請求（某人的寬容或理解）：*I crave your indulgence on this matter.* 在這件事上我懇請您的包涵。

entreat (*formal*) to ask someone earnestly and persuasively for something（真誠、有説服力地）懇求，乞求：*Treat this matter with the utmost urgency, I entreat you.* 懇請您盡快處理這件事情。

implore (*formal*) to ask someone for something by appealing to their emotions（動之以情地）懇求，哀求：*I implore you to examine your conscience and make a donation to the disaster fund.* 我懇求你憑自己良心為災區募捐。

plead to make an emotional appeal to someone to do something（充滿感情地）請求，懇求：*In tears, she pleaded with her husband not to leave her.* 她流着淚懇求丈夫不要離開她。

➲ see also 參見 **ask**

begin *verb* to happen, or to do something, for the first time or for the first time in the period in question 開始（發生或做某事）；起始：*After a while, it began to rain.* 不久，天就下起了雨。

commence (*formal*) to begin, usually in accordance with a plan or previous arrangement（通常指按計劃或事先安排）着手，開始：*Festivities will commence at 7.30 pm.* 慶祝活動將在晚上 7.30 開始。

inaugurate (*formal*) to begin something, such as a new system or service, officially, especially by means of a ceremony（指新體制或儀式等通過正式典禮）開始：*The President of France travelled to London on the first train to inaugurate the new cross-Channel rail link.* 法國總統乘坐第一班火車到達倫敦，為新的跨海峽鐵路舉行落成典禮。

initiate to begin something, such as a relationship or a discussion, by making the first move（主動）開始，發起（關係或討論等）：*Sunita was too shy to initiate a conversation with a stranger.* 蘇妮塔太害羞了，不敢主動與陌生人說話。

instigate (*formal*) to cause something, especially a troublesome event, to happen 煽動，鼓動（某事）：*The shop steward instigated a walkout in protest against the working conditions.* 工會談判代表發起了抗議惡劣工作環境的罷工。

kick off to start, especially to start a football match by kicking the ball from the centre of the pitch（尤指足球比賽）中線開球，開始比賽：*The game kicks off at three o'clock.* 比賽在 3 點開始。

originate to happen, or cause something to happen, for the first time 起源；開創：*The game of golf originated in Scotland.* 高爾夫運動源於蘇格蘭。

set off to begin a course of action, especially a journey 出發；動身；起程：*We set off for Rome first thing in the morning.* 我們一大早就出發去羅馬了。

start to begin to happen or begin doing something 開始（發生或做某事）：*The baby woke up and started crying.* 寶寶醒來就開始哭鬧。

behaviour *noun* the way that a person behaves 行為；舉止：*Children should be rewarded for good behaviour.* 孩子們表現好就應予以獎勵。

conduct the way that a person behaves, often with reference to morality（常指道德）行為，舉止，操行：*His conduct in the face of severe provocation was admirable at all times.* 他面對嚴峻挑釁時的表現總是令人稱道。

demeanour (*formal*) the way that a person behaves and the impression that gives of their character 外表；風度；行為舉止：*His demeanour is very intimidating.* 他的行為舉止很嚇人。

deportment (*formal*) the way that a person stands and moves 儀態；風度；行為舉止：*She has the elegant deportment of a fashion model.* 她具有時裝模特兒般的端莊優雅。

manners ways of behaving towards other people, especially judged by how much courtesy and consideration a person shows 禮貌;禮儀 : *His good manners won over his new girlfriend's parents.* 他的彬彬有禮征服了新女友的父母。

performance the way that a person behaves in a testing situation 表現;成就 : *Najma was happy with her performance in the job interview.* 納吉瑪對她在求職面試中的表現感到很滿意。

ways a person's characteristic habits or style of behaviour 行為方式,習慣;習性 : *Alex has his own little ways, which some people find eccentric.* 亞歷克斯有他自己特有的一些細微的行為習慣,這在有些人看來卻很怪異。

best *adjective* better than any other 最好的 : *the best holiday I have ever had* 我度過的最美好的假期

> **finest** of the best possible quality 優質的;上乘的 : *made from the finest coffee beans* 用優質咖啡豆磨成的

> **foremost** best, most important, or best-known in a particular field (在某領域) 最重要的,最知名的 : *the foremost philosopher of his time* 在他那個時代最知名的哲學家

> **leading** most important or among the most important in a particular field (在某領域) 最重要的,最傑出的 : *a leading neurosurgeon* 一個傑出的神經外科醫生

> **optimum** most effective or most advantageous 最有效的;最有利的;最優的 : *For optimum benefit, you should exercise for half an hour three or four times a week.* 為達到最佳運動效果,你應該每週鍛煉 3 至 4 次,每次半小時。

> **supreme** the greatest in achievement or power (成就或權利) 至高的,最高的 : *the supreme champion at Cruft's Dog Show* 克拉福特狗展的總冠軍

> **top** the most successful or most important in a particular area of activity (在某活動範圍) 最成功的,最出色的,最重要的 : *the top golfer in the world* 世界頂級高爾夫球手

> **ultimate** being the best possible example of something (範例) 最佳的;極品的 : *the ultimate feelgood movie* 最賞心悅目的電影

> **unsurpassed** having never been bettered 非常卓越的;無法超越的 : *The quality of his workmanship is unsurpassed.* 他的手工無與倫比。

betray[1] *verb* to do something, especially to give information, that enables an enemy to defeat or capture someone who trusts you 出賣,背叛 (某人);洩露 (機密) : *His best friend betrayed him to the secret police.* 他最好的朋友將他出賣給秘密警察。

> **deceive** to make someone believe that you are a friend or supporter in order to betray them 欺騙,蒙騙,誆騙 : *They discovered too late that they had been deceived by a traitor in their midst.* 當他們發現被混雜其間的叛徒蒙騙時,為時已晚。

> **double-cross** (*informal*) to betray an ally by working against them while pretending to be on their side (假意與人結盟暗地裏卻) 欺騙,出賣 (盟友) : *If you double-cross a gangster, you're likely to come to a sticky end.* 如果你出賣歹徒,很可能會落得可悲的下場。

grass on (*informal*) to inform on someone 告發，告密（某人）：*Somebody grassed on me to the cops!* 有人到警察那兒告發我！

inform on to give someone in authority, such as the police, information that incriminates someone（向警察等權威人士）告發，檢舉：*One of the neighbours informed on him for working while claiming benefits.* 他的一個鄰居檢舉他在領取失業救濟金期間仍在工作。

betray² *verb* to show something that was intended to be kept hidden, especially inadvertently（尤指無意間）洩露，流露：*The look on his face betrayed his distaste.* 他臉上的表情流露出他的厭惡之情。

disclose to reveal information that has previously been unknown or kept secret 揭露；透露；洩露：*Details of the tour dates will be disclosed in due course.* 有關旅行日程的詳細情況將在適當時候透露。

divulge (*formal*) to allow something to be known, usually by saying it to someone 透露；洩露：*I am not permitted to divulge the present whereabouts of the prime minister and his wife.* 我無權透露首相夫婦目前的行蹤。

expose to make someone's true character known publicly 使（某人的真面目）公之於眾；揭穿；揭露：*The Minister was exposed in the media as a liar and a cheat.* 部長說謊和搞欺騙的真面目被傳媒揭穿了。

give away to reveal information that was meant to be kept secret 洩露，暴露（本應保密的信息）：*The actress gave her real age away when she said she had been at President Kennedy's inauguration.* 女演員說起她曾出席甘乃迪總統的就職儀式時，洩露了她的真實年齡。

let slip to say something unintentionally that reveals information that was meant to be kept secret 無意中說出（本應保守的秘密）：*She let slip that she had lost her engagement ring.* 她無意中說出她把訂婚戒指弄丟了。

reveal to make visible or known, deliberately or inadvertently, something that has previously been unseen or unknown（有意地或無意地）揭示，顯示，透露：*I am now able to reveal the name of the lucky winner.* 現在我可以透露那個幸運獲獎者的名字了。

biased *adjective* not impartial, showing favour or antipathy to a particular kind of person or thing 有偏見的：*biased in favour of pretty young women* 偏愛年輕貌美的女性

bigoted having a strong irrational dislike of certain people or groups of people 偏執的，頑固的（尤指對某人或某群體抱有強烈的、非理性的嫌惡）：*a man so bigoted he would not even shake hands with a Black person* 一個連和黑人握一下手都不願意的偏執男人

discriminatory unfairly treating one person or one group better than others 區別對待的；不公正的；歧視的：*a discriminatory practice* 不公正的做法

homophobic biased against homosexuals 對同性戀者持有偏見的：*homophobic bullying in the workplace* 在工作場所對同性戀偏見者恃強凌弱的行為

partial favouring one contestant, team, or group over others 偏愛的；偏袒的：*A football referee must not appear to be partial to either side.* 足球裁判絕不能表現出對任何一方有偏袒。

partisan biased in favour of a particular person or group（對特定的人或團體）過分支持的，偏袒的，偏護的：*She is too partisan to judge the competition.* 她過於偏頗，因而不能給這場競賽當裁判。

prejudiced having a preconceived opinion of someone, something, or a group of people（對人、物或群體）帶成見的，有偏見的：*prejudiced against Irish people* 對愛爾蘭人有偏見的

racist holding or betraying the belief that one race is superior to all others 種族主義（者）的：*The broadcaster was fired for making racist remarks on television.* 那位播音員因為在電視節目中發表種族主義言論而被解僱。

sexist holding or betraying the belief that one sex is superior to the other, usually that men are superior to women 性別歧視的：*Ron's female colleagues found his sexist attitude offensive.* 羅恩的女同事覺得他的大男子主義態度令人討厭。

skewed presented in a biased way that distorts the truth 歪曲（事實）的；有偏頗的：*a skewed account of events* 對事件的歪曲報道

slanted showing bias in favour of a particular person, group, or view（對個人、團體或觀點）有傾向性的，偏袒的：*The article was slanted in favour of the rebels.* 這篇文章有偏袒叛亂者的傾向。

big *adjective* above the average in size or amount（在體積或數量上高於平均水平）大的：*a big strong man* 一個身強力壯的大個子男人

bulky big, heavy, and difficult to carry or handle（搬運或操縱起來）大而笨重的：*a bulky parcel* 一個大件包裹

colossal extremely big in size or amount (usually even bigger than 'enormous')（在體積或數量上）巨大的，龐大的（通常甚至比 enormous 還要大）：*a colossal statue as tall as a house* 與房子一般高的巨大雕像

considerable quite large in amount（數量上）相當多的：*a considerable sum of money* 一大筆錢

enormous extremely big in size or amount（在體積或數量上）巨大的，龐大的：*an engagement ring with an enormous diamond* 一枚鑲有巨大鑽石的訂婚戒指

extensive wide and, often, varied 廣泛的；廣闊的；各式各樣的：*She has extensive experience in all aspects of publishing.* 她對出版業的方方面面有着廣泛的經驗。

gigantic extremely large in size（體積上）巨大的，龐大的：*A dinosaur was a gigantic reptile of prehistoric times.* 恐龍是史前時期一種體形龐大的爬行動物。

great large in degree or intensity（在程度或強度上）非常的，強烈的：*a great sense of achievement* 一種強烈的成就感

huge extremely big in size or amount（在體積或數量上）巨大的，極多的：*a huge mansion standing in acres of land* 矗立在一大片空地上的一座大廈

immense very great in size, degree, or intensity（在體積、程度或強度上）極大的，巨大的，強烈的：*They took immense pride in their children's achievements.* 他們對孩子們所取得的成就感到無比驕傲。

large above average in size or amount – also used to describe a size of commercial products（在體積或數量上高於平均水平，也用於描述商品尺寸）大的，大規模的，大量的：*This T-shirt comes in small, medium, and large sizes.* 這件 T 恤有大、中、小三個型號。

massive very great in size, degree, or intensity（在體積、程度或強度上）巨大的：*There has been a massive explosion in the city.* 這個城市曾經發生過大爆炸。

spacious having a lot of space inside（內部空間）寬闊的，寬敞的：*a spacious sitting-room* 一間寬敞的客廳

vast extremely large, especially in extent（尤指範圍上）遼闊的，巨大的：*the vast desert* 大沙漠

blame *verb* to say that someone is guilty of a bad action or responsible for something bad that has happened 把…歸咎於；責怪；指責：*Scott blamed his little sister for scribbling on the wall.* 斯科特責怪他妹妹在牆上亂塗亂畫。

accuse to say that you think someone has done something wrong 譴責；指責；指控：*The teacher accused Sophie of cheating in the test.* 老師指責蘇菲考試作弊。

censure (*formal*) to express disapproval of a person or their behaviour（對個人或其行為）譴責，斥責，指責：*Dr Thomas was officially censured for inappropriate behaviour.* 托馬斯博士因行為失當而遭到正式譴責。

condemn to express severe disapproval of a person or a practice（對個人或其做法）強烈譴責：*The model was condemned for setting a bad example to young girls by using hard drugs.* 那個模特兒吸毒成癮，給年輕女孩造成不良影響而受到譴責。

criticize to express disapproval of a person, their work, or their behaviour（對某人及其工作或行為）批評，指責：*She was fed up with being constantly criticized by her parents.* 她已經受夠了父母無休止的指責。

blemish *noun* a visible mark that spoils the appearance of something, especially a person's skin（外觀，尤其是皮膚上的）斑點，疤痕；污點：*She has soft smooth skin with no blemishes.* 她的肌膚柔嫩光滑、白璧無瑕。

defect an imperfection in something, such as a body part or a machine, that means that it fails to function properly, and that may be in it from the beginning or develop later（指身體或機器等固有的或後來產生的）缺點，缺陷，毛病：*The optician says I have a slight defect in my left eye.* 驗光師說我的左眼有輕微的毛病。

fault a defect in something such as a machine, a system, or a garment（機器、系統或衣物的）故障，缺陷，毛病：*I took the CD player back to the shop because there was a fault in it.* 我把 CD 機退回商店了，因為機器出了故障。

flaw an imperfection that is in something, especially a natural material or an argument or theory, from the beginning（尤指天然材料、論點或理論固有的）裂痕，瑕疵，缺陷：*I think I've discovered a flaw in their argument.* 我認為我已經發現了他們論點中的疏漏。

imperfection a mark or other fault that stops something from being perfect 不完美；缺點；瑕疵：*an antique table with a slight imperfection in the wood* 材質上稍有瑕疵的古董餐桌

mark a visible imperfection that spoils the appearance of something, such as a garment or a piece of furniture (衣物或傢具等的) 污點，痕跡，斑點：*He had a greasy mark on his tie.* 他的領帶上有一塊明顯的油漬。

spot a usually round mark or blotch that spoils the appearance of something, especially a small raised area on the skin (外觀上圓形的) 斑點，污漬；（皮膚上突起的）粉刺：*a teenage boy with spots all over his face* 滿臉長痘的少年

boast *verb* to say things that show that you think that something you own, have done, or are associated with makes you really special or better than other people 自誇；自吹自擂：*He is always boasting about how much he earns.* 他經常炫耀自己豐厚的收入。

blow your own trumpet (*informal*) to tell people how good or successful you are 自我吹噓；自吹自擂：*Tariq's a clever guy but he's always blowing his own trumpet.* 塔里克是個聰明的小伙子，但就是太愛自我吹噓了。

brag to boast 吹牛；自誇：*She liked to brag about her two university degrees.* 她喜歡吹噓自己獲得的兩個大學學位。

crow (*informal*) to make it obvious that you take pleasure in the fact that you have an advantage over someone else (因超越他人而) 得意揚揚，自鳴得意：*I couldn't help crowing when I beat Ewan at bowling.* 我打保齡球贏了尤安，禁不住得意起來。

show off to act in a boastful way, especially by demonstrating to other people how well you can do something 賣弄，炫耀（自己的能力等）：*Stop showing off, you're not the only one who can ride a bike with no hands.* 不要再炫耀了，不是只有你一個人才可以放開手騎自行車的。

sing your own praises to tell people about how clever, talented, etc., you are 自我吹噓；自我誇耀：*I got fed up with Shane singing his own praises all the time.* 我受夠了謝恩無休止的自我吹噓。

➲ see also 參見 **proud**

bold *adjective* easily noticed, especially through having strong colours and a definite outline 醒目的；突出的；輪廓分明的：*Bold patterns are in this season.* 這一季流行輪廓分明的樣式。

bright having a strong shining quality, not pale or dark 鮮豔的；鮮亮的；發光的：*The living room was painted in bright blues and oranges.* 客廳漆成了明快醒目的藍色和橙黃色。

loud extremely bright and lacking subtlety 花哨的；顏色刺眼的；豔俗的：*He was known for his loud ties.* 他以繫花哨俗氣的領帶而聞名。

startling having a strong and somewhat surprising effect 令人震驚的；驚人的：*a rather startling close-up photograph of Picasso* 一幅令人震驚的畢加索特寫照片

striking making a strong impression 惹人注目的；印象深刻的：*a very striking portrait of the Queen* 一幅非常引人注意的女皇肖像畫

strong not weakened or diluted, but intended to convey a definite and powerful impression 強烈的；濃重的；有感染力的：*a strong shade of pink* 濃烈的粉紅色調

vibrant very bright and, sometimes, appearing to glow 色彩鮮明的；鮮豔奪目的：*Diana's wardrobe is full of dresses in vibrant colours.* 戴安娜的衣櫥裏滿是色彩鮮豔的衣服。

vivid very bright in an attractive way 鮮明的；鮮豔的；耀眼的：*a vivid painting of a rainbow* 一幅色彩鮮明的彩虹油畫

➲ see also 參見 **brave**

border *noun* a real or imaginary line marking the edge of something or where two things meet (真實的或想像的) 界線，邊界，邊緣：*Carlisle is close to the border between England and Scotland.* 卡萊爾靠近英格蘭和蘇格蘭的邊界。

borderline the division, often indistinct, between two places or two things, such as activities or emotions (兩地或兩種事物，如行為或情感間模糊的) 分界線：*the borderline between dislike and hatred* 嫌惡和仇恨之間的分界線

boundary a line where two areas of land or property meet (土地或房屋之間的) 界限，分界線：*There is a hedge marking the boundary between our garden and our neighbours'.* 我們和鄰居的花園之間有一道樹籬作為分界線。

edge a line or area forming the outermost part of something beyond which there is usually space 邊；邊緣；邊沿：*There is a slight gap between the edges of the wallpaper.* 牆紙的邊緣之間有細小的空隙。

frontier the border between two countries 國界；邊界；邊境：*the Iran-Iraq frontier* 伊朗和伊拉克的邊界

limits the edges of a particular area, especially a city (特定地區，尤指城市的) 邊緣地帶，界限：*A taxi ride will cost a lot more if you go outside the city limits.* 坐計程車出城花費要大得多。

margin a strip at the edge of something, such as an area of land or a leaf (某地區或樹葉等的) 邊緣地帶，邊緣，邊沿：*the margin of the forest* 森林的邊緣

perimeter the outer edge of an area of land, especially of a large military or civil installation such as an airport (尤指大型軍事或民用設施如機場的) 外緣，邊緣：*The guard walked round the perimeter of the compound.* 警衛沿着圍牆圍住的場地四周巡視。

rim the outside edge of a circular or curved object (圓形或曲線形物體的) 邊沿，邊，緣：*He wore glasses with a gold rim.* 他戴着一副金絲邊眼鏡。

boring *adjective* not interesting or exciting 沒趣的；無聊的：*The lecture was so boring I almost fell asleep.* 這個講座太沒意思了，我差點睡着了。

dreary lacking colour and excitement and rather depressing 單調乏味的；沉悶的：*a dreary drama about domestic violence* 一部關於家庭暴力的沉悶的舞台劇

dull lacking brightness and colour, or not providing any excitement or entertainment 枯燥無味的；無趣的；無聊的：*I don't know what Susan sees in her new boyfriend – he is so dull.* 我不知道蘇珊看上新男朋友甚麼了，他太無聊乏味了。

flat not, or no longer, exciting or excited, usually because the lively element has been taken away 枯燥的；平淡無味的：*The party was really flat after the young people left.* 那些年輕人離開後，這個聚會真是無聊透頂。

humdrum very ordinary and with little variety 非常普通的；缺少變化的：*a little light relief in her humdrum existence* 她平淡無奇的生活中的一絲慰藉

monotonous boring because the same thing happens or you have to do the same thing again and again 單調乏味的：*Working on an assembly line can get very monotonous.* 在裝配線上工作可能會非常單調乏味。

stale uninteresting because not new or original 陳腐的；無新意的：*He told a stale old joke that I had heard a dozen times before.* 他講了一個我以前聽過無數次的老掉牙的笑話。

tedious boring, especially because of going on too long 冗長乏味的：*a tedious journey involving several changes of bus* 中途幾次轉車的乏味旅行

tiresome not simply boring but also annoying 令人厭煩的；討厭的；煩人的：*Her constant chatter is so tiresome.* 她沒完沒了的饒舌，真讓人厭煩。

uneventful in which nothing exciting or remarkable happens, though this is often a relief and not necessarily boring 平淡無奇的；平凡的；無驚人事件的：*Our journey home was entirely uneventful.* 我們回家的旅途平安無事。

brave *adjective* having or showing admirable courage either in taking action or enduring suffering（指採取行動或承受痛苦）勇敢的；有勇氣的：*Nobody was brave enough to stand up and tell the boss he was wrong.* 沒有人能勇敢地站出來指出老闆的錯誤。

bold showing not only courage but also a willingness to take the initiative and take risks and often an imaginative quality as well 大膽的；有膽識的；勇敢無畏的：*It was a typically bold move, intended to take the enemy completely by surprise.* 這是典型的有膽識的行動，旨在出其不意地打敗敵人。

courageous brave, usually in taking action rather than in endurance（尤指行動）勇敢的，有勇氣的：*a courageous attempt to rescue the hostages* 一次大膽的營救人質的嘗試

daring showing a willingness to take risks that other people would not take 敢於冒險的；大膽的；英勇的：*a daring raid into the heart of enemy territory* 一次深入敵人腹地的大膽突襲

fearless having or showing no fear in the face of danger（面對危險）不怕的，無畏的：*a fearless military leader* 一個無所畏懼的軍隊首領

gutsy (*informal*) showing courage and determination 顯示勇氣和決心的；勇敢的：*a gutsy marathon runner who kept going despite aching legs* 一個不顧腿傷繼續比賽的勇敢的馬拉松運動員

have-a-go (*informal*) brave enough to tackle a criminal who is committing a crime（在與罪犯周旋時）勇敢的，大膽進行的：*Have-a-go pensioner, Nancy Smith, single-handedly thwarted a raid on her local post office.* 南茜・史密斯，一個靠養老金生活的老人，非常勇敢，單槍匹馬挫敗了歹徒在她當地郵局的搶劫。

heroic showing great courage, especially in putting your own life in danger to help or rescue other people 有英雄氣概的；英雄的；英勇的：*The way that James risked his own life to save a child from drowning was heroic.* 詹姆斯冒着生命危險營救遇溺小孩的行為很英勇。

intrepid (*formal*) acting in a daring or fearless manner（行為舉止）無畏的，英勇的：*an intrepid explorer* 一個無畏的探險者

plucky (*informal*) showing courage in difficult or challenging situations (在困難或具有挑戰的情況下) 顯示出勇氣的，有膽量的：*a plucky little girl who refused to let her disability rule her life* 一個不讓殘疾主宰自己生活的勇敢小女孩

valiant showing courage and determination, often in a situation where you ultimately fail (常指在最終失敗的情況下仍) 表現勇敢的，英勇的，堅定的：*They made a valiant attempt to fight the fire, but it was out of control.* 他們勇敢地試圖撲滅大火，但火勢已經失去控制。

➲ see also 參見 **bold**

break¹ *verb* to damage something so that it is no longer whole or no longer functions 使破碎；損壞，弄壞 (某物)：*Ben broke his new toy gun within an hour.* 班不到一小時就把他的新玩具槍弄壞了。

crack to damage an object so that a narrow gap or gaps appear in it (使) 破裂，出現裂縫，裂開：*This cup is cracked.* 這個茶杯有裂縫了。

fracture to break a bone in your body 骨折：*I fell off the wall and fractured my arm.* 我從牆上摔下來，折斷了手臂。

sever to cut something, especially a body part, off completely 切斷，割斷，切開 (尤指身體部位)：*My uncle severed his little finger in an industrial accident.* 我的叔叔在一起工傷事故中切斷了小指。

shatter to break something, especially something made of glass, completely, so that it falls into many small pieces (尤指玻璃製品) 破碎，碎裂：*A small stone hit the windscreen and shattered it.* 一小塊石頭打在擋風玻璃上，砸碎了玻璃。

smash to break or shatter an object, usually through some deliberate violent action (通常指故意的暴力行為) 砸碎，打碎，打破：*She used her shoe to smash the window.* 她用鞋打碎了窗戶。

snap to break sharply at a single point with a cracking or popping sound (在某個點上咔嚓一聲突然) 折斷，斷裂：*The plastic fork snapped as soon as I put pressure on it.* 我剛一用力，那塑料餐叉就咔嚓一聲折斷了。

splinter to break a hard substance such as wood or stone into many small sharp pieces 使 (木頭或石頭等硬物) 裂成 (鋒利的) 碎片：*The cannonball splintered the timbers in the ship's side.* 那炮彈把輪船的木質船舷炸成了碎片。

split to divide something into two or more parts 劈開，裂開，分開：*The woodcutter struck the log with an axe, splitting it in two.* 伐木者用斧頭把原木劈成兩半。

break² *noun* a short time away from work or study, for rest or recreation (工作或學習時的) 間歇，短暫休息：*The children played tag during the morning break.* 在上午課間休息時，孩子們玩起了捉人遊戲。

breather (*informal*) a short period of rest 小憩，短暫休息：*After a hard morning's graft, the lads took a breather.* 經過一早上辛苦的樹枝嫁接工作，小伙子們稍事休息了一會兒。

respite a period of time spent away from a difficult situation, such as being a carer for a family member who is elderly or ill 短暫的喘息，暫時的緩解，暫停 (指暫時擺脫困境，如看護家中老人或病人等)：*The social services arranged*

for Bridget to have a week's respite from looking after her disabled daughter.
社會福利部門給布麗奇特安排了一週的喘息時間，暫時不去照顧她殘疾的女兒。

rest a short period of time in which you rest（短暫的）休息：*We had been working non-stop for five hours and badly needed a rest.* 我們一直工作了 5 個小時，非常需要休息一下。

tea break a short period of time during which workers are allowed to stop working in order to drink tea 茶歇；工間休息時間：*At work we have a ten-minute tea break every morning.* 我們每天上午有 10 分鐘的工間休息時間。

⊃ see also 參見 **holiday**

brief[1] *adjective* lasting a relatively small length of time, i.e. a few minutes, hours, days, years, etc. 短時間的；短暫的：*a brief trip to London to see a show* 去倫敦看展覽的短暫旅行

ephemeral (*formal*) existing only for a short time and not important or having a lasting effect 短暫存在的，短命的，瞬息即逝的（指無足輕重或無長效性）：*Much teenage slang is too ephemeral to be entered in a dictionary.* 青少年使用的許多俚語時效性太短暫，不可能編入詞典。

fleeting happening quickly and lasting only for a very short time (*usually when you would prefer it to last longer*) 飛逝的，短暫的，轉瞬即逝的（通常指希望持續較長時間）：*I just caught a fleeting glimpse of her before she disappeared into the building.* 我剛瞥見她一眼，她就消失在那棟大樓裏了。

momentary affecting someone or happening for only a very short time 瞬間的；短暫的；片刻的：*Kemal suffered a momentary loss of confidence.* 肯莫一時失去了信心。

short not long (more often used with the word 'time' than is 'brief') 短期的，短暫的（比 brief 更常與 time 搭配使用）：*We've got a lot to do and only a very short time to do it in.* 我們要做的事很多，但時間卻很短暫。

transitory not permanent, lasting a short time and then passing on 非持久的；暫時的；轉瞬即逝的：*Her feelings of resentment towards her sister were merely transitory.* 她對妹妹的怨恨只是暫時的。

brief[2] *adjective* using few words 簡潔的；扼要的：*I left a brief note saying I'd gone to the post office.* 我留了一張簡短的便條說我去郵局了。

concise expressing something precisely but using few words 簡明的；簡練的：*a concise description of the local attractions* 對當地風景名勝簡明扼要的描述

pithy short, clever, and often witty 精練的；精闢的；言簡意賅的：*Peter's pithy comments make him an ideal dinner guest.* 彼得精闢的評論使他成為最佳宴會賓客。

short consisting of comparatively few words 簡短的；簡略的：*Pat wrote a short article on violence in the workplace.* 帕特寫了一篇關於工作場所暴力行為的短文。

succinct expressing something very aptly but using few words 簡潔的；簡明扼要的：*a succinct summing-up of the points discussed at the meeting* 對會上討論的觀點所作的簡明扼要的總結

bright *adjective* shining strongly or having a strong light colour, not dull or dark 明亮的；鮮豔的：*a bright light* 明亮的燈光；a *bright* green 翠綠色

brilliant radiating intense light or colour 閃耀的；燦爛的：*The sun was shining in a brilliant blue sky.* 太陽在蔚藍的天空下閃着耀眼的光芒。

colourful brightly coloured or having many different colours 顏色鮮豔的；五彩繽紛的；色彩豔麗的：*clowns in colourful costumes* 穿着豔麗服裝的小丑

dazzling so bright as to make you temporarily unable to see 眼花繚亂的；令人目眩的：*The dazzling headlights of the oncoming car caused me to swerve.* 迎面駛來的汽車的刺眼燈光使我突然轉向。

glowing shining and usually having a colour associated with fire or heat 熾熱的；發紅光的；色彩鮮明的：*glowing reds and yellows* 鮮亮的紅黃色

luminous giving off light, especially so as to be clearly seen in the dark 發光的，明亮的（尤指黑暗中能清楚看到的）：*The children wear luminous armbands so that motorists will be able to see them on dark winter mornings.* 孩子們都戴着明亮的臂章，好讓司機在漆黑的冬天早晨能清楚地看見他們。

⊃ see also 參見 **bold; clever**

build¹ *verb* to make a building or a similar fairly permanent structure using strong materials（用堅固的材料）建造，建築（房屋）：*Our house was built in 1901.* 我們的房子是 1901 年建成的。

assemble to make something, such as furniture or a model, by fitting together the parts 組裝，裝配（傢具或模型等）：*a computer chair that you have to assemble yourself* 須由你自己裝配的電腦椅

construct to build something, such as a structure or a machine 構築，建造（建築物或機器等）：*The Eiffel Tower is constructed from wrought iron.* 埃菲爾鐵塔是由鍛鐵構築而成的。

erect to build something upright, such as a tall building or a monument 建立，建造，豎立（高樓大廈或紀念碑等）：*A statue of the prime minister was erected in the city centre.* 首相的雕像矗立在市中心。

fashion to form something with care (*and often artistic skill*) or over a period of time（常指用技藝精心地或長時間地）塑造，製作（某物）：*Her skilful fingers fashioned the lump of clay into a tall elegant pot.* 她靈巧的手指把那塊泥土製作成一個雅致的大陶罐。

form to create something by giving a material form or shape（按模型）做成，塑造（某物）：*The children formed the plasticine into animal shapes.* 孩子們用橡皮泥捏成各種動物形狀。

put together to build something from different parts or materials 裝配；組裝成整體：*Tony put together a bookcase from leftover lengths of wood.* 東尼用剩餘的一段段木料組裝了一個書櫃。

put up (*informal*) to build something such as a wall or another structure that may be either permanent or temporary 建造（圍牆等永久或臨時的建築物）：*The new block of flats was put up very quickly.* 那幢新大廈很快就建好了。

build² *noun* the size and shape of a person's, especially a man's, body（尤指男人的）體格，體型，身材：*He has an athletic build.* 他有健壯的體格。

body a person's body with reference to its appearance or physical fitness 身體；軀體：*He likes to look after his body by going to the gym four times a week.* 他喜歡健身運動，每週 4 次到健身房鍛煉。

figure the size and shape of a person's, especially a woman's, body（尤指女子的）身材，體形，身段：*a woman with a very shapely figure* 一個身材勻稱的女子

form a person's body, with reference to shape 形體；身材：*He is an admirer of the female form.* 他十分欣賞女性的身材。

frame the structure and size of a person's body 骨架；體格：*The coat looked huge on her slight frame.* 那件外套穿在她瘦小的身上顯得太大了。

physique a person's, especially a man's body, with reference to muscularity（尤指肌肉發達的男子的）體格，體形：*a boxer with a powerful physique* 一個體格健壯的拳擊手

shape the outline of a person's, especially a woman's, body（尤指女子的）身段，體形：*a tight-fitting dress that shows your shape to good advantage* 突顯身段的一件緊身連衣裙

  ⊃ see also 參見 **make**

business[1] *noun* activities or work involved in the buying and selling of goods or services 商務（活動）；生意：*She gave up teaching for a career in business.* 她棄教從商。

commerce the buying, selling, and distribution of goods or services, especially on a large scale（尤指大宗）商業貿易，買賣：*commerce between America and Asia* 亞洲和美洲間的商貿

dealings business transactions with a person or a company（尤指個人或公司間的）買賣，交易：*We have had dealings with this company in the past.* 以前我們與那家公司有過生意往來。

industry the production of goods, especially in factories, or a particular branch of manufacturing（尤指工廠或製造業部門的）工業，產業：*the steel industry* 鋼鐵工業

trade the buying, selling, and exchange of goods or services, or a particular area of trading 貿易；買賣：*There has been a backlash against the fur trade in some countries.* 一些國家一直抵制皮貨貿易。

business[2] *noun* an organization, large or small, concerned with the production or the buying and selling of goods or services 商行；公司；商店：*Stephen has his own plumbing business.* 史提芬擁有自己的管道設備企業。

big business very large and important companies considered as a group 大企業；集團公司：*the alleged corruption of politics by big business* 集團公司涉嫌的政治腐敗

company a group of people organized as a business, especially a corporation 公司；商號；商行：*the chairman of an insurance company* 保險公司董事長

concern (*formal*) a business 公司；商行；企業：*The company is a small family concern, but very successful.* 該公司是一家小型家族企業，但是非常成功。

corporation a business organization that is recognized in law as having a separate existence, rights, and responsibilities from the individuals who make it up 法人團體；（總）公司：*The company has grown into a huge multinational corporation.* 這家公司已經發展成為大型的跨國公司。

enterprise a business, especially a small one（尤指小型）企業，公司：*She runs a small knitwear enterprise from her own home.* 她經營着一家小型的家族式針織企業。

establishment (*formal*) a shop or other business and the premises that it occupies 公司；商業機構：*We expect the highest standards from the staff in our establishment.* 我們對公司員工寄予厚望。

firm a company 公司；商號；商行：*The supermodel has a contract with one of the large cosmetics firms.* 這位超級模特兒與其中一家大型化妝品公司簽訂了合同。

outfit (*informal*) a business organization 商業機構；營業所：*He got involved with a dodgy moneylending outfit.* 他與一家不可靠的放貸公司糾纏不清。

busy¹ *adjective* working hard or having a lot of work to do 忙碌的；有大量工作要做的：*I have been busy all day cleaning the house.* 我整天忙着打掃房間。

diligent working hard and conscientiously 用功的；勤奮的；勤勉的：*The detective was diligent in his search for clues.* 偵探勤於收集線索。

engaged* not free to speak to someone because you are speaking to someone or doing something else 忙着的；繁忙的：*Mike is engaged at the moment. Shall I ask him to phone you when he's free?* 邁克此時正忙。我讓他有空給你打電話好嗎？

* In British English a telephone line is said to be *engaged* when someone is speaking on it; in US English, it is said to be busy. 電話佔線在英國英語中用 engaged；在美國英語中則用 busy。

engrossed having your attention totally occupied by an activity 全神貫注的：*I was so engrossed in my work that I didn't notice it was lunchtime.* 我全神貫注地工作，竟然沒注意到已是午餐時間。

occupied having your time and attention taken up by an activity 沒空的；忙碌的；佔用的：*Can you keep the children occupied while I cook dinner?* 我做晚飯時，你能照顧一下孩子嗎？

rushed off your feet (*informal*) extremely busy, with no time to rest 馬不停蹄的：*We've been rushed off our feet all day in the café.* 我們整天在酒吧裏忙個不停。

busy² *adjective* filled with work or activities 忙的；沒空的：*I have had a very busy day looking after my sister's five children.* 我一整天都忙着照顧姐姐家的 5 個孩子。

eventful in which a number of important events take place 多事的；充滿大事的：*With the wedding and the football match, it was a very eventful weekend.* 參加婚禮、觀看足球比賽，這個週末活動頗多。

full in which you have little spare time because you have so many things to occupy you 滿的；充滿…的；有很多事情的：*We have a very full schedule* *between now and the end of November.* 從現在到 11 月底，我們的日程排得滿滿的。

hectic extremely busy and rushed 極其忙碌的；忙亂的；繁忙的：*During exam time things get pretty hectic in the departmental secretary's office.* 考試期間，系秘書辦公室裏一片忙亂。

tiring involving so much work as to cause you to feel tired 令人睏倦的；使人疲勞的；勞累的：*After a tiring day at the office, I like to put my feet up when I get home.* 在辦公室勞累了一天，我喜歡回家後就休息。

busy³ *adjective* not quiet or empty, but full of people or activity 熱鬧的；繁忙的；繁華的：*This road is very busy at rush hour.* 這條道路在上下班時間非常繁忙。

bustling full of people who are very busy and energetic 熙熙攘攘的；活躍的：*There is a wide variety of stalls in the bustling marketplace.* 熙熙攘攘的市場上有各式各樣的貨攤。

crowded filled with so many people that it is difficult to move about or be comfortable 擁擠的；擠滿人的：*It's easy to get lost in the crowded streets of central London.* 在倫敦市中心擁擠的街道很容易迷路。

swarming crowded with people who, you feel, make the place unpleasant to be in 擠滿人的；密集的；擁擠不堪的：*Don't go during the festival, the city's bound to be swarming with tourists.* 別在節日期間去，城裏肯定擠滿了遊客。

teeming containing great numbers of people, animals, or things (*which may be either a good thing or a bad thing*) 充滿⋯的；擁擠的；龐雜的：*In summer the resort is teeming with holidaymakers, and the hotels do really good business.* 夏天，旅遊勝地度假者雲集，酒店着實生意興隆。

vibrant full of interesting activity and excitement 充滿生機的；生氣勃勃的；激動的：*New York is such a vibrant city.* 紐約是如此充滿活力的城市。

⊃ see also 參見 **active**

buy *verb* to get something, usually in a shop, in exchange for money（常指在商店）購買（某物）：*Melanie bought a jacket with the money she got for her birthday.* 梅拉妮用生日得來的錢買了一件短外套。

acquire to gain possession of something, often by buying it（常指通過購買）得到，獲得（某物）：*Over the years I have acquired every single Beatles album.* 多年來，我購得了披頭四的每一張唱片。

come by to buy or obtain something, often after searching for it（常指通過尋找後）買到，獲得（某物）：*Exotic foods are hard to come by if you live in a village.* 你如果住在鄉下很難買到異國風味的食品。

obtain (*formal*) to gain possession of something, sometimes by buying it（有時指通過購買）獲得，得到：*Neil succeeded in obtaining a first edition of Seamus Heaney Poetry.* 尼爾終於買到了第一版的《謝默斯・希尼詩集》。

pick up to buy something that you happen to find on a casual shopping trip, rather than after looking specifically for it（逛商店時不經意地）碰巧買到：*I wandered round the market and managed to pick up a few bargains.* 我在市場上閒逛，碰巧買到一些便宜貨。

procure (*formal*) to buy something that is difficult to obtain（設法）買到，得到（某物）：*The country's army is trying to procure the special equipment needed to build nuclear weapons.* 該國的軍隊正在設法購置製造核武器需要的特殊設備。

purchase (*formal*) to obtain something in exchange for money 買，購買：*A home is the most expensive item that most people will ever purchase.* 房子是大多數人都想購買的最昂貴的商品。

C

calculate *verb* to discover the answer to a sum by using mathematics 計算，核算（總數）：*Will someone calculate how much each person's share of the bill is?* 誰來算一算每人分攤的費用有多少？

assess to work out the amount or size of something, such as a payment or damage, either by calculating or estimating 評定，評估，估算（金額或費用）：*My accountant has assessed the amount of income tax I am liable to pay.* 我的會計師已估算出我應支付的所得稅額。

compute to calculate an amount or figure mathematically or using a computer（用數學方法或計算機）計算，估計（數量或數字）：*The votes have been counted, and we're just computing the percentage share of the vote gained by each candidate.* 選票已經清點，我們正在計算每位候選人的得票百分比。

count to add up a number of things, people, or figures 數（數）；清點（總數）：*I counted the number of people ahead of me in the queue.* 我數了數排在我前面的人數。

estimate to make an approximate calculation of a figure or amount 估計，估算（數字或數量）：*The garage mechanic estimated that the repair would cost about £90.* 汽車修理廠的修理工估計維修費約 90 英鎊。

gauge to work out an approximate figure, often involving some guesswork 估量，估計，估算（數字）：*I would gauge the crowd to have numbered about 2000.* 我估計這群人共計 2000 左右。

reckon to add up roughly a number of things, people, or figures（粗略地）估算…的總數：*I reckon the bill will come to about £60.* 我粗略估算賬單總計約 60 英鎊。

work out to calculate something by thinking it through carefully（仔細地）核算，計算出：*I'm trying to work out whether I have enough money to go to the club and take a taxi home.* 我正想辦法計算出我是否有足夠的錢去俱樂部並坐計程車回家。

calm[1] *adjective* quiet and normal in manner and behaviour, not worried, angry, or excited 鎮靜的；沉着的；一如常態的：*He stayed calm in the face of danger.* 他面對危險鎮定自若。

composed in control of your emotions in difficult situations（在困難的形勢下）鎮定自若的：*The prime minister must remain composed in a crisis.* 首相在危機關頭必須保持鎮靜。

cool in control of your emotions, or not showing an emotional reaction when one would normally be expected 冷靜的；平靜的；反應冷漠的：*The murderer stayed cool even when questioned by the police.* 這個殺人犯甚至在警察質問時也保持鎮靜。

laid-back (*informal*) having a very relaxed and nonchalant attitude or a relaxed and informal atmosphere 悠閒自在的；放鬆的；隨便的：*Mary is so laid-back, nothing seems to worry her.* 瑪麗是那樣的悠然自得，似乎沒有甚麼讓她煩惱。

placid having an even temper, not easily upset or angered（性情）溫和的，平和的，安寧的：*She was a very placid child, unlike her brother, who demanded constant attention.* 她是一個很安靜的孩子，不像她弟弟，整天要人照顧。

relaxed being at ease and feeling no tension 放鬆的；不拘謹的：*A good hostess knows how to make her guests feel relaxed.* 一個優秀的女主人知道如何讓客人感到輕鬆自在。

serene at peace with yourself, and often detached from what is going on around you 安詳的，平靜的，寧靜的（常指不受外界影響）：*The bride remained serene and gracious throughout the ceremony.* 新娘在整個婚禮上始終保持着寧靜而和藹的神情。

unflappable (*informal*) always in control of your emotions, however serious the situation is 臨危不亂的；鎮定自若的：*My mum is unflappable – even when we bring friends to stay without warning, it doesn't bother her.* 母親總是應付自如，即使我們不打招呼帶朋友留宿家中，她也不會惱怒。

calm² *adjective* undisturbed by noisy or violent activity on the part of nature or human beings 不受（自然界或人類活動）干擾的，平靜的：*The sea was as calm as mill pond.* 海面靜如池水。

peaceful calm and quiet, usually through a comparative lack of human activity 寧靜的，平靜的，靜謐的（通常指人類活動相對較少）：*a peaceful village in the Scottish Highlands* 蘇格蘭高地上一個寧靜的村莊

still not moving at all 靜止的；不動的：*The wind died away, and suddenly everything was still.* 風逐漸減弱，突然間萬籟俱寂。

tranquil (*usually used to describe natural settings*) peaceful（常用於描述自然界）寧靜的，安靜的，平靜的：*We had a picnic in a tranquil spot by the lake.* 我們在湖邊一個安靜的地方野餐。

➲ see also 參見 **patient**

capture *verb* to take someone or something by force and keep them under your control（用武力）俘獲，捕獲，奪取（人或物使其處於控制中）：*He was captured by enemy soldiers and made a prisoner of war.* 他被敵軍抓獲，成了戰俘。

apprehend (*formal*) said about the police to catch and arrest someone suspected of committing a crime（警方）逮捕，拘押（疑犯）：*The police apprehended the suspect as he was about to board the ferry to Ireland.* 警方在疑犯正準備登上開往愛爾蘭的渡船時逮捕了他。

arrest said about the police: to catch someone suspected of committing a crime and take them to the police station（警方）逮捕，拘留（疑犯）：*The motorist was arrested for drink-driving.* 那個司機因酒後駕駛被拘留。

catch to get a person or an animal under your control, especially after chasing or hunting them (尤指經過追逐或搜捕) 捕捉，捕獲，抓住 (人或動物)：*We went fishing and I caught three trout.* 我們去釣魚了，我釣到 3 條鱒魚。

nick (*informal*) to arrest someone suspected of committing a crime 逮捕，拘留 (嫌犯)：*Jamie got nicked for joy-riding.* 傑米因駕駛偷來的車兜風被捕。

seize to capture or arrest someone 捕獲，逮捕，捉拿 (某人)：*The drug smugglers were seized at the airport.* 毒販走私在機場被捉拿。

take captive to capture someone and keep them as a prisoner or a hostage 劫持，挾持，俘虜 (某人作為戰俘或人質)：*The gunman took a little girl captive and held her for five hours.* 持槍歹徒挾持了一名小女孩作為人質 5 個小時。

trap to use a trap to catch an animal, or to put a person in a position from which they cannot escape 設陷阱捕捉 (動物)；使 (人) 陷入困境：*We were trapped in the lift for two hours when the power failed.* 停電時，我們被困在電梯裏兩個小時。

careful[1] *adjective* taking sensible precautions and not taking risks 小心翼翼的；謹慎的：*Be careful when crossing the road.* 過馬路的時候要謹慎小心。

cautious being very careful to avoid danger or harm, especially by moving slowly or only taking action when you have checked that it is safe to do so 謹慎行事的；小心的；謹慎的：*a cautious driver* 一個謹慎小心的司機

chary nervous about doing something in case it causes you problems 提心吊膽的；謹小慎微的：*I would be chary of actually meeting up with someone I only knew through contacting them on the Internet.* 如果真的要和那些我只是在網上認識的人見面的話，我會小心謹慎的。

prudent wise and careful, especially with money (尤指投資理財) 精明的，謹慎的，慎重的：*She made a prudent investment with her redundancy payment.* 她用自己的裁員補償費做了一筆審慎的投資。

vigilant (*formal*) watchful and alert because you expect that there might be danger or problems (因擔心出現危險或問題而) 警惕的，警戒的，謹慎的：*Be vigilant in the city – there are lots of pickpockets.* 在城裏要提高警惕 —— 扒手可是相當多的。

wary careful and suspicious 小心的；警戒的；機警的：*The old Lady has been wary of door-to-door salesmen ever since she was robbed by one.* 那位老婦人自從被一個上門推銷的銷售員搶劫之後就注意提防這種人了。

watchful making sure that you keep your eyes open and look carefully so that you do not miss any signs of danger or trouble (對危險或麻煩) 注意的，警戒的，提防的：*The invigilator keeps a watchful eye on the students in case they try to cheat during the exam.* 在考試時監考人密切注視考生動向以防他們作弊。

careful[2] *adjective* paying attention so that you do not miss anything or make any mistakes 細緻的；仔細的：*a careful examination of the facts* 對實情的仔細查驗

fastidious paying great or sometimes excessive attention to detail, especially to make sure that everything looks right 過分講究的；挑剔的；一

絲不苟的：*She is fastidious about always wearing matching lipstick and nail polish.* 她對於塗抹相配的唇膏和指甲油過分講究。

meticulous paying very close attention to every small detail to make sure that what you are doing is done perfectly 一絲不苟的；非常注意細節的；周密的：*The painter was meticulous about showing every line on the old man's face.* 畫家一絲不苟地勾畫出老人臉上的每條皺紋。

painstaking done in a very careful way and with an extra effort to get it right (*not usually used to describe people*) 極度細心的，煞費苦心的；辛苦的（通常不用以指人）：*a painstaking search for clues* 對線索煞費苦心的搜索

particular very careful to make sure that everything is just as you want it to be 挑剔的；苛求的；講究的：*She is very particular about eating meat with no fat whatsoever on it.* 她十分講究，絕不吃任何含有脂肪的肉類。

punctilious (*formal*) very careful to make sure that you always behave correctly and that other people behave correctly too 循規蹈矩的；一絲不苟的；謹小慎微的：*punctilious about timekeeping* 絕對守時

thorough very careful to make sure that when a piece of work is done it is properly finished and there are no mistakes in it 周到細緻的；工作縝密的：*Lesley is very thorough – she always checks and rechecks her work.* 萊斯利非常周到細緻，她對自己的工作總是查了又查。

careless *adjective* not paying enough attention to what you are doing, or caused by someone not paying enough attention to what they are doing 粗心的；粗枝大葉的；疏忽的：*Misspelling 'separate' was just a careless mistake.* 把 separate 拼錯只是疏忽造成的錯誤。

hasty done too quickly and without taking sufficient care 匆忙的；草率的：*a hasty decision* 草率的決定

inaccurate not conforming to fact, reality, or the actual state of affairs, or containing mistakes about facts, measurements, etc. 與（事實）不符的；不準確的；不確切的：*His estimate of how long the job would take to finish was wildly inaccurate.* 他對完成這個工作要花費的時間估計極不準確。

lax not taking enough care to make sure that you or other people obey rules or maintain proper standards 不嚴格的；不嚴密的；馬虎的：*The canteen staff are very lax about food hygiene.* 食堂員工對食品衛生馬馬虎虎。

offhand doing something, or done, in a way that suggests that you do not care about it very much or about what people think of it 漫不經心的；不在乎的；隨隨便便的：*His speech was delivered in an offhand manner.* 他的演講是信口開河。

slapdash doing something, or done, very quickly and casually, without enough attention to getting it right 倉促馬虎的；毛躁的；草率的：*Ethan is so slapdash in his attitude that his work is always full of mistakes.* 伊桑非常草率馬虎，所以他的工作總是錯誤百出。

slipshod done badly, without proper care and attention 敷衍了事的；不細心的；馬馬虎虎的：*The refurbishment of the shop was a slipshod job.* 店舖的重新粉飾只是敷衍了事。

sloppy (*informal*) showing little care or commitment, especially by being untidy or inaccurate 馬虎的；凌亂的；草率的：*He's a very sloppy dresser –*

his clothes never seem to fit, and they're usually dirty. 他不修邊幅，衣服好像從來都不合身，而且還總是髒兮兮的。

carry *verb* to move something or someone from one place to another, especially by lifting then holding them 攜帶；運送；搬運：*The old Lady was struggling up the hill carrying a heavy bag.* 老婦人背着沉重的袋子艱難地往山上爬。

bear (*formal or literary*) to carry something or someone 攜帶；運輸；運送：*The Magi came bearing gifts for the infant Jesus.* 東方三博士來了，帶着給初生基督的禮物。

bring to move something or someone from another place to here (從別處) 拿來，帶來：*I've brought you this book, I thought you might like to read it.* 我把這本書給你帶來了，我想你可能會想讀。

cart (*informal*) to carry something heavy or awkward 搬運，運送，載運 (笨重物品)：*I carted this TV all the way home, and it doesn't even work!* 我把這台電視機一路搬回家，它竟然是壞的！

convey (*formal*) to move people or things from one place to another in a form of transport (用運輸工具) 運輸，輸送：*A luxury limousine will swiftly convey you from the airport to your hotel.* 高級豪華轎車將很快把您從機場送到您下榻的酒店。

lug (*informal*) to carry or drag something heavy or awkward (費力地) 拉，拽，搬運 (笨重物品)：*The taxi didn't turn up, so I had to lug my suitcase all the way to the station.* 出租車沒來，我只好一路上把行李箱拖到車站。

take to move something or someone from here to another place 帶走；拿走：*Will you take your grandmother home after dinner?* 晚餐後將你祖母帶回家好嗎？

transport (*formal*) to move people or things from one place to another in a form of transport (使用運輸工具) 輸送，傳送：*Pupils are transported from outlying areas in the school bus.* 校車接學生們離開偏遠地區。

cause[1] *noun* something that makes something else happen (導致某事發生的) 原因，緣故：*The cause of death was heart failure.* 死亡的原因是心臟衰竭。

grounds circumstances that provide someone with an acceptable reason for believing something or doing something, especially taking legal action (相信或做某事，尤其是採取法律行動的) 充分理由，根據：*Unreasonable behaviour is grounds for divorce.* 不理智的行為是離婚的緣由。

justification a fact that justifies a course of action (證明某行為的) 正當理由，辯護，辯解：*There is no justification for a man hitting a woman.* 男人打女人是天理不容的。

motivation something that causes you to want to do something (做某事的) 動機：*His only motivation for wanting the job is to earn more money.* 他想要那份工作的唯一動機是賺更多的錢。

motive a person's reason for doing something, especially for committing a crime (尤指犯罪的) 動機，原因，目的：*Jealousy was her motive for murdering her husband.* 嫉妒是她謀殺丈夫的動機。

occasion (*formal*) a cause for doing something, especially a provocation for a bad action (*usually used with a negative*)（尤指引起惡劣行為的）原因，理由：*You had no occasion to be rude to her.* 你沒理由對她粗暴無禮。

origin something, often an event, in the past that has caused or created something（事情發生的）由來，起因：*The origin of the industrial dispute was the unfair dismissal of an employee.* 勞資糾紛起因於對一個僱員不公平的解僱。

reason an explanation for why someone does something or believes something, or for why something happens（某種行為、相信某人或某事發生的）解釋，理由，原因：*My reason for going to Paris is to study art.* 我去巴黎是為了學習美術。

root the basic cause, which is not always obvious at first, of an unpleasant situation（不愉快境遇的）根源，起因：*The root of her discontent is a thwarted ambition to be an actress.* 她的不滿歸根到底是因為想當演員的願望落空。

source something or someone that is the starting point from which something developed（事物發展的）起源，根源，起因：*We're trying to trace the problem back to its source.* 我們正在設法追溯問題的起因。

cause² *verb* to make something happen, or make someone do something 引起；使發生；促使：*The customer caused a fuss because the steak was too well done.* 那位顧客因為牛排做得太老而小題大做。

bring about to take action that causes a particular situation to exist 致使；使發生；造成：*She brought about a reconciliation between her husband and his father.* 她促成了丈夫和他父親之間的和解。

create to cause something, such as a feeling or situation, to exist 引起，造成，產生（某種情緒或狀況）：*Angela's promotion has created tension among her colleagues.* 安傑拉的晉升導致了她的同事之間的緊張關係。

effect (*formal*) to take action that causes something, such as a change or development, to take place 引起，招致，產生（變化或發展等）：*The Women's Movement effected major changes in women's rights.* 婦女解放運動使女權發生了重大變化。

generate to create or produce something abstract, for example discussion, excitement, or interest 創造，產生，引起（抽象事物，如討論、興奮或興趣等）：*Chat-show appearances by the stars generated a lot of interest in the film.* 有明星露面的訪談節目引發了人們對該影片的極大興趣。

produce to cause something, such as a reaction or a result, to happen or exist 導致，產生，引起（某種反應或結果）：*You can never be quite certain that an action will actually produce the effect that you intended.* 你永遠都無法確定一次行動是否真的會產生預期的效果。

provoke to produce a particular reaction in people, usually a strong or an adverse one 激起，引起，引發（強烈或不利的反應）：*The management's decision to have a pay freeze provoked an angry response.* 管理層凍結薪水的決定犯了眾怒。

trigger to be the direct cause of something happening（直接）引起，觸發：*Her father's death triggered a bout of depression.* 她父親的死使大家籠罩在一片愁雲慘霧之中。

➲ see also 參見 **basis**

chance *noun* a possibility that something may happen, or that you will be able to do something（事情發生的）可能性；（能夠做某事的）機會：*Sean stands a good chance of winning the contest.* 肖恩很有可能贏得比賽。

break (*informal*) a piece of luck, especially one that gives you an opportunity to show your abilities（尤指展現才能的）機會，機遇：*She got her first big break when she was invited to exhibit her work at the Tate Gallery.* 她受邀在泰特美術館展出作品是她人生中第一次重要機會。

likelihood the degree to which it is possible that something may happen（事情發生的）可能性：*There is little likelihood of snow this weekend.* 這個週末幾乎沒有下雪的可能性。

occasion a situation that enables you to do something（能夠做某事的）時機，機會：*I had hoped to ask Maria for some advice, but the occasion didn't arise.* 我本想徵求一下瑪麗亞的意見，但一直沒有機會。

opening an opportunity to achieve something or to show your abilities（取得成就或展現才能的）良機，機遇：*Claire was asked to take over while her boss was away on sick leave, which gave her an opening to show her organizational skills.* 克萊爾受命在老闆病假期間接管他的工作，這給了她展示組織才能的好機會。

opportunity a situation that enables you to do something that you want to do or to make progress（做想做的事或取得進步的）時機，機會：*I have been given the opportunity to work in Paris for six months.* 我得到了在巴黎工作 6 個月的機會。

possibility the fact that something might happen, although it is equally likely that it might not happen（事情發生與否的）可能，可能性：*There's a possibility that the president will visit the scene of the disaster.* 總統有可能視察災難現場。

probability the fact that something is more likely to happen than not to happen 很可能發生的事；很有可能：*There's a probability that you will need an operation.* 你很可能需要動手術。

prospect the fact that something is quite likely to happen in the future（將來發生某事的）可能性，希望，期望：*The family faced the prospect of losing their home.* 這家人可能面臨流離失所的命運。

change[1] *noun* an instance of becoming different or making something different 變化；改變：*There has been a change in the weather.* 天氣變了。

adjustment a minor alteration or rearrangement（細微的）變更；調整；調節：*The computer technician made a few adjustments to my settings, and that fixed the problems.* 電腦工程師對我的設置作了一些調整，從而解決了問題。

alteration a change, especially a change made to something such as a garment or figures（尤指對衣着或數字等的）改變，變動，更改：*The bride's* *dress needed some alterations after she lost weight.* 新娘瘦了以後，婚紗需要改一下。

amendment a small change that improves something, especially a written document（尤指對書面文件做少許的）修改，修訂，修正：*I have made an amendment to your bill to correct the error.* 我把你票據上的錯誤作了修正。

conversion a major change to the form or function of something, such as a building（對建築物等的形式或功能的）改變，轉變，轉換：*The builders are working on a barn conversion.* 施工人員正在改建穀倉。

makeover a set of major changes that are intended to improve the appearance of something, especially a person or a room（尤指對人或房間的外觀進行的一系列）改變，改頭換面：*After she had a makeover, the TV presenter's career was revived.* 這位電視節目主持人改變外型後，事業又蒸蒸日上了。

modification a minor change to make something work better or more efficiently（為使某事物更完善或更有效率而作輕微的）修改，改進，變動：*I have made modifications to the filing system which speed up the process considerably.* 我對文件歸檔系統作了些改進，大大加快了文件處理的速度。

reversal a change in something that makes it the opposite of what it was before 逆轉；顛倒；反轉：*The Minister has had a complete reversal of opinion on local taxation.* 部長對地方稅收的看法發生了大逆轉。

revolution a major change, for example in working methods, that means that everything is done in a new way（劇烈的）變革；革命：*The introduction of computer technology brought about a revolution in animated films.* 電腦技術的應用帶來了動畫片大變革。

transformation a major or complete change in the appearance or nature of something or someone（外觀或本質的徹底）改變，轉變，改觀：*There has been a transformation in Tony's appearance since he got married.* 東尼結婚後外表煥然一新了。

change² *verb* to become different or to make something different 改變；使轉變：*I've decided to change the time of the meeting.* 我決定更改會議時間。

adjust to make a minor alteration or rearrangement to something（輕微地）調節；調整；變更：*I adjusted my watch so that it showed the same time as the clock on the town hall.* 我校準了手錶以便和市政廳的時鐘一致。

alter to change, especially to make changes to something such as a garment or figures（尤指對衣着或數字等）改變，變動，更改：*I altered the 'a' to an 'e' and the 'v' to an 'r', so that the word reads 'here' instead of 'have'.* 我把 a 變成了 e，把 v 變成了 r，這樣這個詞就讀作 here 而非 have 了。

amend (*formal*) to improve something, especially a written document, by making usually small changes to it（尤指對書面文件小幅度地）修改，修訂，修正：*I have amended the final paragraph to make it easier to read aloud.* 我對結尾段作了修改，使其琅琅上口。

convert to change something so that it has a new form or function 改變，轉變，轉換（使具有新的形式或功能）：*I have converted amounts in zlotys to amounts in Euros.* 我將波蘭幣兌換成了歐元。

modify to make minor changes to something so that it works better or more efficiently（輕微地）修改，改進，變動（使其更完善或更有效）：*They modified the design of the exhaust system to reduce the emission of harmful gases.* 他們修改了排氣系統的設計以減少有害氣體的排放。

reverse to change something, for example a decision, so that it becomes the opposite of what it was before 顛倒；逆轉；廢除（決定等）：*A higher court may reverse a judgment made in a lower court.* 高級法院可推翻初級法院的判決。

revolutionize to change a way of doing something completely, and usually for the better（常指朝好的方向）徹底變革，根本改變：*The advent of the computer revolutionized the way in which data is stored.* 電腦的出現徹底改變了數據存儲的方式。

transform to cause a major or complete change in the appearance or nature of something or someone（使外觀或性質完全地）改變，轉變，改觀：*By sheer hard work and business skill they transformed a failing company into a highly successful enterprise.* 他們完全憑着艱苦卓絕的努力和經營才能把一個瀕臨倒閉的公司變成了非常成功的企業。

character *noun* the collection of psychological and moral qualities that makes someone the kind of person that they are（人的心理和道德）品質，品德，性格：*He is not a bad man, but there is a weakness in his character.* 他不是個壞人，但性格上有缺陷。

disposition a person's usual frame of mind 心境，性情，性格：*The little girl has such a sunny disposition that she always makes us smile.* 這小女孩兒開朗的性格使我們笑口常開。

image the nature of a person, organization, or commercial product as it is presented to, or perceived by, the public（人、組織或商品在公眾中的）形象，印象：*The Minister likes to play up to his image as a family man.* 部長喜歡把自己塑造為一個居家男人的形象。

make-up the collection of qualities that are seen by other people as being typical of a person's character（外在的）性格，氣質：*Jealousy is not in her make-up.* 妒忌不是她的個性。

nature the basic character of a person, especially the traits that they are born with, which determines how they behave（尤指與生俱來的）本性，天性，性格：*It is not in his nature to forgive and forget.* 不念舊惡不是他的本性。

persona (*formal*) the version of your character that you present to other people（展現給他人的）表面形象，表象人格，假象：*Often a celebrity's public persona is quite different from his true personality.* 名人的公眾形象常常與其真實性格相去甚遠。

personality a person's character, especially with regard to whether they are lively and interesting（尤指是否活潑、有趣等）個性，性格：*What he lacks in looks he makes up for in personality.* 他的性格彌補了他長相上的缺陷。

temper the kind of nature that a person has, particularly with regard to how easily they become angry 性情；脾氣；情緒：*Juliet has a very even* *temper – nothing much seems to bother her.* 朱麗葉性情平和，似乎沒有多少事情讓她煩心。

temperament the kind of nature that a person has, with regard to how emotional or calm their reactions are 氣質；性情；稟性：*This film is not suitable for people of a nervous temperament.* 這部電影不適合性情焦躁的人觀看。

characteristic *noun* one of the qualities that, combined, make up the nature of a person or thing (構成人或事物本質的) 特徵，特性，特點：*Kieron's sincerity is his most attractive characteristic.* 基隆的真誠是他最具魅力的特徵。

attribute a quality that someone or something has, especially a positive quality (尤指良好的) 特性，性質，屬性：*One of the main attributes of his paintings is his vivid use of colour.* 他的繪畫作品的主要特色之一就是鮮明的色彩運用。

feature a distinctive aspect of a person, thing, or place (人、物、地與眾不同的) 特色，特徵，特點：*The Eiffel Tower is Paris's most easily recognizable feature.* 埃菲爾鐵塔是巴黎最具標誌性特色的建築。

idiosyncrasy an unusual character trait or habit (特別的) 習性，癖性，個性：*Wearing a bow tie is one of his little idiosyncrasies.* 打煲呔是他的小癖好之一。

peculiarity a distinctive or unusual feature (與眾不同的) 特徵，特性，特點：*Cartoonists pick out peculiarities of their subjects and exaggerate them.* 漫畫家捕捉所表現對象與眾不同的特徵並進行誇張處理。

quality a distinguishing characteristic, especially a positive one (尤指好的) 特性，品質，素質：*Ahmed has all the qualities needed to be a good doctor.* 艾哈邁德擁有做一個好醫生所需要的全部素質。

quirk a slightly strange character trait or habit 怪異的性格特徵 (或習性)；怪癖：*She found some of her husband's quirks very hard to live with.* 她發現她丈夫的一些怪癖讓人很難容忍。

trait one of the qualities that make up someone's personality (構成個人性格的) 特徵，特性，特質：*Arrogance is a trait he seems to have inherited from his father.* 傲慢似乎是從他父親那裏遺傳來的性格。

cheap *adjective* not costing a lot of money to buy or use, although often not of very good quality 花錢少的，便宜的，廉價的 (通常指價低質劣)：*You can't expect top-quality service in a cheap hotel.* 在廉價的旅館裏你不能指望高品質的服務。

affordable (*usually used to describe commercial goods and services*) within a price range that most people can afford (常指商品或服務的價格) 負擔得起的：*'Three-piece suites at affordable prices.'* "價格公道的三件式套裝"

budget (*usually used to describe commercial goods and services*) designed to be sold at a relatively low price (常指商品或服務) 經濟的，便宜的，價格低廉的：*a company that deals in budget holidays* 經營經濟式假日旅遊的公司

dirt-cheap (*informal*) costing very little indeed 非常便宜的；廉價的：*I bought this watch at the flea market – it was dirt-cheap!* 我在跳蚤市場買的這隻手錶，太便宜了！

economical (*usually used to describe machines and vehicles*) not costing much to use（常指機器或交通工具）經濟的，節約的：*an economical car with low petrol consumption* 經濟節能型汽車

inexpensive not costing a lot of money (often used to avoid the possible negative sense of 'cheap') 不昂貴的，便宜的，廉價的（常用該詞代替 cheap，以避免可能引起的負面含義）：*an inexpensive family restaurant* 一家廉價的家庭式餐館

low-cost (*used only in business contexts*) costing comparatively little（只用於商業中）成本相對較低的，廉價的：*low-cost car hire* 廉價的汽車租用

no-frills (*informal*) not expensive because only a basic service is offered（因只提供基本服務而）不昂貴的，便宜的：*We flew with a no-frills airline, which does not offer in-flight meals.* 我們乘坐的是不提供飛機餐的經濟航班。

on special offer sold for a limited period of time at a lower price than usual, often with specific conditions（在特定情況下）限時特賣：*Melons are on special offer – buy one, get one free.* 西瓜限時特賣，買一送一。

reasonable being offered at a price that seems very fair（價格）合理的，公道的：*a shop that sells designer clothing at reasonable prices* 一家價格公道、出售名牌服裝的商店

cheat *verb* to behave in a dishonest way to prevent someone from getting something that they ought rightfully to have 欺騙，欺詐（指採用不誠實手段阻止他人得到理應得的東西）：*Philip cheated me out of my share of the money.* 菲利普施展伎倆，不讓我拿到我應得的那份錢。

con (*informal*) to trick someone or steal from someone after gaining their trust（尤指在獲取信任後）欺詐，哄騙：*A couple posing as charity workers conned people into giving them donations.* 一對假稱是慈善工作者的夫婦騙取了人們的捐款。

deceive to make someone believe in something that is false or unreal, usually in order to gain an advantage over them（通常指為利用某人而）蒙騙，誤導，使人誤信：*We were deceived by his honest appearance and professions of good faith.* 我們被他誠實的外表和自我標榜的誠懇所蒙騙。

defraud (*formal*) to get money from someone by dishonest or illegal means（通過不誠實或非法手段）騙取，詐取（錢財）：*The singer was defrauded by his agent, who took a huge percentage of his earnings.* 這位歌手被他的經紀人騙了，他的絕大部分收入都被經紀人拿走。

dupe to fool someone into believing something that is not true 哄騙，欺騙，愚弄（某人）：*We were all duped into believing her sob story about being robbed.* 我們都上她的當了，相信了她被搶劫的悲傷故事。

rip off (*slang*) to deliberately overcharge someone or cheat them out of money 敲詐；訛詐；敲竹杠：*The hotel tried to rip us off by charging for the minibar, which we hadn't used.* 這家旅館對我們並未使用過的小冰箱索價，試圖敲我們一筆。

swindle to get money from someone by dishonest or illegal means（使用不誠實或非法手段）詐取，詐騙（錢財）：*Many people were swindled in unreliable pension schemes.* 許多人被不可靠的退休金計劃所欺騙。

trick to use clever, amusing, or dishonest means to deceive someone or make them do something that puts them at a disadvantage（通過要花招或不誠實手段）哄騙，欺騙，詐騙（使某人處於劣勢）: *Computer users can be tricked into giving away personal information that can be used in crimes against them.* 電腦用戶可能被騙取個人資料，用於對其不利的犯罪。

check *verb* to make sure that something is as it should be 檢查；檢驗；核實: *Always check your spelling before you post a letter.* 在寄信之前總是檢查一下你的拼寫是否正確。

double-check to check your work and then check it again 覆核；覆查；仔細審核: *Chris is very meticulous – she double-checks every document before she files it.* 克麗絲非常細心 —— 她總是在歸檔之前仔細核查每一份文件。

examine to look carefully at something or someone to check whether they are all right（仔細地）檢查，檢驗（物或人以確認是否正常）: *The doctor examined the girl's foot to see if there was a broken bone.* 醫生仔細檢查女孩的腳以確認是否骨折。

give the once-over (*informal*) to look someone or something over quickly but carefully（快速而仔細地）打量，看一眼: *He gave the new girl the once-over and liked what he saw.* 他匆匆打量了一下這個新來的女孩，對她產生了好感。

investigate to examine facts in order to discover the truth about something, such as a crime 調查，偵察（犯罪等）: *The police are investigating a bank robbery.* 警方正在調查一宗銀行搶劫案。

scrutinize to examine something or someone very closely, often in order to discover information about them 仔細查看；細緻審查；認真檢查: *I scrutinized his face for signs of distress.* 我仔細端詳他的臉，尋找悲傷的跡象。

test to try something or someone out in order to discover information about them 實驗，測試，試驗（以發現更多的信息）: *New drugs must be tested thoroughly before they can be licensed for use.* 新藥在獲准使用之前必須接受全面的試驗。

verify to check the truth of some information 核實，查證，證實（信息的真實性）: *You must always verify your facts before you publish them.* 你在公佈事實之前一定要反覆查證。

➾ see also 參見 **inspect**

choose *verb* to decide that you want something or someone (or a number of different people or things) when there are various alternatives on offer（在可供選擇的人或事物中）挑選，選取，選擇: *Would you like to choose a dessert from the trolley?* 在手推餐車裏挑選一份甜點好嗎？

elect to choose someone to hold an official position, for example as an MP or a chairperson, by voting for them（投票）選舉，推選（某公職，如議員或主席等）: *Tony Blair was elected leader of the Labour Party in 1994.* 貝理雅在1994年被選為工黨領袖。

go for (*informal*) to choose something (*usually one particular thing*) 選擇，寧願要（通常為某一具體東西）: *I'd go for the chicken korma, if you want a curry that's not too hot.* 如果你要一份不太辣的咖喱飯，我寧願要腰果滑汁雞。

opt to choose one thing, such as a particular course of action, in preference to other options（傾向於）選擇，挑選（某種特別的行為過程）: *Given the choice of driving or walking, we opted to walk.* 倘若在開車和步行二者中選擇，我們傾向於步行。

pick to choose something or someone (*or a number of different things or people*), especially to choose something that you can take in your hand or to select the members of a team 選擇，挑選（自己可以掌控的事物或隊員）: *Pick a card, look at it, but don't tell anyone what card it is.* 挑一張牌看一看，但不要告訴別人是甚麼牌。

plump for (*informal*) to choose one person or thing, usually after careful consideration（通常指經過慎重考慮之後）挑選，篩選: *We weighed up the pros and cons of a holiday in Spain or Italy and in the end we plumped for Spain.* 我們權衡了在西班牙和意大利度假的利弊之後，最終選擇了西班牙。

select to make a careful choice from among several options, especially to choose the people who are going to make up a team 挑選，選拔，選擇（隊員等）: *He's been selected to be in the national squad for the World Cup.* 他被選入國家隊參加世界盃比賽。

settle on to come to a decision about whom or what you are going to choose, usually after spending a lot of time considering various alternatives（通常指經過長時間考慮）選定，決定: *They have finally settled on a date for the wedding.* 他們最終確定了婚期。

single out to choose one person or thing from a group for special attention（從一組中）單獨挑出，特別選出: *The other students were resentful because Kimberley appeared to have been singled out for special treatment.* 其他同學都感到氣憤，因為金伯利似乎受到特殊的待遇。

> ➲ see also 參見 **decide**

clean *adjective* free from dirt 無灰塵的；乾淨的: *She put clean sheets on the bed.* 她在牀上鋪上了乾淨的被單。

hygienic very clean and free from anything that might be dangerous to health 衛生的；乾淨的: *It's important for kitchen staff to work in hygienic conditions.* 廚房工作人員在乾淨衛生的條件下工作是很重要的。

immaculate extremely clean, with no trace of dirt 特別整潔的；潔淨無瑕的: *He was wearing an immaculate white shirt.* 他穿着一塵不染的襯衫。

pristine (*formal*) extremely clean or in very good condition, as if new 特別乾淨的；嶄新的: *one microwave for sale, in pristine condition* 一個待售的嶄新微波爐

pure free from contamination, or not having anything else mixed with it 未受污染的；不含雜質的；純淨的: *pure spring water* 純淨的泉水

spick and span (*informal*) very clean and neat 乾淨整潔的；清清爽爽的: *Make sure you leave the apartment spick and span.* 一定要保證公寓乾淨整潔。

spotless kept very clean 極清潔的；一塵不染的: *They may be poor, but their house is always spotless.* 他們雖然貧窮，屋子裏卻一塵不染。

sterile absolutely clean and treated with something that kills all germs 無菌的；消過毒的：*Surgical operations must be performed in sterile conditions.* 外科手術必須在無菌環境中進行。

clear *adjective* easy to see, perceive, or understand 顯而易見的；容易理解的；明白易懂的：*It was clear to me that the man was lying.* 對我來説很明顯，這個男人在説謊。

apparent able to be perceived or noticed 顯而易見；顯然的：*It soon became apparent that she was totally unsuitable for that kind of work.* 她完全不適合那種工作，這一點很快就顯露無疑了。

blatant (*used to describe something bad or immoral*) obvious, often because no attempt is made to hide it (用以指不好或不道德的事) 明目張膽的，公開的：*He said he had found the wallet in the street, but that was a blatant lie.* 他説他在街上發現的這個錢包，但這完全是彌天大謊。

conspicuous standing out from its surroundings and so able to be easily seen 顯著的；突出易見的；惹人注意的：*a conspicuous landmark* 顯眼的路標

evident that can be seen by the evidence, for example by somebody's facial expression or body language (基於某些跡象，如面部表情或身體語言等) 顯然的，明白的：*With evident distaste he changed the baby's nappy.* 他給嬰兒換尿布時表現出明顯的不悦。

obvious very easy to see, perceive, or understand 顯而易見的；明白易懂的；容易理解的：*It's obvious from the way he looks at her that Tom is attracted to Julie.* 湯姆看朱莉的眼神明白無誤地表明他被她迷住了。

patent (*formal*) (*used to describe behaviour or abstract things*) obvious (行為舉止或抽象事物) 顯而易見的，明顯的：*For the Minister to preach about family values while cheating on his wife was patent hypocrisy.* 這位部長一面鼓吹家庭價值觀，一面背叛他的妻子，顯然很虛偽。

plain clear and leaving no room for doubt 清楚的；明白無誤的：*I thought I had made my feelings on this subject plain.* 對於這個問題的感受，我想我已經説得很明白了。

clever *adjective* having or showing above average intelligence or skill 聰明的，聰穎的 (指智力和能力過人)：*a clever plan* 一份聰明的計劃

astute having a sharp mind and wise judgment 有敏鋭判斷力的；精明的；機敏的：*an astute judge of character* 對性格特徵的敏鋭判斷

brainy (*informal*) very intelligent and knowledgeable 十分聰明的；知識淵博的；有才智的：*You're brainy – will you help me with my homework?* 你很聰明，你能幫我做功課嗎？

bright quick to learn and having lots of ideas 主意多的；悟性高的；聰慧的：*Melanie is a very bright pupil but lacks concentration.* 梅拉妮是個悟性很高的學生，只是注意力不夠集中。

brilliant extraordinarily intelligent 極其聰明的；才華橫溢的：*a brilliant scientist* 一個才華橫溢的科學家

gifted born with a high degree of skill or intelligence 有天賦的；天資聰慧的：*a school for gifted children* 為天才兒童開辦的學校

ingenious showing an unusual kind of cleverness and originality 機靈的；有獨創性的：*an ingenious invention* 具有獨創性的發明

intelligent having or showing an ability to learn, think, or understand effectively, especially with relation to serious subjects (尤指在嚴肅的問題上) 有才智的，悟性高的；聰明的：*an intelligent conversation* 機智的會談

shrewd having or showing practical intelligence based on experience of life and people's behaviour (基於人生經驗和別人的行為) 精明的，有判斷力的，精於盤算的：*a shrewd assessment of their chances of success* 對於他們成功可能性的準確估計

smart* (*informal*) having or showing intelligence and quick thinking 反應快的；機敏的；聰明的：*a smart answer* 機智的回答

* Smart is very commonly used to describe people who are clever in US English, but is less commonly used about people in British English. Smart 在美國英語中常用以形容人聰明，而在英國英語中較少用於形容人。

➲ see also 參見 **able; shrewd**

climb *verb* to move towards the top of something by using your feet or your hands and feet (用腳或手腳並用地) 攀登，爬：*The boys amused themselves by climbing trees.* 男孩們爬樹玩。

ascend (*formal*) to move upwards, or to go up something 上升；攀登：*They ascended the staircase to the bedroom.* 他們上樓來到臥室。

clamber to use your hands and feet to get up something that is usually quite low and easy to climb (手腳並用) 攀爬 (地勢較低、容易到達的地方)：*The children clambered all over the climbing frame in the park.* 孩子們在公園的攀爬架上爬來爬去。

mount to climb onto something that you are going to ride, such as a horse or a motorcycle, or to go up something, such as steps or a hill 騎上 (馬或摩托車等)；登上，攀登 (台階或山)：*The cowboy mounted his horse and rode off.* 牛仔騎上馬離開了。

scale to climb to the top of something high, such as a wall or a hill 攀登，爬上，登上 (如牆或山等高處)：*Sir Edmund Hillary scaled Mount Everest in 1953.* 埃德蒙·希拉里爵士在 1953 年登上了珠穆朗瑪峰。

scramble to climb with difficulty or awkwardness (吃力或笨拙地) 爬，攀登：*We scrambled up the sand dunes on our hands and knees.* 我們手和膝蓋並用爬上了這座沙丘。

shin up to climb up something narrow and tall, such as a rope or a pole, by using your hands and knees (手和膝蓋並用地) 爬上 (窄而高的東西，如繩索或竿子等)：*When I locked myself out, I had to shin up the drainpipe and climb in through the bedroom window.* 我把自己鎖在了門外，只好順着排水管從臥室的窗戶爬進去。

swarm up to climb quickly up something, such as a rope or a mast, by gripping with the knees and pulling yourself up by the hands (指雙膝夾緊、用手快速地) 爬上 (如繩子或桅桿等)：*The sailor swarmed up the mainmast.* 這水手迅速地爬上了主桅。

➲ see also 參見 **rise**

close[1] *adjective* (to rhyme with dose) a short distance away 短距離的；近的：
Our house is very close to the church. 我家離教堂僅幾步之遙。

adjacent (*formal*) right next to something, but usually not joined to or
touching it 相臨的，鄰近的（但並未相連）：*Our premises are located on a
prime site adjacent to the city centre.* 我們的營業場所座落在臨近市中心的一個
黃金地段。

adjoining right next to something and usually joined to or touching it 緊挨
的；相連的；毗連的：*a suite of adjoining rooms* 房間緊挨着的一個套房

handy (*informal*) situated conveniently close to something 在附近的；方
便的；便利的：*My office is very handy for the station.* 我的辦公室離車站
很近。

near a short distance away in space or time（在空間或時間上）接近的，不遠
的：*in the near future* 在不久的將來

nearby* situated a short distance away from where you are 離所在地不遠
的；附近的：*We could see a light in the window of a nearby cottage.* 我們可以
看見附近農舍窗戶裏透出來的燈光。

* Not used with more or most. 不與 more 和 most 連用。

neighbouring (*usually used to describe buildings or large areas*) right next
to each other（常用於形容建築物或大片區域）緊臨的，臨近的，毗鄰的：
Spain and Portugal are neighbouring countries. 西班牙和葡萄牙是鄰國。

nigh (*old-fashioned*) close in time（時間上）接近的：*I saw a man with a
placard saying 'The end of the world is nigh'.* 我看見一個人舉着告示牌，上面
寫着"世界末日就要來臨了。"

on your doorstep (*informal*) very close to your home 家門口的；離家不遠
的：*When we lived in the city, we had shops, restaurants, and cinemas right on
our doorstep.* 我們住在城市時，一出門就有商店、飯館和電影院。

close[2] *verb* (to rhyme with doze) to move something, such as a door or a
window, so that it is no longer open 關閉（門或窗等）：*Close the gate so that the
sheep don't escape.* 把門關好，別把羊放跑了。

bolt to fasten a door securely with a bolt 上門閂；鎖門：*I locked and bolted
the doors before I went to bed.* 我鎖好門，然後上牀睡覺。

fasten to close a belt, buckle, or other fastening device 扣緊，拴緊，繫緊（帶
子等）：*Fasten your seat belts.* 繫好安全帶。

push to to push a door or a gate so that it is almost closed 把（門）掩上：
Push the door to, but don't shut it, in case the cat wants to come in. 把門掩上，
但不要關緊，説不定貓要進來。

seal to close something, such as an envelope or a container, very tightly 密
封（信封或容器等）：*The jam is put in jars, which are then sealed so that they
are airtight.* 把果醬裝進罐子，然後密封保存。

secure to close or fasten something tightly, for example with a rope or a
lock, to prevent it from moving or being opened（用繩或鎖等）拴牢，固定，
扣緊：*He moored the boat and secured it with a rope.* 他泊好船，並用繩子繫
好。

shut to move something, such as a door or window, so that it is no longer open 把（門窗等）關上：*Don't shut the window, we need some fresh air in here.* 別關窗，屋裏需要新鮮空氣。

slam to close a door or window with a loud bang, often because you are angry（常因為生氣）砰地關上（門或窗）：*She stormed out in a temper, slamming the door.* 她氣沖沖地衝出去，砰地一聲把門關上了。

clumsy *adjective* moving about or doing things in a way that is not graceful or coordinated, so that you often drop things or bump into them 行動笨拙的；跌跌撞撞的：*Phil is very clumsy, always knocking things over.* 菲爾笨手笨腳的，老是把東西撞翻。

awkward not graceful in the way you move or position your body and not skilful in handling objects, but unlikely to cause damage（行動、形態等）笨拙的，不靈巧的（但不至造成損失）：*His jacket was too tight for him, and every time he moved his arms he looked awkward and uncomfortable.* 他的外套太小了，所以他每次伸動胳膊都顯得笨拙而不舒服。

bungling (*informal*) irritatingly clumsy and inefficient（極其）拙劣的，低效率的：*You bungling idiot! You've ruined our plan!* 你這個蠢貨！把我們的計劃全搞砸了！

gauche (*formal*) not good at talking to or dealing with people in social situations, because of inexperience or shyness（因缺乏經驗或害羞等）不善交際的，不苟言談的，笨拙的：*a gauche young man who always seems to say the wrong thing* 似乎總是説錯話的笨拙的年輕人

ham-fisted (*informal*) very clumsy or incompetent 愚笨的；笨手笨腳的；不能勝任的：*Some ham-fisted mechanic had broken the fan belt while attempting to tighten it.* 某個笨手笨腳的機修工本想把風扇皮帶繃緊，卻把它弄壞了。

heavy-handed using or showing too much force or effort and too little skill 粗手粗腳的；魯莽的：*his heavy-handed attempts at humour* 他試圖表現幽默，卻笨手笨腳的

lumbering large, heavy, and moving awkwardly 笨重的；行動遲緩的：*a lumbering giant* 動作遲緩的巨人

uncoordinated moving awkwardly and without smoothness, especially unable to use two or more parts of your body together in a smooth and rhythmic way（動作或肢體）不協調的，不靈活的，笨拙的：*He is too uncoordinated to be a dancer.* 他動作太不協調了，不可能當舞蹈演員。

ungainly showing a lack of grace in movement 動作不雅的；笨拙的：*an ungainly walk* 笨拙難看的步態

cold *adjective* having a low temperature 溫度低的；冷的：*a cold drink* 冷飲

biting (*used mainly to describe the wind*) so cold as to cause a biting or stinging sensation on the skin（主要用以形容風）刺骨的，凜冽的：*a biting wind* 刺骨的寒風

bitter (*used to describe the weather or temperature*) very cold（用以形容天氣或溫度）嚴寒的，刺骨的：*The poor dog was left out in the bitter cold.* 這條可憐的狗被遺棄在刺骨的寒風中。

chilly rather cold 寒冷的 : *It's a bit chilly now that the sun has gone down.* 太陽西下，寒意漸濃。

cool slightly cold, often pleasantly so 涼爽的；涼快的 : *The sun was beating down, but there was a lovely cool breeze.* 烈日當空，但也有愜意的涼風襲來。

freezing extremely cold 嚴寒的；冰凍的 : *The hall was freezing, as the radiators were off.* 因暖氣停了，大廳冷得不得了。

frosty so cold that frost has formed on the ground, trees, and other surfaces 結霜的；霜凍的；嚴寒的 : *I have to scrape the car windscreen on frosty mornings.* 在寒冷的早晨，我得將擋風玻璃上結的霜給刮掉。

frozen feeling extremely cold 極冷的；凍僵的；結冰的 :We were *frozen* by the time the bus arrived, half an hour late. 汽車晚點半個小時，駛來時我們都快凍僵了。

icy so cold as to feel like ice 冰冷的；極冷的 : *Come indoors, your hands are icy.* 快進屋來，你的手是冰冷的。

⊃ see also 參見 **unfriendly**

comfortable *adjective* which makes you feel at ease or relaxed 感覺安逸的；舒適的；放鬆的 : *a comfortable bed* 舒適的牀

comfy (*informal*) comfortable 舒服的；舒適的 : *I always wear my comfy shoes for trudging round the shops.* 我總是穿着舒適的鞋逛商店。

cosy warm and comfortable, because in a small, enclosed space that brings people close together (因空間狹小而封閉) 暖和舒適的；愜意的 : *a cosy little cottage* 溫暖舒適的小屋

relaxing causing you to feel at ease 放鬆的；令人放鬆的 : *a relaxing warm bath* 讓人放鬆的熱水澡

restful causing you to feel rested 休閒的；恬靜的 : *a nice restful evening in front of the TV* 在電視機前度過的恬靜而美好的夜晚

snug small, warm, and comfortable 小而溫暖舒適的 : *a snug little corner by the fire* 爐火旁溫暖舒適的一角

spacious comfortable because containing a lot of room to move around in 寬敞舒適的 : *a spacious apartment* 一套寬敞舒適的公寓

complain *verb* to make negative comments about something or someone 抱怨，埋怨 : *They complained to the manager about the food in the restaurant.* 他們就餐廳的食物問題向經理投訴。

bellyache (*informal*) to complain in a bad-tempered way 氣急敗壞地抱怨；發牢騷 : *Jim is bellyaching about having to do the washing-up.* 吉姆因不得不洗碗而發牢騷。

gripe (*informal*) to complain moodily 發牢騷；嘮嘮叨叨地抱怨 : *Stop griping and just get on with the task!* 別發牢騷了，趕緊幹活！

grumble to mutter about something in a dissatisfied manner（不滿地）嘟囔，嘟嚷，發牢騷 : *Joe was grumbling about the noise of the children playing outside.* 祖嘮叨説外面小孩玩耍的聲音太吵。

make a fuss (*informal*) to complain loudly in a way that attracts attention to you 大吵大鬧；大發牢騷；大驚小怪：*It's only a tiny scratch, there's no need to make a fuss.* 這只是輕微的擦傷，沒有必要大驚小怪。

moan to complain about something in a bad-tempered way 生氣地抱怨：*Brenda is always moaning about the weather.* 布倫達老是抱怨天氣。

protest to object, often formally, to something, such as a plan or a course of action（常指正式）反對，抗議（計劃或行動等）：*Local people protested about plans to open a massage parlour.* 當地居民反對開設按摩院的計劃。

whine to complain about something in a moody or self-pitying way（生氣或自憐地）抱怨；哀訴：*Instead of whining to me about your boss, why don't you talk to him about your grievances?* 與其向我抱怨你的老闆，你幹嘛不直接找他説説你的委屈呢？

whinge (*informal*) to complain in a moody or childish way（生氣或孩子氣地）抱怨，嘟嚷：*I'm fed up listening to you whingeing all the time.* 你一直抱怨個不停，我聽得煩死了。

complete¹ *adjective* with no parts missing 完整的；全部的：*the complete works of Shakespeare* 莎士比亞全集

entire* all of something, such as a time or a place（指時間或地點等）全部的，完整的，整個的：*the entire universe* 整個宇宙
* Only used before a noun. 只用於名詞前。

full with all the space inside taken up, or with no parts missing 充滿的；裝滿的：*a full pack of cards* 一整副撲克牌

intact not broken or damaged 完好無損的；未受損壞的：*The framed picture you sent me arrived intact.* 你寄給我裝裱好的畫已完好無損地收到了。

unbroken not broken or interrupted 未受損害的；完整的；未中斷的：*an unbroken run of success* 接二連三的成功

whole* including every part 所有的；全部的；整個的：*I ate the whole bar of chocolate.* 我吃了整整一塊巧克力。
* Mainly used before a noun. 主要用於名詞前。

complete² (*used* mainly with negative words, but also with some positive words like success) in every respect（主要與含否定意義的詞搭配，也可與 success 等含肯定意義的詞連用）方方面面的，徹底的，完全的：*Their marriage was a complete disaster.* 他們的婚姻完全是場災難。

absolute (*used with negative and positive words*) to the very highest degree（與含否定或肯定意義的詞連用）絕對的，完全的：*It was an absolute pleasure to meet my sporting hero.* 見到我的體育偶像絕對是令人興奮的事。

outright (*used mainly with words like success or victory*) clear and leaving no doubt about the result（主要與 success 或 victory 等詞連用）完全的，徹底的，無保留的：*an outright victory* 徹底的勝利

thorough (*usually used with negative words*) being a strong example of something（通常與含否定意義的詞連用）完全的，徹底的：*They made a thorough mess of trying to organize a party.* 他們試圖組織一次派對，結果卻完全弄得一團糟。

total (*used with negative and positive words*) in every respect（與含否定或肯定意義的詞連用）徹底的，絕對的，全部的：*The child went off with a total stranger.* 這小孩跟着一個完全陌生的人走了。

unmitigated (*used with negative words*) having no good or redeeming features（與含否定意義的詞連用）絕對的，十足的，徹底的：*The man is an unmitigated scoundrel.* 這傢伙是個十足的混蛋。

unqualified (*used with positive words*) having no bad or doubtful features（與含肯定意義的詞連用）完全的，絕對的，無條件的：*The party was an unqualified success.* 晚會百分之百地成功。

utter (*used mainly with negative words*) to the very highest degree（與含否定意義的詞連用）全然的，絕對的：*We stared at the scene in utter disbelief.* 我們全然不信地看着眼前這一幕。

➔ see also 參見 **achieve; finish**

complicated *adjective* (used mainly to describe things, systems, or processes) difficult to understand or deal with because of having many different elements that do not link up or relate to one another in a straightforward way（主要用以描述事物、系統或過程）複雜的，難懂的，難解的：*Carol's life is very complicated, with a full-time job, a family to look after, and her charity work.* 卡羅爾的生活很繁雜，既要全天上班，還要照料家庭和參與慈善事業。

complex (used mainly to describe states or situations, but also people and living things) difficult to understand or deal with as a whole, because made up of many different, sometimes conflicting, elements（主要用以描述狀態或處境，也用以描述人和生物）難懂的，難解的，錯綜複雜的：*Jack was a very complex man – capable of great sensitivity, but also of the most appalling brutality.* 傑克是一個很複雜的人 —— 有時候非常敏感，但有時候也極其殘忍。

difficult causing problems or requiring a lot of effort to deal with or understand 麻煩的；艱難的；難懂的：*a difficult crossword puzzle* 難猜的填字遊戲

elaborate made or planned in a complicated way with a great many, often too many, details 精心策劃的；製作精細的；詳盡的：*A rebel group hatched an elaborate plot to assassinate the president.* 一群叛亂分子精心策劃了暗殺總統的陰謀。

fiddly (*informal*) difficult to handle or accomplish because of involving many small or delicate parts 微小難弄的；精巧難使用的；要求精度高的：*It was a fiddly job to disentangle the fine chain.* 手巧才解得開這根細鏈。

intricate (*used mainly to describe things with a pattern or sequence*) made up of many parts or stages that are linked together in a complicated way（主要用以描述帶圖案或有序列的事物）錯綜複雜的：*an intricate dance routine* 一套複雜的舞步

involved made annoyingly difficult to follow or to do because of being unnecessarily detailed or complicated 複雜難解的；繁雜難處理的；棘手的：*She told us a long involved story about various mishaps that occurred on her way to work to explain why she was late.* 為了解釋遲到的原因，她向我們講述了一段冗長複雜的故事，全是關於她在上班路上發生的種種不幸。

knotty difficult to resolve 難以解決的，棘手的：*a knotty problem* 一道難題
➲ see also 參見 **difficult**

confident *adjective* feeling or showing that you are sure of your own worth or abilities and that you are likely to be able to do something well 有信心的；自信的：*After studying hard for months, Shereen felt confident of passing her exams.* 經過數月的努力學習，謝林有信心通過考試。

assertive firmly stating your opinions or wishes 堅決主張的；堅定自信的；堅信的：*You will have to be more assertive or people will take advantage of you.* 你得更加堅定，不然人們會利用你。

cocky (*informal*) excessively confident to the point of being irritating 過分自信的；自高自大的；自以為是的：*Luke got a little cocky after all the teachers praised him.* 盧克得到所有老師的稱讚之後有點翹尾巴了。

poised sure of yourself in a calm and dignified way 泰然自若的，沉着自信的；鎮定的：*While the other actors were in a state of nerves, the star of the show was perfectly poised.* 當其他表演者都很緊張時，主演卻鎮定自若。

positive tending to expect a favourable outcome 積極樂觀的；有把握的：*Joel's success owes a lot to his positive outlook on life.* 喬爾的成功很大程度上歸因於他積極樂觀的人生觀。

secure feeling no anxiety or self-doubt 放心的；安心的；無後顧之憂的：*The woman stood for election, secure in the knowledge that she had her family's support.* 這位婦女知道家人都支持她，安心地參加了競選。

self-assured feeling or showing that you have no doubts about your ability to do something 有自信的；胸有成竹的：*The singer gave a smooth self-assured performance.* 這位歌手做了一場圓滿而自信的表演。

self-possessed calm and confident 沉着的；鎮靜的；泰然自若的：*When the school went on fire, the teacher remained self-possessed and calmly steered the children to safety.* 學校着火時，老師們鎮定自若，將孩子們帶到了安全的地方。

sure of yourself feeling no doubts about your ability to do something 有信心的；自信的：*David is remarkably sure of himself for a beginner.* 大衛雖是新手，卻非常自信。

➲ see also 參見 **sure**

conflict *verb* (said about things such as opinions or ideas) to be opposed to or in disagreement with something or with each other (指思想或觀點等) 相對立，相抵觸，相衝突：*The interests of the business sometimes conflict with the interests of the family.* 職業利益有時和家庭利益衝突。

be at odds (said about people and ideas, etc.) to disagree with someone, or to conflict with something or each other (指人和想法等) 有分歧，相互衝突：*Joan is always at odds with her mother-in-law on the subject of child care.* 在照料孩子的問題上，瓊總是和婆婆有分歧。

clash to disagree and have a violent argument with someone, or (*said for example about colours*) to be incompatible with each other 發生衝突；(顏色

等) 不協調：*The two co-presenters of the show frequently clashed in private.* 本節目的兩位節目主持人私下裏經常發生口角。

contradict to say something that disagrees with somebody else's account of something and suggests that the other account is wrong 反駁；駁斥；（陳述等）相矛盾，相抵觸：*Your version of events contradicts Jenny's.* 你説的情況和珍妮説的相矛盾。

differ to be different from each other, or to hold a different or opposing point of view（觀點）相異，有區別：*I think we should just agree to differ on this point, because neither of us will change the other's mind.* 我認為在這個問題上我們應該允許持有不同的觀點，因為我們無法改變對方的想法。

go against (said about actions, ideas, statements, etc.) to be contrary to or contradict something（指行為、思想、陳述等）相對立，相矛盾，違背：*This policy goes against everything that the party is supposed to stand for.* 這項政策與該黨所要倡導的各項方針相背離。

⊃ see also 參見 **disagree; fight; oppose; quarrel**

consider *verb* to have a particular idea or image of someone or something, based on your experience of them, that you are reasonably sure is a true one（根據經驗有把握地）認為，料想，斷定：*I consider myself to be a good judge of character.* 我認為自己善於判斷一個人的性格。

believe to have a particular idea or image of someone or something, based on your experience of them, but without being entirely sure that it is a true one（根據經驗卻沒有十足把握地）認為，猜想，料想：*I always believed her to be a good mother, but, of course, you know her better than I do.* 我以前一向認為她是位好母親，不過，你當然比我更了解她。

deem (*formal*) to think of something or someone in the specified way, especially to think about something in terms of how it affects your dignity and status（尤指對尊嚴和身份產生的影響的事）視為，認為，相信：*I would deem it an honour to be invited to your wedding.* 被邀參加你們的婚禮，我將甚感榮幸。

judge to form an opinion about someone or something based on evidence（根據證據）斷定，認為：*Anna was judged to be the best candidate for the job.* 安娜被認為是這份工作的最佳候選人。

rate to think of someone or something in terms of whether they are good or bad, successful or unsuccessful（就好壞或成敗等）評判，評價，鑒定：*The band's comeback concert was rated a huge triumph.* 這支樂隊復出後舉辦的音樂會被看作是巨大的成功。

reckon to have a particular idea or image of someone or something, especially as regards their quality or status 把⋯看作是，把⋯認為是（尤指品質或身份等）：*Gordon is reckoned to be the best table-tennis player in the youth club.* 哥頓被認為是青年俱樂部最優秀的乒乓球選手。

regard as to have a very definite idea of someone or something, usually because of long experience of them（通常根據長期的經驗而明確地）把⋯看成，把⋯當作：*I have always regarded you as one of my dearest friends.* 我一直把你當成我最好的一個朋友。

think to have an opinion about someone or something, which may be based on little evidence or formed very quickly（可能沒有甚麼證據或很快形成的）認為，覺得：*You may think me paranoid, but I prefer not to disclose any personal details over the Internet.* 也許你覺得我多疑，但我不願意將個人詳細資料暴露在互聯網上。

➲ see also 參見 **think**

continuous *adjective* happening without interruption over a period of time 持續的；連續的；不間斷的：*five hours' continuous rain* 5 個小時的持續降雨

constant happening repeatedly, sometimes to the point of irritation 反覆的，持續的（有時達到令人惱火的地步）：*I'm fed up with his constant nagging.* 我受夠了他不停的嘮叨。

continual happening repeatedly, usually at short intervals 反覆的（通常間歇短）；頻繁的：*continual interruptions* 頻繁插話

endless lasting a long time or happening very often, and therefore tedious 無休止的，無止境的，沒完沒了的（因而乏味的）：*her endless boasting about her children's achievements* 她沒完沒了地誇耀孩子的成績

incessant never stopping or pausing, and irritating or tiring because of that 不停的，持續不斷的（因而令人惱火或厭煩）：*their incessant chatter* 他們喋喋不休的談話

nonstop (*informal*) proceeding at a fast pace and never stopping, which may seem energetic or exciting 不間斷的，不停的，馬不停蹄的（顯得精力充沛或令人振奮）：*a nonstop round of social engagements* 應接不暇的社交活動

solid (*used to describe a length of time*) continuing without a break（時間）無間歇的，持續的：*We queued for tickets for three solid hours.* 我們排隊買票排了整整 3 個小時。

uninterrupted continuing without any interruptions 不間斷的；連續的；未受干擾的：*Parents of young babies rarely have a full night's uninterrupted sleep.* 嬰兒的父母很少能不受干擾地睡上一個通宵。

control *verb* to have power to make someone or something do what you want 支配，控制，操縱：*There was a strong police presence to control the crowd.* 有強大的警力控制人群。

command to be in a position of authority over a group of people, especially in the armed forces（尤指在軍隊裏）指揮，命令：*The admiral commanded a destroyer patrol force during the war.* 這位海軍上將在戰爭期間指揮了一支驅逐艦巡邏部隊。

conduct to organize and carry out something, such as an enquiry or a study 進行，組織，實施（調查、研究等）：*The commissioner conducted an enquiry into alleged corruption in the police force.* 專員對警察涉嫌貪污的問題進行了調查。

direct to be in charge of a group of people or an activity 負責；管理：*The agency directed an advertising campaign for the Dairy Council.* 代理商負責為奶製品協會打一輪廣告。

head to be the highest-ranking person in something, such as a business or a department（商家、部門等）主管，領導：*Mr Murphy heads the Accounts Department.* 墨菲先生掌管會計部。

lead to be the person directly responsible for telling or showing a group of people what to do in any sphere of activity from government to business or sport（在政府、商業或體育活動中）領導，率領，掌管：*The captain led his team to victory in the championship.* 隊長率隊在錦標賽中獲得了勝利。

manage to organize and be in charge of a business, or part of a business, or the work of a group of people 掌管；經營；管理：*She manages a fashionable restaurant in the city.* 她在城裏經營一家時尚餐館。

organize to plan something, such as a social occasion or other activity, and be responsible for making sure that it happens according to plan 組織，安排（社交等活動）：*I am organizing a concert for charity.* 我正在組織一場慈善音樂會。

oversee to be in charge of an activity or task to make sure that the work is done satisfactorily 監督，管理，負責（活動、任務等，以確保圓滿完成）：*Your role as Managing Editor is to oversee the work of freelance proofreaders.* 作為執行總編，你的職責是檢查兼職校對員的工作。

run to be in overall charge of a business or an activity 經營，管理，開辦（企業或活動等）：*He runs the family business almost single-handedly.* 他幾乎全憑自己經營着這個家族企業。

supervise to be in charge of a group of people or an activity, especially to be present and watch people to make sure they do what they are supposed to do 管理；（尤指）監督（以確保人們履行職責）：*A teacher must be present to supervise the students who are in detention.* 老師必須在場監督留堂的學生。

convincing *adjective* that makes you believe something, especially something that you did not previously believe 令人信服的；有説服力的：*Sarah is a very convincing liar.* 莎拉説起謊來都讓人信以為真。

believable realistic enough to appear to be true 可信的；真切的：*The star put in a believable performance as a tough detective.* 那影星扮演一個窮追猛打的偵探演得很逼真。

cogent (*formal*) that makes you believe that something is true or correct by presenting strong reasons（通過提供充分理由而）令人信服的：*a cogent argument* 讓人心悦誠服的論證

compelling capable of influencing someone's thoughts or opinions 令人信服的；（對思想、觀點等）有影響力的：*The defence lawyer made a compelling case for her client's innocence.* 辯方律師為證明她的當事人無罪，提出了強有力的辯詞。

credible reasonable enough to be believed 可信的；可靠的：*It was hardly credible that such an unattractive man would have such a beautiful wife.* 這樣一個其貌不揚的男子居然有如此漂亮的妻子，簡直難以置信。

persuasive that persuades you to do something or to believe something 有説服力的；令人信服的：*Michael can be very persuasive when he really wants you to do something for him.* 當米高真的想要你幫他做事情的時候，他會很善於説動你的。

plausible reasonable and likely to be true 有道理的；可信的：*a plausible excuse* 合理的藉口

➲ see also 參見 **persuade; sure**

copy *noun* something made to look like or reproduce something else 拷貝；副本；複製品：*Karen gave me a copy of her notes, as I missed the lecture.* 由於我沒聽這次課，卡倫將她的筆記複印了一份給我。

duplicate an exact copy of something, such as a document, often an unnecessary copy (文件等的) 複製品；完全一樣的東西 (常指沒有必要)：*You can discard this page, as it is just a duplicate of page 5.* 你可以扔掉這一頁，它只是第五頁的翻版。

fax a copy of a document sent electronically from one fax machine to another 傳真：*I sent a fax of my CV to various prospective employers.* 我把我的簡歷傳真給了多位可能的未來僱主。

forgery a copy of something, such as a painting or a banknote, intended to deceive people into thinking that it is an original not a copy (用來以假亂真的) 複製品，贗品 (如繪畫或鈔票等)：*The painting believed to be by Picasso turned out to be a forgery.* 被認為是畢加索真跡的油畫居然是一幅贗品。

imitation something that is made using something else as a model and tries to be like it 仿製品；贗品：*This song is just a poor imitation of a Beatles song.* 這首歌只是對一首披頭四歌曲的拙劣模仿。

photocopy a photographic copy of a document or a picture made on a photocopier machine (文件或圖片等的) 影印本，複印件：*I need to make a photocopy of my phone bill for my tax records.* 我需要複印一份電話費單，留作繳稅記錄。

replica a copy of something three-dimensional (立體的) 複製品：*a replica of an Art Deco statuette* 一幅藝術裝飾雕像的複製品

reproduction a copy of something of historic or artistic value (歷史文物或藝術作品等的) 複製品：*a reproduction of the Book of Kells*《凱爾斯書》的摹本

➲ see also 參見 **imitate**

cowardly *adjective* lacking in courage 膽怯的；缺乏勇氣的：*a cowardly decision* 怯弱的決定

chicken (*informal*) afraid to do something daring 膽小的；害怕冒險的：*Come on, don't be chicken – let's go on the roller coaster!* 快點，別怕，咱們坐過山車去！

craven (*literary*) shamelessly cowardly 畏縮的；怯懦的：*a craven neglect of her duty* 她由於怯懦而疏於職守

faint-hearted nervous about taking action and easily discouraged by difficulties or failure (在困難或失敗面前) 怯懦的；膽怯的：*Liam was too faint-hearted to approach the girl he was interested in.* 利亞姆太怯懦，不敢接近他喜歡的那個女孩。

gutless (*informal*) completely lacking in courage or strength of character 窩囊的；缺乏勇氣的；沒有骨氣的：*He's a gutless coward, picking on somebody half his size.* 他是個窩囊的懦夫，總欺負矮他一半的人。

lily-livered (*literary*) timid and cowardly 懦弱的；膽怯的：*The lily-livered knave abandoned the ladies to the mercies of the bandits.* 膽小怕事的無賴撇下女士們使其任憑這幫強盜的擺佈。

spineless lacking in courage or strength of character 缺乏勇氣的，沒有骨氣的：*Daniel is too spineless to stand up for himself.* 丹尼爾沒有勇氣為自己辯護。

timid lacking in courage and self-confidence and nervous about taking action 缺乏勇氣的；不自信的；羞怯的：*The little boy was too timid to let go of his mother's hand.* 小男孩羞答答的，不敢鬆開媽媽的手。

wimpish (*informal*) having or showing weak character 軟弱的；懦弱的：*Everyone thought he was wimpish for not sticking up for himself.* 由於他沒有為自己辯護，人們都認為他軟弱無能。

yellow (*informal*) very cowardly 怯懦的；膽小的：*He showed his yellow streak when he didn't back me up against the bullies.* 我受欺負時他沒有幫我，這表現出他的怯懦。

➲ see also 參見 **afraid**

crawl *verb* to go somewhere slowly and, sometimes, with difficulty（有時指艱難地）徐徐前進，緩慢行進：*The roads were jammed with holidaymakers, so we were just crawling along.* 路上擠滿了度假的人，我們只得緩慢前行。

creep to go somewhere with slow quiet movements 躡手躡腳地移動；輕聲地緩慢行動：*He crept into the bedroom, trying not to wake his wife.* 他躡手躡腳地進了臥室，盡量不吵醒他的妻子。

ease to move, or to move someone or something, into a place slowly and carefully（緩慢而小心地）移動，挪動：*The nurse gently eased the patient into a sitting position.* 護士輕輕地扶着病人坐起來。

edge to move in a particular direction with small careful movements（小心地）漸進；徐徐移動；漸漸推進：*I had to edge gradually into a tight parking space.* 我只好慢慢開進狹窄的車位。

glide to move slowly and smoothly（緩慢而平穩地）移動；滑行：*The model glided along the catwalk in an elegant evening gown.* 模特兒穿着一身優雅的晚禮服，在 T 型舞台上走着貓步。

inch to go somewhere with small gradual movements 漸進；緩慢移動：*The timid child slowly inched towards the cat and eventually stroked it.* 膽怯的小孩慢慢地靠近那隻貓，最後終於撫摸它了。

worm to make your way somewhere in a slow, indirect, and perhaps devious, manner 曲折行進；緩慢前行；蠕動：*He slowly wormed his way through the crowd right to the front.* 他慢慢穿過人群，一直走到前面。

wriggle to move into or out of a narrow space by making a series of small twisting movements（在狹窄的空間）蜿蜒行進，蠕動而行：*The boy wriggled through the gap in the fence.* 男孩扭動身體從柵欄的狹縫中鑽了過去。

criticize *verb* to express disapproval by saying that someone has behaved badly or that something is bad or faulty 批評（不良行為、過錯等）；責備：*The singer was widely criticized for miming during her stage shows.* 這位歌手因在舞台表演時假裝現場演唱而受到很多人的指責。

cast aspersions on (*formal*) to make unfavourable remarks about someone or something, especially attacking their honour or integrity (尤指對榮譽或誠信等) 中傷，詆毀，誹謗：*How dare you cast aspersions on my family's honour!* 你竟敢詆毀我的家族榮譽！

denounce to make a public statement expressing your strong moral disapproval of a person or their actions 公然抨擊，公開指責，從道德上譴責：*He stood up in court and denounced the proceedings as a travesty of justice.* 他在法庭上站了出來，公開譴責訴訟程序是對公正的嘲弄。

disparage (*formal*) to make remarks that show that you have a low opinion of someone or something, often in an unkind way 貶損，蔑視，貶低：*You shouldn't disparage his efforts, when he's obviously trying his best to please you.* 你不該對他付出的努力表示蔑視，他顯然是在盡全力讓你滿意。

run down (*informal*) to make critical remarks about someone or something in an unkind or humiliating way 毀謗，詆毀，貶低：*She is always running down her husband, but he's actually quite a nice man.* 她老是說老公壞話，其實她老公挺不錯的。

slag off (*informal*) to make very critical and insulting remarks about someone 辱罵，中傷（某人）：*The two rival bands are always slagging each other off.* 兩支競爭的樂隊總是相互詆毀。

slam (*informal*) to criticize a person or their actions severely 猛烈抨擊（人或其行為）：*The manager's team selection was slammed by all the sports journalists.* 球隊教練確定的隊伍人選遭到所有體育記者的猛烈抨擊。

⊃ see also 參見 **attack**[2]; **blame**

cruel *adjective* deliberately causing pain or distress 殘酷的；無情的：*the cruel taunts of the bullies* 惡棍們無情的辱罵

brutal using physical violence or harsh methods to hurt people or achieve your aims 殘忍的；殘暴的：*a brutal beating* 一頓毒打

callous having or showing no compassion for others 冷淡的：*a callous disregard for other people's feelings* 漠視他人的感情

harsh very severe and unpleasant 嚴酷的；嚴厲的：*his harsh treatment of his ex-wife* 他對前妻的殘酷虐待

heartless without mercy or compassion 無情的；殘忍的：*You would have to be heartless not to be moved by the newsreels of the starving children in Africa.* 如果你看了非洲孩子挨餓的新聞片卻不為所動，那就太沒同情心了。

nasty extremely unpleasant in the way you treat someone 卑鄙的；下流的；令人厭惡的：*nasty spiteful remarks* 刻毒的污言穢語

sadistic taking pleasure in making others suffer 虐待狂的；施虐成性的：*He takes a sadistic pleasure in making his girlfriend jealous.* 讓女朋友吃醋讓他感到施虐的快感。

vicious deliberately intending or intended to cause a lot of harm 刻毒的；惡意的：*a vicious attack on a defenceless old lady* 對無助老太太的惡意襲擊

cry *verb* to have tears coming from your eyes and, often, make distressful noises because you feel sadness or some other emotion (常指因傷心等) 哭：*The* *woman cried with relief when her missing child was returned safely.* 當失蹤的孩子安全歸來，這位婦女如釋重負地哭了。

bawl (*informal*) to show distress by crying and making loud noises 嚎哭，大叫，大聲哭叫 (以表示痛苦)：*Vicky is bawling in her room because she is grounded.* 薇姬因為被罰不准出門，在房間裏大喊大叫。

blub or blubber (*informal*) to cry excessively 哭鬧：*For goodness sake, stop blubbing, you've only got a small scratch!* 看在上帝份上，別哭鬧啦，你只不過擦破了點皮！

howl to cry violently and make loud and long noises 嚎叫；嚎啕大哭：*The little boy was howling because he couldn't find his mother.* 小男孩因為找不到媽媽，正在嚎啕大哭。

snivel to cry quietly, with a lot of sniffing, in a way that others might find annoying (令人討厭地) 啜泣，(無聲的) 哭泣：*Ken lost patience with his girlfriend because she was constantly snivelling.* 肯對女朋友失去了耐性，因為她經常哭鼻子。

sob to make distressful noises while taking loud gulps of air 嗚咽；抽泣：*I heard someone sobbing in the next room.* 我聽見有人在隔壁房間裏抽泣。

wail to make a loud long vibrating noise to show sadness or pain (指因悲傷或疼痛) 哀號，慟哭，號啕：*The mothers of children who had been killed in the earthquake were wailing in their grief.* 在地震中死去的孩子們的母親正在傷心痛哭。

weep to shed tears 流淚；哭泣：*My husband caught me weeping at a sad film.* 我丈夫瞧見我正為一部傷感的電影哭泣。

whimper to cry with soft muffled sounds, often because you are afraid (常指因害怕而輕聲) 哭泣，抽泣，嗚咽：*When the police took the gunman away, the hostages were whimpering in the corner.* 當警方把持槍歹徒押走後，那些人質都蜷在角落裏哭泣。

custom *noun* something that is done habitually by a person or in a particular society (人的) 習性；(社會的) 風俗，習俗：*First-footing is a Scottish custom in which it is considered good luck if the first person to cross your threshold at New Year is a tall dark stranger.* 蘇格蘭有"待客履新"的習俗，元旦節第一個訪客，即在新年第一個跨進你家門檻的人，如果是黑皮膚、高個子的陌生人，就會被認為能夠帶來好運氣。

convention a way of doing something that is traditionally accepted as being correct (傳統) 習俗，慣例：*It's a convention that the bride's father gives her away at her wedding.* 新娘的父親在婚禮上將女兒交給新郎是一種傳統習俗。

habit something that a person does regularly (個人的) 習慣，習性：*Brian has a bad habit of biting his nails.* 布賴恩有咬指甲的壞習慣。

norm the usual way of doing something (做事的) 慣例，規範：*Large families used to be the norm in this country, but now they are quite unusual.* 大家庭過去曾是這個國家的慣例，但現在已很少見了。

practice an established way of doing something 通常的做法；慣例；常規：*The practice of cremating dead bodies is common in many societies.* 在許多社會，對死者進行火化的做法已經很普遍了。

ritual an established pattern of behaviour that a person or members of a particular society or religion follow（特定社會或教會的）禮節，規矩，儀式：*Hara-kiri is the ritual of suicide by disembowelment that was practised by Japanese samurai warriors.* 切腹自盡是日本武士曾採用的一種剖腹自殺的儀式。

routine a pattern of behaviour that you follow regularly 常規；例行公事：*A pre-breakfast jog is part of my morning routine.* 早餐前慢跑是我每天早上生活的一部分。

tradition an established pattern of behaviour that has been followed for a long time 傳統；慣例：*There is a long tradition of conflict between the two tribal groups.* 長期以來，兩個部族之間存在衝突。

cut *verb* to separate something, split it into pieces, or damage it, with a sharp implement（用利器）切，砍（某物）：*Cut the meat into small pieces before cooking it.* 烹飪之前，將肉切成碎片。

carve to cut a cooked joint of meat into slices or to form a piece of wood into a shape or design 把（熟肉）切成薄片；把（木頭）雕刻成圖案：*Father traditionally carves the turkey.* 傳統上由父親將火雞切成小塊。

chop to cut something into small pieces with heavy blows, especially using an axe or cleaver（尤指用斧頭、砍刀等）砍，剁碎（某物）：*We chopped the logs into smaller pieces for the fire.* 我們把木材砍成小塊，用來生火。

dice to cut food into small cubes（將食物）切成小方塊：*Dice the vegetables and add them to the pan.* 將蔬菜切成丁，然後放在鍋裏。

gash to injure a part of your body by making a long deep cut in it 劃破，劃傷（身體部位）：*The boy gashed his knee playing football.* 男孩在踢足球時劃破了膝蓋。

lacerate (*formal*) to make many cuts in a part of your body 劃破，劃傷（身體部位）：*The assault victim's face was badly lacerated and required 18 sutures.* 遭到襲擊的受害人面部被嚴重劃傷，縫了 18 針。

slash to make a long cut in something, such as fabric or skin, with a swift stroke from a blade（用刀）砍，割，砍傷（織品或皮膚）：*The vandals slashed the curtains and painted slogans on the walls.* 蓄意破壞者朝窗簾亂砍一氣，還在牆上塗標語。

slice to cut something, especially food, into flat pieces（尤指將食物）切成薄片：*The fishmonger sliced the smoked salmon finely.* 漁商把煙燻過的三文魚切成細細的薄片。

slit to make a small narrow cut in something, such as a piece of fabric or a piece of meat 撕裂（織物等）；切開（肉等）：*Slit the chicken breast in two places and insert a garlic clove in each.* 在雞胸上劃兩道小口，每處塞進一粒蒜瓣。

snip to cut something such as hair or a plant with short quick strokes 剪斷（頭髮或植物等）：*Snip the ends off the flowers before you put them in a vase.* 把花放進花瓶前，要把花枝末端剪掉。

trim to neaten something, such as hair or a hedge, by cutting a little off the edges 修整，修剪（頭髮或樹籬等）：*Bob has a small pair of scissors for trimming his moustache.* 鮑勃有一副修鬍鬚的小剪刀。

➲ see also 參見 **share; shorten**

D

damage *verb* to cause harm or injury that has a bad effect on the appearance of something or makes it work less well, but does not necessarily make it completely unusable 損壞，破壞，損傷 (外表或功能，但不一定使之完全無用)：*My car was badly damaged when another car drove into the back of it.* 我的車遭到另一輛車追尾，嚴重受損。

deface to deliberately spoil the appearance of something, especially by writing or drawing on it (尤指故意亂塗亂畫) 損傷…的外貌：*Vandals have defaced the war memorial with red paint.* 蓄意破壞者在戰爭紀念碑上塗紅漆，毀了它的外觀。

destroy to make something completely unusable (完全) 摧毀，毀壞 (某物)：*The old barn was destroyed by a fire.* 那間陳年穀倉被一場火給毀了。

harm to have a bad effect on someone or something 傷害，妨害，損害：*Revelations about the candidate's private life may harm his political prospects.* 披露那位候選人的私生活可能影響他的政治前途。

hurt to cause someone physical pain or emotional distress 使 (身體) 疼痛；使 (感情) 受到傷害：*These new shoes hurt my feet.* 這雙新鞋穿得我腳痛。

injure to do physical harm to someone or to a part of their body 傷害，損害 (人或身體部位)：*Darren was injured in a car crash.* 戴倫在一次車禍中受了傷。

ruin to damage something, especially a building, beyond repair, or to spoil something completely 毀壞，無可挽回地損壞 (尤指建築物等)：*The guests arrived very late, by which time the dinner was ruined.* 客人們很晚才到，這把晚宴徹底給弄糟了。

spoil to make something less pleasant to experience than it should have been 損壞，弄糟 (心情等)：*The constant arguments spoilt the holiday for me.* 經常爭吵破壞了我度假的心情。

vandalize to damage something, especially a building, for example by breaking windows and writing graffiti on it, for no reason except the fun of doing it 故意破壞，肆意破壞 (尤指建築物，如無端地砸窗戶、亂寫亂畫等)：*Every single telephone box in the main square had been vandalized.* 主廣場上的每一個電話亭都被無端地破壞了。

wreck to damage something, especially a ship or vehicle, beyond repair, or to spoil something completely 毀壞，破壞 (尤指車、船等)；毀滅：*The scandal wrecked her chances of becoming party leader.* 這條醜聞斷送了她當選黨領導人的機會。

➲ see also 參見 **bad²; destroy; hurt**

danger *noun* a situation, or a particular thing, that could easily cause harm to a person or thing 危險；危險因素：*The air-traffic controller guided the aircraft out of danger.* 空中交通管制人員指引飛機脫離了危險。

hazard a particular thing that is likely to have a harmful or deadly effect 危險；危害；危險物：*the health hazards associated with passive smoking* 二手煙造成的健康危害

menace (*often humorous*) something or someone that is likely to cause harm 威脅；危險的人（或物）: *She's a menace to all other road users the moment she gets behind the wheel of a car.* 她一開車就對其他道路使用者構成威脅。

peril (*formal*) danger 危險: *The journey through the mountains was filled with peril.* 翻山越嶺的旅途充滿了危險。

risk the possibility of something harmful happening 冒險；風險: *The firefighter put his own life at risk by going into the burning building to rescue a child.* 消防隊員冒着生命危險衝進熊熊燃燒的房屋去營救一名小孩。

threat the prospect of something frightening or worrying happening 威脅；兇兆: *The threat of redundancy was hanging over their heads.* 裁減冗員的威脅籠罩在他們頭上。

➲ see also 參見 **dangerous**

dangerous *adjective* likely to cause harm, or able to be used to cause harm 有危險的；可能造成傷害的: *a dangerous weapon* 危險的武器

dodgy (*informal*) unsafe or unreliable 危險的；不可靠的: *Watch out for that dodgy rung on the ladder!* 當心梯子的那節橫檔不牢固！

hairy (*informal*) dangerous and frightening 驚險的；可怕的；令人毛骨悚然的: *It was a bit hairy when we skidded on that hairpin bend.* 我們在急轉彎處時車打滑了，真有點驚險。

insecure dangerous because unsteady or not properly fixed 有危險的；不牢靠的；無保障的: *We had to make our way across an insecure rope bridge.* 我們只好從不牢靠的索橋上走過去。

perilous (*formal*) involving serious danger 岌岌可危的；危機四伏的: *a perilous voyage in a lightweight craft* 一次險象環生的輕舟航海之旅

precarious dangerous because there is a strong chance of falling 不穩的；不保險的；危險的: *Be careful on that footpath – the footing is precarious!* 在那條人行道上要當心，走路容易摔跤！

risky involving the possibility of harm or failure 危險的；冒險的；有風險的: *a risky business venture* 冒險的商業投機

treacherous dangerous to move on because there is a chance of slipping or falling（路途）凶險的；有潛在危險的: *Black ice made the roads treacherous.* 路面的薄冰使得道路凶險莫測。

➲ see also 參見 **danger**

dark[1] *adjective* with little or no light, as during the night time（如夜晚）黑暗的；（光線）暗的: *We want to be home before it gets dark.* 我們想在天黑前到家。

dim with little light, so that it is difficult to see things clearly 暗淡的；昏暗的；模糊的: *a dim corridor* 昏暗的走廊

dingy unpleasantly dark and rather dirty 又黑又髒的；骯髒的；邋遢的: *a dingy basement* 又暗又髒的地下室

gloomy with little light and a depressing atmosphere 陰暗的；幽暗的；陰鬱的: *a gloomy winter's day* 一個陰鬱的冬日

murky difficult to see clearly in or through 昏暗的；混濁的：*the murky waters of the pond* 混濁的池水

shady cool and dark because shaded from the sun 成蔭的；陰涼的：*We found a shady spot under some trees.* 我們在樹下找到了一處陰涼的地方。

unlit having no artificial light 無燈光的：*an unlit room* 一間沒有燈光的屋子

dark² *adjective* not pale or bright in colour 深色的：*dark hair* 深色頭髮

black of the darkest possible colour 黑色的：*a black taxi* 一輛黑色出租車

dusky having a fairly dark shade（色調）暗的：*a dusky pink* 暗紅色

swarthy having dark skin and dark hair 頭髮和皮膚顏色深的：*a swarthy stranger* 一個黝黑膚色的陌生人

dead *adjective* no longer alive 死的：*a dead body* 死屍

deceased (*used mainly in official documents*) having died, especially recently（主要用於公文）（尤指最近）已故的：*The deceased woman's son collected her belongings from the hospital.* 這位已故婦女的兒子收拾了她在醫院留下的遺物。

defunct (*not used to describe people*) no longer in existence（不用於描述人）不復存在的：*the now-defunct Whig party* 現已不復存在的輝格黨

departed (*euphemistic or literary*) having died, especially recently（尤指最近）去世的，已故的：*the funeral of her dear departed husband* 她已故丈夫的葬禮

extinct (*not used to describe people*) no longer having any members still living（不用於描述人）絕種的，滅絕的：*The dodo is an extinct species of bird.* 多多鳥是一種已經絕跡的鳥類

gone (*informal*) having just died 剛死不久的：*I rushed to the hospital but my Dad was already gone.* 我匆忙趕到醫院，但我父親已離開人世。

inanimate (*not used to describe people*) never having had life（不用於描述人）死氣沉沉的，無生氣的：*A still life is a painting of inanimate objects.* 靜物畫是無生命體的圖畫。

late (*used before someone's name or a word describing them*) who has died, especially recently（用於人名或稱謂前，尤指最近）已故的：*My late mother was a nurse.* 我母親生前是位護士。

lifeless (*literary*) dead 死的；無生命的：*The murder victim's lifeless body lay in the street.* 被害者橫屍街頭。

decent *adjective* morally acceptable, especially in relation to sex or the way people present themselves in public（尤指在性和當眾表現等方面）正派的，得體的，有分寸的：*Frankly, the way she was dressed was scarcely decent.* 坦率地説，她的穿着不太得體。

decorous (*formal*) conforming to accepted standards of correct behaviour（行為舉止）得體的，正派的，端莊穩重的：*A Lady should conduct herself in a decorous manner at all times.* 女士任何時候舉止都應該端莊穩重。

honourable showing honesty, respect, and fairness to other people 誠實的；表示尊敬的；正直的：*Owning up to your mistake would be the honourable thing to do.* 承認自己的錯誤會是一件光榮的事。

proper conforming to accepted standards of correct behaviour, especially on formal occasions (尤指在正式場合行為舉止) 得體的，正派的：*the proper way to address the Queen* 對女王合乎體統的稱謂

respectable regarded as deserving respect because of moral behaviour or social standing 有名望的；可敬的；德高望重的：*She comes from a very respectable family background.* 她出身名門。

upright behaving in a moral and lawful manner 正直的；規矩的；合乎正道的：*an upright citizen* 誠實守法的公民

well-brought-up taught by your parents or guardians to have good morals and good manners 有教養的；有修養的：*a well-brought-up young man who treats everyone with respect* 一個有禮貌、有教養的年輕人

worthy (*formal*) regarded as deserving respect because of moral behaviour 值得敬重的；可敬的：*a worthy member of the local community* 當地社區值得尊敬的一員

decide *verb* to arrive at a particular idea or choice regarding something after thinking about it (經過思考而) 決定，選擇：*After careful consideration, I decided to accept the job offer.* 仔細考慮之後，我決定接受這個工作。

choose to take a particular course of action after thinking about various alternatives (在考慮多個選項之後) 選定，選擇：*Lisa chose to stay at home to look after the baby, rather than go back to work.* 麗莎決定留在家裏照顧小孩，而不回去工作。

conclude to find what you think is the right answer or course of action after considering evidence or various alternatives (對證據或多個選項進行考慮後) 得出結論，推斷，斷定：*They concluded that their elderly mother needed a home help.* 他們認為老母親需要一個家務女工。

determine (*formal*) to work out what the answer to a problem is or what course of action should be taken 決定；確定：*My friends' support helped me to determine how I should proceed.* 朋友們的支持幫我決定了下一步該如何走。

elect (*formal*) to choose 選定；選擇：*Gareth elected to do the driving for the evening out.* 晚間出去兜風選定加雷思開車。

fix on to agree on or settle on a particular arrangement (對於安排) 決定，選定：*We fixed on 10 December for our next meeting.* 我們決定下一次會議在 12 月 10 日召開。

make up your mind to make a firm decision about something after a period of uncertainty (在猶豫一段時間後) 下定決心：*Once John has made up his mind about something, you will never dissuade him.* 一旦約翰對甚麼事下定了決心，你是無法勸阻他的。

resolve (*formal*) to make a firm decision to do something 斷然決定，決心 (做某事)：*David resolved to stop smoking in the New Year.* 大衛決心在新年裏戒煙。

rule to make or announce a formal decision about something 裁定；裁決；規定：*The government ruled that pubs could serve alcohol up to 24 hours a day.* 政府規定，酒館最多可以全天 24 小時供酒。

decrease *verb* to become fewer in number or less in size, intensity, etc. (數目、尺寸、強度等) 減少，減小，降低：*The programme's viewing figures have decreased significantly over the last few weeks.* 在過去的幾個星期裏，觀看該節目的人數大幅減少。

abate (*said about something violent*) to become less intense (強度) 減輕，緩和，減弱：*The storm gradually abated.* 暴風雨漸漸平息下來。

diminish to become smaller or less effective 變小；(效果) 減弱：*Her intellectual powers sadly diminished with old age.* 令人傷心的是，她的智力隨着她步入晚年而每況愈下。

drop off (*informal*) to become fewer in number or less in amount (數量) 減少：*Sales of videos dropped off after DVDs were introduced.* DVD 推出後，錄像帶的銷量減少了。

dwindle to become gradually less or fewer (逐漸) 縮小，減少：*The money in my bank account is dwindling.* 我銀行賬戶裏的錢越來越少了。

lessen to become less, or make something less 變少；使減少：*The new law lessens the opportunities for companies to avoid paying tax.* 新頒佈的法律減少了公司避稅的機會。

lower to bring something to a lower height or level 減弱；降低 (高度、水平等)：*The age limit for membership of the club has been lowered to 18.* 該俱樂部的會員年齡限制已降至 18 歲。

reduce to become, or to make something smaller in size, number, price, etc. (數量) 減少；(尺寸) 縮小；(價格) 下降：*All dairy goods have been reduced to half price.* 所有奶製品的價格都降了一半。

shrink to become, or to make something, especially a piece of clothing, smaller in size, often accidentally (指尺寸，尤其是衣物意外地) 縮水，縮小：*My sweater has shrunk in the wash.* 我的毛衣洗過之後縮水了。

subside to become less intense 平息；減退；減弱：*I took some medicine, and the pain gradually subsided.* 我吃了一些藥，疼痛漸漸緩解了。

defeat *noun* the act of beating a person, team, or country in a contest, fight, race, etc., or the fact of being beaten (指競賽或戰鬥中) 擊敗，戰勝，失敗：*the defeat of the French fleet by Admiral Nelson at the Battle of the Nile* 法國艦隊在尼羅河戰役中被納爾遜上將打敗

beating the act of defeating a person or team soundly in a contest, race, etc. (指競賽等中) 挫敗，徹底打敗：*The local darts team suffered a thorough beating at the hands of their nearest rivals.* 本地的飛標隊慘敗給與他們旗鼓相當的對手。

conquest the act of beating an enemy in a war or battle and taking control of their country (指戰爭或戰鬥中) 征服，攻克：*the Spanish conquest of Mexico* 西班牙人攻佔墨西哥

fall the loss of power by a leader or government (領導人、政府等) 垮台：*Losing a vote of confidence brought about the fall of the government.* 信任投票的失利導致了政府的垮台。

overthrow the removal of someone or something from power by an act of violence (通過暴力行為) 推翻，顛覆：*the overthrow of a tyrannical regime* 推翻專制政權

rout an overwhelming defeat of an army（軍 隊） 潰 敗：*the rout of the Persian army by the Afghans* 波斯軍隊被阿富汗人擊潰

thrashing (*informal*) a comprehensive defeat of a person or a team in a game or contest（競賽中的個人或團隊）慘敗，徹底失敗：*I gave Derek a thrashing at squash.* 我和德里克打壁球的時候，打得他一敗塗地。

trouncing (*informal*) a comprehensive defeat of a person or a team in a game or contest（競賽中的個人或團隊）慘敗，徹底失敗：*The school football team got a right trouncing on Saturday.* 學校足球隊在星期六遭到慘敗。

➲ see also 參見 **beat²**

defend *verb* to take action to prevent someone or something being harmed or captured when they are attacked 防禦，防衛，防護（使免受傷害或捕獲）：*He defended his wife's good name against attacks in the media.* 他抵禦媒體的攻擊，維護妻子的名譽。

champion to speak in support of a cause or a person 擁護，支持，聲援（事業或人）：*She championed the cause of women's rights.* 她擁護女權主義事業。

guard to keep someone or something safe from harm, especially by being physically present to fight off an attacker（尤指擊退來犯者以）守護，維護，保衛：*They have a large dog guarding the house.* 他們有一條大狗看守着這棟房子。

protect to keep someone or something safe from harm 保護，維護（使免受傷害）：*Use a high-factor sun screen to protect your skin from the harmful rays of the sun.* 要使用防曬係數高的防曬霜，以使皮膚免受太陽有害射線的損傷。

safeguard (*formal*) to take action to keep something safe from harm 維護，捍衛，保衛（安全，使免遭損害）：*Safeguard your computer files by backing up regularly.* 通過定期備份來維護電腦檔案的安全。

shield to protect someone from something, such as a physical threat or unwanted attention 防護，保護（以免遭危險或騷擾等）：*The film star shielded her children from the press photographers.* 那位影星保護着孩子們，不讓新聞攝影師騷擾他們。

speak up for to defend or support someone verbally 辯護；（用言辭）維護：*Danielle spoke up for me when all the others said I was wrong.* 當別人都説我錯的時候，丹妮爾卻替我説好話。

stick up for (*informal*) to give someone strong support（大力）支持，維護（某人）：*Although the brothers argue constantly, they will always stick up for each other against an outsider.* 他們兄弟之間雖然經常爭吵，但在對付外人時他們總是相互支持。

support to express agreement with a person, their point of view, or their aims 支持，贊成，擁護（某人、某人的觀點或目標）：*The committee supported the chairman's proposal.* 委員會擁護主席的提議。

➲ see also 參見 **help; support**

delay¹ *verb* not to do something when you had planned to, but to wait until later 推遲，延遲（執行既定方案等）：*If you delay posting your job application, you may miss the closing date.* 如果你把求職函寄遲了，就可能錯過截止日期。

adjourn to have a break in proceedings and begin again later 休庭；休會；暫時中斷：*I propose that we adjourn the meeting until after lunch.* 我建議現在休會，午餐之後再開。

defer to delay an action, such as paying a bill, until a later time 推遲，拖延（付費等）：*They always defer payment of bills for as long as possible.* 他們總是盡可能推遲付賬。

postpone to cancel an arrangement and rearrange it for a later time 延遲；延期；暫緩：*I had to postpone my driving test because I was unwell.* 因為我不舒服，只好將駕駛考試時間往後移。

procrastinate (*formal*) to keep putting off doing something that you have to do, often because you do not really want to do it at all（因不願意做某事而）拖延，耽擱，推遲：*Kerry keeps procrastinating when she knows she should be revising for her exams.* 克麗知道應該複習備考，可就是一再拖延。

put off not to do something when you should but to wait until later 推遲，延遲（應該做的事）：*Tim put off going to the doctor because he was afraid.* 蒂姆因為害怕，所以遲遲不去看醫生。

reschedule to cancel an arrangement and rearrange it for a later time 重訂（計劃）；改變（時間安排）：*I would like to reschedule my dental appointments because I am going on holiday.* 因為我要去度假，所以希望換個時間看牙醫。

shelve to cancel a planned project completely or postpone it until a much later time 擱置，停止（已計劃的項目）：*We had to shelve our plans to build an extension because we ran out of funds.* 由於資金已經用完，我們不得不將擴建計劃擱置起來。

delay² *verb* to cause someone to be late for something, such as an appointment 耽擱，延誤（約會等）：*Sorry I'm late – I was delayed by a last-minute phone call.* 對不起，我遲到了，在出門之前我接了個電話，所以耽誤了。

detain to hold someone back, for example by talking to them（如通過談話等）阻留，耽擱，留住（某人）：*I was detained by a client who stayed longer than I had expected.* 我被一個客戶拖住了，沒想到他會待那麼久。

hold up to cause someone to be late 阻礙，耽誤，延誤（某人）：*We were held up for an hour in a traffic jam.* 我們遇到交通阻塞，耽誤了一小時。

set back to slow down someone's progress（使進展）放慢，推遲，延誤：*When Richard's computer crashed, it set his schedule back considerably.* 理查德的電腦壞機後，他的日程安排大大延誤了。

delicious *adjective* tasting or smelling very pleasant 美味可口的；芳香的：*a delicious curry* 可口的咖喱

appetizing looking or smelling as if it would taste good 促進食慾的；色香俱全的；開胃的：*the appetizing smell of freshly brewed coffee* 令人饞涎欲滴的剛煮好的咖啡香味

delectable (*formal*) tasting very pleasant indeed 美味可口的；香甜的：*delectable strawberries* 香甜的草莓

luscious tasting very sweet and pleasant 味道甘美的；香甜的：*luscious chocolate truffles* 一塊塊甘美的巧克力軟糖

scrumptious (*informal*) tasting very pleasant indeed 味道極好的：*Mmm, that dinner was really scrumptious!* 嗯，那頓飯菜的味道好極啦！

succulent juicy and sweet-tasting 甘美的；蜜汁般的：*succulent peaches* 味美多汁的桃

tasty having a fairly strong, pleasant, usually savoury, flavour 開胃的；好吃的；可口的：*The lentil soup is very tasty.* 扁豆湯很鮮。

yummy (*informal*) tasting very pleasant 爽口的；美味的：*I had a cup of tea and a yummy cream cake.* 我喝了杯茶，吃了塊爽口的奶油蛋糕。

destroy *verb* to damage something to the extent that it is completely unusable or worthless, or no longer exists 摧毀；毀滅；破壞：*Much of the city was destroyed in the war.* 這座城市在戰爭中幾乎全給毀了。

annihilate to destroy something, such as a place or military force, completely 消滅，殲滅（軍隊）；徹底摧毀（某地方）：*The army was annihilated in the battle.* 那支軍隊在戰鬥中被全部殲滅。

demolish to destroy something, such as a building, by knocking it down 拆毀，拆除（建築物等）：*The block of flats where I lived as a child has been demolished.* 我小時候住過的大樓已被拆除。

knock down to destroy something, such as a building or other structure, by toppling it 推倒，拆掉，拆毀（建築物）：*They're going to knock down all the old houses to make way for the new motorway.* 他們將拆除所有這些舊房屋，修建新的高速公路。

ruin to damage something, especially a building, beyond repair, or to spoil something such as a social occasion 毀壞（尤指建築物等）；擾亂（社交場合等）：*The bride's uncle ruined the wedding by getting drunk and starting a fight.* 新娘的叔叔醉酒打架，把婚宴給擾亂了。

smash to break or shatter an object or a vehicle, sometimes through some deliberate violent action（有時指故意採用暴力）砸壞，砸碎，打碎（物體、車輛等）：*The thief smashed the car window and stole the CD player.* 小偷砸壞車窗偷走了 CD 機。

spoil to greatly reduce the value, quality, or appearance of something（嚴重）損壞，損害（某物的價值、質量或外觀等）：*The rain spoilt her elaborate hairdo.* 這場雨弄亂了她精美的髮型。

wreck to damage something, especially a ship or vehicle, beyond repair, or to spoil something completely 破壞，毀壞（船隻、車輛等）：*A serious car accident in his teens wrecked Peter's career as a footballer.* 彼得在十幾歲時遭遇了一場嚴重的車禍，把他的足球生涯徹底毀了。

⊃ see also 參見 **damage**

deteriorate *verb* to become worse or weaker 惡化；衰退：*The patient's condition has deteriorated rapidly.* 病人的狀況迅速惡化。

decline to become gradually worse 衰落；逐漸惡化：*The former president's health has declined over the last few years.* 在過去幾年裏，前總統的健康每況愈下。

degenerate to become worse, for example in quality or in strength（指質量、實力等）退化，衰退，蛻變：*The discussion degenerated into a slanging match.* 這場討論淪為一場相互對罵。

ebb to become gradually less and less 越來越少 : *Her husband undermined her confidence until it gradually ebbed away completely.* 她的信心受到丈夫的打擊，直至漸漸地喪失殆盡。

go downhill (*informal*) to become worse, weaker, or less successful 每況愈下；走下坡路 : *The old Lady had a stroke last year and has gone downhill since then.* 老太太去年中風了一次，打那以後身體一天不如一天。

wane to become gradually less successful 逐漸衰落；敗落 : *The actor's career has waned since he reached middle age.* 那男演員進入中年後事業就江河日下了。

weaken to become gradually weaker 衰退；逐漸變弱 : *Her singing voice has weakened over the years.* 這些年來，她的歌喉已逐漸衰退。

worsen to become gradually worse 逐漸惡化 : *The standard of his school work has worsened every year as he appears to have lost interest.* 他的學業成績一年不如一年，因為他好像失去了興趣。

determined *adjective* having made a firm decision to do something and showing the courage and will-power needed to do it 堅決的；有決心的 : *She was determined to finish the marathon even though she was exhausted.* 雖然她已跑得筋疲力盡，她還是決心跑完全程馬拉松。

dead set on (*informal*) having a particular aim or plan that no one will be able to persuade you to give up 決意的；下定決心的；主意已定的 : *dead set on going to university* 決意去上大學

focused concentrating your mind and efforts on a particular aim or subject 注意力集中的；目標明確的 : *To be a tennis champion, you have to be really focused.* 要想成為網球冠軍，你必須非常投入。

hell-bent (*informal*) recklessly determined to do something 固執的，拼命的，不顧一切的（做某事）: *He was hell-bent on winning, no matter what it took.* 他執意要贏，不管付出多少代價。

intent having made up your mind to do something 決心的；專心的 : *She seemed to be intent on causing trouble.* 她似乎非得要惹麻煩。

resolute showing courage and firmness in keeping to a decision that you have made 堅決的；斷然的；義無反顧的 : *He was resolute in his refusal to get involved in petty arguments.* 他決不介入瑣碎的爭論。

unflinching firm and strong despite difficulties or opposition 不屈不撓的；不畏困難的；不顧反對的 : *her unflinching support for her husband* 她對丈夫堅定不移的支持

development *noun* the way that something or someone progresses 發展；發育；成長 : *a child's development into an adult* 一個孩子的長大成人

evolution slow gradual change, especially in species of plants and animals over a very long period of time（尤指動植物漫長時間的）進化，演化，演變 : *In the evolution of apes, there is a trend of increase in size.* 在猿的進化過程中，軀幹呈增長的趨勢。

formation the process of developing something, such as an idea or plan（觀點或計劃等的）構成，組成，形成 : *They are working on the formation of a new marketing strategy.* 他們正在醞釀新的營銷策略。

growth the process of becoming gradually larger, more fully developed, or more successful 成長；生長；發育：*There has been a marked population growth in this area over the last ten years.* 在過去的 10 年裏，該地區的人口顯著增長。

progress the process of developing and moving forward 進步；發展；前進：*We have been very impressed with Stacy's progress at school this year.* 我們對斯泰西今年在學校取得的進步留有很深的印象。

devoted *adjective* very loving and loyal towards someone 摯愛的；忠誠的；感情專一的：*a devoted wife* 忠貞的妻子

caring showing kindness or compassion towards people in general 親切的；有同情心的；慈愛的：*a kind and caring neighbour* 一個和藹可親的鄰居

committed having made a statement or promise of your support for a person, a religion, or a cause, and showing loyalty to them（對人、信仰、事業等）忠誠的，效忠的，虔誠的：*a committed Christian* 虔誠的基督徒

dedicated giving a great deal of time and effort to a cause or an activity（為事業或活動等）專心致志的，專注的，投入的：*a dedicated athlete* 一個敬業的運動員

doting excessively fond of someone, often to the point of being blind to their faults 寵愛的；溺愛的：*His doting parents had spoiled him somewhat.* 他父母的溺愛有點把他寵壞了。

faithful unfailingly loyal and supportive 忠實的；守信的：*a faithful companion* 忠誠的伙伴

fond having a liking or affection for someone or something 喜愛的；鍾愛的：*I was very fond of my first car.* 我非常喜愛我的第一輛小汽車。

loving showing love for someone or for each other 親愛的；鍾情的；相愛的：*a loving couple* 一對恩愛夫妻

loyal able to be relied on to support someone or something 忠心的；效忠的；可靠的：*Loyal fans of the singer supported him throughout his court case.* 在這位歌手的法律訴訟案中，忠實的歌迷們始終支持他。

⊃ see also 參見 faithful; reliable

difference *noun* the fact of being unlike someone or something else 差異；區別；差別：*I can't tell the difference between the twins.* 我分不清這對雙胞胎。

contrast a marked difference between two people or things resulting from their being opposites or near opposites（明顯的）差異，反差，對比：*The contrast between yesterday's wind and rain and today's bright sunshine is remarkable.* 昨日的風雨天和今日的豔陽天形成鮮明的對照。

discrepancy a difference between two reports or two sets of figures that suggests that one must be wrong（指報道、數字等的）差異，出入（暗示一方有誤）：*There is a discrepancy between the two boys' accounts of last night's events.* 關於昨晚的事件，兩位男生講的有出入。

disparity (*formal*) a point of difference or an inequality between two things 差異；不同；不均等：*There is disparity in the earnings of men and women.* 男女收入存在差異。

dissimilarity (*formal*) a difference or difference 差別；相異；不同點：*The dissimilarities between the two sisters' characters are more noticeable than the similarities.* 兩姐妹的性格差異比起相似之處來更是顯而易見。

distinction something that enables the difference between two people or things to be perceived (兩個人或事物間的) 差別，區別特徵：*There is a clear distinction between teasing and bullying.* 逗弄與欺辱之間有着明顯的區別。

diversity the fact of existing in many different forms or of consisting of many different elements (*usually used in serious contexts*) 多樣性，多樣化 (多用於嚴肅的語境)：*Religious and ethnic diversity enriches the culture of the nation.* 宗教和種族的多樣性豐富了這個國家的文化。

variation a slight difference 變異；細小的差異：*We found a variation in prices between the supermarkets.* 我們發現超市之間的價格稍有不同。

variety the fact of existing in many different forms or offering a choice of different alternatives 多樣性；多種多樣；不同種類：*We have a variety of entertainments on offer.* 我們提供多種招待服務。

difficult *adjective* not easy to do or to understand 困難的；難懂的：*The exam was really difficult.* 這門考試真難。

awkward requiring great tact or diplomacy 棘手的；難對付的；難處理的：*an awkward situation* 困難的處境

demanding requiring a lot of effort over a long time 費力的；辛苦的：*She has a very demanding job in the city.* 她在城市裏有一份辛苦的工作。

exacting requiring a lot of effort and care 需要付出很大努力的；要求小心細緻的；嚴格的：*Restoring a painting is exacting work.* 修復一幅畫是一項艱苦的工作。

formidable difficult to do because of the size and nature of the task (因任務的規模和性質等而) 難對付的，艱巨的：*Retrieving the bodies from the collapsed building was a formidable task.* 從坍塌的建築物中找回死者屍體是一項艱巨的任務。

gruelling putting a very great strain on your physical or mental strength 使人筋疲力盡的；折磨人的；艱辛的：*a gruelling trek through the mountains* 翻山越嶺的艱苦跋涉

hard difficult, especially because of demanding a lot of physical or mental effort 辛苦的；艱難的；艱苦的：*hard labour* 艱苦的勞動

laborious requiring a lot of effort, especially physical effort, and usually boring or repetitive (通常因乏味或不斷重複而) 辛苦的，費力的：*Stripping the wallpaper is a laborious job.* 剝除牆紙是一件吃力的活兒。

tiring making you feel tired 累人的：*a long tiring journey* 疲憊的長途旅行

troublesome causing problems 麻煩的；棘手的：*troublesome neighbours* 煩人的鄰居

trying annoying and difficult to deal with 煩人的；難以處理的：*I've had a very trying day looking after six five-year-olds.* 因為要照顧 6 個 5 歲的孩子，這一天我過得很累。

uphill very difficult because presenting a lot of resistance 艱難的；費周折的；（如上坡般）費力的：*It's an uphill struggle trying to make conversation with Tom.* 要想和湯姆談話需要費很大的周折。

➲ see also 參見 **complicated; stubborn**

dirty *adjective* not clean, because covered or marked with soil, mud, stains, etc. (因沾有泥土、污點等而) 髒的，骯髒的：*My hands were dirty after gardening.* 在花園裏種植花草後，我的雙手弄髒了。

dusty covered in a layer of dust, or full of dust 沾有灰塵的；積滿灰塵的：*Wipe the top of the table, it's dusty.* 桌面滿是灰塵，把它擦擦吧。

filthy very dirty indeed 污穢的；骯髒的：*The boys came home filthy after playing football.* 這些男孩踢完足球，渾身骯髒地回到家裏。

grimy having a layer of dirt or soot on the surface (指物體表面) 骯髒的，滿是污垢的，滿是煙塵的：*a grimy windowsill* 骯髒的窗台

grubby dirty and shabby 邋遢的；破舊的：*a grubby old raincoat* 破舊的雨衣

messy (*informal*) untidy and dirty 凌亂的；雜亂的；骯髒的：*It's a bit messy in here, because I haven't had time to clear up.* 這裏有點雜亂，因為我一直沒時間整理。

mucky (*informal*) covered in dirt, especially mud 骯髒的；沾有污垢的 (尤指泥漿)：*Take those mucky boots off before you come in the kitchen.* 你進廚房前要脫掉那雙沾着泥土的靴子。

muddy covered in mud, or full of mud 泥濘的；沾滿泥土的：*The path's very muddy after the rain we've had.* 在我們剛經歷的這場雨後，小路沾滿泥濘。

polluted containing waste or harmful chemicals 污染的；弄髒了的 (指含有垃圾、有害的化學物質等)：*polluted water* 污水

soiled (*formal*) marked with soil, mud, or stains 污染的；髒的 (指帶有泥土、污點等)：*soiled bedclothes* 被弄髒的鋪蓋

squalid dirty and unpleasant 骯髒的；齷齪的：*a squalid basement flat* 齷齪的地下公寓

disagree *verb* to have a different opinion from someone else, or think or say that what someone else says is wrong 反對；不同意；不一致；不贊同：*I disagree with his political views.* 我不贊成他的政治見解。

argue to express an opposing opinion to someone, especially in an angry way 爭論；爭吵：*We always argue about where to go on holiday.* 我們總是在關於去哪兒度假的問題上發生爭吵。

differ to hold different opinions or a different opinion from someone else 相異；（觀點）不同；意見相左：*On that point we differ.* 在那一點上我們不一致。

dispute to say that a statement or allegation is wrong (對陳述或主張等) 表示異議；否認；辯論：*I'm not disputing the fact that you did a good job.* 對於你工作幹得不錯的事實，我並不否認。

squabble to argue over something trivial (為瑣事) 爭吵，爭論，發生口角：*The children were squabbling over whose turn it was to use the computer.* 孩子們在爭論該輪到誰玩電腦了。

take issue with to express objections to what someone has said (對某人所說) 表示反對，提出異議，發表相反看法：*I must take issue with your views on capital punishment.* 我不敢苟同你對死刑的看法。

➲ see also 參見 **conflict; fight; oppose; quarrel**

disappear *verb* to cease to exist or stop being visible 消失；不見；不復存在：*Her anxiety disappeared as soon as she saw that her children were safe.* 她看到孩子們都安然無恙，心中的焦慮一下就煙消雲散了。

cease (*formal*) to stop occurring or stop doing something 停止，終止（發生或做某事）：*Ten years have elapsed since the country ceased to be an independent nation.* 自從國家失去獨立，至今已過了 10 個年頭。

die out to gradually stop 逐漸消失；漸漸停息：*Interest in the band has died out over the last few years.* 人們對這支樂隊的興趣在過去的幾年中漸漸消失。

evaporate to become weaker and cease to exist completely （逐漸）消失，衰減，消散：*His self-confidence evaporated the moment he stepped on stage.* 他一登上舞台，自信心便消失了。

fade to become gradually weaker 漸漸變弱：*Hopes of finding the missing girl alive are now fading.* 失蹤女孩能活着找到的希望越來越渺茫。

melt away to become weaker or cease to exist（逐漸）消退，消失：*Her anger with her boyfriend melted away when he apologized sincerely.* 當男友真誠地向她道歉後，她的怒氣便慢慢平息了。

pass to gradually stop existing 漸漸消失：*Your uncertainty will soon pass as you get used to driving on the right-hand side of the road.* 你一旦習慣了在道路的右手邊開車，你的顧慮很快就會消除。

slacken (*off*) to become less intense or busy 鬆弛；減緩：*Business slackened off after the holiday period.* 假期過後，生意變得清淡了。

vanish to be no longer in evidence; to stop existing 消失；不復存在：*When the business tycoon lost all his money, the support of his friends vanished too.* 這位商界大亨傾家蕩產之後，就不再有朋友支持他了。

disapprove *verb* to have or express an unfavourable opinion of something or someone 反對，不贊成，不讚許：*Her parents disapprove of her smoking.* 她的父母不贊成她吸煙。

deplore (*formal*) to disapprove strongly of something or someone（強烈）反對，譴責：*They deplore the enormous waste of food in the West.* 他們譴責西方國家大量浪費糧食。

frown on to consider a practice to be wrong or unacceptable 反對，不贊成，不同意（某種做法）：*The teacher frowns on pupils chewing gum in class.* 老師不允許學生在課堂上嚼香口膠。

look down your nose at (*informal*) to consider someone or something to be inferior 看不起，鄙視，輕視：*She looked down her nose at him because he was a manual worker.* 她瞧不起他，因為他是幹體力活的。

object to feel that something is wrong, often on moral grounds, and be unwilling to do it（常指基於道德）不同意，反對：*He objects to having to tip taxi drivers.* 他反對必須付計程車司機小費的做法。

take a dim view of (*informal*) to disapprove of something or someone 反對；不讚許；對…持否定看法：*He takes a dim view of people who arrive late for their appointments.* 他對那些不按時赴約的人很反感。

take exception to to disapprove of or be offended by someone's words or actions（對某人的話或行為）持異議，生氣，反感：*She took exception to being addressed as 'Miss'.* 她很反感別人稱她“小姐”。

➲ see also 參見 **criticize**

disaster *noun* an event, such as an explosion or an earthquake, that brings death, suffering, or hardship to many people, or something that goes very badly wrong（指致使許多人死亡或受苦的事件，如爆炸、地震等）災難，災禍：*The whole village was in mourning after the mining disaster.* 礦難發生後，整個村子都沉浸在悲痛之中。

accident an unexpected event that usually has harmful effects（通常會帶來傷害的）意外事件，事故：*She was injured in a road traffic accident.* 她在一次道路交通事故中受了傷。

adversity a situation in which things go very badly for you and you have to deal with difficulties, hardship, or suffering 逆境；困境：*They showed great courage in the face of adversity.* 在困難面前他們表現得非常勇敢。

calamity (*usually humorous*) an event that causes a lot of distress 災難；災禍；不幸：*What a calamity – all my luggage went missing!* 多不幸啊，我的行李全不見了！

cataclysm (*formal*) an event, such as an earthquake or a tidal wave, that causes great destruction and loss of life（指地震、潮汐等）大災難：*The tsunami was a cataclysm with devastating effects.* 海嘯是具有破壞性的大災難。

catastrophe an unexpected event that causes a lot of damage and distress, or something that goes badly wrong（導致傷害、痛苦的）突發事件，大災禍，大災難：*Bird flu could threaten to be a major global catastrophe.* 禽流感有可能成為全球性的大災難。

misfortune bad luck, or an event that has bad consequences for you 厄運；不幸；災難：*She has had her share of misfortune.* 倒霉事也輪到過她。

setback an event that spoils your plans or slows down your progress（計劃或進展等受到的）挫折，阻礙：*Losing a key member of staff was a bit of a setback.* 失去一名關鍵的員工多少算是個挫折。

tragedy a very sad event 悲劇；慘案：*Her sudden death at such an early age was a great tragedy.* 她英年早逝，實乃不幸。

discourage *verb* to make someone lose their enthusiasm for something or their wish to do something 使洩氣；使灰心：*The miserable weather discouraged us from going out.* 糟糕的天氣使我們沒了外出的興致。

demoralize to destroy someone's confidence and make them feel that their actions have no purpose 使洩氣；使士氣消沉；使喪失鬥志：*The threat of redundancy had the effect of demoralizing the staff.* 裁員的威脅使員工士氣消沉。

deter to make someone not want to do something 勸阻；阻止；制止：
Many people believe that stiffer sentences are needed to deter violent criminals.
許多人認為需要更嚴厲的判決以制止暴力犯罪。

disappoint to make someone feel sad because something is not as good as
they had hoped 使失望；使掃興：*Stephen's exam results disappointed him, as
they were not good enough to qualify for the course that he wanted to do.* 史提
芬對考試結果感到失望，因為分數不夠理想，他將不能如願參加這個課程的學
習。

dishearten to make someone feel sad because their actions have not had
the effect they hoped for or because they are making no progress 使氣餒；使
灰心：*The teacher was disheartened by her pupils' lack of enthusiasm.* 學生缺
乏積極性，老師感到很灰心。

disillusion to make someone realize that someone or something is not as
good in reality as they imagined them to be 使醒悟；使理想破滅；使不再抱
幻想：*I hate to disillusion you, but she's not as pretty in the flesh as she looks
in the photograph.* 我不想讓你失望，但看她本人沒有照片看上去那麼漂亮。

dissuade to persuade someone not to do something 勸阻：*Harriet's friend
dissuaded her from having a tattoo.* 哈麗雅特的朋友勸她不要紋身。

put off to make someone not want to do or have something 阻止；勸阻；使
打消念頭：*The thought of all the crowds puts me off going to a rock festival.* 一
想到所有那些擁擠的人群，我就不想去參加搖滾音樂節了。

talk out of to persuade someone not to do something by talking to them
about it 勸阻；說服：*Jeremy's wife talked him out of resigning from his job.* 傑
里米的妻子說服他不要辭掉工作。

discussion *noun* the act of talking about a subject, exchanging opinions
on it, and sometimes reaching a decision 商議；討論：*We had a family
discussion about where to go on holiday.* 我們全家人一起商量到哪兒去度假。

chat an informal conversation, often with a friend（常指和朋友）聊天，閒
聊：*The two girls had a cosy chat about boyfriends.* 兩個女孩愜意地談着男友
的事。

confab (*informal*) a casual conversation 談話；閒談：*We must have a confab
soon so that you can tell me all your news.* 我們得馬上聊聊，好讓你告訴我有
關你的全部消息。

conference a formal or serious discussion, often of an academic, political,
or business nature（常指具有學術、政治或商業性等正式或嚴肅的）大會，會
議，討論會：*a conference to discuss climate change* 探討氣候變化的會議

conversation a situation in which two or more people are talking to
one another 交談；會談；談話：*I had an interesting conversation with my
neighbour about his childhood in India.* 我與鄰居就他自己小時候在印度的經歷
作了一次有趣的交談。

debate a discussion, usually a formal one, in which people give their views
on a particular subject, often in the form of speeches（通常指以發言形式就
某一題目進行的正式）討論，辯論：*a debate on the subject of debt relief* 關於
債務免除的辯論

dialogue a conversation or discussion between two or more people or groups, especially between people or groups who are opposed to one another（尤指對立雙方的）談話，對話：*It's important to get a dialogue going between the two opposing sides.* 對立雙方進行對話很重要。

talk a conversation, usually one which has a particular subject or purpose（通常指有主題或目的的）交談，談論，談話：*Barry had a talk with his son about his exam results.* 巴里與兒子針對他的考試成績談了一次話。

disgrace *noun* loss of honour or of respect because lots of people know that you have done something bad 恥辱；丟臉：*His thuggish behaviour has brought disgrace on the family.* 他的暴行給家人帶來了恥辱。

degradation a very low and miserable state in which nobody respects you and you usually have no self-respect either 落魄，潦倒（的境地）；墮落：*This film is a grim portrayal of hopeless addiction and degradation.* 這部電影可怕地描述了不可救藥的嗜毒和墮落。

discredit damage to your reputation 名聲的敗壞；名譽的喪失；丟臉：*It's to her discredit that she let her colleague take the blame for her mistake.* 使她名譽受損的是她讓同事為自己的錯誤承擔責任。

dishonour loss of honour or reputation 恥辱；丟臉；不名譽：*There is no dishonour in coming second out of 1000 contestants.* 在千名參賽者中屈居第二並不丟臉。

disrepute* a state in which the general public has a low opinion of something 壞名聲；不光彩：*The players' drunken antics has brought the game into disrepute.* 選手們醉酒失態讓這場比賽名聲掃地。

* Usually used in the phrase to bring something into disrepute. 通常用於短語 to bring something into disrepute 之中。

humiliation a deeply embarrassing feeling or state and a loss of self-respect that results from people knowing that you have done something bad or have been treated badly 羞辱；蒙羞：*She suffered the humiliation of her husband being pictured in the newspapers with another woman.* 多家報紙刊登了她丈夫與別的女人在一起的照片，這使她感到羞辱。

infamy (*formal*) the state of being well known for shameful reasons 聲名狼藉；臭名昭著：*He achieved infamy after his involvement in a plot to assassinate the president.* 他捲入了一場刺殺總統的陰謀，這讓他臭名昭著。

scandal a shockingly immoral incident or situation 醜聞；醜行：*a scandal involving a government minister and a call girl* 涉及政府部長與應召女郎的醜聞

shame a feeling of embarrassment and humiliation 羞恥；羞愧：*They left the area because they could not live with the shame of their son's conviction for rape.* 他們離開了這個地方，因為兒子被判強姦罪，這使他們沒臉見人。

disgusting *adjective* extremely unpleasant or offensive, usually to the physical senses, but sometimes also to your sense of morality（常指生理反應，但有時也指心理反應）令人討厭的，令人厭惡的：*disgusting personal habits* 令人厭惡的個人習慣

foul extremely unpleasant to the senses of smell or taste 惡臭的；難聞的：*a dark, damp, foul-smelling room* 一間陰暗潮濕、臭氣薰天的房子

ghastly (*informal*) extremely unpleasant or unattractive, or in very bad taste 極其討厭的；很難看的；糟透了的：*He was wearing a ghastly Hawaiian shirt.* 他穿着一件很難看的夏威夷襯衫。

gross (*informal*) nauseating, usually because of some disgusting physical action（常指動作）下流的，令人噁心的：*That film was so gross, especially when the alien burst out of the guy's chest!* 那部電影真噁心，特別是當外星生物從那傢伙的胸膛突然冒出來的時候！

nauseating extremely unpleasant, almost to the point of causing you to feel that you want to vomit 令人噁心的；令人作嘔的：*a nauseating smell* 令人噁心的氣味

offensive causing people to feel upset because their feelings of what is right and proper have been attacked 冒犯的；無禮的：*offensive language* 冒犯的語言

off-putting unattractive, making you not want something or not want to be with someone 討厭的；令人煩惱的：*A price increase is likely to be off-putting for many customers.* 物價上漲可能會令許多消費者煩惱的。

repugnant (*formal*) morally unacceptable or offensive（道德方面）令人反感的，令人厭惡的，討厭的：*I found their racist attitude repugnant.* 我覺得他們的種族主義態度使人反感。

repulsive extremely unattractive in appearance or nature（外表、本性等）極令人厭惡的，使人極反感的：*She found her colleague's advances quite repulsive.* 她對同事再三向她求愛感到厭惡。

revolting extremely unpleasant to the senses 令人作嘔的；令人厭惡的；使人反感的：*a revolting bright blue ice lolly* 一支倒人胃口的鮮藍色冰條

sickening causing you to feel disgusted, usually morally rather than physically（常指道德方面）令人厭惡的，令人作嘔的：*a sickening display of greed* 表現出令人作嘔的貪婪

dishonest *adjective* not acting or done in a way that is morally right 欺騙性的；不誠實的；不正當的：*dishonest politicians* 騙人的政客

corrupt dishonest, especially in being open to bribery 腐敗的；貪污的；受賄的：*a corrupt police officer* 貪污的警察

crooked (*informal*) dishonest, corrupt, or likely to break the law 騙人的；貪污腐化的；違法亂紀的：*a crooked lawyer* 誆人的律師

deceitful giving a false impression, with the intention to deceive 騙人的；欺詐的；蒙蔽人的：*He is sneaky and deceitful and I don't trust him.* 他行為鬼祟、為人欺詐，我不相信他。

deceptive giving a false impression, whether consciously intending to deceive or not 欺騙性的；蒙蔽人的：*Her youthful looks are deceptive.* 她年輕的外表給人以假象。

false not true or genuine 虛偽的；假的；偽造的：*She gave a false impression of being wealthy.* 她給人們留下很富有的假象。

fraudulent intentionally deceiving people, especially indulging in illegal practices to make money from other people（尤指為騙取錢財）欺詐的，欺騙性的；騙人的：*fraudulent benefits claims* 欺詐性的津貼申請

mendacious (*formal*) telling lies, especially habitually 説謊的；撒謊成性的：*I found him to be mendacious and totally untrustworthy.* 我發現他慣於撒謊，根本不值得信賴。

untrustworthy not able to be trusted or believed 靠不住的；不可信的；不能當真的：*an untrustworthy witness* 不可靠的證人

untruthful not consistent with the truth, or not telling the truth 虛假的；説謊的；不真實的：*an untruthful statement* 虛假的陳述

➲ see also 參見 **illegal**

dislike *noun* a feeling of not finding someone or something pleasant or appealing 討厭；不喜歡：*She couldn't hide her dislike of her sister's new boyfriend.* 她無法掩飾對她姐姐新男友的厭惡。

animosity a very strong feeling of hostility and dislike between two people or groups（兩個人或群體間的）仇恨，敵意，憎惡：*The animosity between Trevor and his ex-wife was clear to see.* 特雷弗與前妻之間的仇恨顯而易見。

antipathy (*formal*) a deep-rooted feeling of dislike or opposition to something or someone（根深蒂固的）反感，憎惡：*I must confess to having an antipathy to people who like dogs.* 我得承認我本能地厭惡那些愛狗的人。

aversion a very strong dislike of something or someone, which makes you want to avoid them as far as possible 厭惡；反感；討厭：*I have a deep aversion to public speaking.* 我很不喜歡公開演説。

distaste the fact of finding something or someone unpleasant or disgusting 嫌惡；討厭：*The corners of his mouth turned down in distaste.* 他厭惡地扁扁嘴。

hatred a very powerful and active dislike of someone or something, strong enough that it may make you want to harm or destroy them（強烈的）憎恨，仇恨（以至於希望將其傷害或毀滅）：*In that moment her dislike of him turned to absolute hatred.* 就在那一刻，她對他的厭惡變成了十足的仇恨。

hostility an openly unfriendly attitude towards someone 敵意；不友善：*There is a lot of hostility between the two rival gangs.* 兩個對立的匪幫之間有很深的敵意。

loathing intense hatred（強烈的）憎恨，憎惡：*I had never felt such a strong loathing for anyone as I did for Louis at that moment.* 當時我對路易斯有一種從沒對他人有過的憎惡之情。

➲ see also 參見 **disapprove; hate**

dismay *noun* a usually mild feeling of fear, disappointment, and sadness when something unpleasant happens 沮喪；驚慌；喪氣：*Much to my dismay, the cup slipped out of my hands spilling coffee all over my hostess's best carpet.* 我感到很沮喪的是，杯子從我手中滑落，咖啡在女主人家最好的地毯上灑了一地。

alarm a feeling of anxiety or fear caused by impending danger（因危險迫近產生的）驚恐，恐慌，驚慌：*Try to evacuate the children from the school without causing alarm.* 在不引起恐慌的情況下，設法將孩子們從學校疏散。

disappointment a feeling of sadness because something is not as good as you had hoped 掃興；失望：*Amy could not hide her disappointment when she opened her birthday present.* 艾美打開生日禮物的時候，無法掩飾失望的心情。

distress sorrow or mental suffering 悲痛；憂傷：*It was painful to see the distress of those who had lost loved ones in the incident.* 看到那些人在這一事件中失去親人而悲痛，真令人難過。

sadness a feeling of unhappiness 悲哀；悲傷：*It is with sadness that I have to announce that my father passed away this morning.* 我帶着悲傷的心情告訴大家，我的父親今天早上去世了。

shock a strong sense of surprise and anxiety caused by something that has happened or been said 震驚；驚愕：*It was such a shock to find that we had been burgled.* 我們發現被爆竊，感到非常震驚。

surprise the feeling you have when something happens unexpectedly, whether welcome or unwelcome 吃驚；驚訝：*Imagine my surprise when my Australian cousin turned up without warning!* 我的那位在澳洲的表兄事先不通知就來了，別提我有多驚訝！

upset mental or emotional pain caused by something that has happened or been said 心煩意亂；苦惱；悲痛：*It took the children a long time to get over the upset of their father leaving.* 孩子們過了很久才從父親去世的悲痛中恢復過來。

➲ see also 參見 **frighten; sad; shock; surprise**

disobedient *adjective* not doing as you are told 不聽話的；不服從的：*a disobedient child* 不聽話的孩子

defiant showing that you do not care that someone has said you have done something wrong or opposes you 目中無人的；違抗的；（對批評或反對意見）不服的：*He remained defiant, refusing to apologize to the referee.* 他仍舊不服，拒不向裁判員道歉。

headstrong stubbornly determined to do what you want in spite of warnings against it 一意孤行的；剛愎自用的；任性的：*his headstrong insistence on driving despite dangerous weather conditions* 他不顧惡劣的天氣狀況，硬要駕車

mischievous badly behaved in a playful way 淘氣的；頑皮的；惡作劇的：*The mischievous children hid from their parents when it was time to go home.* 到了回家的時間，淘氣的孩子們躲起來不讓父母找到他們。

naughty badly behaved, but not in a serious way 頑皮的；淘氣的：*The naughty schoolboy threw a snowball at his teacher.* 淘氣的男生把一個雪球扔向他的老師。

rebellious refusing to do what people in authority tell you to do 反叛的；叛逆的：*a rebellious teenager* 一個叛逆的少年

unruly difficult to control 難駕馭的；不馴服的：*an unruly crowd* 一群難以管理的人

wayward behaving badly and being disobedient, but usually in a forgivable way 任性的；倔強的：*Their wayward son came home begging for forgiveness for his past misdemeanours.* 他們任性的兒子回到家裏，乞求寬恕他過去的不端行為。

wilful always doing what you want even if that means disobeying other people or ignoring their advice 任性的；固執的；執拗的：*Sophie was always wilful, even as a child.* 蘇菲總是很任性，童年時已是這樣的了。

disorder *noun* lack of organization or of tidiness in a place 雜亂；混亂；凌亂：*The burglars had ransacked the house and left it in complete disorder.* 盜賊把房子洗劫一空，弄得亂七八糟。

chaos a state of complete confusion and disorganization, sometimes with a jumble of noise 極度混亂；雜亂；嘈雜：*The teacher left the class for five minutes and returned to find the room in chaos.* 老師離開教室才 5 分鐘，回來卻發現教室裏亂作一團。

confusion a state in which things are uncertain or disorganized, sometimes because something unexpected has happened 困惑；（有時指因發生了意想不到的事引起的）混亂狀態：*After the bomb went off, the streets were in a state of confusion, with people running in all directions.* 炸彈爆炸後，人們四處亂跑，街上一片混亂。

disarray a state of disorganization, confusion, or untidiness 混亂；無序：*The managing director's unexpected resignation has left the company in disarray.* 總經理突然辭職使公司陷入混亂。

disorderliness (*formal*) an untidy state, or a state in which things are not where they should be 雜亂；混亂；無秩序：*The disorderliness of the patient's appearance suggested that she might have been attacked.* 從病人凌亂的外表來看，她可能遭到過襲擊。

mess a very untidy, jumbled, or dirty state 雜亂；混亂；髒亂：*My teenage son's bedroom is usually in a dreadful mess, with dirty clothes and old pizza boxes all over the floor.* 我那個未成年兒子的睡房經常凌亂不堪，地板上到處是髒衣服和裝過薄餅的舊盒子。

untidiness lack of neatness or order, especially in a place （尤指某處）雜亂，無序：*The untidiness of the storeroom makes it difficult to find what you are looking for.* 儲物室雜亂無章，很難找到你要找的東西。

➲ see also 參見 **illness; trouble²**

distant *adjective* being a long way away, either in space or time （指時間和空間上）遙遠的，久遠的，遠的：*in the dim and distant past* 在遙遠的過去

far distant, or situated in the extreme part of a place, in any particular direction 遙遠的；（地處）偏遠的：*the Far East* 遠東地區

faraway being a very long way away and usually having an interesting exotic or romantic quality 遙遠的（常含有趣的異國情調、浪漫色彩等）：*a faraway country* 一個遙遠的國度

far-flung (*literary*) being a long way away or spread widely in different places 遙遠的；廣佈的；遼闊的：*a far-flung empire* 遼闊的帝國疆域

far-off faraway 遙遠的：*strangers from far-off lands* 來自遙遠國度的陌生人

outlying being a long way from the centre of a city, country, etc. 邊遠的；偏僻的；遠離市鎮的：*mail for outlying districts* 寄往偏僻地區的郵件

remote being a long way away and very difficult to reach 偏遠的；偏僻的：*a remote part of Tibet* 西藏的偏遠地區

➲ see also 參見 **unfriendly**

disturb *verb* to stop someone from continuing with, or concentrating on, what they are doing 擾亂；打擾；打擾：*I'm sorry to disturb you when you're working, but would you mind helping me for a moment?* 對不起，打擾了您的工作，請幫我一下忙，好嗎？

bother to disturb someone in an annoying way or repeatedly, especially about something that seems trivial to them（尤指因小事不斷）麻煩，煩擾（某人）：*Stop bothering me, I've got a very important letter to write.* 別煩我，我有一封很重要的信要寫。

butt in (*informal*) to interrupt someone by saying something when they are speaking 插話；打斷說話：*I'm trying to explain something to Jane, and he keeps butting in.* 我正試圖向珍解釋事情時，他一個勁地插話。

disrupt to cause trouble and prevent something from happening in an orderly manner 擾亂；使中斷：*Protesters tried to disrupt the meeting.* 示威者試圖擾亂會場。

distract to draw someone's attention to something other than what they are supposed to be concentrating or working on 使分心；使轉移（注意力）：*I was distracted by something that was happening further along the street and didn't notice her.* 我因為街道遠處發生的事情分了心，沒有注意到她。

interrupt to stop something from continuing or to stop someone continuing with something, especially to stop someone from continuing to speak by saying something 插嘴；打斷（發言）：*Please don't interrupt, I'll answer your questions when I've finished what I have to say.* 請別插話，等我把必須說的話說完後再回答你們的問題。

intrude to come into or be in a place where you are not wanted, or disturb someone who wants to be private（未經允許）闖入，侵入，打擾：*You're intruding on a private conversation.* 你是在侵擾私密談話。

pester to disturb someone deliberately and repeatedly in order to get them to do something or pay attention to something 糾纏；煩擾：*She keeps pestering me to write to the council about the state of the pavement outside our house.* 她一直纏着要我給市政廳寫信，反映我們房子外面人行道的情況。

trouble to disturb someone, usually by asking them to do something 打擾；麻煩；煩請：*Sorry to trouble you, but would you mind shutting the window, there's a terrible draught.* 對不起，麻煩你關上窗戶行嗎？這兒風太大。

○ see also 參見 **affect²; hinder; interfere**

doubtful *adjective* not able to be known definitely, or not feeling sure about something and tending to have negative feelings about it 拿不定主意的；不確定的；懷疑的：*It's doubtful whether this birthday card will be delivered on time.* 這張生日賀卡能否按時送到還說不定。

debatable about which people may have differing opinions 可爭議的：*It's debatable whether Jill's presence was a help or a hindrance.* 吉爾的出現是幫忙還是妨礙尚存爭議。

dubious feeling doubtful about something, or questionable 懷疑的；不確定的；可疑的：*I'm dubious about whether the painting is worth the price they are asking for it.* 我懷疑這幅畫是否值他們要的價。

questionable causing you to feel doubt and ask questions, especially as to whether something is good, reliable, or trustworthy（尤指對是否優良、可靠或值得信賴等）有疑問的，不確定的；值得懷疑的：*of questionable morals* 品行有問題的

uncertain doubtful, or not able to make up your mind about something 可疑的；不確定的：*I'm uncertain whether to go or stay.* 是去是留，我還説不準。

unlikely to be expected not to happen rather than to happen 未必的；不太可能的：*It's unlikely that I will be able to go to the party.* 我不一定能參加聚會。

draw *verb* to produce a picture of someone or something, using a pencil or pen（用鉛筆或鋼筆等）繪畫，素描：*The little girl drew a picture of a snowman.* 小女孩畫了一個雪人。

depict (*formal*) to represent a subject in a painting or drawing（用圖）描繪，刻畫，描畫：*The painting depicts a castle on a hillside.* 這幅油畫描繪的是山腰上的一座城堡。

design to draw a detailed plan of something that is yet to be created, such as a building, a garment, or a publication 設計（建築物、服裝或出版物等）：*We're designing a simpler and cheaper model that will appeal to the mass market.* 我們正在設計一個更簡約而廉價的款式，以迎合大眾市場的需求。

doodle to draw absent-mindedly, often while doing something else（常指做其他事時）漫不經心地畫，胡寫亂畫：*Jim always doodles while talking on the phone.* 占姆打電話的時候總是信手亂畫。

illustrate to provide pictures to appear in a book or other publication, especially pictures that show things described in the text（在書籍等出版物中）加插圖説明，圖解：*This book is expensive because it is illustrated in full colour.* 這本書因為配有彩色插圖，所以很貴。

portray to represent a subject, especially a person, in a drawing or painting（用圖）描繪，刻畫，描畫（尤指人）：*The cartoonist portrayed the party leaders as different animals.* 漫畫家把政黨領袖們描畫成各種不同的動物。

scribble to draw or write untidily, as a young child does（如小孩一樣）亂寫亂畫：*When Sally was two years old, she scribbled all over the wall in crayon.* 莎莉 2 歲的時候，用蠟筆在牆上到處亂塗亂畫。

sketch to make a quick and often incomplete drawing of someone or something 勾畫，勾勒（人或物）：*Keith quickly sketched Amber while she was reading her book.* 基思在安伯看書時迅速地為她勾勒了一幅素描。

trace to make a copy of a picture by placing thin transparent paper over it and drawing over the lines with a pencil（用透明薄紙蒙在原圖上用鉛筆）映描，描摹：*The boy traced a picture of a dinosaur from his book.* 男孩照着書本描了一張恐龍圖。

dream *noun* pictures that you see in your mind while you sleep 夢；夢境：*I had a dream about falling off a cliff last night.* 昨晚我夢見自己摔下懸崖。

daydream an instance of imagining pleasant events in a dreamlike way while you are awake 白日夢；幻想：*Julie was having a daydream about travelling to Russia.* 朱莉幻想着去俄羅斯旅遊。

fantasy an instance of imagining a pleasant situation that you would like to happen but which is unlikely to happen 幻想；夢想；空想：*Grant had a fantasy about being a professional footballer.* 格蘭特幻想自己成為一名職業足球員。

hallucination an instance of seeing something that does not really exist, caused by illness or drugs (由疾病或藥品等引起的) 幻覺，幻想：*At the height of his fever he was having hallucinations.* 他發高燒時產生了幻覺。

nightmare a frightening or very unpleasant dream that you have while you sleep 噩夢；夢魘：*The little boy woke up crying because he had been having a nightmare.* 小男孩醒來大哭大叫，因為他做了個噩夢。

reverie (*formal*) an instance of imagining pleasant events in a dreamlike way while you are awake 白日夢；夢想；幻想：*My reverie was interrupted by loud banging on the door.* 響亮的砰砰敲門聲打斷了我的幻想。

vision an instance of seeing something that other people cannot see, sometimes caused by mental illness or drugs (有時由精神疾病或藥品等引起的) 幻象，幻影：*The woman claims to have had a vision of Christ.* 那位婦女稱自己看到過耶穌的幻影。

drink *verb* to take a liquid into your mouth and swallow it 喝；飲：*I drank a cup of tea at breakfast time.* 早餐時間我喝了一杯茶。

down (*informal*) to drink all of something, often quickly (常指一下子) 喝下：*He can down a pint of lager in one go.* 他能一口氣喝下一品脫窖藏啤酒。

gulp to drink something hastily swallowing large amounts at a time 猛喝；一口吞下：*We had to gulp down our drinks before the pub closed.* 我們必須在酒館打烊前把酒水灌下肚。

guzzle (*informal*) to drink something greedily 狂飲；貪婪地喝：*teenagers guzzling cheap cider* 狂飲廉價蘋果酒的青少年

knock back (*informal*) to drink something quickly, usually in one gulp 一下子喝光；一口吞下：*Come on, knock it back in one!* 來，一口乾杯！

quaff (*old-fashioned or humorous*) to drink an alcoholic drink often in large amounts 痛飲；一飲而盡：*They spent the whole night quaffing wine.* 他們整個晚上都在痛飲葡萄酒。

sip to drink something in small mouthfuls 小口地喝；呷：*delicately sipping sherry* 優雅地抿着雪利酒

slug (*informal*) to take a large mouthful of an alcoholic drink 大口地喝 (酒)：*slugging whisky from a hip flask* 大口喝着小扁酒瓶裏的威士忌

swallow to pass liquid from your mouth into your throat and down into your stomach 吞下；嚥下：*Wine tasters don't swallow the wine – they spit it out.* 品酒師不把葡萄酒吞下肚，他們把它吐出來。

swig (*informal*) to drink something quickly and in large amounts 牛飲；痛飲：*The boys were swigging cans of cola.* 那些男孩正在猛喝罐裝可樂。

drunk *adjective* whose behaviour and thinking are affected by having consumed a lot of alcohol 醉的；喝醉了的：*He was so drunk that he couldn't walk in a straight line.* 他喝醉了，走路都走不直了。

inebriated (*formal*) affected by having drunk a lot of alcohol 醉的；喝醉了的：*Everyone was rather inebriated by the end of the office party.* 辦公室聚會結束時，每個人都有幾分醉意。

intoxicated (*formal*) affected by having drunk a lot of alcohol 醉的；喝醉了的：*The TV presenter appeared to be intoxicated.* 電視節目主持人似乎喝醉了。

legless (*informal*) extremely drunk, so that you are unable to walk 爛醉如泥的；酩酊大醉的：*He was absolutely legless and had to be helped home.* 他喝得爛醉如泥，只好被扶回家。

over the limit having drunk more alcohol than is legally permitted if you are going to drive 飲酒過量的 (指超過駕車的法定酒量)：*I will have to leave the car here and take a taxi home because I am over the limit.* 我飲酒過量了，只得把車留在這裏，乘計程車回家。

paralytic (*informal*) extremely drunk so that you are unable to move 爛醉如泥的；酩酊大醉的：*Kevin got paralytic and fell asleep at the bar.* 凱文爛醉如泥，在酒吧睡着了。

smashed (*informal*) extremely drunk 大醉的：*A group of teenage girls staggered out of a club, absolutely smashed.* 一群喝得酩酊大醉的少女搖搖晃晃地走出了夜總會。

tiddly (*informal*) tipsy 微醉的；有點醉意的：*My aunt was quite tiddly after a couple of glasses of sherry.* 我的姑媽喝了幾杯雪利酒後就有些醉了。

tipsy slightly drunk and usually feeling very cheerful as a result 有點醉意的；微醉的：*We had wine with lunch and I felt a little tipsy.* 我們午餐喝了葡萄酒，我感到有點醉了。

duty *noun* something that you are obliged to do, often as part of your work 職責；義務：*Ordering stationery for the department is one of my duties.* 我的職責之一是為系訂購文具。

assignment a task that you are given to do, often as part of your work or studies 任務；作業：*We have to hand in our History assignment tomorrow.* 我們明天必須交歷史作業。

burden a responsibility that is difficult to cope with (責任的) 重擔，負擔：*If Anne gets a part-time job, it will ease the family's financial burden a bit.* 如果安妮找到一份兼職，就會減輕一點家庭的經濟負擔。

chore a task that has to be done regularly, especially in the home, and that you find tedious (尤指單調乏味的) 日常事務，家務，雜務：*Cleaning the bathroom is the least favourite of my household chores.* 打掃浴室是我最不愛做的一件家務。

commission a job, often something creative, that someone has asked you to do for them 受託之事；正式委託：*The artist has a commission for a set of six paintings for the new concert hall.* 畫家受託為新建的音樂廳繪製一套 6 幅的油畫。

function the main duty of a person in a particular job 職責；作用：*The function of a teacher is to educate children.* 教師的職責就是教育孩子。

job a task or duty that you are asked to perform 任務；工作；活兒；職責：*The old Lady next door wants me to do a couple of little jobs around the house for her.* 隔壁的老太太要我幫她幹一些家務。

responsibility a task that you must do and that you can be blamed or punished for not doing 責任；職責：*It's the caretaker's responsibility to lock up the building for the night.* 大樓晚上鎖門是管理員的職責。

task a piece of work that you have to do 任務；作業：*My first task for today is to weed the garden.* 我今天的第一項任務就是給花園除草。

E

eager *adjective* wanting very much to do or to have something 渴望的；渴求的；熱切的：*I was eager to go home.* 我盼着回家。

agog* expecting or watching something in a state of great excitement 興奮期待；急切期盼：*The children were all agog, waiting for Santa Claus to arrive at the party.* 孩子們都興奮不已，急切等待着聖誕老人來到他們的聚會。
* Only used after a verb. 僅用於動詞之後。

anxious wanting very much to do or to have something and slightly nervous in case you cannot (略帶緊張) 急切的；渴望的：*She was anxious to make a good impression on her boyfriend's parents.* 她熱切希望能給男朋友的父母留下良好的印象。

avid very enthusiastically involved in an activity (對某種活動) 熱衷的，酷愛的：*She is an avid reader.* 她是一個酷愛閱讀的人。

enthusiastic having or showing a great interest in something and very positive feelings about it 熱情的；熱心的；積極的：*enthusiastic about golf* 熱衷於高爾夫球

keen wanting very much to do or to have something 渴望的；熱切的；熱衷於：*She is keen to go to university.* 她渴望能上大學。

passionate caring very much about a subject or activity (對某學科或活動) 熱心的，充滿熱情的：*a passionate skier* 一個熱衷於滑雪的人

raring to go (*informal*) very excited about something you are going to do and anxious to start doing it 急切的；渴望的：*I've got my train tickets and now I'm just raring to go.* 我買了火車票，現在急着要走。

zealous strongly committed to a particular cause or religion (對事業、信仰等) 熱衷的，熱情的，充滿激情的：*a zealous campaigner for animal rights* 一個熱衷於動物權益的活動家

earn *verb* to receive money in return for work 賺得，獲得 (錢)：*He earns £30,000 a year.* 他一年賺 3 萬英鎊。

clear (*informal*) to receive a specified amount of money, usually a large sum that you are pleased about, after deductions have been made from your earnings, etc. 淨得，淨賺，獲利 (常指數目可觀的錢)：*With overtime, I cleared £500 that week.* 因為加了班，那個星期我淨賺 500 英鎊。

gross (*usually used in a business context*) to earn a specified amount of money before deductions have been made for tax, etc. (常用於商務場合) 總

收入為，毛收入為：*The film grossed $100 million worldwide.* 這部電影在世界各地的票房收入合計 1 億美元。

make to receive a certain amount of money in wages or salary, or as profit, or when you sell something 賺（工錢或利潤）：*I made a lot more money this year than I did last year.* 與去年相比，我今年賺的錢要多得多。

net (*usually used in a business context*) to receive a specified amount of money in profit after deductions have been made for expenses, etc. （常用於商務場合）淨賺，淨得，實際盈利為：*She didn't net enough to have to pay income tax last year.* 去年她淨賺不多，不必交所得稅。

take home to receive a specified amount of money after deductions have been made from your earnings for tax, etc. 淨得；實得：*The amount he takes home is not enough to support a family.* 他淨賺的錢不夠養家糊口。

easy *adjective* not difficult to do or to understand, especially because requiring little effort 容易的，簡單的（尤指不需多少努力）：*That was an easy question.* 那是個容易回答的問題。

cushy (*informal*) that does not involve hard work 容易的；輕鬆的；不費勁的：*a cushy job* 一份輕鬆的工作

effortless carried out with no effort 容易的；不需費力的：*He gave a seemingly effortless performance.* 他表演起來似乎輕而易舉。

elementary requiring little knowledge and ability to understand, or relating to the most basic facts and principles of a subject (指學科) 基礎的，基本的，初步的：*an elementary course in human biology* 一門人類生物學的基礎課程

foolproof impossible or difficult to get wrong 萬無一失的；十分簡單的：*I'm trying to devise a foolproof method of calculating how much income tax a person owes.* 我在試圖設計一種穩妥的方法，用以計算個人欠繳的所得稅。

simple not difficult to do or to understand, especially through not being complicated 簡易的；簡單的：*simple arithmetic* 簡易算法

straightforward not complicated or difficult 簡單明了的；易懂的：*I was worried about finding my way to the hospital, but it was quite straightforward.* 我還為找去醫院的路擔心，但結果路好找得很。

uncomplicated straightforward and easy to do or to understand 簡單明了的；不複雜的：*an uncomplicated recipe* 一道簡單易做的菜譜

undemanding requiring little effort to do, understand, or appreciate 簡單明了的；難度不大的；易懂的：*an undemanding film* 一部淺顯易懂的影片

eat *verb* to put solid food into your mouth and swallow it 吃：*Vegetarians don't eat meat.* 素食者不吃肉。

bolt (*down*) to eat something quickly, especially by swallowing it without chewing 快速地吃；（尤指）囫圇吞下：*Don't bolt your food – you will get indigestion!* 不要狼吞虎嚥，你會消化不良的！

chew to crush food with your teeth 咀嚼：*Some people find that chewing gum helps them to concentrate.* 有些人發現咀嚼香口膠能幫助他們集中注意力。

consume (*formal*) to eat, drink, or use up something 吃；喝；消耗（掉）：*Members of staff should not consume alcohol while on company premises.* 在公司的場地內，員工們不得飲酒。

devour (*formal*) (*usually said about an animal or someone who eats like an animal*) to eat something greedily（通常用以指動物或如動物般吃食的人）貪婪地吃；狼吞虎嚥：*The lions devoured the carcass of a zebra.* 那幾頭獅子吞食了一隻斑馬的屍體。

gobble to eat something quickly and greedily 狼吞虎嚥；猛吃：*The children were so hungry that they gobbled their food up in no time.* 孩子們餓極了，不一會兒就把食物一掃而光。

munch to eat something noisily 大聲咀嚼：*Adam was munching a packet of crisps.* 亞當大聲嚼着一包薯片。

nibble to take small dainty bites of something 小口咬；一點一點地咬：*Kirsty nibbled her sandwich while she worked.* 姬絲蒂一邊工作一邊啃着三文治。

scoff (*informal*) to eat a large quantity of food quickly and greedily 猛吃；貪婪地吃；狼吞虎嚥：*I thought I had made too much food for the party, but the kids scoffed the lot.* 我還以為晚會的食物準備多了，可沒想到全被孩子們收拾掉了。

swallow to pass food from your mouth into your throat and down into your stomach 吞下；嚥下：*Some people find it difficult to swallow pills.* 有些人覺得吞服藥丸很困難。

wolf (*informal*) to eat a large quantity of something quickly and greedily 狼吞虎嚥；貪婪地吃：*I felt sick after wolfing a whole box of chocolates.* 猛地吃光一整盒巧克力後，我感到不舒服。

eccentric *adjective* (usually only used about people) rather unusual in behaviour or appearance（通常僅用於人的行為或外表等）古怪的，與眾不同的：*an eccentric old Lady who lives with thirty cats* 一個和 30 隻貓生活在一起的古怪老太婆

idiosyncratic being an unusual trait that a particular person has, but no other person does（指個人特性）獨到的，獨具一格的：*her idiosyncratic style of singing* 她獨到的演唱風格

odd different from what is considered normal or ordinary 古怪的；奇特的；反常的：*His behaviour has been rather odd since his illness.* 打他生病以來，他的行為就有點古怪。

peculiar odd 奇特的；特有的：*He has a peculiar way of swinging his arms while he walks.* 他走路時擺動胳膊的方式很奇特。

quirky unusual in an amusing or interesting way 離奇的；怪異的：*a comedian with a quirky outlook on life* 具有離奇人生觀的喜劇大師

unconventional not sticking to the ways of doing things that are usual in society 不拘一格的；不循規蹈矩的；不因循守舊的：*Maria is unconventional, which is probably why she decided to get married in a red dress.* 瑪麗亞不墨守陳規，這可能正是她決定穿紅色連衣裙結婚的原因。

wacky (*informal or humorous*) very unusual, or crazy 古怪的；怪誕的；瘋瘋癲癲的：*All the kids have had problems at school, and some of them are pretty wacky.* 所有這些孩子在學校都有過問題，其中有些性情十分乖僻。

weird very strange, in a puzzling or alarming way 怪異的；不可思議的；離奇的：*This way he looked at me was distinctly weird.* 他這樣瞅着我顯然有些奇怪。

➲ see also 參見 **strange**

empty *adjective* having nothing or no one inside 空的；無人的：*My glass is empty.* 我的玻璃杯是空的。

bare (usually used to describe an enclosed space such as a room, or a shelf) having nothing in it or on it（通常用以描述封閉的空間，如房間、架子等）空的，沒有東西的：*The cupboards were bare.* 櫥櫃是空的。

blank not written on（紙張等）空白的，沒寫字的：*a blank page* 空白頁

deserted in which there are no people 無人居住的；空寂無人的：*a deserted car park* 空無一人的停車場

hollow having an empty space inside 中空的；空心的；空腹的：*a hollow mould* 中空模具

unfurnished containing no furniture 無傢具的：*I rented an unfurnished flat.* 我租了一間沒有傢具的房子。

uninhabited in or on which no one lives 杳無人跡的；無人居住的；無人煙的：*an uninhabited island* 杳無人跡的島嶼

unoccupied not being used or lived in by anybody 空閒的；閒置的；無人佔用的：*an unoccupied room* 空着的房間

vacant unoccupied 空着的；未被佔用的：*This cubicle is vacant.* 這間小臥室空着沒人住。

endanger *verb* to put someone or something in a dangerous position 危及；使處於危險的境地：*People who drink and drive are endangering their own lives and the lives of others.* 人們酒後駕車危及自己和他人的生命安全。

compromise to expose something, such as your safety or your beliefs, to danger or damage（使個人安危、信仰等）面臨不測，陷入危險：*I refuse to compromise my principles in order to fit in with the crowd.* 我決不為迎合眾人而違背我的原則。

expose to leave someone or something open to danger or harm 使面臨，使遭受（危險或傷害等）：*You should not expose your skin to the harmful rays of the sun.* 你不應該讓皮膚接觸到陽光中的有害射線。

imperil (*formal*) to put someone or something in danger 危及；使處於危險：*I urge you not to do anything that might imperil the lives of the troops under your command.* 我勸你不要做任何有可能危及手下將士性命的事情。

jeopardize (*formal*) to make something likely to fail 冒…的危險；危害；危及：*Raymond's infidelity is jeopardizing his marriage.* 雷蒙德的不忠危及到他的婚姻。

put at risk to put someone or something in danger of harm or failure 危及；損害；使陷入（被傷害或遭受失敗等的）危險：*By smoking during pregnancy, you put your unborn child's health at risk.* 你在懷孕期間吸煙可能對未來孩子的健康構成危害。

risk to deliberately put yourself or something, such as your life, in danger in order to do something 冒險，冒着（生命等）危險（做某事）：*The man risked* *his own life to pull a child out of the way of an oncoming car.* 那個男人冒着生命危險拉着一個小孩躲開迎面駛來的汽車。

threaten   to put something, such as a relationship, at risk of failing or being harmed 使（人際關係等）處於危險；危及：*Andy feels his relationship with Pam is threatened by her obsession with work.* 安迪感到帕姆癡迷於工作在危及他們之間的關係。

⊃ see also 參見 **threaten**

enemy *noun* a person who dislikes you and wishes to cause you harm, or a person or force that is opposed to another 敵人；仇敵；敵軍：*The police discovered that the murdered man had several enemies.* 警察發現被害者生前有幾個仇人。

adversary   someone who opposes you in a fight, contest, debate, etc. （戰鬥、競賽、辯論等中的）對手，敵手：*Ian was less than pleased to see his old adversary from university at the interview.* 伊恩在這次面試中見到大學時期的老對手，很不高興。

antagonist   a person who is your adversary, often someone who represents the opposite values to your own（常指價值觀等的）對立者，對抗者，對手：*In certain religions, the Devil is the antagonist of God.* 在有些宗教裏，魔鬼與上帝是敵對的。

foe (*literary*) an enemy 敵人；仇敵：*Dictatorship is the foe of democracy.* 獨裁是民主的敵人。

opponent   someone who is playing against you in a sporting contest or opposing you in a situation similar to a sporting contest（在體育比賽等場合的）對手，競爭者：*The heavyweight champion defeated his opponent in the third round.* 最重量級舉重冠軍在第三輪比賽中戰勝了他的對手。

the opposition   the people, or sometimes the person, opposing you, especially a party opposing a government in a parliament 反對派；反對者；（尤指議會裏的）反對黨：*Before entering any contest, you should try to gauge the strength of the opposition.* 在參加任何比賽前，你應該估計一下對手的實力。

rival   someone with whom you compete for something 競爭者；競爭對手：*Ewan and Jamal are rivals for Abbie's affections.* 尤安與賈馬爾是博取阿比芳心的情敵。

entertain *verb* to do something that makes people laugh or something that gives them pleasure, such as singing or dancing（以歌、舞等）使娛樂，使快樂：*A group of children went to the nursing home to entertain the residents.* 一群孩子去療養院為那裏的人娛樂演出。

amuse   to make someone laugh or keep them occupied in an enjoyable way 逗樂；逗笑；提供娛樂：*There was a clown at the party to amuse the children.* 晚會上有個小丑逗孩子們高興。

delight   to give someone pleasure or enjoyment 使高興；使欣喜：*The speaker delighted the audience with her tales of life as a cabaret singer.* 演講人講述她當酒店歌手時的生活經歷，讓聽眾非常開心。

divert (*old-fashioned*) to amuse someone 取悅；逗樂；使消遣：*The company was diverted by the ladies playing the piano and singing.* 女士們彈奏鋼琴、演唱歌曲，讓這群人得到了消遣。

enthral to hold someone's attention and interest for a long time in an enjoyable way 迷住；迷醉；吸引住：*The actress's great beauty enthralled the audience.* 女演員非常漂亮，迷住了觀眾。

interest to attract someone's attention and give them something to think about 引起注意；使產生興趣：*I found an article in the newspaper that might interest you.* 我在報紙上找到一篇文章，你可能感興趣。

regale to provide people with something, especially interesting and enjoyable stories（通過快樂、有趣的故事等）使娛樂，使享受：*The old sailor regaled us with tales of his naval exploits.* 老水手給我們講了他當海軍時的英雄事跡，逗我們開心。

tickle (*informal*) to make someone laugh 逗笑；使娛樂：*Your sense of humour really tickles me.* 你的幽默感真讓我發笑。

➲ see also 參見 **game; interesting**

err *verb* (formal) to make a mistake, or to do wrong 犯錯；作惡：*He admitted that he had erred in the past.* 他承認過去做過壞事。

be mistaken to be wrong about something 犯錯；弄錯：*I thought the last train was at 11 pm, but I was mistaken.* 我還以為最後一班列車是在晚上 11 點，結果我弄錯了。

blunder to make a stupid mistake 犯大錯；犯荒唐的錯誤：*I really blundered this morning when I called Eric's new girlfriend by his ex-wife's name.* 今天早上我真的犯了個大錯，我將埃里克的新女朋友喊成了他前妻的名字。

boob (*informal*) to make a stupid mistake 犯大錯；犯荒唐的錯誤：*Oops, I've boobed again — that was the wrong number I gave you.* 哎，我又搞錯了，我給你的那個號碼不對。

go wrong to make a mistake and arrive at a bad result, for example in trying to solve a problem or in dealing with people 誤入歧途；（在解決問題、待人接物等方面）犯錯：*Parents whose children end up in serious trouble often ask themselves where they went wrong.* 孩子出了嚴重的問題，家長經常問自己錯在哪兒。

miscalculate to count or estimate something incorrectly 誤算；算錯：*I miscalculated how long it would take to drive to Newcastle.* 我估算錯了駕車到紐卡素需要的時間。

misunderstand to take the wrong meaning out of what someone has said 誤解；誤會：*You misunderstood me. I wasn't arguing with you – I am on your side.* 你誤會了我的意思。我不是在和你爭辯，我是支持你的。

slip up (*informal*) to make a silly or unimportant mistake 疏忽；犯愚蠢的錯誤；出差錯：*Chris slipped up when he posted his application form without signing it.* 克里斯犯了個愚蠢的錯誤，在郵寄申請表的時候忘了簽名。

escape *verb* to get away from a place, especially from captivity（尤指從囚禁之地）逃離，逃脫：*A lion has escaped from the zoo.* 一頭獅子逃出了動物園。

abscond (*formal*) to leave a place, often after committing a crime or to avoid arrest（常指犯罪後或為避抓捕而）潛逃，逃循，逃離：*The company treasurer absconded with the funds.* 公司出納攜款潛逃了。

bolt to run away quickly and suddenly 逃遁；逃跑：*Someone opened the front door, and the dog bolted.* 有人把前門打開，讓那隻狗溜掉了。

break out to get away from a place where you are being kept as a prisoner or are surrounded by enemy forces 逃脫；越獄；突圍：*A convicted murderer has broken out of prison.* 一名被判謀殺罪的兇徒越獄了。

flee to run away, especially from an unpleasant situation 逃離，逃避（尤指不愉快的處境）：*Sally fled to her parents' house to escape an abusive marriage.* 為了逃避屈辱的婚姻，莎莉逃到父母家。

get away to leave a difficult or unpleasant situation 逃脫，逃離，離開（艱苦或不愉快的境地）：*Graham joined the army to get away from a boring job.* 格雷厄姆參軍以逃脫煩悶的工作。

leg it (*informal*) to run away fast 逃跑；開溜：*Here come the cops-quick, leg it!* 警察來啦，快跑啊！

run away to leave a place by running, or to escape from a threatening or unpleasant situation 逃離，離開（危險或不愉快的境地）：*Lisa ran away from home to avoid an unhappy environment.* 麗莎為了躲避不愉快的環境逃離了家。

➲ see also 參見 **avoid**

eternal *adjective* lasting for ever 永恆的；永久的：*a quest for eternal life* 追求永生

ceaseless (*formal*) going on for a long time without stopping 不停的；不斷的：*his ceaseless complaining* 他無休止的抱怨

everlasting lasting for ever, or for the rest of your life 永恆的；持久的：*everlasting love* 永恆的愛

immortal living for ever, never dying 永生的；不朽的：*A god is an immortal being.* 神是永遠不會死的。

infinite having no end or no limits 無窮的；無限的：*infinite time* 無限的時間

limitless having no limits or no restrictions 無限的；無限制的：*for a limitless period* 一段不限長短的時期

perpetual lasting for ever, or going on for a long time without stopping 永久的；永不停息的：*perpetual youth* 永久的青春

undying (*usually used to describe a feeling*) never ceasing or lessening （情感）永恆的，不朽的：*undying admiration* 無盡的讚美

unending going on for a long time without coming to an end 無盡的；永遠的：*a subject of unending fascination* 一個永遠具有魅力的話題

➲ see also 參見 **continuous**

event *noun* something that happens, especially something important 事件；（尤指）重大事件：*a momentous event in history* 歷史上的重大事件

episode an event or a period of time occurring in the course of a longer period 片段；一段經歷：*That was a shameful episode in my past.* 那是我過去的一段丟臉的經歷。

experience something that happens to you 經歷；體驗：*The train crash was a terrifying experience.* 火車發生碰撞事故是一件極其可怕的經歷。

happening something that happens, especially something unusual 事情，發生的事情（尤指不尋常）: *Police asked local residents if they had been aware of any unusual happenings in recent weeks.* 警察問當地居民在最近幾週是否察覺有異常情況。

incident something that happens at a particular time, especially something unpleasant（尤指不愉快的）事變，事件: *a violent incident* 暴力事件

occasion an organized event, especially a celebration of some kind（有組織的）事件，活動事件（尤指慶典等）: *a grand occasion, like a coronation* 一個盛大的場合，比如加冕禮

occurrence something that happens, usually something quite ordinary that may be repeated（通常指可能反覆發生的平凡的）事件: *Mislaying my keys is practically an everyday occurrence.* 我隨手亂放鑰匙實際上是每天都發生的事。

examination *noun* a test of someone's knowledge or skill, especially in school, college, or university（尤指學校對知識、技能等的）考試: *I failed my history examination.* 我歷史考試不及格。

assessment a judgment of someone's progress, for example on a course of study（對某人的進步，如學習等的）評估，評價: *Instead of an end-of-term exam we have continuous assessment of classwork.* 我們沒有期末考試，但有連續性的課堂學業評估。

exam (*informal*) an examination 考試: *I passed all my exams!* 我所有考試都及格了。

interrogation a situation in which someone, especially someone acting in an official capacity, for example a police officer, asks someone else a series of probing questions（尤指警察等行使職權的人）審問: *The police conducted an interrogation of the murder suspect.* 警察對那個謀殺案疑犯進行了審問。

oral (*informal*) a spoken, rather than written, examination 口試: *We have our Spanish oral tomorrow.* 明天我們有西班牙語口語考試。

paper a piece of paper with questions on it, as part of an examination 試卷；考卷: *The first maths paper was easy but the second one was difficult.* 第一份數學試卷容易，但第二份難。

quiz* a set of questions and answers, usually spoken, to test people's knowledge, as a competition（常指口頭的）知識競賽，智力競賽: *The local pub holds a quiz every Thursday night.* 這家當地酒館每逢星期四晚上都舉辦智力競猜。

* In US English a quiz often means a test of school students' knowledge of a particular subject. 在美國英語中，quiz 常指 test，即在校學生的學科測驗。

test a method of assessing someone's knowledge or skill（評定一個人知識或技能等的）測試，測驗: *I am practising for my driving test.* 我正在練習，準備駕駛考試。

excellent *adjective* extremely good 優秀的；極好的: *We had an excellent meal at the new restaurant.* 我們在這家新餐館吃了一頓，飯菜好極了。

brilliant (*informal*) extremely good or enjoyable 極好的；妙極了的: *I had a brilliant holiday.* 我過了一個很爽的假期。

exceptional of an unusually high standard 卓越的；傑出的；出色的：*an exceptional athlete* 一名出色的運動員

exemplary setting a good example for other people 典範的；為人楷模的：*The conduct of the police officers dealing with the incident was exemplary.* 這些警察處理這宗事件的做法堪作楷模。

fantastic (*informal*) extremely good or enjoyable 妙極了的；極好的 ：*Lorraine has got a fantastic new job.* 洛蘭找到了一份很棒的新工作。

first-rate of the highest possible standard 一流的；上乘的：*a first-rate crime writer* 描寫犯罪的一流作家

great (*informal*) extremely good or very enjoyable 很棒的；妙極了的：*I had a great time at the party.* 聚會上我玩得開心極了。

marvellous (*informal*) extremely good or enjoyable 極好的；絕妙的：*a marvellous singer* 一名了不起的歌手

outstanding of exceptionally high quality 突出的；卓越的；出色的：*an outstanding performance* 出色的表演

terrific (*informal*) extremely good or enjoyable 極好的；妙極了的：*We had a terrific time at the wedding.* 婚禮上我們開心極了。

wonderful extremely good or enjoyable 極好的；絕妙的：*a wonderful painting* 一幅美妙的油畫

excited *adjective* full of a lively, bubbly, happy feeling, often because of something good that is going to happen (常因好事即將到來而) 激動的，興奮的：*The little boy was so excited about meeting his soccer hero.* 這小男孩馬上就要見到他心目中的足球英雄，感到非常興奮。

animated acting, talking, or doing something in a lively and excited way (指行為、說話或辦事) 興致勃勃的，生氣勃勃的，活躍的：*After a couple of glasses of wine, Jill became very animated.* 喝完幾杯葡萄酒後，吉爾變得非常興奮。

exhilarated feeling very happy and as if you have much more life and energy than you usually do (指比平時) 興奮的，高興的，激動的：*I felt quite exhilarated when we reached the top of the mountain.* 當我們爬到山頂的時候，我感到興奮不已。

high (*informal*) exhilarated or in a dreamlike happy state, usually as a result of taking drugs or alcohol (通常指由於吸毒或飲酒) 興奮的，飄飄然的：*They were high on Ecstasy.* 他們吃了搖頭丸飄飄欲仙。

hyper (*informal*) overexcited and very active, sometimes as a result of a medical condition or of taking drugs or alcohol (有時指由於體格狀況、吸毒或飲酒等) 亢奮的，精力過旺的：*Little Scott was totally hyper yesterday, running around and yelling nonstop.* 小斯科特昨天亢奮不已，到處亂跑，還不住地喊叫。

overwrought extremely nervous and out of control of your emotions 過度興奮的；極度緊張的；情緒失控的：*Please excuse Alison's behaviour last night – she was a little overwrought.* 請原諒艾利森昨晚的行為，她當時情緒有點失控。

thrilled very happy and excited 激動的；興奮的：*I was thrilled to visit the Parthenon.* 我很興奮地參觀了巴特農神殿。

worked up extremely nervous and overemotional 狂躁不安的；情緒過激的；異常興奮的：*She tends to get all worked up about animal rights.* 談到動物權利的時候，她往往變得異常激動。

exclusive *adjective* restricted to people who are rich or of high social standing 高檔的；奢華的；豪華的：*an exclusive yacht club* 一家高級的遊艇俱樂部

classy (*informal*) having or showing good taste and sophistication 有氣派的；上檔次的：*She was wearing a simple but classy black suit.* 她穿一身簡單但很有派頭的黑色套裝。

elite belonging to a group of people considered special or privileged 精英的；精銳的；特權階層的：*elite troops* 精銳部隊

fashionable stylish and favoured by people of high social standing 流行的；時髦的；有社會地位的人喜愛的：*a fashionable area* 上層人士居住的地區

high-class of superior quality 質量上乘的；高級的：*a high-class establishment* 一流的機構

posh (*informal*) smart and expensive 時髦的；高檔的：*a posh frock* 一件豪華的上衣

select specially chosen 精選的；特地挑選的：*just for the select few* 只針對精選出來的少數幾個

up-market intended for people who are rich or of high social standing 高檔的；高檔消費的：*an up-market restaurant* 一家高檔飯店

⊃ see also 參見 **fashionable**

expect *verb* to be fairly certain that something is going to happen or that you are going to get something 期待；預期（必將發生的事）；指望：*I am expecting a parcel in the post.* 我在等一件郵包。

anticipate to realize that something is likely to happen 預期（可能發生的事）；預見：*Joe had not anticipated such a strong negative reaction to his proposal.* 祖沒想到他的提議會遭到如此強烈的反對。

await to wait for something to happen 等候；等待；期待：*I await confirmation of the booking.* 我在等待預訂的確認。

bank on to be confident that something is going to happen 指望；仰仗：*I am banking on getting your support.* 我指望得到你的支持。

hope for to want something to happen or to get something 期待，希望（某事發生或得到某物）：*The farmers are hoping for rain.* 農民正盼待着下雨。

look forward to to be happy about something that is going to happen（高興地）盼望，期待：*We are really looking forward to going on holiday.* 我們非常盼望去度假。

⊃ see also 參見 **hope**

explain *verb* to give information about something that makes it easier to understand 解釋；說明：*Ray explained the filing system to the new member of staff.* 雷向那位新來的職員解釋了那套文件系統。

clarify to make a statement clearer by giving further information 闡明，澄清（陳述等）：*Can you clarify what you meant in this first paragraph?* 你能闡述一下你的第一段是甚麼意思嗎？

define to describe the meaning of a word or phrase 定義，解釋（詞或短語）：*This dictionary defines over 100,000 words.* 這部詞典為 10 萬多條詞給了釋義。

describe to state what someone or something is like 描述，描寫，形容（人或物）：*This author has often been described as a genius.* 這位作家常常被描述成天才。

elaborate to give further details about something, such as a proposal or a statement 詳細闡述，詳細解釋（提案或聲明等）：*Can you elaborate on this suggestion?* 你能詳細地解釋一下這項建議嗎？

enlighten (*formal*) to make someone understand something better by giving more information 啟發；開導：*Will someone please enlighten me as to how to operate the fax machine?* 誰能教我如何使用這部傳真機？

interpret to explain the underlying meaning of something, such as a statement or a work of art, as you understand it 闡釋，解釋（陳述或藝術作品等的內在含義）：*I interpreted Matthew's words as a threat.* 我認為馬修說的那番話是在威脅。

shed light on to make something easier to understand by giving more information 闡明；交待；說清楚：*Can you shed any light on how the DVD player got broken?* 你能不能說清楚這 DVD 機是怎麼弄壞的？

F

fail *verb* to be unsuccessful in an examination or an endeavour（考試等）不及格；（嘗試等）失敗：*If you don't work hard, you will fail your exams.* 你若不努力學習，考試會不及格的。

bomb (*informal*) to be extremely unsuccessful, especially in the theatre 慘敗；（尤指戲劇）演出失敗，票房極差：*The play bombed in the West End.* 這齣戲在倫敦西區徹底演出失敗了。

collapse to fail suddenly and completely 瓦解；崩潰；突然告吹：*The pay negotiations collapsed when neither side would concede anything.* 雙方都不願意作任何讓步，工資談判就此告吹。

come to grief to end in disaster 慘遭失敗；以徹底失敗而告終：*The boating trip came to grief when the boat capsized.* 小船翻了，水上之旅以失敗告終。

fall through to fail to be achieved 落空；失敗；成為泡影：*Our plans for a skiing holiday fell through.* 我們假期滑雪的計劃泡湯了。

flop (*informal*) to be unsuccessful 失敗；不成功；砸鍋：*The band's first single flopped.* 該樂隊的第一張單曲唱片砸鍋了。

flunk* (*informal*) to fail an examination or test（考試或測驗等）失敗，不及格：*Kay flunked her driving theory test.* 凱的駕駛理論測試沒有通過。

* Common in US English, but not very common in British English. 常見於美國英語中，在英國英語中不很常見。

founder to end unsuccessfully 失敗；以失敗告終：*Their marriage foundered after only six months.* 他們的婚姻僅僅半年就破裂了。

go pear-shaped (*informal*) to go disastrously wrong 不對勁；出大毛病；出大問題：*United were in the lead but it all went a bit pear-shaped in the second half and they ended up 3-1 down.* 聯隊領先，但在後半場就有點不對勁兒了，結果以 1 比 3 敗北。

fair *adjective* treating people properly and equally 公平的；公正的；平等待人的：*If I pay for lunch today and you pay tomorrow, that will be fair.* 如果今天的午餐費由我付，明天由你付，那才算公平。

dispassionate not affected by your own emotions 平心靜氣的；不帶感情的：*As a jury member, you must be dispassionate when reaching your decision.* 作為一名陪審員，你在作決定時不能感情用事。

even-handed treating everyone equally 公平的；一視同仁的：*Teachers must be even-handed in their treatment of the children.* 老師對待孩子們要一碗水端平。

impartial without bias 公正的；不偏袒的：*an impartial judge* 一個公正的法官

just morally right and proper（道德上）正義的；公正的：*a just punishment* 公正的懲罰

kosher (*informal*) generally considered to be right or acceptable 合適的；可接受的：*a kosher excuse* 合適的藉口

objective not affected by personal feelings, preferences, or prejudices 客觀的；不受個人感情（偏好或偏見）影響的：*an objective opinion* 客觀的看法

reasonable sensible and proper 合情合理的；通情達理的：*a reasonable solution* 合理的解決方案

right in accordance with justice, morality, or good treatment of other people 公正的；合法的；公道的：*You shouldn't make fun of people because of their disabilities: it's just not right.* 你不應當因為別人的殘疾就取笑他們，那樣做是不對的。

unbiased not affected by your own interests 客觀的；不帶偏見的：*an unbiased account of events* 對情況的如實敍述

faithful *adjective* not changing your feelings towards someone or doing anything that will have a harmful effect on the good relationship you have with them 守信的；忠實的：*a faithful friend* 忠實的朋友

constant (*literary*) remaining the same, especially in your love or friendship for someone（尤指愛情或友誼等）忠貞不渝的，不變的：*constant in his loyalty* 忠心耿耿

loyal faithful, especially in your friendship with someone or in the support you give to a superior or a cause（尤指對友誼、上司或事業等）忠誠的，忠心的：*Her Majesty's loyal subjects* 為女王陛下效忠的臣民

staunch never wavering in your support 堅定的；忠實可靠的：*a staunch supporter of feminism* 女權運動的堅定支持者

steadfast firmly loyal and supportive, especially in difficult situations（尤指在艱苦的環境中）堅貞不渝的，堅信的，不動搖的：*steadfast support* 堅定的支持

true* faithful or loyal 忠實的；忠誠的：*The party remains true to the principles established by its founders.* 該黨一貫堅持創始人所制定的原則。

* Usually used after a verb in this sense. 作此義解時通常用於動詞後。

unswerving (*literary*) never changing its nature, or never changing your feelings, whatever happens 堅定的；矢志不渝的；始終如一的：*unswerving loyalty* 忠誠不渝

➲ see also 參見 **devoted; reliable; true**

fall *verb* to move downwards towards the ground or a lower level, or to go from a standing position to a position on the ground, usually accidentally 下落；倒下；（常指意外）摔倒：*The old man fell down the stairs.* 老人摔下了樓梯。

collapse to fall down, especially in a faint 倒塌；（尤指）暈倒：*The heat and lack of air in the shop caused a girl to collapse.* 商店裏溫度高又不通風，有個女孩昏倒了。

drop to move downwards, especially suddenly（尤指突然）下落，下墜，下跌：*The apple dropped off the tree.* 蘋果從樹上掉落。

plunge to fall fast and dramatically, usually from a considerable height, either towards the ground or into water 猛跌，驟降，猛落（到地上或水中）：*I heard a shot and saw a bird plunge towards the ground.* 我聽到一聲槍響，看見一隻鳥墮向地面。

sink to move downwards quite slowly, either towards the ground or under water 沉降；徐徐降落（到地面）；沉（入水底）：*A stone hit the boy in the head and he sank to the ground.* 一塊石頭砸到了男孩的腦袋，他慢慢地癱倒在地上。

topple to become unsteady and fall over 坍塌；倒塌：*The vase toppled over and smashed on the floor.* 花瓶倒了，摔在地板上碎了。

trip to stumble over an object or an unevenness in the ground and, sometimes, fall over 絆倒；失足；（有時指向前）摔倒：*Granny tripped over a toy car and broke her hip.* 祖母被玩具車絆倒，臀部骨折。

tumble to fall in an untidy way or head over heels 摔倒；倒塌；栽跟頭：*The child tumbled down the stairs and landed on her head.* 小孩倒栽蔥摔下樓梯。

false *adjective* not true or not correct, often deliberately changed from what is true or correct in order to deceive people 不真實的；不正確的；虛假的（常指故意誤導）：*false information* 虛假的信息

deceptive giving a false impression, sometimes deliberately 欺騙性的；（有時指故意）給人以假象的：*a deceptive smile* 假笑

erroneous (*formal*) incorrect 錯誤的；不正確的：*an erroneous translation of a Hebrew word* 對一個希伯來單詞的錯誤翻譯

inaccurate not conforming exactly to fact, reality, or the actual state of affairs 有誤的；不確切的；與事實不符的：*an inaccurate description* 不確切的描述

incorrect containing or based on a mistake 錯誤的；不正確的：*an incorrect answer* 錯誤的答案

misleading encouraging people to believe something that is untrue or incorrect 引入歧途的；使人誤解的；誤導的：*a misleading statement* 具有誤導性的表述

mistaken involving a failure to understand or recognize what something or someone really is 錯誤的；弄錯的：*a case of mistaken identity* 一件認錯人的事例

untrue not true or not factual 不真實的；虛假的；不屬實的：*The story he told me about his father being a millionaire proved to be untrue.* 他對我講的關於他父親是百萬富翁的故事被證明是編造的。

wrong different from the one that you should have chosen, taken, etc. 弄錯的；選錯的：*We took the wrong turning off the motorway.* 我們下高速公路時拐錯了彎。

➲ see also 參見 **artificial; dishonest**

famous *adjective* known to a lot of people now, or still remembered, for being very good at something or very successful or extraordinary（因某方面的特長或成就等）著名的，出名的，知名的：*a famous pop star* 著名的流行音樂歌星

celebrated well-known and admired, especially for being very talented（尤因才能而）著名的，聞名的，馳名的：*a celebrated concert pianist* 大名鼎鼎的音樂會鋼琴演奏家

distinguished greatly admired and respected 卓越的；著名的；傑出的：*a distinguished military career* 輝煌的軍事生涯

eminent important and highly respected, especially in a certain type of work（尤指在某行業中）傑出的，有名的，顯赫的：*an eminent neurosurgeon* 一個傑出的神經外科醫生

great very well known and highly respected 偉大的；傑出的；了不起的：*the great Surrealist painter, Salvador Dali* 偉大的超現實主義畫家薩爾瓦多·達利

illustrious (*formal*) (*used mainly to refer to people whose fame or good reputation has survived for a long time*) famous（主要指英名已流傳很長時間的人）傑出的，卓越的，著名的：*a member of an illustrious Italian family* 享有盛譽的意大利家族中的一員

infamous well-known for a very bad reason 聲名狼藉的；臭名遠揚的：*the infamous Acid Bath Murderer* 臭名昭彰的酸浴缸謀殺案兇手

legendary having been extremely well-known for a long time 享有盛名的；流芳百世的；傳為佳話的：*the legendary reggae star Bob Marley* 名揚四海的雷鬼樂之父巴布·馬利

notable important or interesting because of a certain characteristic（因某種特點而）著名的，顯著的，重要的：*Venice is notable for its canals.* 威尼斯因其運河而享有盛名。

noted well-known because of a certain characteristic（因某種特點而）著名的，聞名的：*He is noted for his dry sense of humour.* 他以其不形於色的幽默感而聞名。

notorious well-known for a bad reason 臭名昭著的；聲名狼藉的：*a notorious womanizer* 一個臭名昭著的玩弄女性者

renowned (*formal*) well-known and admired for a certain skill or characteristic（因某種技能或特點而）享有盛譽的，著稱的：*a renowned story-teller* 一個享有盛譽的講故事家

well-known known to a lot of people 眾所周知的；有名的：*a well-known television personality* 一個眾所周知的電視圈名流

⊃ see also 參見 **popular**

fashion *noun* a style of dress or behaviour that is popular at a particular time（特定時期的）流行款式，時尚，時興：*the fashion for shoulder pads in the 1980s* 20 世紀 80 年代加墊肩的時尚

craze something that is extremely popular with a great many people, but whose popularity only lasts for a short time and which may not be a very sensible idea（一時的）狂熱；風靡一時的東西：*Why is there this sudden craze for riding tricycles?* 為甚麼突然時興騎三輪車呢？

fad a particular activity, product, etc., that is very popular, but usually only for a short time, and often because people think that it is good for them（一時的）熱門活動（或產品等）；一時的風尚：*the latest fad in diets* 最新的飲食時尚

style a manner of dress, furnishings, etc., that is considered elegant or is popular at a particular time（特定時期服裝、傢具等的）時尚，風格，款式：*She is always dressed in the latest style.* 她穿的總是最新款的。

trend a style of dress or an activity that is in the process of becoming popular or widespread 趨勢；潮流：*The trend is for more and more people to take two holidays a year.* 越來越多的人傾向於每年度兩次假。

vogue a style of dress, music, etc., that is popular at a particular time（特定時期服裝、音樂等的）風行，時尚，時髦：*Punk rock was in vogue in the late 1970s.* 龐克搖滾樂風行於 20 世紀 70 年代後期。

fashionable *adjective* popular at a particular time（特定時期）流行的，時髦的，時興的：*a fashionable nightclub* 新潮的夜總會

all the rage (*informal*) very fashionable for a short time 風靡一時的；（一時）盛行的，走紅的：*Reality TV is all the rage these days.* 時下盛行真人秀電視節目。

chic fashionable, elegant and tasteful 時髦的；雅致的；優雅的：*a chic trouser suit* 時尚的女套裝

cool (*informal*) considered stylish and attractive, especially by young people（尤指年輕人認為）時髦的，帥氣的，酷的：*He was wearing cool shades.* 他戴着一副很酷的太陽鏡。

designer* made by a fashionable designer 由時裝設計師設計的；名牌的：*She wouldn't be seen in anything other than designer clothes.* 如果她穿的不全是時裝設計師設計的服裝，她就不願見人。

* Only used before a noun. 僅用於名詞前。

elegant attractive, stylish, and tasteful, whether or not it is fashionable by current standards 優雅的；漂亮雅致的：*She was wearing an elegant ivory silk evening dress.* 她穿着一身優雅的乳白色絲綢晚禮服。

hip (*informal*) conforming to the latest fashions for young people in clothing, music, etc. (指服裝、音樂等對年輕人來說) 時髦的，時尚的：*a hip new band* 一支時髦的新樂隊

in (*informal*) currently very popular and fashionable (指當前) 時髦的，流行的：*the in thing in sportswear* 流行的運動休閒裝

modern in a style that is currently popular and that looks up to date 新式的；時尚的；摩登的：*a very modern kitchen* 一間非常新式的廚房

sharp (*informal*) very smart and elegant 帥氣的；時髦的：*a businessman in a sharp suit* 身穿時髦衣服的商人

stylish having or showing a sense of style and elegance 打扮入時的；時髦的：*Alison is a very stylish woman – whatever she wears always looks just right.* 艾莉森是一個打扮入時的女人，穿甚麼樣的衣服看上去都很得體。

trendy (*informal*) conforming to the latest fashions 新潮的；入時的：*I've got a trendy new watch.* 我弄到一隻最新潮的新錶。

➔ see also 參見 **exclusive**

fast *adverb* at great speed 迅速地；快速地：*I ran as fast as I could.* 我以盡可能快的速度跑。

briskly at a fairly vigorous pace 輕快地；敏捷地：*Walking briskly is very good exercise.* 步履輕盈地散步是一種很好的鍛煉。

hastily fast because you have little time in which to do something or because you realize that something is urgent 倉促地；匆忙地：*I hastily packed my bags and ordered a taxi to take me to the airport.* 我急忙裝好包，叫了一輛計程車把我送到機場。

hurriedly hastily and sometimes carelessly 匆忙地；倉促地；草率地：*I hurriedly wrote a covering letter and posted it, forgetting to enclose the cheque.* 我匆忙寫完附信就寄了出去，卻忘了把支票裝進去。

like a shot (*informal*) very fast, or without delay 飛快地；立刻：*Alan will be out of there like a shot if you ask him to help with the washing-up.* 如果你讓艾倫幫你洗碗的話，他會立刻跑掉的。

promptly without delay 迅速地；及時地：*Thank you for replying so promptly to my letter.* 謝謝你這麼即時地給我回信。

pronto (*informal*) quickly, or immediately 很快地；急速地；立即：*Go to your room and do your homework – pronto!* 到你的房間裏去做家庭作業，快點！

quickly fast or in a very short time 迅速地；很快地：*The children finished their breakfast quickly so that they could go out to play.* 孩子們很快就吃完了早餐，以便能出去玩耍。

rapidly (*usually used when describing processes that continue or develop over a period of time*) at a fast speed or rate (通常用以描述某段時間內事情的進展) 迅速地，迅捷地，飛速地：*I am rapidly going off him.* 我會很快離開他的。

swiftly (*usually used when describing movement*) fast (通常用以描述運動) 很快地，迅速地，立刻：*moving swiftly on to the next topic* 立刻轉到下一個話題

➔ see also 參見 **quick**

fat *adjective* having too much flesh on your body 肥的；肥胖的：*If you eat too much, you will get fat.* 你要是吃得太多，就會長胖。

chubby (*informal*) slightly fat and rounded 胖乎乎的；豐滿的；圓胖的：*chubby cheeks* 豐滿的臉頰

flabby (*informal*) having a lot of soft, loose excess flesh (肌肉) 鬆弛的；肥胖的：*I'm getting flabby since I stopped going to the gym.* 自從我不再去健身房，肌肉就開始變得鬆弛了。

obese (*often used to describe people whose weight causes medical problems for them*) extremely fat (常用以描述因體重引起健康問題的人) 臃腫的，病態肥胖的，虛胖的：*He is so obese that he can't walk far without a rest.* 他太臃腫了，走不了多遠就要歇歇腳。

overweight weighing too much relative to your height 超重的；過重的：*The doctor said I was a little overweight and he's put me on a diet.* 醫生說我體重有點超標，讓我節食。

plump slightly fat and rounded 豐腴的；微胖的：*the baby's plump little arms* 嬰兒圓鼓鼓的小胳膊

podgy (*informal*) having a lot of excess flesh 胖墩墩的；胖乎乎的：*He's looking a bit podgy around the middle.* 他腰部有點發福。

rotund (*formal*) having a very fat, rounded body 肥圓的；圓胖的：*a rotund elderly gentleman* 一個圓胖的老先生

stout having a fat and rather solid body 肥壯的；肥胖的：*a stout matronly figure* 一個肥壯的中年婦女的身影

tubby (*informal*) having a fat body 肥胖的；胖墩墩的：*You wouldn't think Dave was once a tubby teenager.* 你準想不到戴夫 10 多歲的時候曾是個胖子。

favourite *adjective* that you like best 中意的；最喜愛的：*my favourite film* 我最喜歡的電影

beloved (*often used humorously and usually about other people*) that someone is very or excessively fond of (常帶幽默且通常用以談及他人) 心愛的，鍾愛的：*He won't go anywhere without his beloved pipe.* 他走到哪兒都要帶上心愛的煙斗。

best that you are fonder of than any other 最要好的；最喜歡的：*my best friend* 我最要好的朋友

chosen singled out for special attention 精選的；受到垂愛的：*The other members of staff think Kate is the manager's 'chosen one' because she seems to get privileges that they don't get.* 其他的員工都認為凱特是經理的"紅人"，因為她似乎享有別人無法享有的特權。

dearest that you are very fond of or want more than anything else 最喜愛的；最親愛的：*It has always been my dearest wish to see you happily married.* 看見你們幸福地結成夫婦一直是我最衷心的祝願。

pet that someone is particularly or excessively interested in 寵愛的；珍愛的：*You've got him starting on his pet subject again.* 你又讓他談他偏愛的話題了。

preferred that you always or usually use when you have a choice 首選的；
優先選取的：*E-mail is my preferred method of communication.* 電子郵件是我
用於交流的首選方式。

special that you are particularly fond of 特別喜歡的；親密的：*Dorothy is a
very special friend of mine.* 多蘿西是我非常要好的朋友。

➲ see also 參見 **special**

fear *noun* an unpleasant feeling that you are in danger or might be hurt（對
危險、傷害等的）擔心，害怕：*Isabelle always travels by train because she has a
fear of flying.* 伊莎貝拉總是乘火車旅行，因為她害怕坐飛機。

awe a feeling of wonder or great respect, mixed with fear, caused usually by
someone or something much bigger or more powerful than you（通常由強大
得多的人或事物引起的）驚嘆，敬畏：*Most of the children were in awe of the
head teacher.* 大多數孩子都敬畏他們的校長。

dread a strong feeling of anxiety about something that may happen（指對
可能發生事情的）擔憂，憂慮：*Elizabeth was filled with dread at the prospect
of her in-laws coming to stay.* 伊麗莎白聽說親家要來她這兒住，感到憂心忡忡。

fright a sudden feeling of intense fear（突然的）驚駭，驚恐，驚嚇：*I got
such a fright when a face suddenly appeared at the window.* 當有張臉突然出現
在窗口的時候，我感到非常驚恐。

horror a feeling of fear mixed with strong dislike 恐懼；驚恐；厭惡：*Mark
has a horror of clowns.* 馬克看到小丑就發慌。

panic an acute feeling of fear and anxiety, often one that spreads through a
number of people and makes them act uncontrollably（常指在一些人中傳播
並難以控制的）恐慌，驚慌，驚恐：*The explosion caused panic in the streets.*
爆炸引起街上一片恐慌。

phobia an unreasonable and uncontrollable fear of something（沒有根據且
難以控制的）恐懼，懼怕：*a phobia about spiders* 對蜘蛛的懼怕

scare (*informal*) a fright, or something that causes people to feel frightened
驚嚇；驚恐；引起恐懼之事物：*Sylvia had a cancer scare last year, but the
lump turned out to be benign.* 去年，蘇菲亞害怕自己患了癌症，但腫塊最後證
實是良性的。

terror extreme fear 恐怖；驚駭：*The villagers gazed at the monster in sheer
terror.* 村民們驚恐地盯着那個怪物。

➲ see also 參見 **afraid; anxiety**

feeling *noun* a sensation inside you that may be definable as, for example,
love or anger or may be vague（愛、怒等）感覺，感受，情感：*He couldn't hide
his feelings of frustration.* 他無法掩飾受挫的感受。

emotion a definite feeling, such as love or anger, that is usually quite strong
（愛、怒等強烈的）感情，情感，情緒：*Jealousy is a very destructive emotion.*
嫉妒是一種非常具有破壞性的情緒。

instinct a strong feeling that seems to arise spontaneously and is not easy
to explain in rational terms 本能；天性；直覺：*I just had an instinct that he
was not to be trusted.* 我憑直覺認為他不值得信賴。

intuition an idea or insight that seems to arise spontaneously and is not the result of conscious thought 直覺 : *I had an intuition that all was not well in their relationship.* 我有一種直覺，他們的關係未必完全沒有問題。

passion strong emotion 激情；熱情 : *She always sings with passion.* 她總是帶着激情演唱。

sense a feeling of something or that something is the case 感覺；認識 : *Jenny felt a sense of loss when her best friend emigrated.* 當最好的朋友移民後，珍妮感到失落。

sentiment a particular feeling towards someone else that someone expresses 情感；情緒 : *The sentiments expressed in the card touched my heart.* 咭片上表達的情感打動了我的心。

➲ see also 參見 **opinion**

few *adjective* not many 少數的；不多的 : *Very few people applied for the job.* 很少的人申請了這份工作。

infrequent which does not happen often 稀少的；罕見的；不常發生的 : *our infrequent phone calls* 我們很少接到的電話

insufficient not enough 不夠的；不足的；不充分的 : *an insufficient number of votes to win the election* 不夠當選的得票數

meagre small or insufficient in quantity 貧乏的；少量的；（數量）不足的 : *meagre rations* 不足的定量配給

precious few very few indeed 極少的 : *Precious few people offered to help.* 難得有人主動提出幫忙。

scarce in short supply 缺乏的；短缺的；供應不足的 : *Bananas were scarce during the Second World War.* 二戰期間，香蕉供應短缺。

sparse small in number and spread out 稀少的；稀疏的；零落的 : *sparse trees* 稀少的樹木

thin on the ground (*informal*) sparse, or existing in small numbers only 稀疏的；寥寥無幾的 : *Television sets were thin on the ground in the early 1950s.* 電視機在 20 世紀 50 年代很少見。

fight *noun* a struggle, either physical or verbal, between people, groups, or armed forces （個人、群體或武裝力量之間的）爭鬥，搏鬥，打鬥 : *There was a fight between supporters of the rival teams.* 參賽隊雙方的球迷們打起架來。

battle a fight between armed forces during a war, or an attempt to do or achieve something that involves overcoming opposition of some kind （戰爭中武裝力量之間的）戰鬥，搏鬥 : *They won the battle but lost the war.* 他們打贏了這一仗，但輸掉了這場戰爭。

bout an organized fight between two contestants in a sport such as boxing or wrestling （拳擊、摔跤等的）比賽，較量 : *the heavyweight title bout* 最重量級拳擊冠軍賽

brawl a disorganized physical struggle in which people hit and kick each other 打架；鬥毆；鬧事 : *a drunken brawl* 酒後鬧事

fisticuffs (*old-fashioned or humorous*) a physical struggle in which people punch each other 拳鬥；互毆；打架：*The argument ended in fisticuffs.* 爭吵最後變成了拳頭相向。

scrap (*informal*) a minor physical fight 扭打；打架：*two boys having a scrap in the playground* 在操場上扭打起來的兩個男孩

scuffle a physical fight of short duration (短時間的) 扭打，鬥毆：*A scuffle broke out outside the nightclub.* 夜總會外面發生了鬥毆。

skirmish a minor battle during a war 小衝突；小規模戰鬥：*There were several border skirmishes between the two countries over disputed territory.* 兩國之間因領土爭端發生了好幾次邊境衝突。

➲ see also 參見 **argument; disagree; oppose; quarrel**

fill *verb* to make something, such as a container or a room, full 裝滿，充滿 (容器或房間等)：*We filled our water bottles from the stream.* 我們把水瓶盛滿溪水。

cram to force a lot of things into a tight space, or to fill a space with more things than it can comfortably hold 填滿；塞滿；擠滿：*I crammed my bag full of books.* 我把包塞滿了書。

gorge to overfill yourself with food 貪婪地吃；狼吞虎嚥；塞飽：*The children gorged themselves on party food.* 孩子們狼吞虎嚥地吃聚會上的食物。

jam to force something into a space or container that is really too small for it 塞入，塞進，擠進 (狹小的空間或容器等)：*She tried to jam even more clothes into her already bulging suitcase.* 她設法將更多的衣服塞進那早已鼓鼓囊囊的行李箱。

load to put objects into a container or a vehicle 裝上，裝入 (貨櫃或車輛等)：*I loaded the boot with rubbish to be taken to the dump.* 我把要拿去傾倒的垃圾放在汽車後部的行李箱裏。

pack to put clothes and other belongings into a container, such as a suitcase or bag, before you travel somewhere (外出旅行前) 收拾 (行李)，裝 (箱或包)：*I packed some essentials into an overnight bag.* 我把一些必需品裝進了短途旅行袋中。

replenish (*formal*) to restock something, such as a food cupboard or a refrigerator 重新裝滿，補充，備足 (食櫥、冰箱等裏的東西)：*After our house guests left, we had to replenish our food stocks.* 家裏的客人離開後，我們得補充一些食品備用。

stock to put goods into a shop to be sold, or into something such as a cupboard for storage 備貨；貯存：*The stationery cupboard is fully stocked.* 文具櫃裏裝得滿滿的。

stuff to put large quantities of something into a container or your mouth 填滿，裝滿，塞滿 (容器或口腔等)：*Kyle stuffed a handful of peanuts into his mouth.* 凱爾將一把花生米塞進嘴中。

find *verb* to come upon someone or something that is lost, either by accident or after looking for them (偶然或通過尋找) 找到，發現 (某人或某物)：*I found my other sock in the laundry basket.* 我在洗衣籃裏找到了我的另一隻襪子。

come across to find someone or something by chance 偶遇，偶然發現（某人或某物）: *I was looking for my birth certificate and came across my old school photographs.* 我尋找出世紙時偶然發現自己上學時的一些照片。

detect to discover the presence of something, such as an illness or radiation, by using sensitive equipment or a test (通過高敏度設備或檢測) 發現，查明 (某物，如疾病或輻射等): *The cervical smear test is used to detect precancerous cells.* 子宮頸塗片檢查用於探測癌症前期細胞。

discover to find something, such as a place or scientific information, especially something that has not been previously known or that has been hidden 發現 (某物，如某個地方或科學資料等，尤指曾不為人所知或隱藏的東西): *Christopher Columbus is said to have discovered America in 1492.* 據説克里斯托弗·哥倫布是在 1492 年發現美洲的。

ferret out (*informal*) to discover something by searching hard for it, especially in places where you might not usually look (尤指在不常去找的地方) 搜索出，搜尋出，查獲 (某物): *A journalist ferreted out the names of the politician's former lovers.* 一個新聞記者刨出了這位政客以前情人們的名字。

locate (*formal*) to discover the whereabouts of someone or something 找到，查明 (某人或某物的行蹤): *Police are trying to locate the owner of a blue car that was seen near the scene of the crime.* 犯罪現場附近發現過一輛藍色汽車，警察正在設法查找車主的下落。

stumble across to discover something by accident, often while looking for something else (常指在尋找別的物品時) 偶然發現，不經意地發現: *I stumbled across your phone number while looking for the health centre's number.* 我在找健康中心的號碼時，無意中發現了你們的電話號碼。

track down to find someone or something by searching thoroughly 搜尋到，追捕到，跟蹤找到: *Melanie would not rest until she had tracked down her birth mother.* 梅拉妮要找到自己的生母才會罷手。

uncover to discover something, especially information that has been hidden or kept secret 揭示，揭開 (尤指被隱藏或保密的信息): *The police have uncovered vital evidence that may lead to the identification of the murderer.* 警察發現了可以用來確定殺人兇手的重大證據。

finish *verb* to bring something to an end, or reach the end of something 完成；結束: *Have you finished your homework yet?* 你做完功課了嗎？

close to bring an action or an event to a formal end 閉幕；正式結束 (行動或事件等): *We shall close the service with a hymn.* 我們將唱一首聖詩來結束今天的禮拜。

complete to bring something to an end after doing all that has to be done 圓滿結束；徹底完成；竣工: *I have almost completed my first novel.* 我的第一本小説差不多寫完了。

conclude to bring an event or an action to an end, or to be the final item in something 結束 (行動或事件等)；以⋯結束: *They concluded the concert with a song performed by the whole cast.* 他們以全部演員合唱一首歌曲結束了音樂會。

end to stop something from continuing, or to show that something is finished or complete 終止；結束；結尾：*You should end a formal letter with 'Yours faithfully'.* 正式信函應該用 "您忠實的" 收筆。

finalize to put something such as a plan or arrangement into its final and definite form 把（計劃或安排等）敲定，定案：*We have finalized the wedding arrangements.* 我們已經確定了婚禮安排。

round off (*informal*) to bring something to a satisfying end in a specified manner（以特定方式）完滿結束，圓滿完成：*We rounded off the party with a good old singsong.* 我們最後唱起了一首動聽的老歌圓滿結束了聚會。

terminate (*formal*) to bring something, such as an action or agreement, to an end 結束，終止（行動或協議等）：*The team manager's contract has been terminated.* 球隊主教練的合同已被終止。

wrap up (*informal*) to complete something, such as a meeting or an agreement 完滿結束，圓滿完成（會議或協議等）：*I'm hoping we can wrap up the meeting quickly, as I want to leave early today.* 我希望我們能很快散會，因為我今天想早點離開。

➲ see also 參見 **stop**

fix *verb* to work on something that is broken or not functioning properly in order to bring it back into a satisfactory condition 修理；修復：*The heating engineer fixed our central heating.* 暖氣工程師修理了我們的中央供暖系統。

correct to put right an error or a fault 改正，校正，糾正（錯誤或缺點等）：*Would you read over my letter and correct any spelling mistakes before I post it?* 在我寄出去之前，請您讀一遍我寫的信，並將拼寫錯誤改正過來，好嗎？

mend to make a usually small repair to something, especially something in the home, that is broken or torn 小修小補，修補（尤指家用品）：*Richard's mother mended the split in his trousers.* 理查德的母親把他撕了的褲子補好了。

overhaul to check something thoroughly and make large-scale repairs or changes to something so that it functions properly 大修；徹底檢修：*It's no good tinkering with the system, it needs to be completely overhauled.* 這套系統修補幾下是不起作用的，需要徹底檢修。

patch to mend a hole or a worn part in a garment by putting a small piece of material over it 修補；縫補；打補丁：*I have patched the hole in my sleeve.* 我補好了袖子上的破洞。

patch up (*informal*) to repair something hastily or temporarily 草草修理；臨時修補：*I've patched up the heating system so that it will work for the rest of the winter, but it actually needs a complete overhaul.* 我簡單地修了一下供暖系統，以便它在這個冬天剩餘的時間裏還能運轉，但它其實需要徹底大修。

rectify (*formal*) to put right a mistake or an injustice 矯正，糾正（錯誤或不公平行為等）：*Your name had been left off the list, but that error has now been rectified.* 你的名字沒有列在表上，但這個錯誤現在已經糾正過來了。

renovate to repair and redecorate an old building so that it meets modern standards 修復，翻新（舊建築）：*Now the block of flats has been renovated, the residents have to pay a higher rent.* 現在大樓已經翻新了，住戶得付更高的租金。

repair to work on something that is broken or not functioning properly in order to bring it back into a satisfactory condition 修理；整修；修復：*I have taken my car into the garage to have the suspension repaired.* 我把車弄到修車廠去了，讓他們把懸架修理一下。

restore to return something, usually something valuable such as a historic building or an old piece of furniture, to its former condition 修復（尤指貴重物，如歷史性建築、古老傢具等）；使復原：*The French polisher restored the old scratched table so that it looked as good as new.* 這位法國磨光工匠修復了有刮痕的舊桌子，使它看起來和新的一樣。

➲ see also 參見 **decide**

follow *verb* to go after a person or vehicle, in the same direction 跟隨；追隨；跟在（人、車輛等）後面：*Follow that car!* 跟着那輛車！

chase to run after someone in order to try to catch them 追趕；追逐：*The man chased the thief and caught him.* 那個人追趕小偷，把他抓住了。

hound to follow someone openly, persistently, and in a way that makes them feel harassed, usually in order to get information from them（通常指為了獲得信息公然、不斷地）追蹤，追逐，糾纏：*The press hounded the couple constantly.* 新聞界不斷糾纏這對夫妻。

pursue (*formal*) to go after someone in order to try to catch them or track them down 追趕；追蹤；追擊：*After pursuing him for several years, the police finally tracked down the terrorist.* 那個恐怖分子被警察追蹤了好幾年，終於被逮捕了。

shadow to follow someone in secret 尾隨；悄悄跟蹤；盯梢：*The detective shadowed the murder suspect in the hope of gathering evidence.* 偵探尾隨兇殺案疑犯，希望收集到證據。

stalk to harass someone by following them persistently 跟蹤；糾纏：*A man was arrested for stalking his ex-girlfriend.* 有位男子因糾纏前女友被拘捕。

tail (*informal*) to follow someone who is under suspicion in order to watch what they do 尾隨，跟蹤（以監視嫌疑人等）：*She had a private investigator tail her erring husband.* 她讓私人偵探跟蹤監視她那位行為不軌的丈夫。

track to try to find a person or an animal by following their tracks 追蹤；跟蹤：*The hunters tracked the lion by its prints.* 獵人根據腳印追蹤獅子。

➲ see also 參見 **observe; understand**

fool *noun* a person who lacks intelligence or common sense 愚人；傻瓜：*He was a fool to believe she would change her ways.* 他真蠢，居然相信她會改變她的那些習性。

buffoon (*old-fashioned*) a person whose behaviour is ridiculous 小丑；荒唐滑稽的人：*The man is a blustering buffoon.* 此人是個愛說大話的小丑。

clown (*informal*) a stupid or ineffectual person 蠢貨；無能之輩：*Those clowns at the dry-cleaners ruined my best suit!* 乾洗店的那些蠢貨把我最好的套裝給糟蹋了！

dunce someone who is unintelligent generally or who is not good at a particular subject 笨人；低能兒；遲鈍的學生：*I'm such a dunce when it comes to computers.* 說到電腦，我真是個低能兒。

idiot (*often used humorously*) a stupid or foolish person 白癡；傻瓜：*Don't be an idiot – of course you're not in the way!* 別犯傻了，你當然沒有妨礙別人！

ignoramus (*formal*) an ignorant person 不學無術者；無知的人：*She is such an ignoramus – she thought Paris was the capital of Spain.* 她真是不學無術，居然認為巴黎是西班牙的首都。

imbecile a very stupid or foolish person 低能兒；癡呆；愚蠢的人：*Only an imbecile would shoot himself in the foot.* 只有白癡才會朝自己的腳開槍。

laughing stock someone that people laugh at because of their foolish or strange behaviour（因其愚蠢或奇怪的行為而成為別人的）笑柄，笑料：*He has made himself a laughing stock with his obsessive behaviour.* 他因為執迷不悟成了人家的笑柄。

moron (*often used as a very rude insult*) a very stupid or worthless person（常用作粗魯的侮辱言辭）低能兒，癡呆：*Some moron has desecrated my father's grave.* 有個白癡褻瀆了我先父的墳墓。

twit (*informal*) a rather stupid or foolish person 傻瓜；笨蛋：*I've been a bit of a twit and locked my keys inside the car.* 我有點兒犯傻，把鑰匙鎖在車裏了。

forgive *verb* to set aside feelings or anger or resentment towards someone who has upset you or done something wrong; not hold something against someone 原諒；饒恕；寬恕：*She never forgave her mother for having her adopted.* 她永不原諒母親把她留給別人收養。

absolve to declare that someone is not to blame for some wrongdoing, or to declare that someone's sins have been forgiven 免除⋯的責任；宣告⋯無罪；寬恕：*The social-work department was absolved of all blame for the child's tragic death.* 社會工作部被宣告對這小孩的慘死不承擔任何責任。

condone to find nothing wrong with an action that most other people regard as being wrong 縱容；不咎（過錯）：*If you don't speak out against their actions, it may look as if you condone them.* 如果你不公開反對他們的行為，可能會顯得你在縱容他們。

excuse not to blame someone for doing wrong or condemn their wrongdoing, or to provide an explanation for someone's wrongdoing that makes it seem less bad 原諒，寬恕（過錯、惡行等）；為⋯辯解（或找藉口）：*I know she was upset about splitting up with her boyfriend, but that doesn't excuse her terrible behaviour.* 我知道她因為和男朋友分手心裏很煩，但那並不能為她糟糕的行為開脫。

exonerate (*formal*) to declare that someone is not guilty of any wrongdoing 免除⋯的責任；宣佈⋯無罪：*The pedestrian's death was declared an accident and the driver was completely exonerated.* 行人的死亡被判定為意外事故，司機完全免除責任。

let off to decide not to punish someone for something wrong that they have done 放過；不懲罰：*The police let the boy off with a caution since it was the* *first time he had been in trouble.* 因為這男孩是初犯，警察只是加以警告，便放過了他。

overlook to decide not to punish something wrong that someone has done 對⋯不予懲罰；對⋯不予追究：*I'm prepared to overlook your lateness this time, but don't let it happen again.* 這次我不打算追究你遲到的事，但不要讓這樣的事情再發生。

pardon to forgive someone for some wrongdoing, or, more specifically, to officially declare that someone who has been found guilty of a crime will not, or will no longer, be punished for it 原諒；饒恕；赦免：*Pardon my rudeness – I should have introduced you two.* 請原諒我的無禮，我本應該介紹你們倆的。

turn a blind eye to to pretend not to notice someone's wrongdoing, perhaps in order to avoid having to do something about it 對⋯佯裝不見，隻眼開隻眼閉 (以逃避作出行動等)：*Marion seems to be prepared to turn a blind eye to her husband's affairs as long as he comes home to her.* 瑪麗安似乎準備對她丈夫的風流事隻眼開隻眼閉，只要他還回家和她住在一起。

➲ see also 參見 **mercy**

fortunate *adjective* having good luck 幸運的；交好運的：*They are in the fortunate position of having no money worries.* 他們很幸運，不必為金錢操心。

fortuitous (*formal*) happening by chance, and usually having beneficial results 偶然發生的；(通常指) 巧合的，湊巧的：*Our meeting again after so many years was completely fortuitous.* 我們多年後重逢實屬巧合。

happy happening by good luck 幸運的：*a happy coincidence* 幸運的巧合

lucky having or bringing good fortune 幸運的；吉祥的；好運的：*the lucky winner of the prize draw* 這次抽獎的幸運得主

opportune giving someone an opportunity to do something 幸好的；湊巧的；恰好的：*He just happened to appear on the scene at an opportune moment.* 他恰逢其時地出現在現場。

privileged having certain advantages over other people, especially those of wealth or social standing 受特別優待的，享有特權的 (尤指有財富或地位的人)：*She was in the privileged position of being able to choose whether she wanted to work or not.* 她是有特權的人，能夠選擇要不要工作。

providential (*formal*) happening by chance and having very beneficial results 偶然發生的；巧合的；湊巧的：*the providential discovery of some ancient artifacts* 對一些遠古器物的偶然發現

➲ see also 參見 **happy**

frank *adjective* speaking openly and honestly 坦白的；直率的：*a frank admission of guilt* 坦白認罪

blunt honest and open, almost to the point of rudeness 心直口快的；直言不諱的；生硬的：*Many people find Colin's blunt manner off-putting.* 很多人覺得科林唐突的態度令人討厭。

candid speaking openly, especially about private or intimate matters (尤指對私密事) 坦言的，直率的，直言不諱的：*a candid autobiography* 一部從不諱言的自傳

direct going straight to the point 直率的；直截了當的；開門見山的：*The interviewer was very direct in his line of questioning.* 面試官提問的方式非常直截了當。

forthright saying what you think openly and forcefully, even if it may hurt another person's feelings（儘管可能傷害對方感情）耿直的，直爽的：*My best friend is very forthright but I know I can rely on her to tell me the truth.* 我最要好的朋友説話很直，但我相信她會對我説實話。

open not holding back information 公開的；坦率的：*The actress gave a very open and honest interview about her breakdown.* 女演員非常坦然地接受了關於她精神崩潰的採訪。

outspoken expressing your opinions freely and forcefully 直爽的；暢所欲言的：*She is very outspoken on the subject of benefits cheats.* 她坦誠直言關於福利欺詐的話題。

straightforward direct and without being evasive 坦率的；直率的；直爽的：*a straightforward reply* 直截了當的回答

up-front (*informal*) very open and direct in expressing your views or intentions（觀點或意願等）公開的，坦率的，直爽的：*He is very up-front about the fact that he is motivated by money.* 他對受金錢所驅使這一事實直言不諱。

➲ see also 參見 **sincere**

free¹ *adjective* costing nothing 免費的；不收費的：*a free gift with the magazine* 隨該雜誌贈送的一份免費禮品

complimentary which you do not have to pay for 不需要支付的；免費贈送的：*complimentary tickets for the game* 比賽贈券

on the house offered free by a business such as a pub or restaurant（由酒館或飯店等商家）免費提供的：*These drinks are on the house.* 這些酒水免費。

unpaid done without being paid in return 不收報酬的；義務的；無償的：*unpaid voluntary work* 無償的自願勞動

free² *adverb* without paying anything, or without charging anything 免費地；不收費地：*My bus pass allows me to travel free.* 我的公共汽車通票使我能免費旅行。

for nothing (*informal*) free, especially without being paid 免費；不花錢：*You can't expect the man to work for nothing.* 你別指望那個人白幹活。

gratis (*formal*) free 免費地；不收費地：*Refreshments are provided gratis to members of the club.* 俱樂部成員免費享用茶點。

without charge without expecting to be paid 免費的；不收費的：*The gardener offered his services without charge to his elderly neighbour.* 園丁向鄰居老人提供免費服務。

➲ see also 參見 **release**

friend *noun* someone that you like and have a close relationship with 朋友：*Becky and Sapna have been friends since university.* 貝姬和薩普納在大學就是朋友了。

acquaintance someone that you know, but not very well 相識的人；熟人：
He is not so much a friend of mine as a passing acquaintance. 他算不上是我的
朋友，只是過路的熟人罷了。

ally someone who is on your side when there is difference of opinion 盟友；
支持者：*Andrew was my only ally when all the others ganged up against me.* 其
他人都聯合起來反對我時，只有安德魯支持我。

buddy (*informal*) a friend, especially a senior school pupil who befriends
and looks after a younger pupil 朋友；同伴；（尤指關照低年級學生的）學友：
Rachel has been asked to be a buddy to one of the first-year girls. 雷切爾被要
求與一個一年級的女生結成學友。

chum (*old-fashioned*) a close friend 密友；好友：*I'm going to visit an old
school chum.* 我打算去看望一個老校友。

companion a person who is with you when you go somewhere or do
something 同伴；共事者：*Those two are constant companions.* 那兩個人是忠
實的伙伴。

comrade a friend or companion, especially one with whom you have
shared a difficult experience 朋友；伙伴；（尤指曾患難與共的）同志：*The
two old men were army comrades in the Second World War.* 兩位老人是二戰期
間的戰友。

mate a friend or companion, especially a male friend of a man 朋友；伙伴
（尤指男子的同性伙伴）：*Adam's at the pub with his mates.* 亞當和他的老友在
酒館裏。

pal (*informal*) a close friend 好朋友；密友：*He's acting as if he is my best
pal, just because he wants me to do him a favour.* 他裝出那樣子好像是我最好的
朋友似的，其實只是想要我幫他的忙。

frighten *verb* to make someone feel afraid 使驚嚇；使害怕：*The big dog
that lives next door frightens me.* 隔壁家那條大狗把我給嚇住了。

alarm to make someone feel worried or afraid, usually about something
that might happen in the future（通常指未來可能發生的事）使擔心，使害怕，
使驚恐：*I don't want to alarm you, but we are almost out of petrol and it's a
long way to the next filling station.* 我不想驚動你，但我們汽油快用完了，離下
一個加油站還有很遠的路。

intimidate to deliberately make someone feel afraid, usually so that they
will do what you want（通常指為了做別人想做的事故意）嚇唬，威脅：*They
try to intimidate the younger children by threatening to beat them up after
school.* 他們嚇唬那些小一點的孩子，揚言放學後要揍他們一頓。

panic to make a person or a group of people act uncontrollably because
they are afraid 使驚慌；使驚恐：*The sound of gunfire panicked the crowd into
fleeing in all directions.* 槍聲嚇得這群人四處逃竄。

petrify to make someone feel so afraid that they are temporarily unable to
move 使嚇呆；使嚇呆：*The sight of a snake in the house completely petrified
me.* 看見屋子裏有條蛇，我完全嚇呆了。

scare to make someone feel suddenly afraid or worried 驚嚇；使害怕；使恐
懼：*The sound of fireworks scares cats and dogs.* 煙花的響聲把貓和狗給嚇住了。

startle to cause someone to be surprised and mildly afraid 使驚嚇；使嚇一跳：*Oh, you startled me! I didn't realize you were in the room till you spoke.* 噢，你嚇了我一跳！直到你説話我才知道你在房間裏。

terrify to make someone very afraid 恐嚇；使懼怕：*Rollercoasters terrify me.* 過山車令我心驚肉跳。

➲ see also 參見 **afraid; fear**

full *adjective* having all or most of the space inside taken up 充滿的；裝滿的：*a full carton of milk* 一滿盒牛奶

chock-a-block (*informal*) completely filled with people or vehicles so that it is very difficult to move about 車水馬龍的；塞滿的；擠滿的：*The shops were chock-a-block during the sales.* 在特價促銷活動期間，這些商店擠得水洩不通。

crowded filled with many people so that it is quite difficult to move about in 擁擠的；擠滿人群的：*crowded streets* 擁擠的街道

jam-packed (*informal*) absolutely packed 擁擠不堪的：*The assembly hall was jam-packed for the school concert.* 禮堂裏擁擠不堪，都是來聽學校音樂會的。

loaded carrying a full load 滿載的；滿艙的：*The loaded tanker was low in the water.* 負重的油輪吃水很深。

occupied being used, or having people inside 被佔用的；有人住的：*All the rooms in the hotel are occupied.* 酒店所有房間都已住人了。

packed filled with as many people as it can hold 擠滿人的；擁擠的：*a packed theatre* 擠滿了人的劇場

➲ see also 參見 **busy; complete**

funny *adjective* that makes you laugh, either intentionally or unintentionally 有趣的；令人發笑的：*a funny story* 有趣的故事

amusing quite funny, usually making you smile rather than laugh loudly 風趣的，逗笑的 (通常指令人微笑而非高聲大笑)：*an amusing anecdote* 一件趣聞軼事

comical unusual in way that is amusing or funny 好笑的；滑稽的；有趣的：*She has a comical way of talking.* 她談吐風趣。

droll witty in a slightly unusual way 古怪有趣的；滑稽的；逗趣的：*He has a very droll sense of humour.* 他這人有一種古怪的幽默感。

facetious light-hearted and intended to be amusing 好開玩笑的；逗趣的；滑稽的：*a facetious comment* 滑稽的評述

hilarious extremely funny 引人發笑的；極其滑稽的：*That was the most hilarious film I have ever seen.* 這是我所看過的最搞笑的電影。

humorous written or performed in a style designed to make people laugh (寫作或表現風格等) 富於幽默感的，詼諧的，令人發笑的：*a humorous article* 一篇富有幽默感的文章

side-splitting that makes you laugh a lot 令人笑彎腰的；令人捧腹大笑的：*a side-splitting comedy routine* 一連串令人捧腹大笑的笑料

witty amusing through using words or describing things in a clever way (用詞或描述) 聰穎而詼諧的，風趣的：*a very witty speaker* 一個非常詼諧的演説者

⊃ see also 參見 **strange; unusual**

G

game *noun* an activity that people, especially children, take part in for fun, especially one that has rules or involves make-believe (有規則的) 活動；(尤指小孩玩的) 遊戲：*The children were playing a game of knights and dragons.* 孩子們在玩騎士和龍的遊戲。

amusement something such as a game that is organized or provided to give people, especially children, some fun (遊戲等) 娛樂，消遣：*The hotel doesn't really provide any amusements for the children.* 酒店確實沒有為孩子們提供任何娛樂活動。

diversion (*formal*) something that amuses you 消遣；娛樂：*His chief diversion was teasing his workmates.* 他的主要消遣就是與工友們打趣。

entertainment something provided to give people enjoyment 文娛活動；娛樂活動：*We set out to see what entertainments the town had to offer.* 我們去看看鎮上有哪些娛樂活動。

hobby an activity that you do for enjoyment in your spare time (業餘) 愛好；嗜好：*Alan collects stamps as a hobby.* 艾倫的業餘愛好是集郵。

pastime an activity that you do for enjoyment in your spare time (業餘) 消遣活動，休閒活動：*Bowling is my favourite pastime.* 打保齡球是我最喜愛的消遣活動。

play the activity of taking part in games for fun 玩耍；遊戲：*We watched the children at play.* 我們看着孩子們玩耍。

recreation something that you do for amusement or relaxation 文娛活動；消遣：*My father's chief recreation is fishing.* 我父親主要的消遣方式是釣魚。

sport a physical activity with rules in which individuals or teams compete against each other 運動；體育競技活動：*Taking part in sports keeps you fit.* 參加體育運動使你保持健康。

gather *verb* to come together, or to bring people or things together 聚集；集合；召集：*A small crowd gathered round the speaker.* 一小群人聚在演講者的周圍。

accumulate to acquire a large quantity of something gradually, or to build up into a large quantity gradually 聚積；積累；積少成多：*Over the years they accumulated an impressive art collection.* 這些年來，他們收集了一批令人讚嘆的藝術藏品。

amass to acquire a large quantity of something, especially money, gradually (大量) 積累，積聚 (尤指財富)：*He amassed a fortune in property development.* 他在房地產開發中積累了一筆財富。

assemble to come together or bring people or things together in an orderly or organized way (指有秩序或有組織地) 聚集，召集，集合：*When the fire*

alarm sounded, the staff evacuated the building and assembled in the car park.
當火警響起的時候，員工們撤離了大樓，到停車場集合。

collect to gather, especially to try to acquire a large number of things of the same type that you have a special interest in 收集，收藏（特別感興趣的同一類物品）: *Brian collects foreign coins.* 布賴恩收藏外國硬幣。

congregate (*said about people*) to come together in one place（指 人 ）群集，聚集，集合: *Crowds congregated in the town square to launch the demonstration.* 人群在市鎮廣場集會示威。

hoard to build up a store of something, such as food or money, just for yourself 儲藏，貯藏，囤積（食物或錢財等僅供自己使用）: *David is hoarding sweets in a shoebox under his bed.* 大衛在他牀底下的鞋盒裏藏有糖果。

round up (*informal*) to gather together a group of people 召集；使（人群）聚攏: *Can you round up some parents to help out on the school trip?* 你能召集幾位家長協助這次學校出遊嗎？

stockpile to build up a store of something, such as food or ammunition, for future use 儲備，貯存（食品或彈藥等以備將來之用）: *The country has been stockpiling chemical and biological weapons.* 該國一直在儲備生化武器。

general *adjective* relating to or applied to everything or everyone, not simply to individuals 全體的；普遍的；一般性的: *There has been a general improvement in exam results this year.* 今年的考試成績普遍提高了。

all-purpose having many uses 通用的；多用途的: *an all-purpose cloth* 一塊多用途抹布

broad covering a wide range of things or ideas 廣泛的；寬泛的: *He's a friend in the broad sense of the word.* 他是普通意義上的朋友。

common widely known or shared 廣為人知的；共享的: *It's common knowledge that their marriage is in trouble.* 大家都知道他們的婚姻出了問題。

comprehensive covering every aspect of something 全面的；無所不包的；詳盡的: *a comprehensive survey* 全面的調查

overall taking everything into account 全面的；綜合的；總體上的: *My overall impression of him is a good one.* 我對他的總體印象不錯。

sweeping applied to all without discrimination 全面的；總括的；全盤的: *a sweeping generalization* 全面的概括

genuine *adjective* exactly what it seems or is supposed to be, and not false or fake 貨真價實的；地道的: *a genuine Picasso painting* 畢加索的油畫真品

authentic genuine, especially in being able to be proved to be what it is supposed to be（尤指能被驗證為）真品的，真跡的: *I know it's signed 'Picasso', but is the signature authentic?* 我知道它的署名是"畢加索"，但這個署名是真跡嗎？

bona fide that can be accepted as a genuine example of the thing specified 真正的；名符其實的: *a bona fide rock star* 一個真正的搖滾歌星

legitimate justifiable, or for which there is a good reason 合理的；合法的: *a legitimate complaint* 合情合理的抱怨

original as it was when it was made, not changed and not a copy 原件的；原作的；原版的：*still in its original condition* 仍處於最初的狀態

real actual or genuine, as opposed to apparent or false 真的，真實的（與貌似的或虛假的相對）：*I still don't think we know the real reason why he left.* 我還是覺得我們不知道他離開的真正原因。

true being an excellent example of the thing specified 真正的；標準的：*He is a true gentleman.* 他是真正的紳士。

➲ see also 參見 **sincere; true**

get *verb* to come into possession of something, either by buying it, finding it, or being given it 得到；買到；找到：*I got a new dress for the party.* 我買了一套新的晚宴禮服。

acquire to get something that you did not have before 獲得，學到，得到（以前沒有的東西）：*I seem to have acquired a red pen – did you leave it on my desk?* 我好像拾到一支紅色鋼筆，是你留在我課桌上的嗎？

gain to get something that you did not have before or to get more of something that you already have 得到；賺到；獲得：*Matthew gained a lot of respect when he admitted he had a drink problem and sought help.* 馬修承認了他有貪杯的毛病還為此求助，這樣就得到了高度的尊重。

obtain (*formal*) to get something, usually by making an effort（常指通過努力）得到，獲得：*You can obtain a copy of this leaflet in your local library.* 你可在當地的圖書館獲取一份這種小冊子。

procure (*formal*) to get something, usually with difficulty and by making a special effort（尤指經歷艱辛和努力而）得到，獲得，取得：*My father has somehow procured tickets for the Cup Final.* 我父親想方設法搞到了幾張足總盃決賽的門票。

receive to be given something 接到；接收；收到：*I have received a cheque in the post.* 我收到了一張郵寄來的支票。

secure (*formal*) to manage to get something, such as a job or a business deal, through effort（通過努力）獲得，取得，得到（工作或生意等）：*Olivia has secured a place at Birmingham University.* 奧利維婭已經取得伯明翰大學的學籍。

➲ see also 參見 **achieve; buy; understand**

ghost *noun* the spirit of a dead person that some people believe they can see（死人的）鬼魂，幽靈：*The Blue Lady is a ghost that is believed to haunt the castle.* 有人相信藍衣夫人是經常出沒於城堡的幽靈。

apparition something that appears in a ghostly or spiritual shape 幻影；鬼魂；幽靈：*The girl claimed to have seen an apparition of the Virgin Mary.* 女孩聲稱看見過聖母瑪麗亞顯靈。

ghoul an evil spirit believed to steal dead bodies from graves and eat their flesh 盜墓食屍鬼：*a scary film about flesh-eating ghouls* 一部關於盜墓食屍鬼的恐怖影片

phantom a ghost or a ghostly vision 幽靈；鬼魂；幻影：*I woke up in the middle of the night and thought I saw a phantom in the doorway.* 我半夜醒來，感覺看見門口有個幽靈。

poltergeist a supernatural being that appears to cause disruption, by moving objects or making noises（搬動物體或發出聲響的）促狹鬼：*My friends moved home because they believed there was a poltergeist in their old house.* 我的朋友們都搬家了，因為他們認為原來住的老房子裏有促狹鬼。

spectre a ghost or a ghostly vision, or an idea or situation that haunts or worries you 鬼；幽靈；纏繞心頭的恐懼：*The spectre of death hangs over the starving people.* 死亡的陰影籠罩在這些饑民的頭上。

spirit a ghost or a supernatural being 鬼魂；幽靈；靈魂：*They called in a priest to exorcize their house from evil spirits.* 他們請來牧師驅除屋裏的惡鬼。

spook (*informal*) a ghost or a ghostly figure 鬼；幽靈：*The children dressed up as spooks for Halloween.* 孩子們在萬聖節前夜裝扮成鬼。

gift¹ *noun* something that you give another person, usually for a special occasion, or something that you receive and do not have to pay for（通常指特定場合送的）禮品，禮物：*We all clubbed together to buy a gift for our colleague who was leaving.* 我們一起湊錢買了一件禮物送給即將離開的同事。

bequest (*formal*) a sum of money or some property that someone leaves to another person when they die 遺產；遺贈：*He made a generous bequest to the niece who had looked after him.* 他把一大筆遺產留給了照顧過他的姪女。

bonus an additional payment made by an employer, for example to an employee who has done especially good work 紅利；獎金；津貼：*The workers were offered a bonus if they could finish their work ahead of schedule.* 工人們如果能提前完成工作，就能得到獎金。

contribution a sum of money that you give, along with other people, to pay for something 捐款；籌資：*All the staff made a contribution towards a retirement present for their boss.* 全體員工出資給老闆買了一件退休禮物。

donation a sum of money that you give to a charity（慈善）捐款：*The singer made a large donation to cancer research.* 這位歌手為癌症研究提供了一大筆捐款。

grant a sum of money that the government or another organization sometimes gives to help people to pay for something（政府或其他機構的）補貼，撥款：*The tenants are hoping to get a council grant to help with the cost of their new windows.* 承租人希望得到市政補貼，以幫助解決他們新建窗戶的資金。

gratuity (*formal*) a tip 小費；賞錢：*Gratuities are at the discretion of the customer.* 給不給小費由顧客自行決定。

legacy a sum of money or some property that is left to someone in somebody's will 遺贈；遺產：*My grandmother left me a legacy of £1000.* 祖母留給我 1000 英鎊的遺產。

present a gift given to another person, usually for a special occasion（通常指特定場合送的）禮物，禮品：*I gave my sister a book as a birthday present.* 我送一本書給妹妹作為生日禮物。

reward something that you are given in return for a good deed or an achievement 報酬；獎賞；回報：*The boy received a £20 reward for his honesty* *when he handed in the purse he had found.* 這男孩把拾到的錢包上交後，因為他的誠實而獲得了 20 英鎊的獎賞。

tip a small sum of money that you may give to someone such as a hairdresser or taxi driver, to show that you appreciate what they have done for you （為酬謝某人，如理髮師或出租汽車司機等，而付給的）小費，賞錢：*We gave the taxi driver a good tip because he had helped us with our luggage.* 我們付給出租車司機一大筆小費，因為他幫我們搬了行李。

gift² *noun* a natural ability to do something very well, especially something artistic or entertaining （尤指藝術或文娛等方面的）天賦，天才，才能：*A gift for comedy makes you really popular at school.* 你的喜劇才能使你在學校非常受歡迎。

ability the fact of being able to do something, especially to do it well （尤指辦好事情的）能力，才能，才幹：*Ali has an ability to get on well with most people.* 阿里能夠和大多數人融洽相處。

aptitude an ability to do something easily that many people find difficult （輕易做好別人認為是困難之事的）能力；天賦，天資：*David has an aptitude for learning languages.* 大衛有學語言的天分。

flair an ability to do something well and with style, especially something artistic （尤指藝術方面做得既出色又有風格的）天分，天資，天賦：*She has a flair for flower arranging.* 她有插花的天分。

talent an ability to do something very well, especially something artistic, entertaining, or sporty （尤指藝術、文娛或運動等方面的）天才，才幹，才能：*Val has a talent for imitating people.* 瓦爾有模仿他人的本事。

➲ see also 參見 **reward¹**

give *verb* to hand or present something to someone 給；給予；送給：*Dan gave his girlfriend a diamond ring.* 丹送給女朋友一枚鑽石戒指。

contribute to give something, especially a sum of money, to a common fund （尤指為共同的基金）捐獻，捐助，籌集（款項）：*Would you like to contribute to Jeremy's wedding present?* 你願意湊錢為傑里米買結婚禮物嗎？

donate to give something, such as money or blood, to help other people in need （指向需要的人）捐助，捐贈，捐獻（資金或血液等）：*Hospitals depend on members of the public donating blood for transfusion to patients.* 醫院依靠公眾捐血來維持病人的輸血。

furnish (*formal*) to supply someone with what they need for a particular purpose （指為特定目的）供應，提供：*I feel unable to comment on this matter until I have been furnished with all the facts.* 我認為，在沒有獲得全部事實之前，我無法對這個問題加以評論。

hand to put an object that you are holding into someone else's hand 交給；遞交：*Would you hand me the remote control, please?* 請你把遙控器遞給我，好嗎？

pass to hand an object to someone across a space 傳給；傳遞：*Please pass the salt.* 請把鹽遞過來。

present to give someone a gift or an award, especially in a formal presentation (尤指正式) 贈予，頒發，授予：*The band was presented with an award for Best Album.* 該樂隊被授予最佳音樂專輯獎。

provide to make something, especially an essential such as food or shelter, available to someone 供給，供應，提供 (尤指食物或住宿等必需品)：*Michael's landlady provides all his meals.* 邁克爾的女房東為他提供所有伙食。

supply to give someone something that they need, such as materials or equipment 供給，提供，供應 (材料或設備等所需物品)：*This catering company supplies many pubs in the city with food.* 這家餐飲公司向市裏的許多酒館供應食品。

go *verb* to move away from the place where you are, or to move or progress to a particular place or in a particular direction 去；走；離開：*Go right at the traffic lights!* 在紅綠燈處向右走！

advance to move forward, or to move or progress towards a person or place 前進；行進：*The police marksmen slowly advanced on the besieged building.* 警察狙擊手慢慢靠近被包圍的建築物。

journey (*formal*) to travel a long distance (長途) 旅行；遠行：*Roald Amundsen journeyed from Norway to the South Pole.* 羅爾德‧阿蒙森從挪威一路遠行到南極。

make your way to move towards a particular place 去；前往：*Please make your way to the dining hall, where refreshments will be served.* 請到食堂去，那裏供應茶點。

move to change position and progress to a particular place or in a particular direction 移位；移動：*We moved from the back of the cinema to the middle to get a better view.* 我們從電影院的後排移到中間，以便看得更清楚。

pass to move in a particular direction, or from one place or position to another 行進；通過：*We caught a glimpse of the singer as he passed from the hotel into the waiting car.* 我們一眼瞥見這個歌手從酒店出來，上了一輛正在等候的小汽車。

proceed (*formal*) to move to a particular place or in a particular direction, especially forwards 前往；向前行進：*If the fire alarm sounds, proceed in an orderly manner to the nearest fire exit.* 如果火警響起，要有秩序地向最近的走火出口處跑。

progress (*formal*) to move onwards or forwards 進步；前進：*As we progressed along the coast road, we passed through several picturesque fishing villages.* 我們在海濱路上向前行駛的時候，穿過了幾個風景如畫的漁村。

travel to go on a journey, usually a fairly long one (通常指長途) 旅行，旅遊：*The group of students travelled across Europe by train.* 這群學生乘火車遊歷了歐洲。

walk to go somewhere on foot, usually at a fairly leisurely pace (通常指從容地) 步行走路，散步：*As it was a beautiful day, I left the car at home and walked to work.* 因為天氣不錯，我把車停在家裏，步行去上班。

⊃ see also 參見 **travel; work**[3]

good¹ *adjective* having or showing high moral standards 符合道德的；正派的；高尚的：*good deeds* 高尚的行為

moral committing acts that are generally considered morally right 有道德觀念的；品行端正的：*Ian is a very moral man, who always tries to do the right thing.* 伊恩人品不錯，做起事來總是力求得體。

noble having or showing honour and generosity of spirit 崇高的；高尚的：*Sharing the prize with his helpers was a noble gesture.* 與他的助手們分享這筆獎金是一種高尚的姿態。

virtuous having high moral values, especially in sexual matters（尤指在性方面）有道德觀念的，貞節的，有操守的：*a virtuous young woman* 年輕的貞婦

good² *adjective* having or likely to have positive results, for example for your health（對身體等）有益的，有好處的：*Eating lots of fruit is supposed to be good for you.* 多吃水果會對你有好處。

advantageous likely to help you do or get what you want 有利的；有好處的；有幫助的：*It would be very advantageous to you to have him on your side.* 讓他站在你這邊對你是非常有利的。

beneficial improving your position or your health（對地位或健康等）有利的，有益的：*the beneficial effects of exercise* 鍛煉的益處

favourable likely to help you or bring positive results 有利的；適宜的；有幫助的：*You'll never get a more favourable opportunity to put your plan into action.* 你將無法找到對實施計劃更為有利的時機。

propitious (*formal*) likely to bring positive results in the future 有利的；適宜的；吉利的；吉祥的：*The circumstances seemed propitious for the launch of a new commercial venture.* 這種環境似乎有利於開始一項新的商業投機。

rewarding giving you a sense of satisfaction 有益的；值得的：*a rewarding job* 一份有益的工作

➲ see also 參見 **appropriate;decent; excellent; kind¹; nice**

grand *adjective* large and splendidly decorated so as to seem suitable for very solemn or high-class occasions 盛大的；宏偉的；豪華的：*the grand staircase* 富麗堂皇的樓梯

imposing impressive through being tall or high up and making you feel rather small in comparison 壯觀的；雄偉的；宏偉的：*There was a very imposing archway at the entrance to the house.* 在房子的入口處有一道氣勢雄偉的拱門。

impressive having a strong effect on you and making you admire it 令人難忘的；令人讚嘆的；令人敬佩的：*The singer made an impressive debut.* 那位歌手的初次登場令人難忘。

magnificent impressive in scale or beauty 宏偉壯觀的；壯麗的: *a magnificent view* 壯麗的景色

majestic very impressive and dignified in appearance or manner 宏偉的；威嚴的；壯觀的：*That big black horse is a really majestic animal.* 那匹大黑馬真是威風凜凜。

palatial large and luxurious, like a palace（如宮殿般）富麗堂皇的，豪華的，寬敞的：*a palatial home* 豪華的住宅

regal noble and dignified, like a king or queen（如國王或女王般）威嚴的，莊嚴的：*The mayor has a very regal air about her.* 女市長身上着有非常莊重的氣質。

splendid impressively beautiful and usually quite colourful and showy 壯麗的；輝煌的；色彩絢麗的：*a splendid array of flowers* 一片絢麗的花朵

stately moving in a slow, graceful and dignified manner 緩慢莊嚴的；優雅從容的；氣宇不凡的：*The royal couple continued their stately progress up the aisle of the cathedral.* 這對皇室伉儷繼續沿着大教堂的過道優雅從容地向前走去。

➲ see also 參見 **beautiful**

grateful *adjective* knowing that someone has done for you and having friendly feelings towards them and wanting to thank them 感激的；感謝的：*We were very grateful to the doctors and nurses who took care of our father.* 我們非常感謝曾照料過我父親的醫生和護士。

appreciative showing that you like or approve of something that someone has done for you or given to you 欣賞的；讚賞的；表示感激的：*an appreciative audience* 有鑒賞力的觀眾

beholden feeling that you owe someone something because they have done something to you, and often resenting the fact（因受恩惠而）欠人情的：*I won't accept his help because I don't want to be beholden to him.* 我不願接受他的幫助，因為我不想欠他人情。

glad pleased and thankful 高興的；感激的：*I'm just glad to be out of that terrible situation.* 我真高興擺脫了那種可怕的境地。

indebted owing a debt of gratitude to someone 感恩的；感激的：*We are indebted to everyone who has supported us through this difficult period.* 我們要感激每一個幫助我們度過這段艱難時期的人。

obliged (*formal*) grateful to someone for something that they have done for you（對幫助表示）感激的：*I am much obliged to you for all your assistance and support.* 我非常感謝你們給予的所有協助與支持。

thankful pleased about something that someone has done for you or something good that has happened to you 感謝的；感激的；欣慰的：*Let's just be thankful that the snowstorm was less severe than predicted.* 我們要感到欣慰的是，暴風雪沒有像預報的嚴重。

greedy *adjective* wanting to have more of something, especially money or food, than you need（尤指對金錢或食物等）貪婪的，貪心的：*Don't be greedy with your sweets – share them with your sister.* 你吃糖果不要貪心，分一些給妹妹吃。

acquisitive excessively concerned with acquiring material possessions（對物質財產等）貪求的，渴求的：*Many young people today are too acquisitive – they see something they like and feel they have to have it.* 當今許多年輕人太貪婪，他們見到喜歡的東西就覺得必須擁有。

avaricious excessively concerned with getting money or possessions and keeping them for yourself（對金錢或財產等）過於貪婪的，貪得無厭的：*Tony is too avaricious to give to charity.* 托尼太貪財了，從不捐助慈善。

covetous wanting to have something that belongs to someone else else 豔羨的；垂涎的：*Will is very covetous of his friend's sports car.* 威爾非常豔羨他朋友的那輛跑車。

gluttonous inclined to eat too much and too fast 貪嘴的；貪吃的；暴食的：*It would be gluttonous to eat the whole packet of biscuits.* 想把這一整包餅乾都吃光，那也太貪嘴了。

grasping acquisitive in a nasty way that usually involves taking things away from other people 一味攫取的；貪心不足的：*Most people's image of a tax collector is of someone who is mean and grasping.* 在大多數人的心目中，收稅員的形象是吝嗇貪婪的。

insatiable having an appetite for something, especially food or drink, that is almost impossible to satisfy（尤指對食物或飲料等）貪得無厭的，不知足的：*You've eaten a whole chicken? You are insatiable!* 整隻雞都被你吃了？真是貪得無厭啊！

materialistic more concerned with having money or material possessions than with spiritual matters or human relationships 物質主義的；貪求物質享受的；實利主義的：*Judy is so materialistic – she only goes out with rich men.* 朱迪太貪求物質享受，她只和有錢的男人出去。

miserly reluctant to part with any money 吝嗇的；一毛不拔的：*Eric is so miserly, he never buys a round of drinks.* 埃里克小氣得很，他一巡飲料都沒有買過。

group *noun* a number of people or things gathered together or classed together 群；團體；組：*A group of children were throwing snowballs at each other.* 一群小孩正在打雪仗。

band a number of people acting together 群；夥；幫：*a band of robbers* 一班強盜

bunch a number of things clustered tightly together, or a group of people 束；串；群：*a bunch of grapes* 一串葡萄

class a number of people or things that are regarded as being in the same category because of shared physical, social, or other characteristics 階層；階級；類屬：*a member of the upper classes* 上層社會的一員

clique a small group of friends or associates who exclude other people 派系；私黨；小圈子：*Megan is lonely at her new school because there are already established cliques and she feels left out.* 梅甘在新的學校感到孤獨，因為那裏已經形成了小圈子，她覺得受到了冷落。

gang a group of people who associate together, sometimes for criminal purposes（有時指為犯罪目的結成的）群，夥，幫：*A gang of youths ran rampage through the town centre, causing thousands of pounds' worth of damage.* 一夥年輕人在市鎮中心橫衝直撞，造成數以千計的金錢損失。

pack a group wild animals that live together（野生動物的）群：*a pack of wolves* 一群狼

set a number of people, especially people of high social standing, who associate together（尤指上層社會中結交的）群，幫，夥：*the polo set* 馬球圈子

squad a group of people who work together, especially in the army or police force, or a group of players from whom a team is selected（軍隊的）班；（警察或體育運動的）隊：*the vice squad* 刑警隊

team a group of people who work together or who play together in a competitive sport（一起工作或參加體育競賽的）隊，組：*the international rugby team* 國際橄欖球隊

guard *noun* someone who is employed to protect people or a place or to prevent a prisoner from escaping 保安；守衛；看守：*A woman was stopped by a security guard for shoplifting.* 一個婦女因為店內行竊被保安攔住。

bodyguard someone who is employed to protect the life of an important person（重要人物的）保鏢，護衛：*The president was accompanied by four huge bodyguards.* 總統身邊有 4 個魁梧的保鏢陪同。

escort someone whose job is to accompany and protect an important person（重要人物的）護送者，護衛：*The prime minister arrived at the airport with a police escort.* 首相由警察護送抵達機場。

lifeguard someone who is employed to look after the safety of members of the public at a swimming pool or a beach（游泳池或海灘等的）救生員：*The lifeguard dived in and saved the child from drowning.* 救生員跳進水裏救起了遇溺的兒童。

lookout someone who keeps watch, especially while their accomplices are doing something wrong 監視員；觀察員；（尤指）望風的幫兇：*One man acted as lookout, while the others broke into the shop.* 一個人在望風，其他人則闖進了商店。

night watchman someone who is employed to guard a building, such as a shop or an office building, during the night（商店或辦公樓等的）守夜人：*The night watchman caught two men trying to break into the building.* 巡夜人員抓住了兩個正設法闖進大樓的人。

sentinel (*old-fashioned*) a guard or lookout 哨兵；看守：*A sentinel was posted at the door of the embassy.* 大使館的門口設了一名守衛。

sentry a soldier who is on duty guarding a particular area, especially the entrance to a building or place（尤指某建築物或場地等入口處的）哨兵，崗哨：*The sentry prevented an intruder from entering the palace.* 哨兵阻止闖入者進入宮殿。

warder someone who is employed to supervise the inmates in a prison（監獄）看守；獄吏：*The warders went round locking the cells up for the night.* 監獄看守四處走動，晚上把牢房都上了鎖。

　　➲ see also 參見 **defend**

guess *verb* to form an opinion about something, or state what you think is the answer to a question, without having enough information to know for sure 猜；猜想；認為：*Guess how much these boots cost.* 猜猜這雙靴子花了多少錢。

assume to suppose that something is the case, without proof 假定；假設；假想：*I just assumed that you two had met before.* 我只是假定你們倆以前見過面。

conjecture (*formal*) to guess 推測；猜想：*We can only conjecture as to the cause of the accident.* 我們僅能對事故的起因進行推測。

estimate to calculate a figure or quantity on the basis of a certain amount of information and often in advance of doing something, but without guaranteeing that the calculation is accurate（常指事先根據資料）估算，估計：*The garage estimated that the repair would cost £200.* 修車廠估算修理要花 200 英鎊。

reckon to estimate a figure or quantity roughly（粗略地）估計，估算：*I reckon it's about five kilometres to the nearest supermarket.* 我估計到最近的超市都要走 5 公里路。

speculate to say what you think will happen without knowing the full facts 推測；猜測：*The newspapers are speculating as to when the prime minister might resign.* 多家報紙都在推測首相可能在何時辭職。

surmise (*formal*) to think that something may be the case, based more on intuition than on facts（憑直覺）猜測，臆測，推測：*He is rather less keen on the idea, I surmise, than she is.* 我猜他不像她那麼喜歡這個主意。

guide *verb* to advise and help someone with something that is new to them or difficult for them 指導；引導：*My friend guided me through the installation of my new computer software.* 我的朋友指導我完成了電腦新軟件的安裝。

advise to tell someone what you think they should do about a problem or difficulty 勸告；建議；忠告：*I would advise you to get a good night's sleep before your exam tomorrow.* 我勸你在明天考試前好好睡一宿。

counsel (*formal*) to give someone advice, especially on a serious problem（尤指在重大問題上）勸告，建議：*A minister of the church sometimes has to counsel parishioners with marital problems.* 教會牧師有時必須為教區居民的婚姻問題出謀劃策。

govern to be the factor that controls someone's decisions or actions 統治，管理，控制（某人的決策或行動等）：*Policies have been established to govern the treatment of prisoners.* 已經制定了對待囚犯的管理政策。

influence to persuade someone to act or think in a particular way, either deliberately or because they admire you 影響；左右；支配：*Teenagers are often influenced by their friends' attitudes.* 青少年常常受到朋友們意見的影響。

lead to be the cause of someone's decisions or actions 致使；使得：*What led him to give away all his money?* 是甚麼促使他將所有的錢都捐出去了？

recommend to give someone positive advice on which course of action you think they should take 提議；建議：*The doctor recommended that I stop smoking.* 醫生建議我戒煙。

⊃ see also 參見 **accompany**

H

handle *verb* to touch, hold, or move an object with your hands（用手）觸，拿，搬動（物品）：*'Please do not handle the merchandise!'* "請勿觸摸商品！"

feel to touch an object or fabric with your hands (用手) 觸，摸 (物體或纖物等)：*Feel how soft this sweater is.* 摸摸這毛衣有多柔軟。

finger to touch something with your fingers, sometimes as a nervous reaction (用手指) 觸摸 (有時指緊張時的反應)：*He kept fingering his tie nervously during the interview.* 他在面試時緊張得不停地撥弄自己的領帶。

fondle to touch a person affectionately or sexually (充滿情愛地) 撫弄，撫摸，愛撫：*There was a couple kissing and fondling each other on the bus.* 巴士上有一對情侶在相吻和愛撫。

paw (*informal*) to touch someone roughly or in an unacceptably intimate way (笨拙地) 抓弄；(猥褻地) 摩挲；動手挑逗：*I can't stand the way he paws all the women in the office.* 我無法忍受他在辦公室對所有女性動手動腳。

pick up to lift something, such as food or an ornament, with your hands 提起，拿起 (食物或飾品等)：*You shouldn't pick up food if you are not going to eat it.* 你如果不打算吃，就不要動手拿食物。

touch to make contact with someone or something with your hands (用手) 觸摸，輕碰，接觸：*She touched his cheek lovingly.* 她深情地撫摸他的臉頰。

wield to hold something, such as a weapon or tool, in your hand or hands and move it about 揮舞，揮動 (武器或工具等)：*The mugger was wielding a knife.* 劫匪揮舞着刀。

happiness *noun* a feeling of pleasure and satisfaction because things are going well for you 幸福；快樂；高興：*He finally found happiness running his own antique shop.* 他終於感受到經營自己的古董店的快樂。

bliss a state of extreme happiness 極樂；喜悅；無比幸福：*The young couple are living in wedded bliss.* 這對年輕夫婦新婚燕爾，幸福無比。

cheerfulness a happy and lively quality, especially in a person (尤指生性) 歡樂，快活，快樂：*Meena's cheerfulness always lifts the atmosphere in the office.* 米娜快樂的性情總是讓辦公室裏氣氛活躍。

contentment a state in which you are happy with the way that something is and have no wish to change it 滿意；滿足；知足：*He was a man who never achieved true contentment.* 他是一個從來不會真正知足的人。

delight a feeling of great pleasure produced by something (因某事產生的) 欣喜，喜悅，快樂：*To the delight of her parents, she announced that she was coming home for Christmas.* 令父母欣喜的是，她説她將回家過聖誕節。

ecstasy a state of great happiness, especially a state of such intense happiness that you are no longer in control of your mind or actions 狂喜；入迷；陶醉：*Chloe was in ecstasy when she met her pop idol.* 見到自己的流行歌曲偶像時，克洛艾欣喜若狂。

elation a state of intense happiness and exhilaration, for example, because you have achieved something (因取得成就等而) 欣喜，狂喜：*Skydiving gave me a feeling of sheer elation.* 特技跳傘運動使我感到非常痛快。

euphoria a state of great happiness that is often produced artificially or based on an unrealistic assessment of a situation (常指人為引起或由於對形勢不切實際的判斷產生的) 極度興奮，極度愉快，情緒高漲：*Some drugs produce a temporary feeling of euphoria.* 有些麻醉藥引起暫時的快感。

glee delight, often at someone else's misfortune（常指看到別人倒霉時感到的）高興；幸災樂禍：*The girls laughed in glee as their classmate fell over on the ice.* 女孩們看到同學滑倒在冰上，都幸災樂禍地笑了起來。

joy a feeling of intense happiness 快樂；歡樂；喜悅：*The joy of the newborn baby's parents was clear for all to see.* 新生兒父母的喜悅心情是顯而易見的。

⊃ see also 參見 **happy**

happy *adjective* having a feeling of pleasure and satisfaction, often over a long period, or causing such a feeling（常指長時間）快樂的，幸福的：*a happy marriage* 幸福的婚姻

cheerful happy and lively, with a positive outlook 興高采烈的；快樂的：*a cheerful disposition* 快樂的性情

content happy and satisfied with your circumstances（對境況）愜意的，知足的：*Adam is much more content since he gave up his stressful job.* 亞當自從放棄了緊張的工作後，感到愜意多了。

elated (*usually only used to describe people*) intensely happy and exhilarated, especially because of an achievement or an exciting experience（通常用於描述因成就或激動的經歷而）欣喜的，歡欣鼓舞的：*Caroline was elated when she completed her first marathon.* 卡羅琳第一次跑完馬拉松時，感到歡欣鼓舞。

exuberant (*usually used to describe people*) happy, enthusiastic, and energetic（通常用於描述人）興高采烈的，精力充沛的，生氣勃勃的：*As he grew older, he found it more difficult to cope with children's exuberant behaviour.* 他年紀越大，越感到難以應付孩子的活潑行為了。

joyful feeling or causing intense happiness 令人欣喜的；可喜的；快樂的：*The wedding was a joyful occasion.* 婚禮是歡樂的場合。

merry (*old-fashioned*) feeling, showing, or causing cheerfulness or high spirits 愉快的；歡快的；歡樂的：*merry laughter* 愉快的笑聲

satisfied pleased about the quality or standard of something, or about your circumstances in general（對質量、標準或境況等）滿意的，滿足的：*The inspectors were not satisfied with the standard of cleanliness in the hotel.* 督導員對酒店裏的清潔狀況感到不滿意。

smiling (*usually used to describe people*) showing happiness or friendliness in your facial expression（通常用於描述人）微笑的（以表示高興或友好等）：*One look at her smiling face told me she had been successful in her job interview.* 一看見她的笑臉我就明白了她在求職面試中成功了。

⊃ see also 參見 **fortunate; happiness**

hard *adjective* with a rigid surface that does not yield when you press it, and that may be uncomfortable to sit or lie on 硬的；堅硬的：*a hard bench* 硬長凳

firm resisting pressure but not completely rigid 牢固的；結實的：*a firm mattress* 結實的牀墊

rigid not able to be bent or not able to move 僵直的；不彎曲的；堅硬的：*rigid plastic* 堅硬的塑料

solid hard and not hollow inside 堅硬的；結實的；固體的：*solid rock* 堅硬的岩石

stiff firm and unable to be bent easily 僵硬的；硬的；不易彎曲的：*stiff cardboard* 硬紙板

strong made in such a way that it is difficult to break, smash, etc. 強硬的；結實的；堅固的：*The bridge isn't strong enough to bear the weight of a really big lorry.* 那座橋不太堅固，承受不起一輛大卡車的重量。

tough difficult to tear or cut, or made to withstand rough treatment 不易撕破（或切開）的；堅硬的：*This meat is very tough.* 這肉很難切。

➲ see also 參見 **difficult; harsh**

harsh *adjective* causing, or intended to cause, people to suffer 嚴酷的；殘酷的：*living in harsh conditions* 生活在嚴酷的環境中

austere having no comfort or luxuries 簡樸的；簡陋的；無華飾的：*an austere cell* 簡陋的房間

hard involving a lot of work and unpleasant conditions and very few pleasures 艱苦的；困難的：*a hard life* 艱苦的生活

severe very bad, causing difficulties or hardship for people 嚴峻的；惡劣的；嚴酷的：*severe weather conditions* 惡劣的天氣條件

stark with no soft or gentle qualities and very bare 粗陋的；荒涼的：*a stark landscape* 蕭瑟的風景

tough unpleasant and difficult to cope with 艱難的；棘手的：*They've been having a tough time recently.* 他們最近的日子很難熬。

➲ see also 參見 **cruel**

hate *verb* to have a very strong dislike of someone or something 討厭；恨；不喜歡：*My sister really hates rats.* 我姐姐非常討厭老鼠。

abhor (*formal*) to hate something or someone intensely 痛恨；憎惡；厭惡：*I abhor prejudice in any shape or form.* 我厭惡任何形式的偏見。

despise to regard someone or something with contempt 輕視；鄙視；蔑視：*The officer despised weakness in his men.* 軍官鄙視手下士兵的懦弱。

detest to hate someone or something intensely 極度厭惡；憎惡；討厭：*I really detest liver.* 我極討厭吃動物肝臟。

dislike to find someone or something unpleasant or unappealing 不喜歡；厭煩：*They moved to the country because they disliked the noise in the city.* 因為不喜歡城市裏的噪音，他們搬到鄉下去了。

loathe to hate someone or something intensely 極度厭惡；憎惡：*My father loathes modern art.* 我父親極不喜歡現代藝術。

➲ see also 參見 **dislike**

healthy *adjective* in a good physical and mental state, with no illnesses 健康的；無疾病的：*a healthy baby boy* 健康的男嬰

better having returned to good health after an illness 康復的；痊癒的：*I had flu but I am much better now.* 我患了流感，但現在好多了。

fit in good physical condition, especially as a result of regular exercise（尤指因經常鍛煉而）健康的：*I go to aerobics to keep fit.* 我做有氧運動保持健康。

hale and hearty having good health and lots of energy 精力充沛的；健壯的：*My mother is still hale and hearty in her seventies.* 我母親 70 多歲了仍然精神煥發。

in the pink (*informal*) feeling particularly well 感覺健康的；容光煥發的：*Having lost a stone in weight, I feel in the pink.* 我減了 1 英石的體重後，感覺健康狀況很好。

raring to go (*informal*) feeling very healthy and energetic 精力充沛的；精神抖擻的：*After a good night's sleep, I am raring to go!* 我晚上好好地睡了一覺之後，感覺精神抖擻。

strong physically fit and powerful 健壯的；強壯的：*a strong constitution* 強壯的體格

vigorous strong and energetic 精力充沛的；健壯的：*a vigorous dancer* 精力旺盛的舞蹈演員

well in good health 處於健康狀態的；身體好的：*'How are you?' 'I'm very well, thank you.'* "你身體好嗎？" "我很好，謝謝。"

⊃ see also 參見 **active; vigour**

heavy *adjective* weighing a lot 重的；沉重的：*a heavy bag* 一個很沉的包

bulky large and heavy 大而笨重的：*a bulky parcel* 大而笨重的包裹

hefty (*informal*) large and heavy 沉重的；又大又重的：*a hefty woman* 一個大塊頭女人

overweight weighing too much relative to your height 超重的；過重的：*George is a bit overweight since he stopped playing football.* 佐治自從不再踢足球以來，體重有點超標。

substantial consisting of a strong material or solidly made 堅固的；堅實的；牢固的：*It would be better to cover the hole with something a bit more substantial than a piece of cardboard.* 最好是用比紙板更厚實的東西來封住這個洞口。

weighty (*informal*) heavy 重的；沉重的：*weighty boxes* 沉重的箱子

help *verb* to make it easier for someone to do something 幫助：*Can you help me with my homework?* 你能幫我做家庭作業嗎？

aid (*formal*) to help to achieve something 援助，幫助（以實現某目的）：*To aid recovery, have plenty of bed rest and drink lots of fluids.* 為促進康復，要多臥牀休息，多飲用流體。

assist to help someone, often in a subsidiary position（常處於輔助地位）協助，幫助：*The deputy manager assists the manager.* 副經理協助經理的工作。

do your bit (*informal*) to make a contribution towards a common aim（為共同目標）出一份力：*The women knitted socks to do their bit for the war effort.* 婦女們編織襪子，為戰爭盡她們的一份力量。

lend a hand to help someone to do something 伸出援助之手；幫忙：*The job would get done faster if you would lend a hand.* 如果你幫忙的話，這活兒可能會幹得更快一些。

muck in (*informal*) to help each other as a group 一起幹；合夥幹：*If we all muck in, we can have the room decorated by teatime.* 如果我們一起幹，在下午茶之前我們就能將房間裝飾好。

oblige to do someone a favour 效勞；幫忙：*Would you oblige me by looking after the kids for half an hour?* 能勞駕您幫我照顧孩子們半個小時嗎？

rally round to combine to help and support someone, especially someone who is in a difficult situation（尤指聯合起來）幫助，協助（困境中的人）：*We can rely on our friends to rally round, if Angela has to go into hospital.* 如果安傑拉必須住院，我們可以依靠朋友們齊心協力幫助她。

support to help and encourage someone 支持；幫助：*Stephanie's adoptive parents supported her in her search for her birth parents.* 斯蒂芬妮的養父母支持她尋找親生父母。

hesitate *verb* to pause in uncertainty before speaking or acting（說話或行動前因不確定而）猶豫，遲疑不決：*I hesitated before accepting Brandon's invitation.* 我猶豫了一下，然後接受了布蘭登的邀請。

dither to waste a lot of time hesitating and thinking about what you ought to do before you act or take a decision（行動或作決定前）躊躇不定，猶豫不決：*They dithered so long over the house purchase that someone else got in there before them.* 他們就這棟房子的購買問題遲遲不作決定，讓別人先下手為強了。

falter to hesitate in speech or action through lack or loss of confidence or because of feeling strong emotion（在演講或行動時因缺乏自信或因強烈的情感而）支吾，猶豫，躊躇：*The speaker's voice faltered when he referred to his recently deceased mother.* 提到他剛離世的母親時，那個演講者的聲音發顫了。

pause to stop momentarily in speaking or before acting（講話中或行動前）暫時停頓，猶豫：*The old lady paused uncertainly at the top of the stairs, but a young man came to help her.* 老婦人在樓梯頂部遲疑地停了下來，這時一個年輕人走上來幫助她。

shilly-shally (*informal*) to keep changing your mind about what you ought to do 優柔寡斷；猶豫不決：*Stop shilly-shallying and make up your mind!* 不要再優柔寡斷了，下定決心吧！

stumble to make mistakes when speaking, often through nervousness or emotion（常指講話時因緊張或激動而）出錯，結結巴巴：*The bridegroom was so nervous about making a speech that he stumbled over his words.* 新郎感到十分緊張，講話時結結巴巴的。

think twice to pause to reconsider before taking action（在採取行動前）三思，重新考慮：*If I were you, I would think twice before spending so much money on a second-hand car.* 如果我是你，花如此多的錢買一輛二手車之前我一定會再三考慮的。

vacillate (*formal*) to keep changing your mind about which of various options or decisions you ought to take（在各種選擇或決定上）舉棋不定，猶豫不定：*He vacillated between a desire to travel and a duty to his family.* 對旅遊的渴望和對家庭的責任令他左右為難。

waver to be undecided or unsure about something（對某事）搖擺不定，舉棋不定：*After wavering, Jamie finally decided to accept the job offer.* 猶豫再三，傑米最終決定接受這份工作。

hide *verb* to put an object where it cannot be seen, to prevent people from seeing an emotion or a piece of information, or to put yourself in a place where other people cannot see you 隱藏（物品、情緒或消息等）；躲藏：*My mother used to hide the biscuits so that we wouldn't eat them all at once.* 過去我媽媽常常把餅乾藏起來以防我們一次吃光。

bury to put something out of sight under other things, not necessarily deliberately（不一定是故意地）隱藏，埋藏（某物）：*I found my phone buried under a pile of dirty socks.* 我發現電話埋在一堆髒襪子下面。

camouflage to disguise something, such as a military vehicle, so that it blends into the background and is hard to see 偽裝，掩飾（軍用車輛等）：*The tanks are camouflaged in greens and browns so that they don't show up against the vegetation.* 那些坦克用綠色和棕色偽裝起來，因而在有植物的地方不會被暴露。

cloak (*literary*) (*most often used in the passive*) to hide or cover something（多用於被動語態中）掩蓋，掩藏，掩飾：*The mountains were cloaked in mist.* 群山被籠罩在薄霧中。

conceal to put an object where it cannot be seen or prevent people from seeing an emotion or a piece of information 隱藏，隱蔽（某物）；隱瞞（情感或消息）：*He had concealed his criminal record from his employers.* 他向僱主隱瞞了他的犯罪記錄。

cover to hide something from view by putting something in front of or on top of it 遮蓋；覆蓋：*The footballer covered his face with a newspaper when he saw the waiting photographers.* 那個球員看到攝影師便用報紙把臉遮了起來。

screen to act as a barrier that prevents something from being seen（作為障礙物）阻隔，遮蔽：*A high hedge screens the garden from the road.* 高大的樹籬將花園與道路隔離開來。

secrete (*formal*) to put something out of sight so that other people will not find it（為了不被發現而）隱藏，藏匿（某物）：*He has drugs secreted somewhere on his person.* 他把毒品藏匿在身體某處。

stash away (*informal*) to put something away in a secret store（秘密地）儲存，存放，貯藏：*She has lots of sweets stashed away under her bed.* 她把很多糖果藏在牀下。

high *adjective* (*used to describe objects or buildings, which may be large or broad, but not people*) extending a long way above the ground（用以形容物體或建築物而非人）高的，高大的：*a high wall* 一面高大的牆

elevated raised high above the ground 高出地面的；抬高的：*the elevated railway* 高架鐵路

lofty (*literary*) very high or very tall 高高的；高聳的：*the lofty pine trees* 這些高聳的松樹

soaring rising high up into the air 翱翔的；高飛的：*a soaring plane* 一架翱翔的飛機

steep rising at a very sharp angle 陡的；陡峭的：*a steep hill* 一座陡峭的小山

tall (*used to describe people and objects or buildings that are fairly narrow*) of greater than average height （用以形容人、物體或較狹窄的建築物）高的，高大的：*a tall dark stranger* 一個又高又黑的陌生人

towering rising a very long way above the ground and usually looking impressive （通常指給人深刻印象）高聳的，聳立的，屹立的：*towering mountains* 高聳的群山

⮡ see also 參見 **excited**

hinder *verb* to make it difficult for someone to do something or for something to be done 阻礙，妨礙（某人完成某事）：*The severe weather is hindering the rescue operation.* 惡劣的天氣妨礙着援救工作的開展。

block to prevent someone from reaching a place or from taking a certain action by putting an obstacle in the way （設路障來）阻塞，阻礙，堵塞：*There are barriers blocking the entrance to the stadium.* 障礙物阻塞了體育場的入口。

foil to prevent someone from carrying out a plan, usually a plan to cause harm or destruction 挫敗，阻止，阻撓（通常指引起傷害或破壞的計劃）：*The police foiled the terrorists' plot to plant a bomb.* 警察挫敗了恐怖分子安置炸彈的陰謀。

hamper to make it difficult for someone to move or to take action 阻礙，牽制（進程或行動）：*The completion of my task was hampered by lack of co-operation by my colleagues.* 缺少同事們的合作使我完成任務受阻。

impede (*formal*) to slow down the progress or movement of someone 阻礙，妨礙，阻擋（某人的進步或行程）：*Our progress up the mountain was impeded by thick mist.* 濃霧阻礙了我們登山的進程。

obstruct to block something or make it difficult to pass along or through something, or to hinder someone 阻塞，阻隔，阻斷（通道或人）：*Your car is obstructing the entrance to my garage.* 你的車阻塞了我車房的入口。

prevent to stop something from happening or stop someone from doing something 阻止，妨礙，防止（某事發生或某人做某事）：*Putting the brick there is designed to prevent the car from moving back.* 故意把磚放在那裏是為了防止車往後退。

stymie (*informal*) to make it impossible, or very difficult, for someone to do something 阻止，阻礙（某人完成某事）：*Jackson was stymied in his attempt to break the world record by a pulled hamstring.* 傑克遜的腿筋拉傷使得他打破世界紀錄的企圖化為泡影。

thwart to prevent someone from carrying out a plan 阻撓，妨礙，挫敗（計劃的實施）：*Leanne's plan to live abroad was thwarted by her mother's illness.* 利安娜的媽媽生病了，打破了她到國外居住的計劃。

⮡ see also 參見 **prevent**

hit *verb* to come into contact with an object, usually with a lot of force （通常指用力地）打擊，擊中，撞碰：*The ball hit the window and smashed it.* 球擊中窗戶並砸碎了玻璃。

bump into to accidentally hit someone or something, usually when they are not moving and you are moving fairly slowly（通常指偶然）碰到，撞到（靜止的物體或緩慢移動的人）: *I have a big bruise on my knee from bumping into the coffee table.* 我不小心撞在咖啡桌上，膝蓋出現了大片瘀傷。

collide (*two moving objects, especially vehicles*) to hit one another accidentally（指兩個移動的物體，尤指汽車，意外地）互撞，碰撞: *A bus has collided with a car.* 一輛巴士和一輛汽車相撞了。

crash into to accidentally hit something, usually something that is not moving, when usually in a vehicle that is moving fast or is out of control（通常指快速行駛或失控的車輛）碰撞，撞擊，撞上（某物體，通常為靜止的物體）: *The car skidded off the road and crashed into a wall.* 一輛汽車失控滑出公路，撞到一堵牆。

graze to hit the edge or side of something lightly while moving past it, causing little damage 擦傷；擦破；擦去…的邊緣: *The bullet grazed my cheek.* 子彈擦傷了我的臉頰。

knock to hit something, usually with part of your body or part of an object and with a quick or accidental blow, especially to hit a surface in order to produce a loud noise（通常指用身體或物體的某部位）敲，敲擊: *Someone's knocking on the door.* 有人在敲門。

ram to hit another vehicle deliberately（故意地）撞擊，猛撞（另一車輛）: *One car rammed the other from behind, forcing it off the road.* 一輛汽車故意從後面撞擊另一輛車，迫使它偏離了公路。

smash into to crash into something 碰撞；撞擊；撞上: *The plane went out of control and smashed into a mountain.* 飛機失控撞到了山上。

strike to hit something 擊打；打擊: *Pete swung the bat and accidentally struck Mike on the head.* 皮特揮動球棒，不小心打到邁克的頭上。

⊃ see also 參見 **beat**[1]

hole *noun* an opening in something, or an empty space in something with an opening 洞；孔；開口: *There's a hole in the bucket.* 桶上有一個小孔。

burrow a hollow space dug in the ground, where a small animal lives（小動物在地下挖掘的、供居住的）洞穴，地洞: *The rabbit popped out of its burrow.* 兔子突然從洞穴裏跳了出來。

cavity a hollow space, for example in the body or in a decayed tooth（身體或齲齒等的）腔，洞，孔: *The dentist says I have a cavity that needs a filling.* 牙醫説我的牙洞有個洞需要補一補。

crater a large hollow made in the ground when something explodes or hits it with enormous force（某物爆炸或用力撞擊留下的）大坑，彈坑: *a bomb crater* 彈坑

crevice a narrow crack（狹小的）裂縫，裂隙: *a crevice in the rock* 岩石上的裂縫

gap an opening in something or a space between two things 豁口；缺口；空隙: *a gap in the hedge* 樹籬間的空隙

pit a very deep hole in the ground, especially one dug for mining（尤指採礦後留下的）深坑，礦坑，坑道: *a coal pit* 煤坑

split a long gap in a garment that has been ripped or in material that has cracked（撕裂的衣服或破裂的材料上的）長裂縫，裂口，裂痕：*a split in the wood* 木頭上的裂縫

tear a gap in a garment or in fabric that has been ripped（衣服或織物上的）撕裂處，破處，破縫：*There's a tear in your shirt.* 你的襯衣上有個破縫。

holiday* *noun* a period of time away from work or study, for rest, recreation, or travel 度假；假期；假日：*We went to Austria on a skiing holiday.* 我們去奧地利滑雪度假。

* More commonly used in British English than in US English. 該詞更常用於英國英語而非美國英語。

break a short time away from work or study, for rest, recreation, or travel（工作或學生上課間的）小憩，間歇；短暫的假期：*I am looking forward to having a break from work next week.* 我盼望着下週有一個短暫的休假。

leave time that you are entitled to have away from work（批准的）假期，休假：*We have five weeks' annual leave.* 我們有 5 個星期的年假。

long weekend a weekend when you have an extra day or two days away from work because of a public holiday（3 或 4 天的）週末長假：*They are going to Prague for the long weekend at Easter.* 他們計劃復活節去布拉格度週末長假。

R and R (*informal*) rest and recreation 休閒娛樂；休養：*I'm off to Greece next week for some R and R.* 下週我將去希臘休養一下。

sabbatical a fairly long period of time away from work, especially for a university lecturer, often for research or travel（尤指供大學教師進行學術研究和旅遊的）休假：*My tutor is going on a year's sabbatical to the USA.* 我的導師將去美國休假一年。

time off time away from work or study 休息（指不工作或學習）：*My doctor advised me to take some time off for the sake of my health.* 為了我的健康，醫生建議我休息一段時間。

trip a journey, or some time spent away from home, taken for pleasure（短途）旅行，出行：*The children are going on a school trip to France.* 孩子們將參加學校組織的法國之旅。

vacation* a holiday 度假；假期；休假：*Where did you go on vacation this summer?* 你今年夏天去哪兒度假了？

* In US English a vacation means 'a holiday'；in British English it means specifically a period when normal work stops at a university and the students go on holiday. 在美國英語中，vacation 和 holiday 意思相當；在英國英語中，vacation 特指大學的假期。

honour *noun* the quality of behaving according to what you believe to be right 道義；正直；正義：*The president was widely respected as a man of honour.* 總統因其高尚的品德受到廣泛的尊重。

decency the quality of behaving in a fair and moral way 正派；得體；彬彬有禮：*He has always treated me with decency.* 他總是彬彬有禮地待我。

goodness the quality of being kind and compassionate 善良；仁慈：*She helps at the drop-in centre out of the goodness of her heart.* 她在社會救助站幫忙是出於一顆善良仁慈的心。

honesty the quality of being truthful and trustworthy and doing what is right 誠實；真誠；正直：*The police commended the girl's honesty when she handed in the purse she had found.* 女孩交回拾到錢包時，警察表揚了她的誠實品質。

integrity the quality of being honest and honourable 正直；誠實：*The Minister has conducted himself with integrity throughout this ordeal.* 在這次嚴峻的考驗中，該部長表現出了正直誠實的品質。

morality the quality of behaving according to what is generally considered to be right 道德；道義；倫理：*Many people question the morality of wearing fur.* 許多人對穿戴皮草是否合乎道德提出質疑。

nobility (*formal*) the quality of behaving with honour and generosity of spirit 高貴；崇高；高尚：*There is a certain nobility about these villagers who, though they are living in abject poverty, will always share the little they have with strangers.* 這些村民擁有一種高尚的品質 —— 儘管他們一貧如洗，卻總是樂於與陌生人分享僅有的東西。

hope *noun* a wish for something to happen and a belief that it might well happen 期望；希望；盼望：*What are your hopes for the future?* 你對未來的期望是甚麼？

ambition something that you hope to achieve in the future 抱負；雄心；野心：*Calum's ambition is to be an astronaut.* 卡路姆的抱負是當一名太空人。

aspiration a desire for high achievements （對取得很高成就的）渴望；抱負；志向：*Many young people have aspirations to be famous.* 許多年輕人都渴望成名。

desire a wish to have something or for something to happen （希望擁有某物或希望某事發生的）想望，慾望，渴望：*I have a great desire to go to Egypt some day.* 我非常渴望有一天能去埃及。

dream something that you would very much like to achieve or to have in the future 夢想；嚮往的事；願望：*My dream is to have my own recording studio.* 我的夢想是擁有一間自己的錄音室。

expectation something that you believe will happen or that you will achieve in the future 預料；預期；期待：*The joy of parenthood has exceeded all their expectations.* 做父母的快樂超出了他們所有的預想。

goal something that you aim to achieve 目標；目的：*Helen has set herself a goal of losing five kilograms in weight before her holidays.* 海倫為自己設立了假期前減肥 5 公斤的目標。

intention something that you plan to do 打算；意圖：*I have no intention of resigning.* 我沒有辭職的打算。

plan a method that you have worked out to achieve what you want 計劃；打算；安排：*Tina has a plan to open her own business next year.* 天娜打算明年開辦她自己的公司。

➲ see also 參見 **expect**

hot *adjective* having a high temperature 熱的；溫度高的：*a hot bath* 熱水浴

boiling heated to the temperature at which water turns into steam, or (*informal*) very hot 沸騰的；滾燙的；非常熱的：*Pour boiling water into the teapot.* 把開水倒入茶壺。

burning hot to the touch 灼熱的；燙的：*The sick child's cheeks were burning.* 這個病童的臉頰滾燙。

scalding (*used to describe liquid*) extremely hot so that it will hurt you if you touch it（用以形容液體）滾燙的，灼熱的：*She poured a cup of scalding coffee all over me.* 她把一杯滾燙的咖啡潑了我一身。

scorching (*informal*) very hot and sunny 酷熱的；炎熱的；赤日炎炎的：*a scorching day* 大熱天

sultry hot and humid 悶熱的；濕熱的：*a sultry summer's night* 一個悶熱的夏夜

sweltering uncomfortably hot 熱得難受的；酷熱難耐的：*Come in out of the sweltering heat.* 進來吧，外面酷熱難耐。

tropical in or like the regions of the world close to the equator 熱帶的；似熱帶的：*a tropical climate* 熱帶氣候

➲ see also 參見 **warm**

hungry *adjective* wanting to eat 饑餓的；感到餓的：*Exercise always makes me feel hungry.* 訓練總使我感到餓。

empty having an empty feeling in your stomach because you have not eaten for a while 空腹的；饑餓的：*I feel empty – is it lunchtime yet?* 我感覺餓了，到午飯時間了嗎？

famished (*informal*) very hungry 餓極了的；十分饑餓的：*We were famished after swimming.* 游泳過後，我們餓極了。

malnourished not having had enough healthy food for a long time 營養不良的；營養失調的：*The children were so malnourished that their arms and legs were stick-thin.* 這些孩子營養不良，胳膊和腿瘦得跟木棍似的。

peckish (*informal*) slightly hungry 有點餓的：*If you feel a bit peckish, have an apple.* 如果你感到有點餓，就吃一個蘋果吧。

ravenous very hungry indeed 極其饑餓的：*After missing lunch, I was ravenous by dinnertime.* 由於錯過了午餐，到晚飯時間我餓極了。

starving (*informal*) very hungry 非常餓的；快要餓死的：*'Are you hungry?' 'Yes, starving!'* "你餓了嗎？""我都快餓死了！"

underfed having eaten a less than healthy amount for some time 沒吃飽的：*a poor little underfed dog* 一隻可憐的饑腸轆轆的小狗

voracious very hungry or greedy 狼吞虎嚥的；貪吃的；貪婪的：*a voracious appetite* 胃口極大

hurry *verb* to move quickly 趕緊；匆忙；急趕：*Lisa hurried to answer the phone.* 麗莎急忙去接電話。

accelerate to make something, especially a vehicle, move faster 加快（汽車的）速度；加速：*I accelerated to overtake the car in front.* 我加快速度超過前面那輛車。

dash to run or move somewhere quickly 猛衝；急奔；急馳：*Caroline dashed off to answer the door.* 卡羅琳急匆匆地跑去開門。

fly to go away quickly 快速離開；疾行；飛奔：*I must fly – I'm late for an appointment.* 我得趕快走，約會要遲到了。

get a move on (*informal*) to start to move more quickly 趕快；快點：*Come on, get a move on or we'll miss the bus!* 快點，要不然我們就趕不上巴士了。

hasten to move or act quickly 急忙（行動）；加緊（行動）；加快（步伐）：*The nurse hastened to reassure us that there was no cause for concern.* 護士急忙安慰我們説不必擔心。

rush to move quickly or do something too quickly and, sometimes, without care 倉促行事；草率行事：*Lucy rushed through her homework and made lots of mistakes.* 露茜草草地做完了功課，犯了許多錯誤。

speed to move very quickly, especially to exceed the speed limit when driving 急行；加速；（尤指駕駛）超速：*Darren was caught speeding on his way home from work.* 達倫在下班回家的路上因超速被逮住了。

➲ see also 參見 **run; speed**

hurt *verb* to cause pain or physical damage to someone or part of the body, deliberately or accidentally, or to make someone feel sad or offended（有意或無意地使）受傷，疼痛，傷心，不悦：*Joe hurt his back lifting a heavy weight.* 祖搬重物時弄傷了背。

bruise to hit or knock a part of your body, causing a painful dark mark to appear（使身體部位）挫傷，碰傷，瘀傷：*I bumped into the coffee table and bruised my knee.* 我撞到咖啡桌上，碰傷了膝蓋。

harm to cause pain or physical damage to a person or an animal, usually deliberately（通常指故意地）傷害，損害，危害（人或動物）：*What kind of person would harm an innocent child?* 甚麼樣的人會傷害一個無辜的小孩呢？

impair to make something, such as a person's eyesight or hearing, less good or effective 損害，削弱（視力或聽力等）：*My aunt's eyesight is impaired since she had a stroke.* 我姑姑中風後視力就下降了。

injure to cause someone physical damage（指身體）受傷：*Three people have been seriously injured in a road traffic accident.* 在一次道路交通意外中，3 人受了重傷。

maim to cause someone permanent serious physical damage, such as the loss of a limb 使殘廢；使身體殘缺；使受重傷：*Many people were killed or maimed in the explosion.* 許多人在這次爆炸中喪命或致殘。

pain (*formal*) to cause someone to feel disapproval or irritation 使不快；使惱怒：*It pains me to see that you have still not heeded my warnings.* 你對我的警告依舊置若罔聞，這令我十分不快。

wound to cause someone an injury, especially by breaking the skin（使某人，尤指皮膚）受傷，負傷：*My grandfather was wounded in the war.* 我的祖父在戰爭中負了傷。

➲ see also 參見 **damage**

I

idea *noun* something produced in your mind that can be put into words, especially something that is a starting-point for a thinking process or a plan of action, or a belief or opinion（可用文字表示的）想法，念頭；（尤指）構想：*I have a few ideas for my essay, but I have not started writing it yet.* 我的文章已經有幾點構思了，只是還沒動筆寫。

brainchild (*informal*) an original idea or invention thought up by the person specified（某人的）創見，首創，創造：*The UK National Health Service was the brainchild of Aneurin Bevan.* 英國國民保健制度是安奈林·比萬首創的。

brainwave (*informal*) an inspiration 靈感；妙計：*A student had a brainwave which led to him becoming an Internet millionaire.* 一個學生突發的奇思妙想使他成了互聯網百萬富翁。

concept an idea of what something is（對事物的）概念，觀念：*the concept of democracy* 民主觀念

inspiration a brilliant or creative idea that suddenly occurs to you 靈感；妙想：*I was struggling to write my speech and then I had a sudden inspiration.* 我正在絞盡腦汁撰寫演講稿時突然有了靈感。

notion a usually rather vague idea or belief（通常指不太清晰的）觀念，概念，信念：*I have a notion that she may have mentioned this before.* 我印象中她以前可能提到過此事。

plan something you have thought out carefully as a course of action（經仔細思考制定出的）計劃，方案，打算：*Ruth's plan is to retire to the country.* 魯思打算退休回到鄉下。

suggestion an idea that you offer for consideration 建議；提議：*I would welcome suggestions for the Christmas night out.* 我倒是樂意接受到外面去過聖誕夜的建議。

thought the process of thinking, or an idea 想法，看法；思想：*If you have any thoughts on the subject, perhaps you would let me know.* 如果你對這個題目有甚麼看法，或許可以告知我一聲。

ignorant *adjective* having a lack of knowledge, either generally or about a particular subject（對常識或特定的主題）不了解的；無知的；愚昧的：*Being ignorant of the dangers of sunbathing can lead to skin cancer.* 忽視日光浴的危害有可能導致皮膚癌。

inexperienced having a lack of knowledge or experience, especially of a particular activity or subject（尤指對特定的活動或學科）缺乏經驗的，經驗不足的：*His application for promotion was rejected because he was too inexperienced.* 因為過於缺乏經驗，他的升職申請被拒絕了。

innocent having a lack of knowledge about how things are done in the world, especially about the more unpleasant aspects of life 天真無邪的；不諳世事的；純真的：*With an innocent childlikeness, Tracy tends to trust everyone she meets.* 切麗絲有着孩子般的天真無邪，往往會信任她遇見的每一個人。

unaware not knowing certain information or not realizing that something is happening （對某消息）不知道的；（對正在發生的事）沒有意識到的，未察覺的：*He was unaware of the effects of his smoking on his wife and children.* 他並沒有意識到他抽煙給妻子和孩子們帶來的影響。

unconscious not noticing something or not being aware of something （對某事）未注意的，未意識到的：*The children played amidst the earthquake ruins, happily unconscious of the danger they were in.* 這些孩子在地震後的廢墟上盡情地玩耍，沒有意識到他們正處於危險之中。

ill* *adjective* suffering from a disease or medical condition, feeling that something is physically wrong with you, or generally in poor health 生病的；身體不適的；健康狀況不良的：*My father is seriously ill in hospital.* 我父親正病重住院。

* Always used after a verb. 總是用於動詞後。

indisposed (*formal*) slightly ill 有小病的；身體不適的：*James is indisposed after last night's celebrations.* 昨夜的慶典之後，詹姆斯感覺身體不適。

out of sorts (*informal*) slightly ill 有小病的；不舒服的：*I'm feeling a bit out of sorts – I think I will have a lie-down.* 我感到有些不舒服，我想還是躺下來。

poorly* (*mainly used when speaking to or about children*) ill （主要用於孩子）生病的，不適的，不舒服的：*The baby is poorly – I think she is teething.* 寶寶看起來有些不舒服，我想她是在長牙。

*Always used after a verb. 總是用於動詞後。

queasy feeling as if you are going to vomit 感到噁心的；想吐的：*The sight of blood made me feel queasy.* 看到血使我感到噁心。

seedy feeling slightly ill, especially feeling as if you might vomit 身體不適的；（尤指）感覺噁心的，想吐的：*I felt a bit seedy after the long car journey.* 長途汽車旅行之後，我感覺有點噁心。

sick (*used after a verb*) vomiting, or feeling as if you are about to vomit; (*used before a noun or after a verb*) ill （用於動詞後）想嘔吐的，噁心的；（用於名詞之前或動詞之後）生病的：*Emma has been sick all over the bathroom.* 埃瑪一直在吐，把整個浴室都弄髒了。

under the weather (*informal*) slightly ill （身體）略有不適的，不得勁的：*Dad is a bit under the weather this morning – he may be catching a cold.* 今天早上爸爸有點不舒服，他可能是感冒了。

unhealthy likely to cause people to become ill 不健康的；有損健康的：*an unhealthy diet* 不健康的飲食

unwell* having an illness 染病的；不舒服的：*Pat has been quite unwell with pneumonia.* 帕特得了嚴重的肺炎。

* Always used after a verb. 總是用於動詞後。

illegal *adjective* which is forbidden by law 非法的；違法的：*illegal drugs* 違禁藥品

banned which is officially not allowed 明令禁止的；取締的：*banned substances* 違禁物品

black-market bought or sold illegally 黑市交易的；非法交易的：*black-market ivory* 黑市交易的象牙

contraband smuggled into or out of a country 走 私 的：*contraband cigarettes* 走私香煙

criminal which is a crime, or which commits crimes 有 罪 的；犯 罪 的：*criminal activities* 犯罪行為

crooked (*informal*) illegal or dishonest 不誠實的；欺詐的；不合法的：*crooked dealings* 欺詐性交易

dishonest not truthful or trustworthy, or not conforming to what most people think is morally right 不誠實的；不值得信任的；不正直的：*I don't know whether cheating at cards is illegal, but it's definitely dishonest.* 我不知道打牌作弊是否違法，但這肯定是不誠實的行為。

illicit which is forbidden by law or goes against moral conventions, and which is usually done secretly（通常指暗地裏所幹）非法的，違禁的，不道德的：*She is having an illicit relationship with a married man.* 她與一個已婚男人有不正當關係。

prohibited which is officially not allowed 明令禁止的：*Signs inside the hall said: 'Smoking prohibited'.* 大廳裏的標語寫着"禁止吸煙"。

unlawful which is forbidden by law or not recognized by law 不合法的；非法的；違法的：*unlawful arrest* 非法拘留

➲ see also 參見 **dishonest**

illness *noun* something that affects your physical or mental health and makes your body or mind unable to function normally（身體或精神上的）疾病，病：*a terminal illness* 不治之症

ailment a minor illness 小病；輕病；小恙：*She is always moaning about her ailments.* 她有一點小毛病總是抱怨。

complaint a minor health problem that is troubling someone（引起煩擾、不安的）小毛病，不適：*Backache is a very common complaint.* 背痛是一種常見的毛病。

condition the state of health or ill health of a person, or a problem affecting a particular part of the body 健康狀況；身體不適；（影響身體某部位的）疾病：*a serious heart condition* 嚴重的心臟病

disease a particular kind of serious illness that has recognizable symptoms（有明顯症狀的）病，疾病：*a tropical disease such as malaria* 一種像瘧疾那樣的熱帶疾病

disorder a problem affecting a particular part of the body or a bodily function（影響身體某部位或身體機能的）失調，紊亂：*an eating disorder* 飲食失調

infection a disease caused by a virus or bacteria（由病毒或細菌引起的）傳染病，感染：*a throat infection* 喉部感染

malady (*old-fashioned*) a kind of illness 疾病：*a mysterious malady* 一種神秘的疾病

sickness vomiting, nausea, or illness generally 疾病；噁心；嘔吐：*radiation sickness* 放射病

imitate *verb* to speak or act like someone else, often in order to amuse others, or to try to look or be the same as something else（常指為逗樂而）模仿（他人的言行）；仿效：*Andrew makes his classmates laugh by imitating the teachers.* 安德魯模仿老師逗同學們發笑。

ape to copy the actions of another person, because you want to be like them 模仿（某人的行為）；學（某人）的樣子：*Little Calum apes his older brother.* 小卡路姆學他哥哥的樣子。

copy to do or say the same as someone else, or to make something that is exactly the same as something else 模仿（他人的行為或語言）；複製；仿造：*Babies learn to speak by copying their parents.* 嬰兒通過模仿父母學會說話。

emulate (*formal*) to try to be like someone that you admire or to copy their success 竭力仿效，努力趕上（所敬慕之人或其成就）：*Kelly's ambition is to be a singer and she wants to emulate the success of her idol, Madonna.* 凱莉的夢想是當一名歌手，並希望像她的偶像麥當娜那樣成功。

impersonate to copy a person's speech, actions, or appearance, in order to amuse others or to convince others that you are that person 模仿（他人的言語、行為或外貌）；冒充；假扮：*He was arrested for impersonating a police officer.* 他因假扮警察被逮捕。

mimic to copy a person's speech or actions, often to ridicule them or to amuse others（常指為奚落或取樂而）模仿（他人的言行舉止）：*The school bullies mimicked the new girl's accent.* 這些學生惡霸模仿那位新來女生的口音來取樂。

parrot to repeat another person's words or views unquestioningly 學舌；（機械地）重複，模仿（他人的語言或觀點）：*Jonathan's wife just parrots everything he says.* 喬納森的妻子鸚鵡學舌般地重複他的每一句話。

send up (*informal*) to deliberately speak or act like someone else, usually exaggerating them in order to ridicule them（通常指故意誇張地）滑稽模仿，戲謔：*an impressionist who sends up the Prime Minister* 用滑稽模仿來挖苦首相的印象派畫家

take off (*informal*) to deliberately speak or act like someone else, often in order to amuse others（常指為逗趣而）模仿，學（某人）的樣子：*In her act she takes off several singers and actresses.* 她在表演中滑稽地模仿好幾名歌手和演員。

➲ see also 參見 **copy**

impatient *adjective* getting angry or restless if you have to wait for something or someone, or if someone behaves in a way that annoys or inconveniences you 不耐煩的；惱火的；急躁的：*Many drivers were getting impatient in the traffic jam.* 很多司機在交通擠塞時變得不耐煩了。

agitated very anxious or disturbed and unable to rest or be still 焦躁不安的；煩亂的；躁動的：*The patient became more and more agitated until eventually he had to be sedated.* 病人變得越來越焦躁不安，最後不得不服鎮靜劑。

anxious feeling tense and worried about possible harm that may happen to you or to someone or something else（對可能的傷害感到）焦慮的，憂慮的，

擔 心 的：*I started to feel anxious when my daughter didn't come home from school at the usual time.* 我女兒在正常放學回家的時候沒回來，我就開始擔憂了。

nervous being worried and having physical symptoms such as trembling because of something you are about to do 緊張不安的；焦慮的；惶恐的：*The best man at the wedding was very nervous about having to make a speech.* 伴郎因要在婚禮上發言感到非常緊張不安。

restless feeling bored, impatient, and uncomfortable, and wanting to change position or change your circumstances 坐立不安的；不耐煩的：*As the lecture dragged on and on, the audience started to get restless.* 隨着講座越拖越久，觀眾開始不耐煩。

twitchy (*informal*) feeling anxious and nervous about something, and unable to stay still 緊張的；焦急的；焦慮不安的：*Grace was beginning to get a bit twitchy waiting for her exam results to arrive in the post.* 葛麗絲開始有點緊張不安地等待着考試結果的寄達。

uptight (*informal*) very tense and unable to relax 非常緊張的；無法放鬆的：*I always get a bit uptight about going to the dentist.* 我對看牙醫總是有點忐忑不安。

important *adjective* considered to have a greater effect or more influence, or to need greater or more urgent attention than most things or people 重要的；重大的；有影響力的：*an important event in history* 歷史上的一次重大事件

critical likely to have a decisive influence on the outcome of something, for example, on whether a plan succeeds or fails（對某事的結果，如計劃的成敗等）起決定作用的，至關重要的：*a critical development* 至關重要的發展

crucial critical 關係重大的；決定性的：*at the crucial moment* 在這個決定性的時刻

key on which or whom everything depends 關鍵的；主要的：*the key player in the team* 隊裏的主力隊員

main most important among a number of related things（許多相關事情中）最重要的，主要的：*My main reason for coming to the Louvre is to see the Mona Lisa.* 我來羅浮宮的主要目的是要看蒙娜麗莎。

major very important, standing out among other people or things in the same group（一群人或事物中）主要的，較重要的，突出的：*one of the major 20th-century novelists* 20 世紀重要的小說家之一

momentous being of great and lasting significance 意義重大的；具有重要意義的：*a momentous occasion* 重要時刻

primary (*formal*) main, first in importance 首要的；主要的：*Our primary concern is the children's safety.* 我們最關心的是孩子們的安全問題。

significant having, or likely to have, a considerable effect 有重大影響的；可能產生重大影響的；顯著的：*There's been no significant change in the patient's condition.* 病人的病情沒有顯著改善。

vital very important or necessary, so that you really cannot do without it 至關重要的；非常重要的；必不可少的：*vital information* 至關重要的信息

improve *verb* to become better, or to make something better 改進；改善；改良：*If you practise your golf swing a lot, it will improve.* 如果你多練習一下，高爾夫揮桿的技術就會提高。

advance to make progress in knowledge or learning（在學識方面）取得進步，提高，發展：*He began as a junior editor but he quickly advanced to publishing director.* 他起初只是一個初級編輯，但很快就被提升為出版主管。

ameliorate (*formal*) to make circumstances better 改善，改進（環境）：*We have done everything in our power to ameliorate the circumstances.* 我們已經盡其所能來改進環境狀況。

better yourself to reach a higher position in society or have a better quality of life 提高社會地位；改善生活質量；上進：*Tracy is trying to better herself by going to college.* 切麗絲想通過上大學來提高自己的社會地位。

cure to cause an illness or a problem to disappear 治癒，治好（疾病）；解決（問題）：*Physiotherapy cured my backache.* 物理療法治好了我的背痛。

enhance to add to the beauty or value of something 提高，增加，增進（美或價值等）：*Your sweater enhances the colour of your eyes.* 你的毛衣將你的眼睛襯托得更加神采飛揚。

get better to improve, especially to recover your health after you have been ill（尤指病後健康狀況）改善，好轉：*I've been getting better since I started taking the new medicine the doctor gave me.* 自從我開始服用醫生開的這種新藥後，我的身體狀況逐步好轉。

look up (*informal*) to improve or become more promising 好轉；更有前途；更有希望：*Things are looking up now that I have a permanent job.* 我有了一份穩定的工作，因而情況正在逐步好轉。

make over (*informal*) to make major changes that are intended to improve the appearance of someone or something（使外觀）煥然一新，翻新，徹底改變：*Susan looked ten years younger after she had been made over at the beauty salon.* 蘇珊在美容院美容後看上去年輕了 10 歲。

pick up (*informal*) to get better, for example in health or in sales（健康狀況或銷售等）好轉，改善：*Sales are picking up now after a slow start to the year.* 銷售量在年初緩慢起動，而現在已經開始好轉。

income *noun* money that you receive from any source, for example from working or investments, and that you live on（工作、投資等所得的）收入：*Families on a low income are entitled to state benefits.* 低收入家庭有資格享受國家救濟金。

commission a sum of money that a salesperson earns for every sale that they make（銷售）佣金，提成，回扣：*She has no salary, but works for a commission on all the goods she sells.* 她沒有薪水，但可從售出的每件貨物中得到佣金。

earnings money that you receive in return for work（工作）所得；工資；收入：*He gives a percentage of his earnings to charity.* 他把工資收入的一部分捐給了慈善機構。

pay the money that an employer gives you in return for the work you do（僱主所付的）工資，報酬：*I have had money taken off my pay because I was late one day.* 我因為有一天遲到了被扣了工資。

profits money that you make from a business, selling something, etc., after costs have been deducted from the whole amount that you receive (指扣除成本後的) 利潤，盈利，收益：*Profits are down on this time last year.* 與去年同期相比，利潤額有所減少。

salary the money that you earn by working in a professional position or an office job, which is usually paid monthly (專業人員或辦公室職員按月領取的) 薪水，薪金：*Denis's salary as a bank manager is enough for the family to live on.* 作為銀行經理，丹尼斯的薪水足夠負擔一家人的生活費用。

takings money that is made on sales in a business such as a shop or a pub (商店、酒吧等的) 營業收入，營業額，進賬：*Our takings have gone up over the last few weeks.* 在過去的幾週裏，我們的營業額已有所提高。

wages the money that you earn as an ordinary worker in, for example, a factory or shop, which is usually paid weekly (普通工人按週領取的) 工資，工錢：*I couldn't afford to buy a house on my shop assistant's wages.* 靠我做商店營業員的工資買不起一套房子。

increase *verb* to become, or to make something, bigger or greater in number 增大，增加 (數目)：*Sales have increased since last month.* 自上個月以來銷售額已經增加。

add to to bring more of something of which you already have a certain amount (在已有的數量上) 增添，添加，增加：*You're only adding to my difficulties by trying to help.* 你來幫忙只會給我添更多的麻煩。

amplify to make something, especially sound, greater in intensity 放大，擴大，增強 (尤指聲音)：*We will have to use microphones at the meeting to amplify the sound.* 在會上，我們得使用揚聲器放大聲音。

augment (*formal*) to make something, but not usually a physical object, greater in size or quantity by adding to it 增加，擴大 (尺碼、數量等，但通常不指實物)：*I took an extra job at weekends to augment my salary.* 我週末做了一份額外的工作來增加收入。

boost to make something greater and stronger 促進；增強；提高：*Her success in the exams boosted her self-confidence.* 她考試的成功增強了她的自信心。

enlarge to make something bigger 放大；擴大；擴展：*I am having a photograph enlarged so that I can frame it.* 我正找人把照片放大以便給它裝個框。

expand to become, or to make something, greater in size or scope, especially by moving outwards to occupy more space 增大，擴大 (尺寸、範圍等)：*His waist has expanded by four centimeters.* 他的腰圍增加了 4 厘米。

extend to make something, such as a house, larger or longer by adding something to it 擴充；擴展；使延長：*We are extending the house by adding on a conservatory.* 我們為添建一個溫室正在擴建房子。

go through the roof (*informal*) (*said usually about prices*) to increase by a very large amount (通常指價格) 大幅度增長：*House prices have gone through the roof recently in this area.* 最近這個地區的房價大幅度上漲。

grow to increase in size, number, or intensity, especially to become bigger by a natural process 增加，增長 (體積，數量、強度等)；(尤指在自然進程中)

長大：*Little Annie has grown five centimetres in the last six months.* 最近 6 個月小安妮長高了 5 厘米。

mount (*up*) to increase in amount or number（數量或數目）增長，上升：*The death toll from the earthquake in China continues to mount.* 中國這次地震的死亡人數在持續上升。

multiply to increase in number（數量上）增加：*Out-of-town shopping centres multiplied as car ownership increased.* 郊區購物中心隨着私家車擁有量的增加而增加。

rise to increase in amount or number（數量或數目）上升，上漲：*The price of petrol is likely to rise again.* 汽油價格很可能再次上漲。

⊃ see also 參見 **rise**

inexperienced *adjective* having little or no knowledge or experience, especially of a particular activity or subject（尤指對某一活動或主題）無經驗的，缺乏經驗的：*an inexperienced driver* 一個沒有經驗的司機

amateurish of poor quality through skill or experience 業餘的；蹩腳的：*an amateurish performance* 蹩腳的表演

green (*informal*) inexperienced and often naive 幼稚的，稚嫩的；生的：*I was too young and too green back then to deal with living alone.* 我當時太年輕稚嫩，還無法獨立生活。

inexpert having little skill in a particular activity（對某一特定活動）不熟悉的，不懂行的：*an inexpert cook* 不在行的廚師

new having no previous experience of a particular job or activity 新手的，生手的；無經驗的：*I am new to hang-gliding – this is my first time.* 我對懸掛式滑翔運動不熟悉，這是我第一次接觸。

unaccustomed not used to a particular activity（對某一特定活動）不習慣的：*unaccustomed to using a computer* 不習慣使用電腦

unfamiliar knowing little or nothing about something or unaccustomed to it 不熟悉的；不習慣的：*I was still unfamiliar with the surroundings of my new workplace.* 我對新的工作環境還不熟悉。

untrained having had no formal training in a particular job or activity 未經正式訓練的：*an untrained singer* 一個未經訓練的歌手

⊃ see also 參見 **ignorant**

inferior *adjective* of a low standard or low quality, or of a lower standard or quality than something else（水平或質量）低等的，較低的，較次的：*inferior goods* 次品

hopeless very bad at doing something, or very ineffective（做某事）十分糟糕的，不能勝任的：*I'm absolutely hopeless at maths.* 我對數學簡直一竅不通。

inadequate of lower standard or quality than is required to do something properly 不足的；不夠格的；不適當的：*an inadequate father* 不稱職的父親

mediocre of middle to poor quality, definitely not good enough for you to feel positive about it 平庸的；普通的：*All in all, it was a pretty mediocre performance.* 總之，這是一次相當平庸的表演。

rubbish (*informal*) of a very low standard or quality（水平或質量）極差的，極糟糕的：*She's rubbish at spelling.* 她的拼寫糟糕透了。

second-rate having very little talent or skill 二流的；次等的；平庸的：*He's just a second-rate pub singer.* 他只是個酒吧的二流歌手。

unsatisfactory not of the standard that someone wants or expects 不能令人滿意的；不符合要求的；不合格的：*If your work is unsatisfactory, then you will have to do it again.* 要是你所做的工作未能令人滿意，你就必須重新做過。

useless unable to be used, because damaged, of very poor quality, irrelevant, etc., or (*informal*) very bad at doing something 無用的；無價值的；不擅長的：*His head is full of useless information.* 他滿腦子裝的盡是些無用的東西。

➲ see also 參見 **bad**[4]

informal *adjective* done, or doing things, in a friendly and relaxed way, without strictly following the usual rules of politeness or procedure 非正式的；非正規的；不拘禮節的：*Call me by my first name – we're very informal here.* 直接叫我名字就行，我們這兒不用拘禮。

casual not involving serious matters or feelings, or carried out in a very informal way 隨便的；隨意的；非正式的：*a casual conversation* 隨意的交談

colloquial (*used to describe words or language*) used mainly in informal conversation, rather than in writing（用以形容話語或語言）通俗的，口語化的，非正式的：*'Let the cat out of the bag' is a colloquial expression.* "露馬腳" 是一種口語化的表達。

easygoing not strict, taking a relaxed and good-natured view of what other people do（待人）溫和的，隨和的；隨便的：*an easygoing attitude* 隨和的態度

familiar friendly to an inappropriate degree 過分親密的；隨便的：*Teachers should not be too familiar with their pupils.* 老師不應該跟學生過分親密。

natural behaving in an ordinary, friendly way towards people, not trying to make yourself seem important or special（對人）自然的，不拘束的，不做作的：*Gita is a very natural young girl with no airs or graces.* 吉塔是個舉止自然的年輕姑娘，一點都不矯揉造作。

relaxed with no tension, comfortable and allowing people to feel at ease 放鬆的；輕鬆自在的；不拘束的：*a relaxed atmosphere* 輕鬆的氣氛

unaffected natural in behaviour, or genuine and not pretended 不矯揉造作的；真摯的；自然的：*They greeted the news with unaffected delight.* 聽到這個消息，他們都發自內心的高興。

information *noun* something, usually in the form of statements, numbers, etc, that enables you to know what something or someone is like or what is happening 信息；數據；資料：*I'd like some information on holidays in Turkey.* 我想要一些有關土耳其假日的資料。

data information in the form of facts, numbers, or statistics（以事實、數字或統計為形式的）數據，資料：*The Human Resources Department keeps data on all employees.* 人力資源部保存着所有員工的檔案資料。

facts pieces of information that are proven to be true (準確的) 資料，信息；實情：*I have learned some interesting facts about whales.* 我了解到了有關鯨魚的一些有趣的信息。

info (*informal*) information 信息；消息：*Did you get any info from Grace about her new boyfriend?* 你從葛麗絲那兒聽到有關她新男友的消息了嗎？

intelligence secret information that is discovered by spies about an enemy country（關於敵國的）情報，信息：*He was a government agent gathering intelligence in Germany during the war.* 他曾是政府的情報員，戰爭期間在德國收集情報。

knowledge facts and other information that you have learned, usually about a particular subject（通常指對某一學科的）知識，學問：*George's knowledge of local history is very impressive.* 佐治對當地歷史的了解給人留下了深刻的印象。

material information that can be used as the subject of a written work 素材；材料；資料：*He has collected lots of material for his next comedy series.* 他為下一部系列喜劇收集了大量素材。

news new information about something 新聞；消息：*There is no further news on the missing schoolgirl.* 沒有關於失蹤女生的後續新聞。

statistics information in the form of figures that show the relationship between two or more things 統計情況，統計數據：*Government statistics show a drop in unemployment.* 政府統計數據顯示失業率有所下降。

⊃ see also 參見 **news**

innocent *adjective* not guilty of having committed a crime or done wrong 無罪的；清白的；無辜的：*In the eyes of the law, a person is innocent until proven guilty.* 從法律的角度看，一個人在被證實有罪之前都是清白的。

blameless not responsible for a wrong that has been done or a mistake that has been made 無可責備的；無過錯的：*Jamal is blameless in this situation.* 在這種情形下，買馬爾的行為無可厚非。

faultless having no mistakes or imperfections 無瑕疵的；無缺陷的；完美的：*a faultless portrayal* 一幅完美的畫像

guiltless (*formal*) innocent, not having done anything wrong 無過錯的；無辜的；無罪的：*Any one of us could have stopped her if we had wanted to, so none of us is guiltless in this case.* 如果願意的話，我們任何人原本都是可以阻止她的，所以在這件事上我們都有過錯。

in the clear (*informal*) not suspected or likely to be suspected of having done something wrong 無辜的；無罪的；沒有嫌疑的：*He was abroad at the time when the papers were stolen, so he's in the clear.* 文件被偷時他在國外，所以他是清白的。

irreproachable in which nobody can find anything to blame or any sign of wrongdoing 無可指責的；無可挑剔的；無缺點的：*an irreproachable record* 無可指責的記錄

not guilty found by a court of law not to have committed a crime with which you are charged（法庭裁決）無罪的，無辜的，清白的：*He was found not guilty of murder.* 他被判決未犯謀殺罪。

squeaky-clean (*informal*) very virtuous and innocent, sometimes unattractively so 品行極好的，清廉的，清白的 (但有時並非討人喜歡)：*his squeaky-clean image* 他的清廉形象

⊃ see also 參見 **naive**

insolent *adjective* aggressively insulting and disrespectful in your speech or behavior (語言或行為) 傲慢無禮的，侮慢的，粗野的：*an insolent scowl* 侮慢不悅的神色

brazen knowing that you are doing something that other people disapprove of and not caring what they think 厚顏無恥的：*brazen hypocrisy* 厚顏無恥的虛偽

cheeky mildly disrespectful, sometimes in a charming way 放肆的；無禮的；恃寵而驕的：*You cheeky little monkey!* 你這個放肆無禮的小搗蛋鬼！

defiant boldly resisting authority 公然挑釁的；違抗的；藐視的：*a defiant attitude* 公然挑釁的態度

disrespectful showing no respect or consideration for someone 無禮的；不尊敬的：*Don't be so disrespectful to your mother!* 不要對你媽媽如此無禮！

impertinent disrespectful in your speech or behavior (言談舉止) 不敬的，粗魯無禮的：*an impertinent remark* 無禮的言論

impudent insulting and disrespectful in your speech or behavior, especially towards someone who is older than you or socially superior (尤指對長輩或上級) 放肆無禮的，不尊重的，粗魯的：*an impudent child* 放肆無禮的孩子

presumptuous assuming that you can do something or behave in a particular way, when other people think that you are not really entitled to 自負的；自以為是的：*It was presumptuous of him to take it for granted he would be invited to the wedding.* 他自以為是地認為被邀請參加婚禮是理所當然的。

⊃ see also 參見 **rude**

inspect *verb* to look over something or someone and check that they are in a satisfactory state 視察；檢閱；檢查：*The Queen inspected the troops.* 女王檢閱了部隊。

case (*informal*) to examine a place with a view to committing a crime (為實施犯罪) 踩點，探路：*The burglars cased the joint with a view to breaking in.* 幾個竊賊在入室盜竊前對其進行踩點。

check out (*informal*) to look at someone or something, or to get information about them 檢查；調查：*Check out the guy with the green hair!* 去調查一下那個綠頭髮的傢伙！

eye to look at someone or something in a way that suggests you are interested in them or want them (出於興趣) 注視，審視，察看：*Jim was eyeing the cake, so I quickly offered him a slice.* 占姆眼巴巴地看着那塊蛋糕，所以我趕快給了他一塊。

look over to inspect a person or their work, often quickly (快速) 檢查，查看：*Let me look over your homework.* 讓我檢查一下你的功課。

oversee to supervise a group of people or their work 監督；監視；看管：*As project leader, it is my job to oversee the group's work.* 作為項目組長，監督項目組的工作是我的職責。

review to look back over something that has been done in order to check it 審核；覆查；回顧：*Let's review the progress we have made so far.* 我們回顧一下目前為止我們取得的進展。

take stock of to stop to consider what has been done so far before deciding how to progress（對過去的事情）作出評估，加以總結，進行反思：*When you reach the age of 40, it is common to take stock of your life.* 人到了不惑之年，常常會反思自己的人生。

vet to inspect something or someone carefully 仔細檢查；審查：*People who apply to work with children must be vetted by the authorities.* 申請從事兒童工作的人必須經過權威機構的嚴格審查。

➲ see also 參見 **check**

insult *verb* to say hurtful or offensive things about someone 侮辱；辱罵：*He insulted her by calling her stupid.* 他辱罵她愚蠢。

abuse to speak very harshly and offensively to someone 辱罵；謾罵；詆毀：*The crowd abused the accused as he was hustled into court.* 當被告被推上法庭時，群眾紛紛辱罵他。

call names (*usually said about children*) to describe someone in a hurtful or offensive way（常指孩子）罵人，辱罵：*Children often call each other names in the playground.* 孩子們經常在操場上互相辱罵。

offend to make someone feel that you have no respect for them or the things they consider important 觸怒；冒犯；得罪：*I think I offended Ruth when I called her 'middle-aged'.* 我想我把魯思叫做 "中年婦女" 惹惱了她。

put down to criticize someone in a hurtful and disrespectful way 斥責；教訓：*She often puts her husband down in front of his friends.* 她經常當着丈夫朋友的面斥責他。

slag off (*informal*) to criticize someone in a rude or offensive way（粗魯無禮地）批評，指責，非難：*They are always slagging off other bands in the papers.* 他們總是在報紙上指責其他的樂隊。

slight to be rude or unfriendly to someone or to pay them little attention 怠慢；冷落；輕視：*I felt slighted when my name was omitted from the guest list.* 我的名字從客人名單上漏掉時，我覺得自己被冷落了。

snub to be rude or unfriendly to someone you know or to ignore them completely 故意怠慢；不理不睬；冷落：*When Tim met his ex-girlfriend at a party, he completely snubbed her.* 蒂姆在晚會上遇到他的前女友時對她完全不理不睬。

taunt to tease or mock someone with hurtful or offensive comments 嘲弄；揶揄；奚落：*The bullies cruelly taunted her about being fat.* 那群恃強凌弱的人惡毒地譏諷她的肥胖。

➲ see also 參見 **rude**

intense *adjective* having a very powerful and concentrated quality 強烈的；劇烈的；極度的：*intense pride* 極度驕傲

acute (*used to describe uncomfortable feelings*) strongly and painfully felt（用以描述不舒服的感覺）極度的，強烈的：*acute embarrassment* 極度的尷尬

consuming taking up all your attention and mental energy 令人着迷的；強烈的：*a consuming passion* 無法抗拒的激情

deep sincerely felt and affecting you in a very powerful way 深厚的；深切的；強烈的：*deep shame* 深重的恥辱

extreme of the very strongest kind 極端的；極度的：*extreme irritation* 極端的憤怒

passionate very powerful and directed outwards towards someone or something that you are concerned with 充滿激情的；熱烈的；熱誠的：*passionate love* 熾熱的愛

profound deep 深切的；深厚的：*profound sadness* 深切的憂傷

strong powerful enough to affect your attitude or the way you behave 有巨大影響力的；強大的；強烈的：*strong feelings of jealousy* 強烈的妒忌感

➲ see also 參見 **strong**

interesting *adjective* which attracts or holds your attention 有趣的；引起注意的：*an interesting documentary* 一部有趣的紀錄片

absorbing which holds your attention for a long time（長時間）吸引人的；引人入勝的：*an absorbing book* 一本引人入勝的書

appealing which attracts you 有吸引力的；誘人的：*an appealing idea* 一個誘人的想法

attractive very appealing and worthy of consideration 吸引人的；誘人的；引起興趣的：*an attractive prospect* 誘人的前景

entertaining which holds your attention and amuses you 有趣的；使人愉快的：*an entertaining film* 一部有趣的電影

exciting extremely interesting and eventful 使人激動的；令人興奮的；非常有趣的：*an exciting trip to China* 一次令人激動的中國之旅

fascinating which attracts or interests you very strongly and makes you want to know more about it 迷人的；使人神魂顛倒的；着魔的：*a fascinating conversation* 一次饒有風趣的談話

gripping exciting and dramatic 令人激動的；扣人心弦的：*a gripping adventure story* 一個扣人心弦的冒險故事

intriguing which attracts your attention and is slightly mysterious 饒有興味的；令人好奇的；引人入勝的：*I heard an intriguing snippet of conversation.* 我聽到一段饒有興味的談話。

interfere *verb* to involve yourself in other people's affairs, and often try to change what they are doing, in a way that is irritating to them（以令人不快的方式）介入；干涉，干預：*My mother keeps interfering in our wedding arrangements.* 我媽媽一直在干預我們婚禮的準備工作。

intervene to enter into a situation in order to change it or take control of it 調停；斡旋；干預：*The teacher intervened just in time to prevent the two boys coming to blows.* 老師調解及時，阻止了兩個孩子的打鬥。

meddle   to interfere 干預；干涉；管閒事：*My neighbour is always meddling in other people's business.* 我的鄰居老是愛管閒事。

poke your nose in   (*informal*) to pry or interfere 打探；干預；管閒事：*She can't resist poking her nose in when we're discussing private business.* 我們在討論私事的時候，她總忍不住湊上來打探。

pry   to try to find out information about other people's affairs 打聽，打探，刺探：*Kindly stop prying into my affairs!* 請不要再打探我的私事！

put/shove/stick your oar in   (*informal*) to offer advice or comment on other people's affairs when it is not wanted 插手，橫加干涉，干預：*There's no need for you to stick your oar in – we can sort out our own problems, thanks.* 你不必插手，我們可以解決自己的問題，謝謝了。

snoop   (*informal*) to try to find out information about other people's affairs, especially by underhand means（尤指以不可告人的方式）窺察，窺探：*He snoops around the office when no one is around, looking in people's drawers.* 辦公室空無一人的時候，他四處窺視，翻看別人的抽屜。

➲ see also 參見 **disturb**

invade *verb*   to enter a country with military force, or to go into a place where you are unwelcome 侵略，武力入侵，侵入（某國家或地方）：*The Anglo-Saxons invaded the British Isles in the fifth century.* 盎格魯 – 撒克遜人於公元 5 世紀入侵不列顛群島。

attack   to use force to try to harm or capture someone or something（以武力）傷害，攻擊，進攻：*The capital has been attacked from the air.* 首都遭遇了空襲。

descend on   to arrive in a place in large numbers, in a way that is usually unpleasant for the people who are there（以當地人不喜歡的方式）蜂擁而至，大批來訪：*Hordes of tourists descend on the town from June onwards.* 6 月以來，成批的遊客蜂擁來到這個小鎮。

march into   to invade a country or area 侵略（某國家或地區）；長驅直入：*The army marched into the region and so the war began.* 軍隊長驅直入這一地區，戰爭於是爆發了。

occupy   to station military forces in a country or area to control it after you have conquered it（軍隊）佔領，佔據（某國家或地區）：*The Americans occupied Baghdad and most of northern Iraq.* 美國軍隊佔領了巴格達和伊拉克北部的大部分地區。

overrun   to make a sudden military assault on a country and take possession of it（突然）侵佔，佔領（某國）：*The country was overrun by the invaders.* 這個國家被侵略者佔領了。

➲ see also 參見 **attack**[3]

involve *verb*   to have something as an essential part or element of doing it 包含；含有；涉及：*Being a parent involves a lot of self-sacrifice.* 為人父母包含着大量的自我犧牲。

entail   to have something as a part or consequence 使必要；需要：*What exactly does the job entail?* 這工作到底需要甚麼？

imply to have something as a necessary or logical consequence 必然包含；使有必要；表明：*The title 'Mrs' implies that the person you are referring to is a married woman.* Mrs 這個稱呼表明你提及的那個人是已婚婦女。

include to have something as a part or element, usually as one or more of several parts or elements 包括；包含：*A modern-language degree course includes a year abroad.* 現代語言學位課程包含一年的出國留學。

incorporate (*formal*) to include two or more things within itself, or to make something a part or element of something else 將…包括在內；納入；使合併：*The driving test incorporates a practical exam and a theory exam.* 駕駛考試包括實際操作和理論知識考試。

mean to have something as a consequence 意味着；產生…的結果：*Going back to university will mean a drop in the family income.* 回到大學讀書意味着家庭收入的減少。

necessitate (*formal*) to require 需要；使成為必要：*Accepting this position would necessitate relocation to London.* 接受這個職位就需要搬遷到倫敦。

require to make it necessary to have or do something 要求；需要；使…成為必要：*Being a top-class athlete requires dedication and sacrifice.* 成為一流運動員需要奉獻和犧牲精神。

take in to have two or more things as parts or elements 包括，包含（兩個或以上的因素或組成部分）：*The cat family takes in big cats like lions and tigers as well as the domestic cat.* 貓科動物既包括家養貓，也包括獅子、老虎這樣的大型動物。

J

job *noun* the type of work that you do regularly in order to earn money（為獲取報酬所做的固定的）工作，職業：*She has a job in a bank.* 她在銀行工作。

calling a type of work that you feel as if you are compelled to do, usually one that requires dedication and caring for others（通常指需要奉獻精神和關愛他人的）職業，事業，使命：*Michael had a calling to the priesthood.* 米高肩負傳教士的使命。

career the type of work that you do for most of your life（大半生從事的）職業，事業；生涯：*I would like to have a career in journalism.* 我想從事新聞業。

employment the fact of having a job 就業；受僱；職業：*After being out of work for a few months, it was good to be in employment again.* 失業幾個月後能再找到工作真好。

occupation (*formal*) a job 職業：*Mr Alan Jones, thirty-nine years old, occupation bank manager.* 艾倫・瓊斯先生，39 歲，職業是銀行經理。

position (*formal*) a post 職位：*The position of area manager has become vacant.* 地區經理的職位空缺。

post a job within an organization, which has specified duties, especially a fairly high-status job（機構內部擔負特定責任的）職位；（尤指）要職：*Alan applied for the post of head teacher.* 艾倫申請擔任校長職務。

profession a job, especially one that requires a high level of education and training, such as medicine, teaching, or law（尤指醫學、教學或法律等需要高水平教育和培訓的）職業，行業：*He was an active member of the medical profession.* 他曾是醫療界的活躍分子。

trade a skilled job that requires training（需接受培訓的有技能的）職業，手藝：*If you learn a trade, you'll make much more money than you will as an ordinary labourer.* 如果你學會一門手藝，會比你當普通勞動者多賺些錢。

vocation a type of work that you feel as if you are compelled to do, usually one that requires dedication and caring for others（通常指需要奉獻精神和關愛他人的）職業，工作：*Nursing is generally regarded as a vocation.* 護理通常被看作是一種職業。

work the job or responsibilities of your job that you do regularly to earn money（為獲取報酬所做的固定的）工作：*I usually finish work at 5 pm.* 我通常在下午 5 點下班。

⊃ see also 參見 **duty**

join *verb* to bring two or more things into a position where they are touching one another and fixed together in some way 連接；接合；聯結：*Stand in a circle and join hands.* 站成圈，手拉手。

attach to place something on something else so that it is touching it and remains in that position 黏貼；固定；繫上：*Attach the address label to your suitcase.* 把地址標籤貼在你的旅行箱上。

bind to tie two or more things together firmly 捆緊；綁緊；繫緊：*Bind the plant to the stick so that it grows straight.* 將這株植物綁在枝條上，這樣它就可以長得筆直。

connect to join two or more things together directly, to join them indirectly by means of something else, such as a wire, that is attached to them and enables electric current or a similar force to pass from one to the other, or to be something that connects something to something else（直接）連接；（通過某種方法，如電線等，使電流等間接）相連，聯通：*The amplifier is connected to the loudspeaker.* 擴音器與喇叭相連。

fasten to attach something, usually firmly, to something else 繫牢；拴緊；扣緊：*Fasten the pedometer to your waistband, and it will measure the number of steps you take in a day.* 將計步器緊扣在腰帶上，它就能測出你一天走了多少步。

link to connect 連結；連接：*A walkway links the two buildings.* 一條人行通道將兩座建築連接起來。

unite to come together or bring people or things together 聯合；結合；團結：*The victims' families are united in their grief.* 受害者在悲痛之中聯合起來。

joke *noun* a funny story or a funny comment 笑話；玩笑：*He told me a joke about a talking dog.* 他給我講了一個會說話的狗的笑話。

gag (*informal*) a joke, especially one told by a comedian（尤指喜劇演員的）插科打諢，逗樂的話；噱頭：*The entertainer sang a few songs and told a few gags.* 那個娛樂節目演員唱了幾首歌，講了幾個笑話。

pun a remark that is meant to be funny because the words can have more than one meaning 雙關語 : *He made a pun based on the two meanings of 'bear'.* 他根據 bear 的兩個意思使用了一個雙關語。

quip a witty comment or retort 妙語；俏皮話；巧辯 : *She is always ready with a merry quip.* 她說話總是妙語連珠。

wisecrack a sharp witty remark (尖刻的) 俏皮話；風涼話 : *Sometimes his wisecracks can be quite cutting.* 有時候他說的風涼話特別傷人。

witticism (*formal*) a witty comment 妙語；雋語；詼諧語 : *an article on Oscar Wilde's witticism* 一篇關於奧斯卡・王爾德的詼諧語的文章

jump *verb* to move into the air, with both feet off the ground, and back down again 跳；躍；跳躍 : *Jump over the puddle!* 跳過那個水坑！

bound to move energetically taking big long steps, or to make a big jump that usually covers a long distance rather than goes high into the air (大踏步) 前進；跳躍着跑 : *The dog bounded in from the garden.* 那條狗從花園裏蹦蹦跳跳地跑進來。

hop to jump on one foot 單腳跳 : *When I sprained my ankle, I had to hop to the phone.* 我扭傷了腳踝，不得不單腳跳着去接電話。

leap to take a big jump that either goes high in the air or covers a long distance (大幅度向高處或遠處) 跳，跳躍 : *A salmon leapt right up in the air from the river.* 一條三文魚從河中躍出水面。

skip to jump lightly raising first one foot and then the other, as children do (孩子般輕快地) 蹦，跳；蹦蹦跳跳 : *The little girl skipped right up the path to the house.* 那個小女孩蹦蹦跳跳地走在通往那座房子的小路上。

spring to make a big, sudden jump, often to attack something or someone (常指為攻擊而突然大幅度地) 跳，躍 : *The cheetah sprang from its hiding place onto its prey.* 那隻獵豹從藏身之處躍起，撲向獵物。

vault to jump over something high, sometimes with the help of a pole for support 跳過，躍過 (高處)；(有時指借助撐桿) 跨越 : *The burglar vaulted over the fence and ran off.* 那個竊賊飛身翻越柵欄，逃走了。

K

keep *verb* to continue to have possession of something 保留；保管；保存 : *She has kept all the letters her husband ever sent her.* 她保存着丈夫寫給她的所有信件。

hold to carry something in your hands and look after it 拿着；握着；抱住 : *Will you hold my handbag for me while I have a dance?* 我跳舞的時候你幫我拿一下手提包好嗎？

preserve to maintain something in an unchanged condition 維持，保持 (原狀)；保存 : *We want to preserve this beautiful building for future generations.* 我們想為後代保存這幢美麗的建築物。

retain to keep something in your possession 保留；保存；保持 : *Retain your ticket in case an inspector boards the bus.* 保留你的車票以便巡查員上車驗票。

save to keep something back for later use 保存，留存（以備將來之用）: *After cooking a chicken, I like to save the carcass to make soup.* 我烹完雞後喜歡把雞骨架留下來煲湯。

store to keep goods in a safe place for future use 貯存；貯藏；儲備: *Store the wine in a cool place.* 將葡萄酒貯存在涼爽的地方。

withhold (*formal*) to refuse to give or grant something 拒絕給予；不給；扣留: *He was charged with withholding information pertaining to a crime.* 他被指控拒絕提供有關犯罪信息。

➲ see also 參見 **save**

kill *verb* to end the life of a person or an animal 殺死；殺害；致死: *My brother was killed in a motorcycle accident.* 我哥哥死於電單車意外。

assassinate to murder a well-known or important person 暗殺，行刺: *President Kennedy was assassinated in 1963.* 肯尼迪總統在 1963 年遭到暗殺。

bump off (*informal*) to murder someone 幹掉；謀殺: *The gang boss was bumped off by members of a rival gang.* 該幫派頭目被敵對幫派的人幹掉了。

do in (*informal*) to murder someone 殺掉；幹掉: *She did her old man in with a carving knife.* 她用切肉刀把她老公殺了。

execute to put someone to death as a punishment for committing a very serious crime 處決，處死（罪犯）: *Ruth Ellis was the last woman to be executed by hanging in the UK.* 露絲·埃利斯是英國最後一個被處以絞刑的女人。

massacre to kill large numbers of people in a violent way 大屠殺；（大規模）殘殺: *Troops massacred the entire population of the village.* 軍隊把村莊裏的人都趕盡殺絕了。

murder to kill someone deliberately （故意）謀殺，兇殺: *The woman was murdered by her jealous lover.* 這女人被她醋意大發的情人謀殺了。

put to sleep to end the life of an animal that is suffering, usually by giving it a lethal injection （通常指用注射方法）使（遭受痛苦的動物）安息；使安樂死: *The vet put my cat to sleep because it had cancer.* 我的貓患了癌症，獸醫一針結束了牠的生命。

slaughter to kill an animal for food, or to kill large numbers of people violently 屠宰，宰殺；（大規模）屠殺: *The pigs were transported to the abattoir to be slaughtered.* 這些豬被運往屠宰場等待宰殺。

kind¹ *adjective* helpful to others and considerate of their feelings 體貼的；關照的: *It was kind of you to help me out.* 你真好，幫我解了燃眉之急。

benevolent (*formal*) doing good deeds for those less fortunate than yourself 行善的；樂善好施的；仁慈的: *a benevolent ruler* 仁慈的統治者

charitable inclined to take a kind and tolerant view of others 仁慈的；寬容的: *She always takes a charitable view of people.* 她總是以恩慈待人。

compassionate sympathetic and understanding about others' pain or suffering 富有同情心的；有憐憫心的: *She is a very compassionate woman, who helps out at the homeless shelter.* 她是個富有同情心的女人，常到避難所幫助那些無家可歸的人。

considerate thinking of other people's feelings 替他人着想的；考慮周到的；體諒的：*He is very considerate, always putting other people before himself.* 他總是先人後己，替他人着想。

generous giving, or given, freely 慷慨的；大方的：*a generous gift* 一份厚禮

good pleasant, helpful, and honourable 令人愉快的；有益的；可敬的：*It was good of them to remember my birthday.* 很高興他們還記得我的生日。

helpful keen to do things to benefit others 樂於助人的；有幫助的；有益的：*Thanks for your advice – that was most helpful.* 感謝您的建議，那對我的幫助太大了。

humane having or showing a desire to prevent suffering 仁慈的；人道的：*slaughtering animals for food by humane means so that they don't suffer* 用人道的方法宰殺食用動物以減輕牠們的痛苦

kind² *noun* a number of people or things that have shared characteristics and are regarded as a group 同類；同種：*What kind of film would you like to see – a comedy or a thriller?* 你喜歡看哪種類型的電影，是喜劇還是驚險片？

breed a particular type of dog, cat, cow, etc., that has been bred to have particular physical characteristics（牲畜的）種，品種：*The St Bernard is the largest breed of dog.* 聖伯納德狗是一種體形最大的狗。

category a name or description that can be applied to a particular kind of thing 類別；範疇；種類：*The films are listed in different categories – comedy, horror, adventure, and so on.* 電影分為不同的種類，有喜劇、恐怖片、驚險動作片等等。

sort a kind 類型；種類：*What sort of computer do you have?* 你的電腦是哪種類型的？

style a particular way of doing something 風格；風味；作風：*the Mediterranean style of cooking* 地中海風味的烹飪方法

type a kind 類型；種類：*He is not the jealous type.* 他不是那種有妒忌心的人。

variety a particular kind of something of which there are usually many kinds（同一事物的）多種式樣，不同種類：*an apple of the Granny Smith variety* 名為"青蘋果祖母"的蘋果品種

➲ see also 參見 **group**

knowledge *noun* the information that you store in your memory and use to answer questions, solve problems, etc. 知識；學問；學識：*I have no knowledge of his whereabouts.* 我不知道他的行蹤。

education the knowledge that you acquire at school, college, or university（學校）教育：*You need to have a good education if you want to have a good career.* 如果你要成就一番好的事業，你就需要接受良好的教育。

erudition (*formal*) learning 學問；博學：*He is a man of great erudition.* 他是一個學識淵博的人。

Know-how (*informal*) knowledge of practical or technical matters 實踐知識；實用技術：*I don't have the know-how to install a washing machine.* 我對安裝洗衣機一竅不通。

learning (*formal*) knowledge acquired through extensive study（通過廣泛學習獲得的）學識，學問，知識：*For all his learning, he was unable to answer this one simple question.* 儘管學識淵博，他卻不能回答這個簡單的問題。

scholarship knowledge acquired through extensive study（通過廣泛研究獲得的）學術知識，學問：*She devoted her entire life to scholarship.* 她終生致力於學術研究。

wisdom knowledge acquired through experience of life and people and combined with good judgment（基於人生閱歷和明智的判斷獲得的）智慧，知識：*The elders of the village are respected for their wisdom.* 村裏的這些長輩因其智慧而受人尊重。

➲ see also 參見 **information**

L

lack *noun* the fact of being without something that is needed or desired 缺少；缺乏；欠缺：*Lack of privacy is one disadvantage of fame.* 缺少私隱是成名的唯一不利之處。

absence the fact of not being present in a place or at an event or of not being available 缺席；不在；缺乏：*The absence of hard evidence made a conviction impossible.* 缺少確鑿的證據，因而無法定罪。

deficiency the fact of having less of something than you need 不足；缺少：*An iron deficiency in the blood was causing me to feel fatigued.* 缺鐵性貧血曾使我感覺疲勞。

insufficiency (*formal*) the fact of having less of something than you need 不足；缺少：*We were unable to go ahead with the purchase of the new computing equipment because of an insufficiency of funds.* 由於資金不足，我們無法着手新電腦設備的購買。

need the fact of wanting or having to have something in order to do something, or the state of not having enough of essential things such as money, food, or health care（對基本生活物質的）需求；欠缺：*a charity that helps people in need in the poorest parts of the world* 為世界上最貧窮地區急需援助的人們提供幫助的慈善機構

poverty the state of having little money and few possessions, or a deficiency of something 貧窮；貧乏；缺乏：*If you don't want to live in poverty for the rest of your life, I suggest you start looking for a better-paid job.* 如果你不想貧困潦倒地度過餘生，我建議你着手找一份薪酬較高的工作。

scarcity the fact of not being widely available 稀缺；稀少：*There is a scarcity of bananas at the moment.* 目前香蕉供應短缺。

shortage the fact of having less of something, such as food or money, than you need（錢、食物等的）短缺，缺少：*a severe shortage of skilled workers* 技術工人的嚴重短缺

want the fact of being without something that is needed or desired, especially food or money（尤指食物或金錢的）短缺，缺少：*The people of the village are dying for want of food.* 這個村莊的居民因缺乏食物而生命垂危。

late *adjective* arriving, or happening, after the arranged or expected time 遲的；晚的：*I was late for school this morning.* 今天早晨我上學遲到了。

behind having made less progress than you should have 落後的；落伍的；跟不上的：*I'm a bit behind with my housework.* 我積壓了好些家務事。

belated arriving or happening later than the proper time 遲來的；延遲的；延誤的：*belated birthday greetings* 遲來的生日祝賀

last-minute done or arranged at the last possible moment and therefore obtaining a bargain 最後打折的，最後優惠的：*We are hoping to book a last-minute holiday.* 我們盼望着能預約一個最後打折的休假。

overdue having missed the proper date for some particular action 逾期的；延誤的：*Your library books are overdue.* 你從圖書館借的書逾了期。

tardy (*formal*) arriving, or happening, after the correct or expected time 遲來的；拖延的；拖拉的：*Our dinner guests are a little tardy.* 我們的晚宴客人姍姍來遲。

unpunctual arriving or taking action after the correct or expected time 不準時的；拖延的：*They tend to be unpunctual in paying their bills.* 他們往往是遲遲不付賬單。

➲ see also 參見 **dead**

laugh *verb* to make a sound in your throat because you are amused（因開心而）發出笑聲：*I could hear the children laughing merrily in the garden.* 我可以聽到孩子們在花園裏快樂的笑聲。

cackle to laugh in a loud unattractive manner 嘎嘎地笑：*a group of women cackling* 一群嘎嘎笑的婦女

chortle to laugh quite loudly at something that amuses you 高興地咯咯笑；開懷大笑：*'That's hilarious!' he chortles.* "那太滑稽可笑了！"他樂不可支地說。

chuckle to laugh quietly 低聲輕笑；輕聲地笑：*She sat, chuckling to herself, as she read her magazine.* 她坐着，一面翻看雜誌，一面獨自輕笑。

giggle to give a high-pitched childlike laugh（孩子般）咯咯地笑，尖聲地笑：*The girls started giggling and couldn't stop.* 女孩子們開始咯咯地笑個不停。

guffaw to give a loud deep laugh 哄然大笑；狂笑：*The men were guffawing with laughter at the comedian.* 男人們看到這喜劇演員的表演哄然大笑起來。

roar to give a loud deep hearty laugh（發自內心地）狂笑，放聲大笑：*The audience was roaring with laughter.* 觀眾哈哈大笑起來。

snigger to give a quiet mocking laugh（嘲諷地）竊笑，暗笑：*The rest of the class sniggered at Sam's mistake.* 班上其餘同學都偷偷地嘲笑薩姆的錯誤。

titter to give a high-pitched, embarrassed laugh 尖聲地笑；尷尬地笑：*Some of the children tittered nervously during the sex-education class.* 在性教育課上，一些孩子緊張地嗤嗤笑。

lazy *adjective* disinclined to work or to do anything energetic 懶惰的；懶散的：*She is too lazy to go to the gym.* 她太懶了，不可能去健身房。

bone-idle (*informal*) extremely lazy 極其懶惰的；懶到極點的：*He's bone-idle – his mother does everything for him.* 他懶透了，甚麼事情都是母親給他包了。

idle disinclined to work 懶惰的；遊手好閒的：*Get a move on, you idle layabout!* 趕快，你這個遊手好閒的傢伙！

inactive not doing anything, or not inclined to do much 不活動的；惰怠的；無所事事的：*I have had an inactive day today.* 我今天是無所事事。

indolent (*formal*) disinclined to do anything energetic 懶散的；懶惰的：*He was an incurably indolent and selfish teenager.* 他是一個無可救藥的懶散而自私的少年。

lethargic having little or no energy 無精打采的；無活力的：*I felt very lethargic after the flu.* 流感之後，我感到無精打采。

shiftless disinclined to work and having no motivation 沒志氣的；無進取心的：*a shiftless scrounger* 沒志氣的白食客

sluggish moving or progressing slowly and showing a lack of energy or drive 進展遲緩的；缺少活力的；懶洋洋的：*The housing market is usually very sluggish in winter.* 在冬季房產市場通常都很不景氣。

leader *noun* the person in charge of a group, an organization, or an activity 領導；領袖；負責人：*the leader of the Conservative Party* 保守黨領袖

boss (*informal*) your superior at work 老闆；上司；僱主：*I asked the boss for a rise.* 我要求老闆增加工資。

captain the leader of a team, especially in a sport, or the person who is in charge of a ship or an aircraft （尤指體育運動隊的）隊長；船長；機長：*The captain went up to receive the cup from the chairman of the Football Association.* 隊長走上前去領取足協主席頒發的獎盃。

chief the person in charge of a group of people 首領；領袖；頭目：*the chief of the tribe* 部落首領

head the person in charge of an organization 首長；首腦；領導：*the head of the company* 公司領導

manager the person in charge of a business firm or of a department 經理；經營者；管理人員：*the marketing manager* 市場部經理

principal the person in charge of a school, especially in the USA（尤指美國的）校長：*Go to the principal's office!* 到校長辦公室去！

ringleader the person at the head of a group of criminals or wrongdoers（罪犯或違法分子的）頭目，首惡，魁首：*Max was the ringleader of the bullies.* 馬克斯是惡霸頭目。

supremo (*informal*) the person with most influence or power in a particular organization or field of activity（某機構或活動領域的）最高權威，最高領導人，總管：*the Italian football supremo* 意大利足球掌門人

top dog (*informal*) the most important and influential person in an organization, usually the person in charge 居高位（或要職）者；老闆；當權者：*He's not happy being the top dog's deputy, he wants to be top dog himself.* 他不滿意當老闆的副手，他想自己當老闆。

learn *verb* to gather or receive information or knowledge, usually in a particular subject, into your mind, or to find out how to practise a particular skill 學習，學會（尤指某學科的知識或技能）：*I am learning to drive.* 我正在學開車。

absorb to take in information and store it in your brain 吸納，獲取（信息）: *Children absorb so much information in the first few years of their lives.* 小孩子在一生中的最初幾年裏獲取的信息非常多。

assimilate (*formal*) to absorb information and be able to understand it thoroughly（完全）吸收，消化；（徹底）理解，掌握: *They can repeat what the teacher told them, but have they really assimilated what they've been taught?* 他們可以重複老師教給他們的東西，但他們真正理解了嗎？

master to learn and understand a subject or a skill thoroughly 掌握，精通（學科或技能）: *I have mastered the art of playing the saxophone.* 我已經掌握了色士風的演奏技巧。

memorize to learn something so that it is stored in your memory and you can repeat it exactly in its original form 記住；熟記: *He only needs to see a number for a second to be able to memorize it.* 他只需看一眼數字就能記住它。

revise* to go back over all you have learnt about a subject in order to prepare for an examination or test（為準備考試）溫習，複習: *She's out playing tennis when she should be revising for her history exam.* 她本該溫習功課準備歷史考試，可她卻跑出去打網球。

* Only used in British English; the usual word in US English is review . 只用於英國英語，在美國英語中常用的詞是 review。

study to learn about a subject, especially at school, college, or university（尤指在學校）學習，研修: *Mohammed is studying aeronautics at university.* 穆罕默德在大學學習航空學。

swot (*informal*) to revise a subject for an examination（為準備考試而）苦讀，用功: *Bryony is swotting for her Modern Studies exam.* 布萊奧妮正用功讀書，為 "現代學" 考試做準備。

➲ see also 參見 **knowledge; understand**

lie *noun* an untrue statement that a person makes to deceive someone 謊言，謊話: *He told her he was single, but that was a lie.* 他告訴她自己是單身，但那是謊言。

falsehood (*formal*) an untrue statement 不實之詞: *Someone has been spreading falsehoods about me.* 有人一直在散佈關於我的不實之詞。

fib (*informal*) a lie that is not very serious（無關緊要的）謊言；小謊: *She told a tiny fib about her age.* 關於自己的年齡，她撒了個小謊。

perjury the crime of telling a lie when under oath in a court of law（法庭上的）偽證，偽誓；偽證罪: *The witness has been charged with perjury.* 那名證人被指控作偽證。

porky (pie) (*informal*) a lie 謊話；假話: *He's been found out telling porkies.* 他被查出編造謊言。

tall story a story that someone tells that is difficult to believe, usually because it contains improbably adventurous or romantic events 無稽之談；荒誕不經的故事: *My grandfather used to tell us tall stories about his adventures in India.* 我的祖父過去常向我們吹噓他在印度的歷險奇聞。

untruth (*formal*) an untrue statement 不實之辭；虛假情況：*The newspapers have been known to print untruths.* 眾人皆知這些報紙在刊登虛假消息。

white lie a lie that is told to spare someone's feelings（為不傷害他人感情而說的）善意的謊言：*When she told her friend she liked her new hairdo, that was just a little white lie.* 她對她的朋友說她很喜歡她的新髮型，其實那只是一個善意的小謊言。

whopper (*informal*) a blatant lie 彌天大謊；大謊言：*He said he had a private jet – what a whopper!* 他說他有一架私人噴氣式飛機，真是個彌天大謊！

light *adjective* not weighing much 輕的；不重的：*This bag is very light.* 這個包很輕。

buoyant light enough to float on air or in a liquid 有浮力的；（在空中或液體中）漂浮的：*a buoyant vessel* 一艘浮船

flimsy light and thin, and easy to tear or damage 輕薄的；脆弱的；易損壞的：*a dress made of flimsy material* 用輕薄織物做成的裙子

portable small and light enough to be carried about 輕便的；易攜帶的；便攜式的：*a portable television* 一台便攜式電視機

slight small and light in build（體型）瘦小的，纖弱的；輕微的：*Jockeys must be of slight build.* 賽馬騎師一定要體型瘦小。

underweight weighing too little relative to your height（相對於身高）體重過輕的，重量不足的：*underweight fashion models* 體重過輕的時裝模特兒

weightless weighing nothing 無重量的；失重的：*In space you are weightless because there is no gravity.* 因為沒有地球引力，人在宇宙中處於失重狀態。

list *noun* a series of items such as words, names, or numbers arranged in order, usually written down one below the other 名單；清單：*a shopping list* 一張購物清單

catalogue a long list showing all the items available in something, especially all the goods that you can buy from a firm（尤指商品）目錄，細目：*a mail-order catalogue* 郵購商品目錄

checklist a list of things to attend to, which you tick off as you do them 一覽表；核對表；清單：*I made a checklist of things I need to pack.* 我把需要打包的東西列了一張清單。

directory a list of details such as names, addresses, and telephone numbers 姓名地址錄；電話簿：*a telephone directory* 電話號碼簿

index an alphabetical list at the end of a book showing important items with relevant page numbers 索引：*Look up 'Second World War' in the index.* 在索引中查找"第二次世界大戰"。

inventory a complete list of the items that are in a place such as a flat or house that you are renting, or of the items that a person or business owns, or of the goods that a shop has to sell（所租房屋、個人或企業擁有的）財產清單；（商店的）存貨清單：*We made an inventory of the goods in stock.* 我們列了一份存貨清單。

menu a list of options to choose from in a restaurant or on a computer screen 菜單：*the lunch menu* 午餐菜單

register an official record of something, for example of births, marriages, and deaths or of when children attend school 註冊，登記：*The teacher takes the register every morning before classes begin.* 每天早晨上課前老師都要進行登記。

roll an official list of names and other details of people who are members of something or are entitled to vote（組織成員或選民的）花名冊，名單：*the electoral roll* 選民名冊

listen *verb* to concentrate so that you hear what someone says, music, the radio etc.（注意地）聽；傾聽：*I like to listen to CDs in the car.* 我喜歡在車上聽歌碟。

be all ears (*informal*) to listen very attentively（全神貫注地）聽；傾聽：'*Are you paying attention?*' '*Yes, go ahead – I'm all ears!*' "你在專心聽嗎？""是的，接着說吧，我在洗耳恭聽呢！"

bug (*informal*) to place a secret listening device in a room so that you can listen in to private conversations（在房間）裝竊聽器：*The politician discovered that his room had been bugged.* 那位政治人物發現他的房間被裝了竊聽器。

eavesdrop to listen secretly to a private conversation between other people 偷聽，竊聽：*If you eavesdrop on other people's conversations, you may well hear something you don't like.* 如果你偷聽別人談話，很可能會聽到一些令你不快的事。

hear to register a sound with your ears 聽見；聽到：*I heard a bang.* 我聽到一聲巨響。

overhear to hear by accident a private conversation between other people 無意中聽到；偶然聽到：*I overheard two girls criticizing my best friend.* 我無意中聽到兩個女孩在數落我最要好朋友。

pay attention to give your full attention to what someone is saying 專心地聽：*Are you paying attention at the back of the class?* 你坐在教室後面是在專心聽講嗎？

tap (*informal*) to place a secret listening device in a telephone so that you can listen in to private telephone conversations（在電話上）安裝竊聽器：*The police had tapped the suspect's phone.* 警方在嫌疑人的電話上安裝了監聽器。

long[1] *adjective* lasting for a considerable time 長時間的；長久的；長期的：*a long holiday* 長假

extended lasting for a longer time than usual 延長了的；延期的：*I'm taking an extended break from work.* 我正在休長假。

interminable lasting so long that it seems it will never end and becomes boring 無休止的；沒完沒了的：*an interminable rant about the government* 對政府無休止的責罵

lengthy lasting for a long time, often an inconveniently long time 漫長的；冗長的：*a lengthy wait at the bus stop* 在巴士站漫長的等待

lingering which does not finish quickly but continues slowly for a long time（長時間）逗留的；延期的：*a long lingering death* 漫長的拖延時日的死亡

prolonged lasting longer than planned or expected 延長的；拖延的：*a prolonged visit* 訪期延長了的訪問

protracted proceeding slowly and taking a long time, often an inconveniently long time 曠日持久的；長期的；拖延的：*protracted negotiations* 曠日持久的談判

sustained made to continue for a long time（長時間）持續的；持久的：*a sustained silence* 持久的沉默

time-consuming which takes up a lot of your time 耗時的；費時的：*Washing clothes by hand is very time-consuming.* 用手洗衣物很費時。

long² *extending* for a considerable distance, or for a specified distance 長距離的；長的：*It's a long way from here to London.* 從這裏到倫敦有很長一段路。

extensive extending for a considerable distance and over a wide area 廣闊的；廣大的；廣泛的：*a house with extensive grounds* 有寬敞庭院的房子

in length extending for the specified distance 長度為⋯的：*three metres in length* 長度 3 米

lengthy (*more often used to describe objects than distances*) quite long（常用於描述物體而非距離）相當長的，較長的：*You'll need a lengthy piece of rope to reach to the bottom of the well.* 需要一根較長的繩子才能到達井底。

look *verb* to direct your eyes towards something or someone 看；注視：*Look at this painting!* 看這幅畫！

gaze to look for a long time at someone or something, usually at something you find attractive or fascinating（長時間）凝視，注視（具有吸引力的人或物）：*We gazed at the majesty of the mountains.* 我們凝望着雄偉的山脈。

glance to look quickly or briefly at someone or something or in a particular direction 掃視；瞥見；匆匆一看：*I glanced back over my shoulder to make sure that no one was following me.* 我朝背後瞥了一眼，以確信沒有人在跟蹤我。

glare to look angrily at someone 怒目而視：*John glared at me when I mentioned his wife.* 我提到他妻子時，約翰憤怒地瞪着我。

ogle to look at someone in a way that expresses sexual attraction 送秋波，拋媚眼；色迷迷地看：*She is fed up with being ogled by strange men.* 她極其厭煩被陌生男人色迷迷地盯着看。

peep to have a quick look at someone or something 快速地看；瞥見：*She peeped at him through her fringe.* 她透過額髮瞥了他一眼。

scan to look at the whole of something, especially moving your eyes from side to side, either attentively or swiftly 瀏覽；掃視；審視：*She was anxiously scanning the newspaper to see if her name was mentioned.* 她急切地瀏覽着報紙，看自己的名字有沒有被提到。

stare to look for a long time at someone or something, usually at someone or something you find surprising or remarkable, and sometimes in a rude way（長時間地，有時指無禮地）盯着看，注視：*He could not help staring at her.* 他忍不住盯着她看。

➲ see also 參見 **see; watch**

loud *adjective* having a high level of sound 大聲的；高聲的：*a loud bang* 一聲巨響

blaring making an unpleasantly loud noise 刺耳的，喧鬧的：*The television is blaring.* 電視機發出刺耳嘈雜的聲音。

booming making a loud deep sound 隆隆作響的，（聲音）低沉有力的：*a booming loudspeaker* 發出轟轟聲的擴音器

deafening so loud as to cause temporary deafness 震耳欲聾的；聲音極大的：*a deafening racket* 震耳欲聾的喧鬧

ear-piercing very loud and high-pitched 高聲刺耳的：*an ear-piercing scream* 刺耳的尖叫聲

noisy making an unpleasantly loud sound 吵鬧的；嘈雜的；聒噪的：*a noisy party* 喧鬧的聚會

resonant loud and echoing 嘹亮的，洪亮的，迴響的：*the resonant sound of the church bells* 嘹亮的教堂鐘聲

shrill very loud and high-pitched （聲音）尖厲的；尖聲的：*the shrill screech of a bird* 鳥兒尖厲的鳴叫聲

strident loud and harsh 尖銳刺耳的：*a strident voice* 尖銳刺耳的嗓音

➲ see also 參見 **bold**

love *verb* to feel strong affection for someone or something, or a great liking for doing something 愛；熱愛；喜愛：*I love my parents very much.* 我深愛我的父母。

adore to feel deep love for someone or something 極為喜愛；愛慕：*She adores and looks up to her older sister.* 她愛慕並尊敬姐姐。

be crazy about (*informal*) to be deeply in love with someone 迷戀；癡迷；醉心於：*He is crazy about his new girlfriend.* 他對自己的新女友很癡迷。

be fond of to feel affection for someone or something 喜愛；喜歡：*They are very fond of their dog.* 他們特別喜歡他們的狗。

be infatuated with to feel very strongly attracted to and preoccupied with someone, but in a way that other people do not really approve of or think will last（在他人不看好的情況下）癡迷，迷戀（某人）：*Her husband is infatuated with one of his work colleagues.* 她丈夫迷戀上了一個同事。

care for to feel affection for someone 關心；關懷：*A friend is someone you care for and whose company you enjoy.* 朋友就是你關心並喜歡在一起的人。

dote on to love someone excessively, to a degree that other people think is foolish 寵愛；溺愛；過分喜愛：*They dote on their children to the point of spoiling them.* 他們對自己的孩子溺愛到了嬌慣的地步。

have a crush on (*informal*) to feel a strong, but not necessarily lasting, attraction for someone, especially someone older than you（尤指對比自己年長的人短暫地）迷戀，愛慕：*Natalie has a crush on her art teacher.* 娜塔莉迷戀上了她的美術老師。

worship to love someone very much, to the point of idolizing them 崇拜；仰慕；景仰：*Gerry absolutely worships his wife – she can do no wrong in his eyes.* 格里對妻子崇拜至極，在他的眼裏她不可能做錯任何事。

M

mad* *adjective* unable to understand reality and behave normally or sensibly, or showing a lack of understanding of reality and an inability to behave normally or sensibly 瘋的；瘋狂的；精神錯亂的：*He thought he was going mad.* 他覺得自己快要瘋了。

* It is not usual to describe people with a mental illness as mad when discussing their condition seriously. 在嚴肅談論精神病人的健康狀況時，通常不用 mad 來描述。

barking (*informal*) (*only used to describe people*) completely mad (只用於描述人) 完全發瘋的：*She's absolutely barking, but harmless.* 她完全瘋了，不過她不傷害人。

barmy (*informal*) mad or very foolish 瘋瘋癲癲的；傻裏傻氣的：*He's driving me barmy with all his silly ideas!* 他所有那些愚蠢的想法簡直要把我弄瘋了！

bonkers (*informal*) (*usually used to describe people*) mad (常用於形容人) 瘋狂的，精神不正常的：*Ollie is quite bonkers – you never know what he is going to do next.* 奧利瘋瘋癲癲的 —— 你永遠不知道他下一步要做甚麼。

crazy very foolish or peculiar, or (*informal*) mad 愚蠢的；怪異的；瘋狂的：*a crazy scheme* 一個瘋狂的計劃

demented mad and likely to behave violently or be uncontrollable active 狂亂的；發狂的；失常的：*We've been rushing round as if we were demented, trying to get everything ready in time.* 我們發狂般地東奔西走，試圖按時將一切都準備妥當。

insane having a serious mental illness, or (*informal*) mad 患精神病的；精神失常的；瘋的：*She went insane some years ago and has never fully recovered.* 她幾年前就精神失常了，到現在也沒有完全康復。

mentally ill suffering from a psychological condition that makes you unable to behave normally 患精神病的：*His wife became mentally ill and was confined to a hospital.* 他的妻子精神失常了，被關在醫院裏。

nuts (*informal*) very foolish or peculiar 發狂的；愚蠢的；怪異的：*My friends are all nuts, but they're great fun.* 我的朋友們都瘋瘋癲癲的，不過他們令人非常開心。

of unsound mind (*formal*) not well enough mentally to be considered legally responsible 精神失常的，心智不健全的 (因而無須負法律責任)：*He killed his wife while he was of unsound mind.* 他在精神失常的情況下殺死了妻子。

out of your mind (*informal*) mad 發瘋的；瘋狂的：*Are you out of your mind? This plan could bankrupt the company.* 你瘋了嗎？這個計劃有可能使公司破產。

make *verb* to form, build, or create something 製作；建造；創作：*The little girl made a birthday card for her mother.* 那小女孩給媽媽製作了一張生日賀卡。

assemble to build something, such as furniture or a model, by fitting the parts together 組裝，裝配 (傢具或模型等)：*I tried to assemble my new* *computer chair, but there was a screw missing.* 我試圖組裝我的新電腦椅，但有一個螺絲釘丟失了。

bring into existence to create, produce, or originate something, such as a plan or system 使 (計劃、制度等) 產生，建立 : *National Health Service was brought into existence in the UK in 1948.* 國民保健制度 1948 年在英國建立。

build to create a building or other structure using strong materials 建立；建造 : *We are having an extension built onto our house.* 我們在自己的住宅上進行擴建。

construct to build something, such as a structure or a vehicle 建設，建造 (建築物等結構體或車輛) : *The Empire State Building is constructed from reinforced concrete and steel.* 帝國大廈是用鋼筋混凝土建造的。

fabricate (*formal*) to produce or create something from different materials, especially in a factory (尤指工廠用不同的材料) 製造，製作 : *Dentures, crowns, and bridges are fabricated in a wide variety of materials.* 假牙、齒冠和齒橋是用各種不同的材料製造而成。

manufacture to produce or create goods in a factory, usually in large numbers (常指工廠大批量地) 製造，生產 : *I bought a beautiful chess set that was manufactured in Poland.* 我買了一副產自波蘭的精美的國際象棋。

produce to create or process something, sometimes in a factory (有時指在工廠) 生產，製造，加工 : *The distillery produces the finest single-malt whisky.* 這家釀酒廠生產最好的單一麥芽威士忌。

put together to build or create something from different parts or materials 把…組裝在一起；裝配 : *Ross put together a doll's house for his daughter.* 羅斯為她的女兒搭建了一座玩具房子。

➲ see also 參見 **build**¹

man *noun* an adult male human being 成年男子；男人 : *a big strong man* 強壯的大個子男人

bloke (*informal*) a man 男人；小子；傢伙 : *the bloke in the white T-shirt* 那個穿白色 T 恤衫的傢伙

boy a male child, or (*informal*) a man 男孩子；男青年；小伙子 : *a night out with the boys* 與男孩子們在外度過的夜晚

chap (*informal*) (*sounds slightly old-fashioned and upper-class; usually used to describe a man in an informal but fairly respectful way*) a man (上流社會對男子非正式而略顯過時的尊稱) 傢伙，伙計 : *a decent chap* 一個不錯的傢伙

dude (*informal*) a man, especially a fashionably dressed one (尤指穿着時髦的) 男人 : *a cool dude* 帥哥

fellow (*informal*) a chap 小伙子；傢伙 : *the little fellow* 那個小傢伙

gentleman a man with good manners, or a polite way of referring to a man 紳士；先生 : *Mr Thomson is a real old-fashioned gentleman.* 湯姆森先生是個真正的老派紳士。

guy (*informal*) a man 男人；傢伙；小子 : *He's a really nice guy.* 他是個真正的好小伙子。

male (*used in an impersonal way*) a man or boy (不用以指個人) 男性，雄性 : *a hairdresser for both males and females* 為男女都做頭髮的髮型師

many *adjective* a large number of 許多的：*many years ago* 多年前

countless too many to be counted 無數的；數不盡的：*I have asked you countless times to tidy your room.* 我已經無數次叫你把自己的房間收拾一下。

innumerable (*formal*) too many to be counted 無數的；多得數不清的：*on innumerable occasions* 在無數的場合

loads of (*informal*) a very large number or quantity of 大量的；許多的：*I've got loads of clothes that I will never wear again.* 我有一大堆永遠不會再穿的衣服。

lots of (*informal*) a large number or quantity of 許多的；大量的：*lots of presents* 許多禮物

numerous (*formal*) a very large number of 眾多的；不計其數的：*Numerous people have visited the exhibition.* 許多人參觀了這次展覽。

plenty a sufficiently large number or quantity of 大量的；充足的：*We have plenty of helpers for the jumble sale.* 我們有許多助手參與這次義賣活動。

several a fairly large number of 好幾個的；數個的：*I have several pairs of shoes to choose from.* 我有好幾雙鞋子可以挑選。

mean *adjective* unwilling to spend money or to give to others 吝嗇的；小氣的：*He is too mean to buy a round of drinks.* 他太小氣了，一巡飲料都捨不得買。

grasping excessively concerned with accumulating money and unwilling to spend it 一味攫取的；貪財的：*an unkind grasping man* 一個為富不仁的守財奴

miserly very unwilling to spend money 慳吝的；一毛不拔的：*She is too miserly to buy a poppy for Poppy Day.* 即使在為殘廢軍人募捐的罌粟花日，她也捨不得掏錢買一朵罌粟花。

niggardly (*formal*) parsimonious in character, or very small in amount 小氣的；少量的：*a niggardly amount* 少量

parsimonious (*formal*) unwilling to spend more money than is absolutely necessary 吝嗇的；過分節儉的：*a parsimonious old bachelor* 一個吝嗇的老單身漢

penny-pinching (*informal*) always looking for ways to save money and unwilling to spend it 小氣的；摳門的：*their penny-pinching ways* 他們吝嗇的生活方式

stingy (*informal*) mean 小氣的；摳門的：*Don't be so stingy – we're collecting for a good cause!* 別那麼小氣，我們是為正義事業募捐！

tight-fisted (*informal*) unwilling to spend money or to give to others 摳門的；小氣的：*He is too tight-fisted to buy Christmas presents.* 他太摳門了，聖誕禮物都捨不得買。

meet *verb* to be in the same place as someone, either by accident or by arrangement（偶然或通過安排）會面，見面：*We arranged to meet in the station at four o'clock.* 我們約好 4 點在車站見面。

bump into (*informal*) to meet someone unexpectedly 偶然遇見；碰見：*I bumped into my aunt in town today.* 今天我在城裏碰見了姑姑。

chance upon (*formal*) to meet someone or find something unexpectedly 偶然發現；碰巧遇到：*On holiday we chanced upon some old college friends.* 假期裏，我們偶然遇見了幾個大學的老朋友。

come upon (*formal*) to chance upon 偶然遇見；撞見：*Walking along the seashore, I came upon a crowd of children.* 在海濱漫步時，我撞見了一群孩子。

encounter (*formal*) to meet someone, usually unexpectedly（通常指出乎意料地）遇到，不期而遇：*Jane was shocked to encounter her ex-husband at the party.* 簡在晚會上意外遇到前夫，感到很震驚。

rendezvous to meet someone by arrangement at a particular time（在約定的時間）見面，會面：*One evening he led a patrol to rendezvous with another group of officers.* 一天晚上他帶領巡邏隊與另一隊警官在約定的時間會面。

run into (*informal*) to meet someone unexpectedly 偶然遇見；不期而遇：*I ran into my ex-boss at the conference.* 我在會上偶然遇見了我以前的老闆。

mercy *noun* the act of not punishing or not harming someone who is in your power 仁慈；寬恕；憐憫：*The guards showed no mercy to the prisoners.* 這些看守對犯人絲毫不講仁慈。

clemency (*formal*) the granting of a less severe punishment 寬恕；寬容；仁慈：*The judge rejected their plea for clemency.* 法官拒絕了他們寬恕的乞求。

compassion sympathy and understanding 同情；慈悲；憐憫：*She always treats people with kindness and compassion.* 她待人總是慈悲為懷。

forgiveness the act of excusing someone for some wrongdoing 寬恕；饒恕；原諒：*He begged his wife for forgiveness for his infidelity.* 他乞求妻子原諒自己的不忠。

humanity the quality of being kind and sympathetic to others 人性；仁愛；人道：*The hostages were treated with humanity at all times.* 這些人質一直受到人道的待遇。

kindness the quality of being gentle and helpful to others 善良；仁慈；體貼：*Thank you very much for your kindness and hospitality.* 非常感謝你的體貼和款待。

leniency treating someone less harshly than might have been expected 寬大；寬容；仁慈：*The head teacher showed leniency towards the boy because he was not a persistent troublemaker.* 這個男孩只是偶爾惹是生非，因此校長給予他寬大處理。

pity a feeling, or a show, of kindness towards someone who is suffering 可憐；同情；憐憫：*She took pity on the homeless man and gave him a hot meal.* 她十分同情這個無家可歸的男人，並給他吃了一頓熱飯。

sympathy understanding for someone's feelings, especially the feelings of someone who is suffering 同情；憐憫：*Barry's employers have shown him a great deal of sympathy since his wife died.* 巴里的妻子死後，他的老闆向他表達了極大的同情。

➲ see also 參見 **forgive**

mind *noun* the part of a person that has the power to think, make judgments, imagine, and produce ideas 頭腦；思想；智力：*He had one of the finest scientific minds of the 20th century.* 他是 20 世紀最傑出的科學家之一。

brain the organ of your body, located in your head, that controls your thoughts and bodily functions 大腦；頭腦 : *She has a brilliant brain.* 她有一個聰明的大腦。

brainpower capacity to think and reason 思維能力；智能；智力 : *Use your brainpower to solve the problem.* 用你的智慧來解決這個問題。

head your mind 頭腦；腦筋 : *You think everyone is against you, but it's all in your head.* 你覺得所有人都與你作對，但那只是你的一己之見。

imagination the ability to form mental images of things that you have never experienced 想像力；想像 : *I have never been to Japan, except in my imagination.* 我從未到過日本，只是在想像中去過。

intellect ability to think and reason 智力；理解力；推斷力 : *people of superior intellect* 有高智力的人

intelligence ability to learn, to understand, and to use information and knowledge to solve problems, especially strong ability 智力；才智；智慧 : *He has a keen intelligence.* 他有敏銳的智慧。

mentality a particular way of thinking (特定的) 思維方式；思路；心態 : *I just don't understand the mentality of people who desecrate graves.* 我簡直無法理解褻瀆填墓者的心態。

subconscious the part of your mind that works in ways that you are not conscious of 潛意識；下意識 : *Somewhere in my subconscious I must have been harbouring a resentment that I was not even aware of.* 在我的潛意識中一定懷有自己都不曾意識到的怨恨之情。

mistake *noun* an instance of doing something wrong 錯誤 : *You have made three mistakes in your maths exercise.* 你在數學練習中犯了 3 個錯誤。

bloomer (*informal*) an embarrassing mistake (令人尷尬的) 錯誤 : *I made a real bloomer – I called Eric's wife by the wrong name.* 我犯了一個令人啼笑皆非的錯誤，我把埃里克妻子的名字叫錯了。

blunder (*informal*) a stupid mistake (愚蠢的) 錯誤，大錯 : *Craig made a blunder, which cost the firm a lot of money.* 克雷格犯了個愚蠢的錯誤，使公司損失了一大筆錢。

clanger (*informal*) a stupid or embarrassing mistake (愚蠢或令人困窘的) 錯誤 : *What a clanger – Linda said the capital of Belgium was Amsterdam!* 多麼愚蠢的錯誤，琳達把比利時的首都說成了阿姆斯特丹！

error an instance of getting something wrong 差錯；誤差；錯誤 : *a typing error* 打印錯誤

faux pas (*formal*) an embarrassing social blunder (社交場合的) 失禮，失態，有失檢點 : *I made a terrible faux pas – I asked Margaret how her husband was, and he died last month!* 我太失禮了 —— 我詢問瑪格麗特丈夫的情況，可他上個月已經去世了！

gaffe (*formal*) an embarrassing mistake, especially a social blunder (尤指社交場合的) 失禮，失態，出醜 : *His first gaffe was to use the wrong cutlery at dinner.* 他第一次出醜是在晚餐上用錯了餐具。

inaccuracy an instance of not reporting a fact correctly 失真；不準確 : *There are several inaccuracies in this report.* 這個報道有多處失真。

omission an instance of missing out something that should have been included 遺漏；疏漏；疏忽：*This list is incomplete – there are at least four omissions.* 這個名單不完整，至少有 4 處遺漏。

mix *verb* to put two or more substances together and work on them so that they form one substance or cannot easily be separated again 混合，混雜（使成為一體）：*Mix a few drops of water into the icing sugar to make a smooth paste.* 用少量的水與糖粉混合，調勻成為糊狀。

amalgamate to bring two things, such as organizations, together to form one（指組織機構等）合併，聯合：*The two unions have amalgamated.* 這兩個聯盟合二為一了。

blend to mix ingredients or substances gradually together so that they form one substance（逐漸）混合，融合：*Blend the fruits and yogurt to make a smoothie.* 將水果和酸奶混合製成奶昔。

combine to come together or bring things together to make one thing 結合；聯合；混合：*Combine flour, butter, and milk to make a white sauce.* 將麵粉、牛油和牛奶混合製成白汁。

intersperse to include things at intervals or in separate places among another larger group of things 穿插；散置；點綴：*The essay was interspersed with quotations from other writers.* 這篇文章穿插引用了其他一些作家的雋語。

jumble to mix things up in a haphazard way 使混雜；使亂堆；使雜亂：*Everyone's trainers ended up all jumbled in a pile.* 所有人的運動鞋最後都亂糟糟地堆放在一起。

merge to join two things, such as businesses or pieces of text, together to make one whole thing（使公司或文稿等）併入，合併，結合：*I have merged the two lists into one alphabetical list.* 我將兩份清單按字母順序合併成了一份。

mingle to mix two or more things, such as feelings or smells, together, so that they are experienced at the same time（使各種感覺或氣味等）混合在一起，結合：*I felt excitement mingled with fear.* 我感到既興奮又害怕。

shuffle to mix up a pack of cards so that they end up in a different order 洗牌：*Always shuffle the cards before you deal.* 發牌前總是要先洗牌。

mockery *noun* the act of teasing or ridiculing someone by making hurtful or offensive comments about them or their actions 嘲笑；嘲諷；奚落：*He was just an object of mockery.* 他只是個別人嘲笑的對象。

contempt complete lack of respect, a feeling or behaviour that suggests that someone or something has no value 輕視；鄙視；蔑視：*The lord of the manor treated the servants with contempt.* 這個莊園主對僕人們不屑一顧。

derision the act of showing that you think that something is ridiculous 嘲弄；嘲笑；奚落：*The suggestion was met with shouts of derision.* 這個建議遭到陣陣嘲笑。

disdain dislike and disrespect 輕視；蔑視；嫌惡：*He continued to pursue her even though she treated him with complete disdain.* 儘管她很鄙視他，他仍舊追求她。

jeering the shouting of mocking remarks 嘲笑聲：*There was much jeering and booing from the crowd.* 人群中傳來陣陣嘲笑聲和噓聲。

ribbing (*informal*) the act of teasing someone in a friendly jokey manner 玩笑；戲謔；（善意的）揶揄：*There is always a fair amount of ribbing among the guys in the rugby team.* 橄欖球隊的球員們不時發出陣陣嬉笑聲。

ridicule the act of deliberately making someone appear foolish by laughing at them or making hurtful comments（故意的）嘲笑，奚落，中傷：*She was subjected to much ridicule in the media.* 她受到媒體的惡意中傷。

taunting saying something to someone with the aim of hurting their feelings or making them try to attack you 辱罵；譏笑；嘲弄：*She suffered taunting by bullies about being fat.* 她因肥胖而遭到小混混的譏笑。

modern *adjective* dating from or appropriate to the present time or the recent past 現代的；近代的：*modern literature* 現代文學

contemporary dating from, or being in the style of, the present time 同時代的；當代的：*contemporary art* 當代藝術

current taking place in or relating to the present time 正在發生的；現今的；當前的：*current events* 時事

new which has recently come into fashion or recently become available 新流行的；新近的；新的：*the new fitness craze* 最新流行的健身熱

new-fangled new and unnecessarily complicated 新奇的；（不必要地）複雜的：*a new-fangled device* 一種新奇的裝置

present-day relating to the present time 當今的；現在的：*present-day society* 當今社會

recent that has taken place in or relates to a time shortly before the present 近來發生的；最近的；新近的：*a recent development* 最近的發展

state-of-the-art using the most up-to-date technology 運用最新技術的，最先進的：*a state-of-the-art computer* 運用最新技術的電腦

up-to-date being the newest of its kind 最新的；新式的：*up-to-date technology* 最新技術

➔ see also 參見 **fashionable; new**

money *noun* coins and banknotes that you use to pay for things 錢；貨幣：*I have no money in my purse.* 我的錢包裏沒錢。

capital a large amount of money that you need to start up and run a business 資本；資金：*How can I raise capital to start a hairdressing business?* 我怎麼才能籌資開一家美髮店呢？

cash money in the form of coins and banknotes, rather than cheques, credit cards, etc. 現金；現鈔：*I'm sorry but I haven't got any cash on me at the moment.* 抱歉，此刻我身上沒帶現金。

change a small amount of money in the form of coins 零錢：*Do you have change for the bus fare?* 你有零錢買巴士車票嗎？

currency the type of money used in a particular country or area（某國家或地區通用的）貨幣：*The dollar is the main unit of currency in the USA.* 美元是美國的主要貨幣單位。

dosh (*informal*) money 錢：*He's got loads of dosh.* 他擁有大量金錢。

dough (*informal*) money 錢：*I've run out of dough.* 我把錢花光了。

filthy lucre (*informal and humorous*) money, especially thought of as something sinful or acquired by doubtful means（尤指來歷不明的）錢；不義之財；贓款：*He's moved to Spain to count his filthy lucre.* 他到西班牙清點他的贓款去了。

funds an amount of money saved or collected for a particular purpose（為特定目的籌集的）基金，專款，資金：*I don't have sufficient funds yet to finance a trip to Australia.* 我還沒有賺到足夠的錢去澳洲旅遊。

legal tender a banknote or coin that you can legally use to pay a debt in a particular country 法定貨幣：*I'm not sure that Scottish pound notes are accepted as legal tender in England.* 我不敢肯定蘇格蘭英鎊紙幣在英格蘭是否被接受為法定貨幣。

moving *adjective* causing you to feel strong emotion, especially sadness 令人感動的，感人的（尤指悲傷的感情）：*a very moving speech* 非常感人的演説

affecting causing you to feel strong emotion, especially sadness or pity 強烈情感的；深深打動人的（尤指悲哀或同情的感情）：*an affecting piece of music* 一段動人的音樂

emotional portraying, and arousing, strong emotion, such as sadness or joy 充滿感情的；動感情的；情感的：*an emotional performance* 一場動情的演出

heart-rending causing you to feel great sadness or pity 令人悲痛的；令人傷心的：*a heart-rending story* 令人心碎的故事

heart-warming causing you to feel happiness or satisfaction that something good has happened 令人高興的；使人滿意的：*It was a heart-warming moment in the film when the hero and heroine finally met up again.* 電影中男女主角終於又見面了，那是令人高興的時刻。

poignant causing you to feel strong emotion, especially sadness, regret, or longing 令人傷心的；痛悔的；深切的：*poignant memories* 傷心的回憶

stirring causing you to feel strong positive emotion, such as joy or patriotism 令人振奮的；令人激情澎湃的：*a stirring national anthem* 令人振奮的國歌

tear-jerking (*informal*) deliberately trying to move you to tears 催人淚下的：*a tear-jerking film* 一部催人淚下的電影

touching causing you to feel an emotion such as love, gratitude, or sympathy 動人的；感人的；令人同情的：*Her gratitude was quite touching.* 她的感激之情相當感人。

upsetting causing you to feel distressed or offended 令人心裏難受的；令人苦惱的：*It was upsetting to see the starving children in the news.* 看到新聞裏那些饑餓的兒童令人心裏難受。

➲ see also 參見 **affect²**

mysterious *adjective* strange and unexplained 神秘的；離奇的；無法解釋的：*a mysterious illness* 一種離奇的疾病

baffling very hard to understand or explain 令人費解的；使人困惑的：*His attitude was baffling.* 他的態度令人費解。

enigmatic intriguing and hard to understand 令人不解的；難以捉摸的：*The hero of the film is an enigmatic figure.* 電影中的男主人公是個難以捉摸的人物。

inexplicable unable to be explained 不能解釋的；無法説明的：*for some inexplicable reason* 因為某種無法解釋的原因

inscrutable hard to understand or identify 難以理解的；難以確定的：*an inscrutable facial expression* 難以捉摸的面部表情

mystifying extremely hard to understand or explain 大惑不解的；完全無法解釋的：*I find her hostility mystifying.* 我覺得她的敵意使人無法理解。

puzzling hard to understand or explain 疑惑的；迷惑的；困惑的：*a puzzling question* 令人疑惑的問題

unexplained for which an explanation has not been found 無法解釋的；莫名其妙的：*unexplained infertility* 原因不明的不孕

➲ see also 參見 **strange**

N

naive *adjective* having or showing a very simple and trusting view of the ways in which people behave towards one another, usually because you are inexperienced（通常指由於涉世未深而）天真的，輕信的，幼稚的：*In those days I was too naive to understand what was going on between them.* 當時我太幼稚，不清楚他們之間是怎麼回事。

artless not trying to be clever or sophisticated or to deceive people in any way, and so seeming either refreshingly direct or naive or unsophisticated 單純的；不諳世故的；不詭詐的：*In his artless way he seems to have got straight to the heart of the problem.* 他似乎已經毫不隱諱地觸及到了問題的實質。

credulous *(formal)* too easily and uncritically believing what people say, usually because you are unintelligent or foolish（通常指因愚笨而）輕信的，易受騙的：*Some people are so credulous that they believe anything that is written in the newspapers.* 有些人太容易上當，報紙上寫的任何內容都信以為真。

gullible very easy to deceive and too trusting 易上當的；易受騙的：*You surely don't think I'm gullible enough to fall for that old trick.* 你肯定認為我沒那麼容易上當，不至於連那樣的慣用伎倆都信以為真。

immature not behaving like an adult or having the understanding and judgment of an adult（行為、理解力、判斷力等）不成熟的，幼稚的：*He's twenty-one, but very immature for his age.* 他 21 歲了，但相對於他的年齡還是很幼稚。

ingenuous *(formal)* saying simply what you think or behaving simply in the way you think is right, without realizing that other people are not always so straightforward 坦率的；胸無城府的：*She was too ingenuous herself to* *realize that although other people might be thinking the same things that she was, they were too polite to put their thoughts into words.* 她自己太沒有城府了，意識不到別人可能和她所思略同，只是出於禮貌隻字不提罷了。

innocent not knowing how things are done in the world, especially not knowing about the unpleasant or even wicked ways in which people sometimes treat one another 天真無邪的；不諳世故的：*When it comes to money matters, he's as innocent as a new-born babe.* 談到錢方面的問題時，他單純得像個剛出生的嬰兒。

unsophisticated simple or crude, not clever or subtle in the way you deal with things 不諳世故的；單純的；質樸的：*Country people often seem very unsophisticated when compared with city dwellers.* 與城裏人相比，鄉下人常常顯得很質樸。

unworldly not knowing very much about how things are done in the real world or how people behave in society 不諳世事的；不善處世的：*Scholars sometimes seem unworldly because they spend more time in thinking up theories than in putting their theories into practice.* 學者們投入了大量的時間構想理論，卻疏於花工夫將理論付諸實踐，所以有時顯得不諳世事。

naked *adjective* not wearing any clothes 赤裸的；赤身裸體的：*Do you think he's ever actually seen his wife naked?* 你認為他真的見到過妻子赤身裸體嗎？

bare (*used to describe parts of the body or objects, areas, etc.*) without any covering (用以描述身體部位或物體、地區等) 裸露的，無遮蔽的：*Her arms and shoulders were bare.* 她的胳臂和肩膀都裸露着。

in the nude naked 裸體的；一絲不掛的：*Do you feel embarrassed about appearing on stage in the nude?* 你對赤身裸體登台亮相感到難為情嗎？

in your birthday suit (*informal*) naked 赤條條的；光腚的：*The children were running around in their birthday suits.* 這些孩子光着屁股四處跑着玩耍。

not decent (*informal*) not wearing enough clothes to feel comfortable about being seen by someone else, that is, usually, either naked or in your underwear (通常指赤裸或穿着內衣) 不好見人的；沒穿戴妥當的：*You can't come in – I'm not decent.* 你不能進來，我還沒穿好衣服。

nude (*usually used to describe people represented or appearing in works of art such as paintings, films, or plays*) naked (通常用以描述繪畫、電影或戲劇等藝術作品展現的人物) 裸體的：*a nude reclining figure* 一尊斜躺着的裸體塑像

starkers (*informal and humorous*) naked 赤裸的；光腚的：*They bet me £20 I wouldn't run down the street starkers.* 他們拿 20 英鎊賭我不會光着屁股在街上跑。

stark naked completely and usually dramatically naked 赤條條的；一絲不掛的：*There I was, stark naked, having just got out of the bath, when three armed policemen burst in.* 當時我剛出浴室，身上一絲不掛，3 名武裝警察突然闖了進來。

topless (*usually used to describe women*) with the top half of the body bare (通常用以描述女性) 袒胸露臂的，裸胸的：*topless waitresses* 袒胸露臂的女招待

undressed naked, in your underwear, or in the clothes you wear in bed 未穿衣服的（或只穿着內衣、睡衣的）：*I felt a bit embarrassed about having to* *open the front door while I was still undressed.* 我還沒穿衣服就不得不去開前門，感到有點難堪。

name *noun* a word that identifies someone or something（人或物的）名稱，姓名：*It was not 'borrowing' – let's call it by its right name, it was 'stealing'.* 這不叫"借"，我們確切地説吧，這叫"偷"。

designation (*formal*) a word used to describe something or someone, or the process of using a particular word to describe something or someone 稱號；稱呼：*The status and designation of 'Academy' was granted to the school in 1961.* 這所學校於 1961 年被授予"學院"的身份和稱號。

epithet a descriptive word or expression that is frequently added to substitute for the name of a thing or person 別名；別稱：*Homer almost always uses the epithet 'wine-dark' when he refers to the sea.* 荷馬提到大海時，幾乎總是用"深色葡萄酒"這一別稱。

label a word or expression commonly and often informally used to describe someone or something in addition to or in place of their real name（與真名合用或替代真名的）別號，綽號：*It was so small but so powerful that it soon acquired the label 'The Mighty Midget'.* 它那般渺小，卻又如此強大，很快得到了"強大的侏儒"這一美稱。

nickname a name used to refer to a person informally or humorously, which is often a shortened or modified form of their real name or refers to a habit or characteristic that they have 綽號，外號，諢名：*His nickname at school was 'Beans', because he loved to eat baked beans.* 他在學校的外號是"豆子"，因為他愛吃烘豆。

tag a label or nickname, especially an unflattering one（尤指不中聽的）稱呼，諢名：*I know the National Theatre's production of King John was rather slow, but did it really deserve the tag 'King Yawn'?* 我知道民族劇院的《約翰王》演出進展頗慢，但它真的堪稱"呵欠王"這一罵名嗎？

term a word or expression 説法；術語：*We don't call it a 'lawn-cutter'; the correct term is 'lawnmower'.* 我們不把它叫做"草坪切割機"，正確的名稱是"剪草機"。

title a word by which you address someone or refer to them and which shows their status, for example, Mr, Mrs, Dr, Lord, etc.（表明身份的）稱謂，頭銜：*She's actually Lady Daphne Shufflebotham, but she rarely uses her title.* 她實際上是達夫妮·夏夫波瑟姆夫人，但她很少使用這個頭銜。

necessary *adjective* that you need to have or to do, often in order to be able to do something else（常指為做其他事情所）必要的，必備的，必需的：*It may be necessary for you to prove that you can speak English, if you want to apply for a job in the USA.* 如果你想在美國申請一份工作，可能需要證明你會講英語。

compulsory that you must do, that you are given no choice about 義務的；強制性的；必須的：*Attendance at school is compulsory for all children aged between 5 and 16 who are not being educated at home.* 5 歲至 16 歲沒有在家裏接受教育的孩子都必須上學讀書。

essential extremely important, necessary, or relating to the basic nature of something 至關重要的；必要的；根本的：*Learning to cope with setbacks is an essential part of growing up.* 學會應付挫折是成長過程中不可或缺的一部分。

imperative* (*formal*) necessary and very important 迫切的；重要緊急的：*It is imperative that we act now to prevent the spread of the infection.* 我們現在的當務之急是行動起來，防止傳染擴散。

* Usually used after a verb. 通常用於動詞後。

indispensable that you cannot do without 必備的；不可缺少的：*Harmonious agreement between the member states is an indispensable condition for the European Union to work well.* 成員國之間協調一致是歐盟賴以成功運作的必備條件。

obligatory compulsory 義務的；義不容辭的；必須的：*The government is going to make it obligatory for anyone who wishes to continue driving after the age of 75 to retake the driving test.* 政府將強制規定 75 歲以上希望繼續駕駛的人必須重新考駕照。

required necessary, especially in order to comply with rules or instructions（尤指為遵守規定或指示）必須的；規定的：*Hamlet is required reading for anyone taking the Shakespeare course.* 《哈姆雷特》是選修了莎士比亞課程的學生必讀書目。

requisite (*formal*) required 必備的；必不可少的：*the requisite number of safety personnel* 必須配備的保安人員數

vital extremely important or necessary 至關重要的；必不可少的：*It is vital that this information should not fall into the wrong hands.* 最重要的是，這個信息不能誤入他人之手。

➲ see also 參見 **basic**

new *adjective* not used, owned, or known about before, or recently made, bought, discovered, etc. 新的：*You look very smart in your new suit.* 你穿着這套新西裝很好看。

fresh (*used to describe fruits, vegetables, etc., or cooked things*) recently picked or made and still in best condition; (*used to describe ideas, actions, etc.*) new, sometimes excitingly new, especially now replacing something that previously existed or was previously used and is no longer in best condition（用以描述果蔬、熟食等）新鮮的；（用以描述思想、行為等）新穎的：*The old methods can no longer solve our problems, what we need now is a completely fresh approach.* 這些老方法已經解決不了我們的問題了，我們現在需要的是一種全新的方法。

ground-breaking that does or investigates something that no one has done or investigated before, and makes new developments possible 開創性的；開拓的：*their ground-breaking work in microbiology* 他們在微生物學領域的開創性工作

innovative showing an ability to develop new ways of doing things 創新的；革新的：*In a time of rapid technological change, companies need to be innovative in the way they develop and market their products.* 處於科技高速發展的時代 公司在開發和營銷產品方面必須具有創新性。

novel new and rather unusual or surprising 新奇的；新穎的：*It's a novel way of earning a living, but at least she has no competition.* 這是一條新奇的謀生之道，但至少她沒有競爭。

original that nobody has thought of or done before, or that is not copied from anything or anyone else 首創的；獨創的；有創意的：*Your essay is rather short of original ideas.* 你的文章不太具有新意。

pioneering that is done before anyone else attempts to do the same thing 開拓性的；開創性的：*Their successes would have been impossible without the pioneering work done by their predecessors in the field.* 如果沒有他們的前輩在該領域的開創性工作，他們是不可能成功的。

➲ see also 參見 **modern**

news *noun* information about events that have recently happened 新聞；消息：*Now it's over to James for the rest of the day's news.* 現在由詹姆士報告今日要聞的其他內容。

announcement a written or spoken statement that gives a piece of information to the general public or a particular group of people for the first time (書面或口頭的) 公告，通告，通知：*The Prime Minister will be making an announcement of the date for the general election to Parliament shortly.* 首相不日將發佈議會大選的日期。

article a piece of writing, usually on a serious subject, in a newspaper or magazine (通常指報刊、雜誌中題材嚴肅的) 文章：*I read an article on the subject in today's Times.* 我在今天的《泰晤士報》上看到一篇有關這一話題的文章。

bulletin a news report on television or radio; an official statement giving information (電視、無線電的) 新聞報道，簡報：*In newspapers and television news bulletins around the world, the talk is all about the bombings.* 在世界各地的報紙以及電視新聞報道中，談論的話題都是關於這些轟炸事件的。

headline a statement in large print at the top of a newspaper article or report telling you in a few words what the article or report is about, especially a statement on the front page announcing the main news of the day (報紙的) 大字標題；(尤指) 頭版頭條：*Under the headline GAS BUBBLE BURSTS, the Daily Herald reports on financial problems in the gas industry.* 《每日先驅報》以 "氣泡爆破" 為頭版頭條，報道了煤氣業的財政困難。

message a usually short, written or spoken statement containing news or information, which is intended to be passed on to a particular person or group of people (通常指簡短的) 信息，口信，便條：*He left you a message to say that he wouldn't be able to come to the meeting this evening.* 他給你留了口信，說他今晚不能來開會。

report a written document or spoken statement that is quite long and provides detailed news, information, or discussion of a particular topic 報告；報道：*A report has just come in from our correspondent in Baghdad on the results of the general election in Iraq.* 我們駐巴格達的通訊記者剛發來一份關於伊拉克大選結果的報道。

story an event that the media believe is worth reporting, or an account of an event given in a newspaper or as an item in a news broadcast (報紙、新聞廣播等媒體的) 報道題材，報道：*The story first appeared in the York Evening News and was then taken up by the national newspapers.* 這則報道首現於《約克新聞晚報》，然後被國內各大報紙轉載。

tidings (*old-fashioned*) news 消 息； 訊 息 : *When the king heard the glad tidings, he rejoiced.* 國王聞此喜訊，大悅。

word news or information, especially reported orally by someone 消息；（尤指）傳聞，謠言 : *There's been no word yet on when the wedding will actually take place.* 婚禮究竟何時舉行，現在還沒有消息。

➲ see also 參見 **information**

nice¹ *adjective* (*used to describe things, events, etc.*) arousing generally positive feelings in you, giving you enjoyment or pleasure, or that you like（用以描述事情、活動等）使人高興的，令人愉快的 : *Did you have a nice time at the party?* 晚會上你玩得開心嗎？

agreeable arousing generally positive but not particularly strong feelings, quite pleasant or appealing 使人愉快的；愜意的 : *She found the sea air very agreeable.* 她感覺大海的氣息沁人心脾。

appealing causing you to wish to have it or do it, attractive 吸引人的；令人心動的 : *The idea of not having to get up very early in the morning is very appealing.* 不必一大早就起牀的想法很令人心動。

delightful arousing strongly positive feelings, very pleasant 可喜的；令人開心的 : *How delightful to see you again!* 又見到你了，多好啊！

enjoyable that you enjoyed or can enjoy 令人快樂的；有樂趣的 : *Thank you for this evening: it's been most enjoyable.* 感謝你們舉辦了這場晚會，它讓人非常開心。

good arousing quite strong positive feelings, pleasant or enjoyable, or beneficial 好的；愉快的；有益的 : *I hope you had a good holiday.* 我希望你過了一個愉快的假期。

lovely very pleasant or beautiful 美好的；漂亮的 : *Wouldn't it be lovely if we never had to worry about money ever again!* 如果我們再也不用為錢犯愁，那豈不美哉！

pleasant that gives you pleasure, or makes you feel comfortable and relaxed 令人愉快的；舒適的；合意的 : *It brings back very pleasant memories of my youth.* 它勾起我對青年時期的美好回憶。

nice² *adjective* (*used to describe people*) kind and friendly（用以描述人）友好的，和藹的 : *Be nice to him, because he's not feeling very well.* 因為他感到身體不太舒服，所以對他和氣一點吧。

agreeable friendly and pleasant 友好的；和藹的；討人喜歡的 : *We invited some of our more agreeable neighbours in for a New Year's party.* 我們邀請了幾家比較要好的鄰居到家裏來舉辦新年聚會。

amiable friendly and pleasant to be with, or which makes someone friendly and pleasant to be with 和藹可親的；親切的 : *Our new neighbour seems to be a very amiable sort of man.* 我們的新鄰居像是一個非常和藹的人。

charming having a natural talent for making people like you or feel at ease with you 迷人的；可愛的 : *I expected him to be rather formidable, but he's actually a very charming man.* 我原以為他很令人敬畏，可實際上他挺招人喜歡。

delightful having qualities such as friendliness and good nature that you appreciate very much（因友好和性情溫和而）可愛的，討人喜歡的 : *They're a* *very nice couple, and their children are absolutely delightful.* 他們是一對恩愛夫妻，他們的孩子也非常討人喜歡。

friendly showing that you like someone or that you want them to feel happy and at ease 友好的；友誼的：*a friendly gesture* 友好的手勢

genial friendly and good-natured, especially making people feel relaxed and welcome 和藹可親的；平易近人的：*our genial host* 我們熱情好客的主人

good-natured likely to treat people kindly and not likely to become angry or unfriendly 和善的；性情溫和的：*She's too good-natured to take offence.* 她性情非常溫和，從來不生氣。

likable that is easy to like, or that makes you like someone 可愛的；討人喜歡的：*That is one of his less likable characteristics.* 那正是他不怎麼討人喜歡的特點之一。

O

obedient *adjective* doing what someone tells you to do without questioning their instructions or arguing with them (對某人的吩咐、指示等) 聽從的，服從的：*If all the children were as obedient as she is, the class would be much easier to manage.* 如果每個孩子都像她那樣聽話，這個班管理起來就容易多了。

amenable likely or willing to accept something such as advice, persuasion, or a suggestion (對勸告、勸說或建議等) 順從的，服從的：*They might be more amenable if you offered to repay their expenses.* 如果你提出給他們報銷開支，他們會更順從你。

compliant (*formal*) accepting orders or instructions, or fulfilling obligations, standards, etc., set by someone else (對命令、指示或他人制定的職責、標準等) 遵從的，依從的：*Inspectors check whether restaurant owners maintain standards of cleanliness compliant with regulations under the Health and Safety Act.* 稽查員檢查飯店的老闆是否遵照《衛生與安全法》的規定堅持衛生標準。

docile having a quiet, placid nature and so unlikely to protest or disobey 溫順的；馴良的：*He's a very docile dog – he lets the children climb all over him.* 牠是一條很聽話的狗，讓這些孩子在牠身上爬上爬下。

dutiful conscious of a duty to obey someone, especially your parents (尤指對父母) 恭順的，孝敬的：*a dutiful daughter* 一個孝順的女兒

law-abiding who does not break the law or cause trouble for the authorities 守法的：*The majority of the people in this area are ordinary law-abiding citizens.* 該地區的人大多數都是遵紀守法的普通百姓。

submissive obedient in a way that shows you are humble and acknowledge that others are superior to you or more powerful than you 卑躬屈膝的；唯命是從的：*submissive to the will of the Lord* 遵從上帝的意志

subservient excessively obedient and humble because you want to please people who are superior to you or more powerful than you 屈從的；低聲下氣的；俯首帖耳的：*A good servant knows how to be respectful without being subservient.* 一個好的僕人知道如何做到不卑不亢。

obscure *adjective* difficult to understand through being unclear or through involving knowledge that is not easily available or that not many people possess (由於含混不清或包含深奧的知識而) 晦澀的，費解的：*The meaning of this note is obscure.* 這條註解的意思晦澀難懂。

abstruse (*formal*) very difficult to understand usually because it involves knowledge that very few people possess or very complex ideas (通常指由於包含深奧的知識或複雜的概念而) 深奧的，難解的：*abstruse philosophical arguments* 深奧的哲學觀點

as clear as mud (*informal*) very difficult to understand, usually through not being clearly thought out or expressed (通常指由於思路或表達不清而) 令人費解的：*Can you understand these instructions? They're as clear as mud to me.* 你能看懂這些使用說明嗎？它們對我來說就像一本糊塗賬。

cryptic containing a secret or hidden meaning 含義隱晦的；撲朔迷離的：*The text contains a few brief and cryptic references to the legend.* 正文有幾處簡略而含糊地提到該傳説。

esoteric (*formal*) very obscure and very specialized or secret, often able to be understood or known about only by people who have been given the secret by others who already know it 只有內行才懂的；秘傳的：*Some of their beliefs are esoteric, and ordinary worshippers are kept in ignorance of them.* 他們的有些信仰是秘傳的，普通信徒全然不知。

impenetrable (*formal*) impossible to understand 令人費解的：*If it's impenetrable to someone who knows as much about the subject as Rose, how is the ordinary person supposed to understand it?* 如果它讓像露絲這樣洞悉該領域的人都感到費解，怎麼能要求普通人領會它呢？

recondite (*formal*) that few people possess or know about 艱深的；鮮為人知的：*recondite knowledge* 深奧的知識

unclear not easy to understand or be certain about, usually through containing an element of confusion (通常指由於含有混淆成分而) 含糊的，不清楚的：*It's unclear whether she intended this letter to be read before or after her death.* 現在還不清楚她是想讓人在她生前看這封信還是死後翻看。

observe *verb* to show that you accept something such as a law or rule by doing what it tells you that you must do 遵守，遵照 (法律、規章等)：*Drivers who fail to observe the speed limit can expect to be fined.* 不遵守限速規定的司機可能會被處以罰款。

abide by to accept and obey something such as a decision or a rule 遵守，服從 (決議、規章等)：*We agreed to abide by the referee's decision.* 我們同意服從裁判的裁定。

adhere to (*formal*) to act in accordance with something 堅持；遵守：*We adhered strictly to the terms of the contract.* 我們嚴格遵照合同的各項條款。

conform to to be as something such as a rule or standard says it or you ought to be 符合，遵照 (規章、標準等)：*Does this machinery conform to European safety standards?* 這機器符合歐洲的安全標準嗎？

follow to do what something tells you to do, especially when you are given a series of instructions 遵從，遵循，按照 (一系列的指示説明)：*I followed the* *recipe exactly, but the dish still didn't turn out right.* 我完全是按菜譜做的，可是這道菜還是沒做好。

keep to act in accordance with something, often a rule or an obligation that you have made for yourself 履行，踐行（規章或義務等）: *He promised to be here by seven o'clock, but, of course, he seldom keeps his promises.* 他答應 7 點前到這兒，可是，當然啦，他很少說話算話的。

obey to do what someone, or something such as a law, rule, or order, tells you that you must do 服從，遵守（法律、規章或命令等）: *Would you obey an order from a superior officer even if you knew the order was wrong?* 即使你知道長官的命令有錯，你也會服從嗎？

respect to show that you accept something such as the law or people's rights and do not wish to act in a way that breaks it or interferes with it 尊重（法律或他人的權利等）: *I respect your right to say what you like on any subject, but that doesn't mean I have to agree with what you say.* 我尊重你在任何問題上暢所欲言的權利，但那並不說明我必須同意你的觀點。

⊃ see also 參見 **say; watch**

old *adjective* having lived or been in existence for a long time, or for a specified period of time, usually a specified number of years 老的；古老的；（年齡）大的: *I think you're old enough now to walk to school on your own.* 我覺得你現在已經長大，可以自己走路去上學了。

aged* (*often humorous*) (*usually used to describe people*) old or very old（通常用以描述人）年老的，上了年紀的: *She has to spend a lot of time looking after her aged parents.* 她不得不花大量的時間照顧她年事已高的父母。

* Usually used before a noun. 通常用於名詞前。

ancient (*usually used to describe objects such as buildings or cities*) very old, and usually attractive or interesting through being very old（通常用以描述建築物或城市等）古老的，悠久的；古代的: *an ancient manuscript* 一部古代手稿

antiquated (*usually used to describe objects*) very old-fashioned, completely out of date（通常用以描述物體）陳舊的，過時的，被廢棄的: *antiquated ideas* 陳舊保守的觀念

elderly (*usually used to describe people and thought of as more polite than old*) quite old or old（通常用以描述人，被認為較 old 更禮貌）上了年紀的，年長的: *Most of the residents of these flats are elderly people living on small incomes.* 這些房子裏的大多數住戶都是靠低收入生活的年長者。

middle-aged (*usually used to describe people*) no longer young, usually aged between 40 and 60（通常用以描述人）中年的: *I hate the music that my children listen to, so I must be getting middle-aged.* 我不喜歡兒女們聽的音樂，我一定是步入中年了。

old-fashioned not modern, of a kind commonly used in an earlier time, or (*used to describe people*) behaving or thinking in a way associated with an earlier time 老式的；（用於描述人）守舊的: *He still has an old-fashioned telephone with a dial.* 他現在還有一部帶撥號盤的老式電話。

out-of-date/out of date not modern or fashionable any more, though often only recently having become so 過時的；不再時新的: *I only bought this* *computer three years ago, and it's already out of date.* 我買這台電腦的時間僅僅是在 3 年前，可現在已經過時了。

past its sell-by date (*informal and humorous*) out-of-date or old-fashioned 過期的；過時的：*That joke really is past its sell-by date now.* 那種玩笑現在真的已經不時興了。

past your/its prime no longer young or modern, past the period of being at your/its best 已過盛年的；過了最佳時期的：*She may be a little past her prime, but she's still a very good player.* 她可能略微超過了巔峰期，但仍然還是一名很優秀的選手。

senile (*usually used to describe people*) old and suffering from mental and physical problems that reduce your ability to think, understand or remember things, or look after yourself（通常用以描述人）年老體衰的：*I know who Madonna is, I'm not senile yet!* 我知道麥當娜是誰，我還沒有老態龍鍾！

opinion *noun* an idea or statement that expresses what a particular person or a particular group of people thinks or feels about a subject 意見；看法：*Nothing I've heard so far makes me want to change my opinion that this is a thoroughly bad idea.* 這是一個糟透了的主意，至今我聽到的任何意見還不能讓我想改變這種看法。

attitude the general way a particular person or group of people thinks and feels about something or someone, often shown in the way they behave towards them（常指對人或事物表現出來的）態度，看法：*Your attitude to life changes as you get older.* 你對生活的態度隨着年歲的增長而改變。

belief something that a person believes to be the case 信念；看法：*It's my belief that the victim knew his killer.* 我的看法是，受害者認識兇手。

conviction something that a person is convinced about, or a feeling of certainty about something 信念；確信：*Nothing seems to be able to shake her conviction that someone is following every time she goes out.* 她深信每次外出都有人跟蹤，似乎甚麼都動搖不了她的這一想法。

feeling an impression or opinion, often one that is not entirely clear or that you are not entirely convinced about（常指不太清晰或不太確定的）感覺，印象：*It's just a feeling; I don't have any evidence to support it.* 這只是一種感覺，我還沒有任何證據來證明。

impression an idea that arises from the effect that someone or something has on you 印象；感想：*I got the impression that she knows rather more than she's willing to say.* 我看得出她知道很多，只是不願意多説。

point of view a way of thinking about a subject that results from your particular nature, experiences, and opinions（由特定性情、經歷或意見產生的）觀點，看法：*Try to understand the point of view of the person who is arguing against you.* 要盡量理解你的反對者的觀點。

stance an opinion, or a point of view on a subject, especially one that is deliberately adopted and made public（尤指慎重採取或公之於眾的）觀點，立場，姿態：*There's no sign that the government is likely to change its stance on the question of immigration.* 沒有任何跡象表明政府可能改變對移民入境問題的立場。

view an opinion 觀點；見解：*We all know your views on religion.* 我們都知道你對宗教的見解。

➲ see also 參見 **advice; feeling**

oppose *verb* to disagree with something or someone, and to try to stop something happening or to stop someone doing what they wish or plan to do 反對；阻止；抗拒：*The union will oppose any attempt by the management to increase the working hours of the staff.* 工會將阻止管理層延長職工工作時間的任何企圖。

be against not to be in favour of, or to disapprove of, something 反對；不贊成：*I've always been against capital punishment.* 我始終反對死刑。

confront to show your disagreement with, or opposition to, someone boldly, usually by meeting them face to face（通常指當面公然）對抗，對立：*She decided she was going to confront her boss and ask him to explain his behaviour.* 她決定要與老闆針鋒相對，並要求他對其行為進行解釋。

defy to be bold and determined in refusing to obey someone or something or in challenging someone to do something 公然反對；違抗：*They defied the Security Council and continued with their nuclear programme.* 他們藐視安理會，繼續實施核計劃。

object to be against something, usually because you feel it is wrong or not in your interest, and express your opposition to it（通常指由於認為不對或不感興趣而）反對：*Nobody objected when the Council originally announced its plan to demolish the building.* 政務會最初宣佈拆毀該建築物的計劃時，沒有人表示反對。

resist to take action to defend yourself against someone who is attacking you, or to stop something being done to you 抵抗，反抗（攻擊者或傷害行為等）：*The citizens of the country united to resist the invaders.* 全國的老百姓團結起來共同抵抗侵略者。

stand up to to refuse to be intimidated by someone who is threatening you 勇敢面對，抵抗（威脅者）：*Most bullies are actually cowards, and if you stand up to them, they'll leave you alone.* 多數歹徒實際上都是懦夫，如果你勇敢面對他們，他們就不會惹你。

take issue with to disagree with and argue against something or someone, usually in a polite way（通常指禮貌地）反對，持有異議：*I'd like to take issue with you on that point.* 我在那一點上不敢與你苟同。

➲ see also 參見 **conflict; disagree; fight; quarrel**

order *noun* a spoken or written statement that tells you that you must do something, usually made by someone who has authority over you（上級下達的口頭或書面的）命令：*The colonel gave orders for the regiment to prepare to launch an attack.* 上校下令團部準備發動進攻。

command a spoken order given directly to someone especially by a military officer, or an instruction to a computer to perform a task（尤指軍官的口頭）命令；（電腦操作的）指令：*On the command 'present arms', you will hold your weapon vertically in front of your body.* 一聽到"舉槍致敬"的命令，你就立刻將武器豎握在胸前。

commandment an order or instruction, especially a religious or moral instruction（尤指宗教或道德上的）戒律：*the Ten Commandments* 十戒

decree an official command, especially one issued by the ruler of a country （尤指國家統治者正式頒佈的）王令，政令，敕令：*The decree authorizes the army to take control in an emergency.* 政令授權軍隊在非常時刻採取軍事管制。

demand a request made in a forceful way（迫切的）要求：*If we give in to their demands, they'll ask for even higher wages.* 如果我們答應他們的要求，他們會要更高的工資。

dictate what something such as reason or conscience tells you ought to do （理智、良心等的）支配，要求：*the dictates of conscience* 良心的支配

directive an official instruction given by a non-military organization（ 非軍事機構正式頒佈的）指令，指示：*Head office has issued a directive on the recycling of waste.* 總公司下發了關於廢物回收的指示。

instruction a statement that tells you what you should do or how you should do something（告訴操作內容或方法的）說明，指令：*First read the instructions for setting up the computer.* 首先請閱讀電腦的安裝說明。

request an instance of asking someone to do something 要求；請求；懇求：*We've had a lot of requests from people for us to play this record.* 我們收到了很多份請求，要我們播放這張唱片。

➲ see also 參見 **organize²; rule**

ordinary *adjective* not special, of the kind that people use or experience most often 平常的；普通的；平凡的：*It started out as just an ordinary day.* 剛開始時完全同平日一樣。

average considered as being representative of what most people, things, etc., are like or do, or being at the midpoint between two extremes 平均的；一般的；普通的：*How many cups of coffee do you think the average person drinks in a day?* 你認為一般人一天喝多少杯咖啡呢？

common often seen, done, or experienced 常見的；普遍的；常有的：*It's common nowadays for young people to take a gap year between leaving school and going to university.* 現在年輕人讀完中學後，時隔一年再去上大學是常有的事。

conventional* (*used to describe a method or object*) that is usually used or has been used for a long time; (*used to describe people*) following the normal behaviour and opinions of most people（用以描述方法或事物）常規的，慣例的，習俗的；（用以描述人）傳統的：*Complementary medicine differs from conventional medicine.* 輔助療法與常規療法是不一樣的。

* Only used before a noun. 僅用於名詞前。

everyday* that is seen, used, done very frequently 日常的；平常的：*Artists often try to make people see everyday objects in a new light.* 藝術家常常努力讓人們以新的視角看待日常事物。

* Only used before a noun. 僅用於名詞前。

normal usual or average, especially reassuringly familiar or setting a standard by which you judge that things are different or wrong（尤指）正常

的，標準的：*Temperatures during the day will be around normal for this time of the year.* 今天的溫度將徘徊在一年這時期的正常溫度。

regular* normal 正常的；常規的：*We're just regular people, nothing special.* 我們只是常人，沒甚麼特別的。

* Used more in US English than British English. 多用於美國英語，而非英國英語。

routine very ordinary, not interesting or exciting 平常的；日常的；平凡的：*Computers are good at handling routine tasks.* 電腦善於處理日常工作。

standard ordinary, not having any special features, or being what everybody does or what rules say should be done 通常的；規範的：*It's standard procedure these days to ask for some form of identification before you allow anyone to enter the building.* 目前規範的手續是，在允許任何人進入大樓之前，要求對方提供身份證明。

typical having the characteristics that most things or people of a certain kind possess, or exactly what you would expect of something or someone 典型的；有代表性的：*A typical day in the office begins within an informal meeting of all the staff to make plans, discuss problems, and set targets.* 在辦公室上班，一般每天開頭都有一個非正式的全體員工會議，要制定計劃、討論問題以及設立目標。

usual of the kind that you are familiar with and expect to happen, most often do, etc. 通常的；慣常的：*On that particular day I decided not to walk to work by my usual route.* 正好在那天，我決定不走老路去上班。

organize¹ *verb* to plan something and make the necessary preparations for it to be carried out 組織；籌備：*We're organizing a trip to Stratford-on-Avon for members of the drama club.* 我們正為戲劇社的成員組織一趟莎士比亞故鄉之旅。

arrange to do what is necessary, such as making plans and getting other people to agree to them, to make sure that something happens (指事先通過制定計劃或徵求他人同意等) 安排，籌辦：*I've arranged for a taxi to pick you up from the hotel at seven o'clock.* 我已安排計程車 7 點鐘到酒店接你。

coordinate to make sure that plans or arrangements made by a number of different people work together and do not interfere with one another 協調，配合 (計劃或安排等)：*Your job is to coordinate the efforts of the various departments to improve productivity.* 你的工作是協調各部門的努力，以提高生產力。

deal with to take responsibility for organizing or doing something (負責) 處理，應付：*I'll deal with the financial side of things, and you concentrate on artistic matters.* 由我來處理資金方面的事情，你集中解決藝術方面的問題。

fix (up) (*informal*) to arrange something 打理；安頓：*I've fixed it so that we can pick up the tickets from the theatre box office.* 我已經打理好了，這樣我們就能從劇院票房買到票了。

look after (*informal*) to deal with something 料理，處理：*Who's looking after transport for the delegates to and from the conference hall?* 誰在負責代表們往返會議大廳的交通問題？

make arrangements to arrange something 安 排； 佈 置： *We've made arrangements to meet outside the station at 6.30.* 我們已經約好 6 點半在車站外面碰頭。

see about (*informal*) to take responsibility for doing or getting something 料理；辦理；安排：*Could you see about some chairs for the people who arrived late?* 你能為遲到的人安排一些椅子嗎？

see to (*informal*) to deal with 處理；辦理；料理：*That's being seen to by the cleaning staff.* 那事正由清潔工處理。

organize² *verb* to put things into a state where they are not confused or untidy and have a logical order 佈置，整理（以使清晰、整潔或有條理）：*Could you help me organize these files?* 你能幫我整理一下這些文檔嗎？

arrange to put something into a particular order, shape, or pattern 排列，佈置（以使形成某種順序、形狀或圖案等）：*We arranged the chairs in a circle.* 我們將椅子擺了一圈。

classify to decide what kind of thing something is and put it together with other things of the same kind 分類：*This book is partly fact and partly science fiction, so it's rather difficult to classify.* 這本書既有真實的內容，又有科幻的成分，所以很難歸類。

order to arrange things in a particular sequence or according to a particular system（按特定序列或體系）整理，排列：*Probably the best plan is to order the entries alphabetically.* 或許最好的方案就是將這些詞條按字母順序排列。

put in order to make something tidy, or to order something 整理，佈置（以使整潔或有序）：*We'll start by putting the room in order.* 我們將把房間佈置好。

sort to divide up a number of things into different groups according to what kind of things they are 分類；揀選：*I've sorted your letters into three piles – 'deal with now', 'deal with tomorrow' and 'deal with next week'.* 我已把你的信分成了 3 堆，即"現在處理"、"明天處理"和"下週處理"。

sort out to organize things, especially to put things that are in a confused state into order 整理，清理（尤指混亂的東西）：*It's going to take ages to sort out the mess left by my predecessor.* 我的前任留下的亂攤子要很長時間才能理順。

own *verb* to be in possession of something 擁有：*Do you own your home or is it rented?* 房子是你自己的，還是租來的？

boast to possess or to have achieved something impressive 擁有，獲得（重大事物等）：*The city boasts two cathedrals.* 這座城市擁有兩座天主教堂。

enjoy to be fortunate enough to have something, especially something abstract 享有（尤指抽象事物）：*My mother had always enjoyed good health until she reached her seventies.* 我母親 70 歲之前一直享有健康的身體。

have to be the owner of something 有；擁有：*My parents have a holiday home in Spain.* 我的父母在西班牙有一處度假別墅。

hold to be in possession of something, for example official documents 擁有，持有（如官方文件等）：*Do you hold a current European passport?* 你持有通用的歐洲護照嗎？

keep to continue to have possession of something, sometimes because it is of sentimental value to you (有時指因為有情感價值而) 保存，留存：*Derek keeps the ticket stubs from all the football matches he goes to.* 德里克把他看過的所有足球賽的門票存根都保留下來。

maintain (*formal*) to have possession of or the use of something, such as a vehicle or a home 保養，供養 (車輛或房屋等)：*The family maintains two cars.* 這家人供養着兩輛汽車。

possess to be the owner of something 佔有；擁有：*Sarah possesses fifty pairs of shoes.* 莎拉有 50 雙鞋子。

retain to keep something in your possession 保留；保存：*Please retain your receipt in case you need to return your purchases.* 請留存收據，以備退貨之用。

P

pain *noun* an unpleasant feeling or state that hurts you, which may be physical, caused by an injury or an illness, or may be mental, caused by an event that makes you feel sad (由傷口、疾病等生理原因或傷心事等心理原因引起的) 疼痛，痛苦，痛楚：*Do you feel any pain when I press here?* 我按壓這裏時你覺得痛嗎？

ache a pain in part of your body that continues steadily for a long time, but is usually not very severe (通常指身體局部持續但不太嚴重的) 疼痛，隱痛：*It's not a stabbing pain, doctor, it's more of an ache.* 醫生，那不是一陣刺痛，而更像是隱隱約約的疼痛。

agony a state in which you feel very severe physical or mental pain (生理或心理上極度的) 痛苦，創痛：*I was in agony all night with toothache.* 我整夜牙痛，難受得要命。

cramp a state in which the muscles in part of your body suddenly and painfully tighten up, or a pain caused by this (身體局部肌肉) 抽筋，痛性痙攣：*I woke up with (a) terrible cramp in my right leg.* 我右腿猛地抽起筋來，把我疼醒了。

discomfort a general feeling of being uncomfortable or in pain, sometimes used as a euphemism for pain (有時用作疼痛的委婉語) 不適，不舒服：*If you feel any discomfort, ask the nurse to give you a painkiller.* 如果你感覺不適，就請護士給你一片止痛藥。

itch a small irritating pain on the outside of your body, that usually makes you want to scratch your skin to relieve it 癢，發癢：*My skin feels very dry, and I have a terrible itch.* 我的皮膚感覺很乾燥，癢得難受。

soreness pain that is usually felt when you have a wound or sensitive area on the outside of your body and something rubs against it (通常指傷口或敏感部位受到摩擦時所感到的) 疼痛：*I'll give you some ointment to relieve any soreness where you grazed your leg.* 我會給你一些藥膏來減輕你腿上擦傷部位的疼痛。

stitch (*informal*) a pain, caused by cramp, that you suddenly feel in your side, often when you are running or taking exercise (常指奔跑或鍛煉時由抽

筋引起的肋部突然的）劇痛，岔氣：*I've got a stitch, so I'll have to rest for a minute.* 我岔氣了必須休息一會。

suffering a state in which you experience severe physical or mental pain for a long time（生理或心理上長期的）劇痛，痛楚：*I don't want you to keep him alive if it simply means prolonging his suffering.* 如果僅僅意味着延長他的痛苦，我倒不希望你繼續讓他活着。

twinge a slight but often worrying pain in part of the body（輕微的）陣痛，刺痛：*I feel a twinge every time I bend my knee.* 我每次彎膝的時候都感得一陣刺痛。

⊃ see also 參見 **hurt**

pale *adjective* being a whiter or less intense variety of a particular colour, or showing a whiter colour in your skin than is normal, usually because you are ill or afraid（通常指由於疾病或恐懼等）蒼白的，灰白的，白皙的：*You do look rather pale, perhaps you're sickening for something.* 你看起來確實氣色不太好，也許有甚麼不舒服吧。

ashen having a very pale or greyish complexion, usually as a result of severe illness or a terrible shock or grief（通常指由於重病、驚嚇或悲痛等）面色蒼白的，面如死灰的：*I don't think they should have let him out of hospital – he looked ashen when he got home.* 我認為他們不該讓他出院，他回到家裏的時候看上去面色蒼白。

light (*used to describe a colour*) pale（用以描述顏色）淺的，淡的：*light blue* 淺藍色

pastel (*used to describe a colour*) pale and soft in quality（用以描述顏色）柔和的，淡的：*pastel pink* 淡粉色

pallid pale or lacking a healthy colour 蒼白的；膚色病態的：*a pallid complexion* 蒼白的面色

pasty(-faced) pale and unhealthy looking, especially in the face, usually not as a result of a particular illness, but of an unhealthy lifestyle and a lack of fresh air and exercise（尤指因不健康的生活方式、缺乏新鮮空氣和鍛煉而）面無血色的，臉色發青的：*The pasty-faced ones are the ones who spend more time watching television or playing on their computers than they do running around outside.* 那些面無血色的人花大量的時間看電視、玩電腦，卻很少在戶外四處跑動。

peaky (*informal*) slightly pale and ill 蒼白的；憔悴的；有病容的：*She looks a bit peaky this morning; I don't think she slept very well.* 她今天上午看上去有點憔悴，我認為她是沒睡好覺。

wan (*literary*) pale, usually from grief or illness（通常指由於悲痛或疾病等）臉色憔悴的，面無血色的：*He had the traditional wan and slightly forlorn look of an unhappy lover.* 他看上去宛若傳說中不幸的戀人，憔悴的面容透着一絲淒涼。

white very pale, usually through fear or shock（通常指由於害怕或驚嚇等）面色慘白的：*He went white when I told him the news.* 當我告訴他這個消息時，他臉色煞白。

part¹ *noun* one of several smaller things that go together to make up a larger thing or into which a whole can be divided, or an item that has a particular function within a large machine such as an engine or a vehicle（事物的組成）部分；（發動機或車輛等裝置的）零部件：*I've finished the first part of my essay.* 我完成了作文的第一部分。

bit   a piece, especially a small piece, often of something that has been broken or taken apart（尤指）小塊；（常指破裂或拆開後的）碎塊：*Be careful, I dropped a milk bottle and there are bits of glass all over the kitchen floor.* 小心，我失手把牛奶瓶摔了，廚房地板上到處是玻璃碎片。

chunk   a sizable, three-dimensional piece of a solid material, usually with an irregular shape（通常指大而不規則的）厚塊：*a chunk of metal* 一大塊金屬

fragment   a tiny piece left over after something has been broken or destroyed（破裂或毀壞後的）碎片，殘片：*The glass shattered into fragments.* 玻璃杯摔成了碎片。

lump   an irregularly shaped three-dimensional piece of a hard or soft material（不規則的）塊，團：*My bed was very uncomfortable because there were so many lumps in the mattress.* 我的牀很不舒適，因為牀墊裏面有很多硬塊。

piece   a solid amount of something that is less than all of it and has usually been taken or broken off it（通常指破裂或掰下的）碎塊，片：*Cut the cheese into bite-size pieces.* 把芝士切成一口可以吃下的小塊。

section   one of several parts into which something is deliberately divided（有意分成的）部分，片，段：*The fuselage of the aircraft is made in sections, which are then welded together.* 飛機的機身分段製造，然後焊接在一起。

slice   a thin flat piece, often of food（常指食物的）切片，薄片：*a slice of bread* 一片麵包

part²   *verb* (*said about two or more people*) to leave one another at the end of a relationship or at the end of a period of time together（指兩人或多人之間）告別，分手：*At least we parted on fairly friendly terms.* 至少我們是相當友好地分了手。

divorce or get divorced   (*said about one person or a couple*) to go through the legal process that ends a marriage（指某人或夫妻）離婚：*They lived apart for several years before they finally got divorced.* 他們分居了好些年，最後終於離婚了。

go your separate ways   (*said about two or more people*) to part and go off in different directions, or to end a business or personal relationship（指兩人或多人之間）各奔東西；（私人或業務間）結束往來：*My partner and I decided that we no longer wanted the same things so it was better if we went our separate ways.* 我與合夥人都斷定我們不再有共同的追求，所以最好還是分道揚鑣。

part company (with)   (*formal*) (*said about one person or two or more people*) to leave someone whom you have been accompanying, or to end a relationship（指個人或多人之間）離別，結束關係：*We travelled together as far as Paris, and there we parted company.* 我們一起旅遊到了巴黎，然後在那裏分開了。

say goodbye (to)   to leave someone, or to part, at the end of a period of time together 告辭；離別：*When the time came to say goodbye, it was some* *comfort that we should be seeing one another again quite soon.* 在離別之時，我們知道很快又會相見，因而感到幾分安慰。

separate (*said about a couple*) to stop living together and behaving as a couple, without necessarily getting divorced (指夫妻之間) 分居，分開：*It's a rather odd situation – they say they've separated, but they're still both living in the same house.* 這種情況很奇怪，他們說是已經分居了，但兩人還住在一個房子裏。

split up (with) (*said about a couple*) to separate or end their relationship (夫妻間) 分手，感情破裂：*She split up with Jim, and now she's got a new boyfriend.* 她和占姆分手了，現在有了一個新的男朋友。

take your leave (of) (*formal*) to say goodbye 告辭；辭行：*Well, it has been very pleasant talking to you, but I must now take my leave.* 好啦，和你交談非常愉快，不過我現在得告辭了。

➲ see also 參見 **separate²**

partner *noun* someone who takes part in an activity with you and helps you carry it out, for example someone you dance with, someone who plays a game or sport with you against two other people, or someone with whom you have a formal agreement to share the responsibility and costs of running a business or doing a particular kind of work (舞蹈、遊戲、體育等活動中的) 伙伴；(生意或工作上的) 合夥人：*My business has grown substantially in the last few years, and I'm looking for a partner to help me run it.* 在過去幾年裏我的生意很興隆，我正在尋求合夥人來幫我經營管理。

ally someone, either a person, an organization, or a country, who agrees to support and help you when you are fighting together against a common enemy or when you are trying to achieve a common aim (指個人、團體或國家之間的) 聯盟，同盟，結盟者：*When the American colonists were fighting for their independence, they found an ally in the French.* 當美洲殖民地在為獨立而戰時，他們在法國人中找到了一支同盟軍。

associate someone whom you know and whom you do things together with, especially in business (*sometimes used when you do not wish to specify your exact relationship with a particular person*) (尤指生意上的) 合夥人，同事 (有時用於不希望說明與某人的確切關係時)：*A business associate of mine recommended you to me.* 我的一個生意合夥人將你推薦給我。

collaborator someone who works with you, for example, on a particular project 協作者；(項目等) 合夥人：*He had a team of collaborators who did a lot of research for the project.* 他有一支合作團隊，為項目的研究做了大量的工作。

colleague someone who works with you in the same organization or is in the same profession as you (同一機構或職業的) 同事，同僚，同人：*I know her as a friend and colleague.* 我把她當成朋友和同事。

mate someone who acts as an assistant to a skilled worker (熟練工人的) 副手，助手：*a plumber's mate* 水喉匠的助手

opposite number a person in the same job or position as you, but in a different organization (在不同機構但工作或職位相當的) 對等人物：*The*

Secretary of State for Trade and Industry is having talks with her opposite number in the Polish government. 工業與貿易大臣現正在和波蘭的對等官員會談。

⊃ see also 參見 **accompany**

patient *adjective* not getting angry or restless if you have to wait for something or someone, or if someone behaves in a way that causes you trouble or inconvenience (在必須等待或某人的行為引來麻煩或不便時) 耐心的,忍耐的: *If you wouldn't mind being patient for ten more minutes, I'll definitely see you then.* 如果你不介意再耐心等 10 分鐘,我肯定會見你的。

calm quiet and not showing signs of worry or excitement 平靜的;鎮定的: *He had the great ability to remain calm under pressure.* 他有着在壓力下保持鎮定的非凡能力。

composed able to control your feelings, not becoming nervous, angry, or upset 沉着的;鎮定的: *As his confidence at public speaking increased, he became more composed.* 由於對公開演講越來越有信心,他變得更加沉着了。

forbearing (*formal*) not getting angry when people annoy you or cause you trouble (當他人騷擾或引起麻煩時) 忍耐的,克制的: *You're very forbearing – I would have lost my temper with them straight away.* 你很克制,如果是我,準會立刻朝他們發脾氣。

long-suffering experiencing trouble or inconvenience from someone over a long period of time and being forbearing about it (對某人造成的麻煩或不便) 長期忍受的,長期遭罪的: *Her long-suffering parents once again paid her fine.* 她長期忍氣吞聲的父母再一次替她交了罰款。

philosophical calmly accepting that you will not always get what you want and that you will experience difficulties in life (對可欲不可求之事或生活中的艱辛等) 達觀的,處亂不驚的: *He's trying being philosophical about it, but you can see he's bitterly disappointed.* 儘管他嘗試着處之泰然,可你看得出他非常失望。

resigned accepting that something bad will happen to you and that you can do nothing to stop it happening 逆來順受的;屈從的: *He had heard that the company was closing down and was resigned to losing his job.* 他聽說過公司要倒閉,對失去這份工作無可奈何。

stoical bearing pain or hardship without complaining (對痛苦或艱難等) 堅忍的,恬淡寡慾的: *She was so stoical in the way she bore her last long illness.* 她很堅強,上次患病很長時間都挺過來了。

tolerant forbearing, or accepting that other people are different or behave in different ways to you and not trying to change them (對他人不同的思想或行為方式) 容忍的,寬容的: *a tolerant society* 包容的社會

understanding willing to sympathize with our people and accept their explanations for why they do things (對他人及其行為解釋) 予以理解的,諒解的: *He was very understanding when I explained why I was resigning.* 當我解釋辭職的理由時,他十分理解。

pay *verb* to provide the money needed to buy something, or to give money to someone for something (為購買或交換某物) 付錢,支付: *You pay for the food, and I'll pay for the drinks.* 你付食品錢,我付飲料錢。

cough up (*informal*) to pay, or to pay a certain amount of money, often unwillingly（常指不情願地）支付，出錢：*You lost the bet, so you'd better cough up.* 你賭輸了，所以最好還是把錢吐出來吧。

foot the bill to pay for something 付費；買單；結賬：*It's not fair if you damage my car and then expect me to foot the bill for the repairs.* 如果是你弄壞了車，然後卻指望我來付修理費，那是不公平的。

fork out (*informal*) to pay for something, or pay a certain amount of money, often unwillingly（常指不情願地）支付，掏錢：*I had to fork out £50 to get the TV repaired.* 我得付 50 英鎊修理電視機。

invest to use or spend money in a way that you hope will bring you profit or benefit in the future, for example, by buying shares in a company（通過購買公司股票等方式，以期帶來利潤或效益而）投資：*I invested £10,000 in a small company making electronic equipment.* 我在一家生產電子設備的小公司投資了 1 萬英鎊。

meet the cost of (*formal*) to pay for something 抵付，支付：*We shall have to put a certain amount of money aside to meet the cost of maintaining the new equipment after it has been installed.* 我們將不得不預留一筆資金用來支付新設備安裝後的維修費用。

pay back to repay someone or something 償還：*If you lend me £10 now, I'll pay you back on Monday – I promise.* 如果你現在借我 10 英鎊，我星期一就還給你，我保證。

repay to give someone an amount of money that they lent you previously, or to give back an amount of money that you borrowed from someone 還錢給（某人）；還錢：*We can't ask the bank for another loan, until we've finished repaying the loan we took out last year.* 我們要還清了去年那筆貸款才能再向銀行申請新的貸款。

settle (up) to pay someone what you owe them 付還，結清（欠款）：*If you don't mind paying for me now, I'll settle up with you later.* 如果你不介意現在替我付賬，我以後會如數還給你的。

peace *noun* a quiet, restful state without noise or disturbing activity or in which you do not feel anxious or troubled 平靜；安寧；寧靜：*Look, I've been busy dealing with people all afternoon and I just want five minutes' peace.* 瞧，我整個下午一直忙着與人打交道，真想有 5 分鐘安靜一下。

calm a quiet state in which movement or activity is gentle, especially a state in which there are no waves on the sea or there is no wind blowing（動作、行為等的）平和；（尤指沒有海浪或風時的）平靜：*the calm before the storm* 暴風雨前的平靜

hush a state where there is little or no sound, especially after noise ceases（尤指吵鬧過後的）安靜，肅靜：*There was an expectant hush as the president stood up to speak.* 當總統站起來發言的時候，全場安靜地期待着。

serenity a peaceful and happy state 平靜；安詳；寧靜：*She was feeding her baby with a look of complete serenity on her face.* 她正餵着孩子，臉上的表情非常安詳。

silence absence of sound, often a state in which no one is speaking（常指無人説話時的）寂靜 沉默：*The crowd stood in silence for two minutes, remembering the dead.* 人群默哀兩分鐘，緬懷死者。

stillness absence of sound and, often, movement（常指沒有響動時的）沉寂，寂靜：*The stillness was broken only by the occasional cry of a bird.* 沉寂只是被偶爾的鳥啼聲打破。**tranquillity** a peaceful state usually in a place, scene, or period of time（尤指地方、景色或某段時期的）安寧，寧靜：*the tranquillity of the lakeside scene* 湖邊風景的寧靜

➲ see also 參見 **calm**[2]

persuade *verb* to make someone do something, especially by talking to them and giving them good reasons why they should do it（尤指通過曉之以理而）説服，勸説：*I tried to persuade him to give up smoking and go on a diet.* 我設法勸他戒煙節食。

bring round (*informal*) to make someone change their opinion or do something by explaining to them good reasons why they should do it（通過曉之以理而）使改變觀點，使回心轉意：*You know you will never bring him round to your way of thinking unless he is going to benefit from it himself.* 要知道除非他本人可以從中得到好處，否則你永遠無法讓他接受你的思維方式。

convert to make someone change their present belief, opinion, or attitude, especially their religious belief, and adopt a new one 使轉變（信仰、觀點、態度等）；使皈依（宗教）：*They tried to convert him to Christianity.* 他們設法使他皈依基督教。

convince to make someone sure about something by using strong arguments in favour of it（通過運用有力的論據）説服；使信服：*What can I do to convince you this plan will work?* 我怎麼做才能讓你確信這項計劃是可行的呢？

incite to use language, especially emotional language, to make a group of people do something bad or violent（尤指用感人的語言）煽動，教唆，鼓動：*Agitators incited the crowd to tear down the barriers and attack the police.* 煽動者挑起群眾拆毀圍欄並攻擊警察。

induce to make someone do something 促使；使得：*Nothing would induce me to go swimming in that icy water.* 沒有甚麼能讓我去那麼冰冷的水裏游泳。

influence to use the power that you have over someone, for example, because you are older than they are or because they admire you, to try to make them do, think, believe, etc., something（在行為、思想或信念等方面）影響，感化：*You mustn't be influenced by what the newspapers say.* 你不要受報紙上的話影響。

prevail (up)on (*formal*) to succeed in persuading someone to do something 説服；誘使：*Eventually I prevailed upon them to withdraw their objections to the plan.* 最後，我説服他們撤回了對該計劃的反對意見。

sway (*mostly used in the passive*) to influence someone who is undecided about something to change their opinion（多用於被動語態）使受影響；使動搖：*He was easily swayed by the strong opinions of others.* 他很容易被別人有力的觀點所左右。

talk into to persuade someone to do something by talking to them, often when they are at first unwilling to do it or when they regret doing it afterwards（常指當某人起初不願意做某事或做了某事後感到後悔時）説服：*You shouldn't have let him talk you into buying the car if you couldn't really afford it.* 如果你真的買不起車，就不該被他説服去買。

win over to succeed in persuading someone to agree with you or do what you want 贏得⋯的支持；把⋯爭取過來：*I think it was her charm rather than the force of arguments that eventually won him over.* 我認為是她的魅力而不是論據的分量最終贏得了他的支持。

➲ see also 參見 **convincing; urge**

picture *noun* a representation of the appearance of an object, person, scene, etc., made on a flat surface with pencil, paint, etc., or a photograph 圖畫；圖片；照片：*I'll draw you a picture to show you what the house will look like when we've added the extension.* 我來給你畫張圖，讓你知道我們擴建之後的房子是甚麼樣子的。

cartoon a comic or satirical drawing, often on a topical subject（常指喜劇性或諷刺性題材的）漫畫，卡通：*A cartoon in today's newspaper depicts the prime minister as a toothless lion.* 今天報紙上的一幅漫畫將首相刻畫成一頭無牙的獅子。

diagram a simplified drawing, often using symbols, that shows not how something looks, but how its parts are related to or connect with one another（常指用符號表示某物各部分之間關聯而非其外形的）簡圖，示意圖：*a diagram of the wiring in a car engine* 汽車引擎的電路示意圖

drawing a picture made up of lines in pencil, ink, etc. （用鉛筆或鋼筆線條畫的）素描，圖畫：*a drawing of a bull by Picasso* 畢加索畫的一頭公牛素描

illustration a picture, or drawing in a book（書中的）插圖：*The book contains over 300 full-colour illustrations.* 這本書含有 300 多幅全色插圖。

image a reproduction of the appearance of someone or something, either physically created or in the mind, including a picture appearing in a mirror or on a TV or computer screen（繪製的或想像的，包括鏡子、電視或電腦屏幕上的）圖像，映像，意象：*I have a very clear image in my mind of how he looked when I last saw him 20 years ago.* 我清晰地記得我 20 年前最後一次見到他時的模樣。

painting a picture made by putting paint on a surface 油畫；繪畫：*The Mona Lisa is probably the most famous painting in the world.* 《蒙娜麗莎》大概是世界上最著名的畫作。

photograph an image of something captured by a camera and then printed 照片，相片：*Are you sure you don't recognize the man in this photograph?* 你敢肯定沒有認出照片上的這個人嗎？

plan a drawing that shows the layout of something that already exists, for example, the rooms in a building or the streets in a town, or that serves as a guide to someone who is building or laying out something（反映建築物的房間或市鎮街道等佈局的）平面圖，設計圖：*According to the original plans for the house, this corridor led to a small staircase.* 根據最初的房屋設計圖，這條走廊通向一個小樓梯。

portrait a picture of a particular person 肖像，畫像：*a portrait of the Queen* 女王的肖像

sketch a drawing, painting, or diagram made quickly and roughly, often as preparation for a properly finished work or to help you remember something（常指為事前準備或幫助記憶的）草圖，略圖：*I made a sketch of where the vehicles were after the accident.* 我畫了一幅標示事故發生後車輛所在位置的草圖。

place *noun* an identifiable point or area on the earth's surface, or a particular building, village, town, etc. （地面上可以確認的）地點，地方；（某建築物、村莊或市鎮等的）位置：*the place where I was born* 我出生的地方

area a particular portion of horizontal space on the earth's surface, or within a room, building, town, etc. （地面或房間、大樓、市鎮內的）區域，地區：*Which area of town do you live in?* 你住在鎮上哪個區域？

location (*usually used when discussing business or technical matters*) the position of something or someone or a site where something can be built or done（通常用於談及商業或技術問題時）位置，地點，場所：*The business is moving to a new location on the outskirts of town.* 這家企業要向市郊的一處新址搬遷。

position the place where something or someone is（人或物的）位置，方位：*From our position on the roof of the building, we could see the procession winding its way through the streets below.* 從屋頂上我們所處的位置可以看見隊伍在下面的街道上蜿蜒行進。

scene a place where something is happening or happened 現場；場面：*the scene of the crime* 犯罪現場

setting an area or the surroundings in which something happens 背景；環境：*The lakes and mountains make the perfect setting for a relaxing holiday.* 湖泊與高山構成休閒度假的最佳環境。

site the place where something happened in the past, or a place where something can be done, especially where a building can be built 遺址；（尤指可建房屋的）場地：*We're looking for a suitable site for a new office building.* 我們正在尋找適合建造新辦公樓的場地。

situation the position of something, especially a building, in relation to the other things around it（尤指某建築物以周圍其他東西作參照的）位置，方位，環境：*The hotel has a pleasant situation overlooking the beach.* 酒店俯瞰着海濱，擁有怡人的環境。

spot a place, especially a small place and one that it is pleasant to be in（尤指小而宜人的）場所，地點：*I've found the perfect spot for our picnic.* 我找到了野餐的絕妙去處。

surroundings the landscape, buildings, or objects that are around a particular place, building, etc. （某地方或建築物等的）周邊環境：*It's a pretty house, but it's in rather unpleasant surroundings.* 這是一幢漂亮的房子，但周邊環境不太好。

whereabouts the position of someone or something that you are looking for 下落；行蹤：*If you know the whereabouts of this man, you should inform the police immediately.* 如果你知道這個人的下落，應該馬上通知警察。

plan[1] *noun* an idea or a statement of what you intend to do, how you intend to solve a problem, etc., made before you actually do it 計劃；方案：*I have a plan that I think might work.* 我有一個計劃，我想也許行得通。

agenda a list or plan of things that you intend to do, especially that you intend to discuss during a meeting 議程；議事日程：*The next item on the agenda is the Club's annual dance.* 議程表上的下一項是俱樂部一年一度的舞會。

intention something that you decide that you are going to do 意圖；意向，打算：*It was never my intention to do all the work myself.* 我從來就沒有打算一個人做完所有的工作。

method a planned way of doing something（計劃做某事的）方法：*This photocopier uses a new method of producing high-quality copies.* 該複印機使用了一種新的高品質複製方法。

plot a secret plan to do something dramatically bad, such as to kill someone or overthrow a government 陰謀，密謀：*a plot to blow up the king and the parliament* 炸死國王和議會成員的陰謀

project a plan for doing something that will involve work or effort on your part over a period of time（在一定時期內通過努力完成的）項目；工程；方案；計劃：*My project for this year is to redecorate all the bedrooms in the house.* 我今年的計劃是重新裝修屋裏所有的睡房。

proposal a plan or suggestion, especially one that is formal or written down, for others to decide on（尤指正式或書面供他人採納的）提議，提案，建議：*The commission is considering a proposal to help tackle global warming.* 委員會正在考慮一項有助於解決全球變暖問題的提議。

scheme a plan, usually one involving dishonesty or trickery, or (*in British English*) an official organized plan for a particular activity such as training people or saving money for a pension（通常指）陰謀，詭計；（在英國英語中，指人員培訓或養老金儲蓄等）方案：*She wanted you to think George was in love with her – that was part of her little scheme – to get him away from you.* 她就是想你認為佐治在和她談戀愛，這是她施的一點小計，想從你手中把他奪去。

strategy (*usually used when talking about business or military matters*) a plan setting out your goals and how you intend to achieve those goals over a fairly long period of time（通常指商業或軍事等問題的）戰略，策略：*Opening up new markets in developing countries is part of the company's strategy for the next five years.* 在發展中國家開闢新市場是公司今後 5 年戰略的一部分。

plan[2] *verb* to have a plan or the intention to do something, to make plans, or to make a plan for a particular thing, event 計劃，籌劃，打算（某事或活動等）：*We were just planning our holiday for next year.* 我們正在制定明年的假期計劃。

aim to have something as your goal, to want and intend to do something 打算，旨在：*We're aiming to finish the work by the end of next week.* 我們打算在下週末之前完成工作。

contemplate (*formal*) to have a plan to do something in the future, or to think about doing something in the future（為將來）盤算，謀劃：*Before we contemplate expanding our business in Europe, we ought to try to increase our* *share of the UK market.* 在我們謀劃擴大歐洲業務之前，我們應當努力提高在英國的市場份額。

envisage* to have an idea or a plan of what you will do in the future（為將來）設想，構想：*Do you envisage making many changes when you take over as party leader?* 在您接任黨的領導人之後，是否有許多改革的構想？

* In US English the verb envision is often used in this sense. 在美國英語中，動詞 envision 常用作此義。

intend to have decided that you will do something 意欲；打算：*I intend to wait a while before I finally make up my mind.* 我想等一會再作最後決定。

mean to intend to do something, especially (*and often used in the negative*) to have the deliberate intention of doing something bad（常用於否定句）有意，故意（尤指做壞事）：*I didn't mean to hurt you.* 我並不是有意傷害你。

plot to make a plot 密謀：*They were plotting to overthrow the government.* 他們在秘密策劃推翻政府。

propose (*formal*) to intend or plan to do something 意欲；打算；計劃：*And how exactly do you propose to finance this project?* 你究竟打算如何資助這個項目？

scheme to make plans involving dishonesty or trickery or with bad motives（帶有不良動機）圖謀，謀劃：*He was scheming to get himself promoted ahead of me.* 他圖謀在我之前自己先得到提拔。

⊃ see also 參見 **idea; picture**

please *verb* to give pleasure to someone, or to win someone's approval 取悅，討好（某人）：*He'd do anything to please her, but she just doesn't find him attractive.* 只要能夠取悅她，他做甚麼都願意，可她就是覺得他沒有魅力。

cheer up to make someone who has been feeling sad feel happier 使（某人）高興起來：*I tried to cheer him up by taking him out to the pub.* 我帶他去了酒館，設法讓他高興起來。

delight to make someone feel happy or excited 使（某人）欣喜：*The clowns delighted the crowd with their antics.* 那些丑角用滑稽動作逗得眾人非常開心。

gratify (*formal*) (*often used in the passive*) to make someone feel happy or satisfied or proud（常用於被動語態）使高興；使滿足；使自豪：*I was very gratified to find that people still remember me after all these years.* 得知這麼多年後人們還記得我，我感到十分滿足。

humour to do what someone wants, even though you do not particularly want to do it, in order to make them happy or to prevent them becoming angry or sad（為讓某人高興或不讓其生氣、傷心等而）順應，遷就：*Humour him or you'll make his bad mood even worse.* 順着他吧，否則你會使他本來就不好的心情變得更糟。

oblige (*formal*) to please someone and make them feel grateful to you 使（某人）感激；施恩惠於（某人）：*Would you oblige me by fetching my walking stick? It's in the cupboard under the stairs.* 請你幫個忙，把我的手杖拿過來可以嗎？它在樓梯下的壁櫃裏。

polite *adjective* speaking to and behaving towards other people in a way that shows that you respect them or that conforms to the standards of behaviour that people expect in society（對待他人的言語或行為）禮貌的，客氣的：*Remember to be polite and always say 'please' and 'thank you'.* 記住要講禮貌，任何時候都要説"請"和"謝謝"。

civil using polite language and not being rude or hurtful to someone, but often in situations where you actually feel angry with them or contemptuous of them（常指在對某人很生氣或鄙視的情況下所使用的語言）有禮貌的：*She annoys me so much I have great difficulty in remaining civil to her.* 她讓我非常惱火，要一直對她客客氣氣真是太難了。

courteous (*formal*) polite, especially in doing or saying things that show respect for other people（尤指在言行方面對他人）禮貌的，彬彬有禮的：*They may not expect you to reply to their letter, but it would be courteous to reply to it, nonetheless.* 也許他們並沒指望你給他們回信，不過，回封信要禮貌些。

deferential showing great or exaggerated respect for someone, suggesting that you are unimportant compared with them（對他人非常或過於）恭敬的，恭順的，恭謙的：*He's an important man and deserves respect, but he won't like it if you're too deferential to him.* 他是一個要人，也值得尊敬，可是如果你對他過分地畢恭畢敬，他不會喜歡的。

formal observing all the rules that society makes for addressing or behaving towards other people in public（在公共場所稱呼他人或待人接物等方面）正式的，禮節性的：*Don't be so formal; you can call me Sue, not Dr McKenzie.* 不要太拘謹，你可以就叫我休，不用稱麥肯齊博士。

respectful showing respect 恭敬的；尊敬的：*He made a respectful bow and left the room.* 他恭敬地鞠了個躬，離開了房間。

well-behaved behaving in a way that conforms to the standards that people expect in society 行為端正的；彬彬有禮的：*a very well-behaved young man* 一個彬彬有禮的年輕人

well-bred brought up by your family to be polite and well-mannered 有教養的：*A well-bred young gentleman would not leave a young lady to find her own way home.* 一個有教養的年輕紳士是不會讓一個年輕的女士獨自探路回家的。

well-mannered having good manners, behaving in the way that society expects you to behave（行為舉止）得體的，彬彬有禮的：*It's a pleasure to sit down for a meal with such well-mannered children.* 坐下來和這麼有禮貌的孩子們一起共餐是一件樂事。

poor *adjective* in a state where you do not have very much money or very many possessions 窮的，貧窮的：*We're too poor to send our children to private schools.* 我們太窮了，沒錢送孩子們去私立學校讀書。

bankrupt (*used to describe a person or a company, business, etc.*) officially recognized as not having enough money to pay your debts or to continue doing business as normal（人、公司、企業等）破產的：*When the bank refused to extend the loan, the firm went bankrupt.* 由於銀行拒絕延長貸款，這家公司破產了。

broke (*informal*) not having any money or enough money, usually temporarily（通常指暫時）身無分文的，一文不名的：*I'm always broke at the end of the month.* 我在月尾的時候總是身無分文。

destitute having virtually no money or possessions and unable to afford the basic things you need to live 貧困的；一貧如洗的：*She had no money of her own, so, when her husband died, she was left destitute.* 她自己一個錢也沒有，所以丈夫一死，她就變得一貧如洗了。

hard up* (*informal*) fairly poor, not having very much money 經濟困難的；拮据的：*Could you lend me £20? I'm a bit hard up at the moment.* 你能借給我20英鎊嗎？眼下我手頭有點緊。

* Usually used after a verb. 通常用於動詞後。

impoverished (*usually used to describe areas, countries, groups, etc., rather than individuals*) not having much money or many resources（通常用以描述地區、國家、人群等，而非個人）（在資金或資源方面）貧困的，貧瘠的：*The government offered special incentives to firms to set up businesses in impoverished areas.* 政府對公司在貧困地區開辦企業給予了特別的激勵措施。

needy not having the things that most people have, and therefore needing money or help 缺衣少食的；靠接濟的：*She organized a collection for the needy families in the village.* 她為村裏的貧困戶組織了一場募捐。

penniless very poor or destitute 身無分文的；一貧如洗的：*I'm not a penniless student any more – I've got a job!* 我不再是個不名一文的學生了，我找到工作了！

poverty-stricken (*usually used to describe areas or groups rather than individuals*) very impoverished（通常用以描述地區或人群，而非個人）赤貧的，窮困潦倒的：*When the harvest failed again, the poverty-stricken villagers had no choice but to seek work in the towns.* 再次歉收之後，飽經窮困煎熬的村民們別無選擇，只得到城裏找活兒幹。

➲ see also 參見 **bad**[4]

popular *adjective* liked or wanted by many people 受青睞的；受歡迎的：*a popular entertainer* 一個受歡迎的藝人

favourite that a particular person or group likes most（特定的人或群體）最喜愛的：*What's your favourite colour?* 你最喜愛的顏色是甚麼？

in demand wanted by many people, often in order to act in a particular capacity 有需求的；走俏的：*He's very much in demand as an after-dinner speaker.* 他作為餐後講演者很吃香。

in favour being liked by a particular person or particular group（特定的人或群體）青睞的，喜歡的：*It seemed that her career was going nowhere, but now, suddenly, she's back in favour with the general public.* 她的職業生涯當初似乎是窮途末路，但現在突然之間她又受到普通百姓的追捧。

sought-after that many people want to buy or own 很吃香的；走俏的：*Ming vases are quite rare, so they're very sought-after by collectors.* 明代花瓶十分稀罕，所以很受收藏者的歡迎。

widespread happening or found in many different places or among many different people 廣為流傳的；普遍的：*There's a widespread belief that it's* *now too late to do anything about global warming.* 普遍認為，對於全球變暖，現在採取任何措施都為時已晚。

praise *verb* to say things that show that you admire someone or something that they have done 讚揚，稱讚：*You complain about him when he does things wrong, but you never praise him when he does things well.* 他做錯了事情，你抱怨他，可他把事情幹好了，你卻從來不表揚他。

applaud to show that you like what someone has done by clapping your hands, or to praise someone or something（以鼓掌表示）讚許，稱讚：*The audience stood up and applauded at the end of the act.* 表演結束的時候，觀眾站起來拍手喝彩。

commend *(formal)* to praise someone, especially officially, for showing a good quality such as courage or honesty（尤指因某人表現出的勇氣或誠實等品質而正式）表揚，稱讚：*The police commended her for the courage she showed during the attempted robbery.* 警方表揚了她在這搶劫未遂事件中表現出來的勇氣。

compliment to say something nice to someone to show them that you have noticed something about them or something that they did and you like it 恭維；讚美：*It's not often that someone compliments me on my cooking.* 有人誇獎我的廚藝，這樣的事是不常有的。

congratulate to say something *(especially congratulations)* to praise someone who has achieved something（尤指為某人的成就）祝賀，道賀，恭喜：*Let me be the first to congratulate you on your success.* 讓我第一個祝賀你成功。

flatter to praise someone or say nice things about them when they do not really deserve it, often in order to make them like you or to get something from them（常指為了取悅某人或得到某物而）奉承，討好，阿諛：*He tried to flatter her by saying she looked just like Catherine Zeta Jones.* 他極力討好她，説她看起來就像嘉芙蓮・薛達・鍾絲一樣。

pay tribute to to praise someone or something, or express your gratitude to someone, in public and often on a formal occasion 頌揚；讚頌；（常指在正式場合公開）表示感謝：*I'd just like to pay tribute to the men and women of the emergency services who saved so many lives during the recent disaster.* 我想對參加緊急救助工作的先生們和女士們表示感謝，是他們在最近這場災難中挽救了如此多的生命。

praise to the skies *(informal)* to praise someone or something very enthusiastically 吹捧：*The critics praised it to the skies and called it the film of the decade.* 影評把它捧上了天，稱它為十年來的最佳電影。

recognize *(often used in the passive)* to show by saying or doing something, such as giving someone an award, that you know that someone is talented or has done something good（常用被動語態）認可，賞識，表彰：*Her contribution to this vital discovery has never been properly recognized by her fellow scientists.* 她為這項重大發現做出的貢獻一直沒有得到同行科學家們的充分認可。

pretence *noun* acting as if you were someone other than the person you really are or as if you were doing something other than what you are really doing, or an instance of doing this 偽裝；假裝：*He's not really a war hero, it's all pretence.* 他不是真正的戰鬥英雄，這全是假象。

charade an action or event that has no real purpose or meaning 裝模作樣；象徵性的動作：*Everyone knows that the president has all the real power, and that what goes on in parliament is just a charade.* 每個人都知道總統掌握着全部實權，而國會做的任何事情都只是裝腔作勢而已。

cover something, for example a false identity and life history or a legal business, that is intended to prevent people from finding out who someone really is or what they are really doing (用虛假的身份、身世或合法的生意等所做的) 掩護，掩蓋：*Your cover is that you're a businessman attending a trade fair in London.* 你的掩護身份是參加倫敦交易會的商人。

disguise something that changes your appearance, for example a false beard or a different kind of clothes from the ones you usually wear, and is intended to stop people from recognizing you 偽裝物；裝扮用具：*He tried to slip past the police in disguise.* 他喬裝打扮，設法從警察面前溜過去。

façade a pretence that is intended to hide your real nature, situation, or feelings (虛假的) 外表，表面：*Behind the confident façade, she's actually a very frightened woman.* 在自信的外表背後，她其實挺害怕的。

front an activity, especially a legal business, that hides the fact that someone is doing something illegal (掩飾非法勾當的) 幌子：*The gang set up a betting shop as a front for their money-laundering operation.* 那幫人以開賭場為幌子，幹着洗錢的勾當。

show pretence, especially in order to make people believe that you are doing something that you are not really doing 裝出的樣子；假象：*They made a show of ending their quarrel, but everyone knows they still hate one another.* 他們表面上不再爭吵，但誰都知道他們還彼此懷恨在心。

veneer an outward appearance of some good quality that is intended to hide the bad qualities underneath 虛飾；虛假的外表：*a thin veneer of respectability* 道貌岸然

prevent *verb* to cause something not to happen or not to be done, or to cause someone not to do something 防止；阻止：*There must be some way we can prevent the water from leaking out of the tank.* 我們一定要想個辦法防止水箱漏水。

avert to prevent something that seems likely to happen, especially a bad thing such as an accident or crisis, from actually happening 防止，避免 (似乎很可能發生的事，尤指事故、危機等)：*The driver's quick thinking averted a nasty accident.* 司機急中生智，避免了一次嚴重意外的發生。

avoid to succeed in not doing or undergoing something or in preventing something from happening, usually something that is harmful 避免，避開 (通常指有害事情的發生)：*I want to avoid giving offence to any of our foreign visitors.* 我希望避免冒犯我們任何一個外賓。

forestall to take action in advance to try to prevent something from happening or someone from doing something 預先阻止，搶先行動以阻止 (事情發生或某人做某事)：*The government quickly moved troops into the area to* *forestall a possible invasion.* 政府迅速調動部隊進駐該地區，以阻止可能發生的入侵。

keep from to prevent someone or something from doing something 阻止，阻礙：*How can we keep the newspapers from getting hold of the story?* 我們怎樣才能阻礙報紙得到這個消息呢？

nip in the bud to stop something early before it can develop, especially before it can develop into a serious problem 防患於未然；制止於萌芽狀態：*By keeping the group under surveillance, we should be able to nip any trouble in the bud.* 通過對這群人實行監督，我們應該能做到防患於未然。

preclude (*formal*) to make it impossible for something to happen or for someone to do something 使行不通；阻止；妨礙：*Does the fact that he has a criminal record preclude him from being a candidate in the election?* 他犯有前科這一事實妨礙他當候選人嗎？

rule out to make it impossible for something to happen or for someone to do something 使不可能；排除；避免：*The bad weather ruled out any attempt to break the record.* 糟糕的天氣使打破紀錄的任何嘗試都變得不可能。

stop to prevent or preclude 阻止；阻攔：*If they insist on going, there's nothing we can do to stop them.* 如果他們堅持要去，我們就沒有任何辦法阻止。

⊃ see also 參見 **hinder**

problem noun something that causes worry or anxiety, something that needs to be solved or put right in order to enable you to do something effectively, or something that prevents a machine from functioning properly 問題；難題；（機器等的）故障：*He never discusses his personal problems with anyone in the office.* 他從不在辦公室和任何人討論自己的私人問題。

difficulty something that makes it hard to do or achieve something, or a state in which you have problems of various kinds 難處；困難：*You may have difficulty in understanding some of the technical language in this document.* 要理解這份文件中的一些技術性用語，你可能有困難。

disadvantage something that makes a thing less good, useful, etc., than it might otherwise have been 缺點；不利因素；劣勢：*Since the advantages outweigh the disadvantages, I suggest we should go ahead with the plan.* 既然優點多於缺點，我建議我們繼續實施這項計劃。

drawback a disadvantage or a problem that makes something less good than it might have been 弊端；不利條件：*The proposal looks great; the only drawback is the cost.* 這項提議看起來非常好，唯一不足的是成本太高。

hassle (*informal*) problems or difficulties, especially caused by people being unpleasant (尤指討厭之人帶來的) 麻煩，困難：*My boss is giving me a lot of hassle because I'm behind with my work.* 老闆總是煩擾我，因為我沒跟上工作進度。

hitch (*informal*) something that goes wrong and prevents something from happening as it should 故障；障礙：*We're unable to bring you that report from Beirut because of a slight technical hitch.* 因為一個小的技術故障，我們無法將那份報告從貝魯特帶給你。

plight a state in which you are in danger, suffer hardship, or have a serious problem（身陷危險、受苦的）境地，境遇：*The plight of the refugees has been ignored by the government.* 政府對難民們的境遇一直置之不理。

predicament a situation that is difficult to deal with（難以對付的）困境：*I'm in a bit of a predicament here; I can't decide which candidate to choose, because they are equally well qualified.* 我在這裏有點犯難，無法確定選哪一個候選人，因為他們都同樣地非常符合條件。

setback a problem that hinders progress or puts you into a worse state than you were in before（阻礙發展或使某人狀況惡化的）挫折，逆流：*We suffered a serious setback when there was a fire in the office and many important documents were destroyed.* 辦公室着火時，許多重要文件被毀，這使我們遭受了嚴重的挫折。

snag (*informal*) a small problem that makes it difficult to do something 小故障；小麻煩：*We hit a snag when we tried to feed the data into the computer.* 當我們設法將數據輸入電腦時，遇到了小麻煩。

trouble something that causes worry or anxiety, or a state in which you have difficulty in doing something or in dealing with something or someone 麻煩；困難：*I'm having trouble getting my car to start on cold mornings.* 在寒冷的早上，我很難開動我那輛汽車。

promise *verb* to tell someone that you will definitely do something, that something is definitely the case, or that you will definitely give them something 承諾；許諾；保證：*I promised I'd meet her at the station at six o'clock.* 我答應6點鐘到火車站接她。

assure to tell someone that something is definitely the case 向（某人）斷言；向（某人）保證；使（某人）確信：*He assured me that there was no cause for alarm.* 他向我保證根本毋須驚慌。

give your word to promise something solemnly, suggesting that you will lose your reputation as an honest person if you do not keep the promise（拿自己的名譽鄭重地）承諾，保證：*I'll repay every penny; I give you my word.* 我向你保證：我會分文不少如數歸還的。

guarantee to state that someone can quite definitely rely on something happening 擔保；保障；保證：*I guarantee that if you start reading this book you won't be able to put it down until you've finished it.* 我保證你一旦開始讀這本書，就會愛不釋手，直到讀完為止。

pledge to promise solemnly to give something or to do something（鄭重地）承諾，保證（給予或做某事）：*They pledged their support for the cause.* 他們保證支持這項事業。

swear to promise something solemnly, especially calling on God to witness what you are saying（尤指對上帝）鄭重承諾，發誓要：*Do you swear to tell the truth, the whole truth, and nothing but the truth?* 你能發誓講實話，講出全部實話，而且是只講實話嗎？

undertake (*formal*) to accept the responsibility for doing something, often by signing a contract to do it, or to promise to do something（常指通過簽訂合同或承諾）承擔，保證：*The lessee undertakes to maintain the property in* *good condition for the duration of the lease.* 承租人保證在租賃期間使財物保持完好。

vow to promise solemnly or swear to do something 發誓；立誓：*They vowed to avenge their murdered brother.* 他們發誓要為遇害的兄弟報仇。

proud *adjective* feeling very pleased and satisfied, especially about something that you have achieved yourself or that someone connected with you has achieved 自豪的；感到驕傲的：*I'm so proud of you for having the courage to stand up to those bullies.* 我為你有勇氣面對那些惡棍而感到非常自豪。

arrogant feeling that, or behaving as if, you are much better and more important than anyone else and have the right to give them orders 傲慢的；自大的：*He's far too arrogant to think that he needs advice, but he's always quite happy to give it.* 他太傲慢，認為自己不需要忠告，但卻總是非常樂意給別人忠告。

boastful saying things that show that you think that other people should admire and envy things that you do or own 自吹自擂的；自誇的：*I don't like the boastful way she talks about her new house.* 我不喜歡她在談論自己的新房子時那種自吹自擂的方式。

cocky (*informal*) (*used especially to describe young people*) excessively confident that your own ability and knowledge is very great and superior to other people's (尤用以描述年輕人) 過分自信的，自以為是的：*Don't get too cocky and think that, because you did well in one exam, you don't have to work hard for the others.* 尾巴不要翹得太高，別以為一門課考好了，你就不必認真準備其他考試了。

conceited having an excessively high opinion of your own abilities and importance 自負的；驕傲自滿的：*His parents always praise everything he does to the skies, and as a result he's become very conceited.* 他的父母總是過高誇獎他做的每一件事情，結果他變得非常自負。

haughty behaving in a way that suggests you think yourself to be superior to other people, especially socially superior to them, and that you do not really want to have anything to do with them 傲慢的；高傲自大的：*He always had a haughty look in his eyes.* 他的眼睛裏總有一幅傲慢的神情。

pompous self-important and tending to act or, especially, speak in a grand way that other people find inappropriate and rather ridiculous 自命不凡的；(尤指) 言辭浮誇的：*Excessive use of the pronoun one in the sense of 'you' can sound pompous.* 過多地使用代詞 one 表示"你"，聽起來會有點華而不實。

self-important believing yourself to be, and acting as if you were, a very important person, often because of a job or position that you have 妄自尊大的；自命不凡的：*The mayor was a fussy, self-important little man.* 市長是一個難以取悦、自命不凡的小男人。

snobbish valuing people because of their position or reputation, especially their social position, rather than for their personal qualities, so tending to show little respect for ordinary or lower-class people 勢利的；諂上欺下的：*They have a very snobbish attitude towards people who come from the 'wrong' part of town.* 他們對那些來自鎮上 "不對勁兒" 的地方的人態度非常勢利。

vain conceited, especially with regard to your personal appearance（尤指對於外貌）愛虛榮的，自負的：*The fact that I want to look nice when I go out doesn't make me vain.* 我外出時希望打扮得漂亮些並不說明我愛虛榮。

prove *verb* to provide evidence that makes it clear beyond doubt that something is the case 證實，證明（某事屬實）：*The film from the security camera proves she was in the area at the time the crime was committed.* 從監視攝像機取出的膠卷證明她當時在犯罪現場。

authenticate to prove or certify that something is genuine 鑒別，鑒定（某物的真實性）：*The picture has been authenticated by an expert from the National Gallery.* 這幅圖已由國家美術館的專家鑒定為真品。

bear out to provide evidence to support something that someone has said 證實，驗證（某人所言）：*This bears out what I said yesterday about him being unreliable.* 這驗證了我昨天的話，他不可靠。

certify to state definitely that, or to be evidence of the fact that, something is true or correct 證實，證明（某事的真實性或正確性）：*You have to certify on the back of the photograph that it is a true likeness of the person applying for a passport.* 您必須在照片背後簽字證實該照片與護照申請者本人確實相像。

confirm to state something once again in order to make sure that the information someone has is correct, or to corroborate something 確認；核實：*Could you please confirm your name and address?* 請您確認一下您的姓名和地址好嗎？

corroborate (*formal*) to provide additional evidence to show that what someone has said is true or correct 證實，確證（某人所言）：*She has not yet been able to find anyone who will corroborate her story.* 她還沒能找到可以證明自己所講的情況確鑿可靠的人。

demonstrate (*formal*) to show something 表明；展示：*I can demonstrate the water-repellent properties of this material by means of simple experiment.* 我可以通過簡單的實驗展示這種材料的防水性能。

establish to find out about and provide evidence for something 確定；查實：*We're still trying to establish the time of the victim's death.* 我們仍在設法查實受害人死亡的時間。

show to make something clear or prove it to someone 顯示；表明：*This just goes to show that you shouldn't believe everything you read in the newspaper.* 這正說明你不應該對報紙上看到的內容全都相信。

verify to confirm or state something in order to make sure that the information someone has is correct 核實，查實（信息）：*You can check the original documents to verify the accuracy of the information.* 你可以檢查原始資料以核實信息的準確性。

pull *verb* to be in front of something or someone and touching them and use effort to move them either towards you or along behind you（在前面）拉，扯，拖：*Grab hold of my hand, and I'll pull you up.* 抓緊我的手，我把你拉上來。

drag to pull someone or something roughly or forcefully, especially so that they move along in contact with the ground 用力拖，使勁拽：*His foot was* *caught in the stirrup, and he was dragged along behind the horse.* 他的腳卡在馬鐙裏，被馬拖着走。

draw to pull something along or out of something, especially with a steady and even effort（尤指用穩定而均勻的力量）拉，牽引：*a coach drawn by six white horses* 由六匹白馬拖着的四輪大馬車

haul to pull something (*usually something large or heavy*) strongly, steadily, and with effort（用力地）硬拖，強拉（大或重的東西）：*Six of us harnessed ourselves to the sledge to haul it over the ice.* 我們 6 個人套住雪橇，拉着它在冰上跑。

heave to pull or push something with a concentrated burst of effort（使出一股猛力）拽，拉，推：*When the captain gave the signal, they all heaved the cart up the hill.* 隊長一發出信號，他們就一齊用力把手推車推上了山。

tow to use a powered vehicle to pull another unpowered vehicle along（用機動車輛）拖曳，牽引（無動力的車輛）：*The car broke down and had to be towed to the nearest garage.* 小汽車拋錨了，不得不被拖曳到最近的修車廠。

tug to give something a quick, sharp pull 猛拉；用力拖：*I felt someone tugging at my sleeve.* 我感覺有人在使勁扯我的袖子。

yank (*informal*) to pull something roughly or carelessly 猛拉；使勁扯；用力拔：*He yanked the door open and rushed out.* 他猛地拉開門衝了出去。

punish *verb* to do something that hurts or disadvantages someone who has committed a crime or done something wrong 懲罰，處罰：*She's being punished for a crime she didn't commit.* 她正為沒有犯的罪而受到懲罰。

bring to justice (*formal*) to make someone who has committed a crime face trial and punishment by a court（將犯罪者）繩之以法：*We shall not rest until the perpetrators of this heinous act have been brought to justice.* 直到那些罪大惡極的犯罪分子受到法律的制裁，我們才能得以安寧。

convict (*said about a court or jury*) to state that someone is guilty of a crime that they have been charged with（指法庭或陪審團）宣判（被告人）有罪：*If convicted, she'll face a heavy fine or possibly a prison sentence.* 如果被宣判有罪，她將面對巨額罰款，或有可能被處以監禁。

discipline (*usually used in the passive*) to punish someone and keep order in something such as organization or armed force（通常用於被動語態，指為維護機構或軍隊秩序而）懲處，處罰：*He was disciplined for behaving inappropriately at work.* 他因為在工作時行為不當受到了處分。

fine to punish someone by making them pay a sum of money to the authorities 罰款：*I was fined for speeding.* 我因為超速行駛被罰款。

lock up (*informal*) to send someone to prison 關進監獄：*She got away with a fine when I think she ought to have been locked up.* 我覺得她本該被關進大牢的，可是她交了一筆罰金就逃脫掉了。

make pay to take revenge on someone or to punish them, usually not for something that the state regards as a crime（通常指並非因犯法而）懲罰，報復：*She decided that she was going to make him pay for the insult.* 因為受到了侮辱，她決心報復他。

penalize to impose a penalty on someone, usually in a sport or contest, often by giving an advantage to their opponent（通常指運動會或競賽中）判

罰：*You can be penalized for arguing with the referee.* 你會因為與裁判員發生爭執而受到處罰。

sentence (*said about a judge or court*) to state what a person's punishment will be after they have been convicted of a crime (指法官或法庭) 判處，判決，判刑：*He's been sentenced to life imprisonment.* 他被判處無期徒刑。

purpose *noun* the use to which something can be put, or something that you wish to achieve by doing something 目 的；用 途：*The purpose of this meeting is to discuss arrangements for the firm's Christmas party.* 這次會議的目的是討論公司聖誕晚會的安排。

aim what someone wishes to achieve or something is intended to achieve 目標；宗旨：*a statement setting out the aims of the organization* 闡明機構目標的陳述

function the use for which something is made 功能；作用：*A screwdriver won't make holes in wood; that's not its function.* 螺絲批在木頭上鑽不出洞來，那不是它的功能。

goal an aim 目標；目的：*One of my goals in life is to become a millionaire before I'm forty.* 我的人生目標之一就是在 40 歲前成為百萬富翁。

intention something that you decide you are going to do, or the purpose or aim of something 意圖；意向；打算：*I have no intention of resigning.* 我沒有辭職的打算。

object an aim 目標；目的：*The object of the exercise is to find out what sort of advertising is most likely to bring in new customers.* 這個活動的目的是弄清哪種廣告最有可能招攬新顧客。

objective a place or point that you are trying to reach, for example, when you are on a journey or when you are working on something, or an aim, especially one that is part of a bigger process (在旅途或工作等過程中努力想要實現的) 目的；(尤指階段性的) 目標：*My first objective was to persuade my colleagues that my plan would benefit them as much as it would benefit me.* 我的第一個目標是說服同事們相信我的計劃對他們與對我一樣有利。

point the purpose of an action or of something you say (行為或語言的) 意義，作用：*There's no point in applying if there are no vacancies.* 如果沒有空缺，申請也不頂用。

push *verb* to be behind something or someone and touching them and use effort to move them either away from you or along in front of you, or to be above something and use effort to move it downwards (直接接觸對象用力) 推，推動：*She pushed him out of the way.* 她把他推到一邊去了。

drive to be behind something or someone, but not touching them, and use force or urging to make them move away from you or along in front of you, or to push something in or down with great force (不直接接觸對象並用力) 驅使，驅動，推動：*The wind was driving the rain into our faces.* 風將雨水吹打在我們的臉上。

nudge to push someone or something gently, especially to push someone gently in the side with your elbow (尤指用肘) 輕推：*She nudged me and whispered, 'Don't look now, but isn't that David Beckham sitting three rows in* *front of us?'* 她輕輕地用胳膊肘捅了我一下，對我耳語道："現在先別看，隔着三排坐在我們前面的不是大衛・碧咸嗎？"

poke to push something narrow such as your finger or a stick into an opening in something, or to prod something or someone 戳；捅；刺：*Be careful waving that stick about, you nearly poked me in the eye.* 揮棍棒小心點，你差點捅着我的眼睛了。

press to push something downwards or inwards by applying weight or pressure on top of it 按；擠壓：*I pressed the button to ring the bell.* 我按了一下門鈴。

prod to use something narrow such as your finger or a stick to push against something（用手指或棍棒等狹長的東西）戳，捅：*He prodded me in the ribs with his bony finger.* 他用瘦尖的手指戳我的肋骨。

propel to cause something to move, especially rapidly, often by pushing it from behind（尤指迅速地，通常從後面）推進，推動：*He gave me a push that propelled me into the room.* 他一把將我推進了房間。

shove to push or put something or someone somewhere roughly or carelessly（粗魯或粗心地）推搡，推撞，放置：*Just shove a few things into a suitcase, we're only going for two days.* 往旅行箱隨便塞幾樣東西就行了，我們只走兩天。

squeeze to push on something from two or more sides at once, as when you hold something in your hand and close your fingers around it（抓在手裏用手指）捏握，擠壓：*You have to squeeze the bottle to get the sauce out.* 你得按捏瓶子，把醬擠出來。

puzzle *verb* to make it difficult for someone to find an answer, explanation, or solution for something even though they are thinking hard about it 迷惑；困擾：*What puzzles me is why she waited such a long time before she called an ambulance.* 讓我困惑的是，她為甚麼等了那麼久才打電話叫救護車。

baffle to leave someone completely unable to understand, explain, or solve something 使困惑；使迷惑；難住：*The police admit that they are baffled by this apparently motiveless crime.* 警察承認他們被這宗看似沒有動機的罪案難住了。

bewilder to make someone feel confused and helpless 使迷惑；使不知所措：*The speed at which technology advances bewilders many people.* 技術的迅猛發展讓許多人不知所措。

confuse to make someone unable to understand clearly what is happening or what is being said or to distinguish clearly between different things 使糊塗；使混淆：*You're confusing me – is it the brown wire or the blue wire that goes on this terminal?* 你把我弄糊塗了，終端連接線是棕色那根還是藍色那根？

disconcert (*often used in the passive*) to surprise someone and make it difficult for them to react to what has happened in a controlled way（常用於被動語態）使窘迫；使倉惶失措：*I was rather disconcerted when she announced that she was leaving right away.* 當她宣佈馬上就要離開時，我有點不知所措。

faze (*informal*) (*often used in the passive*) to disconcert someone（常用於被動語態）使驚慌失措；使困窘：*He had to face some very hostile questioning,* *but showed no sign of being fazed by it.* 他必須面對一些非常有敵意的質問，但並沒有表現出驚慌失措的樣子。

mystify (*often used in the passive*) to baffle someone（常用於被動語態）使迷惑，使困惑 : *The whole town is mystified by the sudden disappearance of one of its most prominent citizens.* 鎮上最傑出的人中的一個突然消失了，全鎮的人感到迷惑不解。

perplex (*often used in the passive*) to make someone feel anxious or worried because they cannot understand, explain, or solve something（常用於被動語態）使困惑，使茫然 : *The problem that perplexes me most is how we're going to survive financially when Jane has to give up her job.* 最使我茫然的問題是，在珍必須放棄工作之後，我們在經濟上靠甚麼來維持生計。

Q

quarrel *verb* to have an angry disagreement with someone or with each other, usually with someone that you know or have been friends with before and usually without actually exchanging blows（通常指和先前的熟人或朋友）吵架，爭吵 : *They quarrelled with their neighbours over a tree in their neighbours' garden, which they said was blocking the light to their back window.* 因為鄰居花園裏的一棵樹，他們同鄰居吵了起來，說那棵樹擋住了他們家後窗的光線。

argue to disagree with someone about something and try to change their view, sometimes angrily 爭論；爭辯；（有時指）爭吵 : *There's no point in arguing, I've already made up my mind.* 爭論沒有任何意義，我已經打定主意了。

bicker to argue or quarrel about small matters without getting very angry or violent（為小事）爭吵，發生口角，鬥嘴 : *I'd be surprised if their relationship lasts, because they're always bickering with each other.* 要是他們的關係能長久，我倒會感到奇怪了，因為他倆總是拌嘴。

fall out (with) to cease being friends with someone, or to quarrel with someone who was a friend（與朋友）鬧翻，傷和氣 : *They fell out because Roger thought Peter was having an affair with his wife, and, as far as I know, they've never spoken to one another since.* 他們鬧翻了，因為羅傑認為彼得跟他妻子有染，而就我所知，從那以後他們之間再沒有說過話。

fight (*informal*) to quarrel, sometimes exchanging blows as well as angry words 吵架；（有時指）打架 : *We don't fight very often and when we do, it's usually about money.* 我們不經常吵架，而吵的時候通常都是為了錢的事。

have a row (with) (*informal*) to quarrel 爭吵；吵架 : *George had a row with his boss and he's afraid he may lose his job over it.* 佐治和老闆吵了一架，所以他擔心可能會因此而丟掉工作。

squabble to quarrel noisily over a trivial matter（為瑣事）發生口角，爭吵 : *The children are always squabbling over who should sleep in the top bunk.* 孩子們總是為誰該睡上鋪而爭吵。

➲ see also 參見 **argument; conflict; fight; oppose**

question *verb* to express the opinion that something may not be true or trustworthy（對真實性或可信性）表示懷疑，質疑：*I wouldn't question Kay's judgment – she has excellent taste.* 我不會懷疑凱的判斷，她有極高的鑑賞力。

call into question to question something, or to make something appear doubtful or untrustworthy, especially a person's honesty, integrity, or similar qualities（尤指對人的誠實、正直等品質）產生懷疑，質疑：*When my honesty has been called into question, surely I have the right to defend myself.* 當我的誠信遭到懷疑時，我當然有權為自己辯護。

challenge to state definitely that you believe something to be incorrect 斷然懷疑，質疑（正確性）：*In this article she challenges the widely held belief that the answer to our energy crisis is to build more nuclear power stations.* 在這篇文章中，她對普遍持有的觀點提出了質疑，即解決能源危機的辦法是建造更多的核電站。

dispute to express disagreement with something 對⋯表示異議：*Nobody now disputes that global temperatures have risen in the last 50 years.* 現在沒有人否認全球氣溫在過去的 50 年裏升高了。

distrust or **mistrust** to feel that something or someone may not be genuine or good 不信任；懷疑：*I distrust their motives for wanting to buy the company.* 我懷疑他們想購買這家公司的動機。

doubt to feel unsure whether something is true, right, or real 拿不準，懷疑（真實性或正確性）：*I don't doubt that he has talent, but has he got enough talent to make a living as a writer?* 我並不懷疑他有才華，但他有足夠的能力靠寫作為生嗎？

have reservations about to feel that you cannot accept that something is completely true or right or that someone is completely trustworthy 對⋯持保留意見：*I think that most of her arguments are very sound, though I have reservations about the conclusions she draws from them.* 雖然我對她得出的結論持保留意見，可我還是覺得她的論據大多數都是非常合理的。

query to question the accuracy of something, such as a spelling or a price 對（某事的準確性）懷疑，表示疑慮：*We queried our telephone bill, as it was unusually high.* 我們對電話費單表示懷疑，因為它高得出奇。

⮕ see also 參見 **ask**

quick *adjective* taking comparatively little time to do, or doing something in a very short time（做事）快的，迅速的：*I had a quick wash and then went down to dinner.* 我很快地洗了洗就下樓吃飯去了。

brisk done at a fairly vigorous pace 輕快的；敏捷的：*a brisk walk* 輕快的步伐

fast going, or able to move, at a high speed（移動）快的，快速的：*a fast car* 一輛開得很快的轎車

hasty acting or done quickly or too quickly because you have little time or because you realize that something is urgent 匆忙的；急促的：*Don't be so hasty. Take a little while to think before you make your final decision.* 別太匆忙了，你還是考慮一會兒再作最後決定吧。

hurried done hastily because you have little time, and sometimes carelessly 匆忙的；（有時指）草率的，倉促的：*I wrote a hurried note explaining why I had to leave.* 我匆忙寫了個便條解釋我為甚麼不得不離開。

prompt done without delay 及時的；迅即的：*Thank you for your prompt reply to my letter.* 謝謝你即時回覆我的信。

rapid at a fast speed or rate 迅猛的；飛快的：*in an era of rapid social change* 在一個社會瞬息萬變的時代

speedy happening or doing something very quickly or without delay 迅速的；立刻的：*We wish you a speedy recovery.* 我們祝願你很快康復。

swift (*usually used to describe movement*) fast or quick（通常用以指運動）快的，快速的：*I wanted to be sure I could make a swift exit at the first sign of trouble.* 我想確保一旦出現麻煩的徵兆，我能馬上離開。

➲ see also 參見 **fast**

quiet *adjective* not producing much noise, or not loud 安靜的；不發出聲響的：*Be quiet when I'm talking to you!* 我對你講話時不要吱聲！

faint very quiet, quite difficult to hear（聲音）低弱的，微弱的：*a faint rustling noise* 微弱的沙沙聲

hushed quieter than usual, especially deliberately made quieter than usual（尤指故意使得比往常更）安靜的，壓低聲音的：*People waited in the church, talking in hushed voices.* 人們在教堂裏等着，一邊低聲地交頭接耳。

inaudible unable to be heard 聽不見的：*There was so much noise in the hall that parts of the speech were almost inaudible.* 大廳裏太吵，所以演講的部分內容幾乎聽不見。

muffled not heard as clearly or not sounding as loud and sharp as usual, because there is something between you and the source of the sound（因聲音源被阻隔而）模糊的，沉悶的：*a muffled explosion* 沉悶的爆炸聲

silent producing no sound at all, or not speaking（因沒有聲響或無人說話而）寂靜的，沉默的：*Everyone in the room fell silent.* 房間裏所有的人都沉默下來。

soft not loud and usually having a gentle quality（尤指音色）輕柔的，輕聲的：*a soft voice* 輕柔的聲音

➲ see also 參見 **calm²**

quite* *adverb* (*can be used for either a positive or a negative assessment of something*) to a certain degree or extent, not very（用作褒貶均可）相當，頗有點兒：*This soup is actually quite good.* 這湯味道還真不錯。

* Not used with comparatives. 不與比較級連用。

a bit (*informal*) to a small degree or by a small amount（程度或量）有點兒，稍微：*I feel a bit tired this evening.* 今晚我覺得有點兒累。

a little to a small degree or by a small amount（程度或量）稍微，有點兒：*If you wouldn't mind standing a little further back.* 如果你不介意，請再往後站一點。

fairly* (*usually used for neutral or positive assessments*) not completely or very, but to some degree（通常用作中性或褒義）相當，算得上：*I'm fairly* *certain that's what he meant, even if he didn't actually say it.* 我相當清楚那就是他的本意，儘管他沒有明説出來。

* Not used with comparatives. 不與比較級連用。

moderately* (*usually used for neutral or positive assessments*) not completely or very, but to some degree (通常用作中性或褒義) 適度地，適中地：*a moderately priced CD player* 一台價格適中的 CD 機

* Not used with comparatives. 不與比較級連用。

rather (*usually used for neutral or positive assessments*) to some extent (通常用作中性或褒義) 相當，頗：*It's rather unusual to see daffodils in flower this early in the year.* 一年裏這麼早就看見水仙開花還相當少見。

reasonably* (*usually used for neutral or positive assessments*) not completely or very, but to a usually satisfactory degree (通常用作中性或褒義) 尚可，過得去：*We're reasonably happy with the way things turned out.* 我們對事情發展的方式還算滿意。

* Not used with comparatives. 不與比較級連用。

slightly by a small extent or amount 稍微；有點兒：*It's only slightly more expensive than the other one.* 它比另外那一個只是稍微貴了點。

somewhat (*formal*) to some extent 稍微；有點兒：*I was somewhat surprised to see him at a political meeting.* 在政治會議上看見他，我感到有點兒驚訝。

➲ see also 參見 **very**

R

rain *noun* drops of water falling from the clouds 雨；雨水：*Rain is forecast for this afternoon.* 預報今天下午有雨。

downpour a heavy fall of rain 瓢潑大雨，傾盆大雨：*I got caught in a downpour as I was coming home from the shops.* 正當我離開商店回家時，遇到了瓢潑大雨。

drizzle a light, but steady fall of rain 細雨；毛毛雨：*After some light drizzle, the day should turn dry.* 淅淅瀝瀝的小雨之後，天氣會變得乾燥起來。

rainfall (*usually used in technical discussions of weather conditions*) the amount of rain that falls (通常用於討論氣候條件) 降雨量：*The rainfall for this month has been about average.* 本月的降水量差不多是常年的平均值。

shower a fall of rain that lasts for a comparatively short time 陣雨：*It's only a shower; it'll be over in a few minutes.* 只是一場陣雨，過幾分鐘就會停的。

storm a period when there is heavy rain accompanied by strong winds and sometimes thunder 暴風雨；暴雨；(有時指) 雷雨：*Those black clouds mean there's going to be a storm.* 那些烏雲意味着將有一場暴雨。

thunderstorm a storm with thunder and lightning 雷雨：*You shouldn't shelter under a tree in a thunderstorm.* 雷雨時不應該躲在樹底下。

refuse[1] *verb* to say that you will not do something or that you do not want something 拒絕（做或接受）: *When I asked her to come with me to the police station, she refused.* 當我要她和我一起去警察局時，她拒絕了。

decline (*formal*) to refuse to do something, or not to take or accept something, usually politely（通常指禮貌地）拒絕，謝絕: *I regretfully had to decline their invitation to their daughter's wedding.* 我不得不遺憾地謝絕了出席他們女兒婚禮的邀請。

deny to say that something is not the case or that you have not done something that someone else says you have done 拒不承認；否認: *He denies that he was in the building at the time the incident took place.* 他矢口否認事件發生時他在大樓裏。

pass up (*informal*) not to accept or take something, usually something beneficial or enjoyable, when it is offered to you 放棄，不接受（有利或快樂之事）: *I had to pass up the chance of going to the theatre with them.* 我不得不放棄那次與他們一起去看戲的機會。

reject to say that you do not want something or someone, often suggesting that they are not good enough for you（常指因為不夠好而）拒絕: *My novel has so far been rejected by every single publisher I have sent it to.* 到目前為止，我投出去的小說已經被所有的出版商拒絕了。

say no (to) to refuse something（對…）説不；拒絕；反對: *I wouldn't say no to a cup of tea.* 喝杯茶我是不會拒絕的。

spurn to reject something or someone angrily or with contempt（憤怒或輕蔑地）棄絕，唾棄: *They spurned our offers of financial help.* 他們對我們提供的資助嗤之以鼻。

refuse[2] *verb* to say that you will not give someone something that they want or ask for 拒絕給予: *The authorities refused permission for the company to build on land next to the river.* 當局拒不同意該公司在河邊地帶建房。

deny not to give, grant, or allow someone something 拒絕給予；不允許: *He felt that he'd been denied the chance to tell his side of the story.* 他覺得沒有給他機會講述他自己這一方的情況。

turn down not to accept something such as a request, application, or suggestion, or not to accept someone who wants to join something 拒絕接受（請求、申請、建議等）；拒絕加入: *I applied to join the police force, but they turned me down.* 我申請加入警察隊伍，但被他們拒絕了。

withhold (*formal*) not to allow someone to have something, often temporarily（常指暫時地）拒絕給予: *The mortgage company is withholding part of the loan until we've had the roof repaired.* 抵押貸款公司扣留着部分貸款，要到我們把房頂修好後才給予。

regret *noun* a feeling of sadness about something that has happened, often a bad action, mistake, etc., that you yourself have committed, coupled with a wish that it had not happened 遺憾；歉意；懊悔: *I want to express my regret for any inconvenience you may have suffered.* 我想對您可能感到的任何不便表示歉意。

contrition (*formal*) a feeling of guilt and remorse 悔悟；悔改：*I would be more inclined to forgive him if he showed any sign of contrition.* 如果他有任何悔改的表現，我倒更傾向於原諒他。

grief deep sadness, especially because someone has died（尤指因某人去世引起的）悲痛，悲傷：*We share the grief of those who have lost loved ones in this conflict.* 我們與那些在本次衝突中失去親人的人們同悲傷。

penance something unpleasant you do to show that you realize you have sinned or done wrong and wish to punish yourself in order to make up for it 懺悔；苦修；補贖：*As a penance, he volunteered to clean the toilets for a week.* 作為懺悔，他自願打掃一個星期的廁所。

penitence (*formal*) repentance 悔悟；悔恨：*In order to show penitence, you must first make a full confession of what you have done wrong.* 你必須首先坦白你犯下的所有過錯以表示悔悟。

remorse a feeling of deep and painful sadness because you know that you have committed a bad action 悔罪；悔過：*During all his time in prison, he never expressed any remorse for his crime.* 在他蹲監獄的日子裏，從來沒有表達過任何悔罪之意。

repentance realization that you have committed a crime or sin, sorrow for it, and a wish to behave better in future 悔恨；悔悟：*Do you think her repentance is sincere?* 你認為她的悔悟是真心誠意的嗎？

sorrow a feeling of deep sadness, regret, or disappointment, or something that causes someone to feel sad 痛惜；傷心；傷心事：*Times of joy are almost inevitably followed by times of sorrow.* 快樂的時光過後，幾乎不可避免地有悲傷的日子跟隨。

release *verb* to allow someone or something that is held, captured, etc., to be free or move freely again 釋放，放走（被囚、被俘的人或動物）：*The animals are nearly ready to be released into the wild.* 這些動物差不多馬上就要被放生了。

deliver (*literary*) to save or rescue someone from something bad 解救；拯救；營救：*'Deliver us from evil' is a line in the Lord's Prayer.* "拯救我們於邪惡吧" 是一句對主的禱告詞。

discharge to officially allow a person to leave a hospital or the army, air force, etc. 准許（某人）離開（醫院、軍隊等）：*The patient was discharged from hospital.* 病人獲准出院了。

emancipate (*formal*) to free someone from slavery or a similar condition 使不受（奴隸制等的）束縛；解放：*An Act of Parliament was passed emancipating all the slaves in British territories.* 一部關於解放英屬地區所有奴隸的《議會法案》被通過了。

free to release a person or animal that is in captivity, to release something that is held, tied, or stuck, or to remove a restriction or burden from someone 釋放；解除；使自由：*I managed to free my right arm and then tried to untie the ropes that were binding my legs.* 我先設法讓右臂脫了出來，然後努力解開捆綁着雙腿的繩子。

let go to stop holding or gripping something, or to release someone or something 放開；鬆開；釋放：*Let go of my arm – you're hurting me.* 放開我的胳臂，你把我弄痛了。

liberate to release someone who is a prisoner or slave, or to enable a country or area that has been under the control of an enemy to govern itself again 釋放（囚犯或奴隸等）；解放（敵佔區或國家等）：*This was one of the first villages to be liberated when Allied forces landed in France.* 這是盟軍登陸法國後最先解放的村莊之一。

set free to release a person or animal that is in captivity 釋放（被俘獲的人或動物）：*The hostages begged their captors to set them free.* 那些人質乞求挾持者放了他們。

unleash (*usually used figuratively*) to allow something violent that has previously been restrained to operate with full force（通常用作引申意義）激發，發洩（被全力壓抑的強烈情緒）：*The government's attempt to impose new taxes unleashed a storm of protest.* 政府試圖徵收新稅，激發了一場抗議風暴。

relentless *adjective* not stopping and not decreasing the amount of effort that is put into doing something or the amount of pressure put on other people to make them do something 不懈的；不減弱的；不斷的：*the relentless quest for perfection* 對完美的不斷追求

inexorable (*formal*) that cannot be prevented from happening or from doing something 不可避免的；無法阻擋的：*an inexorable fate* 不可避免的命運

insistent demanding that something should be done, and not allowing someone else to ignore the demand 堅持要求的；堅決主張的：*She was most insistent that I should call you straight away.* 她非常堅決地要我立刻給你打電話。

persistent continuing to do something or ask for something, even if people refuse or if you do not succeed at first（儘管他人拒絕或起初沒成功卻）執意的，堅持不懈的：*I wasn't going to go out with him, but he was so persistent that eventually I gave in.* 我並不打算和他一起出去，但他太固執，我最後還是讓步了。

pitiless showing no pity for people or their weaknesses（對他人或其弱點）冷酷的，無憐憫之心的：*pitiless cruelty* 殘酷無情

remorseless continuing without stopping regardless of people's wishes or feelings（不顧他人的願望或感情而）無休止的，不停的：*remorseless questioning* 沒完沒了的詢問

unrelenting not stopping or decreasing 不懈的；堅定的；不停的：*The work continued at the same unrelenting pace.* 工作繼續以相同的步調緊鑼密鼓地進行着。

reliable *adjective* able to be trusted to do what they say they will do or what you want them to do 可信賴的；可靠的：*I'm sorry to hear that John let you down; I don't know what could have happened as he's usually so reliable.* 聽說約翰讓你失望了，我很遺憾，因為他一向很可靠，我不知道可能發生了甚麼事情。

conscientious working hard and being careful and thorough so as to make sure that everything you have to do is done well 認真負責的；勤勤懇懇的：*She's very conscientious and always checks and rechecks her work for mistakes in spelling or grammar.* 她非常認真，總是反覆檢查自己作業中的拼寫或語法錯誤。

dependable able to be trusted to do what they say they will do or what you want them to do 可靠的；可信賴的：*I need someone who is dependable to be my assistant.* 我需要一個可靠的人當我的助手。

honest morally good and trustworthy, especially not likely to steal or to tell lies 誠實的；正直的：*He's too honest to try to cover up any mistakes that he made.* 他很誠實，不會極力掩蓋自己犯的錯誤。

mature showing the qualities expected of an adult, such as good judgment, responsibility, and a serious attitude to life 成熟的；明白事理的；穩重的：*I expect him to be mature enough to understand there are no simple solutions to problems of this kind.* 我期望他很明事理，能夠懂得這類問題沒有簡單的解決辦法。

responsible showing an ability or a willingness to carry out tasks or deal with situations sensibly without needing to be supervised by someone else 有責任感的；負責任的：*Unless you show that you can behave in a responsible way, they'll never make you captain of the team.* 除非你表明能夠擔當起責任，不然他們是不會選你當隊長的。

thorough not leaving out any necessary part of something that has to be done, but dealing fully with every aspect of it 仔細周到的，一絲不苟的：*They were very thorough and read every single document relating to the case.* 他們非常周詳，查閱了與案件有關的每一份文件資料。

trustworthy able to be trusted, not likely either to deceive or cheat you, reveal information that is supposed to be secret or confidential, or fail to do anything that they are supposed to do 值得信任的；可信賴的；可靠的：*She often has access to confidential information and has always shown herself to be completely trustworthy.* 她經常接觸機密情報，自始自終都表明她是完全可以信賴的。

➲ see also 參見 **devoted; faithful**

religious *adjective* to do with the knowledge or worship of God, or showing belief in God or interest in the spiritual side of life 宗教的；篤信宗教的：*We don't go to church, but that doesn't mean we're not religious.* 我們不去教堂做禮拜，但這並不說明我們不信宗教。

devout sincerely believing in and taking your religious duties seriously（對上帝）虔誠的：*Devout Muslims make a pilgrimage to Mecca at least once in their lives.* 虔誠的穆斯林一生中至少有一次去麥加朝聖。

ecclesiastical connected with the Church or churches 與教堂有關的；與教會有關的：*ecclesiastical architecture* 教堂式建築

holy of or like God, set apart for the service of God; spiritually pure; devout 神聖的；聖潔的；虔誠的：*Believers are called to lead a holy life.* 信徒們被要求過聖潔的生活。

pious showing great devotion to God and respect for religious doctrine in the way you behave 虔誠的；篤信宗教的：*Not all medieval monks were pious; some of them were very worldly and ambitious.* 並非所有的中世紀修道士都很虔誠，他們中有些人非常世俗，而且野心勃勃。

reverent showing respect for God or sacred things（對上帝或神聖的東西）深表崇敬的，虔誠的：*a reverent silence* 虔誠的靜穆

sacred considered to be special and to deserve particular care and respect, especially because of being connected with God or religion 上帝的；神的；神聖的：*sacred relics* 神聖的遺物

spiritual not relating to the body or earthly life, but to the soul, religion, or divine beings 精神的；心靈的：*a spiritual experience* 精神體驗

remain *verb* to continue to be in the same place or in the same condition 保持；依然：*We have remained friends ever since our schooldays.* 打從在校讀書時，我們就一直是朋友。

continue to keep happening or existing 繼續，持續（發生或存在）：*The controversy surrounding the Minister's business interests continues.* 圍繞部長的商業權益的論戰仍然在繼續。

endure to continue to exist, or continue to be successful, for a long time, without becoming less 持續；持久：*Their friendship endured for over twenty years.* 他們的友誼持續了 20 多年。

go on to continue to exist or happen 繼續，接着：*His affair with his secretary is still going on.* 他與秘書的風流韻事仍然在繼續。

last to continue to exist for a long time 持續；延續：*The ill will between the two families has lasted since 1975.* 兩家人的冤仇從 1975 年開始一直持續到現在。

persist to continue to exist, especially for a long time 持續存在（尤指很長時間）：*If the pain persists, you should see a doctor.* 如果疼痛一直持續，你應該看醫生。

stay to continue to be in the same place, position, or condition 保持，停留（在同一地方、位置或狀況）：*This song stayed at Number One for three weeks.* 這首歌連續 3 週排行第一。

survive to continue to exist or continue to flourish in spite of difficulties 繼續存在；倖存：*Somehow our local butcher's has survived while many small shops have closed since the large supermarkets moved into the area.* 不知怎的，自從大超市遷到這個地區以後，許多小商店都關閉了，而我們本地肉店卻倖存了下來。

remember *verb* to retain knowledge, information, experience, etc., that you had in the past and be able to bring it back from your memory, or not to forget to do something 回憶；記得：*I can remember things that happened fifty years ago better than I can remember things that happened last week.* 我對 50 年前發生的事情比對上個星期發生的事還要記得清楚。

call to mind to bring something back to your memory 回想起；回憶：*He called to mind how he had seen his mother dying.* 他回想起自己看到母親臨死時的情形。

hark back to think or speak about something that happened in the past, often in a way that other people find irritating or strange（常指以讓人惱火或奇怪的方式）回顧，重提（舊事）：*She keeps harking back to the 1960s.* 她老是叨念 20 世紀 60 年代的事。

look back to remember and think about the events of a particular period in the past 回顧；追憶：*Looking back over your long and distinguished career,* *what do you consider to be your greatest achievement?* 當您回顧過去漫長而卓著的生涯時，您認為您最大的成就是甚麼？

recall to be able to bring something back from your memory 回憶；記起：*I can't quite recall her exact words, but she was very scathing about her brother.* 我記不起她具體說了些甚麼，但她對她的弟弟非常嚴厲。

recognize to be able to identify someone or something that you have seen or known in the past when you see them again（再次見到時）認出：*Would you recognize the man who attacked you if you saw him again?* 如果你再看到攻擊你的那個人，能認出他嗎？

recollect (*formal*) to recall something, or not to forget something 回憶起；記得：*I recollect that, fifty years ago, television was still a relatively new medium.* 我記得，50 年前，電視還是一種相對較新的媒體。

remind to cause someone to remember something, especially to say or do something that helps someone to remember what they intended to do（尤指以言語或行為）提醒，使想起：*Remind me to write a note to Jean thanking her for her present.* 提醒我給瓊寫封短信感謝她送的禮物。

reminisce to talk pleasantly about things that happened in the past, especially with another person who shared the experience（尤指與共同經歷者一起）敘舊，追憶，緬懷：*They were reminiscing about their days in the army.* 他們在一起回憶在部隊的日子。

think of (*informal*) to recall something 想起；記起：*I can't think of his name, but I know it begins with B.* 我想不起他的名字來了，但我知道那是以 B 開頭的。

replace *verb* to act or function instead of something or someone else 取代；替換：*Gary Neville has to miss this game through injury, so Wes Brown replaces him at right back.* 加里・內維爾由於受傷不能比賽，所以韋斯・布朗代替他擔當右後衛。

deputize for to do the job of someone else, usually a more senior person, temporarily 臨時接替；充當…的代理人：*I'm deputizing for the managing director while he's on holiday.* 在總裁度假期間，我臨時代理他的職務。

fill in for (*informal*) to act as a temporary replacement for someone, or deputize for them 臨時補缺；暫時代理：*I can't go to the meeting next week, so would you mind filling in for me?* 下個星期我不能去開會，請你替我去好嗎？

replace with to remove or omit something or someone and use something or someone to do the same job 以…取代；用…替換：*When the ink cartridge is empty, you simply replace it with a new one.* 墨盒用完了，你就直接換個新的吧。

stand in for (*informal*) to act as a temporary replacement for someone, or deputize for them 臨時替代；當替身：*My job is to stand in for the star if she can't perform for any reason.* 如果那位明星因故無法表演，我的工作就是給她當替身。

substitute for to use something or someone instead of something or someone else 代替；取代：*You can substitute 20 grams of breadcrumbs for 20 grams of flour in this recipe to produce a lighter dough.* 在這道食譜中，你可以用 20 克麵包屑代替 20 克麵粉做出更加鬆軟的麵糰。

succeed to be the person who holds a particular position after someone else 繼任；接替：*Paul succeeded his brother Hugh as managing director of the company.* 保羅接替他的兄長曉治擔任了公司總裁。

supersede to replace something that is now obsolete 取代（廢棄之物）：*The word-processor has superseded the old-fashioned typewriter.* 文字處理器已取代了過時的打字機。

supplant (*formal*) to replace someone or something that is not ready to be replaced 排擠；取代：*She hatched an elaborate plot to supplant her rival as the king's favourite mistress.* 她精心策劃了一項陰謀，以取代對手而成為國王的寵妃。

　 ➲ see also 參見 **replace with**

respect *noun* a feeling that something or someone is good or valuable and ought to be treated with care and paid attention to 尊敬；尊重：*You should treat the religious beliefs of other people with proper respect.* 你應該充分尊重他人的宗教信仰。

admiration a feeling that something or someone deserves praise 欽佩；敬佩：*I'm full of admiration for the way you handled the situation.* 我對您應對局勢的方式充滿敬佩之情。

consideration respect for the feelings of other people, usually coupled with kind or lenient treatment（通常指寬厚仁慈）體諒，考慮周到：*Show some consideration for her, as she's not been well.* 對她體諒一些，因為她身體一直不好。

esteem (*formal*) your judgment (*usually favourable*) of the goodness or value of another person（通常指對他人的優點或價值的）評判，好評：*She stands very high in my esteem.* 她在我的心目中地位很高。

estimation (*formal*) your judgment (*good or bad*) of the moral qualities of another person（對他人的道德品質作出好或壞的）評價，評判：*He has gone down in my estimation since he treated his wife so badly.* 鑒於他如此惡劣地虐待妻子，他在我心目中的威信已降低了。

regard a feeling of respect and admiration for someone or something 敬重；仰慕：*My regard for her talents and her personal qualities is as high now as it ever was.* 我自始至終都非常敬重她的才華和人品。

reverence a sense of great respect for God, a great person, or something important（對上帝、偉人或要事的）崇敬，尊重：*We need to rediscover a reverence for the environment.* 我們需要找回對環境的一份尊重。

veneration very deep respect, of the kind you might show to a saint, a sacred object, or a really great person（對聖人、神物或偉人表達的）敬仰，崇拜：*He has a profound veneration for his ancestors.* 他對祖先懷有深深的敬仰之情。

　 ➲ see also 參見 **admire**

responsible *adjective* having the job of dealing with or looking after something and able to be blamed if that job is not done properly 負責的；負責任的：*The captain is responsible for the safety of the ship and its passengers.* 船長要負責輪船及乘客的安全。

accountable responsible or answerable 有責任的；應負責任的：*I can't be held accountable for decisions that were taken by other people.* 我不應該對他人所作的決定負責任。

answerable having to explain and justify your actions to a particular person who has the power to punish you in some way 應負責的；承擔後果的；承擔責任的：*You'll be answerable to me if anything goes wrong.* 如果出了差錯，你必須給我一個交代。

at fault (*formal*) having acted wrongly（因出差錯而）應受責備的，應負責任的：*The committee concluded that the director had been at fault in authorizing the project without proper consultation.* 委員會議定，董事未經充分協商就授權該項計劃，應當承擔責任。

guilty proved to have committed a crime or done something wrong, or feeling sorry and worried because you know you have done something wrong 有罪的；內疚的：*I was guilty of poor judgment, not of any crime.* 我無罪可究，錯就錯在判斷不足。

in charge (of) being the person who controls a particular operation or particular group of people 主管，負責（業務或團體等）：*She left her deputy in charge while she was abroad on business.* 她在國外出差期間，讓她的副手代為負責。

liable legally obliged to pay a particular sum of money, for example, as tax or compensation 有法律義務的（如繳納稅金或補償金等）：*liable for income tax* 有義務繳納所得稅

to blame having caused something that did harm or was wrong 有過錯的；應受到責備的：*Nobody was really to blame for the accident.* 沒有人真正應該對這件事故負責任。

➲ see also 參見 **reliable; sensible**

restrain *verb* not to allow something, someone, or yourself to become too violent or forceful or to express themselves openly, or to prevent someone, for example a prisoner, from behaving violently by holding them, handcuffing them, etc. 抑制，遏制（以防變得過於激烈、強硬或直白）；（通過拘留、上手銬等方式）阻止，限制（囚犯等的暴力行為）：*I couldn't restrain myself any longer and burst out laughing.* 我再也忍不住，突然大笑起來。

control not to allow something, someone, or yourself to act freely, especially to limit or restrain something or someone（尤指）限制，限定（行動自由）：*Government efforts to control immigration have so far failed.* 政府限制外來移民的努力迄今未獲成功。

curb to keep something under strict control and, usually, to reduce it 嚴格控制；抑制：*He should try to curb his enthusiasm and act more rationally.* 他應該設法抑制自己的衝動，做事更理智一些。

hold back to restrain something such as tears or laughter, or to stop something from progressing or developing as fast as it would like 抑制（淚水或笑聲等）；阻止（某事的進程或發展）：*Business is being held back by government restrictions.* 商業正受到政府限制性政策的制約。

inhibit to prevent an event or process from developing 約束，阻止（事件或過程的發展）：*Does the Internet encourage or inhibit learning?* 互聯網是促進還是妨礙學習呢？

keep under control to control 控制：*If you can't keep your children under control, you'll have to take them out.* 你要是管不住自己的小孩，就必須把他們帶出去。

limit not to allow something to exceed a particular amount or extent, or not to allow someone complete freedom 限制，限定（數量、範圍或充分自由）：*You'd be wise to limit the amount of time you spend on each question in the exam.* 在考試中，你要是能限定每道題的答題時間就高明了。

restrict to limit something, especially to allow less of something than something or someone needs or wants 限制，約束（使之不超過需要的範圍）：*The amount that each candidate in the election can spend on publicity will be restricted to $20,000.* 每位候選人用於競選宣傳的開支將被限定在 2 萬美元之內。

suppress to take action to make sure that something cannot operate, show itself, or express itself at all 鎮壓，壓制（以使無法運行或表現出來）：*All opposition to the regime was suppressed.* 所有反對該政權的勢力都遭到了鎮壓。

result *noun* what is produced by a cause or by an action, or the final score in a contest that shows who won, etc.（原因或行為的）結果，後果；（競賽等的）成績：*The only result of your actions has been to make an already difficult situation worse.* 你們行動的結果只能是讓本來已經艱難的處境雪上加霜。

aftermath the period after a dramatic or important event in which the effects of it are felt or assessed（戲劇性或重大事件後的）結局，後果：*In the aftermath of the disaster, many important safety issues had to be reconsidered.* 這場災難之後，許多重大的安全問題必須重新予以考慮。

consequence what something causes, an event that is the result of a previous event（某事引起的）結果，後果：*The inevitable consequence of poor hygiene is that diseases spread more rapidly.* 衛生條件差不可避免的結果就是疾病的傳播更快。

effect something produced by a cause, often a state or reaction（常指某種狀態或反應產生的）結果，效應，影響：*I don't know what effect the book had on other readers, but it depressed me terribly.* 我不知道這本書對其他的讀者產生甚麼影響，但它讓我感到十分沮喪。

outcome what a process leads to, or the result of a contest（某一過程導致的）結果，成果；（競賽等的）成績：*Whatever the outcome of these negotiations, neither side is likely to get everything it wants.* 無論這些談判的結果如何，雙方都不可能完全如願以償。

reaction what someone does as a result of something that happened to them or of what someone else says or does（對發生的事情或他人的言行的）反應，回應：*My first reaction was one of surprise.* 我第一個反應就是感到吃驚。

repercussions results taking place over a period of time that are usually harmful or unfavourable to someone（通常指在一段時間內對某人造成的）負面影響，反響，惡果：*The ban on smoking in public places is bound to have serious repercussions for the tobacco industry.* 禁止在公共場所吸煙的規定必然會對煙草業造成嚴重的負面影響。

sequel what happened after and as a result of a particular event, or a book, film, etc., showing what happened after the events depicted in a previous book, film, etc. 後續的事；（書、電影等的）續篇，續集：*She's writing a sequel to Pride and Prejudice.* 她正在寫《傲慢與偏見》的續篇。

upshot an event that is result of a previous event or process（前一事件或過程的）結果，結局：*The upshot was that we decided to share the costs of the trip.* 最後我們決定分攤旅行開支。

reveal *verb* to make visible or known, deliberately or accidentally, something that has previously been invisible or unknown（指有意或偶然地）透露，顯示，揭示：*The curtains opened to reveal the battlements of the castle at Elsinore.* 窗簾拉開了，眼前展現的是埃爾西諾城堡的牆垛。

bring to light to find and reveal something that was previously hidden or secret 揭露，披露（隱藏物或秘密等）；使重見天日：*The manuscript lay undiscovered in the archives for centuries and has only recently been brought to light.* 幾個世紀以來這部手稿一直在卷宗裏沒有人注意到，只是最近才被披露出來。

display to make something visible, for example, on a screen, especially to put something in a place where it can be easily seen by a lot of people（通過屏幕等）顯示；（尤指）展覽，展出：*a notice displayed in a shop window* 在一家商店的櫥窗裏貼出的佈告

exhibit to display a work of art or something valuable or interesting in a place where the public can see it 展覽，展出（藝術品、貴重的或引起興趣的物品等）：*Her paintings are being exhibited at an art gallery in London.* 她的油畫正在倫敦的一家藝術館展覽。

expose to remove the covering from something, especially something that would normally be kept covered, so that it becomes visible; to find and reveal something that was previously hidden or secret 使顯露；使露出；暴露：*The wallpaper has come off, exposing the bare plaster.* 牆紙脫落了，露出了光禿禿的灰泥。

lay bare to remove the covering from something, especially something that would normally be kept covered, so that it becomes visible; to find and reveal something that was previously hidden or secret 使顯露；裸露；暴露：*The information laid bare the enemy's true intentions.* 這個情報顯露出敵人的真正意圖。

show to allow or enable someone to see something 出示；展示：*You haven't shown us your wedding photos yet.* 你還沒有把你們的結婚照給我們看呢。

uncover to remove the covering from something, especially something that is meant to be shown at least occasionally 揭開蓋子；（尤指）揭露，揭發：*Don't uncover the sandwiches until we're ready to eat them.* 等我們準備吃三文治的時候再打開蓋子。

unveil to show something such as a statue or a plaque publicly for the first time at a special ceremony in which a cover is removed from it, or to display or announce something such as a new car or a set of plans for the first time 為（雕像、牌匾等）揭幕；（首次）推出（新車等）；將（方案等）公諸於眾：*A plaque commemorating the royal visit was unveiled by Her Majesty the Queen.* 一塊紀念王室來訪的牌匾由女王陛下親自揭幕。

➲ see also 參見 **betray²**

revenge *noun* a punishment that is given to someone for having harmed you, defeated you, etc., especially a punishment that you give them personally

（尤指親自進行的）報復，復仇，雪恥：*She had her revenge the following year, when she knocked the same opponent out in the first round of the competition.* 在接下來那一年，她在第一輪比賽中就擊敗了上次的對手，報了一箭之仇。

redress (*formal*) the putting right of a wrong that has been done to you（對冤屈等的）糾正，洗雪：*In a civilized society people seek redress through the courts; they do not revenge their injuries personally.* 在文明社會裏，人們不會因為受到傷害就自行報復，而是通過法院尋求解決辦法。

reprisal an action carried out, especially by an army, to punish someone who has attacked or harmed them（尤指軍隊因為受到了攻擊或傷害而採取的）報復行動：*Troops were ordered not to take reprisals against the civilian population.* 軍隊被命令不准對平民採取報復行動。

retaliation the act of attacking or harming someone who has previously attacked or harmed you（對曾經攻擊或傷害過自己的人採取的）報復，復仇：*The terrorists say they took the hostages in retaliation for the attack on the base.* 恐怖分子聲稱，他們綁架人質是對基地遭到攻擊採取的報復行動。

retribution some form of compensation for the fact that a crime has been committed against you, such as the punishment of the person who committed the crime 報應；懲罰：*Society is surely entitled to demand retribution when a person deliberately breaks the law.* 當一個人知法犯法時，社會當然有權要求他受到懲罰。

vendetta a long-lasting situation between two or more people or groups in which one harms the other, the other retaliates, the first retaliates for that attack, etc.（人與人之間或團體之間的）積怨，宿怨，長期不和：*The unfortunate lovers are caught up in the vendetta between their two families.* 這對不幸的情侶被捲到兩家的世仇之中。

vengeance (*usually used in describing dramatic feelings and situations*) revenge（通常用以描述強烈的情感或動人的情景）報仇，復仇：*He vows he will exact vengeance on those who had him falsely imprisoned.* 他發誓要向那些將他誣陷入獄的人報仇。

reward[1] *noun* something, especially a sum of money, that you receive in return for some achievement or for a good deed（尤指因某一成就或善行獲得的）獎賞，報酬，回報：*The police are offering a substantial reward for any information leading to the arrest of the murderer.* 警方重金懸賞任何能使兇犯緝拿歸案的線索。

award something that you are presented with to honour some achievement 獎勵；獎品；獎狀：*Archie won an award for the best-kept garden in the village.* 阿奇獲得了村裏的最佳園林維護獎。

benefit a regular payment made by the government to a person who needs financial help because of unemployment, illness, etc.（政府定期向失業人員、病人等發放的）救濟金，補助費，撫恤金：*The family has been living on benefits since the father lost his job.* 自從父親失去工作後，這家人就一直靠救濟金生活。

bonus a single, or sometimes an annual, payment made by an employer to an employee who has done especially good work, or as a share in the profits

（僱主發給僱員的）獎金；（有時指年度）紅利：*On top of the salary, the job offers a profit-sharing bonus.* 除了薪水之外，這份工作還提供分紅。

premium a sum of money paid in addition to the usual payment for something, for example in addition to a salary or a price 補貼；額外費用；附加費：*Solo travellers often have to pay a premium for a single room.* 獨自旅行的人常常得額外付費才能入住單人房。

prize something, such as a sum of money or a trophy, that you are given to honour some achievement, or in return for winning a competition or sporting event（因取得成就或贏得比賽而獲得的）獎金，獎品，獎賞：*The prize for winning this competition is a holiday for four in Florida.* 贏得這場競賽的獎勵是 4 人一行到佛羅里達州去度假。

prize money a sum of money that you win in a competition or a sporting event（競賽或體育運動贏得的）獎金：*Contestants in this quiz show can win up to one million pounds in prize money.* 參加本次智力競猜節目的選手有機會獲得高達 100 萬英鎊的獎金。

profit money that you gain, for example from a business deal, when the amount that you receive is more than you have spent（指生意等的）利潤，收益，盈利：*Because property prices have increased enormously since we bought our house, we made a huge profit when we sold it.* 自從我們買房以來地產價格大幅上漲，所以我們賣房子後賺了一大筆錢。

reward² *verb* to give someone a sum of money or a gift in return for some achievement or for a good deed（以現金或禮品等）酬謝，獎勵（某人的成績或善行）：*The girl was rewarded for her honesty by the person who had lost the wallet that she found and handed over to the police.* 這位女孩撿到錢包，將它交給了警察，由於她拾金不昧，得到了失主的酬謝。

honour to pay tribute to someone who is held in high esteem 給予表揚（或獎勵）；授予稱號：*The veteran actor was honoured by the British Academy with a lifetime achievement award.* 這位老演員被英國電影學院授予終身成就獎。

pay to give money to someone in return for work or for something else that they have done for you 付給（某人工資或報酬等）：*The old lady pays her neighbour's son to look after her garden.* 老太太付錢僱用鄰居家的男孩照顧她的花園。

recompense (*formal*) to give something, especially money, to someone in return for their efforts or to compensate for injury, loss, or inconvenience 酬謝；賠償，補償（傷害、損失或不便等）：*The airline apologized for the long delay and assured us that we would be recompensed.* 航空公司就長時間延誤表示道歉，並保證給我們以賠償。

remunerate (*formal*) to pay someone money in return for work 付酬勞；付報酬：*Anyone who is prepared to work over the weekend will be well remunerated for their efforts.* 願意在週末加班的任何人都會因辛勤付出而得到豐厚的報酬。

tip to give a small sum of money to someone such as a waiter or hairdresser, to show that you appreciate what they have done for you 付小費（給服務員、理髮師等）：*I was happy to tip the waitress handsomely, since the service had been excellent.* 因為服務非常周到，我很樂意付給女服務生優厚的小費。

rich *adjective* having a lot of money and possessions 有錢的；富有的：*They must be rich if they can afford two houses and three cars.* 如果他們買得起 2 幢房子和 3 輛小汽車的話，他們一定很有錢。

affluent rich, or in which most people are comparatively rich 富裕的；富足的：*the affluent society* 富足的社會

better off having more money and possessions than before, or comparatively rich 更富裕的；更寬裕的：*We're definitely better off now than we were three years ago.* 我們現在比 3 年前明顯優裕多了。

loaded (*informal*) very rich 很富有的：*Of course she has nice things – her parents are loaded.* 她當然有吸引人的地方，她的爹媽很有錢。

prosperous doing well in life or business and having or earning lots of money (生活) 繁榮富足的；(生意) 興隆的：*a prosperous company* 一家景氣的公司

rolling in it or rolling in money (*informal*) very rich 非常富有的：*If they own a private jet, they must be absolutely rolling in it.* 如果他們擁有一架私人噴氣式飛機，他們絕對是腰纏萬貫。

wealthy rich 富有的；充裕的：*a wealthy country* 富饒的國家

well off fairly rich, or having many advantages, compared to other people 富裕的；殷實的：*You no longer have to be well off to own a car.* 你不需要很富裕就能擁有一輛車了。

well-to-do (*old-fashioned*) (*only used to describe people*) having more money than most ordinary people (僅用以描述人) 富裕的，寬裕的：*She comes from a well-to-do family.* 她出身於殷實人家。

➔ see also 參見 **wealth**

ridiculous *adjective* contrary to common sense and ordinary behaviour in a way that might make people laugh scornfully, or very foolish or funny 荒謬的；荒唐可笑的；滑稽的：*You look absolutely ridiculous in that hat.* 你戴那頂帽子看上去太滑稽了。

absurd contrary to reason and common sense, ridiculous and odd 荒謬的；荒誕的：*It's absurd to suggest that she might have been involved in the plot.* 認為她可能捲入到這場陰謀之中實在是荒唐。

farcical absurd and often making the people involved look very foolish 鬧劇性的；荒唐的：*We ended up in a farcical situation where everybody knew the secret but nobody knew that anyone else knew it.* 我們鬧劇般地收場，到頭來人人都知道這一秘密，但誰也沒想到別人也都知道這一秘密。

laughable* not to be taken seriously because ridiculous 荒唐可笑的：*The idea that people will actually benefit from having to pay higher taxes is simply laughable.* 認為人們必須多納稅才能切實獲益的想法簡直可笑。

* Most often used after a verb. 最常用於動詞後。

ludicrous absurd 荒唐的；荒謬的：*He came up with the absolutely ludicrous idea of extracting energy from moonbeams.* 他提出了從月光裏吸取能量這種荒謬無比的想法。

nonsensical that does not make sense, that is nonsense 無意義的；荒唐的：*a nonsensical suggestion* 一個荒唐的建議

rise *verb* to move or lead upwards, to become higher, or to be tall or high 上升；增長：*The sun rises tomorrow morning at 6.00 am precisely.* 明天日出時間是在早晨 6 點正。

ascend (*formal*) to go upwards 登高；升高：*a pillar of smoke ascending a few hundred metres into the air* 空中升起一股數百米高的煙柱

climb (*said especially about an aircraft*) to fly upwards to a greater height (尤指飛機等) 爬升，攀升：*The aircraft took off and then climbed steeply to 2000 metres.* 飛機起飛後陡升到兩千米的高空。

loom (up) to be tall or high and look rather threatening 赫然聳現：*As we turned the corner, the mountain loomed into view.* 我們一拐過彎，大山便赫然聳現在我們眼前。

soar to fly or rise up high into the air 直衝雲霄；高飛：*The eagle soars above the mountain tops.* 鷹在山頂的上空翱翔。

swell (up) to become bigger and higher as its surface expands because of the material collecting inside 腫脹；膨脹；高漲：*My ankle has swollen because an insect bit me.* 我的腳踝被昆蟲咬了，所以腫起來了。

tower to be very tall, especially to be much taller than something standing next to it or things standing around 屹立；高聳：*He towers over his wife, who's rather short and dumpy.* 他高出又矮又胖的妻子一大截。

➲ see also 參見 **climb; increase**

road *noun* a way with a specially hardened surface that vehicles can travel along (車輛行駛的) 道路，大道：*They're digging up the road again outside our house.* 他們又在我們屋子外面挖路。

avenue a street, usually a fairly wide street in a smart area of town (通常指市鎮繁華區域的) 大街，林蔭大道：*We strolled down the avenue.* 我們在大街上閒逛。

bypass a road built to carry traffic around a town or village (繞過市鎮或村莊的) 旁道：*The bypass was built to reduce the amount of traffic passing through the town centre.* 旁道的修建是為了減少穿越市中心的交通量。

footpath a way, which may or not be paved, intended for people who are walking, especially in the country (尤指鄉間的) 小路，人行小道：*Follow the footpath through the next field until you come to a stile.* 你沿着這條小路走完下一壟田，一直走到籬笆牆的台階。

high street* the most important street in a town (*but not usually in a very big city*), often where most of the shops, businesses, and public buildings are (通常指市鎮商業區，但非特大城市裏，最繁華的) 大街，主街：*There's a bank in the high street, next door to the library.* 商業區大街上有一家銀行，就在圖書館的隔壁。

* Only used in British English. The equivalent in US English is main street. 僅用於英國英語，美國英語的對應詞是 main street。

lane a narrow road, especially in the country, or a specially marked section of a road for traffic moving in a particular direction (尤指鄉間的) 小路；(道路上專設的) 單向行車道：*Take the right-hand lane as you come up to the traffic lights.* 你到了紅綠燈，就走右手邊的車道。

motorway* a specially built road for high-speed traffic that usually does not run through towns and village and has a limited number of places where you drive onto it or off it 高速公路 : *It only takes an hour to get to London on the motorway.* 走高速公路到倫敦只需一個小時。

* Only used in British English. The equivalent in US English is superhighway . 僅用於英國英語，美國英語的對應詞是 superhighway 。

pavement* an area at the side of a road or street, reserved for pedestrians （馬路或街道旁的）人行道 : *Cyclists aren't supposed to ride along the pavement.* 騎自行車者不得在人行道上行駛。

* Only used in British English. The equivalent in US English is side-walk. 僅用於英國英語，美國英語的對應詞是 sidewalk 。

ring road a circular road that runs all the way around a town or city （環繞市鎮或城市的）環城路，環形公路 : *I can get to my mother's house quicker by going round the ring road than by going through the centre of town.* 我走環形公路到我媽媽家比穿過市中心要快。

street a road in a town, usually with buildings on each side of it （通常指市鎮上兩旁都有建築物的）街道 : *They live just across the street from us.* 他們就住在我們家的街對面。

track a way for vehicles or walkers that does not have a paved surface （供車輛或行人使用但沒有鋪設的）小道，路徑 : *The house was at the end of a rough track that was not really meant for motor vehicles.* 這房子在一條崎嶇不平的、非真正的機動車道的盡頭。

rough¹ *adjective* not smooth, having a surface that has small things sticking out of it 粗糙的；不光滑的 : *His cheek felt rough because he had not shaved.* 他的臉頰感覺不光滑，因為他沒有刮臉。

bristly having short stiff hairs on it or in it （毛髮、鬍鬚等）短而硬的；鬍子拉碴的 : *a bristly beard* 鬍茬子

bumpy having an uneven surface with quite large rises and falls 道路顛簸的；崎嶇不平的 : *a bumpy road* 顛簸的馬路

coarse having a surface or texture with quite large lumps or bumps in it （表面或紋理）粗糙的，高低不平的 : *coarse sandpaper* 粗砂紙

gnarled having an uneven surface with irregular lumps and twists in it 節節疤疤的；彎彎曲曲的 : *the gnarled trunk of an old tree* 一棵彎彎曲曲的老樹幹

lumpy having many small solid pieces in it instead of a smooth texture 不勻細的；多塊狀物的 : *lumpy porridge* 不勻的粥

rugged not smooth or even, but having a strong look 崎嶇的；凹凸不平是；粗獷的 : *rugged rocks* 嶙峋的岩石

uneven not level and smooth 參差不齊的；高低不平的 : *The lawn is too uneven for us to play bowls on it.* 草地凹凸不平，我們無法在上面打保齡球。

rough² *adjective* quickly made and not intended to be complete or completely accurate 粗糙的；粗略的 : *I'll just give you a rough idea of what's involved.* 我想就相關問題給你說一下粗淺的想法。

approximate not completely accurate, but close to the exact number, time, etc. (數量、時間等) 約莫的，大概的：*These figures are only approximate.* 這些數字僅僅是個大概。

estimated calculated in advance before you know the exact figures, amounts, etc. (預先對數目、數量等) 估算的，估計的：*Our estimated time of arrival is 15.30.* 我們預計的抵達時間是下午 3 點半。

general relating to the main or basic features of something, but not including details 籠統的；大致的：*I think she's got the general idea of what's wanted.* 我想她已大致清楚了需要甚麼。

hazy not knowing something exactly or accurately and therefore vague (因不確知而) 矇矓的，模糊的：*I'm a bit hazy about the details of this job.* 我不太了解這份工作的詳情。

sketchy not complete, lacking in detail 粗略的；概要的：*Their account is rather sketchy and fails to mention some of the most important events that took place during this period.* 他們説的情況相當粗略，對這段時間發生的一些最重要的事件都沒有提及。

vague not precise or completely clear, or not knowing or expressing something precisely or very clearly 含糊的；不明確的：*I have a vague memory of him saying something of the sort.* 我約莫記得他説過這類話。

rude *adjective* showing a lack of respect for someone, impolite, or (*often used to describe words or language*) indecent (對人) 粗魯無禮的；(常用以描述談吐) 粗俗的，下流的：*It's rude to interrupt when somebody's talking.* 在別人談話時插話是不禮貌的。

abusive forcefully expressing the idea that someone is bad, ugly, worthless, etc., especially when that person is present (尤指當着對方的面) 謾罵的，惡聲惡氣的：*abusive language* 惡言惡語

crude offensive; referring to sex or parts of the body in an unpleasant way 粗野的；粗俗的；下流的：*crude jokes* 粗俗的笑話

derogatory (*formal*) expressing the idea that someone is bad, ugly, worthless, etc. 貶低的；毀謗的：*a derogatory remark* 貶損的評論

discourteous (*formal*) impolite 失禮的；粗魯的：*It would be discourteous of us not to go after we have accepted the invitation.* 我們接受邀請後不去赴約有失禮貌。

ill-mannered very impolite or badly behaved 無禮的；舉止粗野的：*When children are so ill-mannered, it's usually the parents who are to blame.* 當孩子這麼不講禮貌時，應該受到指責的通常是他們的家長。

impolite not conforming to the usual standards in society for how you should behave towards other people (對他人) 不禮貌的，粗魯的：*I hope you don't think it impolite of me to ask, but how old are you?* 我希望你不要認為我的問題不禮貌，請問你多大年齡？

indecent referring or relating to things, especially sex or bodily functions, that people usually do not mention for fear of offending others 猥褻的；有傷風化的：*People shouldn't talk about their sex lives in public; it's indecent.* 人們不應該當眾談論自己的性生活，那樣有傷風化。

insulting making someone feel that you think they are bad, ugly, worthless, etc. 侮辱的；誣衊的；出言不遜的：*It's so insulting to be treated like an absolute ignoramus.* 把人當成十足的不學無術之輩，真是太侮辱人了。

offensive causing people to feel angry and upset by showing no respect for their feelings, beliefs, etc. (對他人的感情、信仰等) 冒犯的，唐突的：*Are you deliberately trying to be offensive?* 你是存心要惹人生氣嗎？

pejorative (*formal*) (*used to describe words or language*) expressing the opinion that someone or something is bad (用以描述言辭) 貶義的，貶抑的：*I was not using the word in its pejorative sense.* 我並非在用這個詞的貶義。

➲ see also 參見 **insolent; insult**

rule *noun* a statement that tells people how they must behave in a particular situation, for example, when playing a game or sport (遊戲或體育等活動中的) 規則，準則：*It's against the rules to hit the ball twice.* 兩次擊球是犯規的。

condition something that you have to do in order for something else to happen or for you to have something (發生某事或擁有某物的) 條件，前提：*It's a condition of his appointment that he should successfully pass a medical examination.* 任命他的先決條件是，他應該順利通過體檢。

decree a statement saying that something must happen made by a ruler or by a judge or court (統治者頒佈的) 詔令，政令；(法官或法庭下達的) 判決書：*The king issued a decree banning the sale of alcohol anywhere in his kingdom.* 國王頒佈全國上下禁止售酒的詔令。

guidelines instructions or advice on how to do something 指導方針；準則：*Clear guidelines have now been issued to all staff on how to claim expenses.* 明確的報銷標準現在已向全體員工印發。

law a rule made by the state that all citizens have to obey 法律，法規：*a new law allowing pubs to stay open twenty-four hours a day* 一部允許酒館全天 24 小時營業的新法律

(the) law what the state commands or forbids, or all the laws considered together, or all the laws relating to a particular subject (國家的) 法律；(總稱) 法律；(某領域的) 法律：*You can't drive a motor vehicle without a licence, that's the law.* 你不可無牌駕駛車輛，那是法律規定。

regulation an official rule, made by a government or other authority, dealing with a particular activity or a matter such as health and safety (政府或其他管理部門制定的) 法規，規章制度：*It says in the building regulations that you have to fit an extractor fan in a toilet that does not have a window.* 建房制度規定，沒有窗戶的衛生間必須安裝抽氣扇。

statute a written law made by a law-making body such as a parliament (議會等立法機構制定的) 成文法，法令：*a statute from the reign of Edward III* 愛德華三世統治時期的一部法令

➲ see also 參見 **order**

run *verb* to move on legs at a fast pace 跑；奔跑：*I had to run to catch the bus.* 我不得不跑着去趕巴士。

bolt to run very fast, especially in fear（尤指害怕地）拼命逃竄，狂奔：*Running for his life, he bolted down the road.* 為了逃命，他沿路狂奔。

charge to rush towards an enemy to attack them, or to move fast and determinedly in a particular direction regardless of anything or anyone who might be in your way（向敵人）猛衝，衝鋒；横衝直撞：*He charged down the corridor shouting at people to get out of his way.* 他在走廊裏猛衝過來，大聲喝着要人們讓道。

dart to move very quickly and suddenly 飛奔；猛衝：*A small animal darted across the path in front of us.* 在我們前方有隻小動物竄到小路的對面去了。

dash (*informal*) to run very fast, usually because you are in a hurry, or to leave hurriedly（通常因為匆忙而）猛衝；匆匆離開：*He quickly gathered up his things and dashed out of the room.* 他趕緊收拾好東西，衝出了房間。

gallop (*usually said about a horse or rider, but sometimes also about a person running*) to run very fast（通常指馬或騎手，但有時也指奔跑的人）飛奔，疾馳：*The horse galloped across the field towards us.* 那匹馬穿過田野，朝我們飛奔而來。

jog to run at an easy pace, especially for exercise（尤指為了鍛煉而）慢跑：*I jogged around the track a couple of times to warm up for the race.* 我為賽跑熱身圍着跑道慢跑了幾圈。

race to run or move very fast, or (*said about a machine, engine, etc.*) to function at a much faster rate than normal 快速移動；快速運動；（機器、引擎等）快速運轉：*My heart was racing, and every hair on my body seemed to be standing up on end.* 我的心在急速跳動，身上的每根毛髮似乎都豎了起來。

rush to move very fast, often because you are in a hurry（常因匆忙而）迅速移動，飛奔：*She rushed into my office waving a message that had just come through on the fax.* 她急忙跑進我的辦公室，手裏揮着一份剛發來的傳真。

sprint to run very fast, especially over a short distance（尤指短距離）疾跑，猛衝：*She came around the final bend and sprinted for the finishing line.* 她轉過最後一道彎，衝向終點線。

tear (*informal*) to move very fast and often carelessly or dangerously（常指粗心或冒失地）猛衝，瞎撞：*He leapt onto his motorbike and tore off down the road.* 他跳上電單車，沿路猛衝而去。

trot (*usually said about a horse or rider, but sometimes also about person on foot*) to run at a fairly easy pace with regular short steps（通常指馬或騎手，但有時也指步行者）小跑：*The children from the local riding school came trotting down the lane.* 當地騎術學校的孩子們沿着跑道一遛小跑過來了。

➲ see also 參見 **control; hurry; work³**

S

sad *adjective* feeling or showing emotional distress or pain 悲痛的；傷心的：*a sad song* 一首悲傷的歌

dejected (*usually only used to describe people*) in a sad state of mind, usually only for a short period of time (通常僅用以描述人) 情緒低落的，垂頭喪氣的：*He looked a bit dejected, so I tried to cheer him up.* 他看上去情緒有點兒低落，於是我設法讓他高興起來。

depressed feeling sad over a longer period of time, or suffering from a mental condition that makes you feel hopeless and unable to react normally to people and events (長時期) 沮喪的，消沉的，患憂鬱症的：*I get depressed just thinking about the amount of work I still have to do.* 我一想到還得幹那麼多的工作，就感到沮喪。

disappointed sad because something that you hoped would not happen or that you expected to happen has not happened 失望的；感到掃興的：*She was very disappointed when she wasn't picked for the hockey team.* 她沒有被選入曲棍球隊時感到很失望。

dismal unpleasant and causing people to feel sad and hopeless 淒涼的；陰沉的；令人憂鬱的：*The weather has been pretty dismal for the last few days.* 近些天來，天氣一直陰沉沉的。

downcast (*usually only used to describe people*) dejected, especially because of disappointment about something (通常僅用以描述人，尤指因失望而) 垂頭喪氣的，沮喪的，氣餒的：*There's no need to be downcast because you didn't win. You tried your best.* 沒有必要輸了就灰心喪氣，你已經盡力了。

melancholy feeling, showing, or causing a usually mild degree of sadness, which is sometimes not entirely unpleasant (令人) 憂鬱的，悲哀的，傷感的：*The garden in winter is a melancholy place.* 冬天的花園是一處令人傷感的地方。

miserable feeling very sad, or unpleasant, and causing great sadness (令人) 苦惱的，痛苦的，難受的：*He feels utterly miserable at being let down by his best friend.* 最好的朋友辜負了他，他感到十分痛心。

mournful expressing or showing grief in a very obvious way 悲痛的；悲傷的；悽楚的：*I expected the funeral to be a mournful occasion, but it was actually quite jolly.* 我原以為葬禮是悲悽的場合，但實際上挺歡樂的。

unhappy in a sad state of mind, usually over a long period, or causing pain and distress (通常指長時期) 不愉快的，不快樂的，不幸的：*an unhappy love affair* 不幸的戀愛

upset (*usually only used to describe people*) feeling sad and sometimes angry because of something that has happened (通常僅用以描述人) 苦惱的；(有時指) 氣惱的，生氣的：*Naturally, I'm upset that they didn't even bother to phone me.* 他們連電話都懶得給我打，我自然感到悻然不快。

wistful feeling or showing mild sadness mixed with longing for something 依依不捨的；留戀的：*The boy looked at the toys in the shop window with a wistful expression.* 男孩望着商店櫥窗裏的那些玩具，露出戀戀不捨的神情。

➲ see also 參見 **dismay**

safe *adjective* not harmed or injured or in further danger 安全的；平安的：*They were in the hotel when the bomb went off, but they're all safe, thank heaven.* 炸彈爆炸時他們正在酒店裏，可是謝天謝地，他們全都安然無恙。

alive and well not hurt, ill, or in trouble (*used especially when no news has been heard from someone for a long time*)（尤用於某人長時間杳無音信時）平安無事的：*He sent an e-mail to say he was alive and well, but his mobile phone had been stolen.* 他發了一封電子郵件説自己平安無事，只是手機被人偷了。

all right (*informal*) not hurt, ill, or in trouble 一切都好的；安然無恙的：*I'm all right, but Martha's leg was broken.* 我還好，可是瑪莎的腿斷了。

in one piece (*used to describe people and things*) not harmed or damaged（用以描述人或事物）完好的，未損壞的，未受傷的：*I dropped my best china teapot, but, luckily, it's still in one piece.* 我把我那最好的瓷茶壺摔了，但幸運的是，它還一點沒摔壞。

out of danger not likely to be harmed or to die, especially not likely to die as a result of a medical condition（尤指因為得到醫治）脱離危險的，轉危為安的：*The doctor said her condition improved during the night, and she's now out of danger.* 醫生説她的情況在昨夜有了好轉，現在已脱離危險。

unscathed not harmed or injured, especially after being involved in an accident or disaster（尤指事故或災難後）未受傷的：*If you had seen the state of the car, you'd say it was a miracle they got away unscathed.* 如果你看見了那輛小汽車的狀況，你準會説他們安然逃生真是奇跡。

sarcastic *adjective* using words that mean the opposite of what they literally say in order to ridicule or humiliate someone 挖苦的；嘲諷的：*Before you say anything sarcastic, let me just remind you that it's my first attempt at painting anyone's portrait.* 趁你還沒有挖苦我，還是讓我提醒你一下，這是我第一次嘗試畫別人的肖像。

caustic openly and often cruelly critical of people or their behaviour（對人或其行為）尖酸刻薄的，挖苦的：*She refused to speak to reporters after the caustic comments some of them made about her acting.* 在幾名記者對她的表演發表刻薄的評論之後，她拒絕與記者説話。

derisive showing open mockery and contempt, for example, because what someone says is obviously ridiculous or hypocritical（因某人説的話明顯荒唐或偽善而）嘲諷的，嘲弄的，取笑的：*His promise to do better next time was greeted with derisive laughter.* 他許諾下一次做得更好，這引來了嘲諷的笑聲。

ironic(al) using words that mean the opposite of what they literally say for humorous effect（為達到幽默效果）用反語的，反話的：*When I said I'd never been happier than when I was in prison, I was being ironic.* 我説蹲監獄期間是我最快樂的日子，那是我故意説的反話。

mocking showing, usually openly and in an unkind way, that you think that someone or something is ridiculous（通常指公然刻薄地）嘲弄的，嘲笑的：*a mocking laugh* 嘲弄的笑聲

sardonic showing, usually in a quiet, superior way that you think that someone or something is ridiculous（通常指以平靜而傲慢的方式）譏諷的，嘲弄的：*He listened to the policeman's clumsy attempts to question the suspect with a sardonic smile.* 他聽着那個警察笨拙地試圖審問疑犯，臉上露出挖苦的笑。

scornful showing openly that you reject or despise someone or something (公然表示) 輕蔑的，鄙夷的：*'I wouldn't marry you, if you were the last man on earth', was her scornful reply.* "哪怕世上就你一個男人了，我也不會嫁給你。"她輕蔑地回答。

snide (*informal*) trying, usually in an indirect and sneering way, to make someone appear ridiculous (通常指以婉轉或譏笑的方式) 暗諷的，挖苦的，嘲弄的：*Instead of making snide comments about the new recruits, why don't you help them?* 不要對那些新招進來的人冷嘲熱諷，你何不幫他們一把呢？

save *verb* to prevent someone or something from being harmed, destroyed, or lost when they are in trouble or threatened by something 挽救；拯救；保全：*a campaign to save the tiger* 一場拯救老虎的運動

deliver (*literary*) to free someone from something, especially a moral danger or evil (尤指從道德危機或邪惡中) 拯救，解救：*We pray to be delivered from the consequences of our past sins.* 我們祈求從往日罪孽的惡果中得到救贖。

preserve to keep something that is considered to be valuable, often something historic such as an old building or an ancient custom, when it is in danger of being lost or destroyed 維護，保存，保留 (常為具有歷史價值的東西，如古老的建築、風俗等)：*The original façade was preserved, but the rest of the building was demolished.* 建築物的當街正面保留着原樣，但其他部分都已拆毀。

recover to find or get back something that has been lost 找回；挽回；恢復：*The flight recorder has been recovered from the wreck of the aircraft.* 飛行記錄儀已經從飛機的殘骸中找到了。

redeem to save someone or something from being considered very bad, by being good 挽回；補救；彌補：*She only redeemed herself by working extra hard for the rest of the day.* 在那天剩餘的時間裏，她格外努力地工作只是挽回了影響。

rescue to save someone or something, especially after an accident or disaster (尤指在事故或災難後) 營救，搭救，救援：*The fishermen were rescued by helicopter after their boat sank.* 漁民們在船沉後被直升機營救上來。

salvage to recover material that can be reused from the scene of an accident or disaster (從事故或災難現場) 搶救，打撈 (可用物資等)：*After the floodwaters went down, people were allowed back into their houses to try to salvage their personal belongings.* 在洪水退去之後，人們被允許回到家裏取回自己的私人物品。

⊃ see also 參見 **save**

say *verb* to use particular words or express particular ideas when speaking or writing 説；寫道；表達：*I couldn't understand a word he was saying.* 他説的話我一個字都聽不懂。

comment to say something in relation to a particular subject (就特定主題) 進行評論，發表意見：*Prime Minister, there have been reports in the press that you may be thinking of resigning. Would you care to comment?* 首相先生，新聞界已有報道稱您可能在考慮辭職，您想就此發表評論嗎？

declare to say something in a formal or official way or in a way that suggests that you think that what you are saying is important (正式或鄭重地) 宣佈，聲明：*I declare this meeting closed.* 我宣佈會議到此結束。

mention to speak the name of a particular person, thing, or subject, or to say something about them, when discussing something 提到；説起；談及：*He did discuss the question of payment, but he didn't mention any particular sum.* 他的確談論過酬金問題，但沒有提及任何金額。

observe (*formal*) to express an opinion or state a fact 評論；評述；發表看法：*I merely observed that it was cold for the time of year.* 我只是説，就一年的這個時候而言，天氣還很寒冷。

point out to make people aware of something by saying something about it 指出；指明：*I just wished to point out that the proposed changes will affect the tenants as much as the landlords.* 我只想説明一下，提出的變動方案對房客的影響一點都不亞於對房東的影響。

refer to to make someone or something the subject of something you are saying either by mentioning them directly or by showing indirectly that you are thinking of them 提及；談到；涉及：*She didn't mention him by name, but there was no doubt about whom she was referring to.* 她沒有提他的名字，但她指的是誰卻是毋庸置疑的。

remark to say something that conveys a particular piece of information or expresses a particular opinion, often in a fairly casual way (常指較隨意地) 説，評論：*I just happened to remark that she was looking rather pale and she took it as a deadly insult.* 我只是碰巧説説她看上去臉色蒼白，她卻把這句話當成是極大的侮辱。

state to say something in a definite way for other people to take note of 説明；聲明；闡明：*I wish to state my objections to the proposal.* 我希望闡明我對這項提議的反對意見。

➲ see also 參見 **speak; tell**

scatter *verb* to throw things, or to make people or things move, in different directions so that they are not grouped together but cover a wide area with spaces in between them 撒；使分散：*Scatter the seed over the flowerbed.* 把種子撒播在花圃裏。

break up to divide a mass or group into separate parts or units 解散，驅散，消散 (群眾或團體等)：*They broke up the business and sold off the most profitable parts.* 他們解散了公司，變賣了最有利潤的部分。

dispel to drive away something, especially something unpleasant such as negative feelings 驅散，消除 (尤指令人不快的東西，如消極情緒等)：*What she said dispelled all my doubts about whether the plan would work.* 她的一席話打消了我對這項計劃是否可行的疑慮。

disperse to make something go away, especially a crowd of people or a mass of something such as fog or gas, by taking action to break it up 疏散，驅散 (人群等)；使 (霧或毒氣等) 消散：*Police used tear gas to disperse the crowd.* 警察使用催淚氣驅散了人群。

dissipate to use up a resource, e.g., money, wastefully on a number of different things until there is none left 消耗，揮霍掉 (資金等資源)：*By the* *age of thirty, his entire fortune had been dissipated.* 到 30 歲時，他的全部財富已經揮霍一空。

separate to move things or people so that they are apart from one another（將人或物）分開，分隔：*We separated the books into two piles.* 我們把書分成了兩堆。

spread to move something so that it covers something else in a layer 撒；分佈，攤放：*Spread the compost over the flowerbed.* 給花圃施肥。

search¹ *verb* to examine a place, often in a systematic way, in order to try to find something（常指系統地）搜查（某處）：*Police searched the house, looking for stolen goods.* 警察搜查房子，尋找被盜贓物。

comb to search an area very carefully and systematically（非常仔細、系統地）搜尋（某一區域）：*Police combed the woods for any trace of the missing child.* 警察在林子裏四處搜尋失蹤孩子的任何蹤跡。

go through to examine a place or, especially, a collection of things or something made up of separate parts, in order to try to find something 搜查（某處）；（尤指）翻查（一系列物品或零散部件）：*I went through the whole document again, but I still couldn't find the paragraph you mentioned.* 我再次翻遍了整個文件，但還是沒能找到你提到的那段話。

look around to examine a place, usually in a casual way（通常指隨意地）在（某處）四下尋找：*I looked around the garden, but I couldn't find your ball.* 我在花園裏到處尋找，但沒能找到你的球。

rummage to search a usually small place in an unsystematic and untidy way（通常指在一個很小的地方）翻尋，亂翻，查找：*I rummaged around in the cupboard and found an old shirt I thought I'd thrown away.* 我翻遍了衣櫥，找到一件我以為已經扔掉了的舊襯衫。

scour to search an area in a very active and thorough way 四處搜索，細查（某一區域）：*We scoured the second-hand bookshops looking for a copy of Great Expectations.* 為了找到一本《孤星血淚》，我們尋遍了舊書店。

search² *verb* (*search for*) to make a usually serious and systematic attempt to find someone or something, which may be either a physical object or something abstract（通常指認真、系統地）搜查（某人），搜索，探求（具體或抽象的事物）：*We're still searching for the answer to this question.* 我們仍在探求這個問題的答案。

forage to search an area intensively looking for something, especially food to eat（在某一區域）搜尋（尤指食物等）：*The children were well trained in the art of foraging for food in the forest.* 孩子們訓練有素，掌握了在森林裏搜尋食物的本領。

hunt to search for someone or something in a very active and serious way（積極認真地）尋找，搜尋：*Police are hunting the killer of 6-year-old Jimmy Briggs.* 警察正在尋找殺害 6 歲男童吉米·布里格斯的兇手。

look for to try to find something or someone, often in a fairly casual way（常指較隨意地）找，尋找：*I'm looking for the tin-opener – have you seen it?* 我在找開罐器，你見到它沒有？

seek to look for or ask for something abstract, or (*literary*) to search for a person or thing 探求，尋求（抽象事物）；尋找（人或物）：*They sought guidance from an expert in legal matters.* 他們尋求了法律問題專家的指導。

sift to examine something such as documents, evidence, or memories closely and thoroughly to try to find something significant 細查，詳查，探究（文件、證據或回憶錄等）: *The officials sifted through the archives to find the missing photograph.* 官員們仔細清查檔案，以便找到那張缺失的照片。

secret *adjective* deliberately not made known to other people 秘密的；保密的: *a secret plan* 一項秘密計劃

confidential (*said about information*) to be kept private, not public（指信息）機密的，私密的: *The report was marked 'Strictly confidential' and was to be seen only by the top executives.* 這份報告標有 "嚴格保密" 字樣，只有高層人員才能見到。

covert carried out secretly, usually because it would be dangerous or cause trouble if people knew what was happening（通常指如果被人發現就可能帶來危險或麻煩，因而）隱秘的，暗中的，偷偷摸摸的: *covert military operations* 秘密的軍事行動

discreet done in a way that does not attract attention to what you are doing 慎重的；謹慎的: *to make discreet enquiries* 進行慎重的調查

furtive showing a wish that other people should not see or know about what you are doing 偷偷摸摸的；鬼鬼祟祟的；賊頭賊腦的: *a furtive glance* 偷偷的一瞥

private concerning only one person or a particular group of people, not the general public 個人的；非公開的；私下的: *It's a private matter between me and my wife.* 這是我和妻子之間私下的事情。

stealthy acting, moving, or done very quietly and slowly in the hope that no one will notice what is happening（行為、動作等）偷偷摸摸的，躡手躡腳的: *He began to hear stealthy footsteps from down the corridor.* 他開始聽見沿着樓道悄悄走動的腳步聲。

surreptitious (*formal*) (*usually used about a bad action*) done in a stealthy way（通常指不良行為）偷偷摸摸的，鬼鬼祟祟的: *the surreptitious removal of documents from the safe* 從保險櫃偷偷取走文件

undercover using disguise and deception to avoid danger and obtain information（為避免危險或獲取信息等）暗中進行的，秘密進行的: *an undercover police office* 秘密警察局

underground (*usually used to describe activities hostile to a government*) done or operating in secret（通常用以描述敵視政府的活動）不公開的，秘密的，地下的: *an underground resistance movement* 地下抵抗運動

see *verb* to perceive someone or something with your eyes 看見: *You can sometimes see the French coast from the cliffs of Dover.* 有時候，從多佛爾的峭壁上可以看見法國的海岸。

catch sight of to see someone or something that has previously been invisible to you, often suddenly or unexpectedly（常指突然或意外地）見到，看見（先前看不見的人或物）: *I caught sight of him again as I left the wood and began climbing the path up the hill.* 當我離開樹林，沿着小路往山上爬的時候，我再次看到了他。

discern (*formal*) to see something in difficult conditions by looking carefully 看出；覺察出: *Peering through the fog, I was barely able to discern* *the taillights of the car ahead.* 透過煙霧看去，我勉強能辨認出前方小汽車的尾燈。

glimpse or catch a glimpse of to see someone or something very briefly, or not clearly or completely 瞥一眼：*I caught a glimpse of her through the shop window as she hurried by.* 在她匆匆走過的時候，我透過商店的櫥窗一眼瞥見了她。

make out to be able to recognize or understand something that is difficult to see clearly 辨認出；弄懂：*I can make out a few words, but most of the text is completely illegible.* 我能辨認出幾個單詞，可是文中大部分完全無法辨認。

notice to see something or someone and register in your mind that you have seen them 注意到；覺察到；看到：*Now you mention it, I did notice a man of that description standing outside the house yesterday afternoon.* 現在你提起這事兒，我昨天下午還真看到過那種模樣的人站在屋外呢。

perceive (*formal*) to become aware of something through one of the senses or with the mind（通過感官或心智）認識到，意識到，覺察到：*Such small objects in the night sky are difficult to perceive even with the aid of a telescope.* 在夜空中，這麼小的物體即使借助望遠鏡也很難發現。

sight to see someone or something that you have been looking out for 看到，瞧見，發現（一直期待的人或物）：*We finally sighted land after thirty days at sea.* 海上航行 30 天之後，我們終於見到了大陸。

spot to see someone or something that you have been looking for or that may be hidden or not very noticeable 發現，發覺，認出（一直所尋找的，或隱藏着的，或不太引人注意的人或物）：*Did you spot the deliberate mistake?* 你發現那個故意留下的錯誤了嗎？

witness to be present when an action or an event, especially an important one, takes place, or to see someone doing something 目擊，當場看到（某種行為或事件，尤指重大事件的發生）：*We were in London on that day and witnessed the unveiling of the statue.* 那天我們正好在倫敦，親眼目睹了這座雕像的揭幕儀式。

➲ see also 參見 **look; watch**

selfish *adjective* unpleasantly concerned with your own needs and wishes and ignoring those of other people, especially in everyday matters（尤指在日常問題上）自私的，利己的：*Don't be selfish, let your sister have a turn.* 別只顧自己，讓你妹妹也輪一回吧。

egoistic believing in or acting on the principle that your main concern should be to get what you want or need 利己主義的；自我主義的；自私自利的：*You expect artists to be egoistic; it comes with being dedicated to their art above everything else.* 你會認為藝術家們都是以自我為中心，這與他們獻身藝術、並視藝術高於一切的境界分不開。

egotistic(al) vain about your own abilities and achievements and tending to talk about them a lot (*a more condemnatory word than egoistic*) 自負的，自高自大的（該詞比 egoistic 更具貶意）：*It's very difficult to have a proper conversation with someone who's so thoroughly egotistical and boasts about all they've done the whole time.* 與一個極其自負並總是吹噓自己一切成就的人進行真正意義的對話是非常困難的。

inconsiderate rather selfish in not paying proper attention to other people's needs or wishes 不為別人着想的；不體諒別人的：*Young people can be very inconsiderate of the difficulties faced by the old.* 年輕人可能會體諒不到老年人面對的種種困難。

self-absorbed focusing your attention on your own thoughts and feelings 自我專注的；只關心自己感受的：*If you hadn't been so self-absorbed, you might have noticed how unhappy your brother has been these last few weeks.* 如果你不是那麼只關心自己的話，你或許就注意到了弟弟在最近幾週裏是多麼的不愉快。

self-centred always concerned only with yourself and your own interests 自我中心的；只顧自己的；自私自利的：*Living alone for all these years has made him rather self-centred.* 這些年來一直獨居使他變得頗有些自私自利了。

self-seeking trying to gain money or advantages for yourself at the expense of other people 追逐私利的；損人利己的：*She denied that her actions had been self-seeking, and pointed out that she had given nearly half the money she had raised to charity.* 她否認她的行為是追求私利，並指出她已將所籌集到的近一半的款項捐給了慈善機構。

thoughtless not paying proper attention to other people's needs or wishes 不替他人着想的；不顧及他人的；粗心的：*It was very thoughtless of him to forget to send you a birthday card.* 他太粗心了，居然忘記給你寄張生日賀卡。

sell *verb* to give someone something in exchange for payment 賣；出售：*I'm sorry, we sold the last copy yesterday.* 對不起，我們昨天把最後一本都賣了。

carry (*said usually about for example a shop*) to stock (通常指商店等) 備貨，儲貨：*There's very little demand for typewriter ribbons nowadays, so we don't carry them.* 目前對打字機色帶的需求很小，所以我們沒有進貨。

deal in to run a business that sells a particular kind of goods 經營；交易：*He deals in second-hand books.* 他經銷舊書。

hawk to sell things by knocking on people's doors and asking them to buy (逐家逐戶) 推銷，兜售：*I sold a few copies of my novel by hawking them around local bookshops.* 我在當地幾家書店附近兜售我的小說，賣掉了幾本。

peddle to sell goods while travelling from place to place (沿途) 叫賣，兜售：*Gypsy women traditionally used to peddle clothes' pegs and sprigs of lucky white heather.* 吉卜賽婦女以前常常沿途叫賣帶來幸運的白石楠枝條和衣夾。

retail (*said about a business*) to sell goods to the people who will own and use them (指商家) 零售：*The shop is licensed to retail wines and spirits.* 這家商店獲准零售葡萄酒和烈酒。

sell off (*said about a business*) to sell something that you no longer want, usually at a lower price than usual (指商家) 降價銷售 (存貨)：*We're selling off our winter goods to make way for new spring lines.* 我們正在削價銷售冬季存貨，以便騰出空間讓春季新款上櫃。

stock (*said usually about for example a shop*) to have a particular kind of goods available on the premises ready to be sold (通常指商店等) 備有，供應 (商品等)：*We actually stock six different brands of trainers.* 我們實際上銷售 6 種品牌的跑鞋。

send *verb* to arrange for a person or thing to go or be transported to a place 派遣；發送：*She sent a message to say that she was too ill to come to the meeting.* 她送來口信稱病得很厲害，不能來開會。

consign (*formal*) (*used especially in the context of business*) to send goods to someone（尤用於商務語境）運送，發送：*a shipment of raw materials consigned to a factory in Belgium* 發往比利時一家工廠的一批船運原材料

direct to send something, usually by post, to a particular person or address（通常指）把（郵件等）交予，寄至：*Letters of complaint should be directed to the Customer Services Department at our head office.* 投訴信函應寄到我們總部的客戶服務部。

dispatch (*mainly used in the context of business*) to send something such as goods from the place where they are made or stored（主要用於商務語境，指從產地或存放處）發送（貨物等）：*Goods are usually dispatched within 24 hours of receipt of order.* 通常在接到訂單後 24 小時內發貨。

forward to send something received at one address onward to another address 轉遞；轉交；轉發：*The people who bought our house agreed to forward any mail to our new address.* 購買了我們房子的人家同意將所有郵件轉寄到我們的新住址。

mail * to send something such as a letter or parcel using an official postal service 郵寄（信件或包裹等）：*I think I mailed the letter to your old address by mistake.* 我想我是錯把那封信寄到你原來的地址了。

* Used in US English and, though less commonly, in British English. 用於美國英語，較少用於英國英語。

post * to mail something 郵寄：*I posted it yesterday, so you should get it tomorrow.* 我昨天就把它寄出去了，所以你明天應該收到。

* Only used in British English. 僅用於英國英語。

remit to send money to someone, especially to send money earned abroad to your home country 匯，寄（尤指在國外賺的錢）：*He remits most of his wages to his wife and children in India.* 他將工資的大部分都寄給了在印度的妻子和兒女。

sensible *adjective* showing good judgment and an understanding of how to deal with people and situations effectively 明智的；合情合理的：*That's very sensible advice, and I think you should take it.* 那可是個很合理的忠告，我覺得你應該採納。

down to earth (*usually used to describe people*) realistic and practical, and not using fancy language or advocating fancy ideas（通常用以描述人）務實的，實事求是的：*The doctor's very down to earth, he won't try and blind you with science.* 這位醫生很實在，他不會設法用專業知識矇蔽你。

level-headed (*usually used to describe people*) behaving or reacting calmly and showing good judgment 清醒的，頭腦冷靜的：*I thought she was too level-headed to get involved in such a crazy scheme.* 我原以為她很沉穩，不至於參與這項瘋狂的計劃。

practical good at or good for dealing with situations that occur in real life 有實際經驗的；實用的：*What we need is a practical solution to the problem.* 我們需要的是切實解決這個問題的方案。

prudent wise and careful, especially with money（尤指對錢）審慎的；精明的：*It would be a prudent use of your money to invest it more widely.* 投資更廣一些就是在巧用你的資金。

rational using reason rather than emotion when dealing with an issue or problem（在處理問題時）理性的，理智的：*a rational approach to the question* 處理問題的合理方法

realistic showing an understanding of what is possible in real life 現實的：*Be realistic, we'd never be able to raise £50,000.* 現實一點吧，我們永遠不可能籌集到 5 萬英鎊。

reasonable based on reason or showing an ability to use reason and good judgment, especially in not expecting too much of other people 講道理的；（尤指）通情達理的：*Our demands are perfectly reasonable, and we know that the management can afford to pay what we are asking.* 我們的要求完全合理，我們也知道管理部門有能力按我們的要求進行賠付。

responsible able to carry out tasks and deal with situations in a sensible manner 有責任感的；認真負責的：*Is she responsible enough to be left in charge of three small children?* 她有足夠的責任感，可以讓她照顧 3 個小孩嗎？

sound (*usually used to describe ideas, arguments, etc.*) based on clear thinking and good judgment and difficult to argue against（通常用以描述思想、論點等）正確的，合理的，明智的：*These are three sound reasons for not going ahead with the plan.* 有 3 條合理的理由不執行這項計劃。

wise showing good judgment, often based on long experience（常指基於長期的經驗）英明的，明智的：*I think you were wise not to insist on having your own way in this matter.* 我認為你在這個問題上不固執己見是明智的。

⊃ see also 參見 **careful**

sentimental *adjective* showing or producing tender or romantic feelings, often too easily 動情的；（常指）多愁善感的：*a sentimental love song* 一首深情的愛情歌曲

emotional showing strong feeling, especially of the kind associated with sadness 動感情的；情緒激動的；（尤指）傷感的：*He gets very emotional when he has to say goodbye to people.* 在他必須向人們道別的時候，總是十分傷感。

mawkish exaggeratedly or unpleasantly sentimental, very obviously intended to produce a great deal of tender feeling 過於傷感的；自作多情的；無病呻吟的：*The description of the heroine's death was positively mawkish.* 對女主人公之死的描寫確實是過於煽情。

nostalgic showing a great affection or longing for the past 戀舊的；懷舊的：*a nostalgic look back to the Paris of the 1950s* 對 20 世紀 50 年代的巴黎的懷念

soft-hearted (*used to describe people*) easily made to sympathize with or feel pity for other people（用以描述人）仁慈的，心軟的：*You're too soft-hearted, I never give money to beggars.* 你太仁慈了，我可從來不給乞丐錢。

soppy (*informal*) that makes you cry or makes you feel very tender and romantic 多愁善感的；易傷感落淚的：*a soppy love story* 一個催人淚下的愛情故事

tender showing gentleness and care or affection for other people 溫柔體貼的；情意綿綿的：*This is one of the few tender moments in what is basically a very violent film.* 在一部總的來説是非常暴力的電影裏，這可是難得的溫情時刻。

touching causing you to feel an emotion such as gratitude or sympathy 感人的；令人同情的：*It's very touching that the dog is so obviously devoted to the children.* 那條狗對孩子們忠誠可鑒，非常感人。

separate[1] *adjective* not joined to or included with something else, or not shared with someone else 隔開的；單獨的；各自不同的：*They were sitting at separate tables.* 他們坐在各自的餐桌旁。

detached not attached to something else, especially not built beside another house and sharing a dividing wall with it（尤指房屋牆體）獨立的，分離的：*The house we are buying is detached and surrounded by a lovely garden.* 我們要買的房子是獨立屋，周圍是漂亮的花園。

different not the same as, or not of the same type as, something or someone else 相異的；不同種類的：*The view from the back of the house is different.* 從屋後看到的景色是不一樣的。

distinct clearly divided from, or clearly not the same as, something else 有明顯區別的；截然不同的：*The book is divided into two distinct sections.* 該書被分為截然不同的兩個部分。

independent separate from and not under the control of something or someone else 獨立的；自主的：*Formerly part of Czechoslovakia, Slovakia became an independent republic in 1993.* 斯洛伐克先前是捷克的一部分，1993年成為獨立的共和國。

individual consisting of one single and separate item, or for only one person or thing 個別的；單獨的：*Each student receives individual tuition.* 每一個學生都享受一對一的授課。

isolated existing or happening as single and separate instances of something that are not connected with one another 隔離的；孤立的：*There have been isolated cases of bird flu, but there is no sign of an epidemic.* 有一些禽流感的個案病例，但沒有蔓延的跡象。

particular not general but special, referring or relating to one thing or person or a distinct group 特定的，特殊的，獨特的（事物、個人或群體）：*I have a particular reason for not wanting to travel on that date.* 我有特殊原因不想在那天出遊。

unconnected having no link or relationship with something else or with each other 無聯繫的；不相干的：*Although the two crimes have some similar features, the police believe they are unconnected.* 雖然這兩宗罪案有一些相似的特點，但警察認為兩者沒有聯繫。

unrelated unconnected, or not belonging to the same family as someone else 不相干的；無血緣關係的：*We have the same surname, it's true, but we're unrelated.* 我們同姓，這倒是真的，可我們並無親緣關係。

separate[2] *verb* to put something or someone in a position where they are not attached to or not with something or someone else, or to become separate（使）

分開，隔開：*We separate the more able from the less able pupils and teach them in different classes.* 我們把能力較強和能力較差的學生分開，對他們進行分班教學。

come apart to break or divide into separate pieces 破碎；裂開：*If you hold both ends and twist gently, the pen should come apart quite easily.* 如果你抓住兩端輕輕地扭，這支筆可能很容易摔開。

detach to remove something or part of something from a thing that it is joined to 拆卸；使分開；使分離：*Detach the yellow strip before putting the ink cartridge into the printer.* 在將墨盒裝入打印機前，先揭去黃色封條。

disconnect to make something no longer physically attached or joined to something else 使分離；斷開：*Disconnect the appliance from the electricity supply before attempting to repair it.* 在嘗試修理電器前，先切斷電源。

dismantle to take something made from a number of different parts, such as an engine, and remove all of its parts one by one 拆開，拆卸（機器等）：*Surely you don't have to dismantle the whole engine just to repair an oil leak!* 僅僅為了修理滲油口，你大可不必拆開整台發動機。

divide to cut or separate something into a number of parts 分割；切分；劃分：*It's rather difficult to divide a cake into seven equal parts.* 很難把一塊蛋糕切成 7 等份。

fall apart to break or divide into separate pieces in a way that you did not intend or that causes damage to something 破碎；破裂；拆散：*I did not break the chair – it just fell apart when I sat on it.* 不是我把椅子弄壞的，我坐上去的時候它就散架了。

sever to cut something or cut it off, or to end something such as a link or connection between two or more things 切斷，割斷，中斷（聯繫或連接等）：*His right arm was severed in an industrial accident.* 他的右臂在一次工業意外中被切斷。

take apart to dismantle something, usually something that is constructed in a fairly simple way 拆卸，拆開（通常為構造較為簡單之物）：*If the shelves in the bookcase you made aren't level, you'd better take the whole thing apart and start again.* 如果你做的書櫃櫃架不平，最好把它全部拆掉，然後重新開始做。

➲ see also 參見 **alone; part²**

serious *adjective* not showing amusement, or not intending or intended to cause amusement 嚴肅的；認真的：*Please be serious for a moment and tell me what you really think.* 請你嚴肅一會兒，告訴我你的真實想法。

grave showing that something very sad or with very important bad consequences has happened（因極度傷心的事或非常嚴重的後果發生而）沉重的，嚴肅的：*The doctor came back into the room, and his expression was grave.* 醫生回到房間，其表情十分沉重。

grim showing a mixture of seriousness and a fierce, determined, or threatening quality 嚴厲的；嚴酷無情的：*The captain told us with a grim smile that there were no reinforcements and our orders were to fight to the last man.* 上尉冷笑着告訴我們，根本沒有增援部隊，我們得到的命令是堅持戰鬥到最後一個人。

pensive thinking deeply about something 沉思的；心事重重的：*He looked pensive, so I asked him what was on his mind.* 他看上去心事重重，於是我問他擔心甚麼。

preoccupied thinking and worrying about something very important or threatening, or showing that you are doing this 憂心忡忡的；全神貫注的：*She had obviously been too preoccupied to hear what I was saying to her.* 她顯然是在出神，沒有聽見我對她說的話。

sober not excited or affected by emotion; serious and realistic 冷靜的；審慎的：*I asked him for a sober assessment of our chances of escape.* 我要他冷靜地估算一下我們逃脫的機會有多大。

solemn very serious, quiet, and dignified 鄭重的；莊嚴的；一本正經的：*His face wore a solemn expression more suitable for a funeral than a wedding.* 他的臉上流露出莊嚴的神情，更像是在參加葬禮，而不是婚禮。

sombre suggesting that sad or worrying things are happening 憂鬱的；悶悶不樂的：*The atmosphere at the meeting was rather sombre, since everybody had already heard the bad news.* 會場氣氛十分陰鬱，因為所有人都已聽到這個壞消息。

stern showing that you expect people to be serious and will not be pleased if they try to be funny 嚴厲的；嚴肅的：*Our teacher could be very stern, if she thought we were trying to play tricks on her.* 如果老師認為我們是想戲弄她，她可能會非常嚴厲的。

thoughtful thinking rather than reacting to what is happening, or showing that you are thinking 沉思的；若有所思的：*He's very thoughtful today, do you think there's something wrong?* 他今天總是若有所思，你認為有甚麼不對勁嗎？

➲ see also 參見 **important**

shake *verb* to move quickly from side to side or up and down while remaining basically in the same position, or to make something do this 搖晃；抖動：*Shake the tablecloth before you fold it up and put it away.* 把桌布抖一抖，再摺疊起來擱到一邊去。

jiggle to shake something small in a light or casual way 輕搖：*He has an irritating habit of jiggling the keys on his keyring while he's talking to you.* 他有一個讓人心煩的習慣，談話時總愛晃動鑰匙圈上的鑰匙。

quake (*often humorous*) to tremble violently, usually through fear（常指因害怕而）劇烈抖動，顫抖：*The sound of his footsteps on the stairs would make us quake and hide under the blankets.* 他上樓的腳步聲會嚇得我們發抖，都躲到毛毯下面去了。

quiver to shake with many fast small movements, sometimes through fear or alarm（有時指因害怕或驚慌而）顫動：*The arrow stuck, quivering, in the very centre of the target.* 箭正好射中靶心，還顫動着。

shiver (*usually said about a person*) to quiver, especially with cold（通常指人，尤指因寒冷而）顫抖，哆嗦：*Don't stand shivering on the doorstep, come in!* 別站在門口直哆嗦，進來吧！

shudder to shake once violently or with a few violent movements, sometimes through horror（有時指因恐懼而）劇烈抖動，戰慄：*The thought* *of how close we came to being killed makes me shudder even now.* 即使現在想起我們當時險些斃命，我還不寒而慄。

sway to make large and often fairly slow side to side or up and down movements 搖晃；擺動：*The branches were swaying in the wind.* 樹枝在風中搖曳。

tremble (*usually said about a person*) to quiver, especially with fear or emotion (通常指人，尤指因害怕或情緒激動而) 發抖：*Her hand was trembling so badly that she nearly spilt her coffee when she tried to drink it.* 她的手不停地顫抖，甚至在她要喝咖啡時差點把咖啡潑了出來。

vibrate (*said about things*) to shake with many fast, small movements (指物體) 振顫，顫動：*The strings of a violin or piano vibrate to produce sound.* 小提琴或鋼琴的琴弦都是振動發音。

share *noun* a part or amount of something that is given to one person or group when something is divided up equally or systematically between two or more people or groups 部分；份兒；份額：*What are you going to do with your share of the money?* 你打算用你的那份兒錢去做甚麼？

allocation (*formal*) an amount of something, especially money, provided from a central fund to a particular person or group or for a particular purpose (尤指資金的) 配額，配給：*We've already spent most of our allocation from the budget for this year.* 我們已經將今年的預算配額花掉了絕大部分。

cut (*informal*) an amount that someone takes as their share of something, especially a sum of money, that is being divided up informally or illegally (尤指資金的非正式或非法) 分贓，份額：*By the time everyone else has taken a cut, there'll be very little left for us.* 其他所有人都分贓後，留給我們的就很少了。

portion a part or amount of something such as food or money that is being divided up 一部分，一份 (食物或資金等)：*You shouldn't have given them such large portions, now we're running out of stew.* 你本不該給他們分那麼多的，現在我們燉菜快沒了。

quota an amount that someone is officially given or allowed to take (由官方配給或允許的) 定額，限額：*If fishermen exceed their quotas, they have to throw the surplus fish back into the sea.* 如果漁民捕魚超過了限額，他們就得將多出來的魚放回海裏。

ration an amount of something that is scarce, for example food or petrol, that a person is allowed to have (如糧食或汽油等匱乏時的) 配給量，供應量：*Our weekly ration is just 500 grams of bread, 100 grams of fat, and 200 grams of meat.* 我們每週的配給量只有 500 克麵包、100 克油和 200 克肉。

shock *verb* to make someone suddenly and unexpectedly feel a strong and distressing emotion 使震驚；使驚愕：*The scenes of violence were intended to shock viewers.* 那些暴力場面是為了震撼觀眾。

appal (*mostly used in the passive*) to fill someone with a strong negative feeling such as horror or disgust (多用於被動語態) 使驚駭，使反感：*All right-thinking people are appalled by such horrendous crimes.* 所有頭腦正常的人都被如此駭人的罪行嚇得心驚肉跳。

horrify (*mostly used in the passive*) to fill someone with horror or with a strong negative feeling (多用於被動語態) 使恐懼，使厭惡：*I was horrified to* *think that I might have been indirectly responsible for the accident.* 想到可能對這事故負有間接責任，我感到非常害怕。

offend to make someone feel angry or disgusted because things they value highly, such as religious beliefs or moral principles, are being attacked 冒犯，得罪（某人，因某人珍視的東西，如宗教信仰、道德原則等受到侵害）: *You didn't stop to think that you might offend people by using bad language.* 你就沒有停下來想一想，自己說粗話或會冒犯別人的。

outrage (*mostly used in the passive*) to fill someone with anger, especially because they think a wrong or injustice has been done（多用於被動語態，指因為不公正）使憤慨，激怒: *The decision to demolish the historic building outraged conservationists.* 拆除那棟歷史建築的決議使自然環境保護者們感到憤慨。

scandalize (*mostly used in the passive*) to shock someone by doing something that they think is immoral or improper（多用於被動語態）使震驚，使反感（因認為別人做的事不道德或不得體）: *In those days the neighbours would have been scandalized by people living together before they were married.* 在那個時代，婚前同居準會讓鄰居們感到震驚。

unsettle to make someone feel mildly distressed or worried, or to make them lose their self-confidence 使心緒不寧；使動搖: *Something seems to have unsettled him: he can't concentrate on his work.* 好像有甚麼事使他心神不定，他無法專心工作。

upset to cause a fairly strong and distressing feeling in someone 使心煩；使苦惱: *It really upset your mother that you decided not to come home for Christmas.* 你決定聖誕節不回家，真讓你母親心裏不安。

➲ see also 參見 **dismay; surprise**

shorten *verb* to make something less long 縮短；使變短: *Can you shorten the legs of these jeans for me, please?* 請把我這條牛仔褲的褲腿弄短一點行嗎？

abbreviate to make a word less long by missing out the less important letters 縮短，縮寫（詞語等）: *Trinitrotoluene is usually abbreviated to TNT.* Trinitrotoluene 通常被縮寫成 TNT。

abridge to make a piece of writing such as book less long by leaving out some less important passages 刪節，縮短（書籍等作品）: *He refused to allow anyone to abridge his novel, arguing that every single word of the text was important.* 他拒不讓任何人對他的小說進行刪節，辯解說原文的每一個詞都重要。

condense to express something using fewer words, which usually involves not only leaving things out but also rewriting certain things 壓縮（文字篇幅等）；使簡潔: *She wants me to condense a 2000-word essay into an article containing just 500 words.* 她要我把一篇 2000 詞的文章縮寫成只含 500 個詞的短文。

curtail (*formal*) to make something that would normally go on longer finish in a shorter time 縮短；截短；提前結束: *We shall have to curtail our discussions, as the minister has a further meeting at four o'clock.* 我們將提前結束我們的討論，因為部長在 4 點還有一個會議。

cut to make something, especially a piece of writing or a performance, less long by removing or omitting parts of it, or to remove or omit part of something in order to make the whole thing shorter（尤指將作品或表演等）刪節，縮短：*The play lasts five hours, so, of course, directors usually cut it.* 這部戲要演 5 個小時，當然啦，導演們通常都進行刪剪。

dock to shorten or remove the tail of an animal 剪短（動物的尾巴等）：*The sheep look different because their tails have been docked.* 這些綿羊看上去不同，因為牠們的尾巴給剪了。

prune to shorten the branches or stems of a plant, or to cut a text 修剪，修整（植物或枝幹等）；刪節（文本）：*The roses will need to be pruned before next spring.* 這些玫瑰在明年春季前需要修剪。

trim to make something, especially hair or a plant, a little shorter by cutting off a small amount 修剪，修整（尤指毛髮或植物等）：*He trimmed his beard.* 他修了鬍鬚。

　⊃ see also 參見 **cut; decrease**

shout *verb* to speak or say something more loudly than usual because you want people to hear you 喊叫；大聲講：*There's no need to shout; I can hear you perfectly well.* 你沒必要大聲喊叫，我能聽得一清二楚。

bawl to shout very loudly and in an angry, rude, or frightening way 大聲叫罵；吆喝：*Jim's idea of maintaining discipline is to go and bawl at the kids if they're naughty.* 占姆認為維持紀律的辦法就是，如果孩子們調皮，就上前大聲喝止。

bay (*usually said about a large group of people*) to make very loud, angry, and threatening noises like wild animals（通常指一大群人像野獸一樣）大聲叫喊，大聲怒吼：*By the end of the match the crowd were baying for the referee's blood.* 在比賽結束時，人們怒吼着要找裁判算賬。

bellow to shout in a loud deep voice, often angrily or in pain（常指生氣或痛苦地）吼叫：*'Get out of my way', he bellowed.* "別擋我的路！" 他吼道。

call (out) to try to attract someone's attention or tell them something by shouting in their direction 呼喚；叫喊；大聲説出：*Call me if the phone rings while I'm in the garden.* 我在園子裏時，如果電話響了就叫我。

cry (out) to speak in a loud voice suddenly, usually because you feel pain or a strong emotion（通常指因痛苦或激動而突然）大聲叫喊，大聲地説：*'Why are you tormenting me like this?' she cried out.* "你為甚麼要這樣折磨我啊？" 她大聲叫喊道。

raise your voice to start to speak more loudly than usual, especially as a sign that you are getting angry 提高嗓門，高聲喊叫（尤表生氣）：*He's one of those rare people who can keep order in a classroom without ever having to raise his voice.* 在教室裏不用提高嗓門就能維持秩序的人是很少的，他就是其中一個。

roar to shout in a very loud voice that may be fierce or threatening or may show enthusiasm or pleasure 咆哮；吼叫；大聲歡呼：*The crowd roared their approval of the judge's choice.* 人群歡呼説他們支持評委的選擇。

scream to make a very loud high-pitched sound that usually suggests fear or pain, or to shout something in a loud high-pitched voice 尖聲叫喊（通常

表示害怕或痛苦）：*People were screaming for help from the upper floors of the burning building.* 燃燒着的樓房上面幾層有人在大聲呼救。

shriek to make a very loud high-pitched sound (*even shriller and more disturbing to hear than a scream*) that usually suggests panic, or to shout something in that kind of voice 尖叫（比 scream 更刺耳難聽，通常表示驚慌）：*'There's a spider running up my leg!' she shrieked.* "一隻蜘蛛爬到我腿上來了！" 她尖叫道。

yell to shout very loudly and usually in an uncontrolled way （通常指失控地）叫喊，叫嚷：*Stop yelling and I'll give you what you want.* 別叫了，你要甚麼我給你就是。

➲ see also 參見 **cry**

shrewd *adjective* having or showing practical intelligence based on experience of life and people's behaviour 機靈的；敏銳的；精明的：*She's shrewd enough to know when it's best not to interfere.* 她很精明，知道甚麼時候最好不要干預。

calculated (*used to describe actions*) done after thinking carefully about the advantages and disadvantages （用以描述行為）深思熟慮的，精心計劃的，蓄意的：*Taking over a nearly bankrupt company was a calculated risk.* 接管一家瀕臨破產的公司是經過深思熟慮的冒險。

calculating (*used to describe people disapprovingly*) thinking carefully about the advantages and disadvantages for yourself of any action （用以描述人，含貶義）攻於心計的，精於算計的：*a cold calculating villain* 一個攻於心計的冷酷之徒

crafty shrewd and knowing how to get an advantage over other people, usually by acting quietly and carefully, and sometimes by using tricks or deception 詭計多端的，狡詐的，善於騙人的：*He's a crafty old devil, so he's probably not telling us everything he knows.* 他是個詭計多端的老東西，所以他未必會把知道的每件事情都告訴我們。

cunning (*used approvingly and disapprovingly*) crafty, usually ingenious, and often involving an element of secrecy or deception （可用作褒義和貶義）詭詐的，機靈的，巧妙的：*I've worked out a cunning plan to avoid paying any tax on the deal.* 我想出了一個避免支付這筆交易稅的妙招。

knowing showing that you know something that other people do not and that you therefore have an advantage over them 知情的；會意的：*a knowing smile* 會意的微笑

perceptive (*used approvingly*) showing an ability to notice what is happening or what people are feeling or thinking （用作褒義）有理解力的，有洞察力的：*His book is a study full of perceptive insights.* 他的書是一部充滿洞察力的專題研究。

sharp very observant and aware of what is going on and able to think quickly 敏銳的；機智的：*She's very sharp, so she's bound to have noticed the mistake.* 她很精明，所以肯定注意到了這個錯誤。

sly (*mainly used disapprovingly*) done or doing things in a crafty, secretive, or underhand way （主要用作貶義）詭詐的，詭秘的，狡詐的：*You notice how,* *while praising Geoffrey, she slipped in a sly reference to her own contribution to his success.* 你注意吧，她在稱讚傑弗里時，神不知鬼不覺地就把話題轉到她自己對他的成功所起的作用上。

wily (*usually to describe people*) shrewd and careful, knowing a lot about tricks and deception and sometimes using them（通常用以描述人）老謀深算的，狡猾的，詭計多端的：*He's far too wily to be taken in by a simple trick like that.* 他太狡猾了，決不會被那樣的簡單伎倆所騙。

➲ see also 參見 **clever**

shy *adjective* nervous about meeting and talking to people or appearing in public 害羞的；腼腆的：*I asked him to play his violin, but he's too shy.* 我請他演奏小提琴，但他太腼腆了。

bashful (*used mainly to describe young people*) shy, modest, lacking in self-confidence, and usually likely to blush or become confused（主要用以描述年輕人）羞怯的，忸怩的：*Don't be bashful; tell us a little more about yourself.* 別羞答答的，再多給我們講一些你自己的情況吧。

coy shy or unwilling to be frank, but usually in a way that does not seem entirely genuine, as if you were trying to attract attention by appearing to avoid it or as if you had something to hide 忸怩作態的；羞羞答答的；假裝害羞的：*He's rather coy about revealing exactly how much he earns.* 他有點羞於透露自己到底賺多少錢。

diffident modest and usually rather shy 謙卑的；羞怯的：*She's not an easy person to interview because she's so diffident.* 她這個人不容易採訪，因為她很謙卑。

inhibited unable to express your feelings or desires or to enjoy yourself fully because of psychological restraints 羞澀的；拘謹的；內向的：*I'm far too inhibited to take my clothes off in public.* 我太害羞，不敢當眾脫掉衣服。

modest not boasting about your own abilities or achievements, but tending to suggest that they are not very great 謙虛的；謙遜的：*You're too modest; it was a really excellent performance.* 你太謙虛了，你的表演確實非常出色。

reserved unwilling to be frank and open when talking to people and rather quiet and shy in manner 拘謹緘默的；矜持的：*He's usually so reserved, but today he really opened up to me.* 他平日裏緘默寡言，但今天確實對我敞開心扉了。

reticent hesitant and cautious about revealing information or expressing opinions 緘默的；說話有保留的：*They're understandably rather reticent when it comes to discussing their plans for the future.* 談到將來的打算時，他們頗有保留，這是可以理解的。

retiring preferring to live a quiet life avoiding much contact with the public or the media, or with other people in general 離群索居的；孑身獨處的：*They were very pleasant when you met them, but because they were a rather retiring couple, you didn't meet them very often.* 見面時他們很和善，但因為他們夫妻倆不太喜歡社交，所以你不常遇到他們。

self-conscious shy and awkward because you think too much about what other people might be thinking about you（因顧慮別人對自己的看法而）拘

謹 的 ， 怕 難 為 情 的 : *He was so self-conscious about his appearance that he seldom went out.* 他對自己的外貌感到十分難為情，所以很少出去。

self-effacing preferring not to talk about yourself or to take credit for your achievements 自謙的；不喜出風頭的 : *He made light of his achievements in his usual self-effacing way.* 他一貫不事張揚，對自己的成績輕描淡寫。

timid showing a great lack of confidence in social situations and often unable to act through nervousness and shyness 膽小的；膽怯的；羞怯的 : *He was too timid even to ask her what her name was.* 他太羞怯，甚至不敢問她叫甚麼名字。

withdrawn very unwilling to be with or communicate with people, so that they think you may be ill 離群索居的；孤僻的 : *He's become very withdrawn since his wife died.* 他自從妻子死後就變得十分內向。

sign *noun* something that represents or expresses something else, such as that something exists, that something is happening, or what someone is thinking or feeling 標誌；符號 : *When the baby seems irritable, it's usually a sign that he's getting tired.* 嬰兒顯得急躁時，通常表示他睏了。

demonstration an action or event that shows what someone or something can do 示範；演示 : *a demonstration of the awesome power of the sea* 大海威力的展示

evidence signs or pieces of information that show that something has happened or is the case, for example that someone has committed a crime (犯罪等的) 證據 : *There's no evidence that connects her with the murder.* 沒有證據表明她與這宗謀殺案有牽連。

gesture a deliberate movement of part of the body that conveys a wish, command, or what someone is thinking or feeling (表達意願、指令或思想感情的) 手勢，示意動作 : *He held up his hand as a gesture to us to be silent.* 他舉起手示意我們安靜下來。

indication something, often a small thing, that shows that something has happened, is happening, or will happen 指示；跡象 : *Is there any indication that she's likely to change her mind?* 有沒有跡象表明她可能會改變主意呢？

mark something, usually an action, that is intended to show a feeling or attitude (通常指表達情感或態度的) 示意動作 : *We removed out hats and stood in silence as a mark of respect for the dead.* 我們摘帽默立，以示對死者的尊重。

signal an action, gesture, word, etc., that is meant to communicate a message to someone or make them do something 信號；訊號 : *Don't move until I give the signal.* 不要動，直到我發信號。

symbol something that represents something else, especially an object or a design that stands for something abstract (代表某物，尤指抽象事物的) 符號，標誌，象徵 : *The dove is a symbol of peace.* 鴿子是和平的象徵。

symptom a sign of something bad, especially of an illness (尤指疾病的) 症狀，徵兆 : *A sore throat and a runny nose are the usual symptoms of a cold.* 喉嚨痛和流鼻涕是常見的感冒症狀。

token something, often a small object, that is given to someone as a sign of your feelings or attitude towards them (送給他人以表達情感或態度的)

信物，紀念品：*Please accept this gift as a token of our gratitude for all you have done for us.* 請接受這份禮物，我們以此對您為我們所做的一切表示感激。

silly *adjective* not sensible or wise, but usually not causing great harm or damage 傻的；愚蠢的 (但通常無大礙)：*It was silly of me to come out without an umbrella.* 我真傻，不帶傘就出來了。

foolish not sensible or wise (*usually in a more serious context and implying stronger condemnation than silly*) 愚蠢的，傻的 (通常用於更嚴肅的場合，含有比 silly 更強的責備之意)：*I made a very foolish mistake when I trusted him with my money.* 我犯了一個非常愚蠢的錯誤，信任他並把我的錢給了他。

imprudent not thinking enough about the possible bad consequences of your actions insofar as they affect yourself (就行動後果對自己產生的影響而言) 輕率的；魯莽的：*Isn't it rather imprudent to invest so much money in a product for which there is no obvious market?* 將這麼多錢投放到一款沒有明顯市場的產品中去，難道不有點輕率嗎？

irresponsible not showing enough concern for the possible bad consequences of your actions insofar as they affect other people (就行動後果對別人產生的影響而言) 不負責任的，不計後果的：*It would be downright irresponsible to teach your daughter to sail before you've taught her how to swim.* 你還沒有教會你的女兒游泳，就教她駕帆船，完全是不負責任。

misguided acting on wrong principles or assumptions 被誤導的；被引入歧途的：*a misguided attempt to save the company some money* 想為公司省些錢的錯誤企圖

rash acting hastily, without thinking properly about what you are doing 輕率的；倉促的：*I made a rash promise to finish the work by tomorrow.* 我貿然承諾明天前完成工作。

reckless completely disregarding the possible bad consequences of your actions for yourself and other people 魯莽的；疏忽大意的：*reckless driving* 疏忽大意的駕駛

senseless done without a good reason and producing no good results 無謂的；不明智的；愚蠢的：*a senseless waste of resources* 資源的無謂浪費

unwise not showing good judgment 不明智的；不審慎的：*It would be unwise to invest all your money in a single venture.* 將你全部的錢投到單個經營項目上是不明智的。

➲ see also 參見 **stupid**

simple *adjective* not made, written, or decorated in an elaborate way (製作、書寫或裝飾等) 簡單的，簡易的：*Try to write in simple sentences.* 盡量用簡單的句子寫作。

classic simple and elegant in style, not trying to follow the fashion of any particular time 質樸的；傳統式樣的：*a classic tweed jacket* 一件傳統式樣的粗花呢外套

everyday not intended for special occasions or to impress people 平常的；平凡的：*This dress is perfectly good for everyday wear.* 這件衣服最適合平時穿。

homely of a kind that you have at home 家常的：*a restaurant that specializes in plain homely fare* 專做普通家常菜的餐館

no-nonsense avoiding complicated techniques or fashionable theories 直截了當的；講求實際的；不花巧的：*a no-nonsense approach to the teaching of grammar* 一種簡單直接的語法教學法

plain without decoration 樸素的；沒有裝飾的：*a plain white tablecloth* 一張純白色的桌布

unpretentious not trying to impress people by being elaborate, clever, or fashionable 不矯飾的；樸實無華的：*an unpretentious lifestyle* 一種質樸的生活方式

unsophisticated (*usually used disapprovingly*) lacking highly developed skills or techniques（通常用作貶義）不精細的，簡單的：*Using a megaphone is a rather unsophisticated method of communicating with the workforce.* 使用擴音器與職工對話是一種欠缺技巧的做法。

➲ see also 參見 **easy; ordinary**

sincere *adjective* meaning what you say when you say it, or expressing real feelings or opinions 真誠的；誠摯的：*Was he being sincere when he said I deserved the promotion more than he did?* 他說我比他更應該晉升時，是真心的嗎？

fervent expressing real and strong emotion 熱心的；熱烈的：*fervent prayers for his recovery* 熱切祈求他的康復

frank openly expressing what you think or feel 坦率的；真誠的：*We had a frank discussion about the problems we are having in our relationship.* 我們開誠佈公地討論了我們的關係中存在的問題。

genuine real or that someone really feels 真實的；誠懇的：*I think she felt genuine remorse for what she had done.* 我認為她已經為她做過的事情真正感到懊悔了。

heart-felt deeply and strongly felt 衷心的；由衷的：*We should like to offer you our heart-felt sympathy for your loss.* 對你的損失，我們謹向你表示深切的同情。

honest truthful, especially about what you think or feel 誠實的；坦誠的：*To be absolutely honest with you, I never expected the plan to succeed.* 對你説句大實話吧，我從沒指望過這項計劃會成功。

straightforward not trying to hide what you think or feel but expressing it directly and truthfully 直率的；坦率的；直截了當的：*I don't think you're being entirely straightforward with me.* 我覺得你對我不太耿直。

truthful telling the truth 實話實説的：*a truthful answer* 如實的回答

unaffected speaking or behaving naturally and not trying simply to impress other people 率真的；不矯揉造作的：*It's rare to find a politician who seems so unaffected when speaking to ordinary people.* 很少見到哪位政治家在對普通老百姓説話時顯得如此隨和。

unfeigned (*literary*) genuine 真實的；不做作的：*Party members greeted the new policy with unfeigned enthusiasm.* 黨員們以滿腔熱情迎接新的方案。

wholehearted (*usually used to describe positive emotions*) really and strongly felt（通常用以描述積極的情感）赤誠的，全心全意的：*I'm willing to offer you my wholehearted support.* 我願給予你全身心的支持。

➲ see also 參見 **frank**

size *noun* (*used in relation to physical objects and abstract things*) how big or small something is, especially a commercial product, or bigness as such（用以指具體物體和抽象事物，尤指商品的）尺寸，大小：*The sweaters come in all sizes from small to extra large.* 毛衣從細碼到加大碼的尺寸都有。

area (*used in relation to physical objects*) the amount of horizontal space covered by something（用以指具體物體）面積：*How do you work out the area of a circle?* 你怎樣計算出一個圓的面積？

bulk (*used in relation to physical objects and bodies*) bigness combined with heaviness and, usually, awkwardness（用以指具體物體或身體）巨大的體積，笨重的軀體：*He heaved his vast bulk out of the chair.* 他拖着肥碩的身體從椅子上站起來。

dimensions (*used in relation to physical objects and abstract things*) size, especially the height, length, and breadth of something（用以指具體物體和抽象事物）尺寸，大小：*I need to know the dimensions of the room to work out how much wallpaper will be needed.* 我需要知道房間的尺寸，以便算出需要多少牆紙。

extent (*used in relation to physical objects and abstract things*) how far something reaches or how much of something there is 範圍，程度：*The insurance company sent a representative to assess the extent of the damage.* 保險公司派了一名代表來評估受損程度。

magnitude (*formal*) (*used mainly in relation to abstract things or to the brightness of stars*) bigness（主要用以指抽象事物的）巨大，重大；（星體的）亮度，等級：*We are not really equipped to deal with a problem of this magnitude.* 我們確實沒有能力解決這麼重大的問題。

proportions (*used in relation to physical objects and abstract things*) size, especially the height, length, and breadth of something big（用以指具體物體和抽象事物，尤指大物體的）面積，容積，體積：*a figure of larger proportions than I had ever seen before* 我見過的最大的形體

range the number of different types of something that exist or are available 範圍；一系列：*Students can choose from a range of essay topics.* 學生可以從一系列作文題目中進行選擇。

scale (*used mainly in relation to abstract things*) extent or size, especially in relation to other examples of the same thing（主要用以指抽象事物，尤指同類事物相比較時）範圍，大小，規模：*We had not fully realized the scale of the task that we were faced with.* 我們當初沒有充分意識到我們面臨的任務有多大規模。

scope the range or number of subjects that something such as an enquiry or investigation is able or allowed to deal with（查詢、調查等的）範圍：*The government broadened the scope of the enquiry to include the effects of the disaster as well as its causes.* 政府擴大了調查範圍，包括這場災難的前因後果。

sleep *verb* to rest in an unconscious state 睡眠；睡覺：*We don't have a spare bed, so I hope you won't mind sleeping on the sofa.* 我們沒有多餘的牀鋪，所以我希望你不介意睡沙發。

be asleep to be sleeping 熟睡；睡着：*All the guests were still asleep when the fire started.* 火災發生時，所有客人都還在熟睡。

doze to be in a light sleep for a short time 打盹兒；小睡：*I woke up at five o'clock and then dozed until the alarm went off at six.* 我 5 點鐘就醒了，然後打着盹兒，一直到 6 點鐘鬧鈴響。

drop off (*informal*) to fall asleep 入睡；睡着：*I went to bed feeling very tired, but it took me a long time to drop off.* 我上牀睡覺時感覺很累，可我過了很長時間才入睡。

fall asleep to go into a sleeping state 睡着；入睡：*I fell asleep as soon as my head hit the pillow.* 我一倒在牀上就睡着了。

have or take a nap to have a short sleep 小睡；打盹：*I sometimes take a nap in the afternoon, if I'm going out in the evening.* 有時候，如果我晚上要出去，就在下午小睡一會兒。

have forty winks (*informal*) to have a short sleep 小睡；合一合眼：*He's upstairs having forty winks.* 他正在樓上小睡。

nod off (*informal*) to fall asleep, especially when you are trying to, or are supposed to, stay awake (尤指設法或應該保持清醒時) 小睡：*Several people nodded off during the sermon.* 好幾個人在聽講道時打瞌睡。

rest to be inactive, and either conscious or unconscious, so that your body can recover its vitality 休息；歇息：*I was resting on the bed, but not asleep.* 我正躺在牀上休息，但沒睡着。

snooze (*informal*) to doze 打盹兒；小睡：*No snoozing after the alarm clock goes off!* 鬧鈴響後不要再打瞌睡了！

slow *adjective* going, or only able to move, at a low speed 慢的；緩慢的：*Progress so far has been slow.* 至今一直進展緩慢。

gradual proceeding slowly and in steps or stages or by adding or subtracting small amounts 逐漸的；逐步的：*a gradual increase in production* 產量的逐步增加

leisurely moving in a relaxed way without attempting to hurry 悠閒的；不慌不忙的：*a leisurely walk along the side of the lake* 沿着湖邊休閒的散步

measured kept reasonably slow so that something can be done carefully 慢而穩的；從容不迫的：*Don't rush your speech; a measured delivery will ensure that everyone hears and understands clearly what you are saying.* 你演講不要太快，從容的陳述將確保每個人都能清楚地聽見並且理解你說的話。

ponderous moving or proceeding slowly and giving an impression of heaviness or awkwardness 笨重的；笨拙的：*ponderous footsteps* 笨重的腳步

sluggish moving very slowly and showing a lack of energy or drive 遲緩的；懶散的：*The twig barely moved on the surface of the sluggish stream.* 細枝垂在緩緩的溪流水面上，幾乎一動不動。

unhurried deliberately not going fast 從容不迫的；不慌不忙的：*Despite the crisis, she continued to deal with business at the same unhurried pace.* 即使在危急關頭，她照樣不急不忙地繼續處理事務。

small *adjective* not big; of limited size 小的：*a small portion of vegetables* 一小份蔬菜

compact conveniently small, especially not taking up much space or taking up less space than a full-size version of the same thing 緊湊的；小型的；袖珍的：*The tool can be dismantled and fits inside a compact carrying case.* 該工具可以拆開，然後裝進一個小型的手提箱裏。

little small, often small and pretty, or small in a way that arouses protective feelings 小的（常含嬌小或惹人憐愛之義）：*What a dear little puppy!* 多麼可愛的小狗啊！

mini* (*usually used to describe commercial products*) miniature（通常用以描述商品）微小的，小型的，迷你型的：*a mini car* 小型汽車

* Usually only used before a noun. 通常只用於名詞前。

miniature* made or bred to be a much smaller version of a large object or animal 袖珍的，小型的（物體或動物等）：*a miniature dachshund* 一條小型的達克斯獵犬

* Usually only used before a noun. 通常只用於名詞前。

minute very small indeed 微小的；極小的：*The particles are so minute, they can only be seen with the aid of a microscope.* 粒子小極了，只有借助顯微鏡才能看見。

petite (*usually used to describe women*) short and slim（通常用以描述女性）嬌小的，纖細的：*This dress would only fit someone who was really petite.* 這條連衣裙只適合身材特別小巧的人穿。

pocket small enough to fit inside the pocket of a jacket, etc. 袖珍的；可放在衣袋裏的：*a pocket dictionary* 一本袖珍詞典

short not tall or long 短的；矮的：*a short skirt* 一條短裙

slight small and not usually very significant; (*when used to describe people*) with a slim, light body 無足輕重的；（用以描述人）纖細的：*I think you've made a slight mistake.* 我認為你犯了一個小小的錯誤。

tiny very small (*but larger than minute*) 極小的（但比 minute 大些）：*Just a tiny drop of gin and a lot of tonic, please.* 請只放一點點氈酒，多加一些湯力水。

smell *noun* a quality or flavour given off by something and detected through the nose 氣味：*The house was full of the smell of fried onions.* 屋裏充滿了油炸洋葱的味道。

aroma a pleasant smell 芳香；香味：*What is that beautiful aroma coming from the kitchen?* 從廚房飄來誘人的香味，那是甚麼呀？

bouquet the smell given off by wine 酒香；（酒散發出的）芳香：*a white wine with a very delicate bouquet* 非常清香的白葡萄酒

fragrance a pleasant smell, especially a particular smell given to a commercial product（尤指給商品添加的）香味，香氣：*lavatory cleaner with pine fragrance* 帶有松脂香味的洗手間清潔劑

odour a pleasant or unpleasant smell (*odour is a slightly more refined word than smell*) 氣味 (odour 比 smell 略微優雅一些)：*body odour* 體臭

pong (*informal and humorous*) an unpleasant smell 惡臭；難聞的氣味：*What's that terrible pong? I know, it's your socks!* 甚麼氣味這麼難聞啊？我知道了，是你的襪子！

reek a strong and unpleasant smell 濃烈的氣味；臭氣：*the reek of cigarette smoke* 熏人的香煙味

scent the smell naturally given off by a plant or an animal (動植物本身散發的) 氣味，香味：*The flowers are very colourful, but they have a wonderful scent.* 這些花兒色彩鮮艷，散發出奇妙的香味。

stench a very strong and disgusting smell 惡臭；臭氣：*The body had remained undiscovered for several days, and the stench was almost unbearable.* 屍體好幾天都沒被發現，腐臭味幾乎讓人受不了。

stink (*informal*) a strong and unpleasant smell 臭味；臭氣：*We sprayed the room with air freshener to try to get rid of the stink.* 我們在房間裏噴了空氣清新劑，設法除去異味。

whiff a slight smell of something pleasant or unpleasant (微弱的) 一股，一陣 (氣味等)：*I thought I smelt a whiff of gas.* 我感覺聞到了一股煤氣的氣味。

smile *verb* to curve your mouth to express amusement or pleasure 微笑：*He's the only person on the photograph who's not smiling.* 他是照片中唯一一沒有笑的人。

beam to *smile* broadly in a way that expresses great and genuine happiness 面帶笑容；臉露喜色：*When I said how pretty she looked, she absolutely beamed.* 當我說她長得好漂亮時，她臉上笑開了花。

grin to smile broadly and show your teeth in a way that may express real pleasure or amusement, may be artificial, or may express some unpleasant emotion 露齒而笑；強顏歡笑：*He must have been pleased, he was grinning from ear to ear.* 他一定很高興，笑得嘴都合不攏了。

leer to smile in an unpleasant way that usually expresses sexual desire for someone 色迷迷地笑；奸笑；淫笑：*I don't like the way he keeps leering at my sister.* 我不喜歡他一個勁兒色迷迷地朝我姐姐笑。

simper to smile in an affected or exaggerated way, often while saying something (常指說話時) 扭捏作態地笑，矯揉造作地笑：'*Oh, how very kind of you to say so*', *she simpered.* "噢，你這麼說真是太好了。" 她賣弄風情地笑着說。

smirk to smile in a way that suggests you feel superior to someone or are enjoying the fact that they are in trouble 自鳴得意地笑；幸災樂禍地笑：*Stop smirking and help her clear up the mess.* 別幸災樂禍了，幫她收拾收拾爛攤子吧。

speak *verb* to use your voice to communicate something to someone in words 講話，說話：*I spoke to him about it yesterday.* 我昨天跟他講過這事。

address to direct something you are saying to a particular person or group (對某人或群體) 講話，發表演說：*I wasn't addressing you, I was speaking to my friend Mr Roberts here.* 我沒有對你說話，我是在和我的這位朋友羅伯茨先生說話。

express to communicate something such as an idea or a feeling through words or by some other means 表示，表達（思想感情等）: *I should just like to express my appreciation to everyone who has helped us to organize this event.* 我謹向所有幫助我們組織這項活動的人表示感謝。

pronounce to speak or make a sound in a particular way 發音: *The letters -ough can be pronounced in several different ways in English.* 在英語中，字母組合 -ough 能以幾種不同的方式發音。

say to use particular words or express particular ideas when speaking or writing 説；（口頭或書面）表達: *What did he say when you spoke to him yesterday?* 昨天你和他講話時他説了些甚麼？

state to say something in a definite way for other people to take note of 陳述；説明: *I wish to state my objections to the proposal.* 我希望闡明我對這項提議的反對意見。

talk to speak, especially to exchange words and ideas with another person 交談；談話: *We can't talk here; let's go into my office.* 我們不能在這裏談話，還是到我的辦公室去吧。

tell to communicate something to someone in words 告訴；講述: *I told him all about what happened.* 我把發生的事情全都講給他聽了。

utter to produce a sound with your voice, or to say something 發出（聲音等）；説出: *She uttered a terrible cry and sank unconscious to the floor.* 她發出一聲慘叫，隨即倒在地上不省人事。

voice (*formal*) to express something in speech（用言語）表達，吐露: *He has been known to voice opinions that some people might consider subversive.* 大家都知道他表述過在有些人看來可能有破壞性的意見。

whisper to speak, or say something, in a very quiet voice 低聲説；説悄悄話: *Just whisper it in my ear, if you don't want anyone to hear it.* 如果你不希望別人聽見，就對着我的耳朵低聲説吧。

➲ see also 參見 **say; tell**

special *adjective* different from what is normal or ordinary, usually in being better, more enjoyable, or involving particular ceremonies 特別的，特殊的（通常指與眾不同、更好、更令人愉快或涉及某些儀式的事物）: *a special occasion* 特別場合

distinctive having a particular, noticeable or recognizable quality that makes it different from others 特別的；有特色的；與眾不同的: *She has a very distinctive laugh.* 她的笑聲非常特別。

especial (*formal*) greater than usual 特別的；格外的: *Take especial care to spell her name correctly.* 要特別留意把她的名字拼正確。

exceptional of a kind that is not experienced very often 例外的；異乎尋常的: *He has a quite exceptional talent.* 他具有非常獨特的才幹。

extraordinary very unusual, generally through being either very good or very strange 非凡的；不尋常的；卓越的: *That was an extraordinary thing to say at someone's wedding.* 在別人的婚禮上説這件事很不尋常。

memorable easy to remember, usually through being very good, enjoyable, etc. 難忘的；值得紀念的: *Your kindness to us made our holiday especially memorable.* 您對我們無微不至的關懷使我們的假期尤為難忘。

notable definitely good enough to be worth recording or remembering 值得注意的；顯著的：*a notable achievement* 顯著的成績

noteworthy good or unusual enough to be worth recording or remembering (*often used with a negative*) (通常與否定詞配合使用) 值得注意的，顯著的：*Nobody said anything that was particularly noteworthy.* 沒有人説過特別值得留意的話。

➲ see also 參見 **favourite; important; unusual**

speech *noun* a text that is spoken aloud to a group of people at an occasion such as a meeting or a wedding (在會議或婚禮等場合當眾發表的) 講話，演講：*The prime minister is making an important speech today to the European Parliament.* 首相今天將對歐洲議會發表重要講話。

address a formal speech on an important occasion (在重大場合正式發表的) 演説，講話：*In his televised address to the nation, the king urged people to remain calm and to go about their normal business as far as possible.* 國王在對全國的電視講話中要求人們保持鎮定，並盡可能地跟往常一樣。

lecture a speech made to convey information and teach people, especially students, about a subject 講課，講座：*I missed the professor's lecture on Shakespeare, so can I borrow your notes?* 我錯過了那位教授關於莎士比亞的講座，我能借一下你的筆記嗎？

presentation a lecture, often accompanied by visual material such as slides or charts, given in a business context (常指商務場合伴有幻燈片或圖表等視覺資料的) 陳述，介紹，講座：*Can you do a presentation on the new computer system to a group of Chinese businessmen?* 你能為一批中國商人作一次關於電腦新系統的介紹嗎？

sermon a lecture on a religious or moral subject, usually given by a member of the clergy 佈道，説教：*He took some words from St Paul's Second Epistle to Timothy as the text for his sermon.* 他從聖保羅的《提摩太後書》裏面摘選了一些文字來做他佈道的講稿。

talk an informal speech or lecture (非正式的) 講座，演講：*Mr Brown has kindly offered to give us a short talk on the subject of common garden pests.* 布朗先生好心提出來要給我們作一次有關園林常見害蟲問題的簡短講話。

speed *noun* how fast or slowly something or someone is moving or something is done, or quickness 速度；迅速：*a speed of 20 kilometres per hour* 每小時 20 公里的速度

acceleration the fact of changing from a slower to a faster speed, or the ability to change from a slower to a faster speed 加速；加速能力：*This car has wonderful acceleration.* 這輛車具有很好的加速性能。

momentum the energy possessed by something that is moving that enables it to keep moving even when the force that first made it move is no longer operating 推進力；動力；衝力：*The sledge gained enough momentum running downhill to carry it a long way up the slope on the other side of the valley.* 衝下山坡的滑板獲得了足夠的衝力，使它沿着山谷對面的斜坡向上滑了很長一段。

pace speed, especially of something moving on legs (尤指行走或跑步的) 步速：*He surely won't be able to keep this pace up for four more laps.* 他肯定不能以這個步調再連跑 4 圈。

rapidity quickness, usually in doing something rather than in moving (通常指做事情而非運動的) 迅速：*the great rapidity of technological change* 科技進步之神速

rate speed, especially the speed at which something happens or is done (尤指事情發生或做事的) 速度，速率：*The factory must increase its rate of production to become profitable again.* 這家工廠要想能再有盈利，必須提高生產速度。

tempo speed, especially how fast a piece of music is to be played (尤指音樂的) 節奏，速度：*A more relaxed tempo would suit this piece better.* 節奏再緩一些將更適合這支曲子。

velocity speed, especially in scientific or technical contexts (尤指用於科技領域的) 速度，速率：*The rocket must attain a velocity sufficient to enable it to overcome the pull of Earth's gravity.* 火箭必須達到足夠高的速度才能克服地球引力的束縛。

⊃ see also 參見 **hurry; quick**

steal *verb* to take something of value from someone without their consent 偷；偷竊；偷盜：*Someone broke into our house and stole my computer.* 有人闖入我家偷走了我的電腦。

burgle to break into a building in order to steal 入室盜竊：*The house was burgled while the owners were on holiday.* 主人們外出度假時家裏失竊了。

embezzle to steal money that has been entrusted to you by a person or an organization 挪用；盜用：*While working as a computer operator in a bank, he managed to embezzle £20,000.* 在一家銀行做電腦操作員時，他挪用了 2 萬英鎊。

loot to steal goods in large quantities from shops and businesses during a riot, a war, or some other kind of emergency (在暴亂、戰爭或其他緊急情況時) 打劫，搶劫，劫掠：*There wasn't a single shop in the main street that hadn't been looted.* 在這條商業大街上沒有一家商店未被搶劫過。

make off with to escape taking with you something you have stolen 偷走；順手牽羊：*The gang raided a warehouse and made off with £100,000 worth of cigarettes.* 這幫人打劫了一家倉庫，偷走了價值 10 萬英鎊的香煙。

nick (*informal*) to steal something, usually something small 小偷小摸；偷竊 (小物品)：*I put my watch down on the table for a second, and somebody nicked it!* 我把手錶放在桌上一小會兒就被偷了！

pilfer to steal small things of little value, e.g., from where you work (在工作場所) 偷竊，小偷小摸：*Staff were caught pilfering paper clips.* 員工被發現偷萬字夾。

pinch (*informal, rather old-fashioned*) to steal something, usually something of little value 偷拿 (不值錢的東西)：*I used to pinch things sometimes, when I was a kid.* 當我還是個小孩時我偶爾會偷拿一些東西。

rip off (*informal*) to cheat or rob someone, or to steal something 欺騙；搶劫；偷竊：*If you pay $20 for something that usually costs $10, of course you* *feel you've been ripped off.* 如果你花 20 美元去買價值 10 美元的東西，你當然會感到自己被騙了。

rob* to deprive someone or an organization of something of value 搶劫，搶掠，掠奪：*We were robbed of all our foreign currency before we'd even got out of the airport.* 我們還沒有走出機場，所有的外幣就被搶走了。

* As a general rule, you rob someone and you steal something. 通常，rob 後面接某人，而 steal 後面接某物。

shoplift to take goods from a shop without paying for them 在商店行竊：*People who shoplift often don't need the things they steal.* 在商店行竊的人常常並不需要他們所偷的那些東西。

take to remove something without the owner's consent, to steal（未經物主同意）拿走；偷拿：*The house was broken into, but nothing of real value was taken.* 有人私自闖入屋子，但沒有值錢的東西被拿走。

stop¹ *verb* to come to a standstill after moving, or to make something come to a standstill 停止；停下來：*The car slowed down and then stopped.* 那輛車慢慢減速，然後停了下來。

come to rest (*usually said about an object that is moving, but is not powered or being driven*) to stop moving forward（通常指自然移動的物體）停止，停下來：*The boulder rolled all the way down the slope and came to rest at the bottom.* 巨石順着山坡一路滾下來，到山腳才停了下來。

draw up (*said about a vehicle*) to approach slowly and stop next to a particular place（指車輛在某處緩慢）停下來：*A shining limousine drew up outside the entrance to the hotel.* 一輛閃閃發亮的豪華轎車在賓館入口處停下來。

halt (*formal*) to stop, or to stop something 停止；使停止：*The sentry ordered us to halt and show our papers, before allowing us to proceed.* 哨兵命令我們停下出示證件，然後才給我們放行。

park to stop a vehicle and leave it standing in a place 停車：*The only problem with driving into central London is that it's difficult to find anywhere to park.* 駕車進入倫敦市中心唯一的問題就是很難找到車位。

pull up (*said about a vehicle or its driver*) to stop in a particular place（指車輛或其駕駛員在某處）停下來：*I had to pull up at the side of the road because one of the children was feeling sick.* 我不得不在公路旁把車停下來，因為有個孩子想吐。

stop² *verb* not to do something any more after doing it for a period of time 停止，終止（一直在做的事）：*I've stopped smoking at last, after thirty years.* 我吸了 30 年煙，現在終於戒掉了。

break off to stop, usually suddenly, in the middle of doing or saying something（通常指在說話或做事時）突然停止，中斷：*She broke off in the middle of our conversation to go and answer the door.* 她在我們談話時突然停下來去應門。

call it a day (*informal*) to stop working or engaging in an activity finally, usually after a long period（通常指長時間從事某項活動後）停止，終止；到此為止：*You've been hard at it since eight o'clock this morning, and I think it's* *time to call it a day.* 你從早上 8 點開始就一直在努力幹活，我想今天就幹到這裏吧。

cease (*formal*) to come to an end or stop 停止；終止：*The noise of drilling ceased as suddenly as it had begun.* 鑽孔的噪音就像突然開始一樣又戛然而止。

cut out (*informal*) to stop doing something annoying, or using or consuming something that might be harmful 停止做 (惱人的事)；停止使用，停止食用 (有害的東西)：*I had to cut out butter and cheese in order to lose weight.* 為了減肥，我不得不停止食用牛油和芝士。

discontinue (*formal*) to decide not to go on doing or making something 中斷；終止；停止：*The programme was discontinued because it proved unpopular with viewers.* 這個節目被叫停了，因為它已證明不受觀眾的歡迎。

leave off (*informal*) to stop doing something, often temporarily (常指暫時) 停止：*The rain left off just long enough for me to slip out to the shops.* 雨稍停了一下，我剛溜進商店又下了起來。

quit* (*informal*) to stop doing something, often something annoying 停止，終止 (常指令人討厭的事)：*Will you please quit hassling me!* 你不要再煩我了，好嗎？

* More commonly used in US English than in British English. 在美國英語中比在英國英語更常用。

➲ see also 參見 **abandon; finish; prevent**

story *noun* a description in words of an imaginary or real event or series of events 故事，小說：*Will you tell us a story, before we go to sleep?* 在我們睡覺前給我們講個故事好嗎？

account a description in words of what happened at a particular place or time or to a particular person, which is usually but not always factual 敍述；報道；報告：*Your account of the incident differs in several respects from the accounts given by other witnesses.* 你對這件事的敍述有幾點和其他目擊者的敍述不一致。

anecdote a short and usually amusing account of something that happened 軼事；趣聞；奇聞：*He has a fund of anecdotes from his days in the army.* 他有許多當兵時得來的軼聞趣事。

narrative (*formal*) an account of a series of events, or the plot of a novel (系列事件的) 敍述；(小說的) 情節：*a narrative of events that took place in the year 1865* 對發生在 1865 年的事件的敍述

novel a literary work that is usually quite long and tells a story in prose 小說；長篇故事：*She has finished her novel and is now trying to find a publisher for it.* 她已經完成她的小說，現正設法找出版商出版。

parable a short story that is intended to teach a moral or religious lesson, especially one told by Jesus and recorded in the Bible (尤指聖經中記載耶穌講述的) 寓言故事：*the parable of the Good Samaritan* 行善的撒馬利亞人的故事

plot the series of events in which the characters in a work such as a novel, play, or film are involved, as opposed to the characters themselves, the settings of the events, etc. 故事情節：*There is no plot, the characters just sit* *around and talk to one another.* 沒有故事情節，這些角色只是圍坐在一起相互交談。

saga a long story, or series of stories, describing many characters and events of a long period of time 長篇小説；長篇故事：*It is a saga covering three generations of a farming family in the Highlands of Scotland.* 這是一部長篇小説，講述了蘇格蘭高地一戶農家 3 代人的故事。

short story a literary work that is much shorter than a novel and usually deals with one event or one character 短篇故事；短篇小説：*He has had several short stories published in magazines.* 他已經在雜誌上發表了多篇短篇小説。

tale a story, usually a short, unpretentious, or folksy one, often one written for children 故事；（常指）童話故事：*If these walls could speak, they'd have some interesting tales to tell.* 如果這些牆能説話，它們也會講一些有趣的故事。

yarn (*informal*) a story or account, usually one that is told aloud and often one that is not very credible（常指口頭陳述的，不太可信的）故事；奇談：*He spun me some yarn about helping to catch a lion that had escaped from the zoo.* 他向我胡謅了一通他幫忙捕獲一頭從動物園裏跑出來的獅子的故事。

strange *adjective* not as you would usually expect, or not of a kind that you know about or easily recognize, and so causing you to feel surprise, wonder, or sometimes fear 奇怪的；陌生的；奇異的：*He says he heard strange noises in the night.* 他説他晚上聽到了奇怪的聲音。

bizarre startlingly strange, very unlike what is normal and often grotesque 極其怪誕的；異乎尋常的；離奇怪異的：*Her behaviour was so bizarre that I began to think she might need psychiatric help.* 她的行為如此怪異，我都開始認為她可能需要心理治療了。

curious unusual enough to arouse your interest or make you think 好奇的；引起興趣的：*It's curious that he's never mentioned her before.* 令人好奇的是他以前從來沒有提及過她。

odd curious or strange, sometimes amusingly strange 古怪的；奇特的；怪異的：*Does it make me look odd if I wear a red jacket and a yellow waistcoat?* 如果我穿一件紅外套和黃背心，看起來會古怪嗎？

outlandish strange and ridiculous, often through being exaggerated in some way 稀奇古怪的，奇異的：*He made some outlandish claim about being related to the royal family.* 他稀奇古怪地宣稱他和皇室有關係。

peculiar strange or curious 奇特的；奇異的；奇怪的：*There was a peculiar smell coming from the kitchen.* 廚房裏飄出一股奇特的味道。

queer* strange in a way that is often worrying or unpleasant 奇怪的，古怪的，反常的（以至於讓人感到擔憂或不舒服）：*I had a queer feeling that someone was watching me.* 我有一種奇怪的感覺，總覺得有人在注視着我。

* Be careful about using queer to describe people, as it is also sometimes used informally to mean homosexual. 用 queer 描述人時要慎重，因為該詞有時用以表示 "搞同性戀的"。

surreal very strange and of the kind that you might see in a dream or nightmare 離奇的；夢幻般的；光怪陸離的：*surreal images* 夢幻般的影像

weird very strange, usually in a rather frightening way and often in a way that suggests the supernatural 神秘怪異的；怪誕的；離奇的：*Don't you think it's weird that he went for a walk in the woods one day and just disappeared.* 一天他去樹林散步，然後就消失了，你不覺得這很怪異嗎？

⊃ see also 參見 **eccentric; ugly; unusual**

strict *adjective* making sure that people do exactly as they are supposed to do, or that something is exactly as it is supposed to be 嚴格的；精確的；嚴謹的：*Our teacher's very strict and insists that homework is always handed in on time.* 我們的老師非常嚴格，堅持要求學生按時交功課。

authoritarian using the power that you have, often harshly, to make sure that nobody disobeys you 權力主義的；獨裁主義的；專制的：*an authoritarian regime* 獨裁政體

firm making sure, but not in unkind way, that people do what they are supposed to do or that you get what you want 嚴厲的，嚴厲的 (但非刻薄的)：*The boss is firm but fair in the way he deals with the employees.* 這個老闆對待員工嚴厲卻不失公正。

inflexible very strict, not allowing any changes, excuses, exceptions, etc. 不可動搖的；嚴格的：*It should be an inflexible rule that any player who receives two red cards should be banned from playing for the rest of the season.* 被紅牌警告兩次的球員不允許參加該賽季接下來的比賽，這應是一條硬性規定。

rigorous very strict and thorough, or carried out in a strict and thorough way 非常嚴格的；嚴厲的：*rigorous discipline* 嚴格的紀律

stern showing strictness and disapproval towards anything that is done wrong (對缺點) 嚴厲的；嚴峻的：*My father looked very stern, and I wondered what exactly I had done wrong.* 爸爸看上去非常嚴峻，我不知道到底哪裏做錯了。

stringent (*usually used to describe checks or tests*) very rigorous (通常用以指檢查或測試) 嚴格的，嚴厲的，苛刻的：*Stringent tests must be carried out to make sure that the product is absolutely safe.* 一定要執行嚴格的測試以確保產品絕對安全。

uncompromising unwilling to let rules, standards, or principles be modified or relaxed (對規則、標準、原則的執行) 不讓步的，不妥協的，強硬的：*an uncompromising attitude towards offenders* 對待罪犯的強硬態度

strong *adjective* able to exert a lot of physical force, for example to move or lift things, or able to resist weight, pressure, etc., without breaking or collapsing 強壯的，有力的；不易摧毀的：*We need three strong men to help us move the grand piano.* 我們需要三個壯男人幫我們搬那架三角鋼琴。

beefy (*informal*) (*used to describe people*) big, heavy, and strong-looking (用於形容人) 高大健壯的，結實的，強壯的：*Get a couple of beefy blokes to stand at the door and only let people in if they have proper invitations.* 叫幾個身強力壯的小子守住門口，只允許那些持有正式邀請函的人進來。

brawny (*used to describe people*) with strong muscles (用於形容人) 肌肉發達的；健壯的；強壯的：*He doesn't look brawny enough to be a blacksmith.* 作為鐵匠，他看上去不夠健壯。

forceful exerting physical, intellectual, or moral, force（身體、智力或道義上）強有力的，有力的：*I gave it a rather more forceful shove, and it moved a little.* 我使了更大的勁猛推它，它移動了一點點。

mighty exerting a lot of power and force, or very big and strong 強有力的；強大的；有力的：*He struck it three mighty blows with his hammer.* 他用鐵錘重重地擊了它三下。

powerful having physical, intellectual, or political power, exerting a lot of force（身體、智力或政治上）有力的，強大的，強有力的：*a powerful energy* 強大的能量

resilient able to return to its original shape after being bent, stretched, etc., or able to recover after suffering distress, misfortune, etc. 有彈性的；重新振作的；有適應力的：*She'll get over the loss, she's pretty resilient.* 她很有韌性，會從這次失敗中熬過來的。

robust strongly made so as to be able to resist weight, pressure, etc. or rough treatment 結實的；耐用的；堅固的：*The boxes need to be robust enough to withstand being dropped out of a helicopter.* 這些箱子必須足夠結實，能夠從直升機上空投下來不被損壞。

sturdy strong and usually quite small or short and thick, or robust 健壯的；（常指小或短而粗的東西）強壯的：*sturdy little legs* 細小但強壯有力的腿

➲ see also 參見 **intense**

stubborn *adjective* showing an unwillingness to change your opinion or your course of action even when people try to persuade you to or when it seems reasonable to do so 頑固的；固執的；執拗的：*He can be very stubborn when he doesn't get his own way.* 他在不如意的時候會變得十分固執。

difficult (*informal*) uncooperative and unhelpful 難相處的；難以取悅的；故意刁難的：*She's not really against the plan, she's just being difficult.* 她並非真的反對這個計劃，只是故意刁難人罷了。

dogged showing an admirable determination to achieve something even if it takes a long time and many attempts 頑強的；堅忍不拔的；堅持不懈的：*Their dogged persistence eventually paid off.* 他們頑強的堅持最終獲得了回報。

intransigent (*formal*) completely unwilling to change your mind about something 毫不妥協的；不讓步的：*Senior party members remained intransigent in their opposition to any change in the constitution.* 政黨高層人員仍然堅決反對修訂憲法。

obstinate stubborn and usually unreasonable 執拗的，倔強的，頑固的（通常指不理智）：*Her obstinate refusal to accept a compromise made it impossible for us to reach an agreement.* 她頑固地拒絕接受折衷條件，這使我們達成協義成為泡影。

persistent not stopping what you are doing, or doing the same thing over and over again, in order to achieve something, often in a way that is annoying 堅持的，一再的（常指使人惱火）：*She was so persistent that in the end he had to agree to see her.* 在她一再堅持下，最後他只得答應見她。

uncooperative unwilling to help other people do or get what they want 不願合作的；不願配合的：*The dispute could have been settled much sooner, if* *the unions hadn't been so uncooperative.* 要是工會不這麼不配合的話，這次爭端早就解決了。

stupid *adjective* having or showing a lack of intelligence or common sense, often in a way that causes trouble for yourself or other people 蠢笨的，遲鈍的，傻的（常指引起麻煩）: *How could you be so stupid as to leave your passport at home?* 你怎麼會笨到把護照都丟在家裏了！

dim (*informal*) (*used mainly about people*) unintelligent（主要用以形容人）愚鈍的，缺乏才智的，不聰明的: *He's a perfectly nice chap, just a bit dim.* 他是個非常友善的小伙子，就是腦子遲鈍了點。

dumb* (*informal*) stupid 愚蠢的；傻的；笨的: *That was a really dumb thing to do.* 做那樣的事真是太愚蠢了。

* More commonly used in US English than in British English. 在美國英語中比在英國英語中更常用。

idiotic (usually used to describe actions or attitudes rather than people themselves, often humorously) very stupid or silly（常作幽默語，通常用以指行為或態度而非人本身）非常愚蠢的，白癡般的: *He's come up with some idiotic scheme to make money by selling vegetables on eBay.* 他竟然想出在 eBay 網上賣蔬菜賺錢的愚蠢計劃。

ignorant lacking knowledge, either generally or about a particular subject 無知的；愚昧的；矇昧的: *If you weren't so ignorant, you'd know that Macbeth was written by Shakespeare.* 如果你不是那麼無知，你就知道《麥克白》是莎士比亞的作品。

mindless (*usually used to describe actions or states*) showing a complete lack of thought or purpose（通常用以指行為或狀態）沒頭腦的，盲目的，無目的的: *mindless violence* 盲目的暴行

thick* (*informal*) (*used mainly about people and usually in an unkind way*) unintelligent（通常以不友好的方式指人）遲鈍的，愚笨的: *He's too thick to get into university.* 他腦子太遲鈍了，上不了大學。

* More commonly used in British English than in US English. 在英國英語中比在美國英語中更常用。

unintelligent having or showing a lack of the brain power needed to understand things, solve problems, etc. 缺乏才智的；愚笨的；不聰明的: *You have to be pretty unintelligent not to be able to add up 3 + 3.* 只有非常愚笨的人才算不出 3 加 3 等於幾。

➲ see also 參見 **ridiculous; silly**

subject *noun* a thing or matter that someone talks or writes about, or that a student studies at school or university 題目；主題；學科: *I'm giving a short talk on the subject of organic farming.* 我正在就有機農業這一題目作簡短的演講。

argument a series of linked ideas or statements that express someone's point of view on a subject 論點；論據；理由: *You can delete that paragraph, because it's irrelevant to your main argument.* 你可以將那一段刪掉，因為它與你的主要論點不相干。

issue a particular matter that people discuss, or argue or think about（討論、爭論或考慮的）問題，議題: *Reform of the education system is going to be* *one of the main issues in the election campaign.* 在競選運動中，教育體制的改革將成為主要議題之一。

matter something that someone talks about, writes about, or has to deal with（談論、撰寫或必須處理的）問題，課題，事情：*May I discuss a personal matter with you?* 我能和你討論一個私人問題嗎？

point a particular idea that someone is trying to communicate, or an idea that forms part of an argument 論點；觀點；見解：*He seems to talk endlessly around the subject without ever getting to the point.* 他似乎是沒完沒了地談論這個話題，卻一直說不到重點。

question an issue, or a topic in the form of a grammatical question 問題；疑問：*We were discussing the question of women's rights.* 我們正在討論女權問題。

subject matter the information or material that is communicated in a book, a lecture, etc.（著作、演講等的）主題，題目，主旨：*Do you think this is suitable subject matter for an article in the local newspaper?* 你認為這種文章主題適用於當地報紙嗎？

theme a main subject that is dealt with in a long work or in a series of separate discussions, etc., and unifies the whole（長篇著述或一系列獨立討論等的）題目，主題，主題思想：*I have chosen Repentance as the theme for a series of sermons I shall be giving during Lent.* 在大齋節期間，我選擇了"懺悔"作為將要進行的一系列佈道的主題。

thesis an argument, especially a long argument on an academic subject written to qualify for a doctor's degree at a university 學術論文；畢業論文；（尤指博士）學位論文：*I wrote my thesis on Napoleon's contribution to the French legal system.* 我寫的學位論文探討了拿破崙對法國法律制度的貢獻。

topic a thing or matter that someone talks or writes about, usually smaller in scope than a subject or covering a particular aspect of a subject（常指範圍較小、針對某個方面的）話題，題目，主題：*We finished discussing the state of the club's finances and moved on to another topic.* 我們討論完俱樂部的財政狀況後，繼續探討另一話題。

suggest¹ *verb* to offer an idea, usually an idea for a particular course of action, for other people to accept or reject（常指針對某一行動）建議，提議：*I suggest that you go home and think about it before you make a final decision.* 我建議你先回家仔細想想再做最後決定。

advise to offer someone an idea for what they should do that you think is a good one and will help them 勸告，忠告：*I would advise you not to go to the police until you have more evidence.* 我奉勸你在沒有掌握更多證據之前別去警察那兒報案。

propose to suggest a definite course of action, often in the course of a formal meeting where a proposal would usually be followed by a vote 提議，建議（常指在正式會議上提出，通常需經投票決定的建議）：*I propose that the meeting be postponed until next month.* 我提議這個會議延期至下個月。

put forward to offer something such as an idea or a plan for other people to consider 提出（想法或計劃供他人考慮）：*I'd like to come back to the* *suggestion put forward by Andrew at last week's meeting.* 我想還是回到在上週的會議上安德魯提出的建議上來。

recommend to advise someone in a positive way to do something, usually showing quite strongly that you think it is a good idea (通常指強烈) 勸告，建議，推薦: *The doctor recommended that I should take more exercise.* 醫生建議我多運動。

submit (*formal*) (*mainly used in legal contexts*) to suggest something (主要用於法律文書中) 主張，認為，建議: *I submit that the defendant was in no way to blame for the accident.* 我認為被告絕不該為此次事故負責。

suggest² *verb* to communicate something without stating it directly or making it completely clear what the situation is 暗示；言下之意是: *The evidence suggests that the victim knew her attacker.* 這證據表明被害者認識攻擊她的人。

hint to provide a small piece of information that suggests to someone what the situation is or what you intend to do (透過少許信息以) 暗示，提示: *He hinted that there were more revelations to come.* 他暗示說將會有更多的新發現。

imply to communicate an idea indirectly, by using words that can be understood as having an extra meaning in addition to their obvious one (一語雙關地) 暗示；暗指: *He said that he could not comment now, which probably implies that he will comment later.* 他說他現在不能評論，這或許暗示他以後會發表意見。

indicate to communicate an idea or information either directly or indirectly 表示，指出，表明: *Did he indicate when the elections were likely to take place?* 他是否指出選舉可能在甚麼時候舉行？

insinuate to suggest a negative idea about someone in an underhand way 暗示，含沙射影地說，旁敲側擊地指出: *You seem to be insinuating that I was somehow responsible for her death.* 你似乎在含沙射影地說，我多少該為她的死負責。

intimate (*formal*) to hint or imply 提示；暗示；透露: *She intimated that she would be willing to sell her story if the price was right.* 她透露說，如果價錢合適，她願意出讓她的小說。

➲ see also 參見 **advice; idea**

support *verb* to show your approval of an idea, plan, etc., and help to realize it, or to give help and encouragement to enable someone to achieve something or to cope with a difficult situation 幫助，擁護 (想法、計劃等)；鼓勵 (某人有所成就或擺脫困境): *The Conservative Party supports free enterprise.* 保守黨擁護自由企業制。

back to support someone or something by showing your approval or, sometimes, by giving them money 支持；資助: *If you decide to go ahead with the plan, we'll back you all the way.* 如果你決定推行此計劃，我們會自始至終支持你。

be in favour of to approve of a plan, proposal, idea, etc. 贊同，支持 (計劃、建議、想法等): *I'm in favour of giving parents the right to choose which school they send their children to.* 我同意給予父母為孩子選擇學校的權利。

champion to be an active and leading supporter of a cause 倡導；捍衛：
She championed the feminist cause long before it became fashionable to do so.
早在女權運動成為一股潮流之前，她就是這項事業的倡導者了。

encourage to show your approval of a course of action and advise, or try
to persuade someone to adopt it 鼓動，支持 (某個行動或建議)；勸告；慫恿：
We should be encouraging people to save money for their retirement. 我們應鼓
動人們存錢以備退休後使用。

foster to make it possible or easier for something to develop 助長；培養；
促進：*We hope this visit will foster good relations between our two countries.*
我們希望此次訪問能夠促進兩國之間的友好關係。

promote to take action to bring something to people's attention and
encourage them to do it, buy it, etc. 促進；推動；促銷：*They're promoting a
scheme for employees to buy shares in the company they work for.* 他們正在推
行由員工認購本公司股票的方案。

⊃ see also 參見 **defend; help**

sure *adjective* believing quite strongly that you know something or have done
something or remember correctly what happened 確信的；必定的；無疑的：*Are
you sure this is the right way to Richard's house?* 你確定去理查德家是走這條路嗎？

certain believing very strongly that you know something, etc. 確定的；無
疑的：*I can be absolutely certain about the time, because I looked at my watch
just after I heard the gun go off.* 關於時間我可以確信無疑，因為我剛聽到槍響
就看了錶。

confident able to rely on your own or someone else's ability to do
something, or on something happening 有信心的；有把握的：*You can be
confident that the economic situation will improve next year.* 明年的經濟形勢將
會有所改善，對此你可以充滿信心。

convinced very sure, often as a result of thinking about something for some
time (常指在一段時間的思考之後) 確信的，深信不疑的，堅信的：*The more I
examined the case, the more convinced I became that the police had arrested the
wrong man.* 隨着我對案件調查的深入，我越來越堅信警察抓錯人了。

definite accurate and precise, or clear and unmistakable, in what you say (所
說的話) 準確的，明確的，確切的：*Can you be a bit more definite about the
time that the incident took place?* 對於事件發生的時間你能更確切一點嗎？

positive completely certain 有絕對把握的；確信無疑的；肯定的：*I'm
positive he said ten o'clock, not ten thirty.* 我肯定他當時說的是 10 點正，而不
是 10 點 30 分。

⊃ see also 參見 **confident**

surprise *verb* to shock someone slightly by doing or saying something
unexpected 使…吃驚，使…感到意外：*Well, you do surprise me, I thought the
two of you were very happy together.* 唔，你的確讓我感到意外，我以為你們倆在
一起很幸福。

amaze (*often used in the passive*) to fill someone with wonder (常用於被動
語態) 使…驚奇，使…驚愕：*a discovery that amazed the scientific world* 一個
震驚科學界的發現

astonish (*usually used in the passive*) to surprise or amaze someone greatly (通常用於被動語態) 使…大為震驚，使…十分驚訝：*I'm absolutely astonished, I never thought you'd be able to finish the work so quickly.* 我真是大吃一驚，想不到你那麼快就把工作完成了。

astound (*usually used in the passive*) to surprise or amaze someone very greatly (通常用於被動語態) 使…大吃一驚，使…大為震驚：*We were astounded by the sheer size of the project.* 工程規模如此之大，令我們感到震驚。

stagger (*usually used in the passive*) to shock or surprise someone greatly (常用於被動語態) 使…十分驚訝，使…震驚：*He was staggered by the enormity of the task ahead of him.* 眼前這項浩大的任務把他驚呆了。

startle to shock and frighten someone by suddenly doing something (因突然行事而) 使…受到驚嚇：*I'm sorry, I didn't mean to startle you, the door was open so I came in.* 很抱歉，我無意間嚇着你了，看見門開着，所以我就進來了。

stun (*informal*) (*usually used in the passive*) to surprise someone in a pleasant or unpleasant way, so that they find it difficult to react (通常用於被動語態) 使…目瞪口呆，使…驚愕：*I was stunned when they told me I'd got an Oscar nomination.* 他們告知我獲得奧斯卡提名的時候，我驚得目瞪口呆。

take aback (*usually used in the passive*) to surprise someone, usually in an unpleasant way, so that they find it difficult to react (通常用於被動語態，指以令人不悅的方式) 使…目瞪口呆，使…大吃一驚：*I was taken aback by the rudeness of her reply.* 她粗魯無禮的回答使我目瞪口呆。

➲ see also 參見 **dismay**

T

taste¹ *noun* the impression made by a food when you put it into your mouth, for example whether it is sweet, sour, bitter, etc., or whether you find it pleasant or unpleasant 味道；味覺：*I don't like the taste of goat's milk cheese.* 我不喜歡山羊奶酪的味道。

flavour a distinct, pleasant and usually fairly strong taste (獨特的、使人愉悅的、通常十分強烈的) 味道，滋味，風味：*We need to add something to the soup to give it more flavour.* 我們需要再加點調料給湯提味。

savour (*literary*) a distinctive, pleasing, and usually non-sweet flavour (獨特的、使人愉悅的、通常不帶甜味的) 味道，風味，滋味：*The salad, so delicious the evening before, had lost its savour by the following lunchtime.* 前一天晚上還那麼美味的沙律到第二天中午就失去味道了。

smack a particular taste that you can distinguish in the general flavour of something (能分辨出的特殊的) 味道，氣味：*Do I detect a smack of anchovies?* 我好像聞到一股鯷魚的味道？

tang a strong and sharp or acid taste (濃烈的) 味道；酸味：*the refreshing tang of lemon juice* 檸檬果汁提神爽口的味道

taste² *verb* (*said about people*) to put something, or a small amount of something, into your mouth in order to experience its taste, or (*said about food*) to produce a particular taste 品嚐…的味道；(指食物) 有…的味道：*Would you taste the soup to see if it needs more salt?* 嚐一口湯，看鹽放得夠不夠，好嗎？

sample (*often used in polite invitations or requests*) to try a particular kind of food or drink, or to try several kinds of food or drink to see which one you prefer (常用於禮貌的邀請或請求) 嚐一嚐，嘗試 (以決定取捨)：*I'd love to sample some of your fish stew.* 我想嚐一下你做的燉魚。

savour to consume something slowly taking time to enjoy its flavour 細嚼慢嚥地品味；細品：*The beef was cooked to perfection, and I savoured every mouthful.* 牛肉烹調得太好了，我細細地品味着每一口。

try to taste something, or a small amount of something, to see if you like it 試嚐，品嚐：*How do you know you don't like squid if you've never tried it?* 你從來都沒嚐過，怎麼知道你不喜歡吃魷魚呢？

teach *verb* to pass on knowledge or skill to another person, or to groups of people especially in a school, university, etc. (尤指在學校裏) 傳授，教，講授：*She teaches French to students on the Business Studies course.* 她教商科學生的法語。

coach to help someone, usually one person or a small group, prepare a subject for an exam or test, or to teach someone a special skill (為考試) 輔導，指導，訓練：*We hired someone to coach Lucy for her maths A level.* 我們找了個人給露茜輔導數學高級考試。

drill to teach something by making people repeat it several times (反覆、多次) 訓練，操練：*The teacher drilled the students in preparation for their exams.* 為了迎接考試，老師反覆訓練學生。

educate to pass on knowledge in a variety of subjects and the general skills needed in life to someone 教育，教導 (眾多學科知識或綜合技能)：*She was educated at Grimethorpe High School for Girls and the University of Southampton.* 她先在格賴姆索普女子中學然後在修咸頓大學接受教育。

instruct (*formal*) to pass on knowledge or skill in a particular subject 教授，傳授 (某一門學科的知識或技能)：*Sergeant Jenkins instructs the new recruits in the care and handling of their weapons.* 詹金斯警官教這些新兵如何維護和使用他們的武器。

lecture to teach students, usually in a university, by giving long talks on a subject (通常指大學裏的) 講座，演講，講課：*He lectures in history at Ohio State University.* 他在俄亥俄州立大學講授歷史。

train to pass on a particular skill, or the skills and knowledge needed for a particular task, job, or profession, to someone 訓練，培訓 (任務或工作所需的知識或技能)：*Before you introduce the new machines, you need to train a sufficient number of employees to use them.* 在引進這些新設備前，你需要培訓足夠的人員去使用這些設備。

tutor to coach someone, or to teach one student or a small group of students at a university or school (在學校) 輔導，指導，教授 (一個或一小組學生)：*She tutors us in economic geography.* 她教我們經濟地理。

tell *verb* to give people information about something by speaking or writing to them about it, or to speak or write something such as news or a story so that other people can hear it or hear about it（用言語或文字）告訴，告知，敍述：*You should have told us that you're a vegetarian.* 你本應事先告訴我們你是個吃素的。

communicate (*formal*) to pass on information to someone by speaking to them or by contacting them by telephone, radio, letter, etc. 傳達，交流，溝通：*The pilot communicated his position to the control tower.* 飛行員向指揮塔報告了他的位置。

fill in (*informal*) to tell someone about something, usually about something that they were unable to hear about before for some reason 向（某人）提供（無法事先知道的情況）：*I'll just fill you in on what's been happening while you were away.* 我會把你離開後發生的事情原原本本地告訴你。

inform (*formal*) to give someone a particular piece of information 通知，告知，告訴：*I am writing to inform you that your application has been successful.* 茲函告，你的申請已經獲准。

let know to give someone a particular piece of information 告知，通知：*Let us know when you're arriving, and we'll meet you at the station.* 告訴我們你的到達時間，我們好去車站接你。

notify (*formal*) to inform someone officially about something, or to give a piece of information to someone in authority 通報，通告，通知：*You must notify the tax authorities immediately if you leave your present employment.* 如果你要離職，必須馬上通知稅務當局。

recount (*formal*) to tell a story or describe an event 敍述，講述，描述：*The Gospels recount the story of the life of Jesus Christ.* 福音書敍述了耶穌的生平故事。

relate (*formal*) to recount something 敍述，講述：*The opening chapter relates how a little boy meets an escaped convict in a churchyard.* 開篇講述了小男孩怎樣在墓地裏碰到一個逃犯。

report to give people information about something, especially through the media or in the form of a lengthy written document（尤指通過傳媒或長篇書面形式）報道，報告，敍述：*Our correspondent in Pakistan reports on efforts to bring aid to the survivors of the earthquake.* 我們駐巴勒斯坦的記者報道了積極援助地震倖存者的種種努力。

➲ see also 參見 say; speak

tempt *verb* to arouse the desire to have or do something in someone, or (*when used in the passive*) to feel inclined to do something 勸誘，誘惑，慫恿；（用於被動語態時）想要做：*Can I tempt you to try some of this delicious raspberry meringue?* 我能勸你嚐嚐這美味的黑莓蛋白甜餅嗎？

cajole to use persuasive or flattering language to persuade someone to do something that they are at first unwilling to do（用甜言蜜語）哄騙，引誘，勾引（某人做本不願意做的事）：*He's very charming, but don't let him cajole you into buying something that you don't really need.* 他很有魅力，但是不要被他哄着去買那些你並不需要的東西。

coax to use gentle persuasive methods to gradually persuade someone to do something that they are at first unwilling to do 哄勸，勸誘，哄騙（某人做本不願意做的事）：*The baby was very afraid of the sea, and we had to coax him even to go near enough just to get his feet wet.* 這個嬰兒非常怕海，我們只得哄他盡可能靠近海邊，來到哪怕只能打濕腳的地方。

entice to use something attractive as a method of getting someone to do what you want them to 誘惑，誘使，引誘：*An attractive window display will often entice passing customers into the shop.* 一個充滿誘惑力的櫥窗陳設常常把過路的行人吸引入店。

inveigle (*formal*) to use trickery or underhand methods to persuade someone to do something (利用欺騙手段) 誘騙，引誘，勸誘：*She inveigled him into parting with most of his hard-earned wages.* 她誘騙他花掉了大部分辛苦賺來的工資。

lure to offer something attractive as bait in order to get someone to go somewhere where something bad may happen to them, for example, into a trap, or to do what you want (用誘惑物為誘餌) 引誘，吸引，誘惑 (某人上當等)：*They used the promise of very high returns to lure investors into buying shares that eventually proved to be worthless.* 他們以高回報為引誘投資者去買那些最終證明毫無價值的股份。

sweet-talk (*informal*) to use persuasive, flattering, or tempting language to persuade someone to do something (用甜言蜜語) 勸誘，騙誘，哄騙：*She sweet-talked her father into lending her the money.* 她甜言蜜語地哄騙父親借錢給她。

➲ see also 參見 **persuade**

thief *noun* someone who steals something from someone 小偷；賊：*A thief stole my wallet.* 一個小偷偷走了我的錢包。

burglar someone who enters someone else's house or any building in order to steal things from it (入室行竊的) 竊賊，盜賊：*Burglars broke in and stole all our hi-fi equipment.* 竊賊闖入屋內偷走了我們所有的音響器材。

confidence trickster someone who gains another person's trust, for example, with a promise to help them make money, and then steals any money or property that person gives them (先博得別人的信任，而後騙取錢財的) 騙子：*A group of confidence tricksters set up a phony pension fund.* 一班厚顏無恥的騙子設立了一個虛假養老基金。

con-man/con-artist (*informal*) a confidence trickster (先博得別人的信任，而後騙取錢財的) 騙子：*He was so obviously a con-artist that I can't believe they fell for his scheme.* 顯然他是個騙子，我真不敢相信他們竟然為他的計謀所騙。

mugger (*informal*) someone who threatens or attacks people in the street and robs them 搶劫犯；攔路搶劫者；行兇搶劫者：*I'd only just left the hotel, when a mugger pulled a knife on me and demanded my cash and credit cards.* 我剛剛離開酒店，就有一個劫匪掏出小刀逼着我要現金和信用卡。

pickpocket a person who stealthily removes cash, wallets, purses, etc., from people's clothes, usually in crowded places (通常指在擁擠的場所掏別人腰包的) 小偷，扒手：*Beware of pickpockets when travelling on the underground.* 坐地鐵時小心扒手。

robber a person who robs someone or a place 強盜；搶劫犯：*a gang of bank robbers* 一班銀行劫匪

shoplifter someone who steals goods from a shop（商店裏行竊的）竊賊：*'We prosecute shoplifters.'* "我們將起訴商店竊賊。"

swindler someone who uses dishonest methods or trickery to get money from people, but does not physically rob them（用欺騙手段獲取錢財但並不實施搶劫的）騙子，詐騙犯：*These 'get-rich-quick' schemes are usually run by swindlers.* 這些"發橫財"的計劃往往是騙子們在經營。

thin *adjective* not thick, narrow, or having a body with little flesh on it 薄的；窄的；瘦的：*a piece of thin wire* 一根細電線

anorexic suffering from the disease, anorexia nervosa, or (*informal*) having an extremely thin body 患（神經性）厭食症的；厭食的；極瘦的：*She's not just thin, she's anorexic.* 她不單只是瘦，還患有厭食症。

bony having little flesh, so that you are aware of the bones underneath 瘦骨嶙峋的；骨瘦如柴的；瘦得皮包骨的：*His face was too bony to be really handsome.* 他的臉很瘦削，毫無帥氣可言。

emaciated having a very thin body as a result of starvation or disease 羸弱的，枯瘦的，消瘦的：*the emaciated bodies of the victims of the famine* 饑民們羸弱的身體

gaunt having a face or body that is thin and hollowed as a result usually of hardship or suffering（通常指由於艱難困苦而）消瘦的，瘦削的，憔悴的：*You'd think he must have cancer, because he looks so gaunt.* 你會以為他身患癌症，因為他看起來太憔悴了。

narrow small when measured from side to side or across its width 狹窄的：*a narrow gap* 一條窄縫

scrawny unattractively thin 瘦骨嶙峋的；骨瘦如柴的；瘦巴巴的：*I'd like to wring her scrawny neck!* 我真想把她那瘦巴巴的脖子給擰斷！

skinny (*used mainly to describe children or young people*) having a thin body（主要用以描述孩子或年輕人）極瘦的，乾瘦的，皮包骨的：*a skinny little kid* 一個乾瘦的小孩

slender attractively or gracefully thin 苗條的；纖細的；修長的：*long, slender fingers* 纖細修長的手指

slim attractively thin 苗條的；纖細的：*The easiest way to get slimmer is to eat less.* 變苗條最簡單的方法就是少吃。

svelte having an attractively thin and graceful body 苗條的；身材嬌好的：*You're looking very svelte as usual.* 你還像往常那樣苗條。

think *verb* to use your mind, for example, to produce ideas or to try to solve problems 思考；思索；想：*I have thought long and hard about this question and still haven't found a satisfactory answer.* 對這個問題我冥思苦想了很久，但仍找不到一個令人滿意的答案。

concentrate to focus your mind or your attention on something 聚精會神；全神貫注：*I'm trying to concentrate on my work, and she keeps distracting me.* 我一直努力全神貫注於我的工作，而她卻不停地打擾我。

consider to think carefully, for example, before making a decision（在作決定前）仔細考慮，思考：*Perhaps you like to take a couple of days to consider,* *before you finally make up your mind.* 在下定決心前，你也許需要幾天時間仔細考慮一下。

contemplate to think about something, especially to visualize something and think about it (尤指通過設想、想像) 思考，沉思：*The consequences of such a catastrophe are too awful to contemplate.* 這種大災難的後果可怕得難以想像。

deliberate to think about a matter, often to think about something and discuss it with someone else 考慮；商討；研討：*Members of the jury deliberated for several hours and then announced their decision.* 陪審團成員商討數小時後宣佈了他們的裁決。

mull over to think about something, especially something that happened or was said at a previous time 仔細考慮，認真琢磨 (尤指已經發生或剛提到的事)：*I've just been mulling over what you said yesterday and, actually, I think you're quite right.* 我一直在認真思考你昨天説的話，最後我認為你是對的。

ponder to think deeply about something, usually a serious matter 沉思，深思，仔細考慮 (通常指嚴肅的事)：*pondering the mysteries of life* 思索生命之奧秘

reflect to have a particular thought, or to consider 考慮；思考；反思：*She reflected that nobody had forced her to come; she had come of her own free will.* 她尋思，沒有人強迫她來，是她自願來的。

ruminate to think deeply for a long time (長時間) 沉思，反覆思考：*She can spend weeks ruminating on some profound philosophical question.* 她可以花上數週時間反覆思考某一個深奧的哲學問題。

take stock to think carefully about a situation so that you have a clear idea of what has happened or what you have done in the past 深思，權衡，估量 (以理清思路)：*It's time to take stock of what we have achieved so far, so that we can make realistic plans for the future.* 現在是時候估量一下我們已經取得的成就了，這樣我們才能為將來制定現實的計劃。

weigh up to compare different aspects of something and try to come to a judgment about it 斟酌；權衡；衡量：*I'm trying to weigh up the advantages and disadvantages of working from home.* 我正在努力權衡在家工作的利弊。

⊃ see also 參見 **consider**

threaten *verb* to frighten someone by saying or indicating that you will do something to harm them, unless they do as you wish, or to be a danger that could easily happen to someone or something 恐嚇；威脅；恫嚇：*He threatened to kill me if I moved or made a sound.* 他威脅説，如果我敢動一下或發出聲音，他就殺了我。

bully to threaten or mistreat someone who is weaker than you are persistently 恃強凌弱；欺負：*He says he's being bullied by one of the big boys at school.* 他説他在校一直被一個大個子男生欺負。

cow (*usually used in the passive*) to make someone feel afraid and powerless (通常用於被動語態) 威嚇，嚇唬：*Cowed by the teacher's icy stare, the boys slunk off back to their classrooms.* 老師冷冷的盯視嚇得那些男孩悄悄溜回了教室。

intimidate to deliberately make someone feel afraid, usually so that they will do what you want 脅迫，威迫，要挾：*He can threaten with anything he* *likes, his threats won't intimidate me.* 他可以用任何東西來威脅,但他的威脅嚇不倒我。

lean on (*informal*) to use the power or influence you have over someone, often in a fairly discreet way, to make them do what you want (常指以謹慎的方式、利用權勢或影響力) 威脅,脅迫: *The government obviously leant on the trade unions to make them agree to the plan.* 顯然政府是在脅迫工會同意那個計劃。

menace (*usually used in the passive*) to be a danger that could easily happen to someone or something (通常用於被動語態) 危及,威脅,恐嚇: *The health of the population of Europe is being menaced by a new danger, Asian bird flu.* 歐洲人的健康正受到亞洲型禽流感這一新危險的威脅。

pressurize to persuade someone or something to do something by using the power you have over them or telling them repeatedly what you want them to do (利用權力或通過反覆説服) 逼迫,迫使: *I feel I'm being pressurized to sign up to the scheme, although it's not really in my best interests.* 我感覺我是在被迫參加那個方案,儘管那個方案對我並不是真的最有利。

throw *verb* to make something travel through the air, especially by drawing back your arm, then thrusting it forward while releasing it from your hand 扔;拋;投: *Jenny caught the ball and threw it back to me.* 珍妮接住球,然後回拋給了我。

cast* to throw a fishing line or net into the water in order to catch fish, or (*literary*) to throw 投,擲,拋 (魚網或釣絲等): *He glanced briefly at the letter before casting it aside like the rest.* 他匆匆看了一眼那封信,然後像其他信一樣將它扔到了一邊。

* Used in many metaphorical expressions, such as cast an eye and cast a glance. 用於許多隱喻的表達中,如"瞟一眼"、"瞅一眼"。

catapult to throw or propel something or someone suddenly and with great speed and force (突然猛力地) 射出,彈出: *The impact catapulted me out of my seat.* 巨大的衝擊力把我彈出了座位。

fling to throw or propel something, someone, or yourself forcefully, dramatically, or carelessly (猛力地或隨便地) 投,擲,拋 (某物、某人或自己): *She flung herself down on the bed and burst into tears.* 她一頭撲到牀上,大哭起來。

hurl to throw something with great force 用力投擲;猛投: *He was so frustrated that he picked up the typewriter and hurled it across the room.* 他感到十分沮喪,於是提起打字機用力扔到了房間那頭。

launch to make something leave the ground or leave your hand and begin a journey through the air 投射;投出;發射: *She launched herself off the top diving board.* 她從最高的跳水板一躍而下。

lob to throw or hit something, usually a ball, so that it goes high up in the air before coming down again (向空中) 高拋,高擲,高擊 (球): *I was standing by the net, so he just lobbed the ball over my head.* 我站在網邊,因此他恰好把球拋過了我的頭頂。

propel to use force to make something move in a particular direction, or to be the power source that makes a vehicle move 推進;推動;驅動: *She gave* *me a push in the back that propelled me through the open door and out onto the street.* 她從後面一推，把我從開着的門一卜推到了大街上。

sling to throw something forcefully and often in a careless or casual way （猛力地、隨意地）扔，拋，擲：*He came in, slung his coat on the floor, and flopped down on the sofa.* 他進來後，把大衣隨手扔在地板上，然後一屁股坐到沙發上。

toss to throw something without much force, often in a casual way（不費勁、不經意地）拋，擲，扔：*He screwed up the letter and tossed it into the wastepaper basket.* 他把那封信揉成一團，扔進了廢紙簍。

tired *adjective* feeling the effects of effort or work and needing to rest or sleep 疲勞的；疲倦的；勞累的：*I was so tired coming home from work that I fell asleep on the train.* 在下班回家的途中，我太累了，竟在火車上睡着了。

drained very tired, with no energy 非常疲倦的；精疲力竭的：*He felt very drained at the end of the all-day interviews.* 經過一天的採訪，他感到精疲力竭。

drowsy feeling ready to go to sleep 昏昏欲睡的；睏倦的：*After driving for several hours I began to feel rather drowsy and stopped at a roadside café.* 經過幾小時的駕駛，我開始感到昏昏欲睡，於是在路邊的一家咖啡店旁停下來。

exhausted very tired, having used up your strength completely 疲憊的；筋疲力盡的：*They decided to run all the way home and were exhausted by the time they got there.* 他們決定一路跑回家，到家時已經筋疲力盡了。

jaded lacking energy and freshness and in need of a rest or change, especially after doing the same job for a long period of time（長時間做同樣的工作後）疲憊不堪的，厭倦的，倦怠的：*The management team is looking distinctly jaded, and this is probably a good time to introduce some new talent.* 這個管理小組看起來明顯的疲憊不堪，這或許是引進新人材的好機會。

sleepy (*used more often in everyday contexts and to describe children than drowsy*) feeling ready to go to sleep（較之 drowsy，更常用於日常生活中或用以形容孩子）睏乏的，欲睡的：*We have two sleepy children here, who need to go to bed.* 我們這兒的兩個孩子都睏了，需要上牀休息。

weary (*making you feel*)very tired,expecially because you have been working very hard 疲倦的，令人疲憊的：*He began the long weary journey home.* 他踏上了漫長而令人疲憊的回家之路。

worn out (*informal*) exhausted, especially after working for a long time（尤指經過長時間的工作後）疲憊的，筋疲力盡的：*I was completely worn out, and all I wanted to do was to fall into bed.* 我已經筋疲力盡了，只想上牀睡覺。

zonked (*informal*) exhausted 極度疲倦的；筋疲力盡的：*I must be unfit, because every time I play squash it leaves me completely zonked.* 我一定是身體不行了，因為每次打壁球都會使我筋疲力盡。

top[1] *noun* the uppermost or highest part of something 頂部；頂點；頂端：*We climbed to the top of the tower.* 我們爬上了塔頂。

apex the upper angle of a triangle or a similar figure or shape（三角形或相似形狀的）頂點，頂角，尖頂：*A delta is a roughly triangular area, with its apex towards the mouth of the river.* 三角洲為近似三角形的地帶，其頂角朝向江口。

crest the uppermost edge or part of something, especially a wave, hill, or ridge 波峰；浪尖；山頂；頂峰：*We reached the crest of the ridge and could look down into the valley on the other side.* 我們到達了山頂，可以俯瞰另一側的山谷了。

crown the top part of the head or of a hat 頭頂；帽頂；王冠：*Baldness usually begins at the temples and on the crown of the head.* 禿頂往往最早發生在兩側鬢角和頭頂。

peak the top part of the mountain, especially when it is pointed in shape (尤指有尖頂的) 山頂，頂峰：*a mountain with twin peaks* 一座雙峰山

summit the top of a mountain 山頂；頂峰：*We were only 500 metres from the summit when our oxygen cylinders failed.* 氧氣筒缺氧時，我們離山頂只有 500 米的距離。

tip the very highest or furthest end of something, which is often pointed in shape 尖端；尖頂：*a bud on the tip of the stem* 莖幹頂端的一株嫩芽

top² *(usually the top)* noun the most important position, the most intense level, or the level at which the most important and successful people operate (通常為 the top) 要職，高層，（事業的）頂峰：*She has reached the top of her profession.* 她已經達到了事業的頂峰。

climax the most intense moment in something, which usually follows a gradual build-up of intensity 高潮：*The brass blares out at the climax of the movement.* 銅管樂在樂章的高潮時奏響。

culmination something that marks the successful end or climax of a process (標誌成功或某一過程的) 頂點，巔峰，終點：*the culmination of the week's events* 本週系列事件的最高潮

height the most intense point or period of something 最佳點；最強點；頂點：*While the plague was at its height, more than 1000 people were dying every day.* 瘟疫肆虐最猛烈時，每天有 1000 多人喪命。

peak the topmost point, at which something is at its best or most intense, or someone is at their most successful 最佳點；（事業等的）頂峰，高峰：*She reached the peak of her fitness after completing all the exercises.* 全部訓練結束後，她的身體達到了最佳狀態。

pinnacle the peak of something 頂點；頂峰：*the pinnacle of his career* 他事業的頂峰

summit the highest point of something, or a meeting between leaders of important nations 最高點；頂點；（重要國家間的）首腦會議，峰會：*To become head of her own department was the summit of her ambitions.* 成為她所在部門的主管是她的最高目標。

➲ see also 參見 **best**

travel *verb* to go on a journey, to go from place to place, or to use a particular means of transport to go to a place (借助交通工具) 旅行，旅遊：*I have to travel regularly to Paris and Rome on business.* 我得定期去巴黎和羅馬出差。

backpack to travel or hike carrying the things you need in a large pack on your back 背包旅行；徒步旅行：*She spent part of her gap year backpacking in Thailand.* 她把間隔年的部分時間用於在泰國徒步旅行。

commute to travel regularly between home and work 上下班往返；定期往返：*We're trying to buy a house in town so that I don't have to commute so far every day.* 我們正設法在城裏買一所房子，那樣我就不用每天往返奔波了。

go to move by walking or in a vehicle, to make a journey or trip to a place, or to use a particular means of transport 行走；行駛；前往：*Wouldn't it be quicker to go by taxi?* 坐計程車去不是更快嗎？

journey (*formal*) to travel 旅行；出遊：*We remained in Edinburgh while the rest of the party journeyed on towards Fort William.* 我們留在了愛丁堡，而隊裏其他人則繼續前往威廉堡旅行。

ride to travel while sitting on an animal, especially a horse, or a machine such as a bicycle, or to travel as a passenger in a bus, car, or taxi 騎（馬，單車等）；乘（車）：*I learnt to ride a bike when I was six.* 我 6 歲時就學會騎單車了。

roam to go around from place to place, usually without a fixed plan or timetable 漫游；閒逛；徜徉：*They left us free to roam around the city and see some of the less well-known sights.* 他們任憑我們在這座城市四處閒逛，參觀一些不太知名的景觀。

take a trip to go or travel to a place, usually in order to stay there for a limited period of time 旅遊（通常作短暫停留）：*Why not take a trip to London for the weekend?* 為甚麼不去倫敦度週末呢？

⊃ see also 參見 **go**

trick *noun* an often cleverly planned action that is intended to deceive people or take them by surprise, either in order to cheat them or simply for fun or mischief 詭計；騙局；惡作劇：*My sister played a nasty trick on me, pretending to be asleep and then jumping up and scaring me.* 我妹妹惡意捉弄我，先假裝睡覺，隨後跳起來嚇唬我。

deceit the deliberate intention to deceive or mislead other people, usually thought of and condemned as being a bad quality in a person 欺詐；欺騙；蒙騙：*I didn't think you all people would be capable of such deceit.* 我以為並非你們所有的人都有這種欺詐的能耐。

deception the act of deceiving people, or an action that deceives someone, which may either be condemned as dishonest or admired for its cleverness 欺騙；詐騙；騙術：*The goalkeeper didn't spot the deception and went the wrong way.* 守門員未識破這一計，撲向了錯誤的方向。

dodge (*informal*) an action that is intended to enable you to avoid doing something that you ought to do 逃避的詭計；推脱的計策：*a new dodge to avoid paying tax on his profits* 他逃避所得稅的新花招

manoeuvre an action or movement that is intended to put you in a better position to do what you want 計策；花招；手段：*a manoeuvre to outflank the enemy formation* 從側翼包圍敵軍的計策

ploy an action or manoeuvre that involves deception 計謀；手段；花招：*I think this is just a ploy to make us think they're not interested in taking over the company.* 我認為這只不過是一齣花招，想讓我們相信他們對收購公司不感興趣。

ruse a cunning plan or idea, often involving deception 詭計；花招；騙術：*I've thought of a ruse to get us into the circus without paying.* 我想到一個計策，使我們不花錢就能進入馬戲場。

stratagem (*old-fashioned*) a clever and carefully planned action, often involving deception, that is intended to enable you to get the better of someone 計策，計謀，花招：*Odysseus, the most cunning of all the Grecian lords, devised a subtle stratagem to capture the town of Troy.* 奧德賽，這個最精明的希臘國王，設計出一個巧妙的計謀攻陷了特洛伊城。

subterfuge (*formal*) deception, or a deception, that usually involves secret or underhand methods 欺騙性伎倆；欺詐行為：*When she couldn't achieve her aims by honest means, she would often resort to subterfuge.* 在她採用誠實的手段不能達到目的時，她通常會耍花招。

➲ see also 參見 **cheat**

trouble¹ *verb* to make someone feel worried and anxious or sad, often over a long period of time（常指長時間地）使焦慮，使憂慮，使煩惱：*You look sad: what's troubling you?* 你看上去很憂傷，甚麼事使你焦慮不安？

agitate to make someone worried and unable to rest or be still 使煩惱；使憂慮；使不安寧：*The loud music was agitating the residents of the nursing home.* 吵鬧的音樂聲攪得療養院的居民不得安寧。

bother to make someone feel worried or upset 煩擾；使煩惱；使不安：*Travelling by plane really bothers me.* 乘飛機旅行着實令我不安。

distress to make someone feel very sad 使悲痛；使難過；使憂傷：*The sight of the starving children on the news really distressed us.* 看到新聞裏飽受饑餓之苦的兒童真使我們感到難過。

disturb to make someone feel worried 使擔憂；使煩惱；使不安：*There's no reason to be disturbed: this is just a fire drill.* 沒有理由擔心——這只是一次消防演習。

freak out (*informal*) to shock someone and put them in a panic 使受到驚嚇；使驚慌失措：*It really freaked me out when all the lights suddenly went off.* 所有的燈突然熄滅了，我着實感到驚慌失措。

perturb (*formal*) to make someone worried or anxious 使擔憂；使焦慮；使煩惱：*He continued to believe that the plan would be a success and was not unduly perturbed by reports of early difficulties.* 他仍然相信這個計劃會成功，沒有被報道的初期困難過度困擾。

upset to put someone into a sad or worried state 使不安；使難過；使煩惱：*I didn't mean to upset you by talking about your ex-boyfriend.* 我談及你的前男友並非有意讓你難過。

worry to make someone feel anxious, thinking that something bad might happen 使擔心；使不安；使煩惱：*It worries me that you work such long hours.* 你這樣長時間地工作讓我很擔心。

trouble² *noun* a state or situation characterized by violence and disorder 動亂；糾紛；擾亂：*They always call the police at the first sign of trouble.* 一有騷亂跡象，他們總是叫來警察。

commotion a situation where there is a lot of noise and noisy or sometimes violent activity 喧嘩；騷亂；騷動：*We heard a commotion in the flat downstairs and went to see what was happening.* 我們聽到樓下單位裏一陣喧嘩，便去探個究竟。

disorder a situation in which people behave violently and commit illegal acts 動亂；騷亂；混亂狀態：*The authorities will not tolerate disorder on the streets of our cities.* 當局不會容忍在我們的城市街道上出現騷亂。

disturbance an incident in which someone does something that alarms other people or causes trouble 擾亂；干擾：*Someone reported a disturbance outside the pub, and police were sent to investigate.* 有人舉報酒吧外有騷亂，於是警察被派去調查。

fuss noisy behaviour and complaints, often about a trivial matter（常指因瑣事引起的）吵鬧，爭吵，抱怨：*She made a fuss because she thought the waiter was being rude to her.* 她認為侍者對她無禮而大吵大鬧起來。

riot a situation in which a crowd of people behave very violently, usually attacking and destroying property and also attacking other people or the police and officials（通常指破壞財產、襲人的）暴亂，騷亂，騷動：*There were riots in which shops were looted and vehicles set on fire.* 有多宗暴亂發生，暴亂中，商店被搶、車輛被燒。

unpleasantness (*euphemistic*) trouble, usually an argument or fight 不愉快，紛爭（通常指爭論或打架）：*We don't want any unpleasantness, we're all friends here.* 我們不希望任何不快的事情發生，在這裏我們都是朋友。

unrest a situation in which there is disorder, usually because people are opposed to or angry with the government（通常指因反對政府或對其不滿而產生的）無序狀態，動盪不安：*There is unrest in the southern region of the country and tourists are strongly advised not to travel there.* 這個國家的南部地區動盪不安，強烈建議遊客不要到該地區旅遊。

➲ see also 參見 **disorder;disturb;problem**

true *adjective* being in accordance with the facts, not a lie and not invented 真的；真實的：*Is it true that you used to be a dancer?* 你真的曾經是一個舞蹈演員嗎？

accurate conforming to fact, reality, or the actual state of affairs 準確的；正確的；精確的：*an accurate account of events* 對事件的準確敍述

correct without error 無誤的；正確的：*Is this the correct spelling of 'separate'?* 這是 "separate" 的正確拼寫嗎？

faithful in keeping with the facts, or with the essence of something such as a work of art 符合事實的；如實的；忠實的：*a faithful adaptation for television of a classic novel* 對搬上電視的經典小說的忠實改編

literal (*usually used to describe the sense in which a word or phrase is being used*) being the strictest or most basic 按照字意的，如實的，確確實實的：*Jim's hat wouldn't fit you; he has a big head, in the literal sense.* 占姆的帽子不會適合你，沒有誇張，他的頭真大呢。

veracious (*formal*) telling the truth, or being in accordance with the facts 如實的；說實話的；合乎事實的：*a veracious witness* 一個說實話的目擊者

verifiable possible to be proved true or accurate 可證實的；可核實的：*an article containing verifiable information* 一篇內容可被證實的文章

➲ see also 參見 **accurate;faithful;genuine**

try *verb* to take action in the hope of being able to do or achieve something, but without being sure of success 試；嘗試；試圖：*He tried to put the fire out by pouring water onto the stove, but that only made things worse.* 他試圖往火爐澆水來滅火，但那樣只是使事情變得更糟。

attempt to try (*used in more formal contexts than try*) 嘗試，試圖（較之 try，用於更正式的場合）：*I knew I would be unable to dissuade her, so I did not even attempt to.* 我知道無法勸阻她，所以我甚至連試都沒試。

do your best to do everything that you can in order to achieve something 盡力；盡全力；盡力而為：*I did my best to explain the situation to him, but I don't think he understood what I was saying.* 我盡力向他說明情況，但我覺得他並不明白我的意思。

endeavour (*formal*) to try 努力；盡力；力圖：*I shall endeavour to arrange matters to your satisfaction, sir.* 先生，我將盡力把事情安排得讓您滿意。

have a go/crack/stab (*informal*) to try 試一試；嘗試；盡力：*He had a go at fixing the computer himself, but he had to give up and call in an expert.* 他試了試自己修理電腦，但後來不得不放棄，只好請專家。

make an effort to devote more time and energy than usual to trying to do something 付出（比平常更多的）努力；盡力：*He made a special effort to be on time for the meeting.* 為了準時到會，他做了特別的努力。

seek (*formal*) to try to do or get something 試圖，努力：*The publisher is seeking to recruit a new sales director.* 出版商正試圖招募一名新的銷售主管。

strive (*formal*) to try hard to do something, often against opposition （常指不顧反對）努力，奮鬥，力爭：*He was striving to make himself heard above the noise in the hall.* 他努力讓自己的聲音高過禮堂裏的噪音，讓聽眾聽清楚。

struggle to put a lot of effort into trying to do something, but to have little success 費勁，努力，盡力（但成功的機會很小）：*She was struggling to get the lid off a jar of pickles.* 她正費勁地開淹菜缸的蓋子。

turn¹ *verb* to move, or make something move, in a circle or part of a circle around a central point 轉動；使…轉動；旋轉：*You turn the valve clockwise to let the water in.* 你順時針轉動閥門，使水流進來。

reel to move unsteadily or drunkenly in a winding or circular way 踉蹌；搖晃；蹣跚：*I punched him in the face and sent him reeling back.* 我一拳擊中他的臉部，打得他向後一個搖晃。

revolve to turn in a full circle, usually at a speed that is or seems quite slow （通常指緩慢地）旋轉，環繞，轉動：*The little figure on top of the music box revolves as the music plays.* 音樂盒上的小人兒隨着音樂慢慢地轉動。

rotate to turn, or turn something, usually in a full circle, often fast （通常指快速地）轉動，旋轉：*The blades rotate to provide lift to the helicopter.* 螺旋槳旋轉使直升機盤旋上升。

spin to turn, or turn something, in a full circle or to face in the opposite direction fast（快速）旋轉，轉動：*The croupier span the roulette wheel.* 賭台管理員飛速轉動輪盤。

spiral to move in a circle and upwards or downwards at the same time 螺旋式上升（或下降）；盤旋上升（或下降）：*The plane spiralled downwards out of control.* 飛機失去控制盤旋下落。

swivel to turn something around a fixed central point so that it faces in a different direction（繞軸心）旋轉，轉動：*He swivelled his chair round to face them.* 他把椅子轉過來面向他們。

twirl to turn in a full circle fast and usually in a light-hearted way（通常指輕快地）轉動，旋轉：*She twirled around, showing off her new skirt.* 她輕快地轉動身子，炫耀她的新裙子。

twist to turn, or turn something, through part of a circle 擰；扭；轉動：*If you twist the top, it should come off quite easily.* 如果你轉動頂端，它應該很容易擰開。

whirl to turn, or turn something, in a full circle very fast, often in a way that makes you feel giddy（常指令人眩暈地快速）旋轉，轉動：*Couples whirled across the floor as the music got faster and faster.* 隨着音樂越來越快，一對對在舞池裏飛旋起來。

turn² *verb* to change direction, for example to the right or left, or change the direction in which something is pointing 改變方向；轉向：*Turn right at the next set of traffic lights.* 到下一個交通燈向右轉。

invert (*formal*) to move something so that the part that is usually at the top is at the bottom 顛倒；使倒轉：*If you invert the letter M, it becomes W.* 如果你將字母 M 倒過來，它就變成 W 了。

reverse to move or change something so that the part that is usually at the front is at the rear or the thing that usually come first comes last（使）反轉，倒轉，次序顛倒：*We reversed the usual order and began at Z.* 我們顛倒了平常的順序，從 Z 開始。

shift to move or move something, often only a small amount, to be in a different position or facing in a different direction（輕微地）轉動，轉向，移動：*She shifted her chair a little to the right so that she could see the television better.* 為了方便看電視，她稍稍向右轉動了一下椅子。

swerve to change direction quickly or unexpectedly, especially to avoid something（尤指為了避讓而快速或出其不意地）改變方向，轉向：*The car swerved to avoid a pedestrian.* 那輛車突然轉向，以避免撞到行人。

turn upside down to invert something 顛倒；使倒置：*The lid wasn't screwed on properly, so when he turned the jar upside down, all the beans fell out.* 這蓋子沒擰好，所以當他將罐子倒過來時，所有的豆子都掉了出來。

veer to change direction, usually to a new direction at an acute angle from the previous one, or to change direction suddenly 急轉（方向）；（突然）轉向：*The wind veered round to the northwest.* 風向突然轉為西北風。

wind to change direction several times 蜿蜒；迂迴；曲折而行：*The path winds up the hill.* 小路沿着山坡蜿蜒而上。

U

ugly *adjective* unpleasant to look at, through being shaped, arranged, or coloured in a way that people do not consider to be beautiful 醜陋的；難看的：*He has an ugly scar on his left cheek.* 他的左臉有一塊難看的傷疤。

deformed (*used to describe a person or part of the body*) that has not developed in the normal way and does not have the usual shape (用於描述人或者人的身體) 畸形的，變形的：*She was born with a deformed foot.* 她生來就有一隻腳畸形。

grotesque ugly and very strange, and also sometimes intended to be funny 奇形怪狀的；醜陋奇異的；怪誕的：*At the site of the crash, the metal rails had been twisted into grotesque shapes.* 在空難事故現場，那些金屬欄杆都扭曲得奇形怪狀。

hideous very ugly, or frighteningly ugly 十分醜陋的；醜陋而可怕的：*a hideous monster* 醜陋的龐然大物

plain (*usually used to describe a woman*) having a face or appearance that either has no interesting or beautiful features or is definitely unattractive (通常用於描述婦女) 相貌平平的，缺少魅力的：*She was always such a plain little girl, so how did she grow up to look so stunning?* 她以前一直是個其貌不揚的小女孩，怎麼長大後竟出落得如此美麗動人呢？

repulsive extremely ugly or unpleasant, so ugly as to drive people away 極端醜陋的；令人厭惡的；令人反感的：*Well, he's not very good-looking, but I wouldn't go so far as to say I find him repulsive.* 不錯，他是其貌不揚，不過我還不至於說我覺得他令人厭惡。

unattractive not having the qualities that appeal to people, especially in appearance (尤指外貌) 不吸引人的，不起眼的，普通的：*I'm not wearing that outfit, as it makes me look so unattractive.* 我沒有穿那套衣服，因為它讓我看起來很不順眼。

unsightly very obviously spoiling the appearance of something (因外表受損而顯得) 難看的，不悅目，不好看的：*George spilt coffee over the carpet, and it's left a very unsightly mark.* 佐治把咖啡潑灑在地毯上，留下了難看的痕跡。

understand *verb* to be able to explain something or someone's character or actions, or to know what something means or what someone is trying to say 理解；了解；懂得：*I can't understand why I didn't think of it before.* 我搞不懂為甚麼之前我沒有想到呢。

catch on (*informal*) to understand the meaning of what someone says or to understand what is happening 理解；明白；了解：*I knew at once what she was hinting at, but it seemed to take everyone else a while to catch on.* 我立即就知道了她在暗示甚麼，不過其他所有人好像是過了一會兒才明白過來。

comprehend (*formal*) to understand 領會；理解；了解：*I fail to comprehend how such a simple mistake could have happened.* 我沒弄明白為甚麼會犯如此幼稚的錯誤。

dawn on to become clear, understandable, or explainable to someone, especially suddenly 恍然大悟；突然明白：*It suddenly dawned on me that there* *was a much simpler solution to our problem.* 我突然明白，有一種更簡單的方法來解決我們的問題。

fathom (*also fathom out*) to understand something after thinking about it carefully（經過仔細思考後）理解，了解，明白：*I can't fathom (out) what happened.* 我不明白發生了甚麼事。

follow to understand an explanation or a description 理解，懂得（某個説明或描述）：*The pictures will help you follow the story.* 這些圖片會幫助你理解這個故事。

get (*informal*) to understand the meaning of something, or understand a joke 了解，懂得（某事或玩笑的含義）：*I don't get it. Why did he murder his aunt if she was going to leave all her money to his sister anyway?* 我還是沒搞懂。既然他姑姑已經準備把所有的錢都留給他妹妹，那他為甚麼還要謀殺姑姑呢？

grasp to understand the meaning of something 領會；掌握；理解：*I'm not sure she fully grasped what I was saying.* 我不能肯定她是否已經完全領會了我説的話。

realize to become aware of or understand something that you were unaware of or did not understand before 認識到；領悟：*I finally realized that I had been approaching the problem in completely the wrong way.* 最後我終於認識到我一直在用完全錯誤的方式處理這個問題。

see to understand or realize 明白；懂；認識到：*I see now why she was so reluctant to come to the party.* 我現在總算明白她為甚麼不願意來參加聚會了。

unfriendly *adjective* showing that you do not like someone or do not want to be with them 不友善的；不友好的：*He was most unfriendly and didn't even ask me to sit down.* 他非常不友好，甚至沒有請我坐下。

aloof not joining in with what people are doing or not seeming to want to be with them or speak to them, sometimes because you feel superior to them（有時指因優越感而）遠離人群的，疏遠的，孤零的：*While the others were chatting, she remained aloof.* 其他人在聊天時，她卻孤零零地站在一邊。

cold not feeling or showing any emotion, especially not showing any friendliness or affection towards people 冷漠的；冷淡的；不熱情的：*Even when he smiles, you can see he has very cold eyes.* 即使在他笑的時候，你也能感覺到他冷漠的眼神。

distant not seeming to want to communicate with other people very much or become involved with them 疏遠的；冷漠的；冷淡的：*He wasn't exactly unfriendly, but he was rather distant.* 他並非真的不友好，只是很疏遠。

hostile showing that you definitely do not like, approve of, or agree with someone or something and would rather act against them than be friends with them 敵意的；敵對的：*She greeted my remark with a hostile stare.* 她對我的評論橫眉冷對。

inhospitable (*used to describe people*) not inviting people to your home or not making them feel welcome when they visit, or (*said about places*) not pleasant to be in 冷淡的；不適宜人居住的：*The South Pole is one of the most inhospitable places on earth.* 南極是地球上最不適宜人居住的地方之一。

unsociable not wanting to be with or talk to other people 不愛交際的；不合群的：*I don't want to seem unsociable, but I think I'd better go as I do have a train to catch.* 我不想讓人覺得我不合群，但因為要趕火車，所以我想我得走了。

unwelcoming not making people feel happy and comfortable 不受歡迎的；令人不舒服的：*Plain white walls and hard wooden chairs create a very unwelcoming atmosphere.* 純白牆面和硬木椅子營造了一種非常令人不舒服的氣氛。

unpredictable *adjective* that cannot be known in advance with any certainty, because very likely to change or do something unusual 不可預知的；變幻莫測的；捉摸不定的：*His moods are very unpredictable and seem to have nothing to do with whether things are going well or badly for him.* 他的情緒捉摸不定，似乎與自己順利與否毫無聯繫。

changeable not likely to continue being the same as it is now 變化無常的；多變的：*The weather is very changeable at this time of year.* 每年的這個時節，天氣都變化無常。

fickle behaving in an unpredictable way, because you are likely to change your mind about things unexpectedly（心情等）變幻無常的，善變的，多變的：*He's too fickle to ever really know what he wants.* 他太善變了，連自己也不清楚想要甚麼。

unexpected that you did not know was going to happen 想不到的；出乎意料的；意外的：*Well, this is an unexpected pleasure!* 啊，這真是意外的驚喜！

unforeseeable impossible to know about in advance 不可預知的；無法預料的：*You can't be blamed if the accident that happened was completely unforeseeable.* 如果事故的發生完全無法預料，你就不該受到責備。

unreliable that you cannot expect to do what he, she, or it is supposed to do 不可靠的；靠不住的：*The bus service is very unreliable in this part of town.* 在城裏這個地區，巴士是很靠不住的。

unstable in a condition in which it is very likely to change, usually into a worse or more dangerous state（狀態）不穩定的，多變的（尤指每況愈下的）：*mentally unstable* 精神狀態不穩定

variable (*often used in mathematics*) changing, able to change, or likely to change, but not necessarily by a large amount（常用於數學上）變量的；可變的；多變的：*a variable quantity* 變量

unusual *adjective* not as you would normally expect 不尋常的；異乎尋常的；不一般的：*It's unusual for him to be late.* 遲到對他來說是不尋常的。

abnormal unusual, often in a way that seems worrying or dangerous 反常的，異常的，不正常的（常指到達令人焦慮或危險的程度）：*Surely that kind of behaviour is abnormal for a child of her age.* 的確，那種行為對她這個年齡的孩子來說是反常的。

extraordinary very unusual and usually very good 非凡的；不同凡響的：*I've had an extraordinary stroke of luck.* 我的運氣異乎尋常地好。

funny rather unusual or strange 奇異的；奇怪的：*I've got a funny feeling I've seen that man before.* 我有一種奇怪的感覺，似乎以前見過那個男人。

out of the ordinary unusual, especially unusual enough to be worth mentioning or commenting on 不尋常的，非凡的，不同凡響的 (以至於值得提及或評論)：*Nothing out of the ordinary happened.* 沒有甚麼不尋常的事發生。

remarkable unusual and usually impressive 顯著的，非凡的，卓越的：*a remarkable achievement* 非凡的成就

surprising causing you to be surprised 令人驚訝的：*It's surprising how much you can get done in an hour if you really set your mind to it.* 如果你真正專心投入，你在 1 小時之內可以幹的事情會令人驚訝。

uncommon not found very often, or happening rarely 罕有的；罕見的；難得的：*Red squirrels are very uncommon nowadays in most parts of England.* 如今紅松鼠在英格蘭的大多數地方已十分罕見了。

unorthodox not what most people would have or use or would assume to be correct 非正統的；異端的；非正規的：*It's an unorthodox method of opening a can, but it seems to be quite effective.* 雖然這不是開罐頭的常規方法，但看來很有效。

⊃ see also 參見 **eccentric; strange**

urge *verb* to advise someone very strongly to do something, or to use strong emotional pressure to persuade someone to do something 敦促；力勸；強烈要求：*I urge you to act now before it is too late.* 我勸你馬上採取行動，否則就來不及了。

egg on to encourage someone to do something bad 慫恿；煽動；攛掇：*It's not like him to behave so badly, I expect the bigger boys egged him on.* 看來他的行為不會那麼惡劣，我想都是那些大孩子慫恿他的。

encourage to try to build up someone's confidence so that they feel able to do something 鼓勵；激勵：*She encouraged me to try again when I was feeling really depressed about my prospects.* 當我為自己的前途感到灰心喪氣的時候，她鼓勵我再努把力。

goad to tease or taunt someone in order to make them do something (通過戲弄、奚落的手段) 驅使，唆使，刺激：*She goaded him into hitting the other fellow by calling him a coward.* 她稱他膽小鬼，刺激他去打了另一個人。

spur on to make someone more eager or determined to achieve something 激勵；鼓勵；鞭策：*We were spurred on by the shouts of the crowd.* 我們被人群的呼喊聲所激勵。

will to wish very hard for something to happen or for someone to do something in the hope that the power of your wish will bring the result you want 決心；(運用意志力以) 驅使 (某人做某事)：*I was willing you to say yes.* 我希望你會同意。

⊃ see also 參見 **persuade**

useful *adjective* helping you to be able to do what you want to do 有用的；有益的；有幫助的：*I thought you might find this useful if you've got a lot of decorating to do.* 如果你還有大量裝飾工作要做，我想你可能會用得上這東西。

constructive giving you positive advice on what you ought to do or how you can improve 建設性的，有裨益的，積極的：*constructive criticism* 建設性的批評

handy useful and easy to hold and use 便利的；易使用的；唾手可得的：*a handy little gadget* 好用的小工具

helpful useful 有用的；有益的；有幫助的：*helpful hints for newly married couples* 對新婚夫婦有益的提示

practical that you can use to help you deal with real-life tasks and situations, not theoretical 實際的；實用的：*a practical guide to setting up your own business* 創業的實用指南

profitable bringing you either financial profit or some other kind of benefit 有利潤的；有利可圖的；有益的：*Surely there are more profitable ways of spending your time than reading comics.* 當然有比看漫畫書更有益的事來打發時間。

worthwhile worth the time, effort, etc., that you spend doing it 值得（花時間、精力）的：*You get a real sense of achievement when you finish the course, and that makes all the hard work and study worthwhile.* 修完這門課程，你會有一種真正的成就感，讓你覺得所有的艱苦努力都是值得的。

useless *adjective* not helping to achieve anything or bringing any benefit 無用的；無益的；無濟於事的：*It's useless to complain.* 抱怨是沒有用的。

fruitless producing no result 無效的；徒勞的：*All attempts to trace the missing child proved fruitless.* 為追尋失蹤孩子所做出的所有努力都是徒勞的。

futile not serving any purpose or having any chance of success 無用的；徒勞的；無效的：*Resistance is futile and will only lead to more bloodshed.* 抵抗是徒勞的，只會造成更多的傷亡。

ineffective not producing the desired result or effect 無效的；不起作用的：*Antibiotics are ineffective against diseases caused by viruses.* 抗生素對於病毒引起的疾病是無效的。

in vain (*formal*) fruitless 徒勞的；白費的：*We tried several times to contact him, but all our efforts were in vain.* 我們好幾次試圖聯繫他，但所有的努力都是徒勞。

pointless useless 無意義的；無用的；無效果的：*Going on would be pointless, since we know that all the mountain passes are blocked by snow.* 既然我們知道所有的山路都被大雪封住了，繼續前進就毫無意義了。

vain producing no result 徒然的；無益的；無結果的：*vain attempts to make the unruly children behave* 想不受管的孩子乖起來的無謂努力

 see also 參見 **inferior**

V

valuable *adjective* worth a lot of money, or very beneficial or important to someone 很值錢的；貴重的；寶貴的：*She gave me some very valuable advice.* 她給了我一些非常寶貴的建議。

costly that has serious bad effects, such as meaning that you have to spend a lot of money, or (*literary*) very valuable and splendid 代價沉重的；損失慘重的；昂貴的；貴重的：*That mistake could prove costly in the long run.* 從長遠看，那個失誤可能會付出沉重代價。

dear (*used mainly to describe everyday items*) expensive (主要用以形容日常用品) 昂貴的，價格高的：*Strawberries are dear because they're out of season.* 現在草莓不合時令，所以賣得很貴。

expensive costing a lot of money to buy 花錢多的；昂貴的：*It's more expensive to eat in restaurants than to cook for yourself at home.* 在餐館吃飯比自己在家做飯花錢更多。

invaluable extremely beneficial or important to someone 極寶貴的；極其重要的：*Your assistance has been invaluable.* 你的幫助是非常可貴的。

precious having great value, either in terms of money or of its importance to a particular person (從金錢或重要性方面對某人) 珍貴的，寶貴的，貴重的：*Those memories are very precious to me.* 那些回憶對我來説十分珍貴。

priceless so valuable that it is impossible to estimate its worth in money or its importance 無價的；極貴重的：*This manuscript is in Shakespeare's own handwriting, and it is quite literally priceless.* 這是莎士比亞的親筆手稿，是真正的無價之寶。

treasured that a particular person loves and values greatly 珍愛的，珍惜的：*one of my most treasured possessions* 我最珍愛的收藏之一

very *adverb* more than usually, to a greater extent or degree than normal 非常；很；十分：*It's very hot in here.* 這裏很熱。

awfully (*informal*) extremely 非常；很；極其：*I'm awfully sorry, I forgot.* 非常抱歉，我忘了。

exceedingly (*formal*) (*usually used with positive words*) extremely (通常與表示肯定的詞語搭配) 非常，極度地：*I'd be exceedingly grateful for any advice you could offer me.* 你能給我的任何建議我都會感激不盡的。

excessively to a greater degree than is needed 過分地；過度地：*I think they're being excessively cautious, since the risks to them are fairly slight.* 我認為他們過於謹慎了，因為這點風險對他們來説是很小的。

extremely to a much greater extent or degree than normal 極端地；極其；非常：*He's extremely angry about it.* 他對此感到極其憤怒。

highly (*used only with certain adjectives*) to a greater degree than normal (僅與某些形容詞搭配) 極度地，極其，非常：*a highly dangerous mission* 一項極其危險的任務

quite* completely 完全地；徹底地；十分：*'Are you quite sure that those were her exact words?' 'Quite sure.'* "你完全肯定那些是她的原話嗎？""完全肯定。"

* Used mainly with emphatic adjectives to avoid confusion with the commoner sense of quite ('fairly'). 主要與語氣強的形容詞搭配以避免與 quite (相當) 的常見意義相混淆。

really (*often used to emphasize your personal feeling that something is the case*) very or genuinely (常用以強調個人感受) 非常，確實，真正地：*I don't care what they think, I think he's a really nice guy.* 我不在乎他們怎麼想，我認為他是個真正的好人。

terribly (*informal*) extremely 非常，極其：*She's terribly upset.* 她難過極了。

thoroughly in every respect 完 全 地； 徹 底 地：*I think you should feel thoroughly ashamed of yourselves.* 我認為你應該為自己感到萬分羞愧。

truly (*often used to emphasize your personal feeling that something is the case*) very, genuinely, or sincerely (常用以強調個人感受) 非常，真正地，誠摯地：*For what we are about to receive, may the Lord make us truly grateful.* 感謝上帝所賜，願主讓我們心懷誠摯的感激之情。

vigour *noun* a combination of strength and energy that enables you to do things in a brisk and powerful way 體力；精力；活力：*If you put a bit more vigour into it, you'd get the job done in half the time.* 如果你多投入一點精力的話，只用一半的時間你就可以把這工作做完。

animation liveliness, especially in a group activity (尤指團體活動中) 活潑，有生氣，活躍：*It was only when the conversation turned to politics that people began talking with real animation.* 只是當談話轉向政治話題時，人們才開始真正活躍地交談起來。

energy a usually physical force that is used in performing actions and doing work (做事的) 精力，體力，活力：*Some days I feel as if I haven't got enough energy even to get out of bed.* 有幾天我感到好像連起牀的力氣都沒有了。

liveliness an energetic and excited quality, often combined with a sense of enjoyment 活潑；有生氣；快活：*Anna organized some party games, which added greatly to the liveliness of the occasion.* 安娜組織了幾個派對遊戲，大大活躍了晚會的氣氛。

stamina the ability to continue doing something that requires strength and energy, for example running or working, for a long time 毅力；持久力；耐力：*Does she have the stamina to run a long-distance race?* 她有這個耐力參加長跑比賽嗎？

strength the ability to exert a lot of physical force, for example to move or lift things, or to resist weight, pressure, etc., without breaking or collapsing 體力，力氣，力量：*I haven't the strength to lift this on my own.* 憑我一個人的力氣，我抬不起這個東西。

vitality a combination of energy, eagerness to do things, and enjoyment of being alive and active 活力；生命力；生機：*She has so much vitality.* 她是那樣的生氣勃勃。

zest a combination of vigour and enjoyment shown when you do something 熱情；熱忱；樂趣：*He's fully fit again now and beginning to make plans for the company's future with his usual zest.* 他現在已經完全恢復了，並且開始以他一貫的熱情投入到公司未來的籌劃之中。

➲ see also 參見 **active; healthy**

violent *adjective* using force to cause harm or damage, or showing uncontrolled force or power (力量) 猛烈的；強烈的；兇暴的：*a violent storm* 一場猛烈的風暴

aggressive showing a wish to attack someone 好鬥的；攻擊性的；咄咄逼人的：*Then he got really aggressive, and I was frightened that he was going to hit me.* 然後他變得咄咄逼人，我嚇得要命，唯恐他要打我。

fierce suggesting that someone or something may become angry or violent and attack you (因有攻擊性而) 兇猛的；猛烈的；憤怒的：*The lion let out a fierce roar.* 那頭獅子兇猛地咆哮起來。

powerful having or showing a great deal of strength or ability to do things 強大的；有力的；強有力的：*a powerful blow* 有力的一擊

rough not gentle, careless or violent in the way you handle things or people 粗暴的；粗魯的；粗糙的：*You're too rough, you'll hurt him.* 你太粗魯了，會傷着他的。

savage very violent and very uncontrolled 殘暴的；殘忍的：*a savage attack* 兇猛的攻擊

vicious deliberately intending or intended to cause a lot of harm 惡意的；惡毒的；惡狠狠的：*Don't go near that dog, he looks vicious.* 那條狗看上去很兇猛，別靠近牠。

W

wait *verb* to remain where you are or take no action because you are expecting something to happen 等候；等待：*I waited for half an hour at the bus stop and then decided to walk home.* 我在車站等了半個小時，然後決定步行回家。

bide your time to take no action, especially because you think a favourable opportunity to do something will soon arise 等待良機；等待有利時機：*I'm just biding my time until the share price falls a little lower.* 我只是在等待股價小幅下挫的時機。

hang around (*informal*) to stay in a place doing very little, usually waiting for someone or something (通常指等待而在某地) 逗留，閒逛，轉悠：*I hung around for hours outside the station, but she didn't show up.* 我在車站附近轉悠了幾個小時，但是她一直沒有出現。

hang on (*informal*) to wait, or to stop what you are doing and wait 等一下；(放下手頭的活) 等待：*Hang on, I'll be with you in a minute.* 請稍候，我馬上就來。

hold on (*informal*) to wait, or to stop what you are doing and wait 等一下；(放下手頭的活) 等待：*Now just hold on a minute, I didn't tell you could go.* 稍等一會兒，我還沒讓你走。

kick your heels (*informal*) to wait unwillingly or frustratingly (不情願地) 等待；空等；苦等：*He left me kicking my heels in the hotel lounge while he went off to discuss business with somebody.* 他出去和人談生意，留下我一個人在酒店大廳裏苦等。

linger to remain in a place, often doing something in a leisurely or relaxed way (常指悠閒放鬆地) 逗留，漫步，閒蕩：*We lingered by the shore, just chatting and enjoying the view.* 我們在海邊漫步，一邊聊天，一邊欣賞美景。

walk *verb* to move, or to go somewhere, on your legs at a fairly slow pace, as opposed to running or riding in a vehicle 走路；步行；漫步：*The bus service is* *so unreliable that it's often quicker to walk to work.* 巴士太不可靠,步行上班往往還要快些。

amble to walk in a leisurely way, especially for pleasure (悠閒、愉快地) 漫步,溜達,緩行:*The couple ambled slowly along the promenade.* 那對夫婦沿着步行大道悠閒漫步。

hike to walk a long distance, usually for recreation (通常指為娛樂而) 遠足,徒步旅行:*We spent our holiday hiking in the Swiss Alps.* 我們假期在瑞士的阿爾卑斯山作徒步旅行。

march to walk in a disciplined and coordinated fashion, often in a group, or to walk in a determined and forceful way 列隊行進,齊步前進;行軍:*The soldiers marched across the parade ground.* 士兵們從閱兵場上列隊走過。

plod to walk with slow heavy steps 沉重而緩慢地行走;步履艱難地行走:*She strode off in front, and the rest of us plodded along behind.* 她大踏步地走在前面,我們餘下的人步履艱難地跟在後面。

saunter to walk in a casual, carefree manner 悠閒地走;閒逛;漫步:*A group of elegant young gentlemen were sauntering in the park.* 一群優雅的年輕紳士在花園裏悠閒地漫步。

stride to walk with long energetic steps 大步行走;闊步行走:*He strode into the room and started giving orders straight away.* 他大步走進屋子,一進屋便開始發號施令。

stroll to walk in a leisurely way, especially for pleasure (悠閒、愉悅地) 漫步,閒逛,溜達:*We strolled along the Champs Elysées looking in shop windows.* 我們沿着香榭麗舍大道閒逛,瀏覽商店的櫥窗。

strut to walk in a proud or arrogant way 趾高氣昂地走;高視闊步;大搖大擺地走:*From the way he struts around, you'd think he owned the whole estate.* 他大搖大擺走路的姿勢會讓你覺得這整個莊園都為他擁有。

traipse to walk in a tired or reluctant way, often for a long distance 疲憊地行走;長途跋涉;磨蹭:*I traipsed all the way to the post office, only to find it was shut.* 我一路磨蹭到郵局,結果卻發現郵局已經關門了。

wander to walk about casually, not having a clear direction or purpose (漫無目的地) 遊蕩,徘徊,閒逛:*They spent the afternoon wandering around the shops.* 他們一下午都在商店閒逛。

warm *adjective* having a fairly high temperature 溫暖的;暖和的:*Are you warm enough, or shall I switch the heating on?* 你夠暖和嗎?要不要我把暖氣打開?

balmy (*used to describe weather conditions*) pleasantly warm and relaxing (用以形容天氣) 溫暖的,溫和的,和煦的:*a balmy summer's evening* 一個溫和的夏夜

lukewarm (*used to describe substances, especially fluids*) not cold, but not at a high enough temperature to be described as warm (用以形容物質,尤其是液體) 溫度適中的,不冷不熱的,溫熱的:*The milk for the baby should be just lukewarm.* 給嬰兒喝的牛奶應剛好溫度適中。

mild (*used to describe weather conditions*) fairly warm (用以形容天氣) 溫和的,溫暖的:*It's actually quite mild for a winter's day.* 就冬日而言,這算得上是相當溫暖了。

sunny when the sun is shining 陽光充足的；晴朗的：*a sunny day* 陽光明媚的一天

tepid (*used to describe substances, especially fluids, sometimes disapprovingly*) lukewarm (用以形容物質，尤其是液體) 微溫的，溫吞的 (有時含貶義)：*The soup was tepid, and the main course was stone cold when it arrived at the table.* 湯是微溫的，而主菜端上桌時已經冰涼了。

temperate having both cold and warm periods, but neither extreme heat or extreme cold 氣候溫和的；溫帶的；不冷不熱的：*a temperate climate* 溫和的氣候

waste *verb* to use or consume something such as money, time, or resources in a way that produces no benefit for anyone 浪費，消耗，耗費 (金錢、時間或資源)：*They wasted thousands of pounds on a luxury car that they don't really need.* 他們花了幾千英鎊買了一輛他們根本不需要的豪華轎車。

fritter away to use something up little by little on useless objects or activities (在無用的東西或活動上漸漸) 浪費，耗盡，揮霍：*I didn't save all that money for you to fritter it away by gambling on fruit machines.* 我省下那些錢可不是讓你全都揮霍在吃角子老虎機上。

misspend to spend time or sometimes money in an unprofitable way 浪費，揮霍 (時間或金錢)：*my misspent youth* 我虛度了的青春

squander to waste something, especially money 浪費，揮霍 (尤指金錢)：*The government is squandering taxpayers' money on more expensive equipment for the army.* 政府將納稅人的錢浪費在為軍隊購買更貴的裝備上。

throw away not to make good use of something valuable that you have or that is offered to you 丟棄，放棄，浪費 (有價值的東西)：*He had the chance of really successful acting career and he just threw it away.* 他曾經有機會發展成功的演藝事業，但是他卻放棄了。

watch *verb* to look at something or someone or what someone is doing for a period of time, sometimes as a way of protecting or supervising them 觀察；監視；守護：*Now watch carefully while I show you how to do it.* 現在仔細觀察我是怎麼做的。

keep an eye on to watch someone or something, especially in order to protect or supervise them 照顧；看管；密切注視：*Do you mind keeping an eye on my suitcase while I go to the toilet?* 我去洗手間時，請幫我看一下行李好嗎？

keep tabs on (*informal*) to keep an eye on 照顧；看管；密切注視：*Keep tabs on him – don't let him slip away into the crowd.* 好好看着他，別讓他溜進人群跑了。

keep under surveillance to watch something continuously, usually in order to detect or prevent crime (通常指為了偵查或防止犯罪) 監督，監視：*The police suspected that the house was being used by drug smugglers and had kept it under surveillance for several weeks.* 警方懷疑那所房子裏住着毒品走私犯，對它實施監視已經好幾個星期了。

keep watch to look out for possible danger, usually while someone else is doing something or you are guarding something 放哨；望風；值班：*You three can go to sleep, and I'll keep watch.* 你們三個可以去睡覺了，我來值班。

look on to watch something happen without attempting to take part in it or get involved in it 觀看；旁觀 : *Three people were doing the actual work, and another three were just standing around looking on.* 有三個人在幹活，另外三個只是站在一旁看着。

monitor to watch something continuously or check it regularly in order to make sure that there are no problems with it 監控；監督；監視 : *This machine monitors the patient's heartbeat.* 這台機器監控病人的心跳情況。

observe (*formal*) to see or watch someone or something, especially to watch something in order to learn from it （尤指為了學習而）觀察，察看，觀摩 : *Medical students are sometimes allowed to observe while the surgeons are carrying out operations.* 醫科學生有時可以在外科醫生進行手術時在旁觀察。

weak *adective* having little strength or energy or unable to resist much weight, pressure, etc. 薄弱的；軟弱無力的；不堪重負的 : *We think we've found the weak point in their defences.* 我們認為已經找到了他們防守中的薄弱環節。

delicate thin, light, or fine and often beautiful or graceful, but easily damaged 精細的；精密的；脆弱的；纖弱的 : *It's better to wash delicate fabrics by hand rather than in the washing machine.* 輕薄的布料用手洗比用機洗好。

faint (*used to describe a colour, sound, or quality*) having little intensity and difficult to see or hear (*used to describe someone*) feeling unsteady because they are hungry or very ill （用以形容顏色、聲音、質量）模糊的，微弱的，暗淡的；（用以形容人因饑餓或疾病）虛弱的，眩暈的 : *He heard a faint voice coming from behind the door.* 他聽到門後傳來微弱的聲音。

feeble (*often used scornfully*) showing a lack of strength or effectiveness （常用於輕蔑的語氣中）無力的，虛弱的，缺乏效力的 : *her feeble attempts at humour* 她對幽默蹩腳的嘗試

flimsy made of weak materials or not strongly constructed 易壞的；脆弱的；不牢固的 : *The strong wind soon blew down their flimsy shelter.* 強風很快吹倒了他們搖搖欲墜的住處。

fragile that can easily be broken 易碎的；脆的；易損壞的 : *This box is full of fragile ornaments.* 盒子裏裝滿了易碎裝飾品。

frail weak and in poor health, or flimsy （身體）虛弱的；脆弱的；易壞的 : *He's getting very old and frail.* 他漸漸變得年老而虛弱。

puny (*formal*) (*often used scornfully*) having very little strength or power, and often small （常用於輕蔑的語氣中，表示力量或能力）弱小的，微弱的，微不足道的 : *What can their puny forces do against our magnificent war machine?* 他們弱小的力量怎能與我們強大的戰爭武器相抗衡？

wealth *noun* the money and other possessions that someone owns, especially a large amount of money and possessions, or the fact of having a large amount of money and possessions 財富；財產；富有 : *We wish you health, wealth, and happiness in your future life together.* 我們希望你未來的生活健康、富裕和幸福。

affluence a state in which someone has plenty of money and is able to live relatively comfortably 富裕；富有；富足 : *The affluence of most people in the West contrasts starkly with the poverty of the vast majority of people in Africa* *and Asia.* 西方國家大多數人的富裕與亞非國家絕大多數人的貧窮形成鮮明的對比。

fortune a very large amount of money 大筆錢；財富；（大量的）財產：*He made a fortune from that invention.* 那項發明讓他賺了一大筆錢。

luxury a state in which you have a very easy and comfortable life and use the best and most expensive kinds of goods and services 奢侈；奢華；豪華：*If you win the lottery, you'll be able to live in luxury for the rest of your life.* 如果你中了彩票，你的餘生就可以過上奢華的生活了。

means money that you have available or can use to live on 收入；財產；財力：*Obviously, if you live beyond your means, you will end up in debt.* 顯然，如果你入不敷出，你將會債務纏身。

prosperity a state in which things are going well for you and you have lots of money（景況）順利；富足；繁榮：*In the days of his prosperity he would think nothing of spending £500 on a night out.* 在他富裕的日子，他根本不把外出一夜消費五百英鎊當回事。

riches (*formal*) money and other valuable objects or products, or wealth 財富；財產：*The riches obtained from the rubber trade built these splendid mansions.* 從橡膠業貿易中獲得的財富構築了這些富麗堂皇的大廈。

treasure a collection of valuable objects such as jewels and coins, especially when hidden away or buried（尤指被隱藏或埋葬的）財寶，珠寶，珍品：*He dug up an old wooden chest full of treasure.* 他挖出一個裝滿珍寶的舊木箱子。

⊃ see also 參見 **rich**

wet *adjective* covered in, or having absorbed, a lot of liquid, especially water, or (*used to describe the weather*) rainy 濕的；潮濕的；多雨的：*I wore rubber boots so as not to get my feet wet.* 我穿了一雙膠靴，這樣腳就不會弄濕。

damp rather wet, especially to the touch, but not usually showing liquid on the surface（尤指摸上去相當）濕的，潮濕的（但通常表面無水跡）：*Wipe the surface with a damp cloth.* 用濕布擦拭表面。

drenched (*usually used to describe people*) very wet, usually because they have been in the rain（通常用以形容人）濕透的，淋濕的：*I got drenched on the way home from work.* 我在下班回家的路上被雨淋濕了。

humid (*used to describe weather conditions*) where there is quite a lot of moisture in the air（用以形容天氣）潮濕的，有濕氣的，濕潤的：*It's terribly hot and humid in the jungle.* 叢林裏的天氣炎熱而潮濕。

moist (*often used in an approving way*) containing a certain amount of liquid inside itself, but less wet than something that is damp（常用作褒義）濕潤的，微濕的：*a nice moist sponge cake* 一塊美味鬆軟的蛋糕

rainy characterized by frequent rain 多雨的；下雨的：*a rainy day* 雨天

showery characterized by frequent showers 陣雨的；多陣雨的：*showery weather* 陣雨天氣

soaked (*usually used to describe people*) very wet, usually because they have been in the rain（通常用來形容人）淋濕的，濕透的：*You're soaked, come in and get dry.* 你都濕透了，進來吹乾吧。

soaking wet very wet 濕透的：*The clothes have just come out of the washing machine and are still soaking wet.* 衣服剛從洗衣機裏取出，還很濕。

sodden containing as much liquid as it can hold, so very wet and soft 浸透的；濕透的：*The pitch is absolutely sodden, you can't possibly play on it today.* 球場濕透了，你們今天肯定不能在場上玩球了。

soggy having a very soft and yielding texture through containing large amounts of liquid (因包含大量水分而) 鬆軟的；浸水的：*The biscuits will go soggy if you don't keep them in an airtight tin.* 你如果不把餅乾放在密封的罐子裏，它們會變得鬆軟。

woman *noun* an adult female human being 女人；婦女：*There are only two women on the committee.* 委員會裏只有兩名女性。

bitch (*informal and very rude*) an unpleasant or spiteful woman 潑婦；惡婦；婊子：*The bitch took all my money and ran off with another man.* 那婊子拿走了我所有的錢和另一個男人私奔了。

chick* (*informal*) (*used mainly by men*) a young woman, especially an attractive one (主要為男性所用，尤指有魅力的) 少女，少婦，小妞兒：*Who's that good-looking chick over there by the bar?* 那邊吧台旁那個靚妞是誰？

* Usually thought to be offensive. 通常被認為是犯忌的言辭。

female (*used in an impersonal way*) a woman or girl (不用以指個人的) 女性，雌性：*The number of households consisting of a single female has increased markedly in the past decade.* 在過去的十年間，由單身女性組成的家庭的數量明顯增加。

girl* a female child, or (*informal*) a woman 小女孩；女人：*a night out with the girls* 和女孩們在外共處的一夜

* Sometimes felt to be patronizing. 有時給人以優越的感覺。

lady a woman from the upper classes or who has very good manners, or a polite word for a woman (有良好教養的或上層社會的) 女子，夫人；(對女性的尊稱) 女士：*Go and ask that lady if she'd mind if we opened the window.* 去問一下那個女士是否介意我們打開窗戶。

lass (*informal and old-fashioned*) a young woman 少女；女孩；姑娘：*She's a really nice lass, that daughter of yours.* 你的那個女兒，可真是個好姑娘。

work¹ *noun* activity that involves physical or mental effort and is intended to produce a result (體力或腦力的) 工作：*There's still a lot of work to be done before the house is finished.* 在房子完工前還有許多工作要做。

drudgery boring and repetitive work that is also often physically tiring 無聊的苦工；單調乏味的苦差事：*the drudgery of washing clothes and cleaning the house* 洗衣和打掃房間的苦差事

effort the use of energy to produce a result, or an instance of using energy or a considerable amount of energy in order to achieve something 努力；盡力；費力的事：*With a bit more effort, he could do really well.* 再努把力，他會做得非常好。

exertion the use of physical energy to do something (體力上的) 費力，盡力，努力：*The slightest exertion makes her feel really tired.* 稍微幹一點活兒她就覺得很累。

labour (*formal*) hard work, especially work that involves using your hands and body, or workers generally (尤指體力) 勞動；勞工；工人：*Machines have reduced the amount of labour involved in many household tasks.* 機器減少了許多家務的勞動量。

toil (*formal*) hard, usually physical, work that goes on for a long time (尤指長時間的) 體力活，苦工，勞累的工作：*It took hours of back-breaking toil to clear the ground so that it could be ploughed.* 需要花數小時繁重的勞動來平整土地，然後才能耕地。

work² *verb* to do work, especially in order to earn money (尤指為了賺錢) 工作：*I work in an office.* 我在辦公室工作。

be busy to be involved in doing something, especially work 忙於 (工作)；忙碌：*I'm afraid I can't talk to you now, as I'm too busy.* 現在我恐怕不能和你交談了，因為我太忙了。

be employed to work for someone who pays you money, or (*formal*) to be engaged in doing something 受僱於；從事於：*For the last three years I have been employed in a bakery.* 最近三年，我一直受僱於一家麵包店。

earn your living to make the money you need to live on by working 謀生：*She earns her living as a secretary.* 她以做秘書工作為生。

labour (*formal*) to do hard work, especially works that uses your hands and body, or to use a lot of effort in doing something (辛苦地) 勞動；幹苦力；苦幹：*labouring on a building site* 在建築工地幹苦力

toil (*formal*) to do hard, usually physical, work for a long time (通常指長時間) 苦幹，辛苦勞動：*After toiling all day in the fields, he felt he deserved a rest.* 在田地裏辛苦勞動一整天之後，他感覺自己應當休息了。

work³ *verb* (*said about a machine*) to be carrying out a task, especially to be doing what it is designed to do effectively (指機器) 運轉，運行：*The computer's not working, because you forgot to switch it on.* 電腦沒有運行，因為你忘了開機。

function (*formal*) to work 運行；起作用：*In order to function effectively, the machine needs regular maintenance.* 機器需要定期維修以保證有效地運行。

go (*informal*) to operate 運轉；運行；開動：*I gave the lawnmower a kick to see if that would make it go.* 我踢了一腳剪草機，看能否讓它運轉起來。

operate (*said about a machine*) to be using power and performing the task it was designed to do, or (*said about a person*) to control a machine (指機器) 運行，運轉；操縱，控制 (機器)：*The brakes are operated by pushing the foot pedal.* 這些煞制器是通過踩腳踏板來控制。

run to operate, or to use a certain kind of energy in order to operate (使) 運轉，運行；操作：*This engine runs on diesel.* 發動機靠柴油運作。

➲ see also 參見 **job**

worry *verb* to have anxious thoughts about someone or something 擔心；發愁；擔憂：*I always worry about the children if I don't know where they are.* 只要不知道孩子們的行蹤，我就總是為他們擔心。

agonize to experience a lot of anxiety and distress in trying to do something such as reach a decision（因作決定而）焦慮，痛苦，苦悶：*I agonized for a week over whether or not I should accept the offer.* 我為該不該接受這項交易苦苦思索了一個多星期。

be concerned to feel anxious about something 擔心；掛念；關心：*They should have been back three hours ago, and we're concerned about their safety.* 他們本該在三小時前就回來的，我們很擔心他們的安全。

be on tenterhooks (*informal*) to feel very tense and anxious, usually while waiting for news of something（通常指等待消息時）坐立不安，焦慮不安，如坐針氈：*We were on tenterhooks waiting to hear whether she'd passed the exam.* 我們提心吊膽地等待着她是否通過考試的消息。

fret to worry, and to show you are worried by being restless and complaining 煩惱；焦慮不安；焦急：*I told her not to fret, we'd soon have the damage repaired.* 我告訴她不要着急，我們很快就會讓人把受損部分修好。

have butterflies (in your stomach) (*informal*) to be very nervous about something you have to do 緊張；害怕：*I always have butterflies in my stomach before I have to speak in public.* 在公眾場合講話前我總是很緊張。

lose sleep (*informal*) to be unable to sleep through being worried（因焦慮、擔心而）睡不着覺，失眠：*I wouldn't lose any sleep over it, everything's sure to turn out all right.* 我不會為此擔心得睡不着覺，所有事情最終一定會順利的。

➲ see also 參見 **anxiety; trouble**[1]

write *verb* to put words on paper with a pen or pencil, or to compose a document, letter, novel, play, etc. 書寫；寫作；寫：*I'm just writing a postcard to my sister.* 我正在給妹妹寫明信片。

jot down to write something down quickly or in a brief form 草草寫下；簡單扼要地記下：*I jotted down a few points that I'd like you to raise at the meeting.* 我大致列了幾個要點，希望你在會上提出來。

make a note of to write something down briefly to help you remember it, or to pay special attention to something so that you remember it 記下，寫下，特別注意：*I made a note of his name and address, so that I can contact him again if necessary.* 我記下了他的姓名和地址以便需要的時候能再與他聯繫。

note down to write something as a brief record of what has happened or of information that you have been given（粗略、簡要地）記下，記錄：*I noted down the car's registration number so that I could pass it on to the police.* 我記下了汽車的車牌號以便向警察局報告。

pen (*formal*) to write something 寫：*I sat down straight away and penned a letter to the editor of the local newspaper.* 我立刻坐下來給當地報紙的編輯寫了一封信。

put in writing to write something down, especially an agreement that you have made verbally with someone, in order to make it official（正式）寫下，簽署，簽訂（尤指合同、協議）：*I'm happy with the agreement we've just reached on the phone and I'd be grateful if you could put it in writing to me.* 我很高興我們剛才在電話裏達成了協議，如果你能夠以書面形式記下給我，我會非常感激。

scribble to write something hastily or carelessly, often in a way that is difficult to read, or to make meaningless marks on something with a pencil, pen, etc. 潦草地寫；匆忙地寫；胡亂書寫：*I scribbled a note in my diary.* 我在日記裏匆匆做了一個記錄。

sign to write your name in your own handwriting on a document, especially at the end of it, to show that it is from you or that you agree with its contents 簽名；署名；簽署：*You forgot to sign the cheque.* 你忘了在支票上簽名。

write down to put something on paper as a deliberate act, especially as a record of something or to help you remember it 寫下；記下：*If you get a good idea, write it down straight away. Don't simply rely on your memory.* 你如果有了好主意，立刻把它記下來，不要只靠腦子記。

Y

young *adjective* having lived only a relatively short time 年輕的；年紀小的：*You were too young then to understand what was going on.* 你那時太年輕，還不懂發生了甚麼事。

adolescent* past childhood, but not yet fully adult 青春期的：*the fantasies of adolescent boys* 青春期男孩的幻想

* Usually used before a noun. 通常用於名詞前。

immature not having fully developed, especially not having the experience of life, the good sense, or the knowledge of how to behave that an adult has 未發育完全的；不成熟的：*That sort of behaviour shows just how immature she is.* 那種行為表明她多麼的不成熟。

juvenile (*formal*) young, or silly 少年的；幼稚的：*juvenile delinquents* 少年罪犯

little (*informal*) (*used mainly when talking to or about children*) very young 幼小的，年少的：*Did you use to tell me stories when I was little?* 在我小時候，你經常給我講故事嗎？

teenage* aged between 13 and 20, or connected with people of that age(十三至二十歲之間的) 青少年的；有關青少年的：*teenage fashions* 青少年的時尚

* Usually used before a noun. 通常用於名詞前。

youthful having the appearance or the vitality of a young person 年輕的；朝氣蓬勃的：*I hope I still look as youthful as you do when I'm forty.* 我希望在四十歲時看上去仍然像你那麼年輕。